Good Det...

FAKES & FORGERIES

Judy Hindley

Illustrated by: **Colin King**

Consultants: **Donald Rumbelow
and Ruth Thomson**

Series Editor: **Heather Amery**

About this book

A forgery is a copy made to cheat people.
All kinds of things can be faked and forged—
from coins and bank notes to rare stamps or
famous paintings. Crooks also lay false trails,
wear false moustaches, and plant false clues.

To spot fakes, you must always be on guard.
You must be watchful, quick-witted and
sharp-eyed. You must be trained to notice the
smallest differences between real things and
fakes. This book is full of tips and puzzles to
help you practise.

It helps if you know some of the crooks'
secrets, too. This book shows you many of the
sneaky tricks that forgers use—and how a good
detective can uncover them.

First published in 1979 by
Usborne Publishing Ltd.
20 Garrick Street,
London WC2 9BJ, England

© Usborne Publishing Ltd
1979

Printed in Spain by
Gráficas Reunidas, S. A., Madrid.

Good Detective Guide
FAKES & FORGERIES

Contents

Know Your Crooks

Forgers are sometimes very skilful—and extremely sneaky. You will have to work hard to outwit them and trap them.

Counterfeit Money

To detect fake money and hunt down the forgers, you will need to use all your senses. You must train your eyes and ears, your nose and fingers. Later you will find some tips on practising.

Phoney Works of Art

CROOK MAKING FAKE 'ANTIQUE' STATUE

Some crooks forge anything valuable, from stamps to paintings. To detect this sort of fake, you need to know quite a lot about the real thing. (Later you will find some starting-points.)

They will fake or forge anything that might help them cheat people and get things that don't belong to them. Here are some examples.

Forged Signatures

CROOK PRACTISING FORGING SIGNATURE

To get people's money, crooks try to copy their writing and the way they sign their names. Later you will find out how to study handwriting and detect forged signatures.

Fake Clues

CROOK WALKING BACKWARDS TO LEAVE FALSE TRAIL

A crook may even leave fake clues, or lay false trails, in hope of fooling you.

Even footprints may be faked—if a crook thinks it will help him get away with a crime.

Detecting Counterfeits

Forged money (counterfeit money) is probably the most common fake. Few people realise how many special marks there are on a real bank note, and what a complicated pattern it has. To begin your detective training, check these points on some real bank notes.

First, find the signature and serial number. Any real bank note shows the signature of someone important in the bank that had it printed.

Each note is numbered in order, as it is printed. (This is the serial number.) If you find two with the same number, one of them is a forgery.

Hold it to the light to look for a watermark. This is a pattern pressed into the paper. It looks like a ghostly picture—often a face. It shows up on both sides, but only when the note is held to the light.

In most notes there is also a very thin strip of metal. In the light, it looks like a dark line. Sometimes, in a very tattered old note, you can see it glinting through the paper, where the edge is worn.

Now, carefully examine the pattern on each side. Use a magnifying glass, if possible. Notice how complicated the pictures are—and the different colours in them. Each colour is printed separately onto the paper.

Usually you will find a picture of someone famous—notice how clearly you can see each hair. You may also find tiny figures in the background and words hidden in the pattern. They are all traps for forgers.

7

Detection Training

As a detective, you must be ready to act quickly—you may not have time to examine every note and coin. A good detective can identify fake notes and coins without even looking at them. These pages show some ways to train yourself.

Remember that even the paper used to make money is a special kind—crooks sometimes steal it to make forged bank notes. There may be tiny coloured threads in the paper, as well as strips of metal. It is so different from ordinary paper that it is possible to detect a real note by the sound it makes when snapped between your fingers. The ink used to print it is special, too—notice the funny smell new bank notes have.

Touch Identification

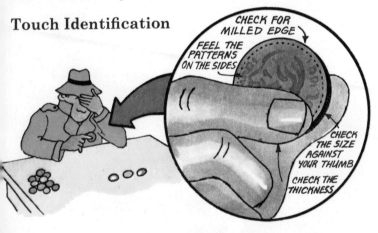

Collect several kinds of coin and test whether you can tell them apart with your eyes closed. Try to place them in order, from the most valuable to the least valuable.

Notice that coins made with some silver often have a milled edge (tiny ridges on the edge). You can feel it if you rub your finger along the edge of the coin.

Money Sensitivity Training

Make some phoney notes from different kinds of paper, using a real note as a pattern. Fold them up and crumple them, and scruff the corners. (This will make them feel more like real money.)

Number the phoney notes. Then get a partner to shuffle a real note among them while you are not looking. Try to pick out the real one by touch and sound alone. Then guess the numbers of the others.

Noise Identification

You can train yourself to pick out fake coins by the sound they make when they are dropped. To practise, work with a partner, like this. One person drops coins and fakes, one by one, on to a hard, flat surface, like a table. The other person (with his eyes closed or wearing a blindfold) tries to work out which are fakes.

Inside a Forgers' Den

This is the scene found by detectives Dodd and Trapper when they broke the Five-Star Forgery Case. It is a good example of what you might find in a forgers' den. The next pages show how forgers work.

PRINTING PRESS

STOCK OF PAPER AND INK

MACHINE TO PREPARE 'PLATES' FOR PRINTING PRESS

'PLATES' HUNG UP TO DRY

How Forgers Work

Here is the main equipment for making forged bank notes. Examine it carefully so that you will recognize it if you see it. The printing press and camera could be used for innocent business. But a plate or film showing pictures of money is evidence of forgery.

The forger in the dark room is just starting to make a new counterfeit. He is taking photographs of a £50 note. (This is against the law.)

Here is the sort of camera forgers like. It can take pictures that show each colour separately, and it uses film as big as a note.

The forger had taken a separate photograph of each colour used on the note, as well as the pattern on the back.

Here is a bit of the film (the photographic negative). Notice that on the negative the pattern is transparent.

This machine shines light through the transparent bits onto a thin sheet of metal called a 'plate'. The light prints the pattern on the plate. There must be a separate plate for the back of the note and for each colour. (Only one colour can be printed at a time.)

This is the best sort of printing press to use for making money. The ink is put on the plate by the rollers on top.

The inky plate presses the money-pattern on to the blanket roller. The blanket roller prints it on the paper.

Tracking Forgers

If you are on the trail of a team of forgers, look first for any building where they would have enough space to work in—and where they could try to hide what they are doing.

Keeping a Look-Out

GLIMPSE OF LIGHT BURNING THROUGH THE NIGHT

NOTICE THE EXTRA CABLE AND DRAINPIPE

CAR LEFT OUT IN SNOW

Look for suspicious changes in a building, like new pipes and cables ... or other signs that it is being used for a hidden purpose.

1 Clues

OILY RAGS

PAPER USED IN TEST RUNS

Look for suspicious rubbish, such as ink-stained rags or badly printed paper.

2

Watch out for any scrap of paper that might show even a tiny bit of money pattern.

14

If you find a likely-looking site, watch it secretly for a few days to note down suspicious activities. Then look for the clues shown at the bottom of these pages.

LOOK-OUT

LOTS OF TRAFFIC TO AND FROM GARAGE

Notice if the people you see seem to be watchful or suspicious. . . .

And whether there seem to be an unusual number of visitors.

Notice whether you can smell printer's ink, or any other strong chemicals.

CLICK-CLANK-CLICK-CLANK

Listen for the click-clank noise that means there is a printing press in action.

15

Forgery Smugglers

Forgery is often an international crime. To make counterfeits difficult to trace, they are printed in one country and then smuggled across the borders to another country.

Because of this, detectives from different countries work together. They share information and sometimes they even help customs officers check travellers at frontiers.

On the right are some of the tricks that smugglers use. Below you can see how detectives spot smugglers as they go through customs.

They notice if a passenger's behaviour seems out of character.

This is how guilty people often show they are nervous.

They check the lining in suitcases that are heavier than the things inside.

They examine anything that seems much heavier than it should be. It might be gold.

Smuggling in Cars and Lorries

THIS CUTAWAY SHOWS HOW NOTES CAN BE SMUGGLED INSIDE A TANKER

PLASTIC BAGS HUNG FROM SUPPORT

NOTES MAY BE HIDDEN IN HOLLOW PARTS OR SECRET COMPARTMENTS IN A CAR. DETECTIVES CHECK FOR THIS BY LISTENING TO THE SOUND MADE WHEN DIFFERENT AREAS ARE TAPPED

SECRET COMPARTMENTS

Suspicious Behaviour

Smugglers like to go through customs with a crowd. They may hang about for a long time, waiting for the right moment—then try to blend in with a group of other passengers.

If they get through customs, they are often so relieved that they give themselves away. They may wink at an accomplice, or smile knowingly—or just act a bit too happy.

Forged Paintings

Remember that pictures can be forged too. Some crooks have made fortunes by copying famous painters, because collectors want lots of pictures by these painters.

The work of Old Masters (famous painters who lived long ago) is even more valuable. Often many of their paintings are lost or damaged and lots of people want to buy what is left.

These pages show some of the signs of an old painting and how they can be faked. Turn the page to see how the phoneys are detected.

Signs of an Old Painting

It shows long-ago things, and the paint has become dark with age.

The paint is very hard. (It takes 50 years for oil paint to dry out completely.)

MAGNIFYING GLASS

MAGNIFIED VIEW OF CRACKED VARNISH

The canvas it is painted on is old, and often the frame is old, too.

It is covered with shiny varnish. Over the years, the varnish has become a mass of tiny cracks.

18

A Forger's Tricks

One very famous forger worked like this. First, he bought a painting that was very old, but not particularly valuable.

EMPTY FRAME

He carefully took off the paint so that he could use the canvas. (Canvas is tough material, though old age weakens it.)

He studied every piece of work by a certain Old Master, until he knew how to copy every detail.

MINERALS ARE GROUND TO POWDER TO MAKE PAINT

Then he learned how paint was made in the Old Master's time, and mixed it up himself.

He faked a new 'Old Master' and heated it to dry the paint. Then he varnished it and heated it again to dry the varnish.

He rolled the canvas tightly round a tube, to crack the varnish so that it looked old. Then he put the canvas back in its old frame.

19

Detecting a Forged Painting

When the forger has finished his fake painting, he has to invent a story. Somehow he has to explain how he happened to get hold of this 'famous' work—and why no one has heard of it before. He may have to forge old letters and other documents. Any of these may be spotted.

Fake Documents

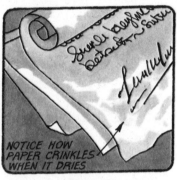

NOTICE HOW PAPER CRINKLES WHEN IT DRIES

Handwriting experts can detect forged writing. Laboratory tests can sometimes even show how old the ink is.

You can make paper look old by soaking it in tea or coffee—try it and see. But it will be blotchy and crinkled.

Fake Worm-Holes

CLOSE UP OF SLICE OF WOOD WITH REAL WORM HOLES

CLOSE UP OF SLICE OF WOOD WITH PHONEY WORM HOLES

Sometimes, forgers make phoney worm-holes in a new frame, to make it seem old.

But holes made by a drill or a needle will be suspiciously straight. Real worms swerve.

The painting itself contains lots of traps. There may be clues in the canvas, frame, paint, varnish—even the dirt. Scientists can detect modern chemicals from a tiny bit of paint or varnish. They can even work out what made the dust in the cracks.

ORDINARY LIGHT SHOWS PAINTING THAT LOOKS VERY OLD

X-RAY PHOTOGRAPH

SHOWS MODERN PAINTING UNDERNEATH

Certain kinds of light rays, such as x-rays, can show up a modern painting hidden under one that looks old.

This is because they show even tiny bits of some colours—and don't show up other colours at all.

Nail Clue

SUPPORT

BACK OF CANVAS

MODERN NAIL

Canvas must be nailed to a frame to make it tight enough to paint on. The nails may be a

clue to when this was done. Nails were not machine-made until about 200 years ago.

Find the Forger's Mistakes

An expert can often detect a faked 'Old Master' by studying the things it shows. This painting was made to look like the work of an artist who lived in Europe 400 years ago, but many things it shows do not belong to that time.

There are at least 20 mistakes in the picture—can you find them? List everything that looks wrong, then turn the page to check. Look carefully and think hard. (You may find you would have made some of the same mistakes.)

The Forger's Mistakes

All the games and many of the toys in the forged picture are actually copied from a real picture painted by an artist named Breughel. Below are the mistakes the forger made.

Paper would not have been used for darts—it was too valuable.

Postmen did not deliver letters from door to door, so there were no letter-boxes.

The first pedal bicycle was made in 1839.

Electricity was not used for lamps and doorbells in ordinary houses until after 1880.

You don't really think they had skateboards—400 years ago—do you?

You would not have found bottles shaped like this, and food was not tinned until after 1810.

Very few people had piped water, and there were no taps or drains like this.

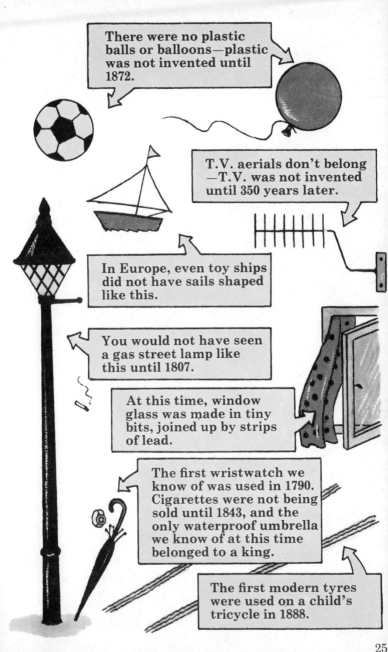

There were no plastic balls or balloons—plastic was not invented until 1872.

T.V. aerials don't belong —T.V. was not invented until 350 years later.

In Europe, even toy ships did not have sails shaped like this.

You would not have seen a gas street lamp like this until 1807.

At this time, window glass was made in tiny bits, joined up by strips of lead.

The first wristwatch we know of was used in 1790. Cigarettes were not being sold until 1843, and the only waterproof umbrella we know of at this time belonged to a king.

The first modern tyres were used on a child's tricycle in 1888.

25

Spot the Fakes

A gang of thieves stole seven antiques from the shop in the picture below. They swapped each with a badly-made fake, hoping the owner would not notice how much was gone. On the right you can see how the shop looked after the raid. How many of the fakes can you spot? (Turn the page upside-down to check what you find.)

These are the mistakes in the fake antiques:
1 The mirror's frame is wrong. 2 The armchair's
legs are straight. 3 The tea and coffee pots are
different. 4 The pistol has no hammer. 5 The suit
of armour has the wrong helmet and has lost a
gauntlet (metal glove). 6 The candle-sticks are
different. 7 There are no birds in the case.

Forgers' Tricks

One of the hardest parts of a forger's job is tricking someone into buying his fakes. But crooks know a lot of ways to fool people. They know how to make cheap things look valuable, and how to convince people that fake things are real. The tricks shown below have fooled a lot of people.

A good detective should learn as much as possible about tricks like these. Remember—the more you know about how forgers work, the better you will be at detecting them.

Fake Discoveries

Sometimes a forger hides things in places where real discoveries might be made.

Then, at just the right moment, he pretends to discover the things he has hidden.

Phoney Expert

Sometimes, crooks work in teams. One pretends
to find something—the other pretends to be an
expert who thinks his 'find' is valuable. (A
really crafty crook may pretend to be the only
expert in the world, in hope of keeping people
from checking up on him.) Below you can see how
a trick like this might work.

Forged Signatures

It is almost impossible to sign someone else's name the way they do it. People write their own names (signatures) so often that they do it without thinking. The way they write their signature may become a scribble with a particular shape, or it may have curls and flourishes.

Try to copy a signature and see what happens. Notice how hard it is to make it look natural. Your hand will hesitate, and make strokes that are too light or heavy. You will probably find that the writing looks stiff and shaky, even if you make each letter perfectly.

Look for things like this when you try the puzzle below. Then turn the page to read more about identifying handwriting.

Spot the Forgeries

One of the signatures above belongs to Iain G. Ashman. The others are forgeries. They were copied (or traced) by crooks trying to get money from him.

Can you spot the forgeries—and pick out the genuine signature? Compare the writing with the sample at the top of the next page. (The answer is at the bottom.)

Handwriting Sample

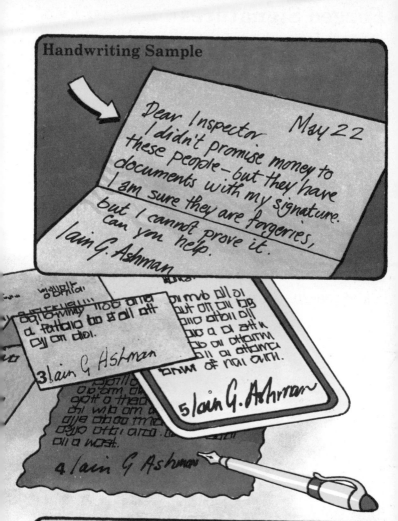

Dear Inspector   May 22
I didn't promise money to
these people—but they have
documents with my signature.
I am sure they are forgeries,
but I cannot prove it.
Can you help.

Iain G. Ashman

3 Iain G Ashman

5 Iain G. Ashman

4 Iain G Ashman

Answer

Number 1 is Iain Ashman's signature. Number
5 was traced—notice the short, unconnected
strokes, like the lines of a drawing rather
than handwriting. The rest were copied.

Handwriting Identification

Being able to identify handwriting may help you trace a criminal or find the writer of an anonymous letter. Read the points below and then try the test on the right.

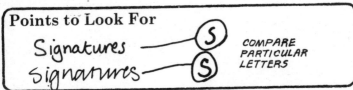

Points to Look For

Signatures

Signatures

COMPARE PARTICULAR LETTERS

First, notice how the writer makes particular letters. Check whether he always makes the letter in the same way. If not, when does he change it?

If possible, compare the writing with a sample from someone who uses the same style. This will help you see some of the tiny differences.

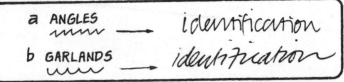

a ANGLES → identification

b GARLANDS → identification

Next, look at how the letters are joined up. (The names of two main ways of joining-up are

shown above.) Are they crowded together or strung out? Which way do they slant?

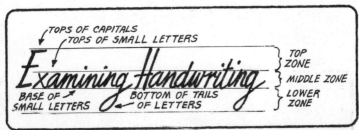

TOPS OF CAPITALS
TOPS OF SMALL LETTERS

Examining Handwriting

TOP ZONE
MIDDLE ZONE
LOWER ZONE

BASE OF SMALL LETTERS
BOTTOM OF TAILS OF LETTERS

Now, draw four lines, like this. The spaces between are 'zones'.

Compare the size of each zone in different samples of writing.

Handwriting Identification Test

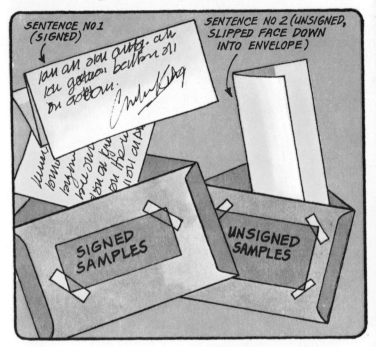

You will need
2 envelopes or small
    boxes
2 slips of paper for each
    person who gives a
    handwriting sample
1 pen or pencil.

First, collect samples of
handwriting from six or
seven people. To do this,
ask each person to copy
two sentences on
separate slips of paper.
Everyone should use the
same sentences and the
same pen (or pencil).

One sentence should be
signed. This is put in
an envelope marked
'signed sample'. The
other sentence, written
secretly and not signed,
should be slipped face
down into a different
envelope.

When you have finished
collecting samples,
shuffle the unsigned
sentences without looking
at them. Then try to
match them to the signed
samples, and work out
who wrote each one.

The Case of Miss Atkins's Will

When Tabitha Atkins died, aged 92, it was expected that her fortune would go to the cats' home owned by her friend Lucy Potter. Miss Atkins had said so, when she made her will. Everyone knew that she had not spoken to her only relative, John Jasper, for many years.

But when her will was opened, it was found that Jasper had inherited her fortune. Miss Potter told detectives that she believed the will had been forged.

At the top of the next page you can see Jasper and Miss Potter, who both thought they should have the fortune. On the right is the will, spread out to show where the important bits are.

NEWSPAPER STORY PRINTED WHEN MISS ATKINS MADE HER FIRST WILL

34

The New Heir

Miss Potter

The will was typewritten except for a few lines Miss Atkins added on the last page. The important bits are circled—below you can read what they say. Do they look suspicious to you? Turn the page to see how the case was solved.

The Will

A Except for the gifts I have put in this will, all of my fortune shall go to the cats at Kitty Korner. It shall belong to them

B for six months only, and then shall become the property of my nephew, John Jasper

C forever.

D To my nephew John Jasper I leave £10, but he must use my gifts to buy a copy of the magazine 'Kitty Kapers' every month as long as he lives.

Checking a Document

When detectives examined the will, they found that Jasper had forged page 3. He had changed the numbers so that the real page 3 became page 4. This completely changed the meaning of what Miss Atkins wrote. The main part of the will should have said: 'My fortune shall go to the cats at Kitty Korner. It shall belong to them forever.'

Here are the clues detectives found.

Watermark

Good stationery often has a watermark that shows what brand it is—you can see it when you hold it to the light. Page 3 had a different watermark from the other pages in the will.

Staple Marks

Pages 1, 2 and 4 had two sets of staple marks, showing that they had been stapled together, and then stapled again when page 3 was added. But page 3 had only one set of staple marks.

Forged Letter

Jasper had forged the letter 's' in the handwritten sentence on the last page. The 's' was crowded in— and a magnifying glass showed how the ink blurred where it crossed the fold in the paper.

CROWDED LETTER

Notice how crowded the letter 's' is.

FEATHERY MARKS AND BLOTS

The crease roughens the paper and makes the ink spread out and blot.

Typewriter Clues

Jasper used a different kind of typewriter on the page he forged. Check the type made by different kinds of machine, and you will see how easily you can tell them apart. With a magnifying glass, you can even see how the type is worn in special ways on a certain typewriter.

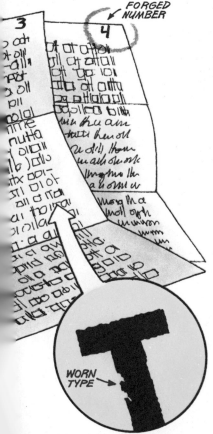

FORGED NUMBER

WORN TYPE

Can Photographs Lie?

Here are some amazing stories, with photographs to prove them. Photographs cannot lie, can they?

Turn the page to see.

MONSTER BIRD ATTACKS LONDONER

UFO OVER CITY

PHOTOGRAPHER SNAPS
MAIDSTONE GHOST

The Secret of the Maidstone Ghost

To make the fake ghost picture, we took an ordinary photograph of a door. Then we had the film developed.

Then we painted a ghostly shape onto the film (you could try it with poster paints) and had it printed.

Fake UFO

The UFO was just a saucer-shaped metal lampshade. One person threw it into the air while another photographed it, using a fast speed on a camera.

Fake Monster Bird

The monster bird and its victim were paper shapes, glued to a window. The photographer who took the picture was standing about a metre away, inside the room.

Faking Monsters

You can use the monster bird trick to photograph fake UFO's, witches on broomsticks, or any flying monster. The windows should be very clean, and there should be no overhead lights on in the room—they might reflect in the window.

Remember that in most cameras, what you see in the viewfinder is a bit different from what the camera 'sees'. This makes it hard to match the paper shape perfectly with the scene outside. Be sure to leave a gap between them.

Detecting Fake Photographs

Always remember that even a truthful photograph only shows part of a scene. Also, it can give you a very false idea of the distance between the things it shows.

When you see a photograph, try to imagine how the scene might have looked if it had been photographed from a different angle. Also, try to work out what might have been happening around it. Below you can see more of the tricks that the camera can play.

Part Pictures

Suppose a photograph shows a scene like this. The person on the left looks threatening and the person on the right looks frightened.

But if you could see the real scene, it might look something like this. (A good detective should double-check everything.)

Action Pictures

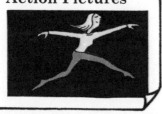

Be suspicious of any action shot that has a black background. This person seems to be making a big leap . . . .

But she is really lying on the ground, on a dark cloth. (In a photograph, you cannot be sure which way is up.)

The Case of the Dirty Burglar

This is the scene found by detectives when they were called about the theft of some rare books. The only witness was a guest of the owner of the books. (His story is shown below.)

Several clues seemed to show that the burglar had entered and left the room through the window. But the detectives were suspicious. Can you see why? Turn the page to see how the case was solved.

43

Detecting Fake Clues

A good detective should always be on guard against phoney clues. A clever crook may have made them to throw you off his track—or to lead you to pin the crime on someone else.

When you are listening to a story, or examining clues, always ask yourself, 'Is it true?' and, 'How did it happen?' Remember that you can often solve a case if you know what questions to ask.

Begin by asking yourself what would have happened if you were the crook. Think about each move he would have made. You might even want to go over each step yourself, to find out what clues you should be looking for.

In the Dirty Burglar Case, the trail of footprints was a fake. Below you can see how this was discovered. Now that you know this, try asking some other questions about the case. Check them with the things the detectives asked. See how close you come to the solution.

How Did it Happen?

To find out whether an outsider would have made the tracks, you have to work out how he might have come through the window. Here are all the most natural ways of getting through the window—none of them would have made the prints that were found.

Backwards

TOES WOULD MARK WALL

PRINTS WOULD FACE WALL

How the Case Was Solved

When the detectives got this far, the witness confessed that he had taken the books. Before this, he had muddied his shoes in the flower bed outside the window, carried them indoors, and placed them under the window. Then he stepped into them, made the tracks, took the books, broke the window, and handed the books and shoes to an accomplice outside.

1 How did the thief climb through the window?

2 If he was tall, how could he jump quickly through a small window?

3 If short, how could he reach the books without the stool? (His tracks go past it.)

4 How did he know which books were valuable—and how was he able to find them without searching the shelves?

5 If he broke the window from outside, why did all the glass fall on the outside sill?

6 How could the witness have seen him take the books? (The door would have been in the way.)

7 Why is the witness fully dressed, but wearing slippers?

Forwards (Slowly)

WOULD LEAVE TOE PRINTS CLOSE TO THE WALL

HEELS WOULD MARK WALL

Forwards (Quickly)

PRINTS WOULD BE FOUND AT A DISTANCE FROM WALL

45

Fake Evidence

'Evidence' is what backs up a story. A good detective always checks that the evidence really fits the story. If it doesn't, it may be fake. Try this case for practice.

The Story

A man who worked for J. G. Jewellers claimed he was robbed while taking their money to the bank. Below is the evidence for his story.

The Evidence

SCRATCH ON FACE

TEAR IN JACKET

"The money was in my right hand. The thief grabbed me from behind, covering my mouth so that I could not call for help."

"Look at the scratch I got from the ring he was wearing. I tore my best jacket trying to stop him —but he got away."

Cracking the Story

Two detectives acted out the story. This showed that:

1 The crook's ring would have scratched the left side of the man's face.
2 The man would probably have torn the sleeve of his free arm (the left) if he had struggled with the crook.

Then the man admitted that he had faked the evidence and hidden the money so that he could keep it himself.

Fake Accidents

Crooks sometimes try to make things look like accidents when they were really done on purpose. Below are pictures of the scene of an 'accident'. Study them to see if it was faked.

The Story

In this case, a crook told his insurance company that he had parked his car to look at a cliff-top view, and it accidentally rolled over the cliff. He said that he had just managed to jump out in time. Do you believe him?

The arrow shows where the car was last seen.

These tracks were found near the cliff edge.

Here is a picture of the wrecked car.

Cracking the Story

The crook had pushed an old car over the cliff so that he could get insurance money and still keep his own car. These are the clues:

1 A sign shows that the cliff is dangerous.

2 The footprints are deep and point outwards— signs of someone pushing something heavy. The toe-prints show where the car began to roll.

3 The crook had taken off the handbrake.

Seeing Through Disguises

Sidney Lurchpast, a well-known criminal, was able to escape detection for many years by using fake identities and clever disguises. Could you have spotted him?

Below are pictures taken by detectives while on his trail. Some are Lurchpast in disguise. Some are innocent people. To work out which is which, think carefully about what can be disguised and what cannot. Then turn the page to find out more about seeing through disguises.

Which of These Are Really Sidney Lurchpast?

884/57   884/57

3

4

7

8

49

Identifying Lurchpast

Lurchpast was a master of disguise. He used false hair and beards, even false eyebrows and often a false nose. But if you trace his head and shoulders, you will find they fit into all but the last pictures in each row.

The man in picture 4 has a different jaw and a longer neck than Lurchpast, and the man in picture 8 has a smaller ear. These are things that cannot be faked or changed.

As a good detective, learn to ignore the showy things that can be faked and keep your mind on the things that permanently identify people. Below are more of the tricks that Lurchpast used. On the right is another case to test your powers of observation.

The Fake Identities of Sidney Lurchpast

Lurchpast used lots of actors' tricks. He knew that what people often notice most about someone is the way he stands and moves about.

In one identity, he slouched and swaggered. In another identity, he always stooped a little. Notice what a difference it makes.

Spot the Imposters

RODERICK ROEHART HOUSEKEEPER FOTHERGILL ROEHART (RODERICK'S UNCLE)

Here is a photograph of Roderick Roehart, taken just before he set out to explore Brazil. Soon after, his expedition was reported lost.

Years later, when his uncle died, all three people shown below claimed the Roehart fortune. Which could be Roderick Roehart?

Which is the Real Roderick Roehart?

HOUSEKEEPER

Obviously, the years have changed Roderick. The hardships he suffered in Brazil have made him thin, bald, and tired.

But you can pick him out from the others by his height, rather short arms, and smallish feet. He is the man on the right.

Finding Hidden Loot

If a forger suspects you are after him, he may hide evidence or stolen loot in secret places in his house or garden. Here are some things you should know about.

Phoney Wall Clues

You can sometimes detect a hollow wall by the sound it makes when you rap your knuckles on it. Learn the different sounds made when you tap on thick main walls, thin dividing walls, and the walls of a cupboard.

If possible, compare the measurements of the rooms and work out how they fit together.

Look for new boards or nails, or fresh paint or plaster, if you think a wall has been boarded up.

DYING SHRUB   WATER TEST

NEW TURF

Buried Loot

If you suspect fresh digging, look for new turf—it will have a slightly different colour from the rest. A plant may wilt if its roots are disturbed by digging.

Remember that water poured on newly-turned earth sinks in faster than it does in packed earth. (To test this, pour lots of water on a bare patch of ground.)

The Farmhouse Forgery Raid

This lonely cottage was used as a hideout by
the team later known as the Farmhouse Forgers.
Thousands of pounds' worth of counterfeit
notes and coins were found in this room. Yet
when detectives entered, this is all they saw.

Do you notice anything suspicious? Where
would you have started looking for the money?
Turn the page for details of the raid.

Discovering the Loot

Below you can see the loot found stashed in the cottage and some of the emergency hiding-places the forgers used.

The forgers were tipped off only minutes before the raid took place. They had to act quickly, hoping the detectives would make only a hasty search. They disguised themselves as an elderly couple to put them off the scent.

The Haul

The main part of the haul was found in the oven, in strong boxes. But notes were also found under the chair cushions and slipped between the picture and its frame. Coins were found in the flower vases, in the stew, and under the gravel in the fishbowl. Other finds are shown below.

High Points of the Raid

The pot turned towards the wall held notes.

Bundles of notes were taped under the table.

But several things looked wrong to the detectives. Did you notice the crooked picture, the disturbed-looking goldfish, and the way the flowers were stuffed into the vases? Most suspicious of all, the dog was barking at his 'mistress' – and not at the strangers at the door.

All this looked very odd to the detectives, so they went ahead and made a thorough search.

Notes were stuffed inside the cut loaf.

Coins were found in the pancake batter.

Famous Fakes

Fakes often succeed only because people want to believe in them. Here are some good examples—would they have fooled you?

Turn the page to read about one of the most famous fakes in history.

Dr. Koch's Sea-Serpent

From 1845 to 1848, crowds of people paid to see this skeleton. Its owner, Dr. Koch, said that it belonged to a sea-serpent. In fact, he had made it himself from bits of much smaller animals.

Dr. Berringer's Fossils

Real fossils are the remains of plants and animals that died long ago and turned to stone.

These fakes were carved by hand. They were brought to Dr. Berringer in about 1725.

Fake Mermaids

This is one of several 'mermaids' shown in London about a hundred years ago. It is really a stuffed monkey with a fish's tail sewn to it.

Dr. Berringer wrote a book about his collection. He was so proud of it that at first he refused to

believe that most of them were fakes—even after the forgers told him what they had done.

Piltdown Man

A human skull dug up at Piltdown, England, in 1912, became world-famous. Experts who examined the skull were very excited – they said it was a two-million-year-old-fossil. For forty years it was displayed as the 'missing link' between modern man and his ape ancestors.

In fact, it was a total fake. The skull was not a fossil and the jaw belonged to an orang-utan. The pieces had been cleverly matched up and faked to look old, probably by being boiled in a kind of acid. Who the forger was, and why he did it, is still something of a mystery.

Complicated tests were made when the forgery was uncovered in 1953. But one of the most glaring bits of evidence came from a simple mistake the forger made—the kind of small detail a good detective should have noticed, if he had really looked.

Teeth Clue

These are the back teeth of Piltdown Man. As you can see, they slant in different directions. They had actually been filed down to make them look like human teeth. (Apes do not chew their food the way we do, so their teeth do not wear down the same way.) A microscope showed the tell-tale scratches.

The top drawing here shows how the bones found at Piltdown were fitted together. Notice that the skull looks like a man's skull, but the jaw looks like an ape's.

Warning!

A good detective should always ask himself, 'Is it true? Or could it be a fake?' He should try to imagine what tricks he might have used, if he were a forger.

When the teeth of the Piltdown Man were finally examined, the scratches looked very suspicious. Yet for forty years, no one bothered to examine them.

Know Your Experts

As a good detective, it is important to know where to go when you need help and who to ask. Below are some useful names to know. Try to learn to say the names correctly—it will help if you need to ask for information.

Get to know your local library and museums too. Some museums have certain days when they will give you advice on things or answer questions. The library can help a lot if you learn how to use it.

Handwriting Expert— Graphologist

DETECTIVES MAY CALL IN EXPERTS TO BACK UP THEIR CASE IN A LAW-COURT

Coin Expert— Numismatist

A SET OF MEDALS WON BY A SINGLE PERSON IS MORE VALUABLE THAN SEPARATE MEDALS

If you collect things like stamps or coins, you could make this a special study and become an expert yourself.

It may be easier than you think to start a collection. Take a look at your old toys and comics—some day they may be valuable. In the future, a set of toy models may be all that is left to show the history of cars at a certain time—or of spacecraft or soldiers' uniforms. Try to make complete sets, if you can.

Stamp Expert— Philatelist

DISPLAY CASES FOR STAMPS

Plant and Animal Expert— Zoologist

Detective Language

Accomplice—A crook's partner, or someone who helps him commit a crime.

Clue—Something that helps you work out part of a mystery, or solve a crime.

Counterfeit—A copy. Forged money is often called counterfeit money.

Documents—Important papers.

Expert—Someone who has special knowledge about certain things, or is particularly skilful.

Fake—Something that is not what it seems to be.

Forger—Someone who makes copies or who changes things in order to trick and cheat people. (A document with words rubbed out or added to change its meaning is said to be forged.)

Imposter—Someone who pretends to be a different person, in order to cheat people.

Lead—A lead is a clue that gives you ideas about where to look for more clues.

Old Master—A famous painter who lived a long time ago.

Plate—The bit that goes into a printing press to make it print a certain pattern.

Solve—To find an answer or work out a problem.

Watermark—A mark pressed into paper when it is made. (It shows up when the paper is wet.)

The Sᴀɴꜰᴏʀᴅ Gᴜɪᴅᴇꜱ are updated annually and published by:

ANTIMICROBIAL THERAPY, INC.

P.O. Box 276, 11771 Lee Highway,
Sperryville, VA 22740-0276 USA
Tel 540-987-9480 Fax 540-987-9486
Email: info@sanfordguide.com   www.sanfordguide.com

Acknowledgements

Thanks to Ushuaia Solutions, SA, Argentina; Alcom Printing, Harleysville, PA and Fox Bindery,
Quakertown, PA for design and production of this edition of the Sᴀɴꜰᴏʀᴅ Gᴜɪᴅᴇ.

Note to Readers

Since 1969, the Sᴀɴꜰᴏʀᴅ Gᴜɪᴅᴇ has been independently prepared and published. Decisions regarding
the content of the Sᴀɴꜰᴏʀᴅ Gᴜɪᴅᴇ are solely those of the editors and the publisher. We welcome
questions, comments and feedback concerning the Sᴀɴꜰᴏʀᴅ Gᴜɪᴅᴇ. All of your feedback is reviewed
and taken into account in updating the content of the the Sᴀɴꜰᴏʀᴅ Gᴜɪᴅᴇ.

Every effort is made to ensure the accuracy of the content of this guide. However, current full prescribing
information available in the package insert for each drug should be consulted before prescribing any
product. The editors and publisher are not responsible for errors or omissions or for any consequences
from application of the information in this book and make no warranty, express or implied, with respect
to the currency, accuracy, or completeness of the contents of this publication. Application of this
information in a particular situation remains the professional responsibility of the practitioner.

Check our website for content-related notices:
http://www.sanfordguide.com

Printed in the United States of America
ISBN 978-1-930808-74-4
Pocket Edition (English)

MIX
Paper from
responsible sources
FSC® C006218
www.fsc.org

MANUFACTURED BY AN
SGP
FACILITY
Sustainable Green Printing Partnership

RAINFOREST ALLIANCE
CERTIFIED

QUICK PAGE GUIDE TO THE SANFORD GUIDE[*]

[*] Adapted from materials provided by Stephanie Troy, M.D., Stanford Univ. Med. Ctr.

—TABLE OF CONTENTS—

ABBREVIATIONS

3TC = lamivudine
AB% = percent absorbed
ABCD = amphotericin B colloidal dispersion
ABLC = ampho B lipid complex
ACIP = Advisory Committee on Immunization Practices
AD = after dialysis
ADR = additive
AG = aminoglycoside
AIDS = Acquired Immune Deficiency Syndrome
AM-CL = amoxicillin-clavulanate
AM-CL-ER = amoxicillin-clavulanate extended release
AMK = amikacin
Amox = amoxicillin
AMP = ampicillin
Ampho B = amphotericin B
AM-SB = ampicillin-sulbactam
AP = atovaquone proguanil
AP Pen = antipseudomonal penicillins
APAG = antipseudomonal aminoglycoside (tobra, gent, amikacin)
ARDS = acute respiratory distress syndrome
ARF = acute rheumatic fever
ASA = aspirin
ATS = American Thoracic Society
ATV = atazanavir
AUC = area under the curve
Azithro = azithromycin
bid = twice a day
BL/BLI = beta-lactam/beta-lactamase inhibitor
BSA = body surface area
BW = body weight
CAPD = continuous ambulatory peritoneal dialysis
CARB = carbapenems (DORI, ERTA, IMP, MER)
CDC = Centers for Disease Control
Cefpodox = cefpodoxime proxetil
Ceftaz = ceftazidime
Ceph = cephalosporin
CFB = ceftobiprole
CFP = cefepime
Chloro = chloramphenicol
CIP = ciprofloxacin; CIP-ER = CIP extended release
Clarithro = clarithromycin; ER = extended release
Clav = clavulanate
Clinda = clindamycin
CLO = clofazimine
CMV = cytomegalovirus
CQ = chloroquine phosphate
Cobi = cobicistat
CrCl = creatinine clearance
CrCl/BSA = CrCl normalized for body surface area (BSA)
CRRT = continuous renal replacement therapy

CSD = cat-scratch disease
CSF = cerebrospinal fluid
CXR = chest x-ray
d4T = stavudine
Dapto = daptomycin
DBPCT = double-blind placebo-controlled trial
dc = discontinue
ddC = zalcitabine
ddI = didanosine
DIC = disseminated intravascular coagulation
div = divided
DLV = delavirdine
Dori = doripenem
DOT = directly observed therapy
DOT group = B. distasonis, B. ovatus, B. thetaiotaomicron
Doxy = doxycycline
DRC = delayed release
DRSP = drug-resistant S. pneumoniae
DS = double strength
EBV = Epstein-Barr virus
EES = erythromycin ethyl succinate
EFZ = efavirenz
ELV = elvitegravir
ENT = entecavir
ER = extended release
ERTA = ertapenem
Erythro = erythromycin
ESBLs = extended spectrum β-lactamases
ESR = erythrocyte sedimentation rate
ESRD = endstage renal disease
ETB = ethambutol
Flu = fluconazole
Flucyt = flucytosine
FOS-APV = fosamprenavir
FQ = fluoroquinolone (CIP, Oflox, Lome, Peflox, Levo, Gati, Moxi, Gemi)
FTC = emtricitabine
G = generic
GAS = Group A Strep
Gati = gatifloxacin
GC = gonorrhea
Gemi = gemifloxacin
Gent = gentamicin
gm = gram
GNB = gram-negative bacilli
grise = griseofulvin
HEMO = hemodialysis
HHV = human herpesvirus
HIV = human immunodeficiency virus
HLR = high-level resistance
H/O = history of
HSCT = hematopoietic stem cell transplant
HSV = herpes simplex virus

IA = injectable agent/anti-inflammatory drugs
ICAAC = Interscience Conference on Antimicrobial Agents & Chemotherapy
IDSA = Infectious Diseases Society of America
IFN = interferon
IMP = imipenem-cilastatin
INH = isoniazid
Inv = investigational
IT = intrathecal
Itra = itraconazole
IVDU = intravenous drug user
IVIG = intravenous immune globulin
Keto = ketoconazole
LAB = liposomal ampho B
LCM = lymphocytic choriomeningitis virus
LCR = ligase chain reaction
Levo = levofloxacin
LP/r = lopinavir/ritonavir
Macrolides = azithro, clarithro, dirithro, erythro, roxithro
M. Tbc = Mycobacterium tuberculosis
mcg = microgram
MER = meropenem
Metro = metronidazole
mg = milligram
Mino = minocycline
Moxi = moxifloxacin
MQ = mefloquine
MSSA, MRSA = methicillin-sensitive/resistant S. aureus
NB = name drug
NF = nitrofurantoin
NAI = not FDA-approved (indication or dose)
NFR = nelfinavir
NNRTI = non-nucleoside reverse transcriptase inhibitor
NRTI = nucleoside reverse transcriptase inhibitor
NSAIDs = non-steroidal
NUS = not available in the U.S.
NVP = nevirapine
O Ceph 1, 2, 3 = oral cephalosporins—see Table 10A
Oflox = ofloxacin
P Ceph 1, 2, 3, 4 = parenteral cephalosporins—see Table 10A
P Ceph 3 AP = parenteral cephalosporins with antipseudomonal activity—see Table 10A
PCR = polymerase chain reaction
PEP = post-exposure prophylaxis
PI = protease inhibitor
PIP = piperacillin
PIP-TZ = piperacillin-tazobactam
po = per os (by mouth)
PQ = primaquine
PRCT = prospective randomized controlled trials
PTLD = post-transplant lymphoproliferative disease

ABBREVIATIONS (2)

Pts = patients
Pyri = pyrimethamine
PZA = pyrazinamide
qid = 4 times a day
QS = quinine sulfate
Quinu-dalfo = Q-D = quinupristin-dalfopristin
R = resistant
RIF = rifampin
RFB = rifabutine
Rick = Rickettsia
RIF = rifampin
RSV = respiratory syncytial virus
RTI = respiratory tract infection
RTV = ritonavir
Rx = treatment
rx = potential synergy in combination with penicillin, AMP, vanco, teico

SA = Staph. aureus
SD = serum drug level after single dose
Sens = sensitive / susceptible
SM = streptomycin
SQV = saquinavir
SS = steady state serum level
STD = sexually transmitted disease
subcut = subcutaneous
Sulb = sulbactam
Sx = symptoms
Tazo = tazobactam
TBc = tuberculosis
TC-CL = ticarcillin-clavulanate
TDF = tenofovir
TEE = transesophageal echocardiography
Teico = teicoplanin
Telithro = telithromycin

Tetra = tetracycline
Ticar = ticarcillin
tid = 3 times a day
TMP-SMX = trimethoprim-sulfamethoxazole
TNF = tumor necrosis factor
Tobra = tobramycin
TPV = tipranavir
TST = tuberculin skin test
UTI = urinary tract infection
Vanco = vancomycin
VISA = vancomycin intermediately resistant S. aureus
VL = viral load
Vori = voriconazole
VZV = varicella-zoster virus
WHO = World Health Organization
ZDV = zidovudine

ABBREVIATIONS OF JOURNAL TITLES

AAC: Antimicrobial Agents & Chemotherapy
Adv PID: Advances in Pediatric Infectious Diseases
AHJ: American Heart Journal
AIDS: AIDS
AIDS Res & HR: AIDS Research & Human Retroviruses
AJG: American Journal of Gastroenterology
AJM: American Journal of Medicine
AJRCCM: American Journal of Respiratory Critical Care Medicine
AJTMH: American Journal of Tropical Medicine & Hygiene
Aliment Pharmacol Ther: Alimentary Pharmacology & Therapeutics
Am J Hlth: The American Journal of Health-System Pharmacy
Amer J Transpl: American Journal of Transplantation
AnEM: Annals of Emergency Medicine
AnIM: Annals of Internal Medicine
Ann Pharmacother: Annals of Pharmacotherapy
AnSurg: Annals of Surgery
Antivir Ther: Antiviral Therapy
ArDerm: Archives of Dermatology
ArIM: Archives of Internal Medicine
ARRD: American Review of Respiratory Disease
BMJ: British Medical Journal
BMT: Bone Marrow Transplantation
Brit J Derm: British Journal of Dermatology
Can JID: Canadian Journal of Infectious Diseases
Canad Med J: Canadian Medical Journal
CCM: Critical Care Medicine
CCTID: Current Clinical Topics in Infectious Disease
CDBSR: Cochrane Database of Systematic Reviews
CID: Clinical Infectious Diseases
Clin Micro Inf: Clinical Microbiology and Infection
CMN: Clinical Microbiology Newsletter
Clin Micro Rev: Clinical Microbiology Reviews
CMAJ: Canadian Medical Association Journal

COID: Current Opinion in Infectious Disease
Curr Med Res Opin: Current Medical Research and Opinion
Derm Ther: Dermatologic Therapy
Dermatol Clin: Dermatologic Clinics
Dig Dis Sci: Digestive Diseases and Sciences
DMID: Diagnostic Microbiology and Infectious Disease
EID: Emerging Infectious Diseases
EJCMID: European Journal of Clin. Micro. & Infectious Diseases
Eur J Neurol: European Journal of Neurology
Eur J Neuropath: European Journal of Neuropathology
Exp Rev Anti Infect Ther: Expert Review of Anti-Infective Therapy
Gastro: Gastroenterology
Hpt: Hepatology
ICHE: Infection Control and Hospital Epidemiology
IDCP: Infectious Diseases in Clinical Practice
IDC No. Amer: Infectious Disease Clinics of North America
IJAA: International Journal of Antimicrobial Agents
Inf Med: Infections in Medicine
J AIDS & HR: Journal of AIDS and Human Retrovirology
J All Clin Immun: Journal of Allergy and Clinical Immunology
J Am Ger Soc: Journal of the American Geriatrics Society
J Chemother: Journal of Chemotherapy
J Clin Micro: Journal of Clinical Microbiology
J Clin Virol: Journal of Clinical Virology
J Derm Treat: Journal of Dermatological Treatment
J Hep: Journal of Hepatology
J Infect: Journal of Infection
J Med Micro: Journal of Medical Microbiology
J Micro Immunol Inf: Journal of Microbiology, Immunology & Infection
J Ped: Journal of Pediatrics
J Viral Hep: Journal of Viral Hepatitis

JAC: Journal of Antimicrobial Chemotherapy
JACC: Journal of American College of Cardiology
JAIDS: JAIDS Journal of Acquired Immune Deficiency Syndromes
JAMA: Journal of the American Medical Association
JAVMA: Journal of the Veterinary Medicine Association
JCI: Journal of Clinical Investigation
JCM: Journal of Clinical Microbiology
JIC: Journal of Infection and Chemotherapy
JID: Journal of Infectious Diseases
JNS: Journal of Neurosurgery
JTMH: Journal of Tropical Medicine and Hygiene
Ln: Lancet
LnID: Lancet Infectious Disease
Mayo Clin Proc: Mayo Clinic Proceedings
Med Lett: Medical Letter
Med Mycol: Medical Mycology
MMWR: Morbidity & Mortality Weekly Report
NEJM: New England Journal of Medicine
Neph Dial Transpl: Nephrology Dialysis Transplantation
Ped Ann: Pediatric Annals
Peds: Pediatrics
Pharmacother: Pharmacotherapy
PIDJ: Pediatric Infectious Disease Journal
QJM: Quarterly Journal of Medicine
Scand J Inf Dis: Scandinavian Journal of Infectious Diseases
Sem Resp Inf: Seminars in Respiratory Infections
Sep: Surgery Gynecology and Obstetrics
SMJ: Southern Medical Journal
Surg Neurol: Surgical Neurology
Transpl: Transplantation
Transpl Inf Dis: Transplant Infectious Diseases
TRSM: Transactions of the Royal Society of Medicine

TABLE 1 – CLINICAL APPROACH TO INITIAL CHOICE OF ANTIMICROBIAL THERAPY*

Treatment based on presumed site or type of infection. In selected instances, treatment and prophylaxis based on identification of pathogens.
Regimens should be reevaluated based on pathogen isolated, antimicrobial susceptibility determination, and individual host characteristics. *(Abbreviations on page 2)*

ANATOMIC SITE/DIAGNOSIS/ MODIFYING CIRCUMSTANCES	ETIOLOGIES (usual)	SUGGESTED REGIMENS* PRIMARY	SUGGESTED REGIMENS* ALTERNATIVE§	ADJUNCT DIAGNOSTIC OR THERAPEUTIC MEASURES AND COMMENTS
ABDOMEN: *See Peritoneum, page 47; Gallbladder, page 17; and Pelvic Inflammatory Disease, page 26*				
BONE: Osteomyelitis. Microbiologic diagnosis is essential. If blood culture negative, need culture of bone. Culture of sinus tract drainage not predictive of bone culture. Review: *Ln 364-369, 2004.* For comprehensive review of antimicrobial penetration into bone, see *Clinical Pharmacokinetics 48:89, 2009.*				
Hematogenous Osteomyelitis				
Empiric therapy—Collect bone and blood cultures before empiric therapy				
Newborn (< 4 mos.)	S. aureus, Gm-neg. bacilli, Group B strep	**MRSA possible: Vanco+ Ceftaz or CFP**	**MRSA unlikely: Natcillin/ oxacillin + (Ceftaz or CFP)**	*Table 16 for dose. Severe allergy or toxicity:* (**Linezolid**^AUI 10 mg/kg IV/po q8h + **aztreonam**). Could substitute **clindamycin** for linezolid
Children (>4 mos.) — Adult: Osteo of extremity	S. aureus; Group A strep, Gm-neg. bacilli rare	**MRSA possible: Vanco** Add **Ceftaz or CFP** if Gm-neg. bacilli on Gram stain. **Adult doses below. Peds Doses: Table 16.**	**MRSA unlikely: Natcillin or oxacillin**	Severe allergy or toxicity: **Clinda** or **TMP-SMX** or **linezolid**^AUI. Adults: **ceftaz** 2 gm IV q8h. **CFP** 2 gm IV q12h. *Peds dosages in Table 16. See Table 10B for adverse reactions to drugs.*
Adult (>21 yrs) **Vertebral osteo ± epidural abscess** (other sites, e.g. *NEJM 355:2012, 2006*)	S. aureus most common but variety other organisms. **Blood & bone cultures essential.**	**MRSA possible: Vanco** 15-30 mg/kg IV q8-12h for trough of 15-20 mcg/ml	**MRSA unlikely: Natcillin or oxacillin** 2 gm IV q4h	**Dx: MRI early to look for epidural abscess.** For comprehensive review of vertebral see *NEJM 362:11, 2010.*
Specific therapy—Culture and in vitro susceptibility results known				
	MSSA	Natcillin or oxacillin 2 gm IV q4h or ceftazolin 2 gm IV q8h	**Vanco** 15-30 mg/kg IV q 8-12h for trough of 15-20 mcg/ml ± **RIF** 300-450 mg po/IV bid	**Other options if susceptible in vitro and allergy/toxicity issues** (see *NEJM 362:11, 2010*): 1) **TMP-SMX** 8-10 mg/kg/d po/IV div q8h + **RIF** 300-450 mg bid; limited data, particularly for MRSA (see *AAC 53:2672, 2009*); 2) (**CIP** 750 mg po bid or **Levo** 750 mg po q24h) + **RIF** 300 mg po bid; 3) Linezolid assoc. with optic & peripheral neuropathy with long-term use (*Neurology 64:926, 2005*); 4) **Fusidic acid**^NUS 500 mg IV q8h + **RIF** 300 mg po bid. (*CID 42:394, 2006*). **Ceftriaxone** 2 gm IV q24h (*CID 54:585, 2012*)
	MRSA— See *Table 6, page 78;* IDSA Guidelines *CID 52:e18-55, 2011; CID 52:285-92, 2011*	**Vanco** 15-30 mg/kg IV q8-12h for trough of 15-20 mcg/ml ± **RIF** 300-450 mg bid	**Linezolid** 600 mg q12h IV/po ± **RIF** 300 mg po/IV bid OR **Dapto** 6 mg/kg 2q 24h IV ± **RIF** 300-450 mg po/IV bid	
Hemoglobinopathy: Sickle cell/thalassemia	Salmonella; other Gm-neg. bacilli	**CIP** 400 mg IV q12h	**Levo** 750 mg IV q24h	Thalassemia: transfusion and iron chelation risk factors. Because of decreasing levels of susceptibility to fluoroquinolones among Salmonella spp. and growing resistance among other gram-negative bacilli, would add a second agent (e.g., third-generation cephalosporin) until susceptibility test results available.
Contiguous Osteomyelitis Without Vascular Insufficiency				
Empiric therapy: Get cultures! Foot bone osteo due to nail through tennis shoe	P. aeruginosa	**CIP** 750 mg po bid or **Levo** 750 mg po q24h	**Ceftaz** 2 gm IV q8h or **CFP** 2 gm IV q12h	See *Skin—Nail puncture, page 56.* Need debridement to remove foreign body.

* **DOSAGES SUGGESTED are for adults** (unless otherwise indicated) with clinically severe (often life-threatening) infections. Dosages also assume normal renal function, and not severe hepatic dysfunction.

§ **ALTERNATIVE THERAPY INCLUDES** these considerations: allergy, pharmacology/pharmacokinetics, compliance, costs, local resistance profiles.

TABLE 1 (2)

ANATOMIC SITE/DIAGNOSIS/ MODIFYING CIRCUMSTANCES	ETIOLOGIES (usual)	SUGGESTED REGIMENS*		ADJUNCT DIAGNOSTIC OR THERAPEUTIC MEASURES AND COMMENTS
		PRIMARY	ALTERNATIVE¹	
BONE/Contiguous Osteomyelitis Without Vascular Insufficiency/Empiric therapy *(continued)*				
Long bone, post-internal fixation of fracture	S. aureus, Gm-neg. bacilli, P. aeruginosa	**Vanco** 15-30 mg/kg IV q 8-12h for trough of 15-20 mcg/ml + (**ceftaz or CFP**). See Comment	**Linezolid** 600 mg IV/po bid^[NAI] + (**ceftaz or CFP**). See Comment	Often necessary to remove hardware after union to achieve eradication. May need revascularization. **Regimens listed are empiric.** Adjust after culture data available. If susceptible Gm-neg. bacillus, **CIP** 750 mg po bid or **Levo** 750 mg po q24h. For other S. aureus options: See Hem. Osteo. Specific Therapy, page 4.
Osteonecrosis of the jaw	Probably rare adverse reaction to bisphosphonates	Infection may be secondary to bone necrosis and loss of overlying mucosa. Treatment: minimal surgical debridement, chlorhexidine rinses, antibiotics (e.g., PIP-TZ), NEJM 355:2278, 2006. Evaluate for concomitant actinomycosis, for which specific long-term antibiotic treatment would be warranted (CID 49:1729, 2009).		
Prosthetic joint	See prosthetic joint, page 33			
Spinal implant infection	S. aureus, coag-neg staphylococci, gram-neg bacilli	Onset within 30 days: culture, treat & treat	Onset after 30 days remove implant, culture & treat	See CID 55:1481, 2012
Sternum, post-op	S. aureus, S. epidermidis, occasionally, gram-negative bacilli	**Vanco** 15-30 mg/kg IV q 8-12h recommended for serious infections. (CID 55:1481, 2012)	**Linezolid** 600 mg po/IV^[NAI] bid	Sternal debridement for cultures & removal of necrotic bone. For S. aureus options: Hem. Osteo. Specific Therapy, page 4. If setting or gram stain suggests possibility of gram-negative bacilli, add appropriate coverage based on local antimicrobial susceptibility profiles (e.g., cefepime, pip-tazo).
Contiguous Osteomyelitis With Vascular Insufficiency				
Most pts are **diabetics** with peripheral neuropathy & infected skin ulcers (see Diabetic foot, page 16)	Polymicrobic (Gm+ cocci (to include MRSA) (aerobic & anaerobic) Gm-neg. bacilli (aerobic & anaerobic))	Debride overlying ulcer & submit bone for histology & culture. Select antibiotic based on culture results & treat for 6 weeks. **No empiric therapy unless acutely ill.** If acutely ill, see suggestions, Diabetic foot, page 16. Revascularize if possible.		**Diagnosis of osteo:** Culture bone biopsy (gold standard). Poor concordance of culture results between swab of ulcer and bone – need bone. (CID 42:57, 63, 2006). Sampling by needle puncture inferior to biopsy (CID 48:888, 2009). Osteo more likely if ulcer >2 cm², positive probe to bone, ESR >70 & abnormal plain x-ray (JAMA 299:806, 2008). **Treatment: (1) Revascularize if possible;** (2) Culture bone; (3) Specific antimicrobial(s). Reviews: BMJ 339:b4905, 2006; Plast Reconstr Surg 117: (7 Suppl):212S, 2006.
Chronic Osteomyelitis: Specific therapy By definition, implies presence of dead bone. **Need valid cultures**	S. aureus, Enterobacteriaceae, P. aeruginosa	**Empiric rx is not indicated.** Base systemic rx on results of culture, sensitivity testing. If acute exacerbation of chronic osteo, rx as acute hematogenous osteo. Surgical debridement important.		**Important adjuncts:** removal of orthopedic hardware, surgical debridement, vascularized muscle flaps, distraction osteogenesis (Ilizarov) techniques. Antibiotic-impregnated cement & hyperbaric oxygen adjunctive. **NOTE: RIF + Vanco or β-lactam)** effective in animal model and in a clinical trial of S. aureus chronic osteo. The contribution of rifampin-containing regimens in this setting is not clear, however (AAC 53:2672, 2009).

Abbreviations on page 2.　　NOTE: All dosage recommendations are for adults (unless otherwise indicated) and assume normal renal function.

TABLE 1 (3)

ANATOMIC SITE/DIAGNOSIS/ MODIFYING CIRCUMSTANCES	ETIOLOGIES (usual)	SUGGESTED REGIMENS* PRIMARY	SUGGESTED REGIMENS* ALTERNATIVE†	ADJUNCT DIAGNOSTIC OR THERAPEUTIC MEASURES AND COMMENTS
BREAST: Mastitis—Obtain culture: need to know if MRSA present. Review with definitions: *Ob & Gyn Clin No Amer 29:89, 2002.*				Review of breast infections: *BMJ 342:d396, 2011.*
Postpartum mastitis (*CID 54:71, 2012*) Mastitis without abscess	S. aureus; less often S. pyogenes (Gp A or B), E. coli, bacteroides species, maybe Corynebacterium sp. & selected coagulase-neg. staphylococci (e.g.: S. lugdunensis)	**NO MRSA: Outpatient: Dicloxacillin** 500 mg po qid or **cephalexin** 500 mg po qid. **Inpatient: Nafcillin/oxacillin** 2 gm IV q4h	**MRSA Possible: Outpatient: TMP-SMX-DS** tabs 1-2 po bid or, if susceptible, **clinda** 300 mg po qid **Inpatient: Vanco** 1 gm IV q12h; if over 100 kg, 1.5 gm IV q12h.	If no abscess, ↑ freq of nursing may hasten response; discuss age-specific risks to infant of drug exposure through breast milk with pediatrician. Corynebacterium sp. assoc. with chronic granulomatous mastitis (*CID 35:1434, 2002*). With abscess, d/c nursing. **I& D standard;** needle aspiration reported successful (*Am J Surg 182:117, 2001*). Resume breast feeding from affected breast as soon as pain allows.
Mastitis with abscess				Smoking and diabetes may be risk factors (*BMJ 342:d396, 2011*). **If subareolar & odoriferous,** most likely anaerobes; need to **add metro** 500 mg IV/po tid. If not subareolar, staph. Need pretreatment aerobic/anaerobic cultures. Surgical drainage for abscess.
Non-puerperal mastitis with abscess	S. aureus; less often Bacteroides sp. peptostreptococcus, & selected coagulase-neg. staphylococci	*See regimens for Postpartum mastitis, page 6.*		
Breast implant infection	Acute: S. aureus, S. pyogenes. TSS reported. Chronic: Look for rapidly growing Mycobacteria	Acute: **Vanco** 1 gm IV q12h; if over 100 kg, 1.5 gm.	Chronic: Await culture results. See Table 12A for mycobacteria treatment.	*Lancet Infect Dis 5:94, 462, 2005.* Coag-negative staph also common (*Aesthetic Plastic Surg 31:325, 2007*).
CENTRAL NERVOUS SYSTEM				
Brain abscess				
Primary or contiguous source In 51 pts, 30 positive by standard culture; using molecular diagnostics, 80 bacterial taxa & many polymicrobics (*CID 54:202, 2012*)	Streptococci (60-70%), bacteroides (20-40%), Enterobacteriaceae (25-33%), S. aureus (10-15%). Rare: Nocardia (see below), Listeria (*CID 40:907, 2005*). See S. aureus Comment	**P Ceph 3** [**cefotaxime** 2 gm IV q4h or **ceftriaxone** 2 gm IV q12h) + (**metro** 7.5 mg/kg q6h or 15 mg/kg IV q12h)] – Duration of rx unclear; treat until response by neuroimaging (CT/MRI)	**Pen G** 3-4 million units IV q4h + **metro** 7.5 mg/kg q6h or 15 mg/kg IV q12h	If CT scan suggests cerebritis or abscesses <2.5 cm and pt neurologically stable and conscious, start antibiotics and observe. Otherwise, surgical drainage necessary. If blood cultures or other clinical data do not yield a likely etiologic agent, aspirate even small abscesses for diagnosis if this can be done safely. Experience with Pen G (HD) + metro without ceftriaxone or nafcillin/oxacillin has been good. We use ceftriaxone because of frequency of isolation of Enterobacteriaceae. **S. aureus rare without positive blood culture; if S. aureus, use vanco until susceptibility known.** Strep. anginosus group esp. prone to produce abscess. Ceph/metro does not cover listeria.
Post-surgical, post-traumatic	S. aureus, Enterobacteriaceae	**For MSSA: (Nafcillin** or **oxacillin)** 2 gm IV q4h + (**ceftriaxone** or **cefotaxime)**	**For MRSA: Vanco** 15-30 mg/kg IV q 8-12h for trough of 15-20 mcg/ml) + (**ceftriaxone** or **cefotaxime)**	Aspiration of abscess usually necessary for dx & rx. If P. aeruginosa suspected, substitute (Cefepime or Ceftazidime) for (Ceftriaxone or Cefotaxime).
HIV-1 infected (AIDS)	Toxoplasma gondii	*See Table 13A, page 146*		

TABLE 1 (4)

ANATOMIC SITE/DIAGNOSIS/ MODIFYING CIRCUMSTANCES	ETIOLOGIES (usual)	SUGGESTED REGIMENS*		ADJUNCT DIAGNOSTIC OR THERAPEUTIC MEASURES AND COMMENTS
		PRIMARY	ALTERNATIVE¹	
CENTRAL NERVOUS SYSTEM/Brain abscess (continued)				
Nocardia: Haematogenous abscess	N. farcinica, N. asteroides & N. brasiliensis	**TMP-SMX:** 15 mg/kg/day of TMP & 75 mg/kg/day of SMX, IV/po div in 2-4 doses + **Imipenem** 500 mg q6h IV. If multiorgan involvement some add **amikacin** 7.5 mg/kg q12h. After 3-6 wks of IV therapy, switch to po therapy. Immunocompetent pts: **TMP-SMX, minocycline or AM-CL** x 3 months. Immunocompromised pts: Treat with 2 drugs for at least one year.	**Linezolid** 600 mg IV or po q12h + meropenem 2 gm q8h	Measure peak sulfonamide levels: target 100-150 mcg/mL, 2 hrs post dose. **Linezolid** 600 mg po bid reported effective (Ann Pharmacother 41;1694, 2007). For in vitro susceptibility testing: Wallace (+1) 903-877-7680 or U.S. CDC (+1) 404-639-3158. In vitro resistance to TMP-SMX may be increasing (Clin Infect Dis 51;1445, 2010), but whether this is associated with worse outcomes is not known. TMP-SMX remains a drug of choice for CNS nocardia infection. If sulfonamide resistant or sulfa-allergic, **amikacin** plus one of: **IMP, MER, ceftriaxone or cefotaxime**. N. farcinica is resistant to third-generation cephalosporins, which should not be used for treatment of infection caused by this organism.
Subdural empyema: In adult 60-90% is extension of sinusitis or otitis media. Rx same as primary brain abscess. Surgical emergency: must drain. Review in LnID 7:62, 2007.				
Encephalitis/encephalopathy IDSA Guideline: CID 47;303, 2008. (For Herpes see Table 14A, page 160 and for rabies, Table 20B, page 215)	In 253 pts, etiol in 52%: H.-simplex (42%), VZV (15%), M. TB (5%), Listeria (10%) (CID 49;1838, 2009). Other: arbovirus, West Nile, rabies, Lyme, Parvo B19, Cat-scratch disease, Mycoplasma, mumps, EBV, HIV-6, and others.	Start IV **acyclovir** while awaiting results of CSF PCR for H. simplex. For amebic encephalitis see Table 13A. Start **Doxy** if setting suggests R. rickettsii, Anaplasma, Ehrlichia, Mycoplasma.		Review of all etiologies: LnID 10;835, 2010. Anti-NMDAR (N-Methyl-D-Aspartate Receptor) encephalitis, autoimmune encephalitis, more common than individual viral etiologies as a cause of encephalitis in the California Encephalitis Project cohort (CID 54;899, 2012).
Meningitis, "Aseptic": Pleocytosis of up to 100s of cells, CSF glucose normal, neg. culture for bacteria (see Table 14A, page 156) Ref: CID 47;783, 2008	Enteroviruses, HSV-2, LCM, HIV, other viruses, drugs (NSAIDs, metronidazole, carbamazepine, TMP-SMX, IVIG), rarely leptospirosis	For all but leptospirosis, IV fluids and analgesics. D/C drugs that may be etiologic. For lepto: **doxy** 100 mg IV/po q12h or **Pen G** 5 million units IV q6h) or **(AMP** 0.5-1 gm q6h). Repeat LP if suspect partially-treated bacterial meningitis. **Acyclovir** 5-10 mg/kg IV q8h sometimes given for HSV-2 meningitis (Note: this entity is distinct from HSV encephalitis where early rx is mandatory).		If available, PCR of CSF for enterovirus. HSV-2 unusual without concomitant genital herpes. For lepto, positive epidemiologic history and concomitant hepatitis, conjunctivitis, dermatitis, nephritis. For list of implicated drugs: Int Med 25;331, 2008.

Abbreviations on page 2.   NOTE: All dosage recommendations are for adults (unless otherwise indicated) and assume normal renal function.

TABLE 1 (5)

ANATOMIC SITE/DIAGNOSIS/ MODIFYING CIRCUMSTANCES	ETIOLOGIES (usual)	SUGGESTED REGIMENS*		ADJUNCT DIAGNOSTIC OR THERAPEUTIC MEASURES AND COMMENTS
		PRIMARY	ALTERNATIVE†	
Meningitis, Bacterial, Acute: Goal is **empiric therapy.** Goal is empiric therapy, then LP, then head CT, then LP. *(NEJM 354:44, 2006; Ln ID 10:32, 2010; IDSA Pract. Guid., CID 39:1267, 2004)* **NOTE:** In children, treatment caused CSF cultures to turn neg. in 2 hrs with meningococci & partial response with pneumococci in 4 hrs *(Peds 108:1169, 2001)*. For distribution of pathogens by age group, see *NEJM 364:2016, 2011.*				
Empiric Therapy—CSF Gram stain is negative—immunocompetent				
Age: Preterm to <1 mo *LnID 10:32, 2010*	Group B strep 49%, E. coli 18% listeria 7%, misc. Gm-neg. 10%, Gm-pos. 10%	**AMP** 100 mg/kg IV q6h + **cefotaxime** 50 mg/kg IV q6h	**AMP** 100 mg/kg IV q6h + **gentamicin** 2.5 mg/kg IV q8h	Regimens active vs. Group B strep, most coliforms, & listeria. If premature infant with long nursery stay & S. aureus, enterococci, and resistant coliforms potential pathogens, **optional empiric regimens (except for listeria): vancomycin + ceftazidime or cefepime). If high risk of MRSA,** use vancomycin. After regimen & after culture/sensitivity data available.
		Intraventricular treatment not recommended. Repeat CSF exam/culture 24–36 hr after start of therapy		
Age: 1 mo– 50 yrs S. pneumo, meningococci, listeria is most common H. influenzae now uncommon, **listeria unlikely if young adult & immunocompetent** (add ampicillin if suspect listeria: 2 gm IV q4h) *(LnID 10:32, 2010)*	S. pneumo, meningococci, H. influenzae now uncommon, **listeria unlikely if young adult & immunocompetent** (add ampicillin if suspect listeria: 2 gm IV q4h)	Adult dosage: **((Cefotaxime** 2 gm IV q4-6h OR **Ceftriaxone** 2 gm IV q12h) + **(dexamethasone)** + **vanco**) **Dexamethasone:** 0.15 mg/kg IV q6h x 2-4 days. **Give with, or just before, 1st dose of antibiotic to block TNF production** (see Comment). See footnote ¹ for Vanco Adult dosage and ² for ped. dosage	**MER** 2 gm IV q8h (Peds: 40 mg/kg IV q8h) + **dexamethasone** + **vanco¹**	Use of **dexamethasone** shown in children (due to H. influenzae and adults with S. pneumoniae in some studies *(NEJM 357:2431 & 2441, 2007; LnID 4:139, 2009).* Decreases markers of inflammation in adults *(CID 49:1387, 2009).* In the Netherlands, adoption of dexamethasone treatment in adult pneumococcal meningitis led to reduced mortality and hearing loss compared with historical control group *(Neurology 75:1533, 2010).* A meta-analysis including all age groups, but mostly from developing world, showed no overall benefit in bacterial meningitis, except possibly in adults over 55 *(Lancet Neurology 9:254, 2010).* For patients with severe **β-lactam allergy,** see below *(Empiric Therapy—positive gram stain and Specific Therapy).*
Age: >50 yrs or alcoholism or other debilitating assoc diseases or impaired cellular immunity	S. pneumo, listeria, Gm-neg. bacilli Note absence of meningo- coccus	(**AMP** 2 gm IV q4h) + (**ceftriaxone** 2 gm IV q12h or **cefotaxime** 2 gm IV q4-6h) + **vanco** + IV **dexamethasone** For Vanco dose, see footnote ¹	**MER** 2 gm IV q8h + **vanco** + IV **dexamethasone** For severe pen. Allergy: See Comment. **Dexamethasone dose:** 0.15 mg/kg IV q6h x 2-4 days, 1st dose before, or concomitant with 1st dose of antibiotic.	For patients with severe β-lactam allergy, see below *(Empiric Therapy—positive gram stain and Specific Therapy)* for alternative agents that can be substituted to cover likely pathogens.
Post-neurosurgery, Ventriculostomy/lumbar catheter, ventriculoperitoneal (atrial) shunt Post-traumatic trauma w/o basilar skull fracture	S. epidermidis, S. aureus, P. acnes. Facultative and aerobic gram-neg bacilli (including P. aeruginosa and A. baumannii (may be multi-drug resistant)	**Vanco** 15 mg/kg IV q8h (to achieve trough level of 15-20 µg/mL) + **Cefepime** or **Ceftaz** 2 gm IV q8h)	• If severe Pen/Ceph allergy, for possible gram-neg, substitute either **Aztreonam** 2 gm IV q6-8h or **CIP** 400 mg IV q8-12h. If IV therapy inadequate, **may need intraventricular therapy:** see Comment. Adult: **Vanco** 10-20 mg, **Amikacin** 30 mg, **Tobra** 5-20 mg, **Gent** 4-8 mg, **Colistin** 10 mg (or 5 mg q12h). **Polymyxin B** 5 mg. Peds: **Gent** 1-2 mg, **Polymyxin B** 2 mg.	• If possible, remove infected shunt or catheter. Logic for intraventricular therapy, goal is to achieve a 10-20 ratio of CSF concentration to MIC of infecting bacteria. For potential toxicities of intraventricular therapy, see *CMR 23:858, 2010.* • Use only preservative-free drug. Clamp/close catheter for 1 hr after 1st dose. • Timing of new V-P shunt *(CID 39:1267, 2004).* • Acinetobacter meningitis *(LnID 9:245, 2009; JAC 61:908, 2008).* • Review of nosocomial bacterial meningitis *(NEJM 362:146, 2010).*
Trauma with basilar skull fracture	S. pneumoniae, H. influenzae, S. pyogenes	**Vanco** 15 mg/kg IV q8h (to achieve trough level of 15-20 µg/mL) + (**Ceftriaxone** 2 gm IV q12h or **Cefotaxime** 2 gm IV q4-6h) **Dexamethasone** 0.15 mg/kg IV q6h x 2-4 d (1st dose with or before 1st antibiotic dose)		

¹ **Vanco adult dose:** 15 mg/kg IV q8h to achieve trough level of 15-20 µg/mL

² **Dosage of drugs used to treat children ≥1 mo of age: Cefotaxime** 50 mg/kg per day IV q6h; **ceftriaxone** 50 mg/kg IV q12h; **vanco** 15 mg/kg IV q6h to achieve trough level of 15-20 µg/mL.

Abbreviations on page 2. NOTE: *All dosage recommendations are for adults (unless otherwise indicated) and assume normal renal function.*

TABLE 1 (6)

ANATOMIC SITE/DIAGNOSIS/ MODIFYING CIRCUMSTANCES	ETIOLOGIES (usual)	SUGGESTED REGIMENS*		ADJUNCT DIAGNOSTIC OR THERAPEUTIC MEASURES AND COMMENTS
		PRIMARY	**ALTERNATIVE†**	
CENTRAL NERVOUS SYSTEM/Meningitis, Bacterial, Acute *(continued)*				
Empiric Therapy—Positive CSF Gram stain				
Gram-positive diplococci	S. pneumoniae	**(ceftriaxone** 2 gm IV q12h or **cefotaxime** 2 gm IV q4-6h) + **vancomycin** 15 mg/kg IV q8h (to achieve 15-20 µg/mL trough) + timed **dexamethasone** 0.15 mg/kg q6h IV x 2-4 days		**Alternatives: MER** 2 gm IV q8h or **Moxi** 400 mg IV q24h. **Dexamethasone** does not block penetration of vanco into CSF *(CID 44:250, 2007).*
Gram-negative diplococci	N. meningitidis	**(Cefotaxime** 2 gm IV q4-6h or **ceftriaxone** 2 gm IV q12h)		**Alternatives: Pen G** 4 mill. units IV q4h or **AMP** 2 gm q4h or **Moxi** 400 mg IV q24h or **chloro** 1 gm IV q6h
Gram-positive bacilli or coccobacilli	Listeria monocytogenes	**AMP** 2 gm IV q4h ± **gentamicin** 2 mg/kg IV loading dose then 1.7 mg/kg IV q8h		**If pen-allergic, use TMP-SMX 5 mg/kg q6-8h or MER 2 gm IV q8h**
Gram-negative bacilli	H. influenzae, coliforms, P. aeruginosa	(**Ceftazidime** or **cefepime** 2 gm IV q8h) ± **gentamicin** 2 mg/kg IV 1st dose then 1.7 mg/kg IV q8h *(See Comment)*		**Alternatives: CIP** 400 mg IV q8-12h; **MER** 2 gm IV q8h; **Aztreonam** 2 gm IV q6-8h. Consider adding intravenous **Gentamicin** to the β-lactam or **CIP** if gram-stain and clinical setting suggest P. aeruginosa or resistant coliforms
Specific Therapy—Positive culture of CSF with in vitro susceptibility results available. Interest in monitoring/reducing intracranial pressure: *CID 38:384, 2004*				
H. influenzae	β-lactamase positive	**Ceftriaxone** 2 gm IV q12h (adult), 50 mg/kg IV q12h (peds)		**Pen. allergic: Chloro** 12.5 mg/kg IV q6h (max. 4 gm/day.); **CIP** 400 mg IV q8-12h; **Aztreonam** 2 gm q6-8h
Listeria monocytogenes *(CID 43:1233, 2006)*		**AMP** 2 gm IV q4h ± **gentamicin** 2 mg/kg IV loading dose, then 1.7 mg/kg IV q8h		**Pen. allergic: TMP-SMX** 20 mg/kg per div q6-12h. **Alternative: MER** 2 gm IV q8h. Success reported with **linezolid** + **RIF** *(CID 40:907, 2005)* after AMP rx for brain abscess with meningitis.
N. meningitidis	Pen MIC 0.1–1 mcg per mL	**Pen G** 4 million units IV q4h or **AMP** 2 gm IV q4h		Rare isolates chloro-resistant, FQ-resistant isolates encountered. **Alternatives: Ceftriaxone** 2 gm IV q12h, **chloro** 1 gm IV q6h.
S. pneumoniae	Pen G MIC			
1. Assumes dexamethasone just prior to 1st dose & x 4 days.	<0.1 mcg/mL	**Ceftriaxone** 2 gm IV q12h or **cefotaxime** 2 gm IV q4-6h or **Pen G** 4 million units IV q4h or **AMP** 2 gm IV q4h		**Alternatives: Cefepime** 2 gm IV q8h or **MER** 2 gm IV q8h.
2. If MIC ≥1, repeat CSF exam after 24-48h.	0.1–1 mcg/mL	**Vanco** 15 mg/kg IV q8h (15-20 µg/mL trough target) + (**ceftriaxone** or **cefotaxime** as above)		**Alternatives: Moxi** 400 mg IV q24h
3. Treat for 10-14 days	≥2 mcg/mL	**Vanco** 15 mg/kg IV q8h (15-20 µg/mL trough target) + (**ceftriaxone** or **cefotaxime** as above)		**Alternatives: Moxi** 400 mg IV q24h; if MIC to ceftriaxone >2 mcg/mL, add **RIF** 600 mg po/IV 1x/day to **vanco** + (**ceftriaxone** or **cefotaxime**)
	Ceftriaxone MIC ≥1 mcg/mL			
E. coli, other coliforms, or P. aeruginosa	**Consultation advised—** need susceptibility results	(**Ceftazidime** or **cefepime** 2 gm IV q8h) ± **gentamicin**		**Alternatives: CIP** 400 mg IV q8-12h; **MER** 2 gm IV q8h. For intraventricular therapy: drug dosing, see *Meningitis, Post-neurosurgery, page 8.*
Prophylaxis for H. influenzae and N. meningitidis				
Haemophilus influenzae type b Household and/or day care contact: residing with index case for 24 hrs in a day. Day care contact or same day care facility as index case for 5-7 days before onset		**Children:** RIF 20 mg/kg po (not to exceed 600 mg) q24h x 4 doses. **Adults (non-pregnant):** RIF 600 mg q24h x 4 days		**Household:** If there is one unvaccinated contact ≤4 yrs in the household, all household contacts (except pregnant women **Child Care Facilities:** With 1 case, if attended by unvaccinated children ≤2 yrs, consider prophylaxis + vaccinate. If all contacts >2 yrs: no prophylaxis. If ≥2 cases in 60 days & unvaccinated children attend, prophylaxis recommended for children & personnel *(Am Acad Ped Red Book 2006, page 313).*

Abbreviations on page 2.

NOTE: All dosage recommendations are for adults (unless otherwise indicated) and assume normal renal function.

TABLE 1 (7)

ANATOMIC SITE/DIAGNOSIS/ MODIFYING CIRCUMSTANCES	ETIOLOGIES (usual)	SUGGESTED REGIMENS* PRIMARY	SUGGESTED REGIMENS* ALTERNATIVE†	ADJUNCT DIAGNOSTIC OR THERAPEUTIC MEASURES AND COMMENTS
CENTRAL NERVOUS SYSTEM/Meningitis, Bacterial, Acute/Prophylaxis for H. influenzae and N. meningitides *(continued)*				
Prophylaxis for Neisseria meningitidis exposure (close contact) NOTE: CDC reports **CIP-resistant group B meningococcus** from selected counties in N. Dakota & Minnesota. **Avoid CIP.** Use **ceftriaxone**. **RIF**, or single 500 mg dose of **azithro** (MMWR 57:173, 2008)		**Ceftriaxone** 250 mg IM x 1 dose (child <15 yrs 125 mg IM x 1) OR [**RIF** 600 mg po q12h x 4 doses. (Children ≥1 mo 10 mg/kg po q12h x 4 doses, <1 mo 5 mg/kg q12h x 4 doses)] OR if not CIP-resistant, **CIP** 500 mg po x 1 dose (adult)		**Spread by respiratory droplets**, not aerosols, hence close contact req, ↑ risk if close contact for at least 4 hrs during wk before illness onset (e.g. housemates, day care contacts, cellmates) or exposure to pt's nasopharyngeal secretions (e.g. kissing, mouth-to-mouth resuscitation, intubation, nasotracheal suctioning).
Meningitis, chronic Defined as symptoms + CSF pleocytosis for 24 wks	M. TBc 40%, cryptococcal 7%, neoplastic 8%, Lyme, syphilis, Whipple's disease	Treatment depends on etiology. No urgent need for empiric therapy, but when TB suspected treatment should be expeditious.		Long list of possibilities: bacteria, parasites, fungi, viruses, neoplasms, vasculitis, and other miscellaneous etiologies—see Bača Clin 28:1061, 2010; Curr Neurol Neurosci Rep 5:429, 2005; Whipple's: JID 188:797 & 801, 2003.
Meningitis, eosinophilic LnID 8:621, 2008	Angiostrongyliasis, gnathostomiasis, baylisascaris	Corticosteroids	Not sure anthelmintic therapy works	1/3 lack peripheral eosinophilia. Need serology to confirm diagnosis. Steroid ref.: LnID 8:621, 2008. Automated CSF count may not correctly identify eosinophils (CID 48: 322, 2009).
Meningitis, HIV-1 infected (AIDS) See Table 11, Sanford Guide to HIV/AIDS Therapy	As in adults, >50 yrs: also consider cryptococci, M. tuberculosis, syphilis, HIV aseptic meningitis, Listeria monocytogenes	If etiology not identified: treat as adult >50 yrs + obtain CSF/serum cryptococcal antigen (see Comments)	For crypto rx, see Table 11A page 118	C. neoformans most common etiology in AIDS patients. H. influenzae, pneumococci, TBc, syphilis, viral, histoplasma & coccidioides also need to be considered. Obtain blood cultures. Listeria monocytogenes risk >60x ↑, % present as meningitis (CID 17:224, 1993).
EAR				
External otitis				
Chronic:	Usually 2° to seborrhea	Eardrops: [(**polymyxin B** + **neomycin** + **hydrocortisone** qid) + **selenium sulfide shampoo**]		Control seborrhea with dandruff shampoo containing selenium sulfide (Selsun) or [(ketoconazole shampoo) + (medium potency steroid solution, triamcinolone 0.1%)].
Fungal	Candida species	**Fluconazole** 200 mg po x 1 dose & then 100 mg po x 3-5 days.		CIP po for treatment of early disease. Debridement usually required. R/O osteomyelitis: CT or MRI scan. If bone involved, treat for 4-6 wks. PIP without Tazo may be hard to find: extended infusion of PIP-TZ (4 hr infusion of 3.375 gm every 8h) may improve kinetics (CID 44:357, 2007).
"Malignant otitis externa" Risk groups: Diabetes mellitus, AIDS, chemotherapy. Ref: Oto Clinics N Am 41:537, 2008	Pseudomonas aeruginosa in >90%	[IMP 0.5 gm IV q6h) or MER 1 gm IV q8h) or CIP 400 mg IV q12h (or 750 mg po q12h)] or (ceftaz 2 gm IV q8h) or (CFP 2 gm q12h) or (PIP 4 gm IV q4-6h + tobra) or (TC 3 gm IV q4h + tobra) (See tobra dose Table 10D)		
"Swimmer's ear" PIDJ 22:299, 2003	Pseudomonas sp., Enterobacteriaceae, Proteus sp. (Fungi rare) Acute infection usually 2° S. aureus	Eardrops: **Oflox** 0.3% **soln bid** or [(**polymyxin B** + **neomycin** + **hydrocortisone**) qid] or (**CIP** + **hydrocortisone bid**) —active vs. gm-neg bacilli. For acute disease: **dicloxacillin** 500 mg po 4x/day. If MRSA a concern, use **TMP-SMX**, **doxy** or **clinda**		Rx includes gentle cleaning. Recurrences prevented (or decreased) by drying with alcohol drops (1/3 white vinegar, 2/3 rubbing alcohol) after swimming, then antibiotic drops or 2% acetic acid solution. Ointments should not be used in ear. Do not use neomycin drops if tympanic membrane punctured.

TABLE 1 (8)

ANATOMIC SITE/DIAGNOSIS/ MODIFYING CIRCUMSTANCES	ETIOLOGIES (usual)	SUGGESTED REGIMENS*		ADJUNCT DIAGNOSTIC OR THERAPEUTIC MEASURES AND COMMENTS
		PRIMARY	ALTERNATIVE¹	
EAR (continued)				
Otitis media—infants, children, adults				
Acute Two PRDB trials indicate efficacy of antibiotic rx if age < 36 mos & definite AOM (NEJM 364:105, 116 & 168, 2011)				
Initial empiric therapy of acute otitis media (AOM) NOTE: In children 6–23 mos, or if < 2 yrs old, afebrile no ear pain, neg./questionable exam — consider analgesic treatment without antimicrobials. Favorable results in mostly afebrile pts with waiting 48hrs before deciding on antibiotic use (JAMA 296:1235, 1290, 2006)	Overall detection in middle ear fluid: No pathogen 4% Virus 70% Bact. + virus 66% Bacteria 92% Bacterial pathogens from middle ear: S. pneumo 49%, H. influenzae 29%, M. catarrhalis 28%. Ref.: CID 43:1417 & 1423, 2006. Children 6 mos–3 yrs, 2 episodes AOM/yrs & 63% are virus positive (CID 46:815 & 824, 2008)	**If NO antibiotics in prior month:** Amox po HD³ **Duration of rx:** <2 yrs old x 10 days; ≥2 yrs x 5–7 days. Appropriate duration unclear, 5 days may be inadequate for severe disease (NEJM 347:1169, 2002) **For adult dosages, see Sinusitis, page 50, and Table 10A**	**Received antibiotics in prior month:** Amox-HD + or AM-CL extra-strength³ or cefdinir or cefpodoxime or cefprozil or cefuroxime axetil For dosage, see footnote⁴. **All doses are pediatric**	**If allergic to β-lactam drugs?** If history unclear or rash, effective oral ceph OK; avoid ceph if IgE-mediated allergy, e.g., anaphylaxis. High failure rate with macrolides if S. pneumo resistant to macrolides. If macrolide: **azithro x 5 days or clarithro x 10 days** (both have ↓ activity vs. DRSP). Up to 50% S. pneumo resistant to macrolides. Rationale & data for single dose azithro, 30 mg per kg: PIDJ 23:S102 & S108, 2004. **Spontaneous resolution occurred in:** 90% pts infected with M. catarrhalis, 50% with H. influenzae, 10% with S. pneumoniae. Overall 80% resolve within 2–14 days (Ln 363:465, 2004). Risk of DRSP ↑ if age <2 yrs, antibiotics last 3 mos, &/or daycare attendance. Selection of drug based on (1) effectiveness against β-lactamase producing H. influenzae & M. catarrhalis & (2) effectiveness against S. pneumo, inc. DRSP. **Cefaclor, loracarbef, & ceftibuten less active vs. resistant S. pneumo.** than other agents listed.
Treatment for clinical failure after 3 days	Drug-resistant S. pneumoniae main concern	**NO antibiotics in month prior to last 3 days:** AM-CL high dose or cefdinir or cefpodoxime or cefprozil or cefuroxime axetil or IM ceftriaxone x 3 days. For dosage, see footnote⁴. **All doses are pediatric** Duration of rx as above	**Antibiotics in month prior to last 3 days:** [IM ceftriaxone or (clindamycin), and/or tympanocentesis] See clindamycin Comments	Clindamycin not active vs. H. influenzae or M. catarrhalis. S. pneumo resistant to macrolides are usually, also resistant to clindamycin. Definition of failure: no change in ear pain, fever, bulging TM or otorrhea after 3 days of therapy. Tympanocentesis will allow culture. **Newer FQs active vs. drug-resistant S. pneumo (DRSP), but not approved for use in children (PIDJ 23:390, 2004). Vanco is active vs. DRSP.** Ceftriaxone IM x 3 days superior to 1-day treatment vs. DRSP (PIDJ 19:1040, 2000). AM-CL HD reported successful for pen-resistant S. pneumo AOM (PIDJ 20:829, 2001).
After >48hrs of nasotracheal intubation	Pseudomonas sp, klebsiella, enterobacter	Ceftazidime or CFP or IMP or MER or PIP-TZ or TC-CL or CIP (For dosages, see Ear, Malignant otitis externa, page 10)		With nasotracheal intubation >48 hrs, about ½ pts will have otitis media with infusion.
Prophylaxis: acute otitis media PIDJ 22:10, 2003		Sulfisoxazole 50 mg/kg po at bedtime or amoxicillin 20 mg/kg po q24h	**Use of antibiotics to prevent otitis media is a major contributor to emergence of antibiotic-resistant S. pneumo!** Pneumococcal protein conjugate vaccine decreases freq. AOM due to vaccine serotypes. Adenoidectomy ± tympanostomy tubes ↓ need for future hospitalization for AOM (NEJM 344:1188, 2001).	

³ **Amoxicillin UD or HD** = amoxicillin usual dose or high dose; **AM-CL HD** = amoxicillin-clavulanate high dose. **Dosages in footnote⁴.** Data supporting amoxicillin HD: PIDJ 22:405, 2003

⁴ **Drugs & peds dosage (all po unless specified) for acute otitis media: Amoxicillin UD** = 40 mg/kg per day div q12h or q8h. **Amoxicillin HD** = 90 mg/kg per day div q12h or q8h. **AM-CL HD** = 90 mg/kg per day of amox component. **Extra-strength AM-CL oral suspension** (Augmentin ES-600) available with 600 mg AM & 42.9 mg CL / 5 mL—dose: 90/6.4 mg/kg per day div q12h. **Cefuroxime axetil** 30 mg/kg per day div q12h. **Ceftriaxone** 50 mg/kg IM x 3 days. **Clindamycin** 20–30 mg/kg per day div q8h (may be effective vs. DRSP but no activity vs. H. influenzae)
Other drugs suitable for drug (e.g., penicillin): sensitive S. pneumo: TMP-SMX 4 mg/kg of TMP q12h. **Erythro-sulfisoxazole** 50 mg/kg per day of erythro div q6-8h. **Clarithro** 15 mg/kg per day div q12h; **azithro** 10 mg/kg per day x 1 & then 5 mg/kg q24h on days 2–5. Other FDA-approved regimens: **cefpodoxime proxetil** 10 mg/kg per day as single dose; **cefaclor** 40 mg/kg per day div q8h; **loracarbef** 15 mg/kg q12h. **Cefdinir** 7 mg/kg q12h or 14 mg/kg q24h.

Abbreviations on page 2.   NOTE: All dosage recommendations are for adults (unless otherwise indicated) and assume normal renal function.

TABLE 1 (9)

ANATOMIC SITE/DIAGNOSIS/ MODIFYING CIRCUMSTANCES	ETIOLOGIES (usual)	SUGGESTED REGIMENS* PRIMARY	ALTERNATIVE[1]	ADJUNCT DIAGNOSTIC OR THERAPEUTIC MEASURES AND COMMENTS
EAR *(continued)*				
Mastoiditis				
Acute				
Outpatient	Strep. pneumoniae 22%, S. pyogenes 16%, **Staph. aureus** 7%, H. influenzae 4%, others <1%	Empirically, same as Acute otitis media, above; need **vanco** or **nafcillin/oxacillin** if culture + for S. aureus.		Has become a rare entity, presumably as result of the aggressive treatment of acute otitis media. Small ↑ in incidence in Netherlands where use of antibiotics limited to children with complicated course at high risk (PIDJ 20:140, 2001). ↑ incidence reported from US also (Arch Otolaryngol Head Neck Surg 127:1, 2001).
Hospitalized		**Cefotaxime** 1-2 gm IV q4-8h (depends on severity) or (**ceftriaxone** 1 gm IV q24h)		Unusual causes of acute mastoiditis: nocardia (AIDS Reader 17: 402, 2007), TB, actinomyces (Ear Nose Throat Journal 79: 884, 2000).
Chronic	Often polymicrobic; anaerobes, S. aureus, Enterobacteriaceae, P. aeruginosa	Treatment for acute exacerbations or perioperatively. No treatment until surgical cultures obtained. Empiric regimens: **IMP** 0.5 gm IV q6h. **TC-CL** 3.1 gm IV q6h, **PIP-TZ** 3.375 gm IV q4-6h or 4.5 gm q8h, or 4 hr infusion of 3.375 gm q8h. **MER** 1 gm IV q8h. If MRSA, add **vanco** to any of the listed agents.		May or may not be associated with chronic otitis media with drainage via ruptured tympanic membrane. Antimicrobials given in association with surgery. Mastoidectomy indications: chronic drainage and evidence of osteomyelitis by MRI or CT. Evidence of spread to CNS (epidural abscess, suppurative phlebitis, brain abscess).
EYE				
Eyelid: Little reported experience with CA-MRSA (See *Cochrane Database Syst Rev 5:CD005556, 2012*)				
Blepharitis	Etiol. unclear. Factors include Staph. aureus & Staph. epidermidis, seborrhea, rosacea, & dry eye	Lid margin care with baby shampoo & warm compresses q24h. Artificial tears if assoc. dry eye (see *Comment*).		Usually topical ointments of no benefit. If associated rosacea, add doxy 100 mg po bid for 2 wks and then q24h.
Hordeolum (Stye)				
External (eyelash follicle)	Staph. aureus	Hot packs only. Will drain spontaneously		Infection of superficial sebaceous gland.
Internal (Meibomian glands): Can be acute, subacute or chronic.	Staph. aureus, MSSA	Oral **dicloxacillin** + hot packs		Also called acute meibomianitis. Rarely drain spontaneously; may need I&D and culture. Role of fluoroquinolone eye drops is unclear. MRSA often resistant to lower conc.; may be susceptible to higher concentration of FQ in ophthalmologic solutions of gati, levo or moxi.
	Staph. aureus, MRSA-CA	**TMP-SMX-DS** tabs ii po bid		
	Staph. aureus, MRSA-HA	**Linezolid** 600 mg po bid possible therapy if multi-drug resistant		
Conjunctivitis: NEJM 343:345, 2000				
Conjunctivitis of the newborn (**ophthalmia neonatorum**): by day of onset post-delivery—all dose pediatric				
Onset 1st day	Chemical due to silver nitrate prophylaxis	None		Usually prophylaxis is erythro ointment; hence, silver nitrate irritation rare.
Onset 2–4 days	N. gonorrhoeae	**Ceftriaxone** 25-50 mg/kg IV x 1 dose (see *Comment*), not to exceed 125 mg		Treat mother and her sexual partners. Hyperpurulent. Topical rx inadequate. **Treat neonate for concomitant Chlamydia trachomatis.**
Onset 3–10 days	Chlamydia trachomatis	**Erythro** base or ethylsuccinate syrup 12.5 mg/kg qdh x 14 days. No topical rx needed.		Diagnosis by antigen detection. Alternative: **Azithro suspension** 20 mg/kg po q24h x 3 days. Treat mother & sexual partner.
Onset 2–16 days	Herpes simplex types 1, 2	Topical anti-viral rx under direction of ophthalmologist.		Also give Acyclovir 60 mg/kg/day IV x 3 doses (Red Book online, accessed Jan 2017).
Ophthalmia neonatorum prophylaxis: **erythro** 0.5% ointment x 1 or **tetra** 1% ointment[NB] x 1 application				
Pink eye (viral conjunctivitis) Usually unilateral	Adenovirus (types 3 & 7 in children, 8, 11 & 19 in adults)	No treatment. If symptomatic, cold artificial tears may help.		Highly contagious. Onset of ocular pain and photophobia in an adult suggests associated keratitis—rare.

Abbreviations on page 2. *NOTE: All dosage recommendations are for adults (unless otherwise indicated) and assume normal renal function.*

TABLE 1 (10)

ANATOMIC SITE/DIAGNOSIS/ MODIFYING CIRCUMSTANCES	ETIOLOGIES (usual)	SUGGESTED REGIMENS*		ADJUNCT DIAGNOSTIC OR THERAPEUTIC MEASURES AND COMMENTS
		PRIMARY	ALTERNATIVE¹	
EYE/Conjunctiva (continued)				
Inclusion conjunctivitis (adult) Usually unilateral	Chlamydia trachomatis	**Azithro** 1 g once or twice weekly (Eye 24:985, 2010 and Am J Ophthal 135:447, 2003)	**Erythro** 250 mg po qid x 1-3 wks	Oculogenital disease. Diagnosis by culture or antigen detection or PCR—availability varies by region and institution. Treat sexual partner. May need to repeat dose of azithro.
Trachoma—a chronic bacterial keratoconjunctivitis linked to poverty	Chlamydia trachomatis	**Azithro** 20 mg/kg po single dose—78% effective in children; Adults: 1 gm po.	**Doxy** 100 mg po bid x minimum of 21 days or **tetracycline** 250 mg po qid x 14 days.	Starts in childhood and can persist for years with subsequent damage to cornea. Topical therapy of marginal benefit. Avoid doxy/tetracycline in young children. Mass treatment works (NEJM 358:1777 & 1870, 2008; JAMA 299:778, 2008).
Suppurative conjunctivitis: Children and Adults				
Non-gonococcal; non-chlamydial Med Lett 50:11, 2008	Staph, aureus, S. pneumoniae, H. influenzae, et al.	Ophthalmic solution: **Gati** 0.3%, **Levo** 0.5%, or **Moxi** 0.5%. All 1-2 gtts q2h while awake 1st 2 days, then q4-8h up to 7 days.	**Polymyxin B + trimethoprim** solution 1-2 gtts q3-6h x 7-10 days. **Azithro** 1%, 1 gtt bid x 2 days, then 1 gtt daily x 5 days.	FQs best spectrum for empiric therapy but expensive: $40–50 for 5 mL. High concentrations ↑ likelihood of activity vs. S. aureus—even MRSA. **TMP** spectrum may include MRSA, Polymyxin B spectrum only Gm-neg. bacilli but no ophthal. prep of only **TMP**. Most S. pneumo resistant to **gent** & **tobra**. **Azithro** active vs. common gm+ pathogens.
Gonococcal (peds/adults)	N. gonorrhoeae	**Ceftriaxone** 25–50 mg/kg IV/IM (not to exceed 125 mg) as one dose in children: 1 gm IM/IV as one dose in adults		
Cornea (keratitis): Usually serious and often sight-threatening. Prompt ophthalmologic consultation essential for diagnosis, antimicrobial and adjunctive therapy! Herpes simplex most common etiology in developed countries; bacterial and fungal infections more common in underdeveloped countries.				
Viral				
H. simplex	H. simplex, types 1 & 2	**Trifluridine** ophthalmic soln, one drop q-2h up to 9 drops/day until re-epithelialized, then one drop q4h up to 5x/day, for total not to exceed 21 days.	**Ganciclovir** 0.15% ophthalmic gel. Indicated for acute herpetic keratitis. One drop 5 times per day while awake until corneal ulcer heals, then, one drop three times per day for 7 days. **Vidarabine** ointment—useful in children. Use 5x/day for up to 21 days (currently listed as discontinued in U.S.).	
Varicella-zoster ophthalmicus	Varicella-zoster virus	**Famciclovir** 500 mg tid or **valacyclovir** 1 gm po tid x 10 days	**Acyclovir** 800 mg po 5x/day x 10 days	Approx. 30% recurrence rate within one year; consider prophylaxis with acyclovir 400 mg bid for 12 months to prevent recurrences (Arch Ophthal 130:108, 2012)

Clinical diagnosis most common: dendritic figures with fluorescein staining in patient with varicella-zoster of ophthalmic branch of trigeminal nerve. |
| **Bacterial** | | | | |
| Acute: No comorbidity | S. aureus, S. pneumo., S. pyogenes, Haemophilus sp. | **All treatment listed for bacterial, fungal, protozoan is topical unless otherwise indicated**
Moxi ophthalmic 0.5%: 1 drop q1h for the first 48h then taper according to response | **Gatt** ophthalmic 0.3%: 1 drop q1h for the first 48h then taper according to response | Moxi may be preferable because of enhanced lipophilicity and penetration into aqueous (Survey of Ophthal 50 (Suppl 1): 1, Nov 2005). Regimens vary: some start rx by applying drops q5 min for 5 doses; some apply drops q15-30 min for several hours; some extend interval during sleep. In a clinical trial, drops were applied q1h for 48-72h, then q2h through day 6; then q2h during waking hours on days 7-9; then q6h until healing (Cornea 29:751, 2010). **Note:** despite high concentrations, may fail vs. MRSA. |

Abbreviations on page 2.   NOTE: All dosage recommendations are for adults (unless otherwise indicated) and assume normal renal function.

TABLE 1 (11)

ANATOMIC SITE/DIAGNOSIS/ MODIFYING CIRCUMSTANCES	ETIOLOGIES (usual)	SUGGESTED REGIMENS*		ADJUNCT DIAGNOSTIC OR THERAPEUTIC MEASURES AND COMMENTS
		PRIMARY	ALTERNATIVE†	
EYE/Cornea (keratitis) (continued)				
Contact lens users	P. aeruginosa	**Tobra** or **Gentamicin** (14 mg/mL) + (**Piperacillin** or **Ticarcillin** eye drops (6-12 mg/mL) q15-60 min around the clock for 24-72h, then slowly reduce frequency depending upon response.	**CIP** ophthalmic 0.3% or **Levo** ophthalmic 0.5%): 1 drop q15-60 min around the clock for 24-72h, then slowly taper based on response.	Recommend alginate swab culture and susceptibility testing.
Dry cornea, diabetes, immunosuppression	Staph. aureus, S. epidermidis, S. pneumoniae, S. pyogenes, Enterobacteriaceae, listeria	**Cefazolin** (50 mg/mL) + **Gent** or **Tobra** (14 mg/mL) q15-60 min around the clock for 24-72h, then slowly reduce frequency depending upon response.	**Vanco** (50 mg/mL) + **Ceftaz** (50 mg/mL) q15-60 min around the clock for 24-72h, then slowly reduce frequency depending upon response. See Comment.	Specific therapy guided by results of alginate swab culture.
Fungal	Aspergillus, fusarium, candida and others.	**Natamycin** (5%): 1 drop every 1-2 hr for several days; then q3-4 hr for several days; can reduce frequency depending upon response.	**Amphotericin B** (0.15%): 1 drop every 1-2 hours for several days; can reduce frequency depending upon response.	Obtain specimens for fungal wet mount and cultures. Numerous other treatment options (1% topical itra to 6 wks, oral itra 100 mg bid for 3 wks, topical voriconazole 1% hourly for 2 wks, topical miconazole bid 5x a day, topical silver sulphadiazine 0.5-1.0% 5x a day) appear to have similar efficacy (Cochrane Database Syst Rev 2:004241, 2012).
Mycobacteria: Post-refractive eye surgery	Mycobacterium chelonae	**Gati** or **Moxi** eye drops: 1 gtt qid, probably in conjunction with other active antimicrobials		Used in conjunction with other topical and/or systemic anti-mycobacterial agents (J Cataract Refract Surg 33:1978, 2007; Ophthalmology 113:950, 2006).
Protozoan Soft contact lens users. Ref: CID 35:434, 2002.	Acanthamoeba, sp.	Optimal regimen uncertain. Suggested regimen: [(**Chlorhexidine** 0.02% or Polyhexamethylene biguanide 0.02%) + (Propamidine isethionate 0.1% or Hexamidine 0.1%)] drops. Apply one drop every hour for 48h, then one drop every hour only while awake for 72h, then one drop every two hours while awake for 3-4 weeks, then reducing frequency based on response (Ref: Am J Ophthalmol 148:487, 2009; Curr Op Infect Dis 23:590, 2010).		Uncommon. Trauma and soft contact lenses are risk factors. To obtain suggested drops: Leiter's Park Ave Pharmacy (800-292-6773; www.leiterrx.com). Cleaning solution outbreak: MMWR 56: 532, 2007.
Lacrimal apparatus				
Canaliculitis	Actinomyces most common. Rarely, Arachnia, fusobacterium, nocardia, candida	Remove granules & irrigate with **pen G** (100,000 mcg/mL). **Child: AM-CL** or **cefprozil** or **cefuroxime** (See dose on Table 16)	If fungi, irrigate with **nystatin** approx. 5 mcg/mL: 1 gtt tid	Digital pressure produces exudate at punctum; Gram stain confirms diagnosis. Hot packs to punctal area qid. M. chelonae reported after use of intracanalicular plugs (Ophth Plast Reconstr Surg 24: 241, 2008).
Dacryocystitis (lacrimal sac)	S. pneumo, S. aureus, H. influenzae, S. pyogenes, P. aeruginosa	Often consequence of obstruction of lacrimal duct. Empiric systemic antimicrobial therapy based on Gram stain of aspirate—see Comment.		Need ophthalmologic consultation. Surgery may be required. Can be acute or chronic. Culture to detect MRSA.

Abbreviations on page 2.   NOTE: All dosage recommendations are for adults (unless otherwise indicated) and assume normal renal function.

TABLE 1 (12)

ANATOMIC SITE/DIAGNOSIS/ MODIFYING CIRCUMSTANCES	ETIOLOGIES (usual)	SUGGESTED REGIMENS* PRIMARY	SUGGESTED REGIMENS* ALTERNATIVE[1]	ADJUNCT DIAGNOSTIC OR THERAPEUTIC MEASURES AND COMMENTS
EYE/Cornea (keratitis) (continued)				
Endophthalmitis: Endogenous (secondary to bacteremia or fungemia) and exogenous (post-injection, post-operative) types				
Bacterial: Haziness of both vitreous and aqueous humor for culture prior to therapy. Intravitreal administration of antimicrobials essential.				
Postocular surgery (cataracts)	S. epidermidis 60%, Staph. aureus, streptococci & enterococci each 5–10%, Grn-neg. bacilli 6%			
Early, acute onset (incidence 0.05%)			**Immediate ophthal. consult.** If only light perception or worse, immediate vitrectomy + intravitreal vanco 1 mg & intravitreal ceftazidime 2.25 mg. No clear data on intravitreal steroid. May need to repeat intravitreal antibiotics in 2–3 days. Can usually leave lens in. Adjunctive systemic antibiotics (e.g., Vancomycin, Ceftazidime, Moxifloxacin or Gatifloxacin[A/B]) not of proven value, but recommended in endogenous infection.
Low grade, chronic	Propionibacterium acnes, S. epidermidis, S. aureus (rare)		Intraocular **vanco**. Usually requires vitrectomy, lens removal.	
Post filtering blebs for glaucoma	Strep. species (viridans & others), H. influenzae		Intravitreal agent (e.g., **Vanco** 1 mg + **Ceftaz** 2.25 mg) and a topical agent. Consider a systemic agent such as **Amp-Sulb** or **Ceftriaxone** or **Ceftaz** (add **Vanco** if MRSA is suspected).	
Post-penetrating trauma	Bacillus sp., S. epiderm.		Intravitreal agent as above + systemic **clinda** or **vanco**. Use topical antibiotics post-surgery (tobra & cefazolin drops).	
None, suspect hematogenous	N. meningitidis, Staph. aureus, Grp B Strep, K. pneumo		(**cefotaxime** 2 gm IV q4h or **ceftriaxone** 2 gm IV q24h) + **vanco** 30-60 mg/kg/day in 2-3 div doses to achieve target trough serum concentration of 15-20 mcg/mL pending cultures. Intravitreal antibiotics as with early post-operative.	
IV heroin abuse	Bacillus cereus, Candida sp.		Intravitreal agent + systemic agent based on etiology and antimicrobial susceptibility.	
Mycotic (fungal): Broad-spectrum antibiotics, often corticosteroids, indwelling venous catheters	Candida sp. or Aspergillus sp.	Intravitreal **ampho B** 0.005-0.01 mg in 0.1 mL. Also see Table 11A, page 116 for concomitant systemic therapy. See Comment.		Patients with Candida spp. chorioretinitis usually respond to systemically administered antifungals (Clin Infect Dis 53:262, 2011). Intravitreal amphotericin and/or vitrectomy may be necessary for those with vitritis or endophthalmitis (Br J Ophthalmol 92:466, 2008; Pharmacotherapy 27:1711, 2007).
Retinitis				
Acute retinal necrosis	Varicella zoster, Herpes simplex, Cytomegalovirus	IV **acyclovir** 10–12 mg/kg IV q8h x 5–7 days, then 800 mg po 5x/day x 6 wks. See Table 14, page 158		Strong association of VZ virus with atypical necrotizing herpetic retinopathy.
HIV+ /AIDS) CD4 usually <100/mm³				Occurs in 5–10% of AIDS patients
Progressive outer retinal necrosis	VZV, H. simplex, CMV (rare)	**Acyclovir** 10-12 mg/kg IV q8h for 1-2 weeks, then (**valacyclovir** 1000 mg po tid, or **famciclovir** 500 mg po tid, or **acyclovir** 800 mg po tid). Ophthalmology consultation imperative: approaches have also included intra-vitreal injection of anti-virals (foscarnet, ganciclovir implant). In rare cases due to CMV use **ganciclovir/valganciclovir** (see CMV retinitis, Table 14A).		Most patients are highly immunocompromised (HIV with low CD4 or transplantation). In contrast to Acute Retinal Necrosis, lack of intraocular inflammation or arteritis. May be able to stop oral antivirals when CD4 recovers with ART (Ocul Immunol Inflammation 15:425, 2007).
Orbital cellulitis (see page 54 for erysipelas, facial)	S. pneumoniae, H. influenzae, M. catarrhalis, S. aureus, anaerobes, (group A strep, occ. Gm-neg. bacilli post-trauma	**Nafcillin** 2 gm IV q4h (or if **MRSA–vanco** 30-60 mg/kg/day in 2-3 div doses to achieve target serum concentration of 15-20 mcg/mL) + **ceftriaxone** 2 gm IV q24h + **metro** 1 gm IV q12h		**If penicillin/ceph allergy: Vanco** + **levo** 750 mg IV once daily + **metro**. Problem is frequent inability to make microbiologic diagnosis. Image orbit (CT or MRI). Risk of cavernous sinus thrombosis. If vanco intolerant, another option for s. aureus is dapto 6 mg/kg IV q24h.

TABLE 1 (13)

ANATOMIC SITE/DIAGNOSIS/ MODIFYING CIRCUMSTANCES	ETIOLOGIES (usual)	SUGGESTED REGIMENS*		ADJUNCT DIAGNOSTIC OR THERAPEUTIC MEASURES AND COMMENTS
		PRIMARY	ALTERNATIVE†	
FOOT				
"Diabetic"—Two thirds of patients have triad of neuropathy, deformity and pressure-induced trauma. IDSA Guidelines *CID 54:e132, 2012.*				
Ulcer without inflammation	Colonizing skin flora	No antibacterial therapy		**General:** 1. Glucose control, eliminate pressure on ulcer 2. **Assess for peripheral vascular disease** 3. Caution in use of TMP-SMX in patients with diabetes, as many have risk factors for hyperkalemia (e.g., advanced age, reduced renal function, concomitant medications) (*Arch Intern Med 170:1045, 2010*).
Mild infection	*S. aureus* (assume *MRSA*), *S. agalactiae* (Gp B), *S. pyogenes* predominate	**Oral therapy:** Diclox or cephalexin or AM-CL (not *MRSA*) Doxy or TMP-SMX-DS (*MRSA*, may not cover strep) CLINDA (covers MSSA, *MRSA*, strep)		**Principles of empiric antibacterial therapy:** 1. Obtain culture; cover for *MRSA* in moderate, more severe infections pending culture data, local epidemiology. 2. Severe limb and/or life-threatening infections require initial parenteral therapy with predictable activity vs. Gm-positive cocci, coliforms & other aerobic Gm-neg. rods, & anaerobic Gm-neg. bacilli. **NOTE:** The regimens listed are suggestions consistent with above principles. Other alternatives exist & may be appropriate for individual patients.
Moderate infection. **Osteomyelitis** See Comment.	As above, plus coliforms possible	**Oral:** As above **Parenteral therapy:** [based on prevailing susceptibilities: (AM-SB or TC-CL or PIP-TZ or ERTA or other carbapenem) plus (**vanco** (or alternative anti-*MRSA* drug as below) until *MRSA* excluded)] *Dosages in footnote⁵*		3. Is there an associated osteomyelitis? Risk increased if ulcer area >2 cm², positive probe to bone, ESR >70 and abnormal plain x-ray. Negative MRI reduces likelihood of osteomyelitis (*JAMA 299:806, 2008*). MRI is best imaging modality (*CID 47:519 & 528, 2008*).
Extensive local inflammation plus systemic toxicity.	As above, plus anaerobic bacteria. Role of enterococci unclear.	**Parenteral therapy: (Vanco** plus β-lactam/β-lactamase inhibitor) or (**vanco** plus [**Dori** or **IMP** or **MER**]). Other alternatives: 1. **Dapto** or **linezolid** for vanco 2. (**CIP** or **Levo** or **Moxi** or **aztreonam**) plus **metronidazole** for β-lactam/β-lactamase inhibitor *Dosages in footnotes⁶,⁷* **Assess for arterial insufficiency!**		
Onychomycosis: See *Table 11, page 120, fungal infections*				
Puncture wound: Nail/Toothpick	P. aeruginosa	Cleanse. Tetanus booster. Observe.		See page 4. *1–2% evolve to osteomyelitis. After toothpick injury (PID) 23:80, 2004*). S. aureus, Strep sp. and mixed flora.

⁵ **TMP-SMX-DS** 1-2 tabs po bid, **minocycline** 100 mg po bid, **Pen VK** 500 mg po qid, (O Ceph 2, 3: **cefprozil** 500 mg po q12h; **cefuroxime axetil** 500 mg po q12h; **cefdinir** 300 mg q12h or 600 mg po q24h; **cefpodoxime** 200 mg po q12h), **Doxy** 750 mg po bid, **Levo** 750 mg po bid, **Diclox** 500 mg po q24h; **Cephalexin** 500 mg po qid; **AM-CL** 875/125 bid. **Doxy** 100 mg bid. **CLINDA** 300-450 mg tid

⁶ **AM-CL-ER** 2000/125 mg po bid, **TMP-SMX-DS** 1-2 tabs po bid, **CIP** 750 mg po bid, **Levo** 750 mg po q24h, **Moxi** 400 mg po q24h, **linezolid** 600 mg po bid.

⁷ **Vanco** 1 gm IV q12h, **parenteral β-lactam/β-lactamase inhibitors: AM-SB** 3 gm IV q6h; **PIP-TZ** 3.375 gm IV q6h or 4.5 gm IV q8h or 4 hr infusion of 3.375 gm q8h;TC-CL 3.1 gm IV q6h); **carbapenems: Doripenem** 500 mg (1-hr infusion) q8h, **ERTA** 1 gm IV q24h; **IMP** 0.5 gm IV q6h, **MER** 1 gm IV q8h, **daptomycin** 6 mg per kg IV q24h, **linezolid** 600 mg IV q12h, **aztreonam** 2 gm IV q8h. **CIP** 1 gm IV q12h, **Levo** 750 mg IV q24h, **Moxi** 400 mg IV q24h, **metro** 1 gm IV loading dose & then 0.5 gm IV q6h or 1 gm IV q12h.

Abbreviations on page 2.   *NOTE: All dosage recommendations are for adults (unless otherwise indicated) and assume normal renal function.*

TABLE 1 (14)

ANATOMIC SITE/DIAGNOSIS/ MODIFYING CIRCUMSTANCES	ETIOLOGIES (usual)	SUGGESTED REGIMENS*		ADJUNCT DIAGNOSTIC OR THERAPEUTIC MEASURES AND COMMENTS
		PRIMARY	ALTERNATIVE†	
GALLBLADDER				
Cholecystitis, cholangitis, biliary sepsis, or common duct obstruction (partial) stone, or stricture. Cholecystitis Ref: NEJM 358:2804, 2008	Enterobacteriaceae 68%, enterococci 14%, bacteroides 10%, Clostridium sp. 7%, rarely candida	**PIP-TZ** or **AM-SB** or **TC-CL** If life-threatening: **IMP** or **MER** or **Dori**	**P Ceph 3** + **metro** or **AP Pen** + **metro** or **CIP†** + **metro** or **Moxi** *Add vanco to these regimens to cover gram-positives. Dosages in footnote¹ on page 16.*	In severely ill pts, antibiotic therapy complements adequate biliary drainage. 15-30% pts will require decompression: surgical, percutaneous or ERCP-placed stent.
GASTROINTESTINAL				
Gastroenteritis—Empiric Therapy (laboratory studies not performed or culture, microscopy, toxin results NOT AVAILABLE) (Ref: NEJM 350:38, 2004)				
Premature infant with necrotizing enterocolitis	Associated with intestinal flora	Antibiotic treatment should cover broad range of intestinal organisms, using regimens appropriate to age and local susceptibility patterns, rationale as in diverticulitis/peritonitis, page 22. See Table 16, page 203 for pediatric dosages.		Pneumatosis intestinalis, if present on x-ray confirms diagnosis. Bacteremia-peritonitis in 30-50%. If Staph. epidermidis isolated, add vanco (IV). For review and general management, see NEJM 364:255, 2011.
Mild diarrhea (≤3 unformed stools/day, minimal associated symptomatology)	Bacterial (see Severe, below), viral (norovirus), parasitic. Viral usually causes mild to moderate disease. For traveler's diarrhea, see page 20.	Fluids only + lactose-free diet, avoid caffeine		**Rehydration: For po fluid replacement,** see Cholera, page 19. **Antimotility:** (Do not use if fever, bloody stools, or suspicion of HUS): Loperamide (Imodium) 4 mg po, then 2 mg after each loose stool to max. of 16 mg per day. Bismuth subsalicylate (Pepto-Bismol) 2 tablets (262 mg) po qid.
Moderate diarrhea (≥4 unformed stools/day &/or systemic symptoms)		Antimotility agents (see Comments) + fluids		
Severe diarrhea (≥6 unformed stools/day, &/or temp ≥101°F, tenesmus, blood, or fecal leukocytes)	Shigella, Salmonella, C. jejuni, Shiga-toxin + E. coli, toxin-positive C. difficile. Klebsiella oxytoca, E. histolytica.	**FQ** (**CIP** 500 mg po q12h or **Levo** 500 mg q24h) times 3-5 days	**TMP-SMX-DS** po bid times 3-5 days. Some resistance to TMP-SMX.	**Hemolytic uremic syndrome (HUS):** Risk in children infected with E. coli O157:H7 is 8-10%. Early treatment with TMP-SMX or FQs ↑ risk of HUS (NEJM 342:1930 & 1990, 2000). Controversial meta-analysis: JAMA 288:996 & 3/10, 2002. **Noroviruses:** Etiology of over 90% of non-bacterial diarrhea
NOTE: Severe afebrile bloody diarrhea & suspicion of Shiga-toxin E. coli O157:H7 & others (MMWR 58 (RR-12):1, 2009).		If recent antibiotic therapy (C. difficile toxin colitis possible) **add: Metro** 500 mg po tid times 10-14 days	**Vanco** 125 mg po qid times 10-14 days	**Other potential etiologies:** Cryptosporidia—no treatment in immunocompetent host (see Table 13A & JID 170:272, 1994). Cyclospora—usually chronic diarrhea, responds to TMP-SMX (see Table 13A, page 141 & AIM 123:409, 1995). For typhoid fever, see page 61 Klebsiella oxytoca identified as cause of antibiotic-associated hemorrhagic colitis (cytotoxin positive): NEJM 355:2418, 2006.
Gastroenteritis—Specific Therapy (results of culture, microscopy, toxin assay AVAILABLE) (Ref: NEJM 361:1560, 2009)				
Norovirus (Norwalk) other virus (EID 17:1381, 2011) — see Norovirus, page 165 NOTE: In 60 hospital pts with unexplained WBCs ≥15,000, 35% had C. difficile toxin present (AJM 115:543, 2003; CID 34:1585, 2002).	If culture negative, probably Aeromonas/Plesiomonas	CIP 750 mg po x3 days.	Azithro 500 mg po once daily x3 days, see Table 13A	Although no absolute proof, increasing evidence for Plesiomonas as cause of diarrheal illness (NEJM 361:1560, 2009).
	Amebiasis (Entamoeba histolytica, Cyclospora, Cryptosporidia (Giardia), see Table 13A	Azithro 500 mg po q24h		**Post-Campylobacter Guillain-Barré:** assoc: 15% of cases (Ln 366:1653, 2005). Assoc with small bowel lymphoproliferative disease; may respond to antimicrobials (NEJM 350:239, 2004). **Reactive arthritis** another potential sequelae. See Traveler's diarrhea, page 20.
	Campylobacter jejuni History of fever in 53-83%. Self-limited diarrhea in normal host.	Erythro stearate 500 mg po qid x 5 days or CIP 500 mg po bid (CIP resistance increasing).		
	Campylobacter fetus Diarrhea uncommon. More systemic disease in debilitated hosts	Gentamicin (See Table 10D)	AMP 100 mg/kg/day IV div q6h or MP 500 mg IV q6h	Draw blood cultures. In bacteremic pts, 32% of C. fetus resistant to FQs (CID 47:790, 2008). Meropenem inhibits C. fetus at low concentrations in vitro.

NOTE: All dosage recommendations are for adults (unless otherwise indicated) and assume normal renal function.

TABLE 1 (15)

ANATOMIC SITE/DIAGNOSIS/ MODIFYING CIRCUMSTANCES	ETIOLOGIES (usual)	SUGGESTED REGIMENS*		ADJUNCT DIAGNOSTIC OR THERAPEUTIC MEASURES AND COMMENTS
		PRIMARY	ALTERNATIVE§	
GASTROINTESTINAL/Gastroenteritis—Specific Therapy *(continued)*				
Differential diagnosis of toxin-producing diarrheas: • C. difficile • Klebsiella oxytoca • Shiga toxin producing E. coli (STEC) • Enterotoxigenic B. fragilis (CID 47:797, 2008)	**C. difficile** toxin positive antibiotic-associated colitis. **C. difficile** po meds okay, WBC <15,000; no increase in serum creatinine.	**Probiotics** (lactobacillus or saccharomyces) inconsistent in prevention of C. difficile (NEJM 359:1932, 2006). **Metro** 500 mg po tid or 250 mg bid x 10-14 days	**Vanco** 125 mg po qid x 10-14 days **Teicoplanin**ᴺᵁˢ 400 mg bid x 10 days	**D/C antibiotic if possible; avoid antimotility agents, hydration, enteric isolation.** Recent review suggests antimotility agents can be used cautiously in certain pts with mild disease who are receiving rx (CID 48: 598, 2009), but others believe there is insufficient data re safety of this approach (CID 48:606, 2009). Relapse in 10-20%. **Nitazoxanide** 500 mg po bid for 7-10 days equivalent to **Metro** po in phase 3 studyᴬᴬᴱ (CID 43:421, 2006)
More on C. difficile: *Treatment review:* CID 51:1306, 2010. *SHEA/IDSA treatment guidelines: ICHE 31:431, 2010;* *ESCMID guidelines:* *Clin Microbiol Infect 15:1067, 2009; AHM 155:839, 2011.*	...more on: Sicker, WBC >15,000, ≥ 50% increase in baseline creatinine	**Vanco** 125 mg po qid x 10-14 days. To use IV **vanco po**, see Table 10A, page 97.		**Vanco** superior to metro in sicker pts. Relapse in 10-20% (not due to resistance: JAC 56:988, 2005). Fidaxomicin had lower rate of recurrence than Vanco for diarrhea with non-NAP1 strains (N Engl J Med 364:422, 2011).
	Post-treatment relapse	**1ˢᵗ relapse** **Metro** 500 mg po tid x 10 days	**Fidaxomicin** 200 mg po bid x 10 days	
		2ⁿᵈ relapse **Vanco** 125 mg po qid x 10-14 days, then immediately start taper (See Comments)		**Vanco** taper (all doses 125 mg po): week 1- bid, week 2 - q24h; week 3 - God, then every 3rd day for 5 doses (NEJM 359, 1932, 2008). Other options: 1) After initial vanco, **rifaximin**ᴺᵁˢ 400-800 mg po daily divided bid or tid x 2 wks (CID 44:846, 2007; rifaximin-resistant C. diff. reported); 2) **nitazoxanide**ᴺᵁˢ 500 mg bid x 10d (JAC 59:705, 2007). **Last resort: stool transplant** (CID 53:994, 2011).
	Post-op ileus; severe disease with toxic megacolon (NEJM 359:1932, 2008).	**Metro** 500 mg IV q6h + **vanco** 500 mg q6h via nasogastric tube (or naso-small bowel tube) ± retrograde catheter in cecum. See comment for dosage.		For vanco installation into bowel, add 500 mg vanco to 1 liter of saline and perfuse at 1-3 mL/min to maximum of 2 gm in 24 hrs (CID 690, 2002). **Note:** **IV vanco not effective. IVIG:** Reports of benefit of 400 mg/kg x 1-3 doses (JAC 53:882, 2004) and lack of benefit (Am J Inf Cont 35:131, 2007). Indications for colectomy, see (ICHE 31:431, 2010. Reported successful use of tigecyclineIV IV to treat severe C. diff. refractory to rx (CID 48:1732, 2009).
E. coli O157:H7 History of bloody stools 63% Shiga toxin producing E. Coli (STEC)		**NO TREATMENT** with antimicrobials or anti-motility drugs. May enhance toxin release and ↑ risk of hemolytic uremic syndrome (HUS) (NEJM 342:1930 & 1990, 2000). Hydration important (Ln 365:1073, 2005).		5-10% of pts develop HUS (approx. 10% with HUS die or have permanent renal failure; 50% HUS pts have some degree of renal impairment) (CID 38:1298, 2004). Non O157:H7 STEC emerging; for lab diagnosis, see MMWR 58 (RR-12), 2009. In the US, infection with non-O157 Shiga toxin producing E. coli was associated with international travel (CID 53: 269, 2011). In 2011, large outbreak centered in Germany of HUS from E. coli O104:H4, an enteroaggregative strain that acquired prophage mediating Shiga toxin 2 (NEJM 365:709, 2011; NEJM 365:718, 2011). Suggested that stopping NSAIDs helps. Ref.: NEJM 355:2418, 2006.
	Klebsiella oxytoca—antibiotic-associated diarrhea	Responds to stopping antibiotic		
(Continued on next page)	**Listeria monocytogenes**	Usually self-limited. Value of oral antibiotics (e.g., ampicillin or TMP-SMX) unknown, but their use might be reasonable in populations at risk for invasive disease (CID 40:1327, 2005; Wien Klin Wochenschr 121:149, 2009). Those with bacteremia/meningitis require parenteral therapy, see pages 9 & 60.		Recognized as a cause of food-associated febrile gastroenteritis. Not detected in standard stool cultures (NEJM 336:100 & 130, 1997). Percentage with invasive diseases varies for various commercial food products (hospitalized during an outbreak, none developed sepsis (NEJM 342:1236, 2000). Populations at ↑ risk of severe systemic disease: pregnant women, neonates, the elderly, and immunocompromised hosts (MMWR 57:1097, 2008).

Abbreviations on page 2.

NOTE: All dosage recommendations are for adults (unless otherwise indicated) and assume normal renal function.

TABLE 1 (16)

ANATOMIC SITE/DIAGNOSIS/ MODIFYING CIRCUMSTANCES	ETIOLOGIES (usual)	SUGGESTED REGIMENS*		ADJUNCT DIAGNOSTIC OR THERAPEUTIC MEASURES AND COMMENTS
		PRIMARY	ALTERNATIVE†	
(Continued from previous page) GASTROINTESTINAL/Gastroenteritis—Specific Therapy (continued)				
	Salmonella, non-typhi— For enteric (enteric) fever, see page 61. Fever in 71–91%, history of bloody stools in 34%	If pt asymptomatic or illness mild, antimicrobial therapy not indicated. **Treat if** < 1 yr old or >50 yrs old, if immunocompromised, if vascular grafts or prosthetic joints, bacteremic, hemoglobinopathy, or hospitalized with severe diarrhea (see typhoid fever, page 61). **CIP** 500 mg po bid or **Levo** 500 mg po once daily x 3 days or **Oflox** 400 mg po bid x 3 days. Alternatives usually active if IV therapy required (see footnote, page 25): ceftriaxone, cefotaxime. Increasing FQ resistance in Asia (AAC 53:2696, 2009). **Primary treatment of enteritis is fluid and electrolyte replacement.**		
		CIP 750 mg po bid x 3 days (14 days if immunocompromised).	**Azithro** 500 mg po once daily x 3 days	Recent expert review recommended adult CIP dose of 750 mg once daily for 3 days (NEJM 361:1560, 2009).
	Shigella Fever in 58%, history of bloody stools 51%	See Comment for peds rx per dose	**Azithro** 500 mg po once daily x 3 days	Infection due to S. flexneri resistant to CIP, ceftriaxone and cefotaxime has been reported (MMWR 59:1619, 2010). **Peds doses: Azithro** 7–10 mg/kg/day once daily x 3 days. For severe disease: ceftriaxone 50–75 mg/kg per day x 2–5 days. CIP suspension 10 mg/kg bid x 5 days. CIP superior to ceftriaxone in children (LnID 3:537, 2003). **Immunocompromised children & adults: Treat for 7–10 days.** Azithro superior to cefixime in trial in children (PIDJ 22:374, 2003).
	Spirochetosis (Brachyspira pilosicoli)	Benefit of treatment unclear. Susceptible to **metro, ceftriaxone,** and **Moxi** (AAC 47:2354, 2003).		Anaerobic intestinal spirochete that colonizes colon of domestic & wild animals plus humans. Case reports of diarrhea with large numbers of the organism present (JCM 39:347, 2001; Am J Clin Path 120:828, 2003). Rarely, B. pilosicoli has been isolated from blood culture (JCM 41:3450, 2003; JCM 41:1348, 2003).
	Vibrio cholerae Treatment decreases duration of disease, volume losses, & duration of excretion (CID 37:272, 2003; Ln 363:223, 2004)	**Primary therapy is rehydration.** Select antibiotics based on susceptibility of locally prevailing isolates. Options include: **Doxycycline** 300 mg po single dose **OR Azithromycin** 1 gm po single dose **OR Tetracycline** 500 mg po qid x 3 days (these options are based on CDC recommendations for 2010 Haiti epidemic)	**For pregnant woman: Azithromycin** 1 gm po single dose **OR Erythromycin** 500 mg po qid x 3 days **For children: Azithromycin** 20 mg/kg po as single dose; for other age-specific alternatives, see CDC website http://www.cdc.gov/haiti/chol era/hcp_goinghaiti.htm	Antimicrobial therapy shortens duration of illness, but rehydration is paramount. When IV hydration is needed, use Ringer's lactate. Switch to PO repletion with Oral Rehydration Salts (ORS) as soon as able to take oral fluids. ORS are commercially available for reconstitution in potable water. If not available, WHO suggests a substitute can be made by dissolving ½ teaspoon salt and 6 level teaspoons of sugar per liter of potable water (http://www.who.int/cholera/technical/en/). For additional practical considerations, see Lancet 363:223, 2004. CDC recommendations for other aspects of management developed for Haiti outbreak can be found at http://www.cdc.gov/haiti/cholera/hcp_goinghaiti.htm. Isolates from this outbreak demonstrate reduced susceptibility to ciprofloxacin and resistance to sulfisoxazole, nalidixic acid and furazolidone.

Abbreviations on page 2. NOTE: All dosage recommendations are for adults (unless otherwise indicated) and assume normal renal function.

TABLE 1 (17)

ANATOMIC SITE/DIAGNOSIS/ MODIFYING CIRCUMSTANCES	ETIOLOGIES (usual)	SUGGESTED REGIMENS* PRIMARY	ALTERNATIVE¹	ADJUNCT DIAGNOSTIC OR THERAPEUTIC MEASURES AND COMMENTS
GASTROINTESTINAL/Gastroenteritis—Specific Therapy (continued)				
	Vibrio parahaemolyticus	Antimicrobial rx does not shorten course. Hydration.		Shellfish exposure common. Treat severe disease: **FQ, doxy, P Ceph 3**
	Vibrio vulnificus	Usual presentation is skin lesions & bacteremia, life-threatening; treat early: **ceftaz** or **doxy**—see page 5¹; **levo** (AAC 46:3580, 2002).
	Yersinia enterocolitica Fever in 68%, bloody stools in 26%	No treatment unless severe. If severe, combine **doxy** 100 mg IV bid + (**tobra** or **gent** 5 mg/kg per day once q24h). **TMP-SMX** or **FQs** are alternatives.		Mesenteric adenitis pain can mimic acute appendicitis. Lab diagnosis difficult: requires "cold enrichment" and/or yersinia selective agar. Desferrioxamine therapy increases severity, discontinue if pt on it. Iron overload states predispose to yersinia (CID 27:1362 & 367, 1998).
Gastroenteritis—Specific Risk Groups—Empiric Therapy				
Anoreceptive intercourse				
Proctitis (distal 15 cm only)	Herpes viruses, gonococci, chlamydia, syphilis. See Genital Tract, page 23			See specific GI pathogens, Gastroenteritis, above.
Colitis	Shigella, salmonella, campylobacter, E. histolytica (see Table 13A)			
HIV-1 infected (AIDS):	G. lamblia			
>10 days diarrhea				
Acid-fast organisms:	Cryptosporidium parvum, Cyclospora cayetanensis			See Table 13A
Other:	Isospora belli, microsporidia (Enterocytozoon bieneusi, Septata intestinalis)			
Neutropenic enterocolitis or "typhlitis" (CID 27:695 & 700, 1998)	Mucosal invasion by **Clostridium septicum**. Occasionally caused by C. sordellii or P. aeruginosa	As for perirectal abscess, diverticulitis, pg 22. Ensure empiric regimen includes drug active vs. Clostridia species. Empiric regimen should have predictive activity vs. P. aeruginosa also.		Tender right lower quadrant may be clue, but tenderness may be diffuse or absent in immunocompromised host. Need surgical consult. Surgical resection controversial but may be necessary. **NOTE:** Resistance of clostridia to clindamycin reported. Broad-spectrum agents such as PIP-TZ, IMP, MER, DORI should cover most pathogens
Traveler's diarrhea, self-medication. Patient usually afebrile (CID 44:338 & 347, 2007)	**Acute:** 60% due to diarrheagenic E. coli; shigella, salmonella, or campylobacter, C. difficile, amebiasis (see Table 13A). **chronic:** cyclospora, cryptosporidia, giardia, isospora	**CIP** 500 mg bid for 1–3 days **OR** **Levo** 500 mg po q24h for 1–3 days **OR** **Oflox** 300 mg po bid for 3 days **OR** **Rifaximin** 200 mg po tid for 3 days **OR** **If Azithro** 1000 mg po once or 500 mg po q24h for 3 days		**For pediatrics:** Azithro 10 mg/kg/day as a single dose for 3 days or Ceftriaxone 50 mg/kg/day as single dose for 3 days. Avoid FQs. **For pregnancy:** Use Azithro. Avoid FQs. **Antimotility agent:** For non-pregnant adults with no fever or blood in stool, add loperamide 4 mg po x 1, then 2 mg po after each loose stool to a maximum of 16 mg per day. **Comments:** Rifaximin approved only for ages 12 and older. Works only for diarrhea due to non-invasive E. coli. Do not use if fever or bloody stool. **References:** NEJM 361:1560, 2009; BMJ 337: a1746, 2008; http://wwwnc.cdc.gov/travel/yellowbook/2012/chapter-2-the-pre-travel-consultation/travelers-diarrhea.htm
Prevention of Traveler's diarrhea	Not routinely indicated. Current recommendation is to take **FQ + Imodium** with 1st loose stool.		Alternative during 1st 3 wks of travel: **Rifaximin** 200 mg bid²⁴ & only if activities are essential. (AnIM 142:805 & 861, 2005).	

Abbreviations on page 2.   NOTE: All dosage recommendations are for adults (unless otherwise indicated) and assume normal renal function.

TABLE 1 (18)

ANATOMIC SITE/DIAGNOSIS/ MODIFYING CIRCUMSTANCES	ETIOLOGIES (usual)	SUGGESTED REGIMENS*		ADJUNCT DIAGNOSTIC OR THERAPEUTIC MEASURES AND COMMENTS
		PRIMARY	ALTERNATIVE†	
GASTROINTESTINAL (continued)				
Gastrointestinal Infections by Anatomic Site: Esophagus to Rectum				
Esophagitis	Candida albicans, HSV, CMV	See SANFORD GUIDE TO HIV/AIDS THERAPY and Table 11A.		
Duodenal/Gastric ulcer; gastric cancer, MALT lymphomas (not 2° NSAIDs).	Helicobacter pylori See Comment Prevalence of pre-treatment resistance increasing	**Sequential therapy** (Rabeprazole 20 mg + amox 1 (gm) bid x 5 days, then (rabeprazole 20 mg + clarithro 500 mg + tinidazole 500 mg) bid for another 5 days. See footnote⁹.	**Quadruple therapy** (10-14 days): Bismuth subsalicylate 2 tabs qid (see footnote⁹); bismuth subcitrate 400 mg bid, + Metro 500 mg qid + tetracycline 500 mg qid + omeprazole 20 mg bid.	**Comment:** In many locations, failure rates with previously recommended triple regimens **(PPI + Amox + Clarithro)** (20%). With 10 days of quadruple therapy (20% vs. 45% eradication) failure rates vary. (2) Outside U.S. can use regimens with each containing **Bismuth subcitrate potassium** 140 mg + **Metro** 125 mg qid + **Tetracycline** 125 mg) and amox 1 (gm) bid x 5 days, eradication rates were 93% in a per protocol population and 80% in an intention-to-treat population, both significantly better than with 7-day triple therapy regimen (PPI + Amox + Clarithro) (Lancet 377:905, 2011). Exercise caution regarding potential interactions with other drugs. Contraindications in pregnancy and warnings for other special populations. For general review, see NEJM 362:1597, 2010. **Dx: Stool antigen**—Monoclonal EIA >90% sens. & 92% specific. (Amer. J. Gastro. 101:921, 2006) Other tests: if endoscoped, rapid urease &/or histology &/or culture; urea breath test, but some office-based tests underperform (CID 48:1385, 2009). **Test of cure:** Repeat stool antigen and/or urea breath test >8 wks post-treatment. **Treatment outcome:** Failure rate of triple therapy 20% due to clarithro resistance. Cure rate with sequential therapy 90%.
Small intestine: Whipple's disease [NEJM 356:55, 2007; LnID 8:179, 2008] See Infective endocarditis, culture-negative, page 30.	Tropheryma whipplei	**Initial 10-14 days:** Ceftriaxone 2 gm IV q24h or Pen G 2 million units IV q4h **Then, for approx. 1 year:** TMP-SMX-DS 1 tab po bid	Pen/Ceph allergic: TMP-SMX-DS 1 tab po tid + Streptomycin 1 gm IM/IV q24h If sulfa-allergic: Doxy 100 mg po bid + hydroxychloroquine 200 mg po tid	Therapy based on empiricism and retrospective analyses. Randomized trial reported that initial therapy with Meropenem 1 gm q8h was comparable to Ceftriaxone 2 gm q24h, each administered for 14 days and then followed by TMP-SMX for 12 months, in maintaining remission of Whipple's disease (Gastroenterology 138:478, 2010; editorial ibid. 138:429, 2010). TMP-SMX, CNS relapses during therapy have been reported (J Antimicrobial Chemother 65:2005, 2010). Cultivated from CSF described (J Antimicrobial Chemother 65:2005, 2010). Late relapses with resistance to TMP-SMX have been reported. For review of Whipple's pathogenesis, see Lancet Infect Dis 8:179, 2008.

⁸ Can substitute other proton pump inhibitors for omeprazole or rabeprazole–all bid: **esomeprazole** 20 mg (FDA-approved), **lansoprazole** 30 mg (FDA-approved), **pantoprazole** 40 mg (not FDA-approved for this indication).

⁹ **Bismuth preparations:** (1) In U.S., **bismuth subsalicylate (Pepto-Bismol)** 262 mg tabs; adult dose for helicobacter is 2 tabs (524 mg) qid. (2) Outside U.S. colloidal bismuth subcitrate (De-Nol) 120 mg chewable tablets; dose is 1 tablet qid. In the U.S. bismuth subcitrate is available in combination with metro only (Pylera; each cap contains bismuth subcitrate 140 mg + Metro 125 mg + Tetracycline 125 mg), given as 3 caps po 4x daily for 10 days **together with a** twice daily PPI.

Abbreviations on page 2. NOTE: All dosage recommendations are for adults (unless otherwise indicated) and assume normal renal function.

TABLE 1 (19)

ANATOMIC SITE/DIAGNOSIS/ MODIFYING CIRCUMSTANCES	ETIOLOGIES (usual)	SUGGESTED REGIMENS*		ADJUNCT DIAGNOSTIC OR THERAPEUTIC MEASURES AND COMMENTS
		PRIMARY	ALTERNATIVE†	
GASTROINTESTINAL/Gastrointestinal Infections by Anatomic Site: Esophagus to Rectum *(continued)*				
Diverticulitis, perirectal abscess, peritonitis *Also see Peritonitis, page 47*	Enterobacteriaceae, occasionally P. aeruginosa, Bacteroides sp., enterococci	**Outpatient rx—mild diverticulitis, drained perirectal abscess:** TMP-SMX-DS bid or (CIP 750 mg bid or **Levo** 750 mg q24h) + **metro** 500 mg q6h. All po x-7-10 days.	**AM-CL-ER** 1000/62.5 mg 2 tabs po bid x 7–10 days **OR Moxi** 400 mg q24h x 7-10 days	Must * cover* both Gm-neg. aerobic & Gm-neg. anaerobic bacteria. **Drugs active only vs. anaerobic Gm-neg. bacilli:** clinda, metro. **Drugs active only vs. aerobic Gm-neg. bacilli:** AP Ag's—P Ceph 2/3/4 (see Table 10A, page 93), aztreonam, AP Pen, CIP, Levo. **Drugs active vs. both aerobic/anaerobic Gm-neg. bacteria:** cefoxitin, cefotetan, TC-CL, PIP-TZ, AM-SB, ERTA, Dori, IMP, MER, Moxi, & tigecycline. **Increasing resistance of Bacteroides species** (AAC 51:1649, 2007):
		Mild-moderate disease—Inpatient—Parenteral Rx: (e.g. focal periappendiceal peritonitis, periverticular abscess, endomyometritis) **PIP-TZ** 3.375 gm IV q6h or 4.5 gm IV q8h **or AM-SB** 3 gm IV q6h **or TC-CL** 3.1 gm IV q6h **or ERTA** 1 gm IV q24h **or MOXI** 400 mg IV q24h	[(CIP 400 mg IV q12h) or **Levo** 750 mg IV q24h)] + **metro** 500 mg IV q6h or 1 gm IV q12h) **OR tigecycline** 100 mg IV 1st dose & then 50 mg IV q12h **OR Moxi** 400 mg IV q24h	% Resistant: Cefoxitin 5-30 / Cefotetan 17-87 / Clindamycin 19-35. **Resistance:** Resistance to metro, PIP-TZ rare. Resistance to FQ increased in enteric bacteria, particularly if any FQ used recently. **Ertapenem** poorly active vs. P. aeruginosa/Acinetobacter sp. **Concomitant surgical management important**, esp. with moderate-severe disease. **Role of enterococci remains debatable.** Probably pathogenic in infections of biliary tract. Probably need drugs active vs. enterococci in pts with valvular heart disease.
		Severe life-threatening disease, ICU patient: IMP 500 mg IV q6h or MER 1 gm IV q8h **or** Dori 500 mg q8h (1-hr infusion)	AMP + metro + CIP [AMP 2 gm IV q6h + **CIP** 400 mg IV q12h or **Levo** 750 mg IV q24h) **OR AMP** 2 gm IV q6h + **metro** 500 mg IV q6h + **aminoglycoside**[10] (see Table 10D, page 109)]	**Severe penicillin/cephalosporin allergy: (aztreonam** 2 gm IV q6h to q8h) + (**metro** (500 mg IV q6h) or (1 gm IV q12h)] **OR** [(**CIP** 400 mg IV q12h) or (**Levo** 750 mg IV q24h) + **metro**)]

[10] **Aminoglycoside = antipseudomonal aminoglycosidic aminoglycoside; e.g., amikacin, gentamicin, tobramycin**

NOTE: All dosage recommendations are for adults (unless otherwise indicated) and assume normal renal function.

Abbreviations on page 2.

TABLE 1 (20)

ANATOMIC SITE/DIAGNOSIS/ MODIFYING CIRCUMSTANCES	ETIOLOGIES (usual)	SUGGESTED REGIMENS* PRIMARY	ALTERNATIVE†	ADJUNCT DIAGNOSTIC OR THERAPEUTIC MEASURES AND COMMENTS
GENITAL TRACT: Mixture of empiric & specific treatment. Divided by sex of the patient. For sexual assault (rape), see Table 15A, page 192 & MMWR 59 (RR-12), 2010.				
Both Women & Men: See Guidelines for Dx of Sexually Transmitted Diseases, MMWR 59 (RR-12), 2010.				
Chancroid	H. ducreyi	**Ceftriaxone 250 mg IM** single dose OR **azithro** 1 gm single dose	**CIP** 500 mg bid po x 3 days OR **erythro base** 500 mg qid po x 7 days.	In HIV+ pts, failures reported with single dose azithro (CID 21:409, 1995). Evaluate after 7 days; ulcer should objectively improve. Symptoms improve in 3 days. All patients with chancroid should be tested for HIV and syphilis. All sex partners in past 10 days with chancroid should be examined and treated if they have evidence of disease or have had sex with index pt within the last 10 days.
Chlamydia et al, non-gono-coccal or post-gonococcal urethritis, cervicitis **NOTE: Assume concomitant N. gonorrhoeae. Chlamydia conjunctivitis, see page 12.**	Chlamydia 50%, Mycoplasma hominis. Other known etiologies (10–15%): tricho-monas, herpes simplex virus, Mycoplasma genitalium. Ref: JID 193:333, 336, 2006.	**[Doxy 100 mg bid po x 7 days]** or **(Azithromycin 1 gm po as single dose).** Evaluate & treat sex partner. **In pregnancy: Azithromycin 1 gm po single dose OR amox 500 mg po tid x 7 days.**	**[Erythro base 500 mg po qid x 7 days]** or **(Ofloxacin 300 mg po x7 days)** or **(Levo 500 mg po q24h x 7 days)** **In pregnancy: Erythro base 500 mg po qid for 7 days. Doxy & FQs contraindicated.**	**Diagnosis:** Nucleic acid amplification tests for C. trachomatis & N. gonorrhoeae on urine samples equivalent to cervix or urethra specimens (AnIM 142:914, 2005). Test all urethritis/cervicitis pts for HIV & syphilis. For additional urethritis retreatment regimens, see MMWR (RR-11), 2006. **Evaluate & treat sex partners.** Re-test for cure in pregnancy. Azithromycin 1 gm was superior to doxycycline for M. genitalium male urethritis (CID 48:1649, 2009), but may select resistance leading to ↑ failure of multi-dose azithromycin retreatment regimens (CID 48:1655, 2009).
Recurrent/persistent urethritis	Occult trichomonas, tetra-resistant U. urealyticum	**Metro** 2 gm po x 1	**Tinidazole** 2 gm po X 1 + **Azithromycin** 1 gm po X 1 (if not used for initial episode)	In men with NGU, 20% infected with trichomonas (JID 188:465, 2003). See above re M. genitalium.
Gonorrhea (MMWR 59 (RR-12); 49, 2010). **FQs no longer recommended for treatment of gonococcal infections** (MMWR 59 (RR-12); 49, 2010).				**Cephalosporin resistance:** JAMA 309:163 & 185, 2013.
Conjunctivitis (adult)	N. gonorrhoeae	**Ceftriaxone** 1 gm IM or IV single dose		Consider one-time saline lavage of eye.
Disseminated gonococcal infection (DGI, dermatitis-arthritis syndrome)	N. gonorrhoeae	**Ceftriaxone** 1 gm IM or IV q24h	**Cefotaxime** 1 gm q8h IV) or **(ceftizoxime** 1 gm q8h IV) – see Comment. FQs may be effective if susceptible organism, **do not use FQs.**	Continue IM or IV regimen for 24hr after symptoms ↓; reliable pts may be discharged 24hr as rx resolve to complete 7 days rx with **cefixime 400 mg po bid.** R/O meningitis; endocarditis. **Treat presumptively for concomitant C. trachomatis.**
Endocarditis	N. gonorrhoeae	**Ceftriaxone** 1–2 gm IV q24h x 4 wks.		Ref: JID 157:1281, 1988.
Pharyngitis	N. gonorrhoeae	**Ceftriaxone** 250 mg IM x 1 PLUS **(Azithro 1 gm po x 1)** or **(doxy** 100 mg po bid x 7 days)	**– (Azithro** 1 gm po x 1) Due to resistance concerns, **do not use FQs.**	Pharyngeal GC more difficult to eradicate. Some suggest test of cure culture after 1 wk. **Spectinomycin, cefixime, cefpodoxime & cefuroxime not effective**
Urethritis, cervicitis, proctitis (uncomplicated) For prostatitis, see page 27. Diagnosis: Nucleic acid amplification test (NAAT) on urine or urethral swab—see AnIM 142:914, 2005. **NO FQs: MMWR 59 (RR-12);49, 2010.**	N. gonorrhoeae (50% of pts with urethritis, cervicitis have concomitant C. trachomatis **–treat for both unless NAAT indicates single pathogen)**	**[(Ceftriaxone 250 mg IM x 1)** or **(doxy** 100 mg po bid x 7 days)] PLUS – (Azithro 1 gm po x 1) or azithro comment. Understanding risk of FQ-resistance, could try FQ therapy with close follow-up.	**PLUS – (Azithro 1 gm po x 1)** or azithro 2 gm po x 1 (Note: not effective for pharyngeal disease); oral cephalosporin use is no longer recommended as primary therapy owing to emergence of resistance. MMWR 61:590, 2012. Other single-dose cephalosporins: ceftizoxime 500 mg IM. **Azithro** 1 gm po x 1 effective for chlamydia but need 2 gm po for GC; not recommended for GC due to GI side-effects, expense & rapid emergence of resistance.	Screen for syphilis. Test alternatives for GC (Test of Cure recommended one week after Rx – if alternatives for GC, use of these approaches listed below): • Cefixime 400 mg po x 1 OR Cefpodoxime 400 mg po x 1 (Note: not effective for pharyngeal disease); oral cephalosporin use is no longer recommended as primary therapy owing to emergence of resistance. MMWR 61:590, 2012. • Other single-dose cephalosporins: ceftizoxime 500 mg IM, cefoxitin 2 gm IM + probenecid 1 gm po. • **Azithro** 1 gm po x 1 effective for chlamydia but need 2 gm po for GC; not recommended for GC due to GI side-effects, expense & rapid emergence of resistance.

** Cefixime oral preparations now available as oral suspension, 200 mg/5 mL, and 400 mg tablets (Lupine Pharmaceuticals). (+1) 866-587-4617). (MMWR 57:435, 2008).

* NOTE: All dosage recommendations are for adults (unless otherwise indicated) and assume normal renal function.

Abbreviations on page 2.

TABLE 1 (21)

ANATOMIC SITE/DIAGNOSIS/ MODIFYING CIRCUMSTANCES	ETIOLOGIES (usual)	SUGGESTED REGIMENS*		ADJUNCT DIAGNOSTIC OR THERAPEUTIC MEASURES AND COMMENTS
		PRIMARY	ALTERNATIVE†	
GENITAL TRACT/Both Women & Men (continued)				
Granuloma inguinale (Donovanosis)	Klebsiella (formerly Calymmatobacterium) granulomatis	**Doxy** 100 mg po bid x 3–4 wks	**TMP-SMX** one DS tablet bid x 3 wks **OR Erythro** 500 mg po qid x 3 wks **OR CIP** 750 mg po bid x 3 wks OR **azithro** 1 gm po q wk x 3 wks	Clinical response usually seen in 1 wk. **Rx until all lesions healed,** may take 4 wks. Treatment failures & recurrence seen with doxy & TMP-SMX. Report of efficacy with FQ and chloro. Ref.: CID 25:24, 1997. Relapse can occur 6-18 months after apparently effective Rx. If improvement not evident in first few days, some experts add gentamicin 1 mg/kg IV q8h.
Herpes simplex virus.	*See Table 14A, page 160*			
Human papilloma virus (HPV)	*See Table 14A, page 166*			
Lymphogranuloma venereum	Chlamydia trachomatis, servovars. L1, L2, L3	**Doxy** 100 mg po bid x 21 days	**Erythro** 0.5 gm po qid x 21 days or **Azithro** 1 gm po qwk x 3 weeks (clinical data lacking)	Dx based on serology: biopsy contraindicated because sinus tracts develop. Nucleic acid ampli tests for C. trachomatis will be positive. In MSM, presents as fever, rectal ulcer, anal discharge (CID 39:996, 2004; Dis Colon Rectum 52:507, 2009).
Phthirus pubis (**pubic lice, "crabs"**)	Phthirus pubis & Sarcoptes scabiei	*See Table 13A, page 151*		
Syphilis (JAMA 290:1510, 2003): **Syphilis & HIV:** MMWR 59 (RR-12): 26, 2010. Review JCI 121:4584, 2011.	T. pallidum			
Early- primary, secondary, or latent <1 yr. Screen with treponemal-specific antibody or RPR/VDRL, see JCM 50:2 & 148, 2012.	NOTE: Test all pts with HIV for latent syphilis.	**Benzathine pen G (Bicillin L-A)** 2.4 million units IM x 1 or **Azithro** 2 gm po x 1 dose (*See Comment*)	**(Doxy** 100 mg po bid x 14 days) or **(tetracycline** 500 mg po qid x 14 days) or **(ceftriaxone** 1 gm IM/IV q24h x 10–14 days). Follow-up mandatory.	If early or congenital syphilis, **quantitative VDRL at 0, 3, 6, 12 & 24 mos** after rx. If 1° or 2° syphilis, VDRL should ↓ 2 tubes at 6 mos, 3 tubes 12 mos, & 4 tubes 24 mos. Update on congenital syphilis (MMWR 59:413, 2010). If early syphilis & treated, 25% will remain RPR seronegative at 12 mos, 24% neg, RPR/VDRL at 1 2-3 yrs (AMM 114:1005, 1991). If titers fail to fall, examine CSF; if CSF (+), treat as neurosyphilis; if CSF is negative, retreat with benzathine Pen G 2.4 mu IM weekly x 3 wks. **Azithro** 2 gm po x 1 dose (equivalent to **benzathine Pen** 2.4 M x 1 dose in early syphilis (N Engl J Med 353:1236, 2005). **Azithro-resistant syphilis** documented in California, Ireland, & elsewhere (CID 44:S130, 2007; AAC 54:583, 2010). NOTE: Use of **benzathine procaine penicillin** is inappropriate!
More than 1 yr's duration (latent of indeterminate duration, cardiovascular, late benign gumma).	For penicillin desensitization method, see Table 7, page 80 and MMWR 59 (RR-12): 26, 2010.	**Benzathine pen G (Bicillin L-A)** 2.4 million units IM q week x 3 = 7.2 million units total	**Doxy** 100 mg po bid x 28 days or **tetracycline** 500 mg po qid x 28 days; **Ceftriaxone** 1 gm IV or IM daily for 10-14 days MAY be an alternative (No clinical data, consult an ID specialist).	No published data on efficacy of alternatives. **Indications for LP (CDC): neurologic symptoms, treatment failure, any eye or ear involvement, other evidence of active syphilis (aortitis, gumma, iritis).**
Neurosyphilis—Very difficult to treat. Includes ocular (retrobulbar neuritis) syphilis		**Pen G** 18-24 million units per day either as continuous infusion or as 3-4 million units IV q4h x 10–14 days.	**Procaine pen G** 2.4 million units IM q24h **+ probenecid** 0.5 gm po qid x 10–14 days—See Comment	**Ceftriaxone** 2 gm IV q IM) q24h x 14 days: 23% failure rate reported (AJM 93:481, 1992). For penicillin allergy, either desensitize to penicillin or obtain infectious diseases consultation. **Serologic criteria for response to rx: 4-fold or greater ↓ in VDRL titer over 6-12 mos.** (CID 28 (Suppl. 1):S21, 1999).
All need CSF exam. HIV infection (AIDS) CID 44:S130, 2007.		Treatment same as HIV uninfected with closer follow-up. Treat early neurosyphilis for 10-14 days regardless of CD4 count. MMWR 56:625, 2007.		See Syphilis discussion in MMWR 59 (RR-12), 2010.

Abbreviations on page 2.   NOTE: All dosage recommendations are for adults (unless otherwise indicated) and assume normal renal function.

TABLE 1 (22)

ANATOMIC SITE/DIAGNOSIS/ MODIFYING CIRCUMSTANCES	ETIOLOGIES (usual)	SUGGESTED REGIMENS*		ADJUNCT DIAGNOSTIC OR THERAPEUTIC MEASURES AND COMMENTS
		PRIMARY	ALTERNATIVE†	
GENITAL TRACT/Both Women & Men (continued)				
Pregnancy and syphilis	T. pallidum	Same as for non-pregnant, some recommend 2nd dose (2.4 million units) **benzathine pen G** 1 wk. after initial dose esp. in 3rd trimester or with 2° syphilis	Skin test for penicillin allergy. Desensitize if necessary as parenteral pen G is only therapy with documented efficacy!	Monthly quantitative VDRL or equivalent. If 4-fold ↑, re-treat. Doxy, tetracycline contraindicated. Erythro not recommended because of high risk of failure to cure fetus.
Congenital syphilis (Update on Congenital Syphilis: MMWR 59 (RR-12): 36, 2010)		**Aqueous crystalline pen G** 50,000 units/kg per dose IV q12h x 7 days, then q8h for 10 day total.	**Procaine pen G** 50,000 units/kg IM q24h for 10 days	Another alternative: Ceftriaxone 250 days old: 75 mg/kg IV/IM q24h (use with caution in infants with jaundice) or > 30 days old 100 mg/kg IV/IM q24h: treat for 10 days. If symptomatic, ophthalmologic exam indicated. If more than 1 day of rx missed, restart entire course. **Need serologic follow-up!**
Warts, anogenital	See Table 14A, page 166			
Women: Amnionitis, septic abortion	Bacteroides, esp. Prevotella bivius; Group B, A streptococci; Enterobacteriaceae; C. trachomatis	[(**Cefoxitin** or **TC-CL** or **Dori**^{AА} or **ERTA** or **PIP-TZ**) **+ doxy**] **OR** [**Clinda** + (**aminoglycoside** or **cefotaxime**)] Dosage: see footnote²	**IMP** or **MER** or **AM-SB**	D&C of uterus. In **septic abortion**, Clostridium perfringens may cause fulminant intravascular hemolysis. **In postpartum patients with enigmatic fever and/or pulmonary emboli, consider septic pelvic vein thrombophlebitis** (see Vascular, septic pelvic vein thrombophlebitis, page 66). After discharge: doxy or clinda for C. trachomatis.
Cervicitis, mucopurulent Treatment based on results of nucleic acid amplification test	N. gonorrhoeae Chlamydia trachomatis	Treat for Gonorrhea, page 23 Treat for non-gonococcal urethritis, page 23	**Note:** In US and Europe, 1/3 of Grp B Strep resistant to clindamycin.	Criteria for diagnosis: 1) (muco) purulent endocervical exudate and/or 2) sustained endocervical bleeding after passage of cotton swab. >10 WBC/hpf of vaginal fluid is suggestive. Intracellular gram-neg diplococci are specific but not insensitive. If in doubt, send swab or urine for culture. EIA or nucleic acid amplification test and treat for both.
Endomyometritis/septic pelvic phlebitis Early postpartum (1st 48 hrs) (usually after C-section)	Bacteroides, esp. Prevotella bivius; Group B, A streptococci; Enterobacteriaceae; C. trachomatis	[(**Cefoxitin** or **TC-CL** or **ERTA** or **IMP** or **MER** or **AM-SB** or **PIP-TZ**) **+ doxy**] or [**Clinda** + (**aminoglycoside** or **cefotaxime**)] Dosage: see footnote²		See Comments under Amnionitis, septic abortion, above
Late postpartum (48 hrs to 6 wks) (usually after vaginal delivery)	Chlamydia trachomatis, M. hominis	**Doxy** 100 mg IV or po q12h times 14 days		Tetracyclines not recommended in nursing mothers; discontinue nursing. M. hominis sensitive to tetra, clinda, not erythro.
Fitzhugh-Curtis syndrome	C. trachomatis, N. gonorrhoeae	Treat as for pelvic inflammatory disease immediately below.	**Doxy** or **ceftriaxone** or clinda or **erythro**	Perihepatitis (violin-string adhesions)
Pelvic actinomycosis; usually tubo-ovarian abscess	A. israelii most common	**AMP** 50 mg/kg/day IV div 3-4 doses x 4-6 wks, then **Pen VK** 2-4 gm/day po x 3-6 mos.		Complication of intrauterine device (IUD). Remove IUD. Can use **Pen G** 10-20 million units/day IV instead of **AMP** x 4-6 wks.

¹² **P Ceph 2** (**cefoxitin** 2 gm IV q6-8h; **cefotetan** 2 gm IV q6-8h; **TC-CL** 3.1 gm IV q4-6h; **AM-SB** 3 gm IV q6h; **PIP-TZ** 3.375 gm q6h or for nosocomial pneumonia: 4.5 gm IV q6h or 4-hr infusion of 3.375 gm q8h; **doxy** 100 mg IV/po q12h; **clinda** 450-900 mg IV/po q8h; **aminoglycoside** (**gentamicin**, see Table 10D, page 109); **P Ceph 3** (**cefotaxime** 2 gm IV q8h, **ceftriaxone** 2 gm IV q24h; **MER** 1 gm IV q8h; **azithro** 500 mg IV q24h; **linezolid** 600 mg IV/po q12h; **vanco** 1 gm IV q12h 2 gm IV q24h); **doripenem** 500 mg IV q8h (1-hr infusion); **ertapenem** 1 gm IV q24h; **IMP** 0.5 gm IV q6h; **MER** 1 gm IV q8h;

Abbreviations on page 2.   NOTE: All dosage recommendations are for adults (unless otherwise indicated) and assume normal renal function.

TABLE 1 (23)

ANATOMIC SITE/DIAGNOSIS/ MODIFYING CIRCUMSTANCES	ETIOLOGIES (usual)	SUGGESTED REGIMENS*		ADJUNCT DIAGNOSTIC OR THERAPEUTIC MEASURES AND COMMENTS
		PRIMARY	ALTERNATIVE§	
GENITAL TRACT/Women *(continued)*				
Pelvic Inflammatory Disease (PID), salpingitis, tubo-ovarian abscess				
Outpatient rx: limit to pts with temp. <38°C, WBC <11,000 per mm³, minimal evidence of peritonitis, active bowel sounds & able to tolerate oral nourishment *CID 44:953 & 961, 2007;* *MMWR 59 (RR-12):63, 2010* *& www.cdc.gov/std/treatment*	N. gonorrhoeae, chlamydia, bacteroides, Enterobacteriaceae, streptococci, especially S. agalactiae Less commonly: G. vaginalis, Haemophilus influenzae, cytomegalovirus (CMV), M. hominis, U. urealyticum, and M. genitalium	**Outpatient rx:** [(ceftriaxone 250 mg IM or IV x 1) ± metro 500 mg po bid x 14 days) + doxy 100 mg po bid x 14 days]. **OR** [cefoxitin 2 gm IM with probenecid 1 gm po both as single dose) plus doxy 100 mg po bid with metro 500 mg bid— both times 14 days]	**Inpatient regimens:** [(cefotetan 2 gm IV q12h or cefoxitin 2 gm IV q6h) + doxy 100 mg IV/po q12h] **OR** [clinda 900 mg IV q8h + gentamicin 2 mg/kg loading dose, then 1.5 mg/kg q8h or 4.5 mg/kg once per day), then doxy 100 mg po x 14 days	Another alternative parenteral regimen: **AM-SB** 3 gm IV q6h + doxy 100 mg IV/po q12h Remember: Evaluate and treat sex partner. FQs not recommended due to increasing resistance (MMWR 59 (RR-12), 2010 & www.cdc.gov/std/treatment). Suggest initial inpatient evaluation/therapy for pts with tubo-ovarian abscess. For inpatient regimens, continue treatment until satisfactory response for ≥ 24-hr before switching to outpatient regimen.
Vaginitis—*MMWR 59 (RR-12):61, 2010 or CID 36 (Suppl 2):S135, 2002* **Candidiasis** Pruritus, thick cheesy discharge, pH <4.5 See Table 11A, page 116	Candida albicans 80–90%. C glabrata, C. tropicalis may be increasing—they are less susceptible to azoles	**Oral azoles: Fluconazole** 150 mg po x 1; **itraconazole** 200 mg po bid x 1 day. For milder cases, Topical Therapy with one of the over the counter preparations usually is successful (e.g., clotrimazole, butoconazole, miconazole, or fluconazole) as creams or vaginal suppositories.	**Intravaginal azoles:** variety of strengths— from 1 dose to 7–14 days. Drugs available (all end in -azole): butocon, clotrim, micon, tiocon, tercon (doses: Table 11A)	Nystatin vag. tabs times 14 days less effective. Other rx for azole-resistant strains: gentian violet, boric acid. If recurrent candidiasis (4 or more episodes per yr), 6 mo. suppression with: fluconazole 150 mg po q week or itraconazole 100 mg po q24h or clotrimazole vag. suppositories 500 mg q week
Trichomoniasis Copious foamy discharge, pH >4.5 Treat sexual partners—see Comment	Trichomonas vaginalis	**Metro** 2 gm as single dose or 500 mg po bid x 7 days **OR** **Tinidazole** 2 gm po single dose **Pregnancy:** See Comment	**For rx failure:** Re-treat with metro 500 mg po bid x 7 days; if 2nd failure: metro 2 gm po q24h x 3–5 days. If still failure, suggest ID consultation and/or contact CDC: 770-488-4115 or www.cdc.gov/std.	**Treat male sex partners (2 gm metronidazole as single dose).** Nearly 20% men with NGU are infected with trichomonas (JID 188:465, 2003). For alternative option in refractory cases, see CID 33:1341, 2001. **Pregnancy:** No data indicating metro teratogenic or mutagenic (MMWR 51[RR-6], 2002). For discussion of treating trichomonas, including issues in pregnancy, see MMWR 59 (RR-12), 2010; CID 44:S123, 2007
Bacterial vaginosis Malodorous vaginal discharge, pH >4.5 Data on recurrence & review: *JID 193:1475, 2006*	Etiology unclear; associated with Gardnerella vaginalis, mobiluncus, Mycoplasma hominis, Prevotella sp., & Atopobium vaginae et al.	**Metro** 0.5 gm po bid x 7 days or **metro vaginal gel**[13] (1 applicator intravaginally) 1x/day x 5 days **OR** **Tinidazole** (2 gm po once daily x 3 days or 1 gm po once daily x 5 days) **OR** **clinda vaginal cream** 5 gm intravaginally at bedtime x 7 days	**Clinda** 0.3 gm po bid x 7 days or **clinda ovules** 100 mg intravaginally at bedtime x 3 days.	Reported 50% 1 h cure rate if abstain from sex or use condoms; CID 44:213 & 220, 2007. Treatment of male sex partner **not** indicated unless balanitis present. Metro extended release tabs 750 mg po q24h x 7 days available, no published data. **Pregnancy:** Oral metro or oral **clinda** 7-day regimens (see Canadian OB GYN practice guidelines in JObstetGynCan 30:702, 2008). Atopobium resistant to metro in vitro, susceptible to clinda (BMC Infect Dis 6:51, 2006); importance unclear.

[13] 1 applicator contains 5 gm of gel with 37.5 mg metronidazole

Abbreviations on page 2.   NOTE: All dosage recommendations are for adults (unless otherwise indicated) and assume normal renal function.

TABLE 1 (24)

ANATOMIC SITE/DIAGNOSIS/ MODIFYING CIRCUMSTANCES	ETIOLOGIES (usual)	SUGGESTED REGIMENS* PRIMARY	SUGGESTED REGIMENS* ALTERNATIVE†	ADJUNCT DIAGNOSTIC OR THERAPEUTIC MEASURES AND COMMENTS
GENITAL TRACT *(continued)*				
Men: **Balanitis**	Candida 40%, Group B strep, gardnerella	**Metro** 2 gm po as a single dose OR **Fluc** 150 mg po x1 OR **Itra** 200 mg po bid x 1 day.		Occurs in 1/4 of male sex partners of women infected with candida. Exclude circinate balanitis (Reiter's syndrome). Plasma cell balanitis (non-infectious) responds to hydrocortisone cream.
Epididymo-orchitis Reviews in Brit J Urol Int 87:747, 2001; Andrologia 40:76, 2008 Age <35 years	N. gonorrhoeae, Chlamydia trachomatis	**Ceftriaxone** 250 mg IM x 1 + **doxy** 100 mg po bid x 10 days		Also: bed rest, scrotal elevation, and analgesics. Enterobacteriaceae occasionally encountered. All patients treated for epididymo-orchitis <35 yrs of age should be tested for HIV and syphilis.
Age >35 years or homosexual men (insertive partners in anal intercourse)	Enterobacteriaceae (coliforms)	[**Levo** 500-750 mg IV/po once daily] OR [(**doxy** 100 mg po bid) or (400 IV or 500 mg po bid)] for 10-14 days.	**AM-SB, P Ceph 3, TC-CL, PIP-TZ** (Dosage, see footnote page 25)	Midstream pyuria and scrotal pain and edema. Also: bed rest, scrotal elevation, and analgesics. NOTE: Do urine NAAT (nucleic acid amplification test) to ensure absence of N. gonorrhoeae with concomitant risk of FQ-resistant gonorrhoeae or of chlamydia if using agents without reliable activity. Other causes include: mumps, brucella, TB, intravesicular BCG, B. pseudomallei, coccidioides, Behcet's (see Brit J Urol Int 87:747, 2001).
Non-gonococcal urethritis **Prostatitis**—Review: C/D 50:1641, 2010.	See Chlamydia et al, Non-gonococcal urethritis, Table 1(20), page 23.			
Acute Uncomplicated (with risk of STD; age <35 yrs)	N. gonorrhoeae, C. trachomatis	(**ceftriaxone** 250 mg IM x 1 OR **cefixime** 400 mg po x 1) then **doxy** 100 mg bid x 10 days.		FQs no longer recommended for gonococcal infections. Test for HIV. In AIDS pts. prostate may be focus of Cryptococcus neoformans.
Uncomplicated with low risk of STD	Enterobacteriaceae (coliforms)	**FQ** (dosage: see Epididymo-orchitis, >35 yrs, above) or **TM-SMX** [1 DS tablet (160 mg TMP) po bid x 10-14 days (minimum)]. Some authorities recommend 4 weeks of therapy		Treat as acute urinary infection, 14 days (not single dose regimen). Some authorities recommend 3-4 wks therapy. If uncertain, do urine test for C. trachomatis and N. gonorrhoeae. If resistant enterobacteriaceae, use ERTA 1 gm IV qd. If resistant pseudomonas, use IMP or MER (500 mg IV q6 or q8 respectively).
Chronic bacterial	Enterobacteriaceae 80%, enterococci 15%, P. aeruginosa	**FQ** [CIP 500 mg po bid x 4-6 wks. **Levo** 750 mg po q24h x 4 wks—see Comment]	**TMP-SMX-DS** 1 tab po bid x 1-3 mos	With treatment failures consider infected prostatic calculi. FDA approved dose of levo is 500 mg.
Chronic prostatitis/chronic pain syndrome (New NIH classification, JAMA 282:236, 1999)	The most common prostatitis syndrome. Etiology is unknown; molecular probe data suggest infectious etiology (Clin Micro Rev 11: 604, 1998).	**α-adrenergic blocking agents are controversial** (AnIM 133:367, 2000).		Pt has sx of prostatitis but negative cultures and no cells in prostatic secretions. Rev. JAC 46:157, 2000. In randomized double-blind study, CIP and an alpha-blocker of no benefit (AnIM 141:581 & 639, 2004).

TABLE 1 (25)

ANATOMIC SITE/DIAGNOSIS/ MODIFYING CIRCUMSTANCES	ETIOLOGIES (usual)	SUGGESTED REGIMENS*		ADJUNCT DIAGNOSTIC OR THERAPEUTIC MEASURES AND COMMENTS
		PRIMARY	ALTERNATIVE¹	
HAND (Bites: See Skin)				
Paronychia				
Nail biting, manicuring	Staph. aureus (maybe MRSA)	Incision & drainage; do culture	TMP-SMX-DS 1-2 tabs po bid while waiting for culture result.	See Table 6 for alternatives. Occasionally—candida, gram-negative rods.
Contact with oral mucosa—dentists, anesthesiologists, wrestlers	Herpes simplex (Whitlow)	Acyclovir 400 mg tid po x 10 days	Famciclovir or valacyclovir should work, see Comment	Gram stain and routine culture negative. Famciclovir/valacyclovir doses used for primary genital herpes should work; see Table 14A, page 160.
Dishwasher (prolonged water immersion)	Candida sp.	Clotrimazole (topical)		Avoid immersion of hands in water as much as possible.
HEART				
Infective endocarditis—Native valve—empirical rx awaiting cultures—No IV illicit drugs	**NOTE: Diagnostic criteria** include evidence of continuous bacteremia (multiple positive blood cultures), new murmur (worsening of old murmur) of valvular insufficiency, definite emboli, and echocardiographic (transthoracic or transesophageal) evidence of valvular vegetations. Refs.: *Circulation* 111:3167, 2005; *Eur Heart J* 30:2369, 2009. For antimicrobial prophylaxis, see Table 15C, page 197.			
Valvular or congenital heart disease but no modifying circumstances See Table 15C, page 197 for prophylaxis	Viridans strep 30-40%, "other" strep 15-25%, enterococci 5-18%, staphylococci 20-35% (including coag-neg staph) staphylococci: CID 46:232, 2008)	[(Pen G 20 million units IV q24h, continuous or div. q4h) or (AMP 12 gm IV q24h, continuous or div. q4h) + (nafcillin or oxacillin 2 gm IV q4h) + gentamicin 1 mg/kg IM or IV q8h (see Comment)]	Vanco 30-60 mg/kg/d in 2-3 divided doses to achieve trough of 15-20 mcg/ml + gentamicin 1 mg/kg IM or IV q8h) OR dapto 6 mg/kg IV q24h	If patient not acutely ill and not in heart failure, wait for blood culture results. If initial 3 blood cultures neg, after 24-48 hrs, obtain 2-3 more blood cultures before empiric therapy started. **Nafcillin/oxacillin + gentamicin** may not cover enterococci, hence addition of penicillin G pending cultures. When positive, can modify regimen to specific therapy for organism. **Gentamicin** used for synergy, peak levels need not exceed 4 mcg per mL. **Surgery indications:** See Ann Thorac Surg 91:2012, 2011.
Infective endocarditis—Native valve—IV illicit drug use ± evidence rt-sided endocarditis empiric therapy	S. aureus/MSSA & MRSA. All others rare	Vanco 30-60 mg/kg per day in 2-3 divided doses to achieve target trough concentrations of 15-20 mcg/mL recommended for serious infections	Dapto 6 mg/kg IV q24h Approved for right-sided endocarditis.	
Infective endocarditis—Native valve—culture positive				
Viridans strep, S. bovis (S. gallolyticus) with penicillin G MIC ≤0.12 mcg/mL	Viridans strep, S. bovis (S. gallolyticus subsp. gallolyticus)	[(Pen G 12-18 million units/day IV divided q4h + gentamicin 1 mg per kg IV q8h both x 2 wks)] OR (Pen G 12-18 million units/day IV divided q4h x 4 wks) OR (ceftriaxone 2 gm IV q24h x 4 wks)	(Ceftriaxone 2 gm IV q24h + gentamicin 1 mg per kg IV q8h x 2 wks) if allergy pen G or ceftriax, use vanco 15 mg/kg IV q12h to 2 gm/day max unless serum levels measured x 4 wks	Target gent levels: peak 3 mcg/mL, trough <1 mcg/mL. If very obese pt, recommend consultation for dosage adjustment. Infuse vanco over ≥1 hr to avoid "red man" syndrome. **S. bovis suggests occult bowel pathology (new name: S. gallolyticus).** Since relapse rate may be greater in pts ill for >3 mos. prior to start of rx, the penicillin-gentamicin synergism theoretically may be advantageous in this group.

TABLE 1 (26)

ANATOMIC SITE/DIAGNOSIS/ MODIFYING CIRCUMSTANCES	ETIOLOGIES (usual)	SUGGESTED REGIMENS* PRIMARY	ALTERNATIVE†	ADJUNCT DIAGNOSTIC OR THERAPEUTIC MEASURES AND COMMENTS
HEART/Infective endocarditis—Native valve—culture positive *(continued)*				
Viridans strep, S. bovis, (S. gallolyticus) with **penicillin G MIC >0.12 to ≤0.5 mcg/mL**	Viridans strep, S. bovis, nutritionally variant streptococci (e.g. Abiotrophia) tolerant strep.[1a]	**Pen G 18 million units/day IV (divided q4h) x 4 wks PLUS Gent 1 mg/kg IV q8h x 2 wks** NOTE: Low dose of Gent	**Vanco** 15 mg/kg IV q12h to max. 2 gm/day unless serum levels documented **x 4 wks**	Can use cefazolin for pen G in pt with allergy, that is not IgE-mediated (e.g., anaphylaxis). Alternatively, can use vanco. (See Comment above on gent and vanco). **NOTE: If necessary to remove infected valve & valve culture neg., 2 weeks antibiotic treatment post-op sufficient** (CID 41:1167, 2005).
For viridans strep or S. bovis with **pen G MIC >0.5** and enterococci susceptible to AMP/pen G, vanco, gentamicin **NOTE:** Inf. Dis. consultation suggested	"Susceptible" enterococci, viridans strep, S. bovis, nutritionally variant streptococci (new names are: Abiotrophia & Granulicatella sp.)	[Pen G 18-30 million units per 24h IV (divided q4h x 4 wks) PLUS gentamicin 1-1.5 mg/kg IV q8h x 4-6 wks)] OR [AMP 12 gm/day IV, divided q4h + gent as above x 4-6 wks]	Vanco 15 mg/kg IV q12h to max 2 gm/day unless serum levels measured PLUS gentamicin 1-1.5 mg/kg q8h IV x 4-6 wks NOTE: Low dose of gent	**4 wks of rx if symptoms <3 mos.; 6 wks of rx if symptoms >3 mos.** Do not give pen cephalosporin for enterococcal endocarditis. Target gent levels: peak 3 mcg/mL, trough <1 mcg/mL. Vanco target serum levels: peak 20-50 mcg/mL, trough 5-12 mg/mL. NOTE: Because of frequency of resistance (see below), all enterococci causing endocarditis should be tested in vitro for susceptibility to penicillin, gentamicin and vancomycin plus β lactamase production.
Enterococci: MIC streptomycin >2000 mcg/mL; MIC gentamicin >500-2000 mcg/mL; no resistance to penicillin	Enterococci, high-level aminoglycoside resistance	Pen G or AMP IV as above x 8-12 wks (approx. 50% cure)	[If prolonged pen G or AMP fails, consider surgical removal of infected valve. See Comment]	10–25%: E. faecalis and 45–50% E. faecium resistant to high gent levels. May be sensitive to streptomycin, check MIC. AMP + Dapto may be another option (Eur J Micro Infect Dis 30:607, 2011). Case report of success with combination of AMP, IMP, and vanco (Scand J Int Dis 29:628, 1997). **Cure rate of 67% with IV AMP 2 gm q4h plus ceftriaxone 2 gm q12h x 6 wks** (AnIM 146:574, 2007). Theory is sequential blocking of PBPs, 455 (Amp) and 283 (ceftriaxone).
Enterococci, intrinsic pen G/AMP resistance pen G MIC >16 mcg/mL; no gentamicin resistance	Enterococci, vanco-resistant, usually E. faecium	Vanco 15 mg/kg IV q12h (check levels if >2 gm) PLUS gentamicin	Teicoplanin active against a subset of vanco-resistant enterococci. Teicoplanin is not available in U.S. Dapto is an option.	Desired vanco serum levels: trough 5-12 mcg/mL. **Gentamicin** used for synergy, peak levels need not exceed 4 mcg/mL.
Enterococci, vanco-resistant, usually E. faecium		No reliable effective rx. Can try quinupristin-dalfopristin (Synercid) or linezolid—see Comment, and Table 5A		**Synercid** activity limited to E. faecium and is usually bacteriostatic, therefore expect high relapse rate. Dose: 7.5 mg per kg IV (via central line) q8h. **Linezolid** active most enterococci, but bacteriostatic. Dose: 600 mg IV or po q12h. Linezolid failed in pt with E. faecalis endocarditis (CID 37:e29, 2003). **Dapto** is bactericidal in vitro; clinical experience in CID 41:1134, 2005. Avoid under dosing (consider 8-10 mg/kg) as resistance may emerge on therapy (CID 52:228, 2011; see also, JAC 65:1126, 2010).
Staphylococcal endocarditis Aortic &/or mitral valve infection—MSSA Surgery Indications: see Comment page 28.	Staph. aureus, methicillin-sensitive **Note: Low dose of gentamicin for only 3-5 days**	**Nafcillin (oxacillin) 2 gm IV q4h x 4-6 wks**	[Cefazolin 2 gm IV q8h x 4-6 wks] **Vanco** 30-60 mg/kg IV in 2-3 divided doses to achieve trough of 15-20 mcg/ml **x 4-6 wks**	If IgE-mediated penicillin allergy, 10% cross-reactivity to cephalosporins (about 1 in 6000 true anaphylaxis). Theoretical concern re: nafcillin in improving outcome is unproven and even low-dose gentamicin for only a few days is nephrotoxic (CID 48:713, 2009); if used at all it should be administered for **no more than 3-5 days.** Cefazolin and **Nafcillin** probably similar in efficacy and Cefazolin better tolerated (AAC 55:5122, 2011).
Aortic and/or mitral valve— MRSA	Staph. aureus, methicillin-resistant	**Vanco** 30-60 mg/kg per day in 2-3 divided doses to achieve target trough concentrations of 15-20 mcg/mL; recommended for serious infections.	**Dapto** 8-10 mg/kg q24h IV (NOT FDA approved for this indication or dose)	In clinical trial (NEJM 355:653, 2006), high failure rate with both vanco and dapto in small subsets of pts. For other alternatives, see Table 6, pg 78. Daptomycin references: JAC 66:1126, 2010; Eur J Clin Micro Infect Dis 30:127, 2011. Reports of success with high dose: AAC 54:5376, 2010; JAC (Jun 8), 2011) and ceftaroline (JAC 67:1267, 2012; J Infect Chemo online 7/14/12).

[1a] Tolerant streptococci = MBC 32-fold greater than MIC

Abbreviations on page 2. NOTE: All dosage recommendations are for adults (unless otherwise indicated) and assume normal renal function.

TABLE 1 (27)

ANATOMIC SITE/DIAGNOSIS/ MODIFYING CIRCUMSTANCES	ETIOLOGIES (usual)	SUGGESTED REGIMENS*		ADJUNCT DIAGNOSTIC OR THERAPEUTIC MEASURES AND COMMENTS
		PRIMARY	**ALTERNATIVE†**	
HEART/Infective endocarditis—Native valve—culture positive (continued)				
Tricuspid valve infection (usually IVDUs): MSSA	Staph. aureus, methicillin-sensitive	Nafcillin (oxacillin) 2 gm IV q4h **PLUS gentamicin** 1 mg/kg IV q8h **x 2 wks. NOTE: low dose of gent**	**If penicillin allergy:** Vanco 15-20 mg/kg IV q8-12h to achieve trough of 15-20 mcg/ml x 4 wks **OR** Dapto 6 mg/kg IV q24h (avoid if concomitant left-sided endocarditis). 8-12 mg/kg IV q24h used in some cases, but not FDA approved.	**2-week regimen not long** enough if metastatic infection (e.g., osteo) or left-sided endocarditis. If **Dapto** is used treat for at least 4 weeks. Dapto resistance can occur de novo, after or during vanco, or after/during dapto therapy. **Dapto** killed by combination of **dapto + TMP/SMX** or nafcillin (AAC 54:5187, 2010; AAC 56:6192, 2012); worked in 7 pts, CID 53:158, 2011).
Tricuspid valve–MRSA	Staph. aureus, methicillin-resistant	Vanco 30-60 mg/kg per day in 2-3 divided doses to achieve target trough concentrations of 15-20 mcg/ml, recommended for serious infections x 4-6 wks	Dapto 6 mg/kg IV q24h x 4-6 wks equiv to vanco for rt-sided endocarditis; both vanco & dapto did poorly in lt-sided endocarditis (NEJM 355:653, 2006). (See Comments & table, page 79)	**Linezolid:** Limited experience (see JAC 58:273, 2006) in patients with few treatment options; 64% cure rate; clear failure in 21%; thrombocytopenia in 31%. Dapto dose of 8-12 mg/kg may help in selected cases, but not FDA-approved.
Slow-growing fastidious Gm-neg. bacilli–any valve	HACEK group (see Comments)	Ceftriaxone 2 gm IV q24h x 4 wks (Bartonella resistant – see below)	AMP 12 gm IV q24h (continuous or div q4h) x 4 wks + gentamicin 1 mg/kg IV/IM q8h x 4 wks.	**HACEK (acronym for Haemophilus parainfluenzae, H. aphrophilus) aggregatibacter, Actinobacillus, Bartonella, Cardiobacterium, Eikenella, Kingella)** H. aphrophilus resistant to vanco, clinda and methicillin. Penicillinase-positive HACEK organisms should be susceptible to AM-SB + gentamicin.
Bartonella species–any valve	B. henselae, B. quintana	[Ceftriaxone 2 gm IV q24h x 6 wks + gentamicin 1 mg/kg IV q8h x 14 days] + doxy 100 mg IV/po bid x 6 wks [f Gent toxicity precludes its use, substitute Rifampin 300 mg IV/po bid]		**Dx:** Immunofluorescent antibody titer ≥1:800; blood cultures only occ. positive, or PCR of tissue from surgery. **Surgery:** Over ½ pts require valve surgery; relation to cure unclear. B. quintana transmitted by body lice among homeless.
Infective endocarditis—"culture negative"				
Fever, valvular disease, and ECHO vegetations ± emboli and neg. cultures				Etiology in 348 cases studied by serology, culture, histopath. & molecular detection: C. burnetii 48%, Bartonella sp. 28%, and rarely, (Abiotrophia elegans (nutritionally variant strep), Mycoplasma hominis, Legionella pneumophila, Tropheryma whipplei—together 1%), & rest without etiology identified (most on antibiotic). See CID 51:131, 2010 for approach to work-up.
Infective endocarditis—Prosthetic valve—empiric therapy (cultures pending) S. aureus now most common etiology (JAMA 297:1354, 2007).				
Early (<2 mos post-op)	S. epidermidis, S. aureus. Rarely, Enterobacteriaceae, diphtheroids, fungi.	Vanco 15 mg/kg IV q12h + gentamicin 1 mg/kg IV q8h + RIF 600 mg po q24h		Early surgical consultation advised especially if etiology is S. aureus, evidence of heart failure, diabetes and/or renal failure, or concern for valve ring abscess (JAMA 297:1354, 2007; CID 44:364, 2007).
Late (>2 mos post-op)	S. epidermidis, S. viridans strep, enterococci, S. aureus			

Abbreviations on page 2.   NOTE: All dosage recommendations are for adults (unless otherwise indicated) and assume normal renal function.

TABLE 1 (28)

ANATOMIC SITE/DIAGNOSIS/ MODIFYING CIRCUMSTANCES	ETIOLOGIES (usual)	SUGGESTED REGIMENS*		ADJUNCT DIAGNOSTIC OR THERAPEUTIC MEASURES AND COMMENTS
		PRIMARY	ALTERNATIVE†	
HEART (continued)				
Infective endocarditis— Prosthetic valve—positive blood cultures Treat for 6 weeks, even if suspect Viridans Strep. **Surgical consultation advised:** Indications for surgery: severe heart failure, S. aureus infection, prosthetic dehiscence, resistant organism, embolic due to large vegetation (JACC 48:e1, 2006). See also, Eur J Clin Micro Infect Dis 38:528, 2010.	Staph. epidermidis.	**(Vanco** 15 mg /kg IV q12h + **RIF** 300 mg po q8h) **x 6 wks** + **gentamicin** 1 mg/kg IV q8h **x 14 days**	If S. epidermidis is susceptible to nafcillin/oxacillin in vitro (not common), then substitute nafcillin (or oxacillin) for vanco.	
	Staph. aureus	Methicillin sensitive: (**Nafcillin** 2 gm IV q4h + **RIF** 300 mg po q8h) **times 6 wks** + **gentamicin** 1 mg per kg IV q8h **times 14 days.** Methicillin resistant: (**Vanco** 1 gm IV q12h + **RIF** 300 mg po q8h) **times 6 wks** + **gentamicin** 1 mg per kg IV q8h **times 14 days.**		Treat for 6 weeks.
	Viridans strep, enterococci Enterobacteriaceae or P. aeruginosa	See *infective endocarditis, native valve, culture positive, page 28.* **Aminoglycoside (tobra** if P. aeruginosa) + (**AP Pen** or **P Ceph 3 AP** or **P Ceph 4**)		In theory, could substitute CIP for aminoglycoside, but no clinical data.
	Candida, aspergillus	*Table 11, page 113*		High mortality. Valve replacement plus antifungal therapy standard therapy but some success with antifungal therapy alone.
Infective endocarditis—Q fever LnID 10:527, 2010. NEJM 356:715, 2007.	Coxiella burnetii	**Doxy** 100 mg po bid + **hydroxychloroquine** 600 mg/day for at least 18 mos (Mayo Clin Pro 83:574, 2008). *Pregnancy: Need long term TMP-SMX (see CID 45:548, 2007).*		**Dx:** Phase I IgG titer >800 plus clinical evidence of endocarditis. Treatment duration: 18 mos for native valve, 24 mos for prosthetic valve. Monitor serologically for 5 yrs.
Pacemaker/defibrillator infections	S. aureus (40%), S. epidermidis (40%), Gram-negative bacilli (5%), fungi (5%).	**Device removal + vanco** 1 gm IV q12h + **RIF** 300 mg po bid	**Device removal + dapto** 6 mg per kg IV q24h[16] ± **RIF** (no data) 300 mg po bid	**Duration of rx after device removal:** For "pocket" or subcutaneous infection, 10-14 days; if lead-assoc. endocarditis, 4-6 wks depending on organism. Device removal and absence of valvular vegetation assoc. with significantly higher survival rate (JAMA 307:1727, 2012).
Pericarditis, purulent— empiric therapy Ref: Medicine 88: 52, 2009	Staph. aureus, Strep. pneumoniae, Group A strep, Enterobacteriaceae	**Vanco + CIP** (Dosage, see footnote[5])	**Vanco + CFP** (see footnote[5])	Drainage required if signs of tamponade. Forced to use empiric vanco due to high prevalence of MRSA.
Rheumatic fever with carditis Ref.: Ln 366:155, 2005	Post-infectious sequelae of Group A strep infection (usually pharyngitis)	ASA, and usually prednisone 2 mg/kg po q24h for symptomatic treatment of fever, arthritis, arthralgia. May not influence carditis.		Clinical features: Carditis, polyarthritis, chorea, subcutaneous nodules, erythema marginatum. *Prophylaxis: see page 61*
Ventricular assist device-related infection Ref: LnID 6:426, 2006	S. aureus, S. epidermidis, aerobic Gm-neg bacilli, Candida sp	After culture of blood, wounds, drive line, device pocket and maybe pump: **Vanco** 15-20 mg/kg IV q12h + (**Cip** 400 mg IV q12h or **levo** 750 mg IV q24h) + **fluconazole** 800 mg IV q24h.		Can substitute **daptomycin** 10 mg/kg/d[44] for **vanco**, **cefepime** 2 gm IV q12h for FQ, and (**vori, caspo, micafungin** or **anidulafungin**) for **fluconazole.** Modify regimen based on results of culture and susceptibility tests. Higher than FDA-approved Dapto dose because of potential emergence of resistance.
JOINT—Also see Lyme Disease, page 58				
Reactive arthritis (See **Comment** for definition)	Occurs wks after infection with C. trachomatis, Campylobacter jejuni, Yersinia enterocolitica, Shigella/Salmonella sp.	Only treatment is non-steroidal anti-inflammatory drugs		Definition: Urethritis, conjunctivitis, arthritis, and sometimes uveitis and rash. Arthritis: asymmetrical oligoarthritis of ankles, knees, feet, sacroiliitis. Rash: palms and soles—keratoderma blennorrhagica; circinate balanitis of glans penis. HLA-B27 positive predisposes to Reiter's.
Reiter's syndrome (see Table 10D, page 109)				

[15] **Aminoglycosides** (see Table 10D, page 109), **IMP** 0.5 gm IV q6h, **MER** 1 gm IV q8h, **nafcillin** or **oxacillin** 2 gm IV q4h; **TC-CL** 3.1 gm IV q6h, **PIP-TZ** 3.375 gm IV q6h or 4.5 gm IV q8h, **AM-SB** 3 gm IV q6h, **P Ceph** 1 (cephalothin 2 gm IV q4h or ceftazidim 2 gm IV q8h), **CIP** 750 mg po bid or 400 mg IV bid, **vanco** 1 gm IV q12h, **RIF** 600 mg po q24h, **aztreonam** 2 gm IV q8h; **CFP** 2 gm IV q12h

Abbreviations on page 2   NOTE: All dosage recommendations are for adults (unless otherwise indicated) and assume normal renal function.

TABLE 1 (29)

ANATOMIC SITE/DIAGNOSIS/ MODIFYING CIRCUMSTANCES	ETIOLOGIES (usual)	SUGGESTED REGIMENS*		ADJUNCT DIAGNOSTIC OR THERAPEUTIC MEASURES AND COMMENTS
		PRIMARY	ALTERNATIVE¹	
JOINT/Reactive arthritis (continued)				
Poststreptococcal reactive arthritis (See Rheumatic fever, above)	Immunologic reaction after strep pharyngitis: (1) arthritis onset in <10 days, (2) lasts months, (3) unresponsive to ASA.	Treat strep pharyngitis and then NSAIDs (prednisone needed in some pts)		A reactive arthritis after a β-hemolytic strep infection in absence of sufficient Jones criteria for acute rheumatic fever. Ref.: *Mayo Clin Proc 75:144, 2000.*
Septic arthritis: Treatment requires both adequate drainage of purulent joint fluid and appropriate antimicrobial therapy. **There is no need to inject antimicrobials into joints.** Empiric therapy after collection of blood and joint fluid for culture; review Gram stain of joint fluid.				
Infants <3 mos (neonate)	Staph. aureus, Enterobacteriaceae, Group B strep	**If MRSA not a concern: (Nafcillin** or **oxacillin)** + **P Ceph 3**	**If MRSA a concern: Vanco + P Ceph 3**	Blood cultures frequently positive. Adjacent bone involved in 2/3 pts. Group B strep and gonococci most common community-acquired etiologies.
Children (3 mos–14 yrs)	Staph. aureus 27%, S. pyogenes & S. pneumo 14%, H. influenzae 3%, Gm-neg. bacilli 6%, other (GC; N. meningitidis) 14%, unknown 36%.	**Vanco + (Cefotaxime, ceftizoxime or ceftriaxone)** until culture results available. *See Table 16 for dosage.* Steroids—*see Comment* *(Dosage, see Table 16, page 203)*		Marked ↓ in H. influenzae since use of conjugate vaccine. **NOTE:** Septic arthritis due to salmonella has no association with sickle cell disease, unlike salmonella osteomyelitis. 10 days of therapy as effective as a 30-day treatment course if there is a good clinical response and CRP levels normalize quickly (*CID 48:1201, 2009*).
Adults (review Gram stain): *See Lyme Disease and page 58 for gonococcal arthritis*				
Acute monoarticular: At risk for sexually-transmitted disease	N. gonorrhoeae (See page 23), S. aureus, streptococci, rarely aerobic Gm-neg. bacilli	**Gram stain negative: Ceftriaxone 1 gm IV q24h** or **cefotaxime 1 gm IV q8h** or **ceftizoxime 1 gm IV q8h.**	If Gram stain shows Gm + cocci in clusters: **vanco 1 gm IV q12h; if >100 kg, 1.5 gm IV q12h.**	For treatment comments, see *Disseminated GC, page 23*
Not at risk for sexually-transmitted disease	S. aureus, streptococci, Gm-neg. bacilli	All empiric choices guided by Gram stain **Vanco + P Ceph 3**	**Vanco + (CIP** or **Levo)** For treatment duration, see Table 3, page 70. For dosage, see footnote page 34 & Table 2 & Table 16	Differential includes gout and chondrocalcinosis (pseudogout). **Look for crystals in joint fluid.** **NOTE:** *See Table 6 for MRSA treatment.*
Chronic monoarticular	Brucella, nocardia, mycobacteria, fungi			
Polyarticular, usually acute	**Gonococci,** B. burgdorferi, acute rheumatic fever, viruses, e.g., hepatitis B, rubella vaccine, parvo B19	Gram stain usually negative for GC. If sexually active, culture urethra, cervix, anal canal, throat, blood, joint fluid, and then: **ceftriaxone 1 gm IV q24h**		If GC, usually associated petechiae and/or pustular skin lesions and tenosynovitis. Consider Lyme disease if exposure areas known to harbor infected ticks. See page 58. Expanded differential includes gout, pseudogout, reactive arthritis (HLA-B27 pos.).
Septic arthritis, post intra-articular injection	MSSE/MRSE 40%, MSSA/MRSA 20%, P. aeruginosa, Propionibacteria, mycobacteria	**No empiric therapy.** Arthroscopy for culture/sensitivity, crystals, washout		Treat based on culture results x 14 days (assumes no foreign body present).

Abbreviations on page 2.   NOTE: All dosage recommendations are for adults (unless otherwise indicated) and assume normal renal function.

TABLE 1 (30)

ANATOMIC SITE/DIAGNOSIS/ MODIFYING CIRCUMSTANCES	ETIOLOGIES (usual)	SUGGESTED REGIMENS*		ADJUNCT DIAGNOSTIC OR THERAPEUTIC MEASURES AND COMMENTS
		PRIMARY	ALTERNATIVE†	
JOINT (continued)				
Infected prosthetic joint (PJI) • Suspect infection if sinus tract or wound drainage, acutely painful prosthesis; chronically painful prosthesis; or high ESR/CRP assoc. w/ painful prosthesis. **Empiric therapy is NOT recommended.** Treat based on culture and sensitivity results. **3 surgical options:** 1) debridement and prosthesis retention (if sx < 3 wks or implantation < 30 days): 2) 1 stage, direct exchange; 3) 2 stage: debridement, removal, reimplantation **IDSA Guidelines:** *CID 56:e1, 2013.*	MSSA/MSSE	**Debridement/Retention:** [(Nafcillin 2 gm IV q4h or Oxacillin 2 gm IV q4h IV) + Rifampin 300 mg po bid] OR (Cefazolin 2 gm IV q8h + Rifampin 300 mg po bid) x 2-6 weeks followed by [(Ciprofloxacin 750 mg po bid OR Levofloxacin 750 mg po q24h) + Rifampin 300 mg po bid] for 3-6 months (shorter duration for total hip arthroplasty) **1-stage exchange:** regimen as above for 3 mos **2-stage exchange:** regimen as above for 4-6 wks	[(Daptomycin 6-8 mg/kg IV q24h OR Linezolid 600 mg po/IV bid) + Rifampin 300 mg po bid]	• **Confirm isolate susceptibility to fluoroquinolone and rifampin:** for fluoroquinolone-resistant isolate consider using other active highly bioavailable agent, e.g., TMP-SMX, Doxy, Minocycline, Amoxicillin-Clavulanate, Clindamycin, or Linezolid • Enterococcal infection: addition of aminoglycoside optional.
	MRSA/MRSE	**Debridement/Retention:** (Vancomycin 15-20 mg/kg IV q8-12h + Rifampin 300 mg po bid) x 2-6 weeks followed by [(Ciprofloxacin 750 mg po bid OR Levofloxacin 750 mg po q24h) + Rifampin 300 mg po bid] for 3-6 months (shorter duration for total hip arthroplasty) **1-stage exchange:** regimen as above for 3 mos **2-stage exchange:** regimen as above for 4-6 wks	(Daptomycin 6-8 mg/kg IV q24h OR Linezolid 600 mg po/IV bid) ± Rifampin 300 mg po bid	• *P. aeruginosa* infection: consider adding aminoglycoside if isolate is susceptible. (but if this improves outcome unclear.) • Prosthesis retention most important risk factor for treatment failure *(Clin Microbiol Infect 16:1789, 2010).* (Linezolid 600 mg + Rifampin 300 mg) may be effective as salvage therapy *(J Infect. Epub ahead of print: Antimicrob Agents Chemother 55:4308, 2011.)*
	Streptococci (Grps A, B, C, D, viridans, other)	**Debridement/Retention:** Penicillin G 20 million units IV continuous infusion q24h or in 6 divided doses OR Ceftriaxone 2 gm IV q24h x 4-6 weeks **1 or 2 stage exchange:** regimen as above for 4-6 wks	Vancomycin 15 mg/kg IV q12h	• If prosthesis is retained, consider long-term, suppressive therapy, particularly for staphylococcal infections; depending on in vitro susceptibility options include TMP-SMX, Doxycycline, Minocycline, Amoxicillin, Cephalexin, Cefadroxil. • Culture yield may be increased by sonication of prosthesis *(N Engl J Med 357:654, 2007).*
	Enterococci	**Debridement/Retention:** Ampicillin 12 gm IV OR Penicillin G 20 million units IV continuous infusion q24h or in 6 divided doses OR **Pen-resistant:** Vancomycin 15 mg/kg IV q12h x 4-6 weeks **1 or 2 stage exchange:** regimen as above for 4-6 wks	Daptomycin 6-8 mg/kg IV q24h OR Linezolid 600 mg po/IV bid	• Other treatment consideration: Rifampin is bactericidal vs. biofilm-producing bacteria. Never use Rifampin alone due to rapid development of resistance.
	Propionibacterium acnes	**Debridement/Retention:** Penicillin G 20 million units IV continuous infusion q24h or in 6 divided doses OR Ceftriaxone 2 gm IV q24h x 4-6 weeks **1 or 2 stage exchange:** regimen as above for 4-6 wks	Vancomycin 15 mg/kg IV q12h OR Clindamycin 300-450 mg po qid	Rifampin 300 mg po/IV tid + Fusidic acid[NUS] 500 mg po/IV bid is another option *(Clin Micro Inf 12(S3):93, 2006).* • Watch for toxicity if Linezolid is used for more than 2 weeks of therapy.
	Gm-neg enteric bacilli	**Debridement/Retention:** Ertapenem 1 gm IV q24h OR other beta-lactam (e.g., Ceftriaxone 2 gm IV q24h OR Cefepime 2 gm IV q12h, based on susceptibility) x 4-6 weeks **1 or 2 stage exchange:** regimen as above for 4-6 wks	Ciprofloxacin 750 mg po bid	
	P. aeruginosa	**Debridement/Retention:** Cefepime 2 gm IV q12h OR Meropenem 1 gm IV q8h + Tobramycin 5.1 mg/kg once daily **1 or 2 stage exchange:** regimen as above for 4-6 wks	Ciprofloxacin 750 mg po bid or 400 mg IV q8h	
Rheumatoid arthritis	**TNF inhibitors** (adalimumab, certolizumab, etanercept, golimumab, infliximab) ↑ risk of TBc, fungal infection, legionella, listeria, and malignancy. *(LnID 8:601, 2008; Med Lett 51:55, 2009).* Treat latent TBc first. Tocilizumab (IL-6 receptor inhibitor) and James kinase inhibitor (tofacitinib) also increase infection risk *(Cell Microbiol 12:301, 2010; Expert Rev Clin Immunol 7:329, 2011).*			Immunosuppression, not duration of therapy, is a risk factor for recurrence. 7 days of therapy may be sufficient for immunocompetent patients undergoing one-stage bursectomy *(JAC 65:1008, 2010).*
Septic bursitis: Olecranon bursitis; prepatellar bursitis	Staph. aureus >80%, M. tuberculosis (rare), M. marinum (rare)	**(Nafcillin or oxacillin** 2 gm IV q4h or **dicloxacillin** 500 mg po qid) if MSSA	**(Vanco** 15-20 mg/kg IV q12h or **linezolid** 600 mg po bid) if MRSA	
		Other doses, see footnote page 34		

Abbreviations on page 2.   NOTE: All dosage recommendations are for adults (unless otherwise indicated) and assume normal renal function.

TABLE 1 (31)

ANATOMIC SITE/DIAGNOSIS/ MODIFYING CIRCUMSTANCES	ETIOLOGIES (usual)	SUGGESTED REGIMENS* PRIMARY	ALTERNATIVE†	ADJUNCT DIAGNOSTIC OR THERAPEUTIC MEASURES AND COMMENTS
KIDNEY, BLADDER AND PROSTATE				
Acute uncomplicated urinary tract infection (cystitis-urethritis) in females				
NOTE: Resistance of E. coli to TMP-SMX approx. 15–20% & correlates with microbiological/ clinical failure. **Recent reports of E. coli resistant to FQs as well.** 5-day **nitrofurantoin** IDSA Treatment Guidelines: *CID* 52:e103, 2011.	Enterobacteriaceae (E. coli), Staph. saprophyticus, enterococci	**<20% of Local E. coli resistant to TMP-SMX & no allergy: TMP-SMX-DS bid** x 3 days; if sulfa allergy, **nitrofurantoin** 100 mg po bid x 5 days or **fosfomycin** 3 gm po x one dose. All plus **Pyridium**	**>20% Local E. coli resistant to TMP-SMX or sulfa allergy:** then 3 days of **CIP** 250 mg bid, **CIP-ER** 500 mg q24h, **Levo** 250 mg q24h, OR **Moxi** 400 mg q24h **OR Nitrofurantoin** 100 mg bid OR single 3 gm dose of **fosfomycin.** All plus **Pyridium**	7-day rx recommended **in pregnancy** (discontinue or do not use sulfonamides (TMP-SMX) near term (2 weeks before EDC) because of potential ↑ in kernicterus). If failure on 3-day course, culture and rx 2 weeks. **Fosfomycin** 3 gm po times 1 less effective vs. E. coli than multi-dose TMP-SMX or FQ. Fosfo active vs. E. faecalis; poor activity vs. other coliforms. **Moxifloxacin** not approved for UTIs. Moxi equivalent to comparator drugs in unpublished clinical trials (on file with Bayer). Therapy of **ESBL producing E. coli and Klebsiella spp.** problematic because of multiple drug resistances: ESBL producers susceptible to fosfomycin, ertapenem, and combo of amox-clav + cefdinir in vitro (AAC 53:1278, 2009). Amox-Clav or an oral cephalosporin are options, but generally less efficacious. **Phenazopyridine (Pyridium)** —non-prescription— may relieve dysuria: 200 mg po tid times 2 days. H-emolysis if G6PD deficient.
Risk factors for STD, Dipstick positive leukocyte esterase or hemoglobin, neg. Gram stain. **Recurrent** (3 or more episodes/ year) in young women	C. trachomatis	**Azithro** 1 gm po single dose	**Doxy** 100 mg po bid 7 days	Pelvic exam for vaginitis & herpes simplex, urine LCR/PCR for GC and C. trachomatis.
	Any of the above bacteria	Eradicate infection, then **TMP-SMX** 1 single-strength tab po q24h long term		A cost-effective alternative to continuous prophylaxis is self-administered single dose rx (TMP-SMX DS, 2 tabs, 320/1600 mg) at symptom onset. Another alternative: 1 DS tablet TMP-SMX post-coitus.
Child: ≤5 yrs old & grade 3–4 reflux	Coliforms	**[TMP-SMX** 8-12 mg/kg/day (based on TMP comp) div q12h] or **(nitrofurantoin** 2 mg per kg po q24h). **CIP** approved as alternative drug ages 1-17 yrs.		
Recurrent UTI in postmenopausal women	E. coli & other Enterobac- teriaceae, enterococci, S. saprophyticus	Treat as for uncomplicated UTI. Evaluate for potentially correctable urologic factors—see *Comment*. **Nitrofurantoin** more effective than vaginal cream in decreasing frequency, but Editors worry about pulmonary fibrosis with long-term NF rx.		Definition: ≥3 culture + symptomatic UTIs in 1 year or 2 UTIs in 6 months. Urologic factors: (1) cystocele, (2) incontinence, (3) ↑ residual urine volume (≥50 mL).
Acute uncomplicated pyelonephritis (usually women 18–40 yrs, temperature >102°F, definite costovertebral tenderness) [NOTE: Culture of urine and blood indicated prior to therapy]. **If male, look for obstructive uropathy or other complicating pathology.**				
Moderately ill (outpatient) NOTE: May need one IV dose due to nausea. Resistance of E. coli to TMP/ SMX (13-45% in collaborative ER study (CID 47:1150, 2008)	Enterobacteriaceae (most likely E. coli), enterococci (Gm stain of uncentrifuged urine may allow identification of Gm-neg. bacilli vs. Gm + cocci)	**FQ** po times 5-7 days: **CIP** 500 mg bid or **CIP-ER** 1000 mg q24h, **Levo** 750 mg q24h, **Ofloxa** 400 mg bid, **Moxi** NAI 400 mg q24h possibly ok—see comment.	**AM-CL, O Ceph,** or **TMP-SMX-DS po.** Treat for 14 days. Dosage in footnote[16] Beta-lactams not as effective as FQs: *JAMA* 293:949, 2005	7 day course of **Cipro** 500 mg bid as effective as 14 day course in women (*Lancet* 380:484, 2012) Since **CIP** worked with 7-day rx, suspect other FQs effective with 7 days of therapy, **Levo** 750 mg FDA-approved for 5 days. Ref: *NEJM* 366:1028, 2012.

[16] **AM-CL** 875/125 mg po q12h or 500/125 mg po tid or 2000 /125 mg po bid; Antipseudomonal penicillins: **AM-SB** 3 gm IV q6h; **PIP** 3 gm IV q4-6h; **PIP-TZ** 3.375 gm IV q4-6h (4.5 gm IV q6h for pseudomonas pneumonia); **TC-CL** 3.1 gm IV q6h; Antipseudomonal cephalosporins: **ceftaz** 2 gm IV q8h; **CFP** 2 gm IV q12h; **aztreonam** 2 gm IV q8h; Carbapenems: **DORI** 0.5 mg IV (1 hr infusion); **ERTA** 1 gm IV q24h; **IMP** 0.5 gm IV q12h (max 4 gm/day); **MER** 1 gm IV q8h; Parenteral cephalosporins: **cefotaxime** 1 gm IV q12h (2 gm IV q6h for severe infections); **ceftriaxone** 2 gm IV q24h; Oral cephalosporins—see, Table 10A page 96; **dicloxacillin** 500 mg po q6h; FQs: **CIP** 400 mg IV q12h; **Gati** NAI 400 mg IV q24h; **levo** 750 mg IV q24h; **gentamicin**—see Table 10D, page 109; **linezolid** 600 IV/po q12h; **metro** 500 mg po q6h or 15 mg/kg IV q12h (max 4 gm/day); **nafcillin/oxacillin** 2 gm IV q4h; **TMP-SMX** 2 mg/kg (TMP component) IV q6h; **vanco** 1 gm IV q12h (if over 100 kg, 1.5 gm IV q12h).

Abbreviations on page 2.   NOTE: All dosage recommendations are for adults (unless otherwise indicated) and assume normal renal function.

TABLE 1 (32)

ANATOMIC SITE/DIAGNOSIS/ MODIFYING CIRCUMSTANCES	ETIOLOGIES (usual)	SUGGESTED REGIMENS*		ADJUNCT DIAGNOSTIC OR THERAPEUTIC MEASURES AND COMMENTS
		PRIMARY	ALTERNATIVE†	
KIDNEY, BLADDER AND PROSTATE: Acute uncomplicated pyelonephritis (continued)				
Acute pyelonephritis—Hospitalized	E. coli most common, enterococci 2nd in frequency	FQ (IV) or (AMP + gentami-cin) or ceftriaxone or PIP-TZ. Treat for 14 days. *Dosages in footnote⁹ on page 34.* Do not use cephalosporins for suspect or proven enterococcal infection	TC-CL or AM-SB or PIP-TZ or ERTA or DORI; 500 mg q8h. Treat for 14 days.	Treat IV until pt afebrile 24–48 hrs, then complete 2-wks course with oral drugs (as Moderately ill, above). **DORI** approved for 10 day treatment. **If pt hypotensive, prompt imaging (Ultrasound or CT) is recommended to ensure absence of obstructive uropathy. NOTE: Cephalosporins & ertapenem not active vs. enterococci.**
Complicated UTI/catheters Obstruction, reflux, azotemia, transplant. R/Foley, catheter-related. R/O obstruction: multi-drug resistant gram-neg bacilli. *For IDSA Guidelines: CID 50:625, 2010.*	Enterobacteriaceae, P. aeruginosa, enterococci, rarely S. aureus	(AMP + gent) or PIP-TZ or TC-CL or DORI or IMP or MER for up to 2-3 wks	For dosing, see Table (Levo/ Ceftaz or CFP for up to 2-3 wks	Not all listed drugs predictably active vs enterococci or P. aeruginosa. **CIP** approved in children (1-17 yrs) as alternative. Not 1st choice secondary to increased incidence joint adverse effects. Peds dose: 6-10 mg/kg (400 mg max) IV q8h or 10-20 mg/kg (750 mg max) **po** q12h.
"Spinal cord injury" below			Switch to **FQ** or **TMP-SMX** when possible *For dosages, see footnote⁹ on page 34.*	Treat for 7 days for catheter-associated UTI if prompt resolution of symptoms and 10-14 days if delayed response; a 3-day course of therapy may be consider for women < 65 years of age (CID 50:625, 2010)
Asymptomatic bacteriuria. *CID 40:643, 2005; U.S. Preventive Services Task Force AnIM 149:43, 2008.*				Diagnosis requires ≥10⁵ CFU per mL urine of same bacterial species in 2 specimens obtained 3-7 days apart
Preschool children		*Base regimen on C&S, not empirical*		Screen monthly for recurrence. Some authorities treat continuously until delivery (stop TMP-SMX 2 wks before EDC); ↑ resistance of E. coli to TMP-SMX.
Pregnancy	Aerobic Gm-neg. bacilli & Staph. hemolyticus	Screen 1st trimester. If positive, rx 3-7 days with **amox, nitrofurantoin. O Ceph, TMP-SMX, or TMP alone**		Clinical benefit of antimicrobial-coated Foley catheters is uncertain (AnIM 144:116, 2006). (CID 60:625, 2010).
Before and after invasive uro-logic intervention, e.g., Foley catheter	Aerobic Gm-neg. bacilli	Obtain urine culture and then rx 3 days with **TMP-SMX DS**, bid. For prevention of UTI: Consider removal after 72 hrs (CID 46:243-250, 2009).		
Neurogenic bladder – see "Spinal cord injury" below		No therapy in asymptomatic patient; intermittent catheterization if possible		Ref: AJM 113(1A):67S, 2002 – Bacteriuria in spinal cord injured patient.
Asymptomatic, advanced age, male or female *Ref CID 40:643, 2005*		No screening or treatment		No therapy indicated unless in conjunction with surgery to correct obstructive uropathy; measure residual urine vol. in females; prostate exam/PSA in males (no screening recommended in men and non-pregnant women (AnIM 149:43, 2008)
Malacoplakia	E. coli	Bethanechol chloride + (CIP or TMP-SMX)		Chronic pyelo with abnormal inflammatory response.
Perinephric abscess Associated with staphylococcal bacteremia	Staph. aureus	If **MSSA, Nafcillin, oxacillin** or **cefazolin** (Dosage, see footnote page 34).	If **MRSA: Vanco** 1 gm IV q12h OR **dapto** 6 mg/kg IV q24h	Drainage, surgical or image-guided aspiration
Associated with pyelonephritis	Enterobacteriaceae	See pyelonephritis, complicated UTI, above		Drainage, surgical or image-guided aspiration
Post Renal Transplant Obstructive Uropathy (CID 46:825, 2008)	Corynebacterium urealyticum	**Vanco** or **Teicoplanin**ᴺᵁˢ		Organism can synthesize struvite stones. Requires 48-72 hr incubation to detect in urine
Prostatitis	See prostatitis, page 27			
Spinal cord injury pts with UTI	E. coli, Klebsiella sp., entero-cocci	**CIP** 250 mg po bid x 14 days		If fever, suspect assoc. pyelonephritis. Microbiologic cure greater after 14 vs. 3 days of CIP (CID 39:658 & 665, 2004); for asymptomatic bacteriuria see AJM 113(1A):67S, 2002.

Abbreviations on page 2.   *NOTE: All dosage recommendations are for adults (unless otherwise indicated) and assume normal renal function.*

TABLE 1 (33)

ANATOMIC SITE/DIAGNOSIS/ MODIFYING CIRCUMSTANCES	ETIOLOGIES (usual)	SUGGESTED REGIMENS*		ADJUNCT DIAGNOSTIC OR THERAPEUTIC MEASURES AND COMMENTS
		PRIMARY	ALTERNATIVE[†]	
LIVER (for spontaneous bacterial peritonitis, see page 47)				
Cholangitis		See Gallbladder, page 17		
Cirrhosis & variceal bleeding	Esophageal flora	**(Norfloxacin** 400 mg po bid or **CIP** 400 mg IV q12h) x max. of 7 days	**Ceftriaxone** 1 gm IV once daily for max. of 7 days	Short term prophylactic antibiotics in cirrhotics with G-I hemorr, with or without ascites, decreases rate of bacterial infection & ↑ survival (Hepatology 46:922, 2007).
Hepatic abscess Klebsiella liver abscess ref.: Ln ID 12:881, 2012	Enterobacteriaceae (esp. Klebsiella sp), bacteroides, enterococci, Entamoeba histolytica, Yersinia enterocolitica (rare), Fusobacterium necrophorum (Lemierre's). For echinococcus, see Table 13, page 150. For cat-scratch disease (CSD), see pages 45 & 57	**Metro** + (**ceftriaxone** or **cefotaxim** or **TC-CL** or **PIP-TZ** or **AM-SB** or **CIP** or **levo**. (Dosage, see footnote[16] on page 34)	**Metro** (for amoeba) + either **IMP, MER** or **Dori** (Dosage, see footnote[16] on page 34)	**Serological tests for amebiasis should be done on all patients;** if neg. surgical drainage or percutaneous aspiration. In pyogenic abscess, ½ have identifiable GI source or underlying biliary tract disease. If amoeba serology positive, treat with **metro** alone without surgery. Empiric **metro** included for both E. histolytica & bacteroides. **Hemochromatosis** associated with Yersinia enterocolitica liver abscess; regimens listed are effective for yersinia. Klebsiella pneumonia genotype K1 associated ocular & CNS Klebsiella infections (CID 45:264, 2007).
Hepatic encephalopathy	Urease-producing gut bacteria	**Rifaximin** 550 mg po bid (take with lactulose)		Refs: NEJM 362:1071, 2010; Med Lett 52:87, 2010.
Leptospirosis	Leptospirosis, see page 60	See page 57		
Peliosis hepatis in AIDS pts	Bartonella henselae and B. quintana			
Post-transplant infected "biloma"	Enterococci (incl VRE), candida, Gm-neg. bacilli (P. aeruginosa 8%), anaerobes 5%	**Linezolid** 600 mg IV bid + **CIP** 400 mg IV q12h + **fluconazole** 400 mg IV q24h	**Dapto** 6 mg/kg per day + **Levo** 750 mg IV q24h + **fluconazole** 400 mg IV q24h	Suspect if fever & abdominal pain post-transplant. Exclude hepatic artery thrombosis. Presence of candida and/or VRE bad prognosticators.
Viral hepatitis	Hepatitis A, B, C, D, E, G	See Table 14F and Table 14G		
LUNG/Bronchi				
Bronchiolitis/wheezy bronchitis (expiratory wheezing)				
Infants/children (≤ age 5) See RSV Table 14A, page 167 Ref. NEJM 368:312, 2006	**Respiratory syncytial virus** (RSV) 50%, parainfluenza 25%, human metapneumovirus	Antibiotics not useful, mainstay of therapy is oxygen. Ribavirin for severe disease: 6 gm vial (20 mg/mL) in sterile H₂O by SPAG-2 generator over 18-20 hrs daily times 3-5 days.		RSV most important. Rapid diagnosis with antigen detection methods. For prevention in humanized mouse monoclonal antibody, **palivizumab**. See Table 14A, page 167. RSV immune globulin is no longer available. Review: Red Book of Peds 2006, 27th Ed.
Bronchitis				
Infants/children (≤ age 5)	≤ Age 2: Adenovirus; age 2-5: Respiratory syncytial virus, parainfluenza 3 virus, human metapneumovirus	Antibiotics indicated only with associated sinusitis or heavy growth on throat culture for S. pneumo., Group A strep, H. influenzae or no improvement in 1 week. Otherwise rx is symptomatic.		
Adolescents and adults with acute tracheobronchitis See Persistent cough, below Ref.: NEJM 355:2125, 2006	Usually viral. M. pneumoniae 5%, C. pneumoniae 5%.	**Antibiotics not indicated.** Antitussive ± inhaled bronchodilators		Purulent sputum alone not an indication for antibiotic therapy. Expect cough to last 2 weeks. If fever/rigors, get chest x-ray. If mycoplasma documented, prefer doxy over macrolides.

Abbreviations on page 2.   NOTE: All dosage recommendations are for adults (unless otherwise indicated) and assume normal renal function.

TABLE 1 (34)

ANATOMIC SITE/DIAGNOSIS/ MODIFYING CIRCUMSTANCES	ETIOLOGIES (usual)	SUGGESTED REGIMENS*		ADJUNCT DIAGNOSTIC OR THERAPEUTIC MEASURES AND COMMENTS
		PRIMARY	ALTERNATIVE†	
LUNG/Bronchi/Bronchitis *(continued)*				
Persistent cough (> 14 days), afebrile during community outbreak: **Pertussis (whooping cough)** 10-20% adults with cough > 14 days have pertussis (*MMWR 54:1283, 2005*). Review: *Chest 130:547, 2006*	Bordetella pertussis & occ. Bordetella parapertussis. Also consider asthma, gastroesophageal reflux, post-nasal drip	**Peds doses: Azithro / clarithro** OR **erythro esto- late**[17] OR **erythro base**[17] OR **TMP-SMX** (*doses in footnote*[17])	**Adult doses: Azithro** po 500 mg day 1, 250 mg q24h days 2-5 OR **erythro estolate** 500 mg po qid times 14 days OR **TMP-SMX DS** tab po bid times 14 days OR **clarithro** 500 mg po bid or 1 gm **ER** q24h times 7 days).	**3 stages of illness:** catarrhal (1-2 wks), paroxysmal coughing (2-4 wks), and convalescence (1-2 wks). Treatment may abort or eliminate pertussis in catarrhal stage, but does not shorten paroxysmal stage. **Diagnosis:** PCR on nasopharyngeal secretions or ↑ pertussis-toxin antibody. Advantage of NP culture is best in early outbreak setting, likelihood of pertussis increased if post-tussive emesis or inspiratory whoop present (*JAMA 304:890, 2010*).
Pertussis: Prophylaxis of household contacts	Drugs and doses as per treatment immediately above			Recommended by Am. Acad. Ped. Red Book 2006 for all household or close contacts, community-wide prophylaxis not recommended.
Acute bacterial exacerbation of chronic bronchitis (ABECB) adults (almost always smokers with COPD) Ref: *NEJM 359:2355, 2008.*	Viruses 20-50%, C. pneumo- niae 5%, M. pneumoniae <1%; role of S. pneumo, H. influenzae & M. catarrhalis controversial. Tobacco use, air pollution contribute. Non-pathogenic H. haemolyticus may be mistaken for H. influenzae (*J/ID 195:81, 2007*).	**Severe ABECB** = ↑ dyspnea, ↑ sputum viscosity/purulence. For severe ABECB: (1) consider chest x-ray, esp. if febrile &/or low O₂ sat.; (2) inhaled anticholinergic bronchodilator; (3) oral corticosteroid; taper over 2 wks (*Cochrane Library 3, 2006*); (4) D/C tobacco use; (5) non-invasive positive pressure ventilation. **Role of antimicrobial therapy debated even for severe disease. For mild or moderate disease, no antimicrobial treatment** or may use amox, doxy, TMP-SMX, or O Ceph or FQs with enhanced activity vs. drug-resistant S. pneumo (Gemi, Levo, or Moxi)	**For severe disease,** AM-CL, azithro/clarithro, or O Ceph or (Gemi, Levo, or Moxi). **Duration** varies with drug: range 3-10 days. Limit Gemi to 5 days to decrease risk of rash. Azithro 250 mg daily x 1 yr modestly reduced frequency of acute exacerbations in pts with milder disease (*NEJM 365:689, 2011*).	
Fever, cough, myalgia during influenza season (See *NEJM 360:2605, 2009* regarding novel H1N1 influenza A)	Influenza A & B	See *Influenza, Table 14A, page 164.*		**Complications: influenza pneumonia, secondary bacterial pneumonia.** Community MRSA and MSSA, S. pneumoniae, H. influenzae.
Bronchiectasis. Ref: *Chest 134:815, 2008* - Acute exacerbation	H. influ, P. aeruginosa, and rarely S. pneumo.	**Gemi, levo,** or **moxi** x7-10 days. *Dosage in footnote*[17].		Many potential etiologies: obstruction, cystic fibrosis, dyskinetic cilia, tobacco, prior severe or recurrent necrotizing bronchitis; e.g. pertussis.
- Prevention of exacerbation	Not applicable	One option: **Erythro** 500 mg po bid or **azithro** 250 mg q24h x 8 wks.		
- Specific organisms	Aspergillus (see *Table 11*) MAI (*Table 12*) and P. aeruginosa (*Table 5A*).			

[17] **ADULT DOSAGE: AM-CL** 875/125 mg po bid or 500/125 mg po bid or 2000/125 mg po bid; **azithro** 500 mg q24h x 4 days or 500 mg po q24h x 3 days: *Oral cephalosporins:* **cefaclor** 500 mg po q8h or 500 mg extended release q12h; **cefdinir** 300 mg po q12h or 600 mg po q24h; **cefditoren** 200 mg po q12h; **cefixime** 400 mg po q24h; **cefpodoxime proxetil** 200 mg po q12h; **cefprozil** 500 mg po q12h; **ceftibuten** 400 mg po q24h; **cefuroxime axetil** 250 or 500 mg po q12h; **clarithro** extended release 1000 mg po q24h; **doxy** 100 mg po bid; **erythro base** 400 mg po q6h or **erythro estolate** 40 mg/kg/day po q6h; *FQs:* **CIP** 750 mg po q12h; **gemi** 320 mg po q24h; **levo** 500 mg po q24h; **moxi** 400 mg po q24h; **TMP-SMX** 1 DS tab po bid.
PEDS DOSAGE: azithro 10 mg/kg/day on day 1, then 5 mg/kg po q24h x 4 days; **clarithro** 7.5 mg/kg po q12h; **erythro base** 40 mg/kg/day div q6h; **erythro estolate** 40 mg/kg/day div q8h;
TMP-SMX (>6 mos of age) 8 mg/kg/day (TMP component) div bid.

Abbreviations on page 2.   NOTE: *All dosage recommendations are for adults (unless otherwise indicated) and assume normal renal function.*

TABLE 1 (35)

ANATOMIC SITE/DIAGNOSIS/ MODIFYING CIRCUMSTANCES	ETIOLOGIES (usual)	SUGGESTED REGIMENS*		ADJUNCT DIAGNOSTIC OR THERAPEUTIC MEASURES AND COMMENTS
		PRIMARY	ALTERNATIVE†	
LUNG/Bronchi (continued)				
Pneumonia: CONSIDER TUBERCULOSIS IN ALL PATIENTS—ISOLATE ALL SUSPECT PATIENTS				
Neonatal: Birth to 1 month	**Viruses:** CMV, rubella, H. simplex; **Bacteria:** Group B strep, listeria, coliforms, S. aureus, P. aeruginosa **Other:** Chlamydia trachomatis, syphilis	**AMP + gentamicin ± cefotaxime.** Add **vanco** if MRSA a concern. For chlamydia therapy, **erythro** 12.5 mg per kg po or IV qid times 14 days.		Blood cultures indicated. Consider C. trachomatis if afebrile pneumonia, staccato cough. IgM >1:8: therapy with erythro or sulfisoxazole. If MRSA documented, **vanco**, **TMP-SMX**, & **linezolid** alternatives. **Linezolid** dosage from birth to age 11 yrs is **10 mg per kg q8h**.
Age 1–3 months Pneumonitis syndrome. Usually afebrile	C. trachomatis, RSV, parainfluenza virus 3, human metapneumovirus, Bordetella, S. pneumoniae, S. aureus (rare)	**Outpatient: po erythro** 12.5 mg/kg q6h x 14 days or po **azithro** 10 mg/kg x dose, then 5 mg/kg x 4 days.	**Inpatient: If afebrile erythro** 10 mg/kg IV q6h or **azithro** 2.5 mg/kg IV q12h (see Comment) **If febrile,** add **cefotaxime** 200 mg/kg per day div q8h.	Pneumonitis syndrome: Cough, tachypnea, dyspnea, diffuse infiltrates, afebrile. Usually requires hospital care. Reports of hypertrophic pyloric stenosis after erythro under age 6 wks: not sure about azithro; bid azithro dosing theoretically might ↓ risk of hypertrophic pyloric stenosis. If lobar pneumonia, give AMP 200–300 mg per kg per day for S. pneumoniae. No empiric coverage for S. aureus, as it is rare etiology.
			For RSV, see Bronchiolitis, Page 36	
Infants and Children, age > 3 months to 18 yrs (IDSA Treatment Guidelines: CID 53:617, 2011)				
Outpatient	RSV, human metapneumovirus, rhinovirus, influenza virus, adenovirus, parainfluenza virus, Mycoplasma, H. influenzae, S. pneumoniae, S. aureus (rare)	**Amox** 90 mg/kg in 2 divided doses x 5 days	**Azithro** 10 mg/kg x 1 dose(max 500 mg), then 5 mg/kg (max 250 mg) x 4 days OR **Amox-Clav** 90 mg/kg (Amox) in 2 divided doses x 5 days	Antimicrobial therapy not routinely required for preschool-aged children with CAP as most infections are viral etiologies.
Inpatient	As above	Fully immunized: **AMP** 50 mg/kg IV q6h Not fully immunized: **Cefotaxime** 150 mg/kg IV divided q8h	Fully immunized: **Cefotaxime** 150 mg/kg IV divided q8h	If atypical infection suspected, add **Azithro** 10 mg/kg x 1 dose (max 500 mg), then 5 mg/kg (max 250 mg) x 4 days. If community MRSA suspected, add **Vanco** 40-60 mg/kg/day divided q6-8h OR **Clinda** 40 mg/kg/day divided q6-8h. Duration of therapy: 10-14 days. Depending on clinical response, may switch to oral agents as early as 2-3 days.
(Continued on next page)				

Abbreviations on page 2.   NOTE: All dosage recommendations are for adults (unless otherwise indicated) and assume normal renal/renal function.

TABLE 1 (36)

ANATOMIC SITE/DIAGNOSIS/ MODIFYING CIRCUMSTANCES	ETIOLOGIES (usual)	SUGGESTED REGIMENS*		ADJUNCT DIAGNOSTIC OR THERAPEUTIC MEASURES AND COMMENTS
		PRIMARY	ALTERNATIVE[1]	
LUNG/Bronchi/Pneumonia (continued)				
Adults (over age 18) — IDSA/ATS Guideline for CAP in adults. Community-acquired, not hospitalized **Prognosis prediction:** CURB-65 score: (AJM 118:384, 2005): C: confusion = 1 pt U: BUN >19 mg/dl = 1 pt R: RR >30 min = 1 pt B: BP <90/60 = 1 pt Age ≥65 = 1 pt If score = 1, ok for outpatient therapy; if >1, hospitalize. The higher the score, the higher the mortality.	Varies with clinical setting. **No co-morbidity:** Atypicals—M. pneumoniae, C. pneumoniae, viral **Co-morbidity:** Alcoholism—S. pneumo, anaerobes, coliforms Bronchiectasis: see Cystic fibrosis, page 43 COPD: H. influenzae, M. catarrhalis, S. pneumo IVDU: Hematogenous S. aureus Post-CVA aspiration: Oral flora, incl. S. pneumo Post-obstruction of bronchi: S. pneumo, anaerobes. Post-influenza: S. pneumo. and S. aureus	**IDSA/ATS Guideline for CAP in adults:** CID 44 (Suppl 2): S27-S72, 2007. **No co-morbidity:** **Azithro** 0.5 gm po times 1, then 0.25 gm per day **OR clarithro-ER** 1 gm po q24h **OR clarithro** 500 mg po bid or **clarithro-ER** 1 gm po q24h **OR** if prior antibiotic within 3 months: **(azithro or clarithro) + (amox or high dose amox, OR high dose** AM-CL) **OR Respiratory FQ** **Duration of rx:** S. pneumo—Not bacteremic: until afebrile 3 days —Bacteremic: 10-14 days C. pneumoniae—Uncleared Legionella—10-21 days Necrotizing pneumonia 2° to coliforms, S. aureus, anaerobes—2 weeks	**Respiratory FQ** (see footnote[19]) **[(azithro or clarithro) + (high dose amox, high dose AM-CL, cefdinir, cefpodox-ime, cefprozil)]** Doses in footnote[20]	**Azithro/clarithro:** Pro: appropriate spectrum of activity; more in vitro resistance than clinical failure; q24h dosing; better tolerated than erythro. Con: Overall S. pneumo resistance in vitro 20-30% and may be increasing. If pen G resist. S. pneumo, up to 50%+ resistance to azithro/clarithro. Increased risk of macrolide resistance with prior use. **Amox:** Pro: Active 90-95% S. pneumo at 3-4 gm per day. Con: No activity atypicals or β-lactamase positive organisms. **AM-CL:** Pro: Spectrum of activity includes β-lactamase positive organisms. Con: No activity atypicals. **Cephalosporins—po:** Cefditoren, cefpodoxime, cefprozil, cefuroxime & others—see footnote[20] Pro: Active 75-85% S. pneumo & H. influenzae. Cefuroxime least active & higher mortality rate when S. pneumo resistant. Con: Inactive vs. atypical pathogens **Doxy:** Pro: Active vs. S. pneumo but resistance may be increasing. Active vs. H. influenzae, atypicals, & bioterrorism agents (anthrax, plague, tularemia). Con: Resistance of S. pneumo 18-20%. Sparse clinical data. **FQs—Respiratory FQs:** Moxi, levo & gemi. Pro: In vitro & clinically effective vs. pen-sensitive & pen-resistant S. pneumo. **NOTE: dose of Levo is 750 mg q24h dosing.** Gemi only available po. Con: Geographic pockets of resistance with clinical failure. Important drug-drug interactions (see Table 22A, page 217). Reversible rash in young females given Gemi for >7 days.
Community-acquired, hospitalized—NOT in the ICU Empiric therapy Treat for minimum of 5 days, afebrile for 48-72 hrs, with good appetite and normal oral intake, and room air O₂ saturation of >90% (CID 20:177, 2007).	Etiology by co-morbidity & risk factors as above. S. pneumo, urine antigen reported (CID 40: 1608, 2005). Legionella urine antigen indicated in sicker pt, the more valuable culture data. Look for S. aureus.	**Ceftriaxone** 1 gm IV q24h + **azithro** 500 mg IV q24h **OR** **Ertapenem** 1 gm q24h plus **azithro** 500 mg IV q24h	**Levo** 750 mg IV q24h or **Moxi** 400 mg IV q24h **Gati** 400 mg IV q24h (gati no longer marketed in US due to hypo- and hyperglycemic reactions)	**Ceftriaxone/Cefotaxime:** Pro: Drugs of choice for pen-sens. S. pneumo, active H. influenzae, M. catarrhalis, & MSSA. Con: Not active atypicals or pneumonia due to bioterrorism pathogens. Add macrolide for atypicals and perhaps their anti-inflammatory effects. **Ceftaroline:** FDA approved at a dose of 600 mg q12h IV for 5-7 days for hospitalized patients with CAP). Pro: Clinical response rates at day 4 and clinical cure rates at days 8-15 post-treatment were similar for ceftaroline and ceftriaxone (see ceftaroline package insert). Con: More expensive; no data for MRSA yet.

Cautions:
1. **If local macrolide resistance to S. pneumoniae >25%, use alternative empiric therapy.**
2. **Esp. during influenza season, look for S. aureus.**

Administration of antibiotic within 6h associated with improved survival in pneumonia and more severe sepsis (Eur Respir J 39:156, 2012); in ER, first dose in ER if diagnosis of pneumonia vague, OK for admitting diagnosis of "uncertain." (Chest 130:16, 2006).

[18] Atypical pathogens: Chlamydophila pneumoniae, C. psittaci, Legionella sp., M. pneumoniae, C. burnetii (Q fever) (Ref.: LnID 3:709, 2003)

[19] Respiratory FQs with enhanced activity vs. S. pneumo with high-level resistance to penicillin: **Gati**[18a] 400 mg IV/po q24h (no longer marketed in US due to hypo- and hyperglycemic reactions). **Gemi** 320 mg po q24h. **Levo** 750 mg IV/po q24h. **Moxi** 400 mg IV/po q24h. Ketolide: **telithro** 800 mg IV/po q24h (physicians warned about rare instances of hepatotoxicity).

[20] O Ceph dosage: **Cefdinir** 300 mg po q12h, **cefditoren pivoxil** 200 mg, 2 tabs po bid, **cefpodoxime proxetil** 200 mg po q12h, **high dose amox** 1 gm po q12h, **high dose AM-CL-ER** 1000/62.5 mg, 2 tabs po bid. **AM-CL**—use **AM-CL-ER**

Abbreviations on page 2.   NOTE: All dosage recommendations are for adults (unless otherwise indicated) and assume normal renal function.

TABLE 1 (37)

ANATOMIC SITE/DIAGNOSIS/ MODIFYING CIRCUMSTANCES	ETIOLOGIES (usual)	SUGGESTED REGIMENS* PRIMARY	ALTERNATIVE†	ADJUNCT DIAGNOSTIC OR THERAPEUTIC MEASURES AND COMMENTS
LUNG/Bronchi/Pneumonia/Adults (over age 18) *(continued)*				
Community-acquired, hospitalized—IN ICU Empiric therapy **NOTE:** Not all ICU admissions meet IDSA/ATS CAP Guideline criteria for severe CAP. Do not believe that all ICU pneumonia in patients need 2 drugs with activity vs. gram-negative bacilli. Hence, 4 example clinical settings are outlined: **severe COPD; post-influenza, suspect gm-neg bacilli; risk of pen-resistant S. pneumo**	**Severe COPD** pt with pneumonia. S. pneumoniae, H. influenzae, Moraxella sp., aureus. Rarely S. aureus. Culture sputum, blood and maybe pleural fluid. Look for respiratory viruses. Urine antigen for both Legionella and S. pneumoniae. Sputum PCR for Legionella.	**Levo** 750 mg IV q24h or **Moxi** 400 mg IV q24h or **Gati** not available in US due to hypo- and hyperglycemic reactions	**[Ceftriaxone** 1 gm IV q24h) **+ azithro** 500 mg IV q24h] **or ERTA** 1 gm q24h IV + **azithro** 500 mg IV q24h (see Comment)	**Various studies** indicate improved outcome when azithro added to a β-lactam (CID 36:389 & 1239, 2003; AJM 164:1837, 2001 & 159:2562, 1999). Similar results in prospective study of critically ill pts with pneumococcal bacteremia (AJRCCM 170:440, 2004). **Ertapenem** could substitute for ceftriaxone: need azithro for atypical pathogens. Do not use if suspect P. aeruginosa. **Legionella:** Not all Legionella species detected by urine antigen; if suspicious culture or PCR on airway secretions. Value of specific diagnosis: CID 46:1356 & 1365, 2008. In patients with normal sinus rhythm and not receiving beta-blockers, relative bradycardia suggests Legionella, psittacosis, Q-fever, or typhoid fever.
		Addition of a macrolide to beta-lactam empiric regimens lowers mortality for patients with bacteremic pneumococcal pneumonia (CID 36:389, 2003). Benefit NOT found with use of FQ or tetracycline for "atypicals" (Chest 131:466, 2007). Combination therapy benefited patients with concomitant shock. (CCM 35:1·5, & 617, 2007).		
Community-acquired, hospitalized—IN ICU Empiric therapy **If concomitant with or post-influenza,** S. aureus, and S. pneumoniae possible.	**If concomitant with or post-influenza,** S. aureus, and S. pneumoniae possible.	**vanco** (CCM 35:1·5, & 617, 2007) + **Levo** 750 mg IV q24h or **Moxi** 400 mg IV q24h)	**Linezolid** 600 mg IV bid + (levo or moxi)	Sputum gram stain may help. S. aureus ref: EID12:894, 2006. Empiric therapy vs. MRSA decreases risk of mortality (CCM 34:2069, 2006)
Community-acquired, hospitalized—IN ICU Empiric therapy	**Suspect aerobic gm-neg bacilli:**(respiratory fluoroquinolone and/or life-threatening infection (see comment). Hypoxic and/or hypotensive "Cover" S. pneumo & Legionella	**Anti-pseudomonal beta-lactam**† (respiratory FQ or aztreonam + **aminoglycoside).** Add **azithro** if no FQ	If severe (g)c-mediated beta-lactam allergy: **aztreonam** + (respiratory FQ or **aminoglycoside + azithro).**	At risk for gm-neg rod pneumonia due to: alcoholism with necrotizing pneumonia, underlying chronic bronchiectasis (e.g. cystic fibrosis), chronic tracheostomy and/or mechanical ventilation, febrile neutropenia and pulmonary infiltrates, septic shock, underlying malignancy, or organ failure.
	Risk of Pen G-resistant S. pneumoniae 2° antibiotic use in last 3 months.	**High dose IV amp (or Pen G) + azithro + respiratory FQ**	Beta-lactam allergy: **vanco + respiratory FQ**	**If Pen G MIC>4 mg/mL, vanco. Very rare event.**
Health care-associated pneumonia (HCAP) Ref: CID 46 (Suppl 4): S296, 2008.	HCAP used to designate large diverse population of pts with many co-morbidities who reside in nursing homes, other long-term care facilities, require home IV therapy or are dialysis pts. Pneumonia in these pts frequently resembles hospital-acquired pneumonia (see next section).			

Drugs and doses in footnote21

[21] Antipseudomonal beta-lactams: **Aztreonam** 2 gm IV q6h; **piperacillin** 3 gm IV q4h; **piperacillin/tazobactam** 3.375 gm IV q4h or 4.5 gm IV q6h or 3.375 gm q8h(high dose for Pseudomonas); **cefepime** 2 gm IV q12h; **ceftazidime** 2 gm IV q8h; **doripenem** (do NOT use to treat pneumonia) 1 gm IV q8h; **imipenem/cilastatin** 500 mg IV q6h; **meropenem** 1 gm IV q8h; **gentamicin or tobramycin** (see Table 10D, page 109). FQ for P. aeruginosa: **CIP** 400 mg IV q8h or **levo** 750 mg IV once daily. **Respiratory FQs: levofloxacin** 750 mg IV q24h or **moxifloxacin** 400 mg IV q24h; **high-dose ampicillin** 2 gm IV q6h; **azithromycin** 500 mg IV q24h; **levo** 750 mg IV q24h; **vanco** 1 gm IV q12h.

Abbreviations on page 2. *NOTE: All dosage recommendations are for adults (unless otherwise indicated) and assume normal renal function.*

TABLE 1 (38)

ANATOMIC SITE/DIAGNOSIS/ MODIFYING CIRCUMSTANCES	ETIOLOGIES (usual)	SUGGESTED REGIMENS*		ADJUNCT DIAGNOSTIC OR THERAPEUTIC MEASURES AND COMMENTS
		PRIMARY	ALTERNATIVE[1]	
LUNG/Bronchi/Pneumonia/Adults (over age 18) (continued)				
Hospital-acquired—usually with mechanical ventilation (VAP) (empiric therapy) Refs: U.S. Guidelines: A/RCCM 171:388, 2005; U.S. Review: JAMA 297:1583, 2007; Canadian Guidelines: Can J Infect Dis Med Micro 19:19, 2008; British Guidelines: JAC 62:5, 2008	Highly variable depending on clinical setting: S. pneumo, S. aureus, Legionella, coliforms, P. aeruginosa, stenotrophomonas, acinetobacter[22], anaerobes all possible	**IMP** 0.5 gm IV q6h or **MER** 1 gm IV q8h[23] plus, if suspect legionella or bioterrorism, **respiratory FQ** (**Levo** or **Moxi**) **NOTE:** Regimen not active vs. **MRSA** — see Comment regarding diagnosis Dosages: See footnote* on page 40. Duration of therapy, see footnote[24]	If suspect P. aeruginosa, empirically start 2 anti-P. are drugs to increase likelihood that at least one will be active, e.g., **IMP** or **CFP** or **PIP-TZ** plus (**CIP** or **Levo**). If suspect legionella, add macrolide or FQ. Ref: CCM 35:1888, 2007	**Dx of ventilator-associated pneumonia:** Fever & lung infiltrates often **not** pneumonia. Quantitative cultures helpful: bronchoalveolar lavage (>10⁴ per mL pos.) or protect. spec. brush (>10³ per mL pos.) Ref: A/RCCM 165:867, 2002; AnIM 132:621, 2000. **Microbiologic etiology:** No empiric regimen covers all possibilities. Regimens listed active vs majority of S. pneumo, legionella, & **most coliforms**. Regimens not active vs. **MRSA, Stenotrophomonas & others;** see below. **Specific therapy when culture results known.** **Ventilator-associated pneumonia—Prevention:** Keep head of bed elevated 30° or more. Remove N-G, endotracheal tubes as soon as possible. If available, continuous subglottic suctioning. Chlorhexidine oral care. Ref: & Chest 130:251, 2006; A/RCCM 173:1297, 1348, 2006. **Misc.: clarithro** accelerated resolution of VAP (CID 46:1157, 2008). Silver-coated endotracheal tubes reported to reduce incidence of VAP (JAMA 300:805 & 842, 2008).
Hospital- or community-acquired, neutropenic pt (<500 neutrophils per mm³)	Any of organisms listed under community- & hospital-acquired + fungi (aspergillus). See Table 11.	See Hospital-acquired, immediately above. Vanco not included in initial therapy unless high suspicion of S. pneumo. Ampho not used unless still febrile after 3 days or high clinical likelihood. See Comment		See consensus document on management of febrile neutropenic pt: CID 34:790, 2002.
Adults—Selected specific therapy after culture results (sputum, blood, pleural fluid, etc.) available. Also see Table 2, page 67				
Acinetobacter baumannii (See also Table 5A) Ref: NEJM 358:1271, 2008	Patients with VAP	Use **IMP** or **MER** if susceptible	If IMP resistant: **colistin** + (IMP or MER): Colistin Dose: Table 10A, page 101.	Subactam portion of AM-SB often active; dose: 3 gm IV q6h. For second-line agents, see Pharmacother 30:1279, 2010; J Inten Care Med 25:343, 2010
Burkholderia (Pseudomonas) pseudomallei (etiology of melioidosis). Can cause primary or secondary skin infection. See Curr Opin Infect Dis 23:554, 2010.	Gram-negative	**Initial parenteral rx:** **Ceftazidime** 30–50 mg per kg IV q6h or **IMP** 20 mg per kg IV q8h. Rx minimum 10 days & improving, then po therapy → see Alternative column	**Post-parenteral po rx:** For children] **TMP-SMX** 5 mg/kg (TMP component) bid + **Doxy** 2 mg/kg bid x 3 mos.	**Children ≤8 yrs old & pregnancy:** For oral regimen, use **AM-CL-ER** 0.000/62.5, 2 tabs po bid times 20 wks. Even with compliance, relapse rate is 10%. Max. daily ceftazidime dose: 6 gm.
				Tigecycline: No clinical data but active in vitro (AAC 50:1555, 2006)
Haemophilus influenzae	β-lactamase negative β-lactamase positive	**AMP** IV, **amox** po, **TMP-SMX, azithro/clarithro, doxy** **AM-CL, O Ceph 2/3, P Ceph 3, FQ** Dosage: Table 10A		25–35% strains β-lactamase positive↑ resistance to both TMP-SMX and doxy. See Table 10A, page 11 for dosages. High % of commensal H. hemolyticus misidentified as H. influenza (JID 165:273, 2011).
Klebsiella sp.—**ESBL pos. & other coliforms**[25]	β-lactamase positive	**IMP** or **MER**, if resistant, **Colistin** + (**IMP** or **MER**) Usually several weeks of therapy.		**ESBL**[25] inactivates all cephalosporins, β-lactam/β-lactamase inhibitor drug activ, not predictable; co-resistance to all FQs & often aminoglycosides.

[22] If Acinetobacter sp., **susceptibility to IMP & MER** may be discordant (CID 41:758, 2005).

[23] **PIP-TZ** for P. aeruginosa pneumonia: 3.375 gm IV over 4 hrs (& repeat q8h) (CID 44:357, 2007) plus **tobra.**

[24] Dogma on duration of therapy not possible with so many variables: i.e. certainty of diagnosis, infecting organism, severity of infection, number/severity of co-morbidities. Agree with efforts to de-escalate & shorten course: Treat at least 7–8 days. Need clinical evidence of response: fever resolution, improved oxygenation, falling WBC. Refs: A/RCCM 171:388, 2005; COID 19:185, 2006.

[25] **ESBL** = Extended spectrum beta-lactamase

Abbreviations on page 2.   NOTE: All dosage recommendations are for adults (unless otherwise indicated) and assume normal renal function.

TABLE 1 (39)

ANATOMIC SITE/DIAGNOSIS/ MODIFYING CIRCUMSTANCES	ETIOLOGIES (usual)	SUGGESTED REGIMENS* PRIMARY	ALTERNATIVE¹	ADJUNCT DIAGNOSTIC OR THERAPEUTIC MEASURES AND COMMENTS
LUNG/Pneumonia/Adults— Selected specific therapy after culture results (sputum, blood, pleural fluid, etc.) available *(continued)*				
Legionella species Relative bradycardia common feature	Hospitalized/ immunocompromised	**Azithro** 500 mg IV or **Levo** 750 mg IV or **Moxi** 400 mg IV. See Table 10A, pages 98 & 100 for dosages. Treat for 7–14 days (CID 39:1734, 2004)	**FQ**, **TMP-SMX**	Legionella website: www.legionella.org. Two studies support superiority of **Levo** over macrolides (CID 40:794 & 800, 2005), although² not FDA-approved.
Moraxella catarrhalis	93% β-lactamase positive	**AM-CL**, **O Ceph 2/3**, **P Ceph 2/3**, **macrolide²⁶**, **FQ**, **TMP-SMX**	**Doxy** another option. See Table 10A, page 93 for dosages	
Pseudomonas aeruginosa	Often ventilator-associated	(**PIP-TZ** 3.375 gm IV q4h or prefer 4-hr infusion of 3.375 gm q8h) + **tobra** 5 mg/kg IV once q24h (see Table 10D, page 109). Could substitute anti-pseudomonal **cephalosporin** or **carbapenem** (**IMP**, **MER**) for **PIP-TZ** if pt. strain is susceptible.	**NOTE: PIP-TZ** for P. aeruginosa (CID 44:357, 2007); other options: **CFP** 2 gm IV q 12h; **CIP** 400 mg IV q8h + **PIP-TZ**. **IMP** 500 mg IV q6h + **CIP** 400 mg IV q12h; if multi-drug resistant, **Colistin** IV + (**IMP or MER**) + **Colistin** by inhalation 80 mg bid.	
Staphylococcus aureus Duration of treatment: 2–3 wks if just pneumonia, 4–6 wks if concomitant endocarditis and/or osteomyelitis. IDSA Guidelines, CID 52 (Feb 1):1, 2011.	Nafcillin/oxacillin susceptible	**Nafcillin/oxacillin** 2 gm IV q4h	**Vanco** 30–60 mg/kg/d iv in 2–3 divided doses or **linezolid** 600 mg IV q12h	Adjust dose of vancomycin to achieve target concentrations of 15–20 mcg/mL. Some authorities recommend a loading dose (actual body weight) in severely ill patients (25–30 mg/kg loading dose) (CID 49:325, 2009). A prospective trial comparing Linezolid to Vanco for MRSA pneumonia
	MRSA	**Vanco** 30–60 mg/kg/d IV in 2–3 divided doses or **Linezolid** 600 mg q12h	**Dapto** probably not an option. Pneumonia developed during dapto rx (CID 49:1286, 2009).	showed higher cure rate (p=0.042) for Linezolid (95/165, 57.6%) than for Vancomycin (81/174, 46.6%) but no difference in mortality (15.7% for Linezolid vs. 17% for Vanco) (CID 54 <621, 2012).
Stenotrophomonas maltophilia		**TMP-SMX** up to 20 mg/kg/day div q6h	**TC-CL** 3.1 gm IV q4h	Potential synergy: **TMP-SMX** + **TC-CL** (JAC 62:889, 2008).
Streptococcus pneumoniae	Penicillin-susceptible	**AMP** 2 gm IV q6h; **amox** 1 gm po tid, **macrolide²⁶**, **pen G**²⁷, **doxy**, **O Ceph 2**, **P Ceph 2/3**. See Table 10A, page 111 for other dosages. Treat until afebrile, 3–5 days (min. of 5 days).		
	Penicillin-resistant, high level	**FQs** with enhanced activity: **Gemi**, **Levo**, **Moxi**, **P Ceph 3** (resistance rare), high-dose IV **AMP vanco** IV—see Table 5A, page 77 for more data. If all options not possible (e.g. allergy), linezolid active. 600 mg IV or po q12h. Dosages Table 10A. Treat until afebrile, 5 days (min. of 5 days). In CAP trial, Ceftriaxone 600 mg IV q12h superior to Ceftriaxone (CID 51:641, 2010).		
Yersinia pestis (Plague) CID 49:736, 2009	Aerosol Y. pestis.	**Gentamicin** 5 mg/kg IV q24h	**Doxy** 200 mg IV times 1, then 100 mg IV bid	TMP-SMX used as prophylaxis for plague pneumonia (CID 40:1166, 2005). Chloro effective but potentially toxic. Cephalosporins and FQs effective in animal models.
LUNG—Other Specific Infections				
Actinomycosis	A. Israelii and rarely others	**AMP** 50 mg/kg/day IV div in 3–4 doses x 4–6 wks, then **Pen VK** 2-4 gm/day po x 3–6 wks	**Doxy** or **ceftriaxone** or **clinda** or **erythro**	Can use **Pen G** instead of AMP: 10-20 million units/day IV x 4-6 wks.

²⁶ **Macrolide** = azithromycin, clarithromycin and erythromycin.
²⁷ **IV Pen G dosage:** no meningitis, 2 million units IV q4h. If concomitant meningitis, 4 million units IV q4h.

Abbreviations on page 2.   NOTE: All dosage recommendations are for adults (unless otherwise indicated) and assume normal renal function.

TABLE 1 (40)

ANATOMIC SITE/DIAGNOSIS/ MODIFYING CIRCUMSTANCES	ETIOLOGIES (usual)	SUGGESTED REGIMENS*		ADJUNCT DIAGNOSTIC OR THERAPEUTIC MEASURES AND COMMENTS
		PRIMARY	ALTERNATIVE†	
LUNG—Other Specific Infections (continued)				

Anthrax
Inhalation (applies to oropharyngeal & gastrointestinal forms):
Treatment
(Cutaneous: See page 51)
 	
Ref: www.bt.cdc.gov
	Bacillus anthracis
	To report possible bioterrorism event:
	770-488-7100
	
	Plague, tularemia:
	See page 45.
	
	Chest x-ray: mediastinal widening & pleural effusion
		Adults (including pregnancy): CIP 400 mg IV q12h **or Levo** 500 mg IV q24h) **or doxy** 100 mg IV q12h **plus clindamycin** 900 mg IV q8h &/or **RIF** 300 mg IV q12h). Switch to po when able & lower CIP to 500 mg po bid or **clinda** to 450 mg po q8h, & RIF 300 mg po bid. Treat times 60 days.	**Children: CIP** 10 mg/kg IV q12h or 15 mg/kg po q12h) or **(Doxy** >8 y/o & >45 kg: 100 mg q12h; >8 y/o, <45 kg: 2.2 mg/kg q12h; <8 y/o: 2.2 mg/kg IV q12h) **plus clindamycin** 7.5 mg/kg IV q6h **and/or RIF** 20 mg/kg (max. 600 mg) IV q24h.
			Treat times 60 days. See Table 16, page 203 for oral dosage.
				1. Clinda may block toxin production
				2. Rifampin penetrates CSF & intracellular sites.
				3. If isolate shown penicillin-susceptible:
				  a. **Pen G** 4 million units q4h IV or
				    Children: Pen G <12 y/o: 50,000 units per kg IV q6h; >12 y/o:
				    4 million units IV q4h
				  c. Constitutive & inducible β-lactamases—do not use pen or amp alone.
				4. Do not use cephalosporins or TMP-SMX.
				5. Erythro, azithro activity borderline; clarithro active.
				6. No person-to-person spread.
				7. Monoclonal antitoxin antibody approved: **raxibacumab** single 2 hr IV infusion
				8. Moxi should work, but no clinical data
				9. Case report of survival with use of anthrax immunoglobulin
				  (CID 44:968, 2007; CID 54:1849, 2012).

Anthrax, prophylaxis	Info: www.bt.cdc.gov	**Adults (including pregnancy) or children >50 kg:** (CIP 500 mg po bid or **Levo** 500 mg po q24h) x 60 days. **Children <50 kg: CIP** 10-15 mg/kg/day div q12h x 60 days or **levo** 8 mg/kg q12h x 60 days	**Adults (including pregnancy): Doxy** 100 mg po bid x 60 days. **Children (see Comment):** Doxy >8 y/o & >45 kg: 100 mg po bid; >8 y/o, <45 kg: 2.2 mg/kg po bid; <8 y/o: 2.2 mg/kg po bid. All for 60 days.	1. Once organism shows suscept. to penicillin, switch to amoxicillin 80 mg per kg per day div. q8h (max. 500 mg q8h); pregnant pt to amoxicillin 500 mg po tid 2. Do not use cephalosporins or TMP-SMX. 3. Other FQs (Gati, Moxi) & clarithro should work but no clinical experience.
Aspiration pneumonia/anaerobic lung infection/lung abscess	Transthoracic culture in 90 pts—% of total isolates: anaerobes 34%, Gm-pos. cocci 26%, S. milleri 16%, Klebsiella pneumoniae 25%, nocardia 3%	**Clindamycin** 300-450 mg po tid OR **Ampicillin-sulbactam** 3 g IV q6h OR **A carbapenem** (e.g., ertapenem 1 g IV q24h)	**Ceftriaxone** 1 gm IV q24h plus metro 500 mg IV q6h or 1 gm IV q12h	Typically an aerobic infection of the lung including aspiration pneumonitis, necrotizing pneumonia, lung abscess and empyema (REF: Anaerobe 18:235, 2012) Other treatment options: PIP-TZ 3.375 g IV q6h (for mixed infections with resistant Gram-negative aerobes) or Moxi 400 mg IV/po q24h (CID 41:764, 2005).
Chronic pneumonia with fever, night sweats and weight loss	M. tuberculosis, coccidioidomycosis, histoplasmosis	See Table 11, Table 12. For risk factors, see CID 41(Suppl 3):S187, 2005.		HIV+, foreign-born, alcoholism, contact with TB, travel into developing countries
Cystic fibrosis **Acute exacerbation of pulmonary symptoms** Ref: AJRCCM 180:802, 2009 (Continued on next page)	S. aureus or H. influenzae early in disease; P. aeruginosa later in disease	**For P. aeruginosa:** (Peds doses) **Tobra** 3.3 mg/kg q8h or 12 mg/kg/day (Peds dose, Table 16). Combine tobra with **(PIP** or **ticarcillin** 100 mg/kg q6h) or **ceftaz** 50 mg/kg IV q8h to max of 6 gm per day. Double-check resistance if CIP/Levo used if P. aeruginosa susceptible. See footnote²⁸ & Comment	**For S. aureus: (1) MSSA** oxacillin/nafcillin 2 gm IV q4h (Peds dose, Table 16). **(2) MRSA—vanco** 1 gm q12h & check serum levels. See Comment	Cystic Fibrosis Foundation Guidelines: 1. Combination therapy for P. aeruginosa infection. 2. Once-daily dosing for aminoglycosides. 3. Need more data on continuous infusion beta-lactam therapy. 4. Routine use of steroid not recommended. For chronic suppression of P. aeruginosa, **inhaled phenol-free tobra** 300 mg bid x 28 days, then no rx x 28 days, then repeat cycle (AJRCCM 167:841, 2003). Aztreonam (Cayston) 75 mg inhaled tid; pre-dose bronchodilator (Chest 135:1223, 2009)

²⁸ Other options: (Tobra + aztreonam 50 mg per kg IV q8h); (IMP 15-25 mg per kg IV q6h); **CIP commonly used in children.** (unless otherwise indicated) and assume normal renal function.

* Other options: (Tobra + aztreonam 50 mg per kg IV q8h);   NOTE: All dosage recommendations are for adults (unless otherwise indicated) and assume normal renal function.

Abbreviations on page 2.

TABLE 1 (41)

ANATOMIC SITE/DIAGNOSIS/ MODIFYING CIRCUMSTANCES	ETIOLOGIES (usual)	SUGGESTED REGIMENS*		ADJUNCT DIAGNOSTIC OR THERAPEUTIC MEASURES AND COMMENTS
		PRIMARY	ALTERNATIVE†	
LUNG—Other Specific Infections (continued)				
(Continued from previous page)	Burkholderia (Pseudomonas) cepacia	TMP-SMX 5 mg per kg (TMP) IV q6h	Chloro 15–20 mg per kg IV/po q6h	B. cepacia has become a major pathogen. Patients develop progressive respiratory failure, 62% mortality at 1 yr. **Fail to respond to** aminoglycosides, piperacillin, & ceftazidime. Patients with B. cepacia should be isolated from other CF patients.
Empyema. Refs.: Pleural effusion review: *CID 45:1480, 2007; IDSA Treatment Guidelines for Children, CID 53:617, 2011.*				
		For other alternatives, see Table 2		
Neonatal	Staph. aureus	See Pneumonia, neonatal, page 38		Drainage indicated.
Infants/children (1 month–5 yrs)	Staph. aureus, Strep. pneumoniae, H. influenzae	See Pneumonia age 1 month–5 years, page 38		Drainage indicated.
Child >5 yrs to ADULT: Diagnostic thoracentesis; chest tube for empyemas	Staph. aureus	Cefotaxime or ceftriaxone‡ (Dosage, see footnote³ page 25)	Vanco	Tissue Plasminogen Activator (10 mg) + DNase (5 mg) bid x 3 days via chest tube improves outcome (*NEJM 365:518, 2011).*
Acute usually parapneumonic: Strep. pneumoniae, Group A strep	MSSA	Nafcillin or oxacillin if MSSA	Vanco or linezolid if MRSA.	Usually complication of S. aureus pneumonia &/or bacteremia.
For dosage, see Table 10B	Check for MRSA			
Microbiologic diagnosis: *CID 42:1135, 2006.*	Staph. aureus	Ceftriaxone	TMP-SMX or AM-SB	Pleomorphic Gm-neg. bacilli. ↑ resistance to TMP-SMX
Subacute/chronic	H. influenzae			
	Anaerobic strep, Strep. milleri, Bacteroides sp., Entero-bacteriaceae, M. tuberculosis	Clinda 450–900 mg IV q8h	Cefoxitin or IMP or TC-CL or PIP-TZ or AM-SB (Dosage, see footnote¹² page 25)	If organisms not seen: treat as subacute. Drainage. R/O tuberculosis or tumor. Pleural biopsy with culture for mycobacteria and histology if TBc suspected
Human immunodeficiency virus infection (HIV+): See SANFORD GUIDE TO HIV/AIDS THERAPY				
CD4 T-lymphocytes <200 per mm³ or clinical AIDS	Pneumocystis carinii most likely; also M. TBc, fungi, Kaposi's sarcoma, & lymphoma.	Rx listed here is for **severe** pneumocystis; *see Table 13A, page 145 for po regimens for mild disease.*		**Diagnosis (induced sputum or bronchial wash) for:** histology or monoclonal antibody strains or PCR. Serum beta-glucan (Fungitell) levels under study (*CID 46:1928 & 1930, 2008).* **Prednisone 40 mg bid po**
Dry cough, progressive dyspnea, & diffuse infiltrate		**Prednisone 1*** (see Comment).		**times 5 days then 40 mg q24h** times 5 days then 20 mg q24h po **times 11 days is indicated with PCP** (pO₂ <70 mmHg), **should be**
Prednisone first if suspect pneumocystis (see Comment)	NOTE: AIDS pts may develop pneumonia due to DRSP or other pathogens—see next box below	**TMP-SMX** [IV: 15 mg per kg per day q8h (TMP component) or po: 2 DS tabs q8h], total of 21 days	**[Clinda** 600 mg IV q8h + **primaquine** 30 mg po q24h] or **[pentamidine isethionate** 4 mg per kg per day IV] times 21 days. See Comment	**given at initiation of anti-PCP rx; don't wait until pt's condition deteriorates.** If PCR studies negative, consider bacterial pneumonia, TBc, cocci, histo, crypto, Kaposi's sarcoma or lymphoma. **NOTE: Pneumocystis resistant to TMP-SMX, albeit rare, does exist.**
			Pentamidine not active vs. bacterial pathogens.	
CD4 T-lymphocytes normal	Strep. pneumoniae, H. influenzae, aerobic Gm-neg. bacilli (including P. aeruginosa), Legionella	Ceftriaxone 1 gm IV q24h (over age 65:1 gm IV q24h) + **azithromycin** 500 mg IV q24h (see Comment)	For HIV+ adults, use **Levo**, or **Moxi** IV as alternative	If Gram stain of sputum shows Gm-neg. bacilli, options include: **P Ceph 3 (Cefotax, CefTZ, AM-CL, IMP,** or **MER.** **FQs: Levo** (750 mg) IV q24h, **Moxi** 400 mg po/IV q24h; Gati not available in US due to hypo- & hyperglycemic reactions.
TBc excluded: Adults				
As above: Children	Same as adult with HIV + lymphoid interstitial pneumonia (LIP)	As for HIV+ adults with pneumonia. If diagnosis is LIP, rx with steroids.		In children with AIDS, LIP responsible for 1/3 of pulmonary complications, usually >1 yr of age vs. PCP which is seen at <1 yr of age. Clinically: clubbing, hepatosplenomegaly, salivary glands enlarged (take up gallium), lymphocytosis.

Abbreviations on page 2.   NOTE: All dosage recommendations are for adults (unless otherwise indicated) and assume normal renal function.

TABLE 1 (42)

ANATOMIC SITE/DIAGNOSIS/ MODIFYING CIRCUMSTANCES	ETIOLOGIES (usual)	SUGGESTED REGIMENS* PRIMARY	ALTERNATIVE§	ADJUNCT DIAGNOSTIC OR THERAPEUTIC MEASURES AND COMMENTS
LUNG—Other Specific Infections *(continued)*				
Nocardia pneumonia Expert Help: Wallace Lab (+1) 903-877-7680; CDC (+1) 404-639-3158 Ref. *Medicine* 88:250, 2009.	N. asteroides, N. brasiliensis	**TMP-SMX** 15 mg/kg/day IV/po in 2-4 divided doses + **imipenem** 500 mg IV q6h for first 3-4 wks then **TMP-SMX** 10 mg/kg/day in 2-4 divided doses x 3-6 mos	IMP 500 mg IV q6h + amikacin 7.5 mg/kg IV q12h x 3-4 wks & then po **TMP-SMX**	**Duration:** 3 mos. if immunocompetent; 6 mos. if immunocompromised. **Measure peak sulfonamide levels:** Target is 100-150 mcg/ml, 2 hrs post po dose. Linezolid active in vitro (*Ann Pharmacother* 41:1694, 2007). In vitro resistance to TMP-SMX may be increasing (*Clin Infect Dis* 51:1445, 2010), but whether this is associated with worse outcomes is not known.
Tularemia Inhalational tularemia Ref. *JAMA* 285:2763, 2001 & www.bt.cdc.gov	*Francisella* tularemia Treatment	**Streptomycin** 15 mg per kg IV (x4) or po bid times 14-21 days or **CIP** 400 mg IV (or 750 mg po) bid times 14-21 days	Doxy 100 mg IV or po bid times 14-21 days or **CIP** 400 mg IV (or 750 mg po) bid times 14-21 days	For pediatric doses, see Table 16, page 203. Pregnancy: as for non-pregnant adults. **Tobramycin** should work.
	Postexposure prophylaxis	Doxy 100 mg po bid times 14 days	CIP 500 mg po bid times 14 days	For pediatric doses, see Table 16, page 203. Pregnancy: As for non-pregnant adults.
Viral (interstitial) pneumonia suspected See Influenza, Table 14A, page 164. Ref. *Chest* 133:1221, 2008.	Consider: Influenza, adenovirus, coronavirus (SARS), hantavirus, metapneumovirus, parainfluenza virus, respiratory syncytial virus	Oseltamivir 75 mg po bid x 5 days or zanamivir two 5 mg inhalations twice a day for 5 days.		No known efficacious drugs for adenovirus, coronavirus (SARS), hantavirus, metapneumovirus, parainfluenza or RSV. Need travel (SARS) & exposure (Hanta) history. RSV and human metapneumovirus as serious as influenza in the elderly (*NEJM* 352:1749 & 1810, 2005; *CID* 44:1152 & 1159, 2007).
LYMPH NODES (approaches below apply to lymphadenitis without an obvious primary source)				
Lymphadenitis, acute Generalized	Etiologies: EBV, early HIV infection, syphilis, toxoplasma, tularemia, Lyme disease, sarcoid, lymphoma, systemic lupus erythematosus, and **Kikuchi-Fujimoto** disease. Complete history and physical examination followed by appropriate serological tests. Treat specific agent(s)			
Regional **Cervical—see cat-scratch disease (CSD), below**	CSD (B. henselae), Grp A strep, Staph. aureus, anaerobes M. TBc (scrofula), M. avium, M. scrofulaceum.	History & physical exam directs evaluation. If nodes fluctuant, aspirate and base rx on Gram & acid-fast stains **Kikuchi-Fujimoto** disease causes fever and benign self-limited adenopathy; the etiology is unknown (*CID* 39:138, 2004).		
Inguinal Sexually transmitted	HSV, chancroid, syphilis, LGV			
Not sexually transmitted	GAS, SA CSD, Y. pestis (plague)	Consider bubonic plague & glandular tularemia.		
Axillary	GAS, SA, CSD, tularemia, Y. pestis	Consider bubonic plague & glandular tularemia.		
Extremity, with associated nodular lymphangitis	Sporotrichosis, leishmania, Nocardia brasiliensis, Mycobacterium marinum, Mycobacterium chelonae.	Treatment varies with specific etiology.		A distinctive form of lymphangitis characterized by subcutaneous swellings along inflamed lymphatic channels. Primary site of skin invasion usually present; regional adenopathy variable.
Nocardia lymphadenitis & skin abscesses	N. asteroides, N. brasiliensis	TMP-SMX 5-10 mg/kg/day based on TMP IV/po div in 2-4 doses	Sulfisoxazole 2 gm po qid or **minocycline** 100-200 mg	**Duration:** 3 mos. if immunocompetent; 6 mos. if immunocompromised. Linezolid 600 mg po bid reported effective (*Ann Pharmacother* 41:1694, 2007).
Cat-scratch disease— immunocompetent patient Axillary/epitrochlear nodes 46%, neck 26%, inguinal 17%. Ref. *Amer Fam Physician* 83:152, 2011.	Bartonella henselae	**Azithro dosage—Adults** (>45.5 kg): 500 mg po x 1, then 250 mg/day x 4 days. **Children** (<45 kg): liquid azithro 10 mg/kg x 1, then 5 mg/kg per day x 4 days. Rx is controversial	No therapy; resolves in 2-6 mos. Needle aspiration relieves pain in suppurative nodes. Avoid I&D.	**Clinical:** Approx. 10% nodes suppurate. Atypical presentation in <5% pts, i.e., lung nodules, liver/spleen lesions, Parinaud's oculoglandular syndrome, CNS manifestations in 2% of pts (encephalitis, peripheral neuropathy, retinitis). FUO **Dx:** Cat exposure. Positive IFA serology. Rarely need biopsy.

Abbreviations on page 2.   NOTE: All dosage recommendations are for adults (unless otherwise indicated) and assume normal renal function.

TABLE 1 (43)

ANATOMIC SITE/DIAGNOSIS/ MODIFYING CIRCUMSTANCES	ETIOLOGIES (usual)	SUGGESTED REGIMENS*		ADJUNCT DIAGNOSTIC OR THERAPEUTIC MEASURES AND COMMENTS
		PRIMARY	ALTERNATIVE¹	
MOUTH				
Aphthous stomatitis, recurrent	Etiology unknown	Topical steroids (Kenalog in Orabase) may ↓ pain and swelling. If AIDS, see *SANFORD GUIDE TO HIV/AIDS THERAPY.*		
Buccal cellulitis Children <5 yrs	H. influenzae	**Cefuroxime** or **ceftriaxone**	AM-CL or TMP-SMX	With Hib immunization, invasive H. influenzae infections have ↓ by 95%. Now occurring in infants prior to immunization.
		Dosage: see Table 16, page 203		
Candida Stomatitis ("Thrush")	C. albicans	Fluconazole	Echinocandin	See Table 11, page 113.
Herpetic stomatitis	Herpes simplex virus 1 & 2	See Table 14		
Submandibular space infection, bilateral (Ludwig's angina)	Oral anaerobes, facultative streptococci, S. aureus (rare)	(**PIP-TZ** or **TC-CL**) or **Pen G IV** + **Metro IV**)	**Clinda** 600 IV q6-8h (for Pen-allergic pt)	**Ensure adequate airway** and early surgical debridement. Add Vanco IV if gram-positive cocci on gram stain.
Ulcerative gingivitis (Vincent's angina or Trench mouth)	Oral anaerobes + vitamin deficiency	**Pen G** po/IV + **Metro** po/IV	Clinda	Replete vitamins (A-D). Can mimic scurvy. Severe form is NOMA (Cancrum oris) (*Ln 368:147, 2006*)
MUSCLE				
"Gas gangrene" Contaminated traumatic wound. Can be spontaneous without trauma	Cl. perfringens, other histotoxic Clostridium sp.	(**Clinda** 900 mg IV q8h) + (**pen G** 24 million units/day div q4-6h IV)	**Ceftriaxone** 2 gm IV q12h or **erythro** 1 gm q6h IV (not by bolus)	Surgical debridement primary therapy. **Hyperbaric oxygen** adjunctive: efficacy debated, consider if debridement not complete or possible. Clinda given to decrease toxin production.
Pyomyositis	Staph. aureus, Group A strep, (rarely Gm-neg. bacilli), variety of anaerobic organisms	(**Nafcillin** or **oxacillin** 2 gm IV q4h) or (**P Ceph 1** (**cefazolin** 2 gm IV q8h)) if **MSSA**	**Vanco** 1 gm IV q12h if **MRSA**	Common in tropics; rare, but occurs, in temperate zones. Follows exercise or muscle injury, see *Necrotizing fasciitis.* Now seen in HIV/AIDS. Add **metro** if anaerobes suspected or proven.
PANCREAS: Review: *NEJM 354:2142, 2006*				
Acute alcoholic (without necrosis) (idiopathic) pancreatitis	Not bacterial	NONE No necrosis on CT		1-9% become infected but prospective studies show no advantage of prophylactic antimicrobials. Observe for pancreatic abscesses or necrosis which require therapy.
Post-necrotizing pancreatitis; infected pseudocyst; pancreatic abscess	Enterobacteriaceae, entero-cocci, S. aureus, S. epider-midis, anaerobes, candida	Need culture of abscess/infected pseudocyst to direct therapy; **PIP-TZ** is reasonable empiric therapy		Can often get specimen by fine-needle aspiration. **Moxi, MER, IMP, ERTA** are all options (*AAC 56:6434, 2012*).
Antimicrobic prophylaxis, necrotizing pancreatitis	As above	If > 30% pancreatic necrosis on CT scan (with contrast), initiate antibiotic therapy. **IMP** 0.5-1 gm IV q6h or **MER** 1 gm IV q8h. No need for empiric Fluconazole. If patient worsens CT guided aspiration for culture & sensitivity. Controversial: *Cochrane Database Sys Rev 2003: CD 002941; Gastroenterol 126:977, 2004; Ann Surg 245:674, 2007.*		
PAROTID GLAND				
"Hot" tender parotid swelling	S. aureus, S. pyogenes, oral flora, aerobic Gm-neg. bacilli (rare), mumps, rarely enteroviruses/ influenza: **Nafcillin** or **oxacillin** 2 gm IV q4h if MSSA; **vanco** if MRSA			Predisposing factors: stone(s) in Stensen's duct, dehydration. Therapy depends on ID of specific etiologic organism.
"Cold" non-tender parotid swelling	Granulomatous disease (e.g., mycobacteria, fungi, sarcoidosis, Sjögren's syndrome), drugs (iodides, et al.), diabetes, cirrhosis, tumors			History/lab results may narrow differential; may need biopsy for diagnosis

Abbreviations on page 2.   NOTE: All dosage recommendations are for adults (unless otherwise indicated) and assume normal renal function.

TABLE 1 (44)

ANATOMIC SITE/DIAGNOSIS/ MODIFYING CIRCUMSTANCES	ETIOLOGIES (usual)	SUGGESTED REGIMENS*		ADJUNCT DIAGNOSTIC OR THERAPEUTIC MEASURES AND COMMENTS
		PRIMARY	**ALTERNATIVE¹**	
PERITONEUM/PERITONITIS: *Reference—CID 50:133, 2010*				
Primary (spontaneous) bacterial peritonitis, SBP) *Hepatology 49:2087, 2009.* Dx: pos. culture & ≥ 250 neutrophils/µL of ascitic fluid	Enterobacteriaceae 63%, S. pneumo 9%, enterococci 6–10%, anaerobes <1%. Extended β-lactamase (ESBL) positive Klebsiella species.	**Cefotaxime** 2 gm IV q8h (if life-threatening, q4h)) or **TC-CL** or **PIP-TZ;** OR (**ceftriaxone** 2 gm IV q24h) or **ERTA** 1 gm IV q24h) If **resistant E. coli/Klebsiella species (ESBL-+),** then **(DORI** or **ERTA** or **IMP** or **MER);** **Moxi** (Dosage in footnote²⁹) Check in vitro susceptibility.	**TMP-SMX** ↓ peritonitis or spontaneous bacteremia from 27% to 3% (AnIM 122:595, 1995). Ref. for CIP: Hepatology 22:1171, 1995	One-year **risk of SBP** in pts with ascites and cirrhosis as high as 29% (Gastro 104:1133, 1993). Diagnosis of SBP: 30-40% of pts have neg. cultures of blood and ascitic fluid. % pos. cultures ↑ if 10 mL of pt's ascitic fluid added to blood culture bottles (JAMA 299:1166, 2008). If Pt bacteremic, Rx for at least 5 days; perhaps longer if non-bacteremic (Pharmacol Therapeutics 34:1261, 2011). **IV albumin** (1.5 gm/kg at dx & 1 gm/kg on day 3) may ↓ frequency of renal impairment (p 0.002) & ↓ hospital mortality (p 0.01) (NEJM 341:403, 1999).
Prevention of SBP [Amer J Gastro 104:993, 2009]: Cirrhosis & ascites *For prevention with UGI bleeding, see Liver, page 36*		**TMP-SMX-DS** 1 tab po 5 days/wk or **CIP** 750 mg po q.wk		
Secondary (bowel perforation, ruptured appendix, ruptured diverticula) *Ref: CID 50:133, 2010 (IDSA Guidelines)* Antifungal rx? No need if successful source control (secondary to visceral perforation. Treat for candida if recurrent surg. perforation(s), anastomotic leaks, necrotizing pancreatitis, liver/pancreas transplant, pure peritoneal culture, candidemia (Ln 21:1437, 1989; Ann Surg 76:159, 2010).	Enterobacteriaceae, Bacteroides sp., enterococci. P. aeruginosa (3-15 %) C. albicans (may contribute with recurrent surgery/immultiple surgeries) If VRE documented, dapto may work (Int J Antimicrob Agents 32:369, 2008).	**Mild-moderate disease—Inpatient—parenteral rx:** (e.g. focal periappendiceal peritonitis, periciverticular abscess). Usually need surgery for source control. **PIP-TZ** 3.375 gm IV q6h or 4.5 gm IV q8h or 4-hr infusion of 3.375 gm q8h **OR TC-CL** 3.1 gm IV q6h **OR ERTA** 1 gm IV q24h **OR MOXI** 400 mg IV q24h ------- **Severe life-threatening disease—ICU patient:** Surgery for source control **IMP** 500 mg IV q6h or **MER** 1 gm IV q8h or **DORI** 500 mg IV q8h (1-hr infusion). See Comments. ------- Concomitant surgical management important.	**(CIP** 400 mg IV q12h or **Levo** 750 mg IV q24h) + **(metro** 1 gm q12h or **metro** 500 mg IV q6h) **+ tigecycline** 100 mg IV times 1 dose, then 50 mg q12h ------- **(CIP** 400 mg IV q12h or **Levo** 750 mg IV q24h) **OR [AMP 2 gm IV q6h + metro + (CIP or Levo** 400 mg IV q8h or **Levo** 750 mg IV q24h)] **OR [AMP 2 gm IV q6h + aminoglycoside** (see Table 10D, page 109) ------- **Doxy** or **ceftriaxone** or **clinda**	Must "cover" both Gm-neg. aerobic & anaerobic bacteria. Empiric coverage of MRSA, enterococci and candida not necessary unless culture indicates infection. Cover enterococci if valvular heart disease. **Drugs active only vs. anaerobic Gm-neg. bacilli:** metro. **Drugs active only vs. aerobic Gm-neg. bacilli:** aminoglycosides, P Ceph 2/3/4, aztreonam, AP Pen, CIP, Levo. **Drugs active vs. both aerobic/anaerobic Gm-neg. bacteria:** cefoxitin, TC-CL, PIP-TZ, DORI, IMP, MER, Moxi. Increasing resistance (R) of Bacteroides species (AAC 51:1649, 2007; AAC 56:1247, 2012): --- Cefoxitin Cefotetan Clindamycin **% R** 5-30 17-87 19-35 Essentially no resistance of Bacteroides to metro. **PIP-TZ.** Case reports of metro resistance to: CID 40:e67, 2005; JCM 42:4127, 2004. Ertapenem not active vs. P. aeruginosa. Acinetobacter species. If absence of ongoing fecal contamination, **aerobic/anaerobic culture** of peritoneal exudate/abscess may be of help in guiding specific therapy. Less need for aminoglycosides. **With severe pen allergy,** can "cover" Gm-neg. aerobes with **CIP** or **aztreonam. Remember DORI/IMP/MER are β-lactams.** IMP dose increased to 1 gm q6h if suspect P. aeruginosa and pt. is critically ill. If VRE documented, daptomycin may work (Int J Antimicrob Agents 32:369, 2008).
Abdominal actinomycosis	A. Israeli and rarely others	**AMP** 50 mg/kg/day IV div in 3-4 doses x 4-6 wks, then **Pen VK** 2-4 gm/day po x 3-6 mos.		Presents as mass +/- fistula tract after abdominal surgery, for ruptured appendix. Can use IV Pen G instead of AMP: 10-20 million units/day IV x 4-6 wks.

²⁹ Parenteral **IV therapy** for peritonitis: **TC-CL** 3.1 gm IV q6h, **PIP-TZ** 3.375 gm IV q6h or 4.5 gm IV q8h or 4-hr infusion of 3.375 gm q8h (See Table 10), **Dori** 500 mg IV q8h (1-hr infusion), **IMP** 0.5-1 gm q6h, **MER** 1 gm q8h, **FQ** (**CIP** 400 mg IV q12h, **Levo** 750 mg q24h, **Moxi** 400 mg q24h), **AMP** 1 gm q6h, **ampho-glucoside** (see Table 10D, page 109), **cefotaxime** 2 gm IV q4-6-8h, **cefoxitin** 2 gm q6-8h, **ceftazidime** 1-2 gm q8h, **ceftriaxone** 1-2 gm q24h, **P Ceph 4 (CFP** 2 gm q12h, **ceftriaxone** 1-2 gm q24h, **P Ceph 3 (cefotaxime** 2 gm q4-8h), **clinda** 600-900 mg q8h, **Metronidazole** 1 gm (15 mg/kg) loading dose IV, then 0.5 gm q6h (Some data suggests once-daily dosing, see Table 10A, page 102), **AP Pen (ticarcillin** 4 gm q6h, **PIP** 4 gm q6h, **aztreonam** 2 gm q6h) NOTE: All dosage recommendations are for adults (unless otherwise indicated) and assume normal renal function.

Abbreviations on page 2.

TABLE 1 (45)

ANATOMIC SITE/DIAGNOSIS/ MODIFYING CIRCUMSTANCES	ETIOLOGIES (usual)	SUGGESTED REGIMENS		ADJUNCT DIAGNOSTIC OR THERAPEUTIC MEASURES AND COMMENTS
		PRIMARY	ALTERNATIVE[1]	
PERITONEUM/PERITONITIS (continued)				
Associated with chronic ambulatory peritoneal dialysis (Abdominal pain, cloudy dialysate, dialysate WBC >100 cell/µL with >50% neutrophils; normal = <8 cells/µL. Ref: Perit Dial Int 30:393, 2010.)	Gm− 45%, Gm+ 15%, Multiple 1%, Fungi 2%, M. TBc 0.1%. (Perit Dial Int 24:424, 2004.)	**Empiric therapy:** Need activity vs. MRSA **(Vanco)** and aerobic gram-negative bacilli **[Ceftaz, CFP, Carbapenem, CIP, Aztreonam, Gent].** Add **Fluconazole** if gram stain shows yeast. Use intraperitoneal dosing, unless bacteremia (rare), then systemic IV dosing. For dosing detail, see Table 19, page 213.		**For diagnosis:** concentrate several hundred mL. of removed dialysis fluid by centrifugation. Gram stain concentrate and then inject into aerobic/anaerobic blood culture bottles. A positive Gram stain will greatly increase chance of "saving" the catheter. Common organisms are S. aureus, S. epidermidis, and aerobic gram-negative bacilli. **If multiple Gm-neg. bacilli cultured, consider catheter-induced bowel perforation and need for catheter removal.** See Perit Dialysis Int 29:5, 2009. Other indications for catheter removal: relapsing/refractory peritonitis, fungal peritonitis, catheter tunnel infection.
PHARYNX				
Pharyngitis/Tonsillitis				
Exudative or Diffuse Erythema Associated cough, rhinorrhea, hoarseness and/or oral ulcers suggest viral etiology. IDSA Guidelines on Group A Strep: CID 55:1279, 2012.	Group A, C, G Strep; Fusobacterium (in research studies); Infectious Mono; Primary HIV; N. gonorrhea; Respiratory viruses	**For Strep pharyngitis: [Pen V** po x 10 days or **Benzathine Pen** 1.2 million units IM x 1 dose] **OR [Cefdinir** or **Cefpodoxime** x 5 days. **Cephalosporin doses in footnote**[30] (adult and peds) (Durations are FDA-approved)]	**For Strep pharyngitis: Pen allergic: Clinda** 300-450 mg po q8h x 10 days. **Azithro, Clarithro** are alternatives, but resistant S. pyogenes reported (JAC 63:242, 2009). Sulfonamides and Tetracyclines have questionable efficacy; FQs not recommended due to resistance	Dx: Rapid Strep test. No need for post-treatment test of cure rapid strep test or culture. Complications of Strep pharyngitis: 1) Acute rheumatic fever 48− follows Grp A S. pyogenes infection, rare after Grp C/G infection. See footnote[31] For prevention, start treatment within 9 days of onset of symptoms. 2) Children age < 2 at risk for post-streptococcal glomerulonephritis. 3) Pediatric autoimmune neuropsychiatric disorder associated with Grp A Strep (PANDAS) infection. 4) Peritonsillar abscess. Suppurative phlebitis are potential complications. Not effective for chronic Grp A Strep infection from chronic Grp A Strep carriage and/or repeat viral infections. Ref: MMWR 61:590, 2012.
Gonococcal pharyngitis		**Ceftriaxone** 250 mg IM x 1 dose + **Azithro** 1 gm po x 1 dose or **Doxy** 100 mg po bid x 7 days	**Cefdinir** or **Cefpodoxime** + **Azithro**. Tonsillectomy not recommended to decrease Strep infections	
Proven S. pyogenes recurrence (Grp A infections >6 in 1 yr; 4 in 2 consecutive yrs)			**AM-CL** or **Clinda**	Hard to distinguish true Grp A Strep infection from chronic Grp A Strep carriage and/or repeat viral infections.
	F. necrophorum (44%) Grp A Strep (33%) Grp C/G Strep (9%) (CID 49:1467, 2009)	**PIP-TZ** or **TC-CL** or **(Metro + Ceftriaxone)**	Pen allergic: **Clinda** IV	**Avoid macrolides: Fusobacterium is resistant.** Reports of beta-lactamase production by oral anaerobes (Anaerobe 9:105, 2003). See jugular vein suppurative phlebitis, page 49.
Peritonsillar abscess – Serious complication of exudative pharyngitis		Surgical drainage plus above		
Other complications		See parapharyngeal space infection and jugular vein suppurative phlebitis (below)		

[30] **Treatment of Group A, C & G strep:** Treatment durations are from approved package inserts. Subsequent studies indicate efficacy of shorter treatment courses. **All po unless otherwise indicated. PEDIATRIC DOSAGE: Benzathine penicillin** 25,000 units/kg to max. 1.2 million units. **Pen V** 250 mg q8h x 10 days; **amox** 1000 mg po once daily x 10 days or **AM-CL** 45 mg per kg per day (max 875 mg) div q12h x 10 days; **cefadroxil** 30 mg/kg once daily x 10 days; **cefpodoxime proxetil** 10 mg per kg per day div q12h x 5 days; **cefdinir** 14 mg per kg div q24h x 10 days; **cefprozil** 15 mg per kg per day. bid x 10 days; **cefadroxil** 30 mg/kg once daily x 10 days; **clarithro** 15 mg per kg per day div. bid x 250 mg once daily x 5 days; **ceftibuten** 20-30 mg per kg per day div. q8h x 10 days. **ADULT DOSAGE: Benzathine penicillin** 1.2 million units IM x 1; **Pen V** 500 mg or 250 mg q6h x 10 days; **cefdinir** 300 mg bid or 250 mg q24h x 10 days; **cefpodoxime** 100 mg bid x 5 days; **cefpodoxime proxetil** 100 mg bid x 10 days; **cefuroxime axetil** 250 mg bid x 10 days; **cefprozil** 500 mg once daily x 10 days. **NOTE: All Ceph 2 drugs** approved for 10-day rx of strep. pharyngitis, increasing number of studies show efficacy of 4-6 days; **clarithro** 250 mg bid x 10 days; **azithro** 500 mg x 1 and then 250 mg q24h x 4 days or 500 mg q24h x 3 days.

[31] Primary rationale for therapy is eradication of Group A strep (GAS) and prevention of acute rheumatic fever (ARF). Benzathine pen in clinical trials to rate of ARF from 2.8 to 0.2%. This was associated with clearance of GAS on pharyngeal cultures (CID 19:1110, 1994). Subsequent studies have been based on cultures, not actual prevention of ARF. Treatment decreases duration of symptoms.

Abbreviations on page 2. NOTE: All dosage recommendations are for adults (unless otherwise indicated) and assume normal renal function.

TABLE 1 (46)

ANATOMIC SITE/DIAGNOSIS/ MODIFYING CIRCUMSTANCES	ETIOLOGIES (usual)	SUGGESTED REGIMENS*		ADJUNCT DIAGNOSTIC OR THERAPEUTIC MEASURES AND COMMENTS
		PRIMARY	ALTERNATIVE[1]	
PHARYNX/Pharyngitis/Tonsillitis (continued)				
Membranous pharyngitis due to Diphtheria Respiratory isolation, nasal & pharyngeal cultures, obtain antitoxin.	C. diphtheriae (human to human), C. ulcerans and C. pseudotuberculosis (animal to human) (rare)	Treatment: antibiotics + antitoxin **Antibiotic therapy:** Erythro 500 mg IV q6 OR Pen G 50,000 units/kg (max 1.2 million units) IV q12h. Can switch to Pen VK 250 mg po q6h when able. Treat for 14 days	**Diphtheria antitoxin:** Horse serum. Obtain from CDC, +1 404-639-2889. Do scratch test before IV therapy. Dose depends on stage of illness: < 48hrs: 20,000-40,000 units in IV membranes: 40,000-60,000 units; > 3 days & bull neck: 80,000-120,000 units	Ensure adequate airway. EKG & cardiac enzymes. F/U cultures post-treatment to document cure. Then, diphtheria toxoid immunization. Culture contacts; treat contacts with either single dose of **Pen G** IM: 600,000 units if age < 6 yrs, 1.2 million units if age ≥ 6 yrs. If Pen-allergic, **Erythro** 500 mg po qid x 7-10 days.
Vesicular, ulcerative pharyngitis (viral)	Coxsackie A9, B1-5, ECHO (multiple types), Enterovirus 71, Herpes simplex 1,2	Antibacterial agents not indicated. For HSV-1, 2: **acyclovir** 400 mg tid po x 10 days.		Small vesicles posterior pharynx suggests enterovirus. Viruses are most common etiology of acute pharyngitis. Suspect viral if concurrent conjunctivitis, coryza, cough, skin rash, hoarseness.
Epiglottitis (Supraglottis) Children	H. influenzae (rare), S. pyogenes, S. pneumoniae, S. aureus (includes MRSA)	**Peds dosage: Cefotaxime** 50 mg per kg IV q8h or **ceftriaxone** 50 mg per kg IV q24h) + **Vanco**	**Peds dosage: Levo** 10 mg/kg IV q24h + **Clinda** 7.5 mg/kg IV q8h	Have tracheostomy set "at bedside." **Levo** use in children is justified as emergency empiric therapy in pts with severe beta-lactam allergy. Ref: Ped Clin No Amer 53:215, 2006.
Adults	Group A strep, H. influenzae (rare) & many others	Same regimens as for children. **Adult dosage:** See footnote[52]		
Parapharyngeal space infection; peritonsillar abscess (Spaces include: sublingual, submaxillary, submandibular (Ludwig's angina), lateral pharyngeal, retropharyngeal, pretracheal) Poor dental hygiene, dental extractions, foreign bodies (e.g., fish bones). Ref: CID 49:1467, 2009	Polymicrobic: Strep sp., anaerobes, Eikenella corrodens. Anaerobes outnumber aerobes 10:1.	**(Clinda** 600-900 mg IV q8h) or (**pen G** 24 million units/day by cont. infusion or div. q4-6h IV + **metro** 1 gm IV load and then 0.5 gm IV q6h)	**Cefoxitin** 2 gm IV q8h or **clinda** 600-900 mg IV q8h or **TC-CL** or **PIP-TZ** (Dosage, see footnote[52])	Close observation of airway, 1/3 require intubation. MRI or CT to identify abscess; **surgical drainage. Metro** also may be given 1 gm IV q12h. Complications: infection of carotid (rupture possible) & jugular vein phlebitis.
Jugular vein suppurative phlebitis (Lemierre's syndrome) LnID 12:808, 2012.	Fusobacterium necrophorum in vast majority	**PIP-TZ** 4.5 gm IV q8h or **IMP** 500 mg IV q6h or (**Metro** 500 mg po/IV q8h + **ceftriaxone** 2 gm IV once daily)	**Clinda** 600-900 mg IV q8h. Avoid macrolides; **fusobacterium are resistant**	Emboli: pulmonary and systemic common. Erosion into carotid artery can occur. Lemierre described F. necrophorum in 1936; other anaerobes & Gm-positive cocci are less common etiologies of suppurative phlebitis post-pharyngitis.
Laryngitis (hoarseness)	Viral (90%)	Not indicated		

[52] Parapharyngeal space infection: **Ceftriaxone** 2 gm IV q24h; **cefotaxime** 2 gm IV q4-8h; **PIP-TZ** 3.375 gm IV q4-8h or 4-hr infusion of 3.375 gm IV q8h; **TC-CL** 3.1 gm IV q4-6h; **TMP-SMX** 8-10 mg per kg per day (based on TMP component) div q6h, q8h, or q12h; **Clinda** 600-900 mg IV q8h; **Levo** 750 mg IV q24h. NOTE: All dosage recommendations are for adults (unless otherwise indicated) and assume normal renal function.

Abbreviations on page 2.

TABLE 1 (47)

ANATOMIC SITE/DIAGNOSIS/ MODIFYING CIRCUMSTANCES	ETIOLOGIES (usual)	SUGGESTED REGIMENS*		ADJUNCT DIAGNOSTIC OR THERAPEUTIC MEASURES AND COMMENTS
		PRIMARY	ALTERNATIVE‡	
SINUSES, PARANASAL **Sinusitis, acute; current terminology: acute rhinosinusitis.** **Obstruction of sinus ostia, viral infection, allergens** Refs: Otolaryngol Head & Neck Surg 130:1, 2004; JAMA 301:1798, 2009; JAMA 307:685, 2012. For rhinovirus infections (common cold), see Table 14A, page 167	S. pneumoniae 33%, H. influenzae 32%, M. catarrhalis 9%, Group A strep 2%, anaerobes 6%, viruses 15% **By CT scans, sinus mucosa inflamed in 87% of viral URIs; only 2% develop bacterial rhinosinusitis**	Reserve antibiotic therapy for pts given decongestants/ analgesics for 7 days then: with persistence of (1) nasal/sinus pain & (2) purulent nasal discharge; (3) low-grade fever; severe illness (pain, fever); treat sooner—usually requires hospitalization. Viral infections should resolve within 10 days. For mild/mod. disease: Ask if recent antibiotic use (recent = in last month)		**Rx goals:** (1) Resolve infection, (2) prevent bacterial complications, e.g. subdural empyema, epidural abscess, brain abscess, meningitis and cavernous sinus thrombosis (LnID 7:62, 2007), (3) avoid chronic sinus disease, (4) avoid unnecessary antibiotic rx. 40-60% rate of spontaneous resolution. For pts with pen/cephalosporin allergy, esp. severe IgE-mediated allergy, e.g. hives, anaphylaxis, treatment options: clarithro, azithro, TMP-SMX, doxy or FQs if under age 18. Do not use Clinda - no activity vs. Haemophilus or Moraxella sp. Dosages in footnote[34], page 50. If allergy just skin rash, po cephalosporin OK.
Meta-analysis of 9 double-blind trials found no clinical signs/symptoms that justify treatment--even after 7-10 days of symptoms (Ln 371:908, 2008).	S. pneumoniae 33%, H. influenzae 32%, M. catarrhalis 9%, Group A strep 2%, anaerobes 6%, viruses 15%, Staph. aureus 10%. CID 45:e121, 2007.	**No Recent Antibiotic Use:** Amox-HD or AM-CL-ER or cefdinir or cefpodoxime or cefprozil *In general, treat 10 days (see Comment). Adult and pediatric doses, footnote[34] and footnote[35], see Comment*	**Recent Antibiotic Use: AM-CL-ER** (adults) or resp. **FQ** (adults). For pen. allergy, see Comments, previous page. Use AM-CL susp. in peds.	**Usual rx 10 days:** but same efficacy with 3-7 days vs. 6-10 days (LnID 8:543, 2008) (meta-analysis). **S. aureus is not considered an etiology of acute uncomplicated sinusitis.** Isolation of S. aureus in pts same incidence as in healthy controls. Hence, empiric therapy is not aimed at S. aureus. NOTE: **Levo** 750 mg q24h x 5 days vs. **levo** 500 mg q24h x 10 days has equivalent microbiologic and clinical efficacy (Otolaryngol Head Neck Surg 134:10, 2006).
Clinical failure after 3 days	As above, consider diagnostic tap/aspirate	**Mild/Mod. Disease: AM-CL-ER** OR (**cefpodoxime**, **cefprozil**, or **cefdinir**) *Treat 5-10 days. Adult doses in footnote[34]*	**Severe Disease: Gati³⁴, Gemi, Levo, Moxi** Adjunctive therapy, footnote[34] & Comment	**Complications:** From acute viral rhinosinusitis--transient hyposmia. From acute bacterial rhinosinusitis--orbital infections, meningitis, epidural abscess, brain abscess & cavernous sinus thrombosis. Adjunctive therapy for cavernous sinus thrombosis: topical decongestant (oxymetazoline) for < 3 d; nasal steroids of possible benefit; antihistamines (minor role), saline irrigation may help.
Diabetes mellitus with acute keto-acidosis; neutropenia; deferox-amine rx: Mucormycosis	Rhizopus sp. (mucor), aspergillus	See Table 11, pages 117 & 122		
Hospitalized + nasotracheal or nasogastric intubation	Gm-neg. bacilli 47% (pseudomonas, acinetobacter, E. coli common), Gm+ (S. aureus) 35%, yeasts 18%, Polymicrobial in 60%	Remove nasotracheal tube if fever persists and ENT available; recommend sinus aspiration for C/S prior to empiric therapy **IMP** 0.5 gm IV q6h or **MER** 1 gm IV q8h. Add **vanco** for MRSA if Gram stain suggestive	(**Ceftaz** 2 gm IV q8h + **vanco**) or (**CFP** 2 gm IV q12h + **vanco**)	After 7 days of nasotracheal or nasogastric tubes, 95% have x-ray "sinusitis" (fluid in sinuses) but on transnasal puncture only 38% culture + (AJRCCM 150:776, 1994). For pts requiring mechanical ventilation with nasotracheal tube for ≥1 wk, bacterial sinusitis occurs in <10% (CID 27:851, 1998). May need fluconazole if yeast on Gram stain of sinus aspirate.

---

[33] **Pediatric doses for sinusitis (all oral): Amox HD** high dose 90 mg per kg per day div. q8h or q12h; **AM-CL-ES** (extra strength) pediatric susp.: 90 mg **amox** component per kg per day div. q12h; **azithro** 10 mg per kg day 1, then 5 mg per kg per day times 3 days. **clarithro** 15 mg per kg per day div. q12h; **cefpodoxime** 10 mg per kg per day (max. 400 mg) div. q12-24h; **cefuroxime axetil** 30 mg per kg per day div. q12h; **cefdinir** 14 mg per kg per day once q24h or divided bid; **cefprozil** 30 mg/kg/day divided bid (max 1 gm/day); **TMP-SMX:** 8-12 mg TMP/40-60 mg SMX per kg per day div. q12h.

[34] **Adult doses for sinusitis (all oral): AM-CL-ER** 2000/125 mg bid. **amox high-dose (HD)** 1 gm tid. **clarithro** 500 mg bid or **clarithro ext. release** 1 gm q24h, **doxy** 100 mg bid, **respiratory FQs** (**Gati** 400 mg q24hUS due to hypo/hyperglycemia. **Gemi** 320 mg q24h (not FDA indication but should work). **Levo** 750 mg q24h x 5 days, **Moxi** 400 mg q24h); **O Ceph** (**cefdinir** 300 mg q12h or 600 mg q24h, **cefpodoxime** 200 mg bid, **cefuroxime** 250-500 mg bid. **TMP-SMX** 1 double-strength (TMP 160 mg) bid (results after 3- and 10-day rx similar).

Abbreviations on page 2.   NOTE: All dosage recommendations are for adults (unless otherwise indicated) and assume normal renal function.

TABLE 1 (48)

ANATOMIC SITE/DIAGNOSIS/ MODIFYING CIRCUMSTANCES	ETIOLOGIES (usual)	SUGGESTED REGIMENS* PRIMARY	SUGGESTED REGIMENS* ALTERNATIVE†	ADJUNCT DIAGNOSTIC OR THERAPEUTIC MEASURES AND COMMENTS
SINUSES, PARANASAL: (continued)				
Sinusitis, chronic **Adults**	Prevotella, anaerobic strep, & fusobacterium—common anaerobes. Strep sp. haemophilus, P. aeruginosa, S. aureus, & moraxella-aerobes. (CID 35:428, 2002)	Antibiotics usually not effective	Otolaryngology consultation. If acute exacerbation, treat as acute sinusitis.	Pathogenesis unclear and may be polyfactorial: damage to ostiomeatal complex during acute bacterial disease, allergy ± polyps, occult immunodeficiency, and/or odontogenic disease (periodontitis in maxillary teeth).
SKIN				
Acne vulgaris (Med Lett Treatment Guidelines 11 (Issue 125): 1, 2013).				
Comedonal acne, "blackheads," "whiteheads," earliest form; no inflammation	Excessive sebum production & gland obstruction. No Propionibacterium acnes	All once-q24h: Topical **tretinoin** (cream 0.025 or 0.05%) or (gel 0.01 or 0.025%)	Topical **adapalene** 0.1% gel OR **azelaic acid** 20% cream or **tazarotene** 0.1% cream	Goal is prevention. ↓ number of new comedones and create an environment unfavorable to P. acnes. Adapalene causes less irritation than tretinoin. Azelaic acid less potent but less irritating than retinoids. **Tazarotene: Do not use in pregnancy.**
Mild inflammatory acne: small papules or pustules	Proliferation of P. acnes + abnormal desquamation of follicular cells	Topical **erythro** 3% + **benzoyl peroxide** 5%, bid	Can substitute **clinda** 1% gel for erythro	In random. controlled trial, topical benzoyl peroxide + erythro of equal efficacy to oral minocycline & tetracycline and not affected by antibiotic resistance of propionibacteria (Ln 364:2188, 2004)
Inflammatory acne: comedones, papules & pustules. Less common: deep nodules (cysts)	Progression of above events. Also, drug-induced, e.g., glucocorticoids, phenytoin, lithium, INH & others.	[Topical **erythro** 3% + **benzoyl peroxide** 5% bid] + oral antibiotic: **doxy** or **minocycline** See Comment for mild acne	Oral drugs: (**doxy** 50 mg bid) or (**minocycline** 50 mg bid). **erythro. TMP-SMX. clinda.** Expensive extended release **once-daily minocycline** (Solodyn) 1 mg/kg/d	Systemic **isotretinoin** reserved for pts with severe widespread nodular cystic lesions that fail oral antibiotic rx: 4–5 mos. course of 0.1–1 mg per kg per day. Aggressive/violent behavior reported. **Tetracyclines** stain developing teeth. (**Doxy** can cause photosensitivity. **Minocycline** side-effects: urticaria, vertigo, pigment deposition in skin or oral mucosa. Rare autoimmunity in children: fever, polyarthralgia, positive ANCA (J Peds 153:314, 2008).
Acne rosacea Ref: NEJM 352:793, 2005.	Skin mite: Demadex folliculorum	**Azelaic acid** gel bid, topical or **Metro** topical cream once daily or q24h	**Doxy** 50 mg po once daily.	Avoid activities that provoke flushing, e.g., alcohol, spicy food, sunlight. Ref: Med Lett 49:5, 2007.
Anthrax, cutaneous, inhalation **To report bioterrorism event:** 770-488-7100; **For info:** www.bt.cdc.gov See JAMA 281:1735, 1999; MMWR 50:909, 2001. Treat as inhalation anthrax if systemic illness.	B. anthracis Spores are introduced into/under the skin by contact with infected animals/animal products. See Lung, page 43.	**Adults (including pregnancy) and children** >50 kg: (**CIP** 500 mg po bid x 60 days. **Children** <50 kg: **CIP** 30 mg/kg/day div q12h po (10 max. 1 gm per day) or **Levo** 8 mg/kg po q24h x 60 days.	**Adults (including pregnancy):** **Doxy** 100 mg po bid x 60 days. **Children: Doxy** >8 y/o & >45 kg: 100 mg po bid; <8 y/o & ≤45 kg: 2.2 mg/kg po bid; ≤8 y/o: 2.2 mg/kg po bid. All for 60 days.	1. If penicillin susceptible, then: **Adults: Amox** 500 mg po q8h times 60 days. **Children: Amox** 80 mg per kg per day div q8h (max. 500 mg q8h) 2. **Usual treatment of cutaneous anthrax: 7–10 days; 60 days in setting of bioterrorism with presumed aerosol exposure.** 3. Other FQs (Levo, Moxi) should work based on in vitro susceptibility data 4. Intestinal anthrax can also occur (NEJM 363:766, 2010). 5. Anthrax vaccine absorbed recommended at 0, 2, 4 wks postexposure to postexposure prophylaxis.
Bacillary angiomatosis: For other Bartonella infections, see Cat-scratch disease lymphadenitis, page 46, and Bartonella systemic infections, page 62. In immunocompromised (HIV-1, bone marrow transplant) patients Also see SANFORD GUIDE TO HIV/AIDS THERAPY	Bartonella henselae and quintana	**Clarithro** 500 mg po bid or **Erythro** 500 mg po qid or ext. release 1 gm po q24h or **azithro** 250 mg q24h (see Comment)	**Erythro** 500 mg po qid or **doxy** 100 mg po bid or (**Doxy** 100 mg po bid + **RIF** 300 mg po bid)	For AIDS pts, continue suppressive therapy until HIV treated and CD >200 cells/µL for 6 mos.

Abbreviations on page 2.   NOTE: All dosage recommendations are for adults (unless otherwise indicated) and assume normal renal function.

TABLE 1 (49)

ANATOMIC SITE/DIAGNOSIS/ MODIFYING CIRCUMSTANCES	ETIOLOGIES (usual)	SUGGESTED REGIMENS*		ADJUNCT DIAGNOSTIC OR THERAPEUTIC MEASURES AND COMMENTS
		PRIMARY	ALTERNATIVE†	
SKIN (continued)				
Bite: Remember tetanus prophylaxis— See Table 20B, page 215 for rabies prophylaxis. For extensive review of microbiology of animal bite caused infections, see CMR 24:231, 2011.				
Bat, raccoon, skunk	Strep & staph from skin; rabies	AM-CL 875/125 mg po bid or 500/125 mg po tid	Doxy 100 mg po bid	In America, **anti-rabies rx indicated:** rabies immune globulin + vaccine. See EClid 13:916, 1999.
Camel	S. aureus, P. aeruginosa, Others	Diclox 250-500 mg po q6h + CIP 750 mg po bid	Cephalexin 500 mg po qid + CIP 750 mg po bid	
Cat: 80% get infected, culture & treat empirically.	**Pasteurella multocida** Streptococci, Staph. aureus, Neisseria, Moraxella	AM-CL 875/125 mg po bid or 500/125 mg po tid	Cefuroxime axetil 0.5 gm po q12h or doxy 100 mg po bid. Do not use cephalexin.	**P. multocida resistant to dicloxacillin, cephalexin, clinda; many strains resistant to erythro** (most sensitive to azithro but no clinical data). P. multocida infection develops within 24 hrs. Observe for osteomyelitis. If culture + for only P. multocida, can switch to pen G IV or pen VK po. See Dog Bite
Cat-scratch disease; page 45		See Comments		+ for only P. multocida, can switch to pen G IV or pen VK po. See Dog Bite Presents as immediate pain, erythema and edema. Resembles strep cellulitis.
Catfish sting	Toxins	See Comments		May become secondarily infected; AM-CL is reasonable choice for prophylaxis.
Dog: Only 5% get infected; treat only if bite severe or bad co-morbidity (e.g. diabetes).	**Pasteurella canis**, S. aureus, Streptococci, Fusobacterium sp, Capnocytophaga	AM-CL 875/125 mg po bid or 500/125 mg po tid	Clinda 300 mg po qid + FQ (adults) or clinda + TMP-SMX (children)	Consider anti-rabies prophylaxis: rabies immune globulin + vaccine (see Table 20B). Capnocytophaga is splenectomized pts may cause local eschar, sepsis with DIC. **P. canis resistant to diclox, cephalexin, clinda and erythro; susceptible to ceftriaxone, cefuroxime, cefpodoxime and FQs.**
Human (For bacteriology, see CID 37:1481, 2003	Streptococci 100%, Staph epidermidis 53%, corynebacterium 41%, **Staph. aureus 29%, eikenella 15%**, bacteroides 82%, peptostrep 26%	Early (not yet infected): AM-CL 875/125 mg po bid times 5 days. Later: Signs of infection (usually in 3-24 hrs): (AM-SB 1.5 gm IV q6h or cefotixin 2 gm IV q8h) or (TC-CL 3.1 gm IV q6h) or (PIP-TZ 3.375 gm IV q6h or 4.5 gm q8h or 4-hr infusion of 3.375 gm q8h)		**Cleaning, irrigation and debridement most important.** For clenched fist injuries, x-rays should be obtained. Bites inflicted by hospitalized pts. consider aerobic Gm-neg. bacilli. **Eikenella resistant to clinda, nafcillin/oxacillin, metro, P Ceph 1, and erythro; susceptible to FQs and TMP-SMX.**
Leech (Medicinal)	Aeromonas hydrophila	Pen allergy: Clinda + (either CIP or TMP-SMX) CIP (400 mg IV or 750 mg po) bid	TMP-SMX DS 1 tab po bid	Aeromonas found in GI tract of leeches. Some use prophylactic antibiotics when leeches used medicinally, but not universally accepted. Necessary (DCP 10:211, 2001). Avoid Amp or 1st gen Cephalosporins (CID 35:e1, 2002). Information limited but infection is common and serious (Ln 348:888, 1996).
Pig (swine)	Polymicrobic: Gm+ cocci, Gm-neg. bacilli, anaerobes, Pasteurella sp.	AM-CL 875/125 mg po bid	P Ceph 3 or TC-CL or AM-SB or IMP	
Prairie dog	Monkeypox	See Table 14A, page 165. No rx recommended		CID 20:421, 1995
Primate, non-human	Herpesvirus simiae	Acyclovir: See Table 14B, page 168		
Rat	Spirillum minus & Strepto-bacillus moniliformis	AM-CL 875/125 mg po bid	Doxy	Anti-rabies rx not indicated. Causes rat bite fever (Streptobacillus moniliformis). Pen G or doxy, alternatively erythro or clinda.
Seal	Marine mycoplasma	Tetracycline times 4 wks		Can take weeks to appear after bite (Ln 364:448, 2004).
Snake: pit viper (Ref. NEJM 347:347, 2002)	Pseudomonas sp. Enterobacteriaceae, Staph. epidermidis.	See Table 14A, page 165	**Primary therapy is antivenom.** Penicillin generally used but would not be effective vs. organisms isolated. Ceftriaxone should be more effective. Tetanus prophylaxis indicated. Ref. CID 43:1309, 2006.
Spider bite: Most necrotic ulcers attributed to spiders are probably due to another cause, e.g. cutaneous anthrax (Ln 364:549, 2004) or **MRSA infection** (spider bite painful; anthrax not painful)	Clostridium sp.	None		May be confused with "acute abdomen." Diazepam or calcium gluconate helpful to control pain, muscle spasm. Tetanus prophylaxis.
Widow (Latrodectus)	Not infectious	None		
Brown recluse (Loxosceles) NEJM 352:700, 2005	Not infectious. Overdiagnosed & self-healing. No therapy of proven efficacy.	Bite usually self-limited & self-healing.	Dapsone 50 mg po q24h often used despite marginal supportive data	Dapsone causes hemolysis (check for G6PD deficiency). Can cause hepatitis; baseline & weekly liver panels suggested.

Abbreviations on page 2.   NOTE: All dosage recommendations are for adults (unless otherwise indicated) and assume normal renal function.

TABLE 1 (50)

ANATOMIC SITE/DIAGNOSIS/ MODIFYING CIRCUMSTANCES	ETIOLOGIES (usual)	SUGGESTED REGIMENS*		ADJUNCT DIAGNOSTIC OR THERAPEUTIC MEASURES AND COMMENTS
		PRIMARY	ALTERNATIVE†	
SKIN (continued)				
Boils—Furunculosis—Subcutaneous abscesses in drug addicts ("skin poppers"). **Carbuncles** = multiple connecting furuncles.				
Active lesions See Table 5a, page 78 Community-associated MRSA widespread. I&D mainstay of therapy. Ref: CID 46:1032, 2008. No difference between TMP-SMX and placebo in peds pts—most with abscess <5 cm (An Emer Med (ePub, Apr 29), 2009	Staph. aureus, both MSSA & MRSA—concern for community-associated MRSA (See Comments) CID 52 (Feb 1);1, 2011.	If **afebrile & abscess <5 cm in diameter: I&D** culture, no packs. No drugs. If **≥5 cm in diameter:** **TMP-SMX-DS** 1 tab po bid times 5–10 days. Alternatives (Adult dosage): **clinda** 300–600 mg po q6-8h or **doxy** or **minocycline** 100 mg po q12h IV therapy.	**Febrile, large &/or multiple abscesses; outpatient care: I&D** culture & abscess & maybe blood, hot packs. **TMP-SMX-DS** 1 tab po bid times 5–10 days + **RIF** 300 mg po bid times 10 days. If no response after 2-3 days, look for complications and consider IV therapy.	Emergency Dept Perspective (IDC N Amer 22:89, 2008). One TMP-SMX-DS tab bid as effective as 2 tabs bid in prospective case control study (AAC 55:5430, 2011). TMP-SMX activity vs streptococci uncertain. Usually clear clinical separation of strep "cellulitis" (erysipelas) from S. aureus abscess. If unclear or strep. use **clinda** or **TMP-SMX** plus **beta-lactam** (eg, **TMP-SMP** alone first. Other options: (1) **Linezolid** 600 mg po bid x 10 days; (2) **Fusidic acid**[NUS] 250-500 mg po q8-12h ± **RIF** (CID 42:394, 2006); (3) **FQs** only if in vitro susceptibility known.
		← Incision and Drainage mainstay of therapy →		
To lessen recurrence of furuncle —decolonization For surgical prophylaxis, see Table 15B, page 193.	MSSA & MRSA. IDSA Guidelines, CID 52 (Feb 1);1, 2011; AAC 56:1084, 2012.	7-day therapy. **Chlorhexidine** (2%) washes daily + **mupirocin** ointment anterior nares 2x daily + (**rifampin** 300 mg bid + **doxy** 100 mg bid).	**Mupirocin ointment** in anterior nares bid x 7 days + **chlorhexidine** (2%) washes daily x 7 days + **TMP-SMX DS** 1 tab po bid + RIF 300 mg po bid x 7 days	Optimal regimen uncertain. In randomized prospective study of combined topical & systemic therapy, negative MRSA cultures at 3 mos. in 74% of treated vs. 32% of not treated (CID 44:178, 2007). Mupirocin trials: CID 48:922, 2009; JAC 64:9-15, 2009. No benefit from decolonizing household contacts (CID 54:743, 2012). Can substitute bleach baths for chlorhexidine (Pediatr Infect Dis J 32:872, 2011). Bacitracin oint. inferior to Mupirocin (ICHE 20:351, 1999).
Hidradenitis suppurativa Not infectious disease, but bacterial superinfection occurs	Lesions secondarily infected: S. aureus, Enterobacteriaceae, pseudomonas, anaerobes	Clinda 1% topical cream	Tetracycline 500 mg po bid x 3 months	Caused by keratinous plugging of apocrine glands of axillary, inguinal, perianal, perineal, infra-mammary areas. Other therapy: antiperspirants, loose clothing and anti-androgens. Dermatol Clin 28:779, 2010.
		Adalimumab 40 mg once weekly beneficial (AnIM 157:846, 2012)		
Burns. For overall management: NEJM 350:810, 2004—step-by-step case outlined & explained Initial burn wound care Clin Infect Dis 37:543, 2003& BMJ 332:649, 2006). Topical burn options: NEJM 359:1037, 2008.	**Not infected** Prophylactic measures.	Early excision & wound closure. Variety of skin grafts and skin substitutes: see JAMA 283:717, 2000 & Adv Skin Wound Care 18:323, 2005; shower hydrotherapy. Role of topical antimicrobics unclear.	**Silver sulfadiazine** cream, 1%, apply 1–2 times per day and skin substitutes: see above. **Silver nitrate** solution or **mafenide acetate** cream. Apply cream.	Marrow-induced neutropenia can occur during 1st wk of sulfadiazine but resolves even if use is continued. Silver nitrate leaches electrolytes from wounds & stains everything. Mafenide inhibits carbonic anhydrase and can cause metabolic acidosis.
Burn wound sepsis	Strep. pyogenes, Enterobacter sp., S. aureus, S. epidermidis, E. faecalis, E. coli, P. aeruginosa. Fungi rare. Herpesvirus rare.	(**Vanco** 1 gm IV q12h) + (**amikacin** 10 mg per kg loading dose then 7.5 mg per kg IV q12h) + (**PIP** 4 gm IV q4h (give ½-1 dose of piperacillin first). Can substitute **Silver nitrate** surgical eschar removal within 12 hours)). Can use **PIP-TZ** if PIP not available.		**Monitor serum levels of Vanco and AMK as T½ of most antibiotics ↓**. Staph. aureus tend to remain localized to burn wound; if toxic, consider toxic shock syndrome. Superinfection rates of colonized burn wounds vary. Pneumonia is the major non-burn infectious complication, often staph. Complications include septic thrombophlebitis at IV sites. Dapto (6-8 mg per kg IV q24h) alternative for vanco.

Abbreviations on page 2.   NOTE: All dosage recommendations are for adults (unless otherwise indicated) and assume normal renal function.

TABLE 1 (51)

ANATOMIC SITE/DIAGNOSIS/ MODIFYING CIRCUMSTANCES	ETIOLOGIES (usual)	SUGGESTED REGIMENS*		ADJUNCT DIAGNOSTIC OR THERAPEUTIC MEASURES AND COMMENTS
		PRIMARY	**ALTERNATIVE†**	
SKIN (continued)				
Cellulitis, erysipelas: Be wary of macrolide (erythro-resistant) Streptococcus sp. Review. *NEJM 350:904, 2004.* **NOTE:** Consider diseases that masquerade as cellulitis (*ArIM 142:47, 2005*)				
Cellulitis, erysipelas, non-diabetic Extremities, non-diabetic *For diabetes, see below.* Practice guidelines *CID 41:1373, 2005.*	Streptococcus sp. (erythro-resistant) Streptococcus sp., Groups A, B, C & G, Staph. aureus, including MRSA (but rare).	Inpatients: Elevate legs. **Pen G** 1–2 million units IV q6h, **or ceftazolin** 1 gm IV q8h. If Pen-allergic: Vanco 15 mg/kg IV q12h. When afebrile: **Pen VK** 500 mg po qid ac & hs Total therapy: 10 days.	Outpatient: Elevate legs. Pen 10 × 500 mg po–qid ac & hs × 10 days. If Pen-allergic: Azithro 500 mg po × 1 dose, then 250 mg po once daily × 4 days (total 5 days). Rarely, might need Linezolid 600 mg po bid (expensive).	Look for tinea pedis as portal of entry. Treat if present. If suspected due to fluctuance or positive gram stain: MSSA: Diclox 500 mg po qid or Nafcillin/Oxacillin 2 gm IV q4h; MRSA: Doxy 100 mg po bid or TMP-SMX-DS 1 tab po bid or Vanco 1 gm IV q12h (inpatient). If S. aureus confirmed, usually need I&D. **Leg elevation is helpful. Note.** TMP-SMX for MRSA but not S. pyogenes; S. pyogenes may fail in vivo even if active in vitro (*Eur J Clin Micro 3:424, 1984*).
Facial, adult (erysipelas)	Strep. sp. (Grp A, B, C & G); Staph. aureus (to include MRSA), S. pneumo.	**Vanco** 1 gm IV q12h; if over 100 kg, 1.5 gm IV q12h	**Dapto** 4 mg/kg IV q24h **or Linezolid** 600 mg IV q12h	**Choice of empiric therapy must have activity vs. S. aureus.** S. aureus erysipelas of face can mimic streptococcal erysipelas of an extremity. Forced to treat empirically for MRSA until in vitro susceptibilities available.
Diabetes mellitus and erysipelas (See *Foot, "Diabetic", page 16*)	Strep. sp. (Grp A, B, C & G); Staph. aureus, Enterobacteriaceae; Anaerobes	**Early mild: TMP-SMX-DS** 1–2 tabs po bid + (**Pen VK** 500 mg po qid or **cephalexin** 500 mg po qid). **For severe disease: IMP, MER, ERTA** or **Dori** IV + (**linezolid** 600 mg IV/po bid or **vanco** IV or **dapto** 4 mg/kg IV q24h). *Dosage, see page 16, Diabetic foot.*		Prompt surgical debridement indicated to rule out necrotizing fasciitis and to obtain cultures. If septic, consider x-ray of extremity to demonstrate gas. **Prognosis dependent on blood supply: assess arteries.** See *diabetic foot, page 16.* For severe disease, use regimen that targets both aerobic gram-neg bacilli & MRSA.
Erysipelas 2° to lymphedema (congenital = Milroy's disease); post-breast surgery with lymph node dissection	Streptococcus sp., Groups A, C, G	**Benzathine pen G** 1.2 million units IM q4 wks		Indicated only if pt is having frequent episodes of cellulitis. Pen V 250 mg po bid should be effective but not aware of clinical trials. In pen-allergic pts: erythro 500 mg po q24h, azithro 250 mg po q24h, or clarithro 500 mg po q24h.
Dandruff (seborrheic dermatitis)	Malassezia species	Ketoconazole shampoo 2% or selenium sulfide 2.5%		See *page 10, chronic external otitis*).
Erythema multiforme	H. simplex type 1, mycoplasma, Strep. pyogenes, drugs (sulfonamides, phenytoin, penicillins)			**Rx: Acyclovir** if due to H. simplex (*Dermatology 207:349, 2003*)
Erythema nodosum	Sarcoidosis, inflammatory bowel disease, M. TBc, coccidioidomycosis, yersinia sulfonamides, Whipple's disease.			**Rx: NSAIDs; glucocorticoids** under certain circumstances. Identify and treat precipitant disease if possible.
Erythrasma	Corynebacterium minutissimum	Localized infection: **Topical Clinda** 2–3 × daily × 7-14 days	Widespread infection: **Clarithro** 500 mg po bid or **Erythro** 250 mg po bid) × 14 days	Dx. Coral red fluorescence with Wood's lamp. If infection recurs, prophylactic bathing with anti-bacterial soap or wash with benzyl peroxide.
Folliculitis	S. aureus, candida, P. aeruginosa common	Usually self-limited, no Rx needed. Could use topical mupirocin for Staph and topical antifungal for Candida.		
Furunculosis	Staph. aureus	See *Boils, page 53*		
Hemorrhagic bullous lesions Hx of sea water-contaminated abrasion or eating raw seafood in cirrhotic pt.	**Vibrio vulnificus** (*CID 52:788, 2011*)	**Ceftazidime** 2 gm IV q8h + **doxy** 100 mg IV/po bid	Either **cefotaxime** 2 gm IV q8h or (**CIP** 750 mg IV po bid or 400 mg IV bid)	Wound infection in healthy hosts, but bacteremia mostly in cirrhotics. Pathogenesis: Open wound exposure to contaminated seawater. Can cause necrotizing fasciitis (*JAC 67:488, 2012*).
Herpes zoster (shingles): *See Table 14*				

Abbreviations on page 2.   NOTE: *All dosage recommendations are for adults (unless otherwise indicated) and assume normal renal function.*

TABLE 1 (52)

ANATOMIC SITE/DIAGNOSIS/ MODIFYING CIRCUMSTANCES	ETIOLOGIES (usual)	SUGGESTED REGIMENS*		ADJUNCT DIAGNOSTIC OR THERAPEUTIC MEASURES AND COMMENTS
		PRIMARY	ALTERNATIVE†	
SKIN (continued)				
Impetigo—children, military				
"Honey-crust" lesions (non-bullous). Ecthyma is closely related. Causes "punched out" skin lesions.	**Group A strep impetigo** (rarely Strept. ssp. Groups B or C); crusted lesions can be Staph. aureus + streptococci. Staph. aureus may be secondary colonizer.	Mupirocin ointment 2% tid or fusidic acid cream[NUS] 2%, retapamulin ointment, 1% bid times 5 days *For dosages, see Table 10A and Table 16, page 203 for children*	Should be no need for oral antibiotics. *For dosages, see Table 10A for children*	In meta-analysis that combined strep & staph impetigo, mupirocin had higher cure rates than placebo. Mupirocin superior to oral erythro. Penicillin inferior to erythro. Few placebo-controlled trials. Ref.: *Cochrane Database Systemic Reviews, 2004 (2): CD003261.* 46% of USA-300 CA-MRSA isolates carry gene encoding resistance to mupirocin (*JID 367:731, 2006*). **NOTE:** Mupirocin resistance & topical mupirocin continues to evolve, over-the-counter triple antibiotic ointment (Neomycin, polymyxin B, Bacitracin) remains active in vitro (*DMID 54:63, 2006*).
Bullous (if ruptured, thin "varnish-like" crust)	**Staph. aureus** MSSA & MRSA strains that produce exfoliative toxin A.	**For MSSA:** po therapy with dicloxacillin, cephalexin. **AM-CL,** azithro, clarithro, or mupirocin ointment or retapamulin ointment	**For MRSA: Mupirocin** po therapy with TMP-SMX-DS, doxy, clinda	**Ecthyma:** Infection deeper into epidermis than impetigo. May need parenteral penicillin. Military outbreaks reported: (*CID 48:1213 & 1220, 2009)(good images).*
		For dosages, see Table 10A		
Infected wound, extremity—Post-trauma *(for bites, see page 52; for post-operative, see below)—* **Gram stain negative**				
Mild to moderate, uncomplicated Debride wound, if necessary.	Polymicrobic: S. aureus (MSSA & MRSA), aerobic strep.	TMP-SMX-DS 1-2 tabs po bid or **clinda** 300–450 mg po bid (see Comment)	Minocycline 100 mg po bid or linezolid 600 mg po bid (see Comment)	**Culture & sensitivity, check Gram stain. Tetanus toxoid if indicated.** **Mild infection:** Suggested drugs focus on S. aureus & Strep species. If suspect Gm-neg. bacilli, add **AM-CL-ER** 1000/62.5 two tabs po bid.
Febrile with sepsis—hospitalized Debride wound, if necessary.	Enterobacteriaceae, C. perfringens, Cl. tetani; Pseudomonas sp., Aeromonas sp. Acinetobacter sp. in soldiers in Iraq (see *CID 47:444, 2008*).	**TC-CL** or **PIP-TZ** or **DORI**[NUS] or **IMP** or **MER** or **ERTA** *(Dosage, page 25)* + **vanco** 1 gm IV q12h (1.5 gm if > 100 kg)	**Vanco** 1 gm IV q12h or **ceftaroline** 600 mg IV/po q12h or **daptomycin** 6 mg/kg IV q24h or **televancin** 10 mg/kg IV q24h) + **CIP** or **Levo** IV—dose in Comment)	If MRSA is erythro-resistant, may have inducible resistance to clinda. **Fever—sepsis:** Another alternative is **linezolid** 600 mg IV/po q12h. If Gm-neg. bacilli & severe pen allergy, **CIP** 400 mg IV/po q12h. Why **TMP-SMX-DS?** See discussion in footnote 1 of Table 6 (*MRSA*) **TMP-SMX** not predictably active vs. strep species.
Infected wound, post-operative—Gram stain positive cocci - see below				
Surgery not involving GI or female genital tract				
Without sepsis (mild, afebrile)	Staph. aureus, Group A, B, or G strep sp.	**TMP-SMX-DS** 1 tab po bid	**Clinda** 300–450 mg po tid	Check Gram stain of exudate. If Gm-neg. bacilli, **add** β-lactam/β-lactamase inhibitor: **AM-CL-ER** po or (**ERTA** or **PIP-TZ** or **TC-CL**) IV. *Dosage on page 25.*
With sepsis (severe, febrile)		**Vanco** 1 gm IV q12h; if >100 kg, 1.5 gm q12h.	**Dapto** 6 mg per kg IV q24h or **televancin** 10 mg/kg IV q24h	Why 1-2 **TMP-SMX-DS?** See discussion in footnote 1 of Table 6 (*MRSA*). **TMP-SMX** not predictably active vs. strep species.
Surgery involving GI tract (includes oropharynx, esophagus) or female genital tract—fever, neutrophilia	MSSA/MRSA, coliforms, bacteroides & other anaerobes	**PIP-TZ** or (**P Ceph 3** + **metro** or **DORI** or **ERTA** or **IMP** or **MER**) + (**vanco** 1 gm IV q12h or **dapto** 6 mg/kg IV q 24h) **If severely ill. Mild infection: AM-CL-ER** 1000/62.5 mg 2 tabs po bid + **TMP-SMX-DS** 1-2 tabs po bid if Gm+ cocci on Gram stain. *Dosages Table 10A & footnote 36, page 56*		For treatment options, see Peritonitis, page 47. Most important: Drain wound & get cultures. Can sub **linezolid** for vanco. Can sub **CIP** or **Levo** for β-lactams. Why **TMP-SMX-DS?** See discussion in footnote 1 of Table 6 (*MRSA*)
Meleny's synergistic gangrene	See Necrotizing fasciitis, page 56			

Abbreviations on page 2.

NOTE: All dosage recommendations are for adults (unless otherwise indicated) and assume normal renal function.

TABLE 1 (53)

ANATOMIC SITE/DIAGNOSIS/ MODIFYING CIRCUMSTANCES	ETIOLOGIES (usual)	SUGGESTED REGIMENS* PRIMARY	SUGGESTED REGIMENS* ALTERNATIVE†	ADJUNCT DIAGNOSTIC OR THERAPEUTIC MEASURES AND COMMENTS
SKIN/Infected wound, post-operative—Gram stain negative *(continued)*				
Infected wound, post-op, febrile patient— **Positive gram stain: Gram-positive cocci in clusters**	S. aureus, possibly MRSA	**Do culture & sensitivity: open & drain wound** Oral: TMP-SMX-DS 1 tab po bid or clinda 300–450 mg po tid (see Comment)	IV: **Vanco** 1 gm IV q12h or **dapto** 4–6 mg/kg IV q24h or **ceftaroline** 600 mg IV q12h (q24?)	Need culture & sensitivity to verify MRSA. Other po options for CA-MRSA include minocycline 100 mg q12h or **Doxy** 100 mg po bid (inexpensive) & linezolid 600 mg po q12h (expensive). If MRSA clinda-sensitive but erythro-resistant, watch out for inducible clinda resistance.
Necrotizing fasciitis ("flesh-eating bacteria") See **Gas gangrene, page 46** & **Toxic shock, page 64**. Refs: CID 44:705, 2007; NEJM 360:281, 2009.	**5 types:** (1) Strep sp. Grp A. (2) clostridia (3) polymicrobic; aerobic + anaerobic (If S. aureus + anaerobic strep = Meleney's synergistic gangrene). (4) Community-associated MRSA. (5) Klebsiella pneumoniae (CID 55:930 & 946, 2012)	For treatment of clostridia, see Muscle, gas gangrene, page 46. The terminology of **polymicrobic** wound infections is not precise: Meleney's synergistic gangrene, Fournier's gangrene, necrotizing fasciitis have common pathophysiology. **All require prompt surgical debridement** + antibiotics. Dx of necrotizing fasciitis req incision & probing. If no resistance to probing subcut with fascial plane involvement (fascial plane), diagnosis = necrotizing fasciitis **Need Gram stain/culture** to determine if etiology is strep, clostridia, polymicrobial, or S. aureus. **Treatment: Pen G** if strep or clostridia. **DORI***** **IMP** or **MER** if MRSA suspected. **NOTE:** If strep necrotizing fasciitis, reasonable to treat with penicillin & clinda. If clostridia ≡ gas gangrene, add clinda to penicillin (see page 46). MRSA ref.: NEJM 352:1445, 2005. See **toxic shock syndrome, streptococcal, page 64.**		
Puncture wound—nail, toothpick	Through tennis shoe. P. aeruginosa	Local debridement to remove foreign body & tetanus prophylaxis; no antibiotic therapy.		Osteomyelitis evolves in only 1–2% of plantar puncture wounds. Consider x-ray if chance of radio-opaque foreign body.
Staphylococcal scalded skin syndrome Ref.: PIDJ 19:819, 2000.	Toxin-producing S. aureus	**Nafcillin** or **oxacillin** 2 gm IV q4h (children: 150 mg/kg/ day div. q6h) x 5–7 days for MSSA, **vanco** 1 gm IV q12h (children 40–60 mg/kg div. q6h) for MRSA.		Toxin causes **intraepidermal split** and positive Nikolsky sign. Biopsy differentiates: drugs cause epidermal/dermal split, **called toxic epidermal necrolysis—more serious.**
Ulcerated skin lesions: Differential Dx	Consider: anthrax, tularemia, insufficiency, venous stasis, and injury	P. aeruginosa (ecthyma gangrenosum), plague, blastomycosis, spider (rarely), mucormycosis, mycobacteria, leishmania, YAWS; arterial		
Ulcerated skin: venous/arterial insufficiency; pressure with secondary infection (infected decubiti)	Polymicrobic: Streptococcus sp. (Groups A, C, G), enterococci, anaerobic strep, Enterobacteriaceae, Pseudomonas sp., Bac-teroides sp., Staph. aureus	Severe local or possible bacteremia: **IMP** or **MER** or **ERTA** or **TC-CL** or **PIP-TZ**. If Gm-pos cocci on gram stain, add **Vanco**.	[**CIP** or **Levo**] + **Metro**] or [**CFP** or **Ceftaz**] + **Metro**] if Gm-pos cocci on gram stain, add **Vanco**.	If ulcer clinically inflamed, treat IV with no topical rx. If not clinically inflamed, consider debridement, removal of foreign body, lessening direct pressure for weight-bearing limbs & leg elevation (if no arterial insufficiency). Topical rx to reduce bacterial counts: silver sulfadiazine 1% or combination antibiotic ointment. **Chlorhexidine & povidone iodine may harm "granulation tissue"—Avoid.**
Whirlpool: (Hot Tub) folliculitis	Pseudomonas aeruginosa	Dosages: see footnotes [4, 6, 7, 12, 15, 36] Usually self-limited, treatment not indicated		Decontaminate hot tub; drain and chlorinate. Also associated with exfoliative beauty aids (loofah sponges). Ref: CID 38:38, 2004.
Whirlpool: Nail Salon, soft tissue infection	Mycobacterium (fortuitum or chelonae)	Minocycline, doxy or CIP		
SPLEEN. For post-splenectomy prophylaxis, see Table 15B, page 193; for Septic Shock Post-Splenectomy, see Table 1, page 63.				
Splenic abscess Endocarditis, bacteremia	Staph. aureus, streptococcal	**Nafcillin** or **oxacillin** 2 gm IV q4h if MSSA	**Vanco** 1 gm IV q12h if MRSA	Burkholderia (Pseudomonas) pseudomallei is common cause of splenic abscess in SE Asia.
Contiguous from intra-abdominal site Immunocompromised	Polymicrobic Candida sp.	**Treat as Peritonitis, secondary page 47** **Amphotericin B** or caspo, see Table 11, page 113	Fluconazole, **caspofungin**	

Abbreviations on page 2. NOTE: All dosage recommendations are for adults (unless otherwise indicated) and assume normal renal function.

TABLE 1 (54)

ANATOMIC SITE/DIAGNOSIS/ MODIFYING CIRCUMSTANCES	ETIOLOGIES (usual)	SUGGESTED REGIMENS*		ADJUNCT DIAGNOSTIC OR THERAPEUTIC MEASURES AND COMMENTS
		PRIMARY	ALTERNATIVE¹	
SYSTEMIC SYNDROMES (FEBRILE/NON-FEBRILE)				
Spread by infected **TICK, FLEA, or LICE**: Epidemiologic history crucial. **Babesiosis, Lyme disease, & Anaplasma (Ehrlichiosis)** have same reservoir & tick vector.				
Babesiosis see *NEJM 366:2397, 2012.* Do not treat if asymptomatic, young, has spleen, and immunocompetent; can be fatal in lymphoma pts.	**Biol.:** *B. microti* et al. **Vector:** Usually *Ixodes* ticks **Host:** White-footed mouse & others	(Atovaquone 750 mg po q12h.) + (azithro 600 mg po) (day 1, then 500-1000 mg/day) times 7-10 days	If severe infection (**clinda** 1.2 gm IV bid or 600 mg po times 7 days + **quinine** 650 mg po tid times 7 days. **Ped. dosage: Clinda** 20-40 mg per kg per day and **quinine** 25 mg per kg per day). **Exchange transfusion-** *See Comment*	**Seven diseases where pathogen visible in peripheral blood smear:** African/American trypanosomiasis; babesia; bartonellosis; filariasis; malaria; relapsing fever. **Dx:** Giemsa-stained blood smear, antibody test available, PCR if available **in severe disease.** May need treatment for 6 or more wks if immunocompromised. Look for Lyme and/or Anaplasma co-infection. **Rx: Exchange transfusions successful adjunct if used early, in severe disease.**
Bartonella infections: Review *EID 12:389, 2006*				
Bacteremia, asymptomatic	B. quintana, B. henselae	**Doxy** 100 mg po/IV times 15 days		Can lead to endocarditis &/or trench fever; found in homeless, alcoholics, esp. if lice/leg rash. Often missed since asymptomatic.
Cat-scratch disease	B. henselae			Or symptomatic only--see *Lymphadenitis, page 45*: usually lymphadenitis, oculoglandular syndrome
Bacillary angiomatosis; Peliosis hepatis--pts with AIDS *MMWR 58(RR-4):39, 2009; AAC 48:1921, 2004.*	B. henselae, B. quintana	**Erythro** 500 mg po qid or **Doxy** 100 mg po bid x 3 months or longer. If CNS involvement: **Doxy** 100 mg IV/po bid + **RIF** 300 mg po bid	**Azithro** 250 mg po once daily x 3 months or longer	**Do not use:** TMP-SMX, CIP, Pen, Ceph. **Manifestations of Bartonella infections:** **HIV/AIDS Patient:** Bacillary angiomatosis Bacillary peliosis Bacteremia/endocarditis/FUO **Immunocompetent Patient:** Bacteremia/endocarditis/FUO encephalitis Cat scratch disease Vertebral osteo Trench fever Parinaud's oculoglandular syndrome
Endocarditis *(see page 28)* *Circ 111:3167, 2005; AAC 48:1921, 2004.*	B. henselae, B. quintana	Regardless of CD4 count, DC therapy after 3-4 mos. & observe. If no relapse, no suppressive rx. If relapse, **doxy, azithro** or **erythro** x 3 mos. Stop when CD4 >200 x 6 mos. *If suspect endocarditis:* **Ceftriaxone** 2 gm IV once daily x 6 weeks + **Gent** 1 mg/kg IV q8h x 14 days + **Doxy** 100 mg IV/po bid x 6 wks Surgical removal of infected valve	*If proven endocarditis:* **Doxy** 100 mg IV/po bid x 6 wks + **Gent** 1 mg/kg IV q8h x 11 days	**Gentamicin toxicity:** If Gent toxicity, substitute Rifampin 300 mg IV/po bid x 14 days. Role of valve removal surgery to cure uncertain. Presents as SBE. Diagnosis: ECHO, serology & PCR of resected heart valve.
Oroya fever (acute) & Verruga peruana (chronic) *(AAC 48:1921, 2004)*	B. bacilliformis	**Oroya fever:** (**Chloro** 500 mg po bid x 14 d or **Doxy** 100 mg po bid) x 14 d. Alternative: **Chloro** 500 mg IV/po q6h + **beta lactam** or **Azithro** 500 mg po q24h	**Verruga peruana: Rif** 10 mg/kg po once daily x 14 d or **Streptomycin** 15-20 mg/kg IM/IV once daily x 10 days or **Azithro** 500 mg po q24h x 7 days	Oroya fever transmitted by sand-fly bite in Andes Mtns. Related Bartonella (*B. rochalimae*) caused bacteremia, fever and splenomegaly (*NEJM 356:2346 & 2381, 2007*. DIP and Chloro preferred due to prevention of secondary Salmonella infections.
Trench fever (FUO) *(AAC 48:1921, 2004)*	B. quintana	No endocarditis: **Doxy** 100 mg po bid x 4 wks; if endocarditis: **Doxy** + **Gentamicin** 3 mg/kg once daily for 1st 2 wks of therapy *(AAC 48:1921, 2004).*		Vector is body louse. Do not use: TMP-SMX, FQs, cefazolin or Pen

Abbreviations on page 2   NOTE: All dosage recommendations are for adults (unless otherwise indicated) and assume normal renal function.

TABLE 1 (55)

ANATOMIC SITE/DIAGNOSIS/ MODIFYING CIRCUMSTANCES	ETIOLOGIES (usual)	SUGGESTED REGIMENS*		ADJUNCT DIAGNOSTIC OR THERAPEUTIC MEASURES* AND COMMENTS
		PRIMARY	ALTERNATIVE†	
SYSTEMIC SYNDROMES (FEBRILE/NON-FEBRILE)/Spread by Infected TICK, FLEA, or LICE (continued)				
Ehrlichiosis. CDC def. is one of: (1) 4x ↑ IFA antibody, (2) detection of Ehrlichia DNA in blood or CSF by PCR, (3) visible morulae in WBC and IFA ≥1:64. New species in *WI, MN (NEJM 365:422, 2011)*. **Human monocytic ehrlichiosis** *(MMWR 55(RR-4), 2006; CID 43:1089, 2006)*	*Ehrlichia* (Ehrlichia chaffeensis (Lone Star tick is vector)	**Doxy** 100 mg po/IV bid times 7–14 days	**Tetracycline** 500 mg po qid x 7–14d. No current rec. for children or pregnancy	30 states: mostly SE of line from NJ to Ill. to Missouri to Oklahoma to Texas. History of outdoor activity and tick exposure. April–Sept. Fever, rash (36%), leukopenia and thrombocytopenia. Blood smears no help. PCR for early dx.
Human Anaplasmosis (formerly known as Human granulocytic ehrlichiosis)	*Anaplasma* (Ehrlichia phagocytophilum (Ixodes sp. ticks are vector). Dog variant is Ehrlichia ewingii *(NEJM 341:148 & 195, 1999)*	**Doxy** 100 mg po or IV times 7–14 days	**Tetracycline** 500 mg po qid times 7–14 days. Not in children or pregnancy. See Comment	Upper Midwest, NE, West Coast & Europe. H/O tick exposure. April–Sept. Febrile flu-like illness after outdoor activity. No rash. Leukopenia, thrombocytopenia common. **Dx:** Up to 80% have visible morulae. Antibody test ↓ sens. Rx successful in pregnancy *(AJ0B 27:213, 1998)*. Not worry about resistance developing. Based on in vitro studies, no clear alternative rx—Levo activity marginal *(AAC 47:413, 2003)*
Lyme Disease NOTE: Think about concomitant tick-borne disease—e.g., babesiosis and ehrlichiosis. Bite by ixodes-infected tick in an endemic area --	*Borrelia burgdorferi* **IDSA Guidelines:** *CID 43:1089, 2006; CID 51:1, 2010.*		**Guidelines:** *CID 43:1089, 2006.*	Prophylaxis study in endemic area: erythema migrans developed in 3% of the control group and 0.4% doxy group *(NEJM 345:79 & 133, 2001).*
Postexposure prophylaxis		If endemic area, if nymphal partially engorged deer tick: **doxy** 200 mg po times 1 dose with food	If not engorged, not deer tick: No treatment	
Early (erythema migrans) See Comment	Western blot diagnostic criteria: **IgM**—Need 2 of 3 positive of kilodaltons (KD): 23, 39, 41	**Doxy** 100 mg po bid, or **amoxicillin** 500 mg po bid or **cefuroxime axetil** 500 mg po bid times 14–21 days. (10 days is good as 20): *See Comment* for peds doses	**Doxy** (see Comments) or **erythro** 250 mg po qid times 14–21 days. *AnM 136:697, 2003.*	High rate of clinical failure with azithro & erythro *(Drugs 57:157, 1999).* **Peds** (all no treatment ≤8 yrs): **Amoxicillin** 50 mg per kg per day in 3 div. doses or **cefuroxime axetil** 30 mg per kg per day in 2 div. doses or **erythro** 30 mg per kg per day in 3 div. doses.
Carditis See Comment	**IgG**—Need 5 of 10 positive in KD: 18, 21, 28, 30, 39, 41, 45, 58, 66, 93	**Ceftriaxone** 2 gm IV (q4h) or **cefotaxime** 2 gm IV q4h or **Pen G** 3 million units IV (q4h) times 14–21 days	**Doxy** (see Comments) 100 mg po bid times 14–21 days or **amoxicillin** 500 mg po bid times 14–21 days.	Lesions usually homogeneous—not target-like *(AnM 136:423, 2002).* First degree AV block: Oral regimen. Generally self-limited. High degree AV block (PR >0.3 sec.): IV therapy—permanent pacemaker not necessary.
Facial nerve paralysis (isolated finding, early)	For chronic Lyme disease discussion see: *CID 51:1, 2010.*	**Doxy** 100 mg po bid or (**amoxicillin** 500 mg po) tid both times 30–60 days	**Ceftriaxone** 2 gm IV q24h times 14–28 days	If suggested excluding central neurologic disease if LP neg., oral regimen OK. If abnormal or not done, suggest parenteral Ceftriaxone.
Meningitis, encephalitis Polyradiculopathy, see Comment		**Ceftriaxone** 2 gm IV q24h times 14–28 days	**Pen G** 20 million units IV q24h in div. doses or (**cefotaxime** 2 gm IV q8h) times 14–28 days	Encephalopathy, memory difficulty, depression, somnolence, or headache, CSF abnormalities. 89% had objective CSF abnormalities. 18/18 pts improved with ceftriaxone 2 gm per day times 30 days *(JID 180:377, 1999).* No compelling evidence that prolonged treatment has any benefit in post-Lyme syndrome *(Neurology 69:91, 2007).*
Arthritis		(**Doxy** 100 mg po bid) or (**amoxicillin** 500 mg po tid), Choice should not include amoxicillin 500 mg po tid times 21 days	(**Ceftriaxone** 2 gm IV q24h) or (**pen G** 20–24 million units per day IV) times 14–28 days. **If pen. allergic: (azithro** 500 mg po qid times 7–10 days) or (**erythro** 500 mg po qid times 14–21 days)	Start with 1 mo of therapy; if only partial response, treat for a second mo.
Pregnant women		None indicated		No benefit from treatment *(CID 51:1, 2010; NEJM 345:85, 2001).*
Post-Lyme Disease Syndromes				

38 In endemic area (New York), high % of both adult ticks and nymphs were jointly infected with both Anaplasma (HGE) and B. burgdorferi. NOTE: *All dosage recommendations are for adults (unless otherwise indicated) and assume normal renal function.*

Abbreviations on page 2.

TABLE 1 (56)

ANATOMIC SITE/DIAGNOSIS/ MODIFYING CIRCUMSTANCES	ETIOLOGIES (usual)	SUGGESTED REGIMENS* PRIMARY	SUGGESTED REGIMENS* ALTERNATIVE¹	ADJUNCT DIAGNOSTIC OR THERAPEUTIC MEASURES AND COMMENTS
SYSTEMIC SYNDROMES (FEBRILE/NON-FEBRILE)/Spread by infected TICK, FLEA, or LICE (continued)				
Relapsing fever Louse-borne (LBRF)	Borrelia recurrentis Reservoir: human Vector: Louse pediculus humanus	Tetracycline 500 mg IV/po x 1 dose	Erythro 500 mg IV/po x 1 dose	Jarisch-Herxheimer (fever, ↑ pulse, ↑ resp., ↓ blood pressure) in most patients (occurs in ~2 hrs). Not prevented by prior steroids. **Dx: Examine peripheral blood smear during height of fever for spirochetes.** Can relapse up to 10 times. Postexposure **doxy** pre-emptive therapy highly effective (NEJM 355:148, 2006) B. miyamoto ref: EID 17:816, 2011.
Tick-borne (TBRF)	No Amer: B. hermsii, B. turicata. Africa: B. hispanica, B. crocidurae, B. duttonii, Russia: B. miyamoto	Doxy 100 mg po bid x 7-10 days	Erythro 500 mg po qid x 7-10 days	
Rickettsial diseases. Review—Disease in travelers (CID 39:1493, 2004)				
Spotted fevers (NOTE: Rickettsial pox not included)				
Rocky Mountain spotted fever (RMSF) Ref: LnID 8:143, 2008 and MMWR 55 (RR-4), 2007)	R. rickettsii (Dermacentor tick vector)	**Doxy** 100 mg po/IV bid times 7 days or for 2 days after temp. normal. Do not use in pregnancy. Some suggest single 200 mg loading dose.	**Chloro** 50 mg/kg/day in 4 div doses. Use in pregnancy.	Fever, rash (88%), petechiae 40-50%. **Rash spreads from distal extremities to trunk.** Rash in <50% pts in 1st 72 hrs. Dx: Immunohistology on skin biopsy: confirmation with antibody titers. Highest incidence in NC and South Central states; also seen in Oklahoma, S. Dakota, Montana. Cases reported from 42 U.S. states. **NOTE: Only 3-18% of pts present with fever, rash, and hx of tick exposure; many early deaths in children & empiric doxy reasonable in severe illness.** (MMWR 49: 885, 2000)
NOTE: Can mimic ehrlichiosis. Pattern of rash important—see Comment				
Other spotted fevers, e.g., Rickettsial pox, African tick fever	At least 8 species on 6 continents (CID 45 (Suppl 1) S39, 2007).	**Doxy** 100 mg po/IV bid times 7 days	**Chloro** 500 mg po/IV qid times 7 days Children <8 y.o. – **azithro** or **clarithro** (if mild disease)	Clinical diagnosis suggested by: 1) fever, intense myalgia, headache; 2) exposure to mites or ticks; 3) localized eschar (tache noire) or rash. Definitive Dx: PCR of blood, skin biopsy or elevated antibody tests.
Typhus group—Consider in returning travelers with fever				
Louse-borne: epidemic typhus Ref: LnID 8:417, 2008.	R. prowazekii (vector is body or head louse)	**Doxy** 100 mg IV/po bid times 7 days, single 200 mg dose 95% effective.	**Chloro** 500 mg IV/po qid 5 days	**Brill-Zinsser disease** (Ln 357:1198, 2001) is a relapse of typhus acquired during WWII. Truncal rash (64%) spreads centrifugally—opposite of RMSF. Louse borne typhus is a winter disease. Diagnosis by serology: R. prowazekii found in flying squirrels in SE US. Delouse clothing of infected pt.
Murine typhus (cat flea typhus): EID 14:1019, 2008	R. typhi (rat reservoir and flea vector): CID 46:913, 2008	**Doxy** 100 mg IV/po bid times 7 days	**Chloro** 500 mg IV/po qid times 5 days	Rash in 20-54%; not diagnostic. Without treatment most pts recover in 2 wks. Faster recovery with treatment. Dx based on suspicion; confirmed serologically.
Scrub typhus	O. tsutsugamushi (rodent reservoir, vector is larval stage of mites (chiggers)	**Doxy** 100 mg po/IV bid x 7 days. In pregnancy: **Azithro** 500 mg po x one dose	**Chloro** 500 mg po/IV qid x 7 days	Asian rim of Pacific. Suspect Dx in endemic area. Confirm with serology. If Doxy resistance suspected, alternatives are **Doxy + RIF** 900 or 600 mg once daily (Ln 356:1057, 2000) or **Azithro.**
Tularemia, typhoidal type Ref: **bioterrorism:** see JAMA 285:2763, 2001; ID Clin No. Amer 22:489, 2008; MMWR 58:744, 2009.	Francisella tularensis. (Vector depends on geography: ticks, biting flies, mosquitoes identified)	Moderate/severe: **(Gentamicin** or **tobra** 5 mg per kg per day div. q8h IV) **or (Streptomycin** 10 mg/kg IV/IM q12h) x 10 days	Mild: (**CIP** 400 mg IV or 750 mg po) bid **or Doxy** 100 mg IV/po bid) x 14-21 days	Diagnosis: Culture on cysteine-enriched media & serology. Dangerous in the lab. Hematogenous meningitis is a complication: treatment is **Streptomycin + Chloro** 50-100 mg/kg/day IV in 4 divided doses (Arch Neurol 66:523, 2009).

Abbreviations on page 2.   NOTE: All dosage recommendations are for adults (unless otherwise indicated) and assume normal renal function.

TABLE 1 (57)

ANATOMIC SITE/DIAGNOSIS/ MODIFYING CIRCUMSTANCES	ETIOLOGIES (usual)	SUGGESTED REGIMENS*		ADJUNCT DIAGNOSTIC OR THERAPEUTIC MEASURES AND COMMENTS
		PRIMARY	ALTERNATIVE¹	
SYSTEMIC SYNDROMES (FEBRILE/NON-FEBRILE): Obtain careful epidemiologic history				
Other Zoonotic Systemic Bacterial Febrile Illnesses: *(continued)*				
Brucellosis Refs: *NEJM 352:2325, 2005; CID 46:426, 2008; MMWR 57:603, 2008; BMJ 336:701, 2008; PLoS One 7:e32090, 2012.*	B. abortus–cattle B. suis–swine B. melitensis–goats B. canis–dogs	**Non focal disease:** **[Doxy** 100 mg po bid x 6 wks **+ Gent** 5 mg/kg once daily for 1ᵃ] x 7 days	**[Doxy** 100 mg po bid **+ RIF** 600–900 mg po once daily] x 6 wks	CiP active in vitro but clinical response not good. Clinical response to ceftriaxone in 20–30%. **Neurobrucellosis:** Usually meningitis. 1% of all pts with brucellosis. Role of corticosteroids unclear; not recommended. **Endocarditis:** Rare but most common cause of death. Need surgery + antimicrobials. **Pregnancy:** TMP-SMX may cause kernicterus if given during last week of pregnancy.
		Spondylitis, Sacroiliitis: **[Doxy + Gent** (as above) **+ RIF]** x min 3 mos	**[CIP** 750 mg po bid **+ RIF** 600–900 mg po once daily] x min 3 mos	
		Neurobrucellosis: **[Doxy + RIF** (as above) **+ ceftriaxone** 2 gm IV q12h until CSF returned to normal *(AAC 56:1523, 2012)*]		
		Endocarditis: Surgery + **[(RIF + Doxy + TMP-SMX)** x 1-1/2 to 6 mos **+ Gent** for 2-4 wks]		
		Pregnancy: Not much data. **RIF** 900 mg po once daily x 6 wks	**RIF** 900 mg po once daily + TMP-SMX 5 mg/kg (TMP comp) po bid x 4 wks.	
Leptospirosis *(CID 36:1507 & 1514, 2003; LnID 3:757, 2003)*	Leptospira–in urine of domestic livestock, dogs, small rodents	Severe illness: **Pen G** 1.5 million units IV q6h or **ceftriaxone** 1 gm q24h. Duration: 7 days	Mild illness: **[Doxy** 100 mg IV/po q12h or **AMP** 0.5–1 gm IV q6h] x 7 days	**Severity varies.** Two-stage mild anicteric illness to severe icteric disease (Weil's disease) with renal failure and myocarditis. **Rx:** Azithro 1 gm once, then 500 mg daily x 2 days: non-inferior to, and fewer side effects than, doxy in standard dose *(AAC 51:3259, 2007)*. Jarisch-Herxheimer reaction can occur post-Pen therapy.
Salmonella bacteremia other than S. typhi–non-typhoidal)	Salmonella enteritidis— a variety of serotypes from animal sources	If NOT acquired in Asia: **CIP** 400 mg IV q12h or **Levo** 750 mg po once daily *(See Comment)*	If acquired in Asia: **Ceftriaxone** 1 gm IV q24h or **Azithro** 1 gm po x 1 dose, then 500 mg once daily x5-7 days. Do NOT use FQs until susceptibility determined. *(See Comment)*	In vitro resistance to nalidixic acid indicates relative resistance to FQs. Bacteremia can infect any organ/tissue: look for infection of atherosclerotic aorta, osteomyelitis in sickle cell pts. Rx duration range 14 days (immunocompetent) to ≥6 wks if mycotic aneurism or endocarditis. Alternative, if susceptible: **TMP-SMX** 8-10 mg/kg/day (TMP comp) divided q8h.

Abbreviations on page 2.   *NOTE: All dosage recommendations are for adults (unless otherwise indicated) and assume normal renal function.*

TABLE 1 (58)

ANATOMIC SITE/DIAGNOSIS/ MODIFYING CIRCUMSTANCES	ETIOLOGIES (usual)	SUGGESTED REGIMENS*		ADJUNCT DIAGNOSTIC OR THERAPEUTIC MEASURES AND COMMENTS
		PRIMARY	ALTERNATIVE†	
SYSTEMIC SYNDROMES (FEBRILE/NON-FEBRILE)				
Miscellaneous Systemic Febrile Syndromes				
Fever in Returning Travelers (NEJM 354:119, 2006; COID 20:449, 2007).	Dengue	Supportive care; see Table 14A, page 156		Average incubation period 4 days; serodiagnosis.
	Plasmodia sp.	Diagnosis: peripheral blood smear		See Table 13A, page 143
	Salmonella sp.	See Table 1, page 60.		Average incubation 7-14 days; diarrhea in 45%.
Kawasaki syndrome 6 weeks to 12 yrs. of age, peak at 1 yr of age: 85% below age 5. Ref: Pediatrics 124:1, 2009.	Acute self-limited vasculitis with ↑ temp., rash, conjunctivitis, stomatitis, cervical adenitis, red hands/feet & coronary artery aneurysms (25% if untreated)	IVIG 2 gm per kg over 8-12 hrs x 1 + ASA 20-25 mg per kg qid THEN ASA 3-5 mg per kg per day po q24h times 6-8 wks	It still febrile after 1st dose of IVIG, some give 2nd dose. In Japan: IVIG + prednisolone 2 mg/kg/day. Continue steroid until CRP normal for 15 days (Lancet 379:1571, 2012).	IV gamma globulin (2 gm per kg over 10 hrs) in pts before 10th day of illness ↓ coronary artery lesions (Ln 347:1128, 1996). See Table 14A, page 11 for IVIG adverse effects. Pulsed steroids of NO value: NEJM 356:659 & 663, 2007.
Rheumatic Fever, acute Ref.: Ln 366:155, 2005.	Post-Group A strep pharyngitis (not Group B, C, or G)	(1) Symptom relief: ASA 80-100 mg per kg per day in children; 4-8 gm per day in adults. (2) Eradicate Group A strep: Pen times 10 days (see Pharyngitis, see below)		
Primary prophylaxis: Treat S. pyogenes pharyngitis		**Benzathine pen G** 1.2 million units IM (see Pharyngitis, p. 48)	**Penicillin** for 10 days prevents rheumatic fever even when started 7-9 days after onset of illness (see page 48). Alternative: Penicillin V 250 mg po bid or sulfadiazine (sulfisoxazole) 1 gm po q24h or erythro 250 mg bid.	
Secondary prophylaxis (previous documented rheumatic fever)		**Benzathine pen G** 1.2 million units IM q3-4 wks	Duration? No carditis: 5 yrs or until age 21, whichever is longer; carditis without residual heart disease: 10 yrs since last attack; carditis with residual valvular disease: 10 yrs since last episode or until age 40 whichever is longer (PEDS 96:758, 1995).	
Typhoidal syndrome (typhoid fever, enteric fever) (Ln 366:749, 2005; LnID 5:623, 2005) Global susceptibility results: CID 50:241, 2010.	Salmonella typhi, S. paratyphi A, B, C & S. choleraesuis. NOTE: In vitro resistance to nalidixic acid predicts clinical failure of CIP (FQs). Do not use empirically if Asia-acquired infection. Need susceptibility results. AAC 54:5201, 2010; BMC ID 5:37, 2009.	If NOT acquired in Asia: CIP 400 mg IV q12h or Levo 750 mg po/IV q24h x 7-10 d (See Comment) In children: CIP superior to ceftriaxone	If acquired in Asia: (Ceftriaxone 2 gm IV daily x 7-14 d) or (Azithro 1 gm po x 1 dose, then 500 mg po daily x 5 d) Chloro 500 mg po/IV q6h x 14 d) (See Comment)	Dexamethasone: In controlled trial, mortality lower than in pts given Chloro+ dex vs. Chloro alone (NEJM 310:82, 1984). No data on dex + FQs or Ceftriaxone. Use in severely ill pts: 1st dose just prior to antibiotic, 3 mg/kg IV, then 1 mg/kg q6h x 8 doses. Complications: perforation or terminal ileum &/or cecum, osteo, septic arthritis, mycotic aneurysm (approx. 10% over age 50. AJM 110:60, 2001), meningitis.
Sepsis: Following suggested empiric therapy assumes pt is bacteremic; mimicked by viral, fungal, rickettsial infections and pancreatitis (Intensive Care Medicine 34:17, 2008; IDC No Amer 22:1, 2008).				
Neonatal—early onset <1 week old	Group B strep, E. coli, klebsiella, enterobacter, Staph. aureus (uncommon), listeria (rare in U.S.)	AMP 25 mg per kg IV q8h + cefotaxime 50 mg per kg q12h	AMP + gent 2.5 mg per kg IV/IM q12h or (AMP + ceftriaxone 50 mg per kg IV/IM q24h)	Blood cultures are key but only 5–10% +. Discontinue antibiotics after 72 hrs if cultures and course do not support diagnosis. In Spain, listeria produces late-onset disease, salmonella in developing countries. Use cellular IgG. If penicillin-allergic, alternatives include: erythro & clinda; report of slow beta-lactam allergy; alternatives include: erythro & clinda; report of clinda resistance at 38% & erythro resistance at 51% (AAC 56:739, 2012).
Neonatal—late onset 1-4 weeks old	As above + H influenzae & S. epidermidis	(AMP 25 mg per kg IV q8h + cefotaxime 50 mg per kg q8h) or (AMP + ceftriaxone 75 mg per kg IV q24h)	AMP + gent 2.5 mg per kg q8h IV or IM	If MSSA/MRSA a concern, add vanco.

NOTE: All dosage recommendations are for adults (unless otherwise indicated) and assume normal renal function.

Abbreviations on page 2.

TABLE 1 (59)

ANATOMIC SITE/DIAGNOSIS/ MODIFYING CIRCUMSTANCES	ETIOLOGIES (usual)	SUGGESTED REGIMENS* PRIMARY	ALTERNATIVE†	ADJUNCT DIAGNOSTIC OR THERAPEUTIC MEASURES AND COMMENTS
SYSTEMIC SYNDROMES (FEBRILE/NON-FEBRILE)/Sepsis (continued)				
Child; not neutropenic	Strep. pneumoniae, meningococci, Staph. aureus (MSSA & MRSA), H. influenzae now rare	Cefotaxime 50 mg per kg IV q8h or ceftriaxone 100 mg per kg IV q24h) + **vanco** 15 mg per kg IV q6h	Aztreonam 7.5 mg per kg IV q6h + **linezolid** (see Table 16, page 203 for dose)	Major concerns are S. pneumoniae & community-associated MRSA. Coverage for Gm-neg. bacilli included but H. influenzae infection now rare. Meningococcemia mortality remains high (Ln 356:961, 2000).
Adult; not neutropenic; NO HYPOTENSION but LIFE-THREATENING **Source unclear** —consider primary bacteremia, intra-abdominal or skin source. May be **Life-threatening.** Survival greater with quicker, effective empiric antibiotic Rx. (CCM 38:1045 & 1211, 2010).	Aerobic Gm-neg. bacilli, S. aureus, streptococci, others	(**ERTA**† or IMP or MER) + **vanco** Could substitute linezolid for vanco or dapto;	(**Dapto** 6 mg per kg IV q24h) or PIP-TZ or TC-CL *see page 63* however, linezolid bacteriostatic vs S. aureus. *Dosages in footnote***	Systemic inflammatory response syndrome (**SIRS**): 2 or more of the following: 1. Temperature >38°C or <36°C 2. Heart rate >90 beats per min. 3. Respiratory rate >20 breaths per min. 4. WBC >12,000 per mcL or >10% bands **Sepsis:** SIRS + a documented infection (+ culture) **Severe sepsis:** Sepsis + organ dysfunction: hypotension or hypoperfusion abnormalities (lactic acidosis, oliguria, [mental status]) **Septic shock:** Sepsis-induced hypotension (systolic BP <90 mmHg) not responsive to 500 mL IV fluid challenge → peripheral hypoperfusion.
If suspect biliary source (see p.12)	Enterococci + aerobic Gm-neg. bacilli	**PIP-TZ** or TC-CL	**Ceftriaxone + metro.** (CIP or Levo or moxi)	
If community-acquired pneumonia (see page 39 and following pages)	**S. pneumoniae; MRSA; Legionella; Gm-neg. bacillus**	(**Levo or moxi**) + (**PIP-TZ**)	Aztreonam + (Levo or moxi) + linezolid *Dosages—footnote***§	Many categories of CAP: see material beginning at page 39. Suggestions based on most severe CAP, e.g. MRSA after influenza or Klebsiella pneumonia in an alcoholic.
If illicit use IV drugs	S. aureus	**Vanco** if high prevalence of MRSA. **Do NOT use** empiric **vanco + oxacillin** pending organism iD. In vitro nafcillin increased production of toxins by CA-MRSA (JID 195:202, 2007). *Dosages—footnote 36, page 62*		
If suspect intra-abdominal source	Mixture aerobic & anaerobic	See secondary peritonitis, page 47.		
If petechial rash	Meningococcemia	**Ceftriaxone** 2 gm IV q12h (until sure no meningitis), consider Rocky Mountain spotted fever—*see page 59*		
If suspect urinary source, e.g. pyelonephritis	Aerobic Gm-neg. bacilli & enterococci	See pyelonephritis, page 34		
Neutropenic: Child or Adult (absolute PMN count <500 per mm3) in cancer and transplant patients. Guideline: CID 52:427, 2011				
Prophylaxis (UnID 9:97, 2011				
Post-chemotherapy— impending neutropenia	Aerobic Gm-neg. bacilli, viridans strep, pneumocystis (PCP),	**TMP-SMX-DS** 1 tab po once daily—adults; 10 mg per kg per day div bid po—children		Meta-analysis demonstrates substantive reduction in mortality with **CIP** 500 mg po bid (AnIM 142:979, 2005). Similar results in observational studies using **Levo** 500 mg po q24h (CID 40:1087 & 1094, 2005). Also NEJM 353:977, 988 & 1052, 2005.
Post-chemotherapy in AIDS patient	Pneumocystis, aerobic Gm-neg. bacilli	**TMP-SMX** as above + [either **acyclovir** or **ganciclovir**] + **fluconazole**		TMP-SMX DS has prophylactic efficacy vs PCP and E. coli.
Post-marrow ablation, bone marrow transplant	Aerobic Gm-neg bacilli, ↑ risk pneumocystis, herpes viruses, candida	**TMP-SMX** as above + [either **acyclovir** or **ganciclovir**] + **fluconazole**		Combined regimen justified by combined effect of neutropenia and immunosuppression.

** **P Ceph 3** (cefotaxime 2 gm IV q8h, ceftizoxime 2 gm IV q4h; ceftriaxone 2 gm IV q12h). **AP Pen** [piperacillin 3 gm IV q4-6h, ticarcillin 3 gm IV q4h), **TC-CL** 3.1 gm IV q4h, **PIP-TZ** 3.375 gm IV q4h or 4-hr infusion of 3.375 gm q8h, also see comment (CID 56:236, 2013) or for P. aeruginosa 4.5 gm IV q6h, **AMP** 2 gm IV q4h, **clinda** 900 mg IV q8h, **MER** 1 gm IV q8h. **ERTA** 1 gm IV q24h. **Amino glycosides** (see Table 10D, page 109) **IMP** 500 mg IV q6h, **vanco** 1 gm IV q12h, **aztreonam** 2 gm IV q8h, **oxacillin or nafcillin** 2 gm IV q4h; **levo** 750 mg IV q24h, **vanco** 1 gm IV q12h, **ceftazidime** 2 gm IV q8h; **Cefepime** 2 gm IV q8h (q8h if neutropenic), **ceftriaxone** 2 gm IV q12h (q8h if meningitis), **CIP** 400 mg IV q12h. **levo** 750 mg IV q24h. **linezolid** 600 mg IV q24h.

Abbreviations on page 2. NOTE: All dosage recommendations are for adults (unless otherwise indicated) and assume normal renal function.

TABLE 1 (60)

ANATOMIC SITE/DIAGNOSIS/ MODIFYING CIRCUMSTANCES	ETIOLOGIES (usual)	SUGGESTED REGIMENS*		ADJUNCT DIAGNOSTIC OR THERAPEUTIC MEASURES AND COMMENTS
		PRIMARY	ALTERNATIVE†	
SYSTEMIC SYNDROMES (FEBRILE/NON-FEBRILE)/Neutropenia (continued)				
Empiric therapy—febrile neutropenia (≥38.3°C (or > 1 hr or sustained >38°C and absolute neutrophil count <500 cells/µL) (Practice Guidelines: CID 52:427, 2022).				
Low-risk adults Anticipate < 7 days neutropenia, no co-morb., can take po meds.	Aerobic Gm-neg bacilli, Viridans strep	**CIP** 750 mg po bid + **AM-CL** 875/125 mg po bid. Treat until absolute neutrophil count >1000 cells/µL.		**Treat as outpatients with 24/7 access to inpatient care if: no focal findings, no hypotension, no COPD, no fungal infection, no dehydration, age range 16-60 yrs: motivated and compliant pts & family.**
High-risk adults and children (Anticipate > 7 days profound neutropenia, active co-morbidities)	**Aerobic Gm-neg. bacilli; to include P. aeruginosis; cephalosporin-resistant viridans strep; MRSA**	**Monotherapy:** ceftaz or IMP (see Comment) or MER or DORI or CFP or PIP-TZ	**Combination therapy:** (Gent or tobra) + (TC-CL or PIP-TZ)	Increasing resistance of viridans streptococci to penicillins, cephalosporins & FQs (CID 34:1524 & 1524, 2022). **What if severe IgE-mediated β-lactam allergy?** No formal trials, but (aztreonam + cipro or CIP) + aztreonam) ± vanco should work. **IMP:** 0.5 gm q6h achieved MIC90 coverage in only 53%. If GFR OK, dose of 500 mg q4h or 750 mg (over 2 hrs) q6h may be better (AAC 53:785, 2009). If cultures remain neg, but pt afebrile, treat until absolute neutrophil count ± 500 cells/µL.
		Dosages: Footnote⁸ and Table 10B - **Include empiric vanco if:** suspect IV access infected; colonized with drug-resistant S. pneumo or MRSA; blood culture pos. for Gm-pos. cocci; pt hypotensive		
Persistent fever and neutropenia after 5 days of empiric antibacterial therapy—see CID 52:427, 2011.				
	Candida species, aspergillus, VRE, resistant GNB	Add either (**caspofungin** 70 mg IV day 1, then 50 mg IV q24h or **Micafungin** 100 mg IV q24h or **Anidulafungin** 200 mg IV x 1 dose, then 100 mg IV q24h) **OR voriconazole** 6 mg per kg IV q12h times 2 doses, then 3 mg per kg IV q12h		Conventional **ampho B** causes more fever & nephrotoxicity & lower efficacy than lipid-based ampho B; both **caspofungin** and **voriconazole** better tolerated & perhaps more efficacious than lipid-based ampho B (NEJM 346:225, 2002 & 351:1391 & 1445, 2005).
Shock syndromes				
Septic shock: Fever & hypotension **Bacteremia: endotoxin shock** Antimicrobial therapy: Surviving Sepsis Campaign: CCM 36:296, 2008 & Intensive Care Med 34:17, 2008; JAMA 305:1469, 2011.	Bacteremia with aerobic Gm-neg. bacteria or Gm+ cocci	**Proven Therapies:** - Replete intravascular vol. with IV saline; goal is CVP >8 cm within 6 hr of admission - Attempt to correct source of bacteremia. - Blood cultures, then antibiotics appropriate for clinical syndrome. Time to 1ˢᵗ dose crucial (Chest 136:1237, 2009; CCM 38:1045 & 1211, 2009). - If still hypotensive & lactate elevated either nor-epinephrine or dopamine (NEJM 362:779 & 841, 2010).		- Low dose glucocorticoids: data controversial. Currently, consider use if pt still hypotensive & vasopressor dependent after 2+ days of fluids, antibiotics & success w/source control (JAMA 301:2362, 2009; CID 49:93, 2009). Hard to interp. ACTH stim. data. Review: Am J Resp Crit Care Med 185:133, 2012. - Insulin Rx: current target is glucose levels of 140-180 mg/dL. Attempts at tight control (80-110 mg/dL) resulted in excessive hypoglycemia (NEJM 363:2540, 2010). - A polymyxin B fiber column reduced 28 day mortality in pts with intra-abdominal gram-negative infections (not available in U.S.): Ln JID 11:65, 2011.
Septic shock: post-splenectomy or functional asplenia	S. pneumoniae, N. meningitidis, H. influenzae, Capno-cytophaga (DF-2)	**Ceftriaxone** 2 gm IV q24h (1 to 2 gm q12h if meningitis)	(**Levo** 750 mg or **Moxi** 400 mg) once IV q24h - Other management as per Septic shock, above	Howell-Jolly bodies in peripheral blood smear confirm absence of functional spleen. Often results in **symmetrical peripheral gangrene of digits** due to severe DIC. For prophylaxis, see Table 15A, page 192.

Abbreviations on page 2.   NOTE: All dosage recommendations are for adults (unless otherwise indicated) and assume normal renal function.

TABLE 1 (61)

ANATOMIC SITE/DIAGNOSIS/ MODIFYING CIRCUMSTANCES	ETIOLOGIES (usual)	SUGGESTED REGIMENS*		ADJUNCT DIAGNOSTIC OR THERAPEUTIC MEASURES AND COMMENTS
		PRIMARY	ALTERNATIVE†	
SYSTEMIC SYNDROMES (FEBRILE/NON-FEBRILE)/Neutropenia (continued)				
Toxic shock syndrome, Clostridium sordellii Clinical picture: shock, capillary leak, hemoconcentration, leukemoid reaction, afebrile Ref: CID 43:1436 & 1447, 2006.	Clostridium sordellii —hemorrhagic & lethal toxins	Fluids, aq. **penicillin G** 18–20 million units per day div. q4–6h + **clindamycin** 900 mg IV q8h. **Surgical debridement is key.**		Occurs in variety of settings that produce anaerobic tissue, e.g., illicit drug use, post-partum. Several deaths reported after use of abortifacient regimen of mifepristine (RU486) & misoprostol. 2001-2006 standard medical abortion: po mifepristine & then vaginal misoprostol. Since 2006, switch to buccal, instead of vaginal misoprostol, plus prophylactic Doxy resulted in dramatic decrease in TSS (NEJM 361:145, 2009). Mortality nearly 100% if WBC > 50,000/uL.
Toxic shock syndrome, staphylococcal. Review: LnD 9:281, 2009. Colonization by toxin-producing Staph. aureus or of: vagina (tampon-assoc.), surgical/traumatic wounds, endometrium, burns	Staph. aureus (toxic shock—toxin-mediated)	**Naf/cillin** 2 gm IV q4h (if MRSA **vanco** 1 gm IV q12h) + **Clinda** 600–900 mg IV q8h + **IVIG** (Dose in Comment)	**Cefazolin** 1–2 gm IV q8h or (if MRSA **vanco** 1 gm IV q12h OR **dapto** 6 mg/kg IV q24h) Clinda 600-900 mg IV q8h + **IVIG** (Dose in Comment)	**IVIG reasonable** (see Streptococcal TSS) — dose 1 gm per kg on day 1, then 0.5 gm per kg days 2 & 3—antitoxin antibodies present. If suspect TSS, "turn off" toxin production with clinda, report of success with **linezolid** (JID 195:202, 2007). Exposure of MRSA to naf/cillin increased toxin production in vitro (JID 195:202, 2007.
Toxic shock syndrome, streptococcal. NOTE: For Necrotizing fasciitis without toxic shock, see page 56. Ref: LnD 9:281, 2009. Associated with **invasive disease**, i.e., erysipelas, necrotizing fasciitis; secondary strep. infection of varicella. 10% mortality. TSS cases reported (NEJM 335:547 & 590, 1996; CID 27:150, 1998).	Group A, B, C, & G Strep. pyogenes, Group B strep ref: EID 15:223, 2009.	(**Pen G** 24 million units per day IV in div. doses) + (**clinda** 900 mg IV q8h)	**Ceftriaxone** 2 gm IV q24h + **clinda** 900 mg IV q8h	**Definition:** Isolation of Group A strep. hypotension and ≥2 of: renal impairment, coagulopathy, liver involvement, ARDS, generalized rash, soft tissue necrosis. Associated with invasive disease. **Surgery** usually **required.** Mortality with clinda 30–50%, myositis 80%, even with early rx (CID 14:2, 1992). Clinda ↓ toxin production. Use of NSAID may predispose to TSS. For reasons pen G may fail in fulminant S. pyogenes infections (see JID 167:1401, 1993).
IVIG associated with ↓ in sepsis-related organ failure (CID 37:333 & 341, 2003). IVIG dose: 1 gm per kg day 1, then 0.5 gm per kg days 2 & 3. IVIG preps vary in neutralizing antibody content (CID 43:743, 2006). In multicenter retrospect study, no benefit from IVIG—controversial (CID 7:369 & 377, 2009).				
Toxin-Mediated Syndromes—no fever unless complicated				
Botulism CID 41:1167, 2005. As **biologic weapon:** JAMA 285:1059, 2001; www.bt.cdc.gov) Food-borne Dyspnea, dry presentation bad sign (CID 43:1247, 2006)	Clostridium botulinum	For all types: Follow vital capacity, other supportive care. If no ileus, purge GI tract	Heptavalent equine serum antitoxin—CDC (see Comment)	**Equine antitoxin:** Heptavalent currently only antitoxin available (U.S) for non-infant botulism: CDC (+1 404-639-2206 M-F OR +1 404-639-2888 evenings/weekends). For infants, use Baby BIG (human botulism immune globulin): California Infant Botulism Treat & Prevent Program.
Infant (Adult intestinal botulism is rare variant: EIN 18:1, 2012).		Human botulinum immunoglobulin,(BIG) IV, single dose. Call (+1) 510-540-2646. Do not use equine antitoxin.	**No antibiotics:** may lyse C. botulinum in gut and ↑ load of toxin	**Antimicrobials:** May make infant botulism worse. Untested in wound botulism. When used, pen G 10–20 million units per day usual dose. If complications (pneumonia, UTI) occur, avoid antimicrobials with assoc. neuromuscular blockade, i.e., aminoglycosides, tetracycline, polymyxins, phosphate toxicity. West Nile virus.
Wound		Debridement & anaerobic cultures. No proven value of local antitoxin. Role of antibiotics untested.	Trivalent equine antitoxin (see Comment)	**Differential dx:** Guillain-Barré, myasthenia gravis, tick paralysis, organo-phosphate toxicity, West Nile virus. Wound botulism can result from spore contamination of tar heroin. Ref: CID 31:1018, 2000. Mouse bioassay failed to detect toxin in 1/3 of patients (CID 48:1669, 2009).

Abbreviations on page 2.   NOTE: All dosage recommendations are for adults (unless otherwise indicated) and assume normal renal function.

TABLE 1 (62)

ANATOMIC SITE/DIAGNOSIS/ MODIFYING CIRCUMSTANCES	ETIOLOGIES (usual)	SUGGESTED REGIMENS*		ADJUNCT DIAGNOSTIC OR THERAPEUTIC MEASURES AND COMMENTS
		PRIMARY	ALTERNATIVE†	
SYSTEMIC SYNDROMES/Neutropenia *(continued)*				
Tetanus: Trismus, generalized muscle rigidity, muscle spasm. Ref. *AnIM 154:329, 2011.*	C. tetani-production of tetanosporium toxin	**Six treatment steps:** 1–Urgent endotracheal intubation to protect the airway. Laryngeal spasm is common. Early tracheostomy. 2–Eliminate reflex spasms with diazepam, 20 mg/kg/day IV or midazolam. Reports of benefit combining diazepam with magnesium sulfate (*Ln 368:1436, 2006*). Worst cases: need neuromuscular blockade with vecuronium. 3–Neutralize toxin: Human hyperimmune globulin IM. start tetanus immunization–no immunity from clinical tetanus. 4–Surgically debride infected source tissue. Start antibiotics: **(Pen G 3 million units IV q4h or Doxy 100 mg IV q12h or Metro 1000 mg IV q12h) x 7–10 days** 5–Avoid light as may precipitate muscle spasms. 6–Use beta blockers, e.g., short acting esmolol, to control sympathetic hyperactivity.		
VASCULAR				
IV line infection *(See IDSA Guidelines CID 49:1, 2009).*				
Heparin lock, midline catheter, **non-tunneled** central venous catheter (subclavian, internal jugular, peripherally inserted central catheter (PICC) 2008 study found ↑ infection risk/thrombosis if femoral vein used, esp. if *JAMA 299:2413, 2008*). Recent meta-analysis did not confirm an increased risk (*CCM 40: 2479 & 2528, 2012*).	Staph. epidermidis, Staph. aureus (MSSA/MRSA). **Diagnosis:** Fever & either > blood cuff from line & peripheral vein culture **OR** >15 colonies on tip of removed catheter positive 2 hrs earlier than peripheral vein culture.	**Vanco 1 gm IV q12h. Other alternatives—see Comment.** Other rx and duration: **(1) If S. aureus,** remove catheter. Can use TEE result to determine if 2 or 4 wks of therapy (*JAC 57:1172, 2006*). **(2) If S. epidermidis,** can try to "save" catheter. 80% cure after 7–10 days of therapy. With only systemic antibiotics, high rate of recurrence (*CID 49:1187, 2009*). If **leuconostoc** or **lactobacillus** are **Vanco** resistant; need Pen G, Amp or Clinda.		If no response to, or intolerant of, **vanco** switch to **daptomycin** 6 mg per kg IV q24h. **Quinupristin-dalfopristin** an option: 7.5 mg per kg IV q8h via central line. Culture removed catheter. With "roll" method, >15 colonies (*NEJM 312:1142, 1985*) suggests infection. Lines do not require "routine" changing when not infected. When infected, do not insert new catheter over a wire. Antimicrobial-impregnated catheters may ↓ infection risk; the debate is lively (*CID 37:65, 2003 & 38:1287, 2004 & 39:1829, 2004*).
Tunnel type indwelling venous catheters and ports (Broviac, Hickman, Groshong, Quinton), dual lumen hemodialysis catheters (Permacath). For prevention, see below.	Staph. epidermidis, Staph. aureus, (Candida sp.). Rarely leuconostoc or lactobacillus—both resistant to vanco (see Table 2, page 67).	If candida, voriconazole or an echinocandin (anidulafungin, micafungin, caspofungin) if clinically stable. Dosage: see Table 11B, page 124	**[Vanco + (Cefepime or Ceftaz)]** or **(Vanco + Pip-Tazo)** or **IMP** or **[(Cefepime or Ceftaz) + Aminoglycoside]** (Dosage see footnotes³⁶,³⁸ on pages 47 and 62).	If subcutaneous tunnel infected, very low cure rates; need to remove catheter. Beware of silent infection in clotted hemodialysis catheters. Indium scans detect >8% (*J Kid Dis 40:832, 2002*).
Impaired host (burn, neutropenic)	As above + Pseudomonas sp., Enterobacteriaceae, Corynebacterium jeikeium, aspergillus, rhizopus			Usually have associated septic thrombophlebitis; biopsy of vein to rule out fungal. If fungal: surgical drainage, ligation or excision if possible.
Hyperalimentation	As with tunnel, Candida sp. common (see Table 11, resistant Candida species)			Remove venous catheter and discontinue antimicrobial agents if possible. Ophthalmologic consultation recommended. **Rx all patients with + blood cultures.** See Table 11A, Candidiasis, page 113
Intravenous lipid emulsion	Staph. epidermidis Malassezia furfur	**Vanco 1 gm IV q12h** **Fluconazole 400 mg IV q24h**		Discontinue intralipid

Abbreviations on page 2.   NOTE: All dosage recommendations are for adults (unless otherwise indicated) and assume normal renal function.

TABLE 1 (63)

ANATOMIC SITE/DIAGNOSIS/ MODIFYING CIRCUMSTANCES	ETIOLOGIES (usual)	SUGGESTED REGIMENS*		ADJUNCT DIAGNOSTIC OR THERAPEUTIC MEASURES AND COMMENTS
		PRIMARY	ALTERNATIVE¹	
VASCULAR/IV line Infection *(continued)*				
Prevention of Infection of Long-Term IV Lines *CID 52:1087, 2011*	To minimize risk of infection: **Hand washing and** 1. Maximal sterile barrier precautions during catheter insertion 2. Use >0.5% chlorhexidine prep with alcohol for skin antisepsis 3. If infection rate high despite #1 & 2, use either chlorhexidine/silver sulfadiazine or minocycline/rifampin-impregnated catheters or "lock" solutions (see Comment) 4. If possible, use subclavian vein, avoid femoral vessels. Lower infection risk in jugular vs femoral vein if BMI >28.4 (*JAMA 299:2413, 2008*).			**IV line "lock" solutions under study. No FDA-approved product.** Reports of the combination of TMP, EDTA & ethanol (*AAC 55:4430, 2011*). Trials to begin in Europe. Another report: lock soln of sodium citrate, methylene blue, methylparabens (*CCM 39:613, 2011*). Recent meeting abstracts support 70% ethanol.
Mycotic aneurysm	S. aureus (≥ 71%), S. epidermidis, Salmonella sp. (15-24%), M. TBc, S. pneumonia, many others	**Vanco** (dose sufficient to achieve trough level of 15-20 μg/mL) + **(ceftriaxone** or **PIP-TZ** or **CIP)** **Treatment is combination of antibiotic + surgical resection with revascularization.**	**Dapto** could be substituted for Vanco. For GNB: **cefepime** or **carbapenems**. For MDR-GNB, **colistin** in combination therapy	No data for ceftaroline or telavancin. Best diagnostic imaging, CT angiogram. Blood cultures positive in 50-85%. **De-escalate to specific therapy when culture results known.** Treatment duration varies but usually 6 wks from date of definitive surgery.
Suppurative Phlebitis				
Pelvic thrombophlebitis (with or without septic pulmonary emboli) Postpartum or post abortion or post pelvic surgery	Streptococci, bacteroides, Enterobacteriaceae	**(Metro + Cefepime)** or **PIP-TZ**	**(Dapto** 6 mg per kg IV q24h^AA or **linezolid** 600 mg IV q12h) + **ceftriaxone** 2 gm IV q12h	Use heparin during antibiotic regimen. Duration unclear; one study shows benefit of anticoagulation (*Am J Obstet Gyn 181:143, 1999*). Decreasing activity of cefoxitin & cefotetan vs. Bacteroides sp.
		Dosages: Table 10A, page 93		
Cavernous sinus thrombosis	Staph. aureus, Streptococcus sp., H. influenzae, aspergillus/mucor/rhizopus	**Vanco** 1 gm IV q12h + **ceftriaxone** 2 gm IV q12h	**[clinda + (aztreonam or gent)]**	CT or MRI scan for diagnosis. **Heparin** usually used. If, fungal etiology, see specific organism in Table 11.
Other: Femoral, saphenous, internal jugular, subclavian	S. aureus, S. pyogenes, Strep sp. (Group B), Fusobacterium necrophorum (Lemierre's Syndrome)	**Vancomycin** 15 mg/kg IV q12h (normal weight) + **ceftriaxone** 1 gm IV q24h	**Daptomycin** 6 mg/kg IV q12h + **ceftriaxone** 1 gm IV q24h	Retrospective study: 2-3 weeks IV specific therapy + 2 weeks po therapy was efficacious (*CID 49:741, 2008*). If involved vein accessible, surgical I&D or excision may help, esp. if bacteremic pt.

Abbreviations on page 2.   NOTE: All dosage recommendations are for adults (unless otherwise indicated) and assume normal renal function.

TABLE 2 – RECOMMENDED ANTIMICROBIAL AGENTS AGAINST SELECTED BACTERIA

BACTERIAL SPECIES	ANTIMICROBIAL AGENT (See page 2 for abbreviations)		
	RECOMMENDED	ALTERNATIVE	ALSO EFFECTIVE[1] (COMMENTS)
Achromobacter xylosoxidans spp xylosoxidans (formerly Alcaligenes)	IMP, MER, DORI (no DORI for pneumonia)	TMP-SMX. Some strains susc. to ceftaz, PIP-TZ	Resistant to aminoglycosides, most cephalosporins & FQs.
Acinetobacter calcoaceticus—baumannii complex	If suscept: IMP or MER or DORI. For MDR strains: Colistin + (IMP or MER) (no DORI for pneumonia)	AM-SB used for activity of sulbactam (CID 51:79, 2010). Perhaps Minocycline IV	Resistant to aminoglycosides, FQs. Minocycline, effective against many strains (CID 51:79, 2010) (See Table 5A, pg 77)
Actinomyces israelii	AMP or Pen G	Doxy, ceftriaxone	Clindamycin, erythro
Aeromonas hydrophila & other sp.	CIP or Levo	TMP-SMX or (P Ceph 3, 4)	See AAC 56:1110, 2012.
Arcanobacterium (C.) haemolyticum	Erythro; azithro	Benzathine Pen G, Clinda	Sensitive to most drugs, resistant to TMP-SMX (AAC 38:142, 1994)
Bacillus anthracis (anthrax): inhalation	See Table 1, page 43		
Bacillus cereus, B. subtilis	Vancomycin, clinda	FQ, IMP	
Bacteroides sp., B. fragilis & others	Metronidazole or PIP-TZ	Dori, ERTA, IMP, MER, AM-CL	Increasing resistance to: clinda, cefoxitin, cefotetan.
Bartonella henselae, quintana See Table 1, pages 30, 45, 51, 57	Varies with disease entity & immune status. Active: Azithro, clarithro, erythro, doxy & in combination: RIF, gent, ceftriaxone. Not active: CIP, TMP-SMX, Pen, most cephalosporins; aztreonam		
Bordetella pertussis	Azithro or clarithro	TMP-SMX	See PIDJ 31:78, 2012.
Borrelia burgdorferi, B. afzelii, B. garinii (Lyme & relapsing fever)	See specific disease entity		
Brucella sp.	Drugs & duration vary with localization or non-localization. See specific disease entities. PLoS One 7:e32090; 2012.		
Burkholderia (Pseudomonas) cepacia	TMP-SMX or MER or CIP	Minocycline or chloramphenicol	(Usually resist to aminoglycosides, polymyxins) (AAC 37: 123, 1993 & 43:213, 1999; Inf Med 18:49, 2001) (Some resist to carbapenems). May need combo rx (AJRCCM 161:1206, 2000).
Burkholderia (Pseudomonas) pseudomallei Curr Opin Infect Dis 23:554, 2010; CID 41:1105, 2005	Initially, IV ceftaz or IMP or MER, then po (TMP-SMX + Doxy x 3 mos) ± Chloro (AAC 49:4010, 2005).		(Thai, 12–80% strains resist to TMP-SMX). FQ active in vitro. MER also effective (AAC 48: 1763, 2004)
Campylobacter jejuni	Azithro	Erythro or CIP	TMP-SMX, Pen & cephalosporins not active.
Campylobacter fetus	Gentamicin	IMP or ceftriaxone	AMP, chloramphenicol
Capnocytophaga ochracea (DF-1)	Dog bite: Clinda or AM-CL	Septic shock, post-splenectomy: PIP-TZ, Clinda, IMP, DORI, MER	FQ activity variable; aminoglycosides, TMP-SMX & Polymyxins have limited activity. LN ID 9:439, 2009.
Capnocytophaga canimorsus (DF-2)	Dog bite: AM-CL		
Chlamydophila pneumoniae	Doxy	Erythro, FQ	Azithro, clarithro
Chlamydia trachomatis	Doxy or azithro	Erythro	
Citrobacter diversus (koseri), C. freundii	Life threatening illness: IMP, MER, DORI	Non-life threatening illness: CIP or Gent	Emergence of resistance: AAC 52:995, 2007.
Clostridium difficile	Mild illness: Metronidazole (po)	Moderate/severe illness: Vancomycin (po) or Fidaxomicin (CID 51:1306, 2010).	Bacitracin (po); Nitazoxanide (CID 43:421, 2006; JAC 59:705, 2007). Rifaximin (CID 44:846, 2007). See also Table 1, page 18 re severity of disease.
Clostridium perfringens	Pen G ± clindamycin	Doxy	Erythro, chloramphenicol, cefazolin, cefoxitin, AP Pen, carbapenems
Clostridium tetani	Metronidazole or Pen G	Doxy	Role of antibiotics unclear.
Corynebacterium. diphtheriae	Erythro + antitoxin	Pen G + antitoxin	RIF reported effective (CID 27:845, 1998)
Corynebacterium jeikeium	Vancomycin + aminoglycoside	Pen G + aminoglycoside	Many strains resistant to Pen (EJCMID 25:349, 2006).
Corynebacterium minutissimum	Clinda 1% lotion	Clarithro or Erythro	Causes erythrasma
Coxiella burnetii (Q fever) acute disease (CID 52:1431, 2011).	Doxy, FQ (see Table 1, page 31)	Erythro, Azithro, Clarithro	Endocarditis: doxy + hydroxychloroquine (JID 188:1322, 2003; LnID 3:709, 2003; LnID 10:527, 2010).
chronic disease, e.g., endocarditis	Doxy + hydroxy chloroquine	TMP-SMX, Chloro	

TABLE 2 (2)

BACTERIAL SPECIES	ANTIMICROBIAL AGENT *(See page 2 for abbreviations)*		
	RECOMMENDED	ALTERNATIVE	ALSO EFFECTIVE[1] (COMMENTS)
Ehrlichia chaffeensis, Ehrlichia ewubguum Anaplasma (Ehrlichia) phagocytophillium	Doxy	RIF *(CID 27:213, 1998)*, Levo *(AAC 47:413, 2003)*.	CIP, oflox, chloramphenicol also active in vitro. Resist to clinda, TMP-SMX, IMP, AMP, erythro, & azithro *(AAC 41:76, 1997)*.
Eikenella corrodens	AM-CL, IV Pen G	TMP-SMX, FQ	Resistant to clinda, cephalexin, erythro, metro, diclox
Elizabethkingae meningosepticum (formerly Chryseobacterium)	Levo or TMP-SMX	CIP, Minocycline	Resistant to Pen, cephalosporins, carbapenems, aminoglycosides, vancomycin *(JCM 44:1181, 2006)*
Enterobacter species	Recommended agents vary with clinical setting and degree and mechanism of resistance.		
Enterococcus faecalis	Highly resistant. See Table 5A, page 77		
Enterococcus faecium	Highly resistant. See Table 5A, page 77		
Erysipelothrix rhusiopathiae	Penicillin G or amox	P Ceph 3, FQ	IMP, AP Pen (vancomycin, APAG, TMP-SMX resistant)
Escherichia coli	Highly resistant. Treatment varies with degree & mechanism of resistance, see TABLE 5B.		
Francisella tularensis (tularemia) *See Table 1, page 45*	Gentamicin, tobramycin, or streptomycin	Mild infection: Doxy or CIP	Chloramphenicol, RIF. Doxy/chloro bacteriostatic → relapses CID 53:e133, 2011.
Gardnerella vaginalis (bacterial vaginosis)	Metronidazole or Tinidazole	Clindamycin	See Table 1, pg 26 for dosage
Helicobacter pylori	See Table 1, pg 21		Drugs effective in vitro often fail in vivo.
Haemophilus aphrophilus (Aggregatibacter aphrophilus)	[(Penicillin or AMP) + gentamicin] or [AM- SB ± gentamicin]	(Ceftriaxone + Gent) or CIP or Levo	Resistant to vancomycin, clindamycin, methicillin
Haemophilus ducreyi (chancroid)	Azithro or ceftriaxone	Erythro, CIP	Most strains resistant to tetracycline, amox, TMP-SMX
Haemophilus influenzae Meningitis, epiglottitis & other life-threatening illness	Cefotaxime, ceftriaxone	AMP if susceptible and β-lactamase neg, FQs	Chloramphenicol (downgrade from 1st choice due to hematotoxicity).
non-life threatening illness	AM-CL, O Ceph 2/3		Azithro, clarithro, telithro
Klebsiella ozaenae/ rhinoscleromatis	CIP	Levo	Acta Otolaryngol 131:440, 2010.
Klebsiella species	Treatment varies with degree & mechanism of resistance, see TABLE 5B.		
Lactobacillus species	Pen G or AMP	Clindamycin	**May be resistant to vancomycin**
Legionella sp.	Levo or Moxi		Telithro active in vitro.
Leptospira interrogans	Mild: Doxy or amox	Severe: Pen G or ceftriaxone	
Leuconostoc	Pen G or AMP	Clinda	**NOTE: Resistant to vancomycin**
Listeria monocytogenes	AMP + Gent for synergy	TMP-SMX	Erythro, penicillin G (high dose), APAG may be synergistic with β-lactams. Meropenem active in vitro. **Cephalosporin-resistant!**
Moraxella (Branhamella) catarrhalis	AM-CL or O Ceph 2/3, TMP-SMX	Azithro, clarithro, dirithromycin, telithro	Erythro, doxy, FQs
Mycoplasma pneumoniae	Doxy	Azithro	Clindamycin & β lactams NOT effective. Increasing macrolide resistance in Asia (>30% reported in Japan) *(AAC 52:348, 2008)*.
Neisseria gonorrhoeae (gonococcus)	Ceftriaxone,	Azithro (high dose)	FQs and oral cephalosporins no longer recommended: high levels of resistance.
Neisseria meningitidis (meningococcus)	Ceftriaxone	Chloro, MER	Chloro-resist strains in SE Asia *(NEJM 339:868, 1998)* (Prophylaxis: pg 10)
Nocardia asteroides or **Nocardia brasiliensis**	TMP-SMX + IMP	Linezolid	Amikacin + (IMP or ceftriaxone or cefotaxime)
Pasteurella multocida	Pen G, AMP, amox, cefuroxime, cefpodoxime	Doxy, Levo, Moxi, TMP-SMX	Resistant to cephalexin, oxacillin, clindamycin, erythro, vanco.
Plesiomonas shigelloides	CIP	TMP-SMX	AM-CL, Ceftriaxone & Chloro active. Resistant to: Amp, Tetra, aminoglycosides
Propionibacterium acnes (not acne)	Penicillin, Ceftriaxone	Vanco, Dapto, Linezolid	May be resistant to Metro.
Proteus sp, **Providencia sp**, Morganella sp. (Need in vitro susceptibility)	CIP, PIP-TZ; avoid cephalosporins	May need carbapenem if critically ill	Note: Proteus sp. & Providencia sp. have intrinsic resistance to Polymyxins.
Pseudomonas aeruginosa *(ID Clin No Amer 23:277, 2009)*. Combination therapy? *See Clin Micro Rev 25:450, 2012.*	No in vitro resistance: AP Pen, AP Ceph 3, Dori, IMP, MER, tobramycin, CIP, aztreonam. For serious inf., use AP β-lactam + (tobramycin or CIP)	For UTI, if no in vitro resistance, single drugs effective: AP Pen, AP Ceph 3, cefepime, IMP, MER, aminoglycoside, CIP, aztreonam	If resistant to all beta lactams, FQs, aminoglycosides: Colistin + MER or IMP. Do not use DORI for pneumonia.

TABLE 2 (3)

BACTERIAL SPECIES	ANTIMICROBIAL AGENT (See page 2 for abbreviations)		
	RECOMMENDED	ALTERNATIVE	ALSO EFFECTIVE[1] (COMMENTS)
Rhodococcus (C. equi)	Two drugs: Azithro, Levo or RIF	(Vanco or IMP) + (Azithro, Levo or RIF)	Vancomycin active in vitro; intracellular location may impair efficacy (CID 34:1379, 2002). Avoid Pen, cephalosporins, clinda, tetra, TMP-SMX.
Rickettsia species (includes spotted fevers)	Doxy	Chloramphenicol (in pregnancy), azithro (age < 8 yrs)	See specific infections (Table 1).
Salmonella typhi (CID 50:241, 2010; AAC 54:5201, 2010; BMC ID 51:37, 2005)	If FQ & nalidixic acid susceptible: CIP	Ceftriaxone, cefixime, azithro, chloro	Concomitant steroids in severely ill. Watch for relapse (1-6%) & ileal perforation. FQ resistance reported with treatment failures (AAC 52:1278, 2008).
Serratia marcescens	If no in vitro resistance: PIP-TZ, CIP, LEVO, Gent	If in vitro resistance: Carbapenem	Avoid extended spectrum Ceph if possible.
Shigella sp.	FQ or azithro	Ceftriaxone is alternative; TMP-SMX depends on susceptibility.	
Staph. aureus, methicillin-susceptible	Oxacillin/nafcillin	P Ceph 1, vanco, teicoplanin[NUS] clinda ceftaroline	ERTA, IMP, MER, BL/BLI, FQ, erythro, clarithro, azithro, telithro, quinu-dalfo, linezolid, dapto, telavancin.
Staph. aureus, methicillin-resistant (health-care associated) IDSA Guidelines: CID 52 (Feb 1):1, 2011.	Vancomycin	Teicoplanin[NUS], TMP-SMX (some strains resistant), quinu-dalfo, linezolid, daptomycin, telavancin, ceftaroline	Fusidic acid[NUS]. >60% CIP-resistant in U.S. (Fosfomycin + RIF). Partially vancomycin-resistant strains (GISA, VISA) & highly resistant strains now described—see Table 6, pg 78. Also, ceftaroline.
Staph. aureus, methicillin-resistant [community- associated (CA-MRSA)]			CA-MRSA usually not multiply-resistant. Oft resist. to erythro & variably to FQ. Vanco, teico[NUS], telavancin or daptomycin can be used in pts requiring hospitalization (see Table 6, pg 78). Also, ceftaroline.
Mild-moderate infection	(TMP-SMX or doxy or mino)	Clinda (if D-test neg— see Table 5A & 6	
Severe infection	Vanco or teico[NUS]	Linezolid or daptomycin	
Staph. epidermidis	Vancomycin ± RIF	RIF + (TMP-SMX or FQ), daptomycin (AAC 51:3420, 2007)	Cephalothin or nafcillin/oxacillin if sensitive to nafcillin/oxacillin but 75% are resistant. FQs. (See Table 5A).
Staph. haemolyticus	TMP-SMX, FQ, nitrofurantoin	Oral cephalosporin	Recommendations apply to UTI only.
Staph. lugdunensis	Oxacillin/nafcillin or penicillin G (if β-lactamase neg.)	P Ceph 1 or vancomycin or teico[NUS]	Approx. 75% are penicillin-susceptible.
Staph. saprophyticus (UTI)	Oral cephalosporin or AM-CL	FQ	Suscept to most agents used for UTI; occ. failure of sulfonamides, nitrofurantoin reported (JID 155:170, 1987). Resist to fosfomycin.
Stenotrophomonas (Xanthomonas, Pseudomonas) maltophilia	TMP-SMX	TC-CL	Minocycline, tigecycline, CIP, Ceftriaxone, moxifloxacin, ceftaz (LnID 9:312, 2009; JAC 62:889, 2008). [In vitro synergy (TC-CL + TMP-SMX) & (TC-CL + CIP), JAC 62:889, 2008].
Streptobacillus moniliformis	Penicillin G	Doxy	Maybe azithro, clinda, ceftriaxone
Streptococcus, anaerobic (Peptostreptococcus)	Penicillin G	Clindamycin	Doxy, vancomycin, linezolid, ERTA (AAC 51:2205, 2007).
Streptococcus anginosus group	Penicillin	Vanco or Ceftriaxone	Avoid FQs; macrolide resistance emerging
Streptococcus pneumoniae, penicillin-susceptible	Penicillin G, Amox	Multiple agents effective, e.g., Ceph 2/3, Clinda	If meningitis, higher dose, see Table 1, page 9.
penicillin-resistant (MIC ≥2.0)	Vancomycin, Levo, ceftriaxone, Amox (HD), Linezolid		
Streptococcus pyogenes, Groups A, B, C, G: bacteremia	Penicillin G + Clinda	Pen (alone) or Clinda (alone)	JCM 49:439, 2011. Pockets of macrolide resistance
Vibrio cholerae	Doxy, FQ	Azithro, erythro	Maybe CIP or Levo; some resistance.
Vibrio parahaemolyticus	Doxy	Azithro, CIP	If bacteremic, treat as for V. vulnificus
Vibrio vulnificus, alginolyticus, damsela	Doxy + ceftriaxone	Levo	CID 52:788, 2011
Yersinia enterocolitica	CIP or ceftriaxone	TMP-SMX; CIP (if bacteremic)	CIP resistance (JAC 53:1068, 2004), also resistant to Pen, AMP, erythro.
Yersinia pestis (plague)	Streptomycin or Gent	Doxy or CIP	Maybe TMP-SMX (for bubonic, but sub-optimal)

[1] Agents are more variable in effectiveness than "Recommended" or "Alternative." Selection of "Alternative" or "Also Effective" based on in vitro susceptibility testing, pharmacokinetics, host factors such as auditory, renal, hepatic function, & cost.

TABLE 3 – SUGGESTED DURATION OF ANTIBIOTIC THERAPY IN IMMUNOCOMPETENT PATIENTS[1,2]

CLINICAL SITUATION		DURATION OF THERAPY
SITE	**CLINICAL DIAGNOSIS**	**(Days)**
Bacteremia	Bacteremia with removable focus (no endocarditis)	10–14 (CID 14:75, 1992) (See Table 1)
Bone	Osteomyelitis, adult; acute	42
	adult; chronic	Until ESR normal (often > 3 months)
	child; acute; staph. and enterobacteriaceae[3]	21
	child; acute; strep, meningococci, haemophilus[3]	14
Ear	Otitis media with effusion	<2 yrs: 10 (or 1 dose ceftriaxone) ; ≥2 yrs: 5–7
	Recent meta-analysis suggests 3 days of azithro (JAC 52:469, 2003) or 5 days of "short-acting" antibiotics effective for uncomplicated otitis media (JAMA 279:1736, 1998), but may be inadequate for severe disease (NEJM 347:1169, 2002).	
Endo-cardium	Infective endocarditis, native valve	
	Viridans strep	14 or 28 (See Table 1, page 28)
	Enterococci	28 or 42 (See Table 1, page 29)
	Staph. aureus	14 (R-sided only) or 28 (See Table 1, page 29)
GI Also see Table 1	Bacillary dysentery (shigellosis)/traveler's diarrhea	3
	Typhoid fever (S. typhi): Azithro	5 (children/adolescents)
	Ceftriaxone	14 [Short course ‡ effective (AAC 44:450, 2000)]
	FQ	5–7
	Chloramphenicol	14
	Helicobacter pylori	10–14. For triple-drug regimens, 7 days probably adequate (AJM 147:553, 2007).
	Pseudomembranous enterocolitis (C. difficile)	10
Genital	Non-gonococcal urethritis or mucopurulent cervicitis	7 days doxy or single dose azithro
	Pelvic inflammatory disease	14
Heart	Pericarditis (purulent)	28
Joint	Septic arthritis (non-gonococcal) Adult	14–28 (Ln 351:197, 1998)
	Infant/child	Rx as osteomyelitis above. Recent study suggests 10-14 days of therapy sufficient (CID 48:1201, 2009), but not complete agreement on this (CID 48:1211, 2009).
	Gonococcal arthritis/disseminated GC infection	7 (See Table 1, page 23)
Kidney	Cystitis (bladder bacteriuria)	3 (Single dose extended-release cipro also effective) (AAC 49:4137, 2005)
	Pyelonephritis	14 (7 days if CIP used; 5 days if levo 750 mg)
	Recurrent (failure after 14 days rx)	42
Lung	Pneumonia, pneumococcal	Until afebrile 3–5 days (minimum 5 days).
	Community-acquired pneumonia	Minimum 5 days and afebrile for 2-3 days (CID 44:S55, 2007; AJM 120:783, 2007).
	Pneumonia, enterobacteriaceae or pseudomonal	21, often up to 42
	Pneumonia, staphylococcal	21–28
	Pneumocystis carinii in AIDS;	21
	other immunocompromised	14
	Legionella, mycoplasma, chlamydia	7–14
	Lung abscess	Usually 28–42[4]
Meninges[5] (CID 39:1267, 2004)	N. meningitidis	7
	H. influenzae	7
	S. pneumoniae	10–14
	Listeria meningoencephalitis, gp B strep, coliforms	21 (longer in immunocompromised)
Multiple systems	Brucellosis (See Table 1, page 60)	42 (add SM or gent for 1ˢᵗ 7–14 days) (JAC 65:1028, 2010)
	Tularemia (See Table 1, pages 45, 59)	7–14
Muscle	Gas gangrene (clostridial)	7
Pharynx	Group A strep pharyngitis Also see Pharyngitis, Table 1, page 48	10 O Ceph 2/3, azithromycin effective at 5 days (JAC 45, Topic TI 23, 2000; JIC 14:213, 2008). 3 days less effective (Inf Med 18:515, 2001). Single dose extended rel Azithro (2 gm) as effective as 3 days of immediate rel Azithro (CMI 15:1103, 2009). See also 2009 Cochrane Review (www.thecochranelibrary.com).
	Diphtheria (membranous)	7–14
	Carrier	7
Prostate	Chronic prostatitis (TMP-SMX)	30–90
	(FQ)	28–42
Sinuses	Acute sinusitis	5–14[6]
Skin	Cellulitis	Until 3 days after acute inflamm disappears
Systemic	Lyme disease	See Table 1, page 58
	Rocky Mountain spotted fever (See Table 1, page 59)	Until afebrile 2 days

[1] Early change from IV to po regimens (about 72 hrs) is cost-effective with many infections, i.e., intra-abdominal (AJM 91:462, 1991). There is emerging evidence that serum **procalcitonin** level determination (a measure of bacterial or fungal infection) may allow early stopping of empiric therapy (JCM 48:2325, 2010).

[2] The recommended duration is a minimum or average time and should not be construed as absolute.

[3] These times are with proviso: sx & signs resolve within 7 days and ESR is normalized (J.D. Nelson, APID 6:59, 1991).

[4] After patient afebrile 4-5 days, change to oral therapy.

[5] In children relapses seldom occur until 3 days or more after termination of rx. For meningitis in children, see Table 1, page 8.

[6] Duration of therapy dependent upon agent used and severity of infection. Longer duration (10-14 days) optimal for beta-lactams and patients with severe disease. For sinusitis of mild-moderate severity shorter courses of therapy (5-7 days) effective with "respiratory FQs" (including gemifloxacin, levofloxacin 750 mg), azithromycin. Courses as short as 3 days reported effective for TMP-SMX and azithro and one study reports effectiveness of single dose extended-release azithro. Authors feel such "super-short" courses should be restricted to patients with mild-mod disease (JAMA 273:1015, 1995; AAC 47:2770, 2003; Otolaryngol-Head Neck Surg 133:194, 2005; Otolaryngol-Head Neck Surg 127:1, 2002; Otolaryngol-Head Neck Surg 134:10, 2006).

TABLE 4 - COMPARISON OF ANTIBACTERIAL SPECTRA

Editorial Note: Choice of antibacterial agent must be made in consideration of local/institutional patterns of organism susceptibility and drug resistance. Patterns vary considerably based on geography and temporal changes in patterns are continuous. These data are intended to convey a generalized image of susceptibility/resistance to provide a basis for making decisions concerning initial empiric as well as specific antibacterial therapy. These data reflect in vitro susceptibilities, drawn from package inserts and/or reports in the published literature. In vitro susceptibility is not a predictor of in vivo efficacy.

Organisms	Penicillins		Antistaphylococcal Penicillins			Amino-Penicillins			Anti-Pseudomonal Penicillins				Carbapenems				Aztreonam	Fluoroquinolones						
	Penicillin G	Penicillin V	Methicillin	Nafcillin/Oxacillin	Cloxacillin[NUS]/Diclox.	AMP/Amox	Amox/Clav	AMP-Sulb	Ticarcillin	Ticar-Clav	Pip-Tazo	Piperacillin	Doripenem	Ertapenem	Imipenem	Meropenem	Aztreonam	Ciprofloxacin	Ofloxacin	Pefloxacin[NUS]	Levofloxacin	Moxifloxacin	Gemifloxacin	Gatifloxacin
GRAM-POSITIVE:																								
Strep. Group A, B, C, G	+	+	+	+	+	+	+	+	+	+	+	+	+	+	+	+	0	±	±		+	+	+	+
Strep. pneumoniae	+	+	+	+	+	+	+	+	+	+	+	+	+	+	+	+	0	±	±		+	+	+	+
Viridans strep	+	+	+	+	+	+	+	+	+	+	+	+	+	+	+	+	0	0	0	0	±	+	±	+
Strep. milleri	±	±	±	±	±	±	±	±	±	±	±	±	±	±	±	±	0	0	0	0	±	±	±	±
Enterococcus faecalis	+	+	0	0	0	+	+	+	±	±	+	+	+	0	+	±	0	±	±	0	+	+	±	+
Enterococcus faecium	+	+	0	0	0	+	+	+	±	±	±	±	0	0	0	0	0	0	0	0	±	±	±	±
Staph. aureus (MSSA)	0	0	+	+	+	0	+	+	±	+	+	±	+	+	+	+	0	+	+	+	+	+	+	+
Staph. aureus (MRSA)	0	0	0	0	0	0	0	0	0	0	0	0	0	0	0	0	0	0	0	0	0	0	0	0
Staph. aureus (CA-MRSA)	0	0	0	0	0	0	0	0	0	0	0	0	0	0	0	0	0	+	+	+	+	+	+	+
Staph. epidermidis	0	0	±	±	±	0	±	±	±	±	±	±	±	±	±	±	0	±	±	0	±	±	±	±
C. jeikeium	0	0	0	0	0	0	0	0	0	0	0	0	0	0	±	0	0	0	0	0	0	±	±	±
L. monocytogenes	+	+	0	0	0	+	+	+	+	+	+	+	+	±	+	+	0	+	+	0	+	+	+	+
GRAM-NEGATIVE:																								
N. gonorrhoeae	0	0	0	0	0	0	+	+	+	+	+	+	+	+	+	+	+	+[1]	+[1]	+[1]	+[1]	+[1]	+[1]	+[1]
N. meningitidis	+	+	0	0	0	+	+	+	+	+	+	+	+	+	+	+	+	+	+	+	+	+	+	+
M. catarrhalis	0	0	0	0	0	0	+	+	+	+	+	±	+	+	+	+	+	+	+	+	+	+	+	+
H. influenzae	0	0	0	0	0	±	+	+	+	+	+	±	+	+	+	+	+	+	+	+	+	+	+	+
E. coli	0	0	0	0	0	±	+	±	+	+	+	+	+	+	+	+	+	+	+	+	+	+	+	+
Klebsiella sp.	0	0	0	0	0	0	+	+	0	+	+	+	+	+	+	+	+	+	+	+	+	+	+	+
E. coli/Klebs sp ESBL+	0	0	0	0	0	0	0	0	0	0	±	0	+	+	+	+	0	+	+	+	+	+	+	+
E. coli/Klebs sp KPC+	0	0	0	0	0	0	0	0	0	0	0	0	0	0	0	0	0	±	±	±	±	±	±	±
Enterobacter sp.	0	0	0	0	0	0	0	0	±	±	±	±	+	+	+	+	+	+	+	+	+	+	+	+

[1] Prevalence of quinolone-resistant GC varies worldwide from <1% to 30.9% in Europe and >90% in Taiwan. In US in 2006 it was 6.7% overall and as a result, CDC no longer recommends FQs for first line therapy of GC (MMWR 56:332, 2007; JAC 58:587, 2006; CID 40:188, 2005; AnIM 147:81, 2007).

+ = **usually susceptible**; ± = **variably susceptible/resistant**; 0 = **usually resistant**; blank = **no data**
** Most strains ±: can be used in UTI, not in systemic infection

TABLE 4 (2)

Organisms	Penicillin V	Penicillin G	Methicillin	Nafcillin/Oxacillin	Cloxacillin[NUS]/Diclox.	AMP/Amox	Amox/Clav	AMP-Sulb	Ticarcillin	Ticar-Clav	Pip-Tazo	Piperacillin	Doripenem	Ertapenem	Imipenem	Meropenem	Aztreonam	Ciprofloxacin	Ofloxacin	Pefloxacin[NUS]	Levofloxacin	Moxifloxacin	Gemifloxacin	Gatifloxacin
Serratia sp.	0	0	0	0	0	0	0	0	+	+	+	0	+	+	+	+	+	+	+	+	+	+		+
Salmonella sp.	0	0	0	0	0	±	+	+	+	+	+	+	+	+	+	+	+	+	+	+	+	+		+
Shigella sp.	0	0	0	0	0	±	+	+	+	+	+	+	+	+	+	+	+	+	+	+	+	+		+
Proteus mirabilis	0	0	0	0	0	+	+	+	+	+	+	+	+	+	+	+	+	+	+	+	+	+		+
Proteus vulgaris	0	0	0	0	0	0	±	+	+	+	+	+	+	+	+	+	+	+	+	+	+	+		+
Providencia sp.	0	0	0	0	0	0	±	+	0	+	+	+	+	+	+	+	+	+	+	+	+	+		+
Morganella sp.	0	0	0	0	0	0	0	0	0	±	±	±	+	±	+	+	+	+	+	+	+	+		+
Citrobacter sp.	0	0	0	0	0	0	±	+	0	+	±	+	+	+	+	+	+	+	+	+	+	+		+
Aeromonas sp.	0	0	0	0	0	0	0	0	+	+	+	+	+	+	+	+	+	+	+	+	+	+		+
Acinetobacter sp.	0	0	0	0	0	0	0	±	±	±	±	±	±	0	±	±	±	±	±	0	±	±		±
Ps. aeruginosa	0	0	0	0	0	0	0	0	±	+	+	±	+	0	±	±	±	±	±	0	±	±		±
B. (Ps.) cepacia	0	0	0	0	0	0	0	0	±	+	±	±	+	0	0	0	0	±	±		±	±		±
S. (X.) maltophilia	0	0	0	0	0	0	0	0	0	+	±	0	0	0	0	0	0	±	0	0	±	±		±
Y. enterocolitica	0	0	0	0	0	0	±	±	+	+	+	+	+	+	+	+	+	+	+	+	+	+		+
Legionella sp.	0	0	0	0	0	0	0	0	0	0	0	0	+	0	0	0	0	+	+	+	+	+	+	+
P. multocida	+	+	0	0	0	+	+	+	+	+	+	+	+	+	+	+	+	+	+	+	+	+		+
H. ducreyi	±	+	0	0	0	±	+	+	+	+	+	+			+	+	+	+	+	+	+	+		+
MISC:																								
Chlamydophila sp	0	0	0	0	0	0	0	0	0	0	0	0	0	0	0	0	0	+	+	+	+	+	+	+
M. pneumoniae	0	0	0	0	0	0	0	0	0	0	0	0	0	0	0	0	0	+	+	+	+	+	+	+
ANAEROBES:																								
Actinomyces	+	+	0	0	0	+	+	+	+	+	+	+	+	+	+	+	0	±				±		
Bacteroides fragilis	0	0	0	0	0	0	+	+	0	+	+	±	+	+	+	+	0	0	±	0	±	±		±
P. melaninogenica	±	±	0	0	0	±	+	+	+	+	+	+	+	+	+	+	0	±	±	0	±	±		±
Clostridium difficile	+²	+²	0	0	0	+	+	+	+	+	+	+			+	+	0					±		±
Clostridium (not difficile)	±	+	0	0	0	+	+	+	+	+	+	+			+	+	0	+			+	±		±
Fusobacterium necrophorum	+	+	0	0	0	+	+	+	+	+	+	+			+	+	0	±	±		±	±		±
Peptostreptococcus sp.	+	+	±	±	+	+	+	+	+	+	+	+	+	+	+	+	0	±	±		±	+		+

TABLE 4 (3)

CEPHALOSPORINS

Organisms	1st Generation — Cefazolin	2nd Generation — Cefotetan	2nd Generation — Cefoxitin	2nd Generation — Cefuroxime	3rd/4th Generation (including anti-MRSA) — Cefotaxime	Ceftizoxime	Ceftriaxone	Ceftaroline	Ceftazidime	Cefepime	Oral 1st Gen — Cefadroxil	Cephalexin	Oral 2nd Gen — Cefaclor/Loracarbef*	Cefprozil	Cefuroxime axetil	Oral 3rd Gen — Cefixime	Ceftibuten	Cefpodox/Cefdinir/Cefditoren
GRAM-POSITIVE:																		
Strep. Group A, B, C, G	+	+	+	+	+	+	+	+	+	+	+	+	+	+	+	+	+	+
Strep. pneumoniae[3]	+	+	+	+	+	+	+	+	±	+	+	+	+	+	+	+	±	+
Viridans strep	+	+	+	+	+	+	+	+	0	+	0	0	0	0	0	+	0	0
Enterococcus faecalis	0	0	0	0	0	0	0	+	0	0	0	0	0	0	0	0	0	0
Staph. aureus (MSSA)	+	+	+	+	+	+	+	+	±	+	+	+	+	+	+	0	0	+
Staph. aureus (MRSA)	0	0	0	0	0	0	0	+	0	0	0	0	0	0	0	0	0	0
Staph. aureus (CA-MRSA)	0	0	0	0	0	0	0	+	0	0	0	0	0	0	0	0	0	0
Staph. epidermidis	±	±	±	±	±	±	±	+	±	±	±	±	±	±	±	±	±	±
C. jeikeium	0	0	0	0	0	0	0		0	0	0	0	0	0	0	0	0	0
L. monocytogenes	0	0	0	0	0	0	0		0	0	0	0	0	0	0	0	0	0
GRAM-NEGATIVE:																		
N. gonorrhoeae	±			+	+	+	+	+	+	+						+	+	+
N. meningitidis	0			+	+	+	+	+	+	+						±	±	±
M. catarrhalis	±	+	+	+	+	+	+	+	+	+	±	±	±	+	+	+	+	+
H. influenzae	±	+	+	+	+	+	+	+	+	+	0	0	+	+	+	+	+	+
E. coli	+	+	+	+	+	+	+	+	+	+	+	+	+	+	+	+	+	+
Klebsiella sp.	+	+	+	+	+	+	+	+	+	+	+	+	+	+	+	+	+	+
E coli/Kleb sp ESBL +	0	0	0	0	0	0	0	0	0	0	0	0	0	0	0	0	0	0
E coli/Kleb sp KPC+	0	0	0	0	0	0	0	0	0	0	0	0	0	0	0	0	0	0
Enterobacter sp.	0	0	0	0	±	+	+	±	±	+	0	0	0	0	0	+	+	+
Serratia sp.	0	0	0	0	+	+	+	±	+	+	0	0	0	0	0	+	+	+
Salmonella sp.	±	+			+	+	+		+	+	0	0	0	0	0	+	+	+
Shigella sp.	±	+			+	+	+		+	+	0	0	0	0	0	+	+	+
Proteus mirabilis	+	+	+	+	+	+	+	+	+	+	0	0	0	0	0	+	+	+
Proteus vulgaris	0	+	+	0	+	+	+	+	+	+	0	0	0	0	0	+	+	+
Providencia sp.	0	+	+	±	+	+	+	+	+	+	0	0	0	0	0	+	+	+
Morganella sp.	0	±	+	±	+	+	+	+	+	+	0	0	0	0	0	+	+	±

[3] Ceftaz 8-16 times less active than cefotax/ceftriax; effective only vs Pen-sens. strains (AAC 39:2193, 1995). Oral cefuroxime, cefprozil, cefpodoxime most active in vitro vs resistant S. pneumo (PIDJ 14:1037, 1995).

+ = **usually susceptible**; ± = **variably susceptible/resistant**; 0 = **usually resistant**; blank = **no data**

* A 1-carbacephem best classified as a cephalosporin

TABLE 4 (4)

Organisms	CEPHALOSPORINS											Oral Agents						
	1st Generation	2nd Generation			3rd/4th Generation (including anti-MRSA)						1st Generation		2nd Generation			3rd Generation		
	Cefazolin	Cefotetan	Cefoxitin	Cefuroxime	Cefotaxime	Ceftizoxime	Ceftriaxone	Ceftaroline	Ceftazidime	Cefepime	Cefadroxil	Cephalexin	Cefaclor/Loracarbef*	Cefprozil	Cefuroxime axetil	Cefixime	Ceftibuten	Cefpodox/Cefdinir/Cefditoren
C. freundii	0	0	±1	0	+	0	+		0	+	0	0	0	0	0	0	0	0
C. diversus	0	±1	±1	±1	+	+	+		+	+	0	0	0	0	±1	+	+	+
Citrobacter sp.	0	±1	±1	±1	+	+	+		+	+	0	0	0	0	0	+	+	0
Aeromonas sp.	0	+	+	+	+	+	+	+	+	+	0	0	0	0	0	+	+	0
Acinetobacter sp.	0	0	0	0	0	0	0		±1	±1	0	0	0	0	0	0	0	0
P. aeruginosa	0	0	0	0	0	0	0		+	+	0	0	0	0	0	0	0	0
B. (P.) cepacia	0	±1	±1	0	±1	±1	±1		±1	±1	0	0	0	0	0	0	0	0
S. (X.) maltophilia	0	0	0	0	0	0	0		0	0	0	0	0	0	0	0	0	0
Y. enterocolitica	0	±1	±1	0	+	+	+		±1	+	0	0	0	0	0	+	+	+
Legionella sp.	0	0	0	0	0	0	0		0	0	0	0	0	0	0	0	0	0
P. multocida	0	±1	±1	±1	+	+	+		0	+	0	0	+	+	+	+		+
H. ducreyi		+	+	+	+	+	+		+	+		+			+	+		+
ANAEROBES:																		
Actinomyces	0	±4	+							0								
Bacteroides fragilis	0	+	+	+	0	±1	0		0	+	0						0	
P. melaninogenica		+	0	+	+	±1	+		+	+							+	
Clostridium difficile		0	0	0	0	0	0		0	0							0	
Clostridium (not difficile)		+	+	+	0	+	+		+	0							0	
Fusobacterium necrophorum		+	+	+	+	+	+		+	+								
Peptostreptococcus sp.		+	+	+	+	+	+		+	+		+		+	+	+	0	+

+ = **usually susceptible;** ± = **variably susceptible/resistant;** 0 = **usually resistant;** blank = **no data**

4 Cefotetan is less active against B. ovatus, B. distasonis, B. thetaiotaomicron.

* A 1-carbacephem best classified as a cephalosporin.

TABLE 4 (5)

Organisms	Gentamicin	Tobramycin	Amikacin	Chloramphenicol	Clindamycin	Erythro	Azithromycin	Clarithromycin	Telithromycin	Doxycycline	Minocycline	Tigecycline	Daptomycin	Vancomycin	Teicoplanin^NUS	Telavancin	Fusidic Acid^NUS	Trimethoprim	TMP-SMX	Nitrofurantoin	Fosfomycin	Rifampin	Metronidazole	Quinupristin-dalfopristin	Linezolid	Colistimethate (Colistin)
GRAM-POSITIVE:																										
Strep Group A, B, C, G	O	O	O	+	+	±	±	±	+	±	+	+	+[6]	+	+	+	±	+	+[5]	+		+	O	+	+	O
Strep. pneumoniae	S	O	O	+	+	±	±	±	+	+	+	+	+	+	+	+	±	±	+[5]	+	±	+	O	+	+	O
Enterococcus faecalis	S	S	S	±	O	O	O	O	±	O	O	+	+	+	+	+	+	O	O	+		±	O	O	+	O
Enterococcus faecium	S	S	S	±	O	O	O	O	O	O	O	+	+	±	±	+		+	+	+		O	O	+	+	O
Staph. aureus (MSSA)	+	+	+	+	+	+	+	+	+	±	±	+	+	+	+	+	+	±	+	+		+	O	+	+	O
Staph. aureus (MRSA)	O	O	O	O	O	O	O	O	O	±	±	+	+	+	+	+	+	±	+	+		+	O	+	+	O
Staph. aureus (CA-MRSA)					±	±	+	+	+	+	+	+	+	+	+	+	+	±	±			+	O	+	+	O
Staph. epidermidis	±	±	±	O	O	+	O	O	O	O	O	+	+	+	±	+	+	O	O	O		+	O	+	+	O
C. jeikeium	O	O	O	O	O	O	O	O	O	O	O	+	+	+	+	+	O	+	+			+	O	+	+	O
L. monocytogenes	S	S	S	+		+	+	+	+	+	+	+	±	+	+	+	+					+	O	+	+	O
GRAM-NEGATIVE:																										
N. gonorrhoeae	O	O	O	+	O	±	±	+	+	±	±	+	O	O	O	O	+	O	±	+	+	+	O	O	O	O
N. meningitidis	O	O	O	+	O	+	+	±	+	+	+		O	O	O	O	+	±	+			+	O	±	±	O
M. catarrhalis	+			+	O	±	+	+	+	+	+	+	O						±			+	O	+	+	
H. influenzae	O	+	+	+	O				+	+	+	+	O	O	O	O		±	+	±	±	O	O	O	O	
Aeromonas	+	+	+	+			±			+	+	+	O	O	O	O			±			O	O	O	O	
E. coli	+	+	+	±	O	O	O	O	O	+	+	+	O	O	O	O	O	+	±	±	+	O	O	O	O	+
Klebsiella sp.	+	+	+	±	O	O	O	O	O	±	±	+	O	O	O	O	O	±	±	±		O	O	O	O	+
E. coli/Klebs sp ESBL+	+	+	+						O	±	±	+	O	O	O	O	O	±			±	O	O	O	O	+
E. coli/Klebs sp KPC+												+	O	O	O	O	O					O	O	O	O	+
Enterobacter sp	+	+	+	O	O	O	O	O	O	O	O	+	O	O	O	O	O	±	±	+		O	O	O	O	+
Salmonella sp.	+	+	+	+			O	O	O	±	±	+	O	O	O	O	O	±	±	+		O	O	O	O	
Shigella sp.	+	+	+	+		±	±	±	O	+	+	+	O	O	O	O	O	±	±	+		O	O	O	O	

+ = usually susceptible;   ± = variably susceptible/resistant;   0 = usually resistant;   blank = no data

Antimicrobials such as azithromycin have high tissue penetration & some such as clarithromycin are metabolized to more active compounds, hence in vivo activity may exceed in vitro activity.

** Vancomycin, metronidazole given po active vs C. difficile; IV vancomycin not effective.   S = Synergistic with cell wall-active antibiotics.

[5] Although active in vitro, TMP-SMX is not clinically effective for Group A strep pharyngitis or for infections due to E. faecalis.

[6] Although active in vitro, daptomycin is not clinically effective for pneumonia caused by strep pneumonia.

TABLE 4 (6)

Organisms	MISCELLANEOUS — Colistimethate (Colistin)	MISCELLANEOUS — Linezolid	MISCELLANEOUS — Quinupristin-dalfopristin	MISCELLANEOUS — Metronidazole	MISCELLANEOUS — Rifampin	AGENTS URINARY TRACT — Fosfomycin	AGENTS URINARY TRACT — Nitrofurantoin	TMP-SMX	Trimethoprim	Fusidic Acid[NUS]	GLYCO-/LIPOGLYCO-/LIPO-PEPTIDES — Telavancin	GLYCO- Teicoplanin[NUS]	GLYCO- Vancomycin	GLYCO- Daptomycin	GLYCYL-CYCLINE — Tigecycline	TETRA-CYCLINES — Minocycline	TETRA-CYCLINES — Doxycycline	KETOLIDE — Telithromycin	MACROLIDES — Clarithromycin	MACROLIDES — Azithromycin	MACROLIDES — Erythro	Clindamycin	Chloramphenicol	AMINO-GLYCOSIDES — Amikacin	AMINO-GLYCOSIDES — Tobramycin	AMINO-GLYCOSIDES — Gentamicin
Serratia marcescens	o	o		o	o	±	o	±	o	o	o	o	o	o	+	o	o	o	o	o	o	o	O	+	+	+
Proteus vulgaris	o	o		o	o	±	o	O	o	±	o	o	o	o	±	o	o	o	o	o	o	±	±	+	+	O
Acinetobacter sp.	+	o	o	o	o			±	o	o	o	o	o	o	±	o	o	o	o	o	o	o	o	±	±	+
Ps. aeruginosa	+	o		o	o			o	o	o	o	o	o	o	o	o	o	o	o	o	o	o	o	+	+	+
B. (Ps.) cepacia	O	o		o	o			+	+	o	o	o	o	o	±	o	+	o	o	o	o	o	+	+	o	o
S. (X.) maltophilia	±	o		o	o			+	+	±	o	o	o	o	±	+	+	o	o	o	o	o	+	o	o	o
Y. enterocolitica		o		o				+			o	o	o	o	+	+	+	o	+	+	+	o	+	+	+	+
F. tularensis		o		o				+			o	o	o	o		+	+						+			±
Brucella sp.				o	±			±	+		o	o	o	o	+	+	+		+	+	+		+	+	+	
Legionella sp.				o	+			±	+		o	o	o	o	+	+	+	+	+	+	+	±	+			
H. ducreyi											o	o	o	o					+	+	+	o				
V. vulnificus									o						o	+	+		o	+	+	±	±			±
MISC.:																										
Chlamydophila sp.		+	+	o	+	o	o		o	o					+	+	+	+	+	+	+	+	+	o	o	o
M. pneumoniae		+	+							o					+	+	+	+	+	+	+	±	±	o	o	o
Rickettsia sp.								o		o					o	+	+		o	o	o	o	+	o	o	o
Mycobacterium avium	±	±		o	+			o	+	+	o	o	o		+	±	±	+	+	+	±	±	+	+	+	o
ANAEROBES:																										
Actinomyces		±	±	o	+				+	+	+	+	+		+	±	±		±	±	±	±	±	o	o	o
Bacteroides fragilis		±	±	+			o	+	+	+	o	o	o		+	+	+		+	+	+	+	+	o	o	o
P. melaninogenica		±	+	+			o		+	+	o	o	o		+	+	+		+	+	+	+	+	o	o	o
Clostridium difficile		±		+	+			+	+	+	+	+	+		+	±	±		±	±	±	±	+	o	o	o
Clostridium (not difficile)**		±±	±	+				+	+	+	o	+	o		+	+	+		±	±	±	±	+	o	o	o
Fusobacterium necrophorum		±±	±±	+				+	+	+	+	+	+		+	+	+		±	±	±	±	+	o	o	o
Peptostreptococcus sp.		+	+	+				+	+	+	+	+	+		+	+	+	+	±±	±±	±±	+	+	o	o	o

+ = **usually susceptible**; ± = **variably susceptible/resistant**; O = **usually resistant**; blank = no data

Antimicrobials such as azithromycin have high tissue penetration & some such as clarithromycin are metabolized to more active compounds, hence in vivo activity may exceed in vitro activity.

** Vancomycin, metronidazole given po active vs C. difficile; IV vancomycin not effective. S = Synergistic with cell wall-active antibiotics.

TABLE 5A – TREATMENT OPTIONS FOR SYSTEMIC INFECTION DUE TO SELECTED RESISTANT GRAM-POSITIVE BACTERIA

ORGANISM	RESISTANT TO	PRIMARY TREATMENT OPTIONS	ALTERNATIVE TREATMENT OPTIONS	COMMENTS
Enterococcus sp.	Vancomycin, Ampicillin, Penicillin, Gentamicin	No clearly effective therapy. Can try **Daptomycin** 8-12 mg/kg IV q24h but monitor for emergence of resistance (NEJM 365:892, 2011).	**Quinupristin-dalfopristin** 22.5 mg/kg/day IV divided q8h (see E. faecium activity) OR **Linezolid** 600 mg IV/po q12h	Activity of quinupristin/dalfopristin is limited to E. faecium (CID 33:816, 2001). Linezolid bacteriostatic with 40% relapse rate in endocarditis (AnIM 138:133, 2003). Role of televancin unclear
Staphylococcus aureus (See also Table 6 for more details)	Vancomycin (VISA or VRSA) and all beta lactams (except Ceftaroline)	**Daptomycin** 6-10 mg/kg IV q24h or **Quinupristin-dalfopristin** 7.5 mg/kg IV q8h	**Linezolid** 600 mg IV/po q12h	Confirm dapto susceptibility as VISA strains may be non-susceptible. If prior vanco therapy (or persistent infection on vanco) there is significant chance of developing resistance to dapto (JAC 66:1696, 2011). Addition of an anti-staphylococcal beta-lactam (ASBL) may restore susceptibility against Dapto-resistant MRSA (AAC 54:3161, 2010). Combination of Dapto + ASBL has been successful in clearing refractory MRSA bacteremia (CID 53:158, 2011). Other possibilities: televancin, ceftaroline.
Streptococcus pneumoniae	Penicillin G (MIC ≥ 4 μg/mL)	If no meningitis: **Ceftriaxone** 2 gm IV once daily OR **Ceftaroline** 600 mg IV q12h OR **Linezolid** 600 mg IV/po q12h	Meningitis: **Vancomycin** 15 mg/kg IV q8h OR **Meropenem** 2 gm IV q8h	**Ceftriaxone** 2 gm IV q12h should also work for meningitis.

TABLE 5B: TREATMENT OPTIONS FOR SYSTEMIC INFECTION DUE TO SELECTED MULTI-DRUG RESISTANT GRAM-NEGATIVE BACILLI

The suggested treatment options in this Table are usually not FDA-approved. Suggestions are variably based on in vitro data, animal studies, and/or limited clinical experience.

ORGANISM	RESISTANT TO	PRIMARY TREATMENT OPTIONS	ALTERNATIVE TREATMENT OPTIONS	COMMENTS
Acinetobacter baumannii	All Penicillins, All Cephalosporins, Aztreonam, Carbapenems, Aminoglycosides and Fluoroquinolones	**Polymyxin E (Colistin) + (Imipenem or Meropenem)** See Table 10A, page 101, for guidance on Colistin dosing.	**Polymyxin E (Colistin) + Rifampin** 300 mg IV q12h or 600 mg IV q24h. Another option (if active in vitro): **Minocycline** (IDCP 20:184, 2012) (in vitro synergy between minocycline and imipenem)	Refs: Int J Antimicrob Agts 37:244, 2011; BMC Inf Dis 11:109, 2011. Detergent effect of colistin reconstitutes antibiotic activity of carbapenems and other drugs. Do not use colistin as monotherapy.
E. coli, Klebsiella pneumoniae, or other Enterobacteriaceae producing extended spectrum beta-lactamase producing organisms (ESBLs)	All Cephalosporins, TMP-SMX, Fluoroquinolones, Aminoglycosides	**Imipenem** 500 mg IV q6h OR **Meropenem** 1 gm IV q8h OR **Doripenem** 500 mg IV q8h (CID 39:31, 2004) (Note: **Dori** is **not** FDA approved for treatment of pneumonia).	Perhaps high dose **Cefepime** 2 gm IV q12h. **Polymyxin E (Colistin)** in combination with carbapenem. For dosing, see Table 10A, page 101.	For UTI: Fosfomycin, nitrofurantoin (AAC 53:1278, 2009). Resistant to ceftidinr, but combination of ceftidinr with amox-clav active in vitro (AAC 53:1278, 2009).
Carbapenemase producing gram-negative bacilli	All Penicillins, Cephalosporins, Aztreonam, Carbapenems, Aminoglycosides, Fluoroquinolones	**Polymyxin E (Colistin)** in combination with carbapenem. See Table 10A, page 101, for guidance on Colistin dosing.	Combination of Colistin and Rifampin.	See Table 10A, page 101, for guidance on Colistin dosing.
Pseudomonas aeruginosa	All beta-lactams, Aminoglycosides, Fluoroquinolones	**Polymyxin E (Colistin)** in combination with carbapenem. See Table 10A, page 101, for guidance on Colistin dosing.	Inhaled **Colistin**™ 50-75 mg in 3-4 mL saline via nebulizer + **Colistin** IV + carbapenem.	See Table 10A, page 101, for guidance on Colistin dosing.
Stenotrophomonas maltophilia	All beta-lactams except Ticar-Clav, Aminoglycosides, Fluoroquinolones	**TMP-SMX** 8-10 mg/kg/day IV divided q8h/q8h/q12h (based on TMP component)	**Ticar-Clav** 3.1 gm IV q4-6h	

TABLE 6 – SUGGESTED MANAGEMENT OF SUSPECTED OR CULTURE-POSITIVE COMMUNITY-ASSOCIATED METHICILLIN-RESISTANT S. AUREUS INFECTIONS
(See footnote[1] for doses)

IDSA Guidelines: CID 52 (Feb 1)1, 2011. With the magnitude of the clinical problem and a number of new drugs, it is likely new data will require frequent revisions of the regimens suggested. (See page 2 for abbreviations).
NOTE - Distinction between community and hospital strains of MRSA blurring.

CLINICAL ILLNESS	ABSCESS, AFEBRILE & IMMUNOCOMPETENT: OUTPATIENT CARE	ABSCESS(ES) WITH FEVER; OUTPATIENT CARE	PNEUMONIA	BACTEREMIA OR POSSIBLE ENDOCARDITIS OR BACTEREMIC SHOCK	TREATMENT FAILURE (See footnote[2])
Management Drug doses in footnote	TMP-SMX-DS or doxycycline or minocycline or clindamycin (CID 40:1429, 2005 & AAC 51:2628, 2007). NOTE: I&D alone may be sufficient	TMP-SMX-DS or doxycycline plus incision and drainage. Note: Hospital associated MRSA strains are often resistant to Clindamycin.	Vanco IV or linezolid IV	Vanco IV or Dapto IV. Dapto not inferior to vanco in bacteremia trial (NEJM 355:653, 2006). No apparent benefit adding RIF to VANCO, maybe harm (AAC 52:2463, 2006).	Confirm adequate vanco troughs of 15-20 µg/mL and vancomycin susceptibility, search for deep foci of infection. Switch to alternative regimen if vanco MIC ≥ 2 µg/mL. Dapto resistance reported after vanco exposure & prior to dapto therapy (CID 45:601, 2007). Dapto appears safe at doses of up to 12 mg/kg/d (AAC 50:3245, 2006).
Comments continue on next page	Culture abscess & maybe blood. I&D. Hot packs. Close follow-up.			Target Vancomycin troughs of 15-20 µg/mL (CID 52:975, 2011). Vancomycin MICs ≥ 2 µg/mL associated with treatment failure in serious infections but whether this is mediated by insensitivity to vancomycin per se or to other factor unclear (CID 204:340, 2011). If patient has slow response to vancomycin and isolate has vancomycin MIC ≥ 2 µg/mL do not add rifampin but rather change therapy. An agent other than vancomycin should be used for infections caused by isolates with MICs ≥ 4 µg/mL	Data extremely limited concerning salvage regimens for treatment failures. Addition of aminoglycoside or rifampin to vancomycin not effective in one retrospective study (0% success), whereas linezolid with or without a carbapenem was effective (88% success in patients with bacteremia due to pneumonia, vascular catheter or graft infection; no patient had endocarditis) (CID 49:395, 2009). Options: For endocarditis or complicated bacteremia dapto 10 mg/kg IV once daily plus gentamicin 1 mg/kg (ideal body wt) IV every 8 hours or plus gentamicin daily, linezolid + a second agent (JAC 58:273, 2006 & JAC 56:923, 2005); quinupristin-dalfopristin (Q-D) ± with vanco. Case reports of success with Telavancin for MRSA failure (JAC 65:1315, 2010; AAC 54:5376, 2010; JAC (Jun 8), 2011). Options: For endocarditis or complicated bacteremia dapto 10 mg/kg IV once daily plus gentamicin 1 mg/kg IV every 8 hours or plus RIF 300-450 mg twice daily. Case reports of success with Telavancin 10 mg/kg/d for MRSA failure (JAC 65:1315, 2010; AAC 54:5376, 2010; JAC 66:2186, 2011) OR ceftaroline 600 mg q8h (JAC 67:1267, 2012 and J Infect Chemother online Jul 14, 2012).

¹ **Clindamycin:** 300 mg po tid. **Daptomycin** 6 mg/kg IV q24h is the standard dose; higher doses (10 mg/kg) and use of combination therapy recommended for vancomycin treatment failures. **Doxycycline or minocycline:** 100 mg po bid. **Linezolid:** 600 mg po/IV bid. **Quinupristin-dalfopristin (Q-D):** 7.5 mg/kg IV q8h (dedicated line). Long term use (e.g. endocarditis) may require switch to oral drug, dosing 600 mg po q24h; however, frequency of nausea less with 300 mg po bid. **TMP-SMX-DS:** Standard dose 8-10 mg/kg per day. For 70 person = 700 mg TMP component per day. **TMP-SMX** contains 160 mg TMP and 800 mg SMX. The dose for treatment of CA-MRSA skin and soft tissue infections (SST) is 1 DS tablet twice daily. **Vancomycin:** 1 gm IV q12h; up to 45-60 mg/kg/day in divided doses may be required to achieve target concentrations of 15-20 mcg/mL recommended for serious infections

² The median duration of bacteremia in endocarditis is 7-9 days in patients treated with vancomycin (AnIM 115:674, 1991). Longer duration of bacteremia, greater likelihood of endocarditis (JID 190:1140, 2004). Definition of failure unclear. Clinical response should be factored in. **Unsatisfactory clinical response especially if blood cultures remain positive beyond 5-7 days is an indication for change in therapy.**

TABLE 6 (2)

CLINICAL ILLNESS	ABSCESS, AFEBRILE; & IMMUNOCOMPETENT: OUTPATIENT CARE	ABSCESS(ES) WITH FEVER; OUTPATIENT CARE	PNEUMONIA	BACTEREMIA OR POSSIBLE ENDOCARDITIS OR BACTEREMIC SHOCK	TREATMENT FAILURE (See footnote⁷)
Comments	Effective dose of TMP-SMX-DS is unclear. IV dose is 8-10 mg/kg/d; roughly equivalent to 2 tabs po bid. Anecdotally, most pts respond to I&D and 1 tab bid although failures may occur (see footnote⁷) particularly in obese patients and 2 DS tabs bid recommended for those with BMI > 40. **Fusidic acid** 500 mg tid (not available in the US) + **rifampin** also an option (J Antimicrob Chemother 61: 976, 2008 and Can J Infect Dis Med Microbiol: 17(Suppl C): 4C, 2006); do not use rifampin alone as resistance rapidly emerges. One retrospective study (Peds 123: e959, 2009) in children reports increased risk of treatment failure with TMP-SMX compared to other agents for undrained, uncultured skin and soft tissue infections; presumably these were mainly cellulitis, which could reflect less activity of this agent against Group A streptococcus.	Note: Increasing frequency of strains with inducible resistance to clindamycin. Some authorities recommend addition of rifampin to TMP-SMX: do not use rifampin alone as resistance rapidly emerges. Patients not responding after 2-3 days should be evaluated for complicated infection and switched to **vancomycin**.	Prospective study of **Linezolid** vs **Vanco** showed slightly higher cure rate with Linezolid, no difference in mortality (CID 54:621, 2012).	Efficacy of IV TMP-SMX vs CA-MRSA uncertain. IV **TMP-SMX** was inferior to IV **vanco** for bacteremic MSSA (AnIM 117:390, 1992). **Dapto** failures associated with development of **dapto** resistance (NEJM 355:653, 2006)	Do not add **linezolid** to **vanco**: no benefit & may be antagonistic (AAC 47:3002, 2003). **Ceftaroline** is approved for MSSA pneumonia but not MRSA pneumonia. MRSA was an exclusion in the clinical trials (CID 51:1395, 2010).

TABLE 7 - DRUG DESENSITIZATION METHODS

Penicillin. Oral route (Pen VK) preferred. 1/3 pts develop transient reaction, usually mild. **Perform in ICU setting. Discontinue β-blockers. Have IV line, epinephrine, ECG, spirometer available.**
Desensitization works as long as pt is receiving Pen; allergy returns after discontinuance. History of Steven-Johnson, exfoliative dermatitis, erythroderma are contraindications. Skin testing for evaluation of Pen allergy: Testing with major determinant (benzyl Pen polylysine) and minor determinants has negative predictive value (97-99%). Risk of systemic reaction to skin testing <1% (Ann Allergy Asth Immunol 106:1, 2011). General refs: CID 35:26, 2002; Am J Med 121:572, 2008; Curr Clin Topics ID 13:131, 1993.
- **Method:** Prepare dilutions using **Pen-VK** oral soln, 250 mg/5mL. Administer each dose @ 15 min intervals in 30 mL water/flavored bev. After Step 14 observe pt for 30 min, then give full therapeutic dose by route of choice. Ref: Allergy, Prin & Prac, Mosby, 1993, p. 1726

Step	Dilution (mg/mL)	mL Administered	Dose/Step mg	Dose/Step units	Cumulative Dose Given mg	Cumulative Dose Given units
1	0.5	0.1	0.05	80	0.05	80
2	0.5	0.2	0.1	160	0.15	240
3	0.5	0.4	0.2	320	0.35	560
4	0.5	0.8	0.4	640	0.75	1,200
5	0.5	1.6	0.8	1,280	1.55	2,480
6	0.5	3.2	1.6	2,560	3.15	5,040
7	0.5	6.4	3.2	5,120	6.35	10,160
8	5	1.2	6	9,600	12.35	19,760
9	5	2.4	12	19,200	24.35	38,960
10	5	4.8	24	38,400	48.35	77,360
11	50	1	50	80,000	98.35	157,360
12	50	2	100	160,000	198.35	317,360
13	50	4	200	320,000	398.35	637,360
14	50	8	400	640,000	798.35	1,277,360

TMP-SMX. Perform in hospital/clinic. Refs: CID 20:849, 1995; AIDS 5:311, 1991.
- **Method:** Use **TMP-SMX** oral susp. (40 mg TMP/200 mg SMX)/5 mL. Take with 6 oz water after each dose. Corticosteroids, antihistaminics NOT used.

Hour	Dose (TMP/SMX) (mg)
0	0.004/0.02
1	0.04/0.2
2	0.4/2
3	4/20
4	40/200
5	160/800

Penicillin. Parenteral (Pen G) route. Follow procedures/notes under Oral (Pen-VK) route.
Ref: Allergy, Prin & Prac, Mosby, 1993, p. 1726.
- **Method:** Administer **Pen G** IM, IV or sc as follows:

Step	Dilution (units/mL)	mL Administered	Dose/Step (units)	Cumulative Dose Given (units)
1	100	0.2	20	20
2		0.4	40	60
3		0.8	80	140
4	1,000	0.2	200	340
5		0.4	400	740
6		0.8	800	1,540
7	10,000	0.2	2,000	3,540
8		0.4	4,000	7,540
9		0.8	8,000	15,540
10	100,000	0.2	20,000	35,540
11		0.4	40,000	75,540
12		0.8	80,000	155,540
13	1,000,000	0.2	200,000	355,540
14		0.4	400,000	755,540
15		0.8	800,000	1,555,540

Ceftriaxone. Ref: Allergol Immunopathol (Madr) 37:105, 2009.
- **Method:** Infuse **Ceftriaxone** IV @ 20 min intervals as follows:

Day	Dose (mg)
1	0.001, then 0.01, then 0.1, then 1
2	1, then 5, then 10, then 50
3	100, then 250, then 500
4	1000

Desensitization Methods for Other Drugs (References)
- **Imipenem-Cilastatin.** See Ann Pharmacother 37:513, 2003.
- **Meropenem.** See Ann Pharmacother 37:1424, 2003.
- **Daptomycin.** See Ann All Asthma Immun 100:87, 2008.
- **Ceftazidime.** See Curr Opin All Clin Immunol 6(6): 476, 2006.
- **Vancomycin.** Intern Med 45:317, 2006.

TABLE 8A – RISK CATEGORIES OF ANTIMICROBICS IN PREGNANCY

DRUG	FDA CATEGORIES*
Antibacterial Agents:	
Aminoglycosides:	
Amikacin, gentamicin, isepamicin[NUS], netilmicin[NUS], streptomycin & tobramycin	**D**
Beta Lactams	
Penicillins; pens + BLI; cephalosporins; aztreonam	B
Imipenem/cilastatin	C
Meropenem, ertapenem, doripenem	B
Chloramphenicol	C
Ciprofloxacin, oflox, levo, gati, gemi, moxi	C
Clindamycin	B
Colistin	C
Daptomycin	B
Fosfomycin	B
Fidaxomicin	B
Fusidic acid†	See Footnote†
Linezolid	C
Macrolides:	
Erythromycins/azithromycin	B
Clarithromycin	C
Metronidazole	B
Nitrofurantoin	B
Polymyxin B	C
Quinupristin-Dalfopristin	B
Rifaximin	C
Sulfonamides/trimethoprim	C
Telavancin	C
Telithromycin	C
Tetracyclines, tigecycline	**D**
Tinidazole	C
Vancomycin	C

DRUG	FDA CATEGORIES
Antifungal Agents: *(CID 27:151, 1998)*	
Amphotericin B preparations	B
Anidulafungin	C
Caspofungin	C
Fluconazole (150 mg SD for vaginal candidiasis)	C
Fluconazole (other regimens, uses)	D
Itraconazole, ketoconazole, flucytosine	C
Micafungin	C
Posaconazole	C
Terbinafine	B
Voriconazole	D
Antiparasitic Agents:	
Albendazole/mebendazole	C
Artemether/lumefantrine	C
Atovaquone/proguanil; atovaquone alone	C
Chloroquine	C
Dapsone	C
Eflornithine	C
Ivermectin	C
Mefloquine	B
Miltefosine	
Nitazoxanide	B
Pentamidine	C
Praziquantel	B
Proguanil	C
Pyrimethamine/pyrisulfadoxine	C
Quinidine	C

DRUG	FDA CATEGORIES
Antimycobacterial Agents:	
Quinine	X
Capreomycin	C
Clofazimine/cycloserine	"avoid"
Dapsone	C
Ethambutol	B
Ethionamide	C
INH, pyrazinamide	"safe"
Rifabutin	B
Rifampin	C
Thalidomide	"do not use" X
Antiviral Agents:	
Abacavir	C
Acyclovir	B
Adefovir	C
Amantadine	C
Atazanavir	B
Cidofovir	C
Cobicistat	C
Darunavir	C
Delavirdine	C
Didanosine (ddI)	B
Efavirenz	**D**
Elvitegravir/cobicistat/emtricitabine/tenofovir	
Emtricitabine	B
Enfuvirtide	B
Entecavir	C
Etravirine	B
Famciclovir	B

DRUG	FDA CATEGORIES
Antiviral Agents: *(continued)*	
Fosamprenavir	C
Foscarnet	C
Ganciclovir	C
Indinavir	C
Interferons	C
Lamivudine	C
Lopinavir/ritonavir	C
Maraviroc	B
Nelfinavir	B
Nevirapine	B
Oseltamivir	C
Raltegravir	C
Ribavirin	**X**
Rilpivirine	B
Rimantadine	C
Ritonavir	B
Saquinavir	B
Stavudine	C
Telbivudine	B
Tenofovir	B
Tipranavir	C
Valacyclovir	B
Valganciclovir	C
Zalcitabine	C
Zanamivir	C
Zidovudine	C

* **FDA Pregnancy Categories: A**—studies in pregnant women, no risk; **B**—animal studies no risk, but human not adequate or animal toxicity but human studies no risk; **C**—animal studies show toxicity, human studies inadequate but benefit of use may exceed risk; **D**—evidence of human risk, but benefits may outweigh; **X**—fetal abnormalities in humans, risk > benefit

† **Fusidic acid**[NUS]: potential for neonatal kernicterus

TABLE 8B – ANTIMICROBIAL DOSING IN OBESITY

The number of obese patients is increasing. Intuitively, the standard doses of some drugs may not achieve effective serum concentrations. Pertinent data on anti-infective dosing in the obese patient is gradually emerging. Though some of the data needs further validation, the following table reflects what is currently known.
Obesity is defined as ≥ 20% over Ideal Body Weight (Ideal BW) or Body Mass Index (BMI) ≥ 30. Dose = suggested body weight (BW) for dose calculation in obese patient, or specific dose if applicable.

Drug	Dose	Comments
Acyclovir	Use **Ideal BW** Example: for HSV encephalitis, give 10 mg/kg of Ideal BW q8h	Unpublished data from 7 obese volunteers (Davis, et al., ICAAC abstract, 1991).
Aminoglycosides	Use **Adjusted BW** Example: Critically ill patient, Gentamicin or Tobramycin (not Amikacin) 7 mg/kg of Adjusted BW IV q24h (See Comment)	Adjusted BW = Ideal BW + 0.4(Actual BW – Ideal BW). Ref: Pharmacother 27:1081, 2007. Follow levels so as to lower dose once hemodynamics stabilize.
Cefazolin (surgical prophylaxis)	No dose adjustment needed: 2 gm x 1 dose (repeat in 3 hours?)	Conflicting data; unclear whether dose should be repeated, or if an even higher dose is required. Patients with BMI 40-80 studied. Refs: Surg 136:738, 2004; Eur J Clin Pharmacol 67:985, 2011; Surg Infect 13:33, 2012.
Cefepime	Modest dose increase: 2 gm IV q8h instead of the usual q12h	Data from 10 patients (mean BMI 48) undergoing bariatric surgery; regimen yields free T > MIC of 60% for MIC of 8μg/mL. Ref: Obes Surg 22:465, 2012.
Daptomycin	Use **Actual BW** Example: 4-12 mg/kg of Actual BW IV q24h	Data from a single-dose PK study in 7 obese volunteers. Ref: Antimicrob Ag Chemother 51:2741, 2007.
Flucytosine	Use **Ideal BW** Example: Crypto meningitis, give 25 mg/kg of Ideal BW po q6h	Date from one obese patient with cryptococcal disease. Ref: Pharmacother 15:251, 1995. »
Levofloxacin	**No dose adjustment** required Example: 750 mg po/IV q24h	Data from 13 obese patients; variability in study findings renders conclusion uncertain. Refs: Antimicrob Ag Chemother 55:3240, 2011; J Antimicrob Chemother 66:1653, 2011.
Moxifloxacin	**No dose adjustment** required Example: 400 mg po/IV q24h	Data from 12 obese patients undergoing gastric bypass. Ref: J Antimicrob Chemother 66:2330, 2011.
Oseltamivir	**No dose adjustment** required Example: 75 mg po q12h	Data from 10 obese volunteers; unclear if applicable to patients >250 kg (OK to give 150 mg po q12h) Ref: J Antimicrob Chemother 66:2083, 2011.
Vancomycin	Use **Actual BW** Example: in critically ill patient give 25-30 mg/kg of Actual BW IV load, then 15-20 mg/kg of Actual BW IV q8h-12h (infuse over 1.5-2 hr). No single dose over 2 gm. Check trough levels.	Data from 24 obese patients; Vancomycin half-life appears to decrease with little change in Vd. Ref: Eur J Clin Pharmacol 54:621, 1998.
Voriconazole	**No dose adjustment** required Example: 400 mg po q12h x2 doses then 200 mg po q12h. Check trough concentrations (underdosing common with Voriconazole).	Data from a 2-way crossover study of oral voriconazole in 8 volunteers suggest no adjustment required, but data from one patient suggest use of adjusted BW. Recommended IV voriconazole dose based on actual BW (no supporting data). Refs: Antimicrob Ag Chemother 55:2601, 2011; Clin Infect Dis 53:745, 2011.

TABLE 9A – SELECTED PHARMACOLOGIC FEATURES OF ANTIMICROBIAL AGENTS

For pharmacodynamics, see Table 9B; for Cytochrome P450 interactions, see Table 9C. Table terminology key at bottom of each page. Additional footnotes at end of Table 9A, page 91.

DRUG	REFERENCE DOSE/ROUTE	PREG RISK	FOOD EFFECT (PO)[1]	ORAL %AB	PEAK SERUM LEVEL (µg/mL)	PROTEIN BINDING (%)	VOL OF DISTRIB (Vd)	AVER SERUM T½, hrs[2]	BILE PEN (%)[3]	CSF/ BLOOD (%)	CSF PEN[4]	AUC (µg•hr/mL)	Tmax (hr)
PENICILLINS: Natural													
Benz Pen G	1.2 million units IM				0.15 (SD)						Yes: Pen-sens S. pneumo		
Penicillin G	2 million units IV	B								500	5-10			
Penicillin V	500 mg po	B	Tab/soln no food	60-73	5-6 (SD)	65		0.5						
PEN ASE-RESISTANT PENICILLINS													
Cloxacillin^AUS	500 mg	B	Cap no food	50	7.5-14 (SD)	95	0.1 L/kg	0.5						1-1.5
Dicloxacillin	500 mg	B	Cap no food	37	10-17 (SD)	98	0.1 L/kg	0.7	5-8					1-1.5
Nafcillin	500 mg	B			30 (SD)	90-94	27.1 Vss	0.5-1	>100	9-20	Yes	18.1	
Oxacillin	500 mg	B			43 (SD)	90-94	0.4 L/kg	0.7	25	10-15	Yes		
AMINOPENICILLINS													
Amoxicillin	500 mg po	B	± food	80	5.5-7.5 (SD)	17	0.36 L/kg	1.2	100-3000	13-14	Yes	22	1-2
Amoxicillin ER	775 mg po	B	Tab + food		6.6 (SD)	20		1.2-1.5				29.8	3.1
AM-CL	875/125 mg po	B	Cap/tab/susp ± food	80/30-98	11.6/2.2 (SD)	18/25		1.4/1.1	100-3000			AM: 26.8 - CL: 5.1	
AM-CL-ER	2 tabs [2000/125 mg]	B	Tab + food		17/2.1 (SD)	18/25		1.3/1.0				AM: 71.6 - CL: 5.3	AM: 1.5 CL: 1.03
Ampicillin	2 gm IV	B			100 (SD)	18-22	0.29 L/kg	1.2	100-3000	13-14	Yes	AM: 120- SB 71	
AM-SB	3 gm IV	B			109-150(48-88 (SD)	28/38		1.2					
ANTIPSEUDOMONAL PENICILLINS													
PIP-TZ	3/.375 gm IV	B			242/24 (SD)	16-48	PIP: 0.24 L/kg	1.0	>100			PIP: 242 - TZ: 25	
TC-CL	3.1 gm IV	B			330/8 (SD)	45/25	TC: 9.7 Vss	1.2/1.0				TC: 485 - CL: 8.2	
CEPHALOSPORINS—1st Generation													
Cefadroxil	500 mg po	B	Cap/tab/susp ± food	90	16 (SD)	20	0.31 L/kg V/F	1.5	22			47.4	
Cefazolin	1 gm IV	B			188 (SD)	73-87	0.19 L/kg	1.9	29-300	1-4	No	236	
Cephalexin	500 mg po	B	Cap/tab/susp ±	90	18 (SD)	5-15	0.38 L/kg V/F	1.0	216			29	1

Preg Risk: FDA risk categories: A = No risk. **B** = No risk – human studies. **C** = toxicity in animals - inadequate human studies. **D** = human risk, but benefit may outweigh risk. **X** = fetal abnormalities – risk > benefit. **Food Effect (PO dosing): ±** food = take with or without food. **± food** = take with food. **no food** = take without food. **Oral % AB** = % absorbed. **Peak Serum Level: SD** = after single dose. **SS** = steady state after multiple doses; **Volume of Distribution (Vd): V/F** = Vd/oral bioavailability. **Vss** = Vd at steady state. **Vss/F** = Vd at steady state/oral bioavailability. **CSF Penetration:** therapeutic efficacy comment based on dose, usual susceptibility or target organism & penetration into CSF. **AUC** = area under drug concentration curve; **24hr** = AUC 0-24; **Tmax** = time to max plasma concentration.

TABLE 9A (2) (Footnotes at the end of table)

DRUG	REFERENCE DOSE/ROUTE	PREG RISK	FOOD EFFECT (PO)	ORAL %AB	PEAK SERUM LEVEL (μg/mL)	PROTEIN BINDING (%)	VOL OF DISTRIB (Vd)	AVER SERUM T½ hrs	BILE PEN (%)³	CSF/ BLOOD (%)	CSF PEN⁵	AUC (μg*hr/mL)	Tmax (hr)
CEPHALOSPORINS—2nd Generation													
Cefaclor	500 mg po	B	Cap/susp ± food	93	13 (SD)	22-25	0.33 L/kg V/F	0.8	≥60			20.5	0.5-1.0
Cefaclor-ER	500 mg po	B	Tab + food		8.4 (SD)	22-25		0.8	≥60			18.1	2.5
Cefotetan	1 gm IV	B			158 (SD)	78-91	10.3 L	4.2	2-21			504	
Cefoxitin	1 gm IV	B			110 (SD)	65-79	16.1 L Vss	0.8	280	3	No	25.7	
Cefprozil	500 mg po	B	Tab/susp ± food	95	10.5 (SD)	36	0.23 L/kg Vss/F	1.5				150	
Cefuroxime	1.5 gm IV	B			100 (SD)	33-50	0.19 L/kg Vss	1.5	35-80	17-88	Marginal	150	
Cefuroxime axetil	250 mg tabs po	B	Susp + food; Tab ± food	52	4.1 (SD)	50	0.66 L/kg V/F	1.5				12.9	2.5
CEPHALOSPORINS—3rd Generation													
Cefdinir	300 mg po	B	Cap/susp ± food	25	1.6 (SD)	60-70	0.35 L/kg V/F	1.7				7.1	2.9
Cefditoren pivoxil	400 mg po	B	Tab + food	16	4 (SD)	88	9.3 L Vss/F	1.6				20	1.5-3.0
Cefixime	400 mg tabs po	B	Tab/susp ± food	50	3-5 (SD)	65	0.93 L/kg V/F	3.1	800			25.8	4
Cefotaxime	1 gm IV	B			100	30-51	0.28 L/kg	1.5	15-75	10	Yes	70	
Cefpodoxime proxetil	200 mg po	B	Tab + food Susp ± food	46	2.3 (SD)	40	0.7 L/kg V/F	2.3	115			14.5	2-3
Ceftazidime	1 gm IV	B			69 (SD)	<10	0.24 L/kg Vss	1.9	13-54	20-40	Yes	127	
Ceftibuten	400 mg po	B	Cap/susp no food	80	15 (SD)	65	0.21 L/kg V/F	2.4				73.7	2.6
Ceftizoxime	1 gm IV	B			60 (SD)	30	0.34 L/kg	1.7	34-82			85	
Ceftriaxone	1 gm IV	B			150 (SD), 172-204 (SS)	85-95	5.8-13.5 L	8	200-500	8-16	Yes	1006	
CEPHALOSPORIN—4th Generation and Anti-MRSA													
Cefepime	2 gm IV	B			164 (SD)	20	18 L Vss	2.0	10-20	10	Yes	284.8	
Ceftaroline	600 mg IV	B			21.3	20	20.3 Vss	2.7				56.3	
Ceftobiprole^plus	500 mg IV	B			33-34.2 (SD)	16	18 L Vss	2.9-3.3				116	
CARBAPENEMS													
Doripenem	500 mg IV	B			23	8.1	16.8 L Vss	1	117 (0-611)			36.3	
Ertapenem	1 gm IV	B			154	95	0.12 L Vss	4	10			572.1	
Imipenem	500 mg IV	C			40	15-25	0.27 L/kg	1	minimal	8.5	+⁶	42.2	
Meropenem	1 gm IV	B			49	2	0.29 L/kg	1	3-300	Approx. 2	+	72.5	

Preg. Risk: FDA risk categories: A = no risk. **B** = No risk- human. **C** = toxicity in animals - inadequate human studies. **D** = human risk, but benefit may outweigh risk. **X** = fetal abnormalities - risk > benefit. **Food Effect (PO dosing): + food** = take with food. **± food** = take with or without food. **Oral % AB** = % absorbed. **Peak Serum Level: SD** = after single dose. **SS** = steady state after multiple doses. **Volume of Distribution (Vd): V/F** = Vd/oral bioavailability. **Vss** = Vd at steady state/oral bioavailability. **CSF Penetration:** therapeutic efficacy comment based on dose, usual susceptibility or target organism & penetration into CSF. **AUC** = area under drug concentration curve; **24hr** = AUC 0-24; **Tmax** = time to max plasma concentration.

TABLE 9A (3) *(Footnotes at the end of table)*

DRUG	REFERENCE DOSE/ROUTE	PREG RISK	FOOD EFFECT (PO)[1]	ORAL %AB	PEAK SERUM LEVEL (µg/mL)	PROTEIN BINDING (%)	VOL OF DISTRIB (Vd)	AVER SERUM T½, hrs[2]	BILE PEN (%)[3]	CSF/BLOOD (%)	CSF PEN[4]	AUC (µg·hr/mL)	Tmax (hr)
MONOBACTAM													
Aztreonam	1 gm IV	B			90 (SD)	56	12.6 L Vss	2	115-405	3-52	±	271	
AMINOGLYCOSIDES													
Amikacin, gentamicin, kanamycin, tobramycin—see Table 10D, page 109, for dose & serum levels		D				0-10	0.26 L/kg	2.5	10-60	0-30	No; intrathecal dose: 5-10 mg		
Neomycin	po	D	Tab/soln ± food	<3	0								
FLUOROQUINOLONES[5]													
Ciprofloxacin	750 mg po q12h	C	± food	70	3.6 (SS)	20-40	2.4 L/kg	4	2800-4500			31.6 (24 hr)	1-2
	400 mg IV q12h	C	± food		4.6 (SS)	20-40		4	2800-4500	26	1 µg/mL inadequate for Strep. sp. (CID 31:1131, 2000)	25.4 (24 hr)	
	500 mg ER po q24h	C	± food		1.6 (SD)	20-40		6.0				8 (24 hr)	1.5
	1000 mg ER po q24h	C	± food		3.1 (SS)	20-40		6.3				16 (24 hr)	2.0
Gemifloxacin	320 mg po q24h	C	Tab ± food	71	1.6 (SS)	55-73	2-12 L/kg Vss/F	7				9 (24 hr)	0.5-2.0
Levofloxacin	500 mg po/IV q24h	C	Tab ± food	99	5.7/6.4 (SS)	24-38	74-112 L Vss	7		30-50		PO:47.5, IV 54.6 (24 hr)	PO: 1.3
	750 mg po/IV q24h	C	Tab ± food; Oral soln: no food	99	8.6/12.1 (SS)	24-38	244 L Vss	7				PO 90.7, IV 108 (24 hr)	PO: 1.6
Moxifloxacin	400 mg po/IV q24h	C	Tab ± food	89	4.2-4.6/4.5 (SS)	30-50	2.2 L/kg	10-14		>50	Yes (CID 49:1080, 2009)	PO 48, IV 38 (24 hr)	PO: 1-3
Ofloxacin	400 mg po/IV q24h	C	Tab ± food	98	4.6/6.2 (SS)	32	1-2.5 L/kg	7				PO 82.4, IV 87 (24 hr)	PO: 1-2
MACROLIDES, AZALIDES, LINCOSAMIDES, KETOLIDES													
Azithromycin	500 mg po	B	Tab/Susp: ± food	37	0.4 (SD)	7-51	31.1 L/kg Vss/F	68	High			4.3	2.5
	500 mg IV	B			3.6 (SD)	7-51		12/68				9.6 (24 hr, pre SS)	
Azithromycin-ER	2 gm po	B	Susp no food	≈30	0.8 (SD)	7-50		59	High			20	5.0
Clarithromycin	500 mg po q12h	C	Tab/Susp: ± food	50	3-4 (SS)	65-70	4 L/kg	5-7	7000			20 (24 hr)	2.0-2.5
	1000 mg ER po q24h	C	Tab + food	≈50	2-3 (SS)	65-70							5-8

Preg Risk: FDA risk categories: **A** = no risk. **B** = No risk - human studies. **C** = toxicity in animals - inadequate human studies. **D** = human risk, but benefit may outweigh risk. **X** = fetal abnormalities – risk > benefit. **Food Effect (PO dosing): + food** = take with food, **no food** = take without food, **± food** = take with or without food; **Oral % AB** = % absorbed; **Peak Serum Level: SD** = after single dose, **SS** = steady state after multiple doses; **Volume of Distribution (Vd): V/F** = Vd/oral bioavailability. **Vss** = Vd at steady state/oral bioavailability; **CSF Penetration:** therapeutic efficacy comment based on dose, usual susceptibility or target organism & penetration into CSF. **AUC** = area under drug concentration curve; **24hr** = AUC 0-24; **Tmax** = time to max plasma concentration.

TABLE 9A (4) *(Footnotes at the end of table)*

DRUG	REFERENCE DOSE/ROUTE	PREG RISK	FOOD EFFECT (PO)[1]	ORAL %AB	PEAK SERUM LEVEL (µg/mL)	PROTEIN BINDING (%)	VOL OF DISTRIB (Vd)	AVER SERUM T½, hrs	BILE PEN (%)[3]	CSF/BLOOD (%)	CSF PEN[e]	AUC (µg·hr/mL)	Tmax (hr)
MACROLIDES, AZALIDES, LINCOSAMIDES, KETOLIDES *(continued)*													
Erythromycin Oral (various)	500 mg po	B	Tab/Susp no food DR Caps ± food	18-45	0.1-2 (SD)	70-74	0.6 L/kg	2-4		2-13	No		Delayed Rel: 3
Lacto/glucep	500 mg IV	B				70-74		2-4					
Telithromycin	800 mg po q24h	C	Tab ± food	57	3-4 (SD) 2.3 (SS)	60-70	2.9 L/kg	10	7			12.5 (24 hr)	1
Clindamycin	150 mg po / 900 mg IV	B / B	Cap ± food	90 / 90	2.5 (SD) 14.1 (SS)	85-94 / 85-94	1.1 L/kg	2.4 / 2.4	250-300 / 250-300		No / No		0.75
MISCELLANEOUS ANTIBACTERIALS													
Chloramphenicol	1 gm po q6h	C	Cap ± food	High	18 (SS)	25-50	0.8 L/kg	4.1		45-89	Yes		
Colistin (Polymyxin E)	150 mg IV	C			5-7.5 (SD)	92	0.34 L/kg	2-3	0		No (AAC 53:4907, 2009)		
Daptomycin	4-6 mg/kg IV q24h	B			58-99 (SS)	92	0.1 L/kg Vss	8-9		0-8		494-632 (24 hr)	
Doxycycline	100 mg po	B	Tab/cap/susp ± food		1.5-2.1 (SD)	93	53-134 L Vss	18	200-3200		No (26%)	31.7	2
Fosfomycin	3 gm po	–	Sachet ± food		26 (SD)	<10	136.1 L Vss/F	5.7				150	
Fusidic acid[NUS]	500 mg po		Tab ± food	91	30 (SD)	95-99		5-15	100-200			315	2-4
Linezolid	600 mg po/IV q12h	C	Tab/susp ± food	100	15-20 (SS)	31	40-50 L Vss	5		60-70	Yes (AAC 50:3971, 2006)	PO 276/IV 179 (24 hr)	PO: 1.3
Metronidazole	500 mg po/IV q6h	B	ER tab no food, Tab/cap ± food		20-25 (SS)	20	0.6-0.85 L/kg	6-14	100	45-89		560 (24 hr)	Immed Rel: 1.6 ER: 6.8
Minocycline	200 mg po	D	Cap/tab ± food		2.0-3.5 (SD)	76	80-114 L Vss	16	200-3200		No	48.3 (24 hr)	2.1
Polymyxin B	2 mg/kg IV	C			1-8 (SD)	78-92	0.07-0.2 L/kg	4.3-6				31.8 (24 hr)	
Quinu-Dalfo	7.5 mg/kg IV q8h	B			3.2/8 (SS)		0.45/0.24 L/kg Vss	1.5					
Rifampin	600 mg po	C	Cap no food		4-32 (SD)	80	0.65 L/kg Vss	2-5	10,000			58	
Rifaximin	200 mg po	C	Tab ± food	<0.4	0.004-0.01 (SD)								1.5-2
Tetracycline	250 mg po	D	Cap no food		1.5-2.2 (SD)		1.3 L/kg	6-12	200-3200		No (7%)	30 (24 hr)	2-4
Telavancin	10 mg/kg q24h	C			108 (SS)	90	0.13 L/kg	8.1	Low			780 (24 hr)	

Preg Risk: FDA risk categories: **A** = no risk, **B** = No risk – human studies, **C** = toxicity in animals – inadequate human studies, **D** = human risk, but benefit may outweigh risk, **X** = fetal abnormalities – risk > benefit. **Food Effect (PO dosing):** + **food** = take with food, **no food** = take without food, ± **food** = take with or without food. **Oral % AB** = % absorbed; **Peak Serum Level:** **SD** = after single dose, **SS** = steady state after multiple doses; **Volume of Distribution (Vd): V/F** = Vd/oral bioavailability, **Vss** = Vd at steady state/oral bioavailability, **Vss/F** = Vd at steady state; **CSF Penetration:** therapeutic efficacy comment based on dose; usual susceptibility of target organism & penetration into CSF; **AUC** = area under drug concentration curve; **24hr** = AUC 0-24; **Tmax** = time to max plasma concentration.

TABLE 9A (5) *(Footnotes at the end of table)*

DRUG	REFERENCE DOSE/ROUTE	PREG RISK	FOOD EFFECT (PO)[1]	ORAL %AB	PEAK SERUM LEVEL (μg/mL)	PROTEIN BINDING (%)	VOL OF DISTRIB (Vd)	AVER SERUM T½, hrs	BILE PEN (%)[2]	CSF/BLOOD (%)[3]	CSF PEN[4]	AUC (μg*hr/mL)	Tmax (hr)
MISCELLANEOUS ANTIBACTERIALS *(continued)*													
Tigecycline	50 mg IV q12h	D			0.63 (SS)	71-89	7-9 L/kg	42	138		No	4.7 (24 hr)	
Trimethoprim (TMP)	100 mg po	C	Tab ± food	80	1 (SD)		100-120 V/F	8-15					1-4
TMP-SMX-DS	160/800 mg po q12h / 160/800 mg IV q8h	C	Tab/susp ± food	85	1-2/40-60 (SS) / 9/105 (SS)		TM: 100-120 L / SM: 12-18 L		100-200 / 40-70	50/40			TMP PO: 1-4 / SMX IV: 1-4
Vancomycin	1 gm IV q12h	C			20-50 (SS)	<10-55	0.7 L/kg	4-6	50	7-14			
ANTIFUNGALS													
Amphotericin B:													
Standard	0.4-0.7 mg/kg IV	B			0.5-3.5 (SS)		4 L/kg	24		0	No	17	
Lipid (ABLC)	5 mg/kg IV	B			1-2.5 (SS)		131 L/kg	173				14 (24 hr)	
Cholesteryl complex	4 mg/kg IV	B			2.9 (SS)		4.3 L/kg	39				36 (24 hr)	
Liposomal	5 mg/kg IV	B			83 (SS)		0.1-0.4 L/kg Vss	6.8 ± 2.1			Yes	555 (24 hr)	PO: 1-2
Fluconazole	400 mg po/IV / 800 mg po/IV	B / D	Tab/susp ± food / Tab/susp ± food	90 / 90	6.7 (SD) / Approx. 14 (SD)	10	50 L V/F	20-50 / 20-50		50-94	Yes		
Itraconazole	200 mg po soln	C	Soln no food	Low	0.3-0.7 (SD)	99.8	796 L	35		0		29.3 (24 hr)	2.5 Hydroxy: 5.3
Ketoconazole	200 mg po	C	Tab ± food	75	1-4 (SD)	99	1.2 L/kg	6-9		<10	No	12	1-2
Posaconazole	200 mg po	C	Susp + food		0.2-1.0 (SD)	98-99	1774 L	20-66			Yes /JAC 56;745, 2005	15.1	3-5
Voriconazole	200 mg po q12h	D	Tab/susp no food	96	3 (SS)	58	4.6 L/kg Vss	6		22-100	Yes /CID 37;728, 2003	39.8 (24 hr)	1-2
Anidulafungin	200 mg IV x 1, then 100 mg IV q24h	C			7.2 (SS)	>99	30-50 L	26.5			No	112 (24 hr)	
Caspofungin	70 mg IV x 1, then 50 mg IV qd	C			9.9 (SD)	97	9.7 L Vss	9-11			No	87.3 (24 hr)	
Flucytosine	2.5 gm po	C	Cap ± food	78-90	30-40 (SD)	<20	0.6 L/kg	3-6		60-100	Yes		
Micafungin	150 mg IV q24h	C			16.4 (SS)	>99	0.39 L/kg	15-17			No	167 (24 hr)	2
ANTIMYCOBACTERIALS													
Bedaquiline	400 mg po qd	ND	Tab + food	ND	3.3 (Wk 2)	>99	~ 60x total body water Vss	24-30	ND	ND	No	22 (24hr)	5
Capreomycin	15 mg/kg IM	C		ND	25-35 (SD)	ND	0.4 L/kg	2-5	ND	<10	No	ND	1-2
Cycloserine	250 mg po	C	Cap, no food	70-90	4-8 (SD)	<20	0.47 L/kg	10	ND	54-79	Yes	110	1-2
Ethambutol	25 mg/kg po	Safe	Tab ± food	80	2-6 (SD)	10-30	6 L/kg/F	4	ND	10-50	No	29.6	2-4

Preg Risk: FDA risk categories: A = No risk, **B** = No risk - human studies, **C** = toxicity in animals - inadequate human studies, **D** = human risk, but benefit may outweigh risk, **X** = fetal abnormalities - risk > benefit. **Food Effect (PO dosing): + food** = take with food, **no food** = take without food, **± food** = take with or without food; **Oral % AB** = % absorbed; **SD** = after single dose, **SS** = steady state after multiple doses; **Volume of Distribution (Vd): V/F** = Vd/oral bioavailability; **Vss** = Vd at steady state/oral bioavailability; **Peak Serum Level: SD** = after single dose; **Oral bioavailability. CSF Penetration:** therapeutic efficacy comment based on dose, usual susceptibility of target organism & penetration into CSF; **24hr** = AUC 0-24; **Tmax** = time to max plasma concentration.

TABLE 9A (6) *(Footnotes at the end of table)*

DRUG	REFERENCE DOSE/ROUTE	PREG RISK	FOOD EFFECT (PO)[i]	ORAL %AB	PEAK SERUM LEVEL (µg/mL)	PROTEIN BINDING (%)	VOL OF DISTRIB (Vd)	AVER SERUM T½, hrs[2]	BILE PEN (%)[3]	CSF[4]/BLOOD (%)	CSF PEN[a]	AUC (µg*hr/mL)	Tmax (hr)
ANTIMYCOBACTERIALS *(continued)*													
Ethionamide	500 mg po	C	Tab ± food	90	2.2 (SD)	10-30	80 L	1.9	ND	∞100	Yes	10.3	1.5
Isoniazid	300 mg po	C	Tab/syrup no food	100	3-5 (SD)		0.6-1.2 L/kg	0.7-4	ND	Up to 90	Yes	20.1	1-2
Para-aminosalicylic acid (PAS)	4 gm po	C	Gran + food	ND	20 (SD)	50-73	0.9-1.4 L/kg (V/F)	0.75-1.0	ND	10-50	Marg	108	8
Pyrazinamide	20-25 mg/kg po	C	Tab ± food	95	30-50 (SD)	5-10		10-16		100	Yes	500	2
Rifabutin	300 mg po	B	Cap ± food	20	0.2-0.6 (SD)	85	9.3 L/kg (Vss)	32-67	300-500	30-70	ND	8.6	2.5-4.0
Rifampin	600 mg po	C	Cap no food	70-90	4-32 (SD)	80	0.65 L/kg Vss	2-5	10,000	7-56	Yes	58	1.5-2
Rifapentine	600 mg po q72h	C	Tab ± food	ND	15 (SS)	98	70 L	13-14	ND	ND	No: Intrathecal: 5-10 mg	320 over 72hrs	4.8
Streptomycin	1 gm IV	D			25-50 (SD)	0-10	0.26 L/kg	2.5	10-60	0-30			
ANTIPARASITICS													
Albendazole	400 mg po	C	Tab + food		0.5-1.6	70							Sulfoxide: 2-5
Artemether/Lumefantrine	4 tabs po: 80/480 mg	C	Tab + food		Art: 9 (SS), D-Art 1, Lum: 5.6-9 (not SS)			Art: 1.6, D-Art: 1.6, Lum: 101					Art: 1.5-2.0 Lum: 6-8
Atovaquone	750 mg po bid	C	Susp + food	47	24 (SS)	99.9	0.6 L/kg Vss	67		<1	No	801 (750 mg x1)	
Dapsone	100 mg po q24h	C	Tab ± food	100	1.1 (SS)		1.5 L/kg	10-50					
Ivermectin	12 mg po	C	Tab no food		0.05-0.08 (SD)		9.9 L/kg						4
Mefloquine	1.25 gm po	C	Tab + food		0.5-1.2 (SD)	98	20 L/kg	13-24 days					17
Miltefosine	50 mg po tid	X	Cap + food		31 (SD)	95		7-31 (long) AAC 52:2855, 2008					
Nitazoxanide	500 mg po tab	B	Tab/susp + food		9-10 (SD)	99						41.9 Tizoxanide	Tizoxanide: 1-4
Proguanil	100 mg	C	Tab + food	75	No data	75	1600-2000 L/F	96					
Pyrimethamine	25 mg po	C	Tab ± food	"High"	0.1-0.3 (SD)	87	3 L/kg						2-6
Praziquantel	20 mg per kg po	B	Tab ± food	80	0.2-2.0 (SD)		8000 L/F	0.8-1.5				1.51	1-3
Tinidazole	2 gm po	B	Tab + food	48	48 (SD)	12	50 L	13				902	1.6

Preg Risk: FDA risk categories: **A** = no risk; **B** = No risk - human studies, **C** = toxicity in animals - inadequate human studies, **D** = human risk, but benefit may outweigh risk; **X** = fetal abnormalities - risk > benefit; **Food Effect (PO dosing):** **+ food** = take with food, **no food** = take without food, **± food** = take with or without food; **Oral % AB** = % absorbed; **Peak Serum Level: SD** = after single dose, **SS** = steady state after multiple doses; **Volume of Distribution (Vd): V/F** = Vd/oral bioavailability, **Vss** = Vd at steady state, **Vss/F** = Vd at steady state/oral bioavailability; **CSF Penetration:** therapeutic efficacy comment based on dose, usual susceptibility of target organism & penetration into CSF; **AUC** = area under drug concentration curve; **24hr** = AUC 0-24; **Tmax** = time to max plasma concentration.

TABLE 9A (7) *(Footnotes at the end of table)*

89

DRUG	REFERENCE DOSE/ROUTE	PREG RISK	FOOD EFFECT (PO)[1]	ORAL %AB	PEAK SERUM LEVEL (µg/mL)	PROTEIN BINDING (%)	VOL OF DISTRIB (Vd)	AVER SERUM T½, hrs[2]	BILE PEN (%)[3]	CSF/BLOOD (%)	CSF PEN[4]	AUC (µg*hr/mL)	Tmax (hr)
ANTIVIRAL DRUGS– NOT HIV													
Acyclovir	400 mg po bid	B	Tab/cap/susp ± food	10–20	1.21 (SS)	9–33	0.7 L/kg	2.5–3.5				7.4 (24 hr)	
Adefovir	10 mg po	C	Tab ± food	59	0.02 (SD)	≤4	0.37 L/kg Vss	7.5				0.22	1.75
Boceprevir	800 mg po q8h	B	Cap + food		1.7 (SS)	75	772L (Vss/F)	3.4	ND	ND	ND	5.41 (8 hr)	
Cidofovir w/Probenecid	5 mg/kg IV	C			19.6 (SD)	<6	0.41 L/kg (VSS)	2.2	ND	0	No	40.8	1.1
Entecavir	0.5 mg po q24h	C	Tab/soln no food	100	4.2 ng/mL (SS)	13	>0.6 L/kg V/F	128–149				0.14	0.5–1.5
Famciclovir	500 mg po	B	Tab ± food	77	3–4 (SD)	<20	1.1 L/kg*	2–3	No			8.9 Penciclovir	Penciclovir: 0.9
Foscarnet	60 mg/kg IV	C			155 (SD)	4	0.46 L/kg	<1				2195 µM*hr	
Ganciclovir	5 mg/kg IV	C			8.3 (SD)	1–2	0.7 L/kg Vss	3.5	ND	ND	ND	24.5	
Oseltamivir	75 mg po bid	C	Cap/susp ± food	75	0.065/0.35* (SS)	3	23–26 L/kg Vss*	1–3	ND	ND	ND	5.4 (24 hr) Carboxylate	ND
Peramivir	600 mg IV	?			35–45 (SD)	<30	ND	7.7–20.8	ND	ND	ND	90–95	ND
Ribavirin	600 mg po	X	Tab/cap/soln + food	64	0.8 (SD)		2825 L V/F	44	ND	ND	ND	25.4	2
Rimantadine	100 mg po	C	Tab ± food		0.05–0.1 (SD)	25	17–19 L/kg	25				3.5	6
Telaprevir	750 mg po	B	Tab + food (high fat)		3.51 (SS)	59–76	252L (V/F)	4.0–4.7 (SD)	ND	ND	ND	22.3 (8 hr)	
Telbivudine	600 mg po q24h	B	Tab/soln ± food		3.7 (SS)	3.3	>0.6 L/kg V/F	40–49				26.1 (24 hr)	2
Valacyclovir	1000 mg po	B	Tab ± food	55	5.6 (SD)	13–18	0.7 L/kg	3				19.5 Acyclovir	
Valganciclovir	900 mg po q24h	C	Tab/soln + food	59	5.6 (SS)	1–2	0.7 L/kg	4				29.1 Ganciclovir	Ganciclovir: 1–3

Preg Risk: FDA risk categories: A = no risk, **B** = No risk – human studies, **C** = toxicity in animals - inadequate human studies, **D** = human risk, but benefit may outweigh risk, **X** = fetal abnormalities - risk > benefit; **Food Effect (PO dosing): + food** = take with food, **± food** = take with or without food, **no food** = take without food. **Oral %AB** = % absorbed; **Peak Serum Level: SD** = after single dose, **SS** = steady state after multiple doses; **Volume of Distribution (Vd): V/F** = Vd/oral bioavailability, **Vss** = Vd at steady state, **Vss/F** = Vd at steady state/oral bioavailability; **CSF Penetration:** therapeutic efficacy comment based on dose, usual susceptibility of target organism & penetration into CSF; **AUC** = area under drug concentration curve; **24hr** = AUC 0–24; **Tmax** = time to max plasma concentration.

TABLE 9A (8) (Footnotes at the end of table)

DRUG	REFERENCE DOSE/ROUTE	PREG RISK	FOOD EFFECT (PO Prep)	ORAL %AB	PEAK SERUM LEVEL (µg/mL)	PROT BIND (%)	VOL DISTRIB (Vd)	AVER SERUM T½, hrs²	INTRA CELL T½, HOURS	CSF/BLOOD (%)	CSF PEN⁶	AUC (µg*hr/mL)	Tmax (hr)
ANTI-HIV VIRAL DRUGS													
Abacavir (ABC)	600 mg po q24h	C	Tab/soln ± food	83	4.3 (SS)	50	0.86 L/kg	1.5	12-26	Low	No	12 (24 hr)	
Atazanavir (ATV)	400 mg po q24h	B	Cap + food	Good	2.3 (SS)	86	88.3 L/F	7		Intermed	?	22.3 (24 hr)	2.5
Darunavir (DRV)	(600 mg +100 mg RTV) bid	B	Tab + food	82	3.5 (SS)	95	2 L/kg	15		Intermed	?	116.8 (24 hr)	2.5-4.0
Delavirdine (DLV)	400 mg po tid	C	Tab ± food	85	19 ± 11(SS)	98		5.8				180 µM*hr	1
Didanosine (ddI)	400 mg EC² po	B	Cap no food	30-40	?	<5	308-363 L	1.4	25-40	Intermed	?	2.6	2
Efavirenz (EFV)	600 mg po q24h	D	Cap/tab no food	42	4.1 (SS)	99	252 L/F	52-76		Intermed	?	184 µM*hr (24 hr)	3-5
Elvitegravir (with cobicistat, TDF and FTC, as Stribild)	150 mg	B	Tab + Food		1.7	98-99		12.9				23	4
Emtricitabine (FTC)	200 mg po q24h	B	Cap/soln ± food	93	1.8 (SS)	<4		10	39	Intermed	?	10 (24 hr)	1-2
Enfuvirtide (ENF)	90 mg sc bid	B		84	5 (SS)	92	5.5 L	4				97.4 (24 hr)	
Etravirine (ETR)	200 mg po bid	B	Tab + food	No data	0.3 (SS)	99.9		41	No data	Intermed	?	9 (24 hr)	2.5-4.0
Fosamprenavir (FPV)	(700 mg po+ 100 mg RTV) bid	C	Boosted ped susp + food Adult susp no food	65	6 (SS)	90		7.7		Intermed	?	79.2 (24 hr)	2.5
Indinavir (IDV)	800 mg po tid	C	Boosted cap + food, Cap alone no food	65	9 (SS)	60	1.3 L/kg	1.2-2		High	Yes	92.1 µM*hr (24 hr)	0.8
Lamivudine (3TC)	300 mg po	C	Tab/soln ± food	86	2.6 (SS)	<36		5-7	18-22	Intermed	?	11	
Lopinavir/RTV (LPV/r)	400 mg po bid	C	Soln ± food	98-99	9.6 (SS)	98-99		5-6 (LPV)		Intermed	?	186 LPV	LPV: 4
Maraviroc (MVC)	300 mg po bid	B	Tab ± food	33	0.3-0.9 (SS)	76	194 L	14-18		Intermed	?	3 (24 hr)	0.5-4.0
Nelfinavir (NFV)	1250 mg po bid	B	Tab/powd + food	20-80	3-4 (SS)	98	2-7 L/kg V/F	3.5-5		Low	No	53 (24 hr)	
Nevirapine (NVP)	200 mg po bid	C	Tab/susp ± food	>90	2 (SD)	60	1.2 L/kg Vss/F	25-30		High	Yes	110 (24 hr)	
Raltegravir (RAL)	400 mg po bid	C	Tab ± food	?	5.4 (SS)	83	287 L Vss/F	9		Intermed	?	28.6 µM*hr (24 hr)	3
Rilpivirine	25 mg po	B	Tab + food	?	0.1-0.2 (SD)	99.7	152L	45-65	ND	Low	No	2.4 (24 hr)	
Ritonavir (RTV)	600 mg po bid	B	Cap/tab + food	65	11.2 (SS)	98-99	0.41 L/kg V/F	3-5		Low	No		Soln: 2-4
Saquinavir (SQV)	(1000 +100 RTV) mg po bid	B	Tab/cap + food	4	0.37 min (SS conc)	97	700 L Vss	1-2		Low	No	29.2 (24 hr)	

Preg Risk: FDA risk categories: **A** = no risk, **B** = No risk in animals - inadequate human studies, **C** = toxicity in animals - human studies, **D** = human risk, but benefit may outweigh risk, **X** = fetal abnormalities - risk > benefit. **Food Effect (PO dosing):** **+ food** = take with food, **no food** = take with or without food; ± **food** = take with or without food; **Oral % AB** = % absorbed; **Peak Serum Level; SD** = after single dose, **SS** = steady state after multiple doses; **V/F** = Vd/oral bioavailability, **Vss** = Vd at steady state/oral bioavailability; **CSF Penetration:** therapeutic efficacy comment based on dose, usual susceptibility of target organism & penetration into CSF; **24hr** = AUC 0-24; **Tmax** = time to max plasma concentration.

TABLE 9A (9) (Footnotes at the end of table)

DRUG	REFERENCE DOSE/ROUTE	PREG RISK	FOOD EFFECT (PO Prep)	ORAL %AB	PEAK SERUM LEVEL (μg/mL)	PROT BIND (%)	VOL DISTRIB (Vd)	AVER SERUM T½, hrs²	INTRA CELL T½, HOURS	CSF²/BLOOD (%)	CSF PEN⁶	AUC (μg*hr/mL)	Tmax (hr)
ANTI-HIV VIRAL DRUGS (continued)													
Stavudine (d4T)	40 mg bid	C	Cap/soln ± food	86	0.54 (SS)	<5	46L	1	7.5			2.6 (24 hr)	1
Tenofovir (TDF)	300 mg po	B	Tab ± food	25	0.3 (SD)	<1-7	1.3 L/kg Vss	17	>60	Low	No	2.3	1
Tipranavir (TPV)	(500 + 200 RTV) mg po bid	C	Cap/soln + food		47-57 (SS)	99.9	7.7-10 L	5.5-6		Low	No	1600 μM*hr (24 hr)	3
Zidovudine (ZDV)	300 mg po	C	Tab/cap/syrup ± food	60	1-2	<38	1.6 L/kg	0.5-3	11	High	Yes	2.1	0.5-1.5

1   Food decreases rate and/or extent of absorption. For adult oral preps; not applicable for peds suspensions.

2   Assumes CrCl >80 mL per min.

3   Peak concentration in bile/peak concentration in serum x 100. If blank, no data.

4   CSF levels with inflammation

5   Judgment based on drug dose & organism susceptibility. CSF concentration ideally ≥10 above MIC.

6   Concern over seizure potential; see Table 10B.

7   Take all po FQs 2-4 hours before sucralfate or any multivalent cations: Ca^{++}, Fe^{++}, Zn^{++}

8   Given with atovaquone as Malarone for malaria prophylaxis.

9   Oseltamivir/oseltamivir carboxylate.

10 EC = enteric coated.

Preg Risk: FDA risk categories: **A** = no risk, **B** = No risk – human studies, **C** = toxicity in animals - inadequate human studies, **D** = human risk, but benefit may outweigh risk. **X** = fetal abnormalities - risk > benefit. **Food Effect (PO dosing):** ± **food** = take with or without food; **no food** = take without food; + **food** = take with food. **Oral % AB** = % absorbed; **Peak Serum Level:** **SD** = after single dose, **SS** = steady state after multiple doses; **Volume of Distribution (Vd):** **V/F** = Vd/oral bioavailability. **Vss** = Vd at steady state/oral bioavailability, **Vss/F** = Vd at steady state & penetration into CSF. **AUC** = area under drug concentration curve; **24hr** = AUC 0-24; **Tmax** = time to max plasma concentration. **CSF Penetration:** therapeutic efficacy comment based on dose, usual susceptibility or target organism & penetration into CSF.

TABLE 9B – PHARMACODYNAMICS OF ANTIBACTERIALS*

BACTERIAL KILLING/PERSISTENT EFFECT	DRUGS	THERAPY GOAL	PK/PD MEASUREMENT
Concentration-dependent/Prolonged persistent effect	Aminoglycosides, daptomycin, ketolides, quinolones, metro	High peak serum concentration	24-hr AUC/MIC
Time-dependent/No persistent effect	Penicillins, cephalosporins, carbapenems, monobactams	Long duration of exposure	Time above MIC
Time-dependent/Moderate to long persistent effect	Clindamycin, erythro/azithro/clarithro, linezolid, tetracyclines, vancomycin	Enhanced amount of drug	24-hr AUC/MIC

* Adapted from Craig, WA. IDC No. Amer 17:479, 2003 & Drusano, GL: CID 44:79, 2007

Cytochrome P450 isoenzyme terminology:
e.g., 3A4: 3 = family, A = subfamily, 4 = gene; PGP = an intestinal drug transporter; P = glycoprotein; UGT = uridine diphosphate glucuronosyltransferase

TABLE 9C - CYTOCHROME P450 INTERACTIONS OF ANTIMICROBIALS

DRUG	Substrate	Cytochrome P450 interactions Inhibits	Induces
Antibacterials			
Azithromycin (all)		PGP (weak)	
Chloramphenicol		2C19, 3A4	
Ciprofloxacin (all)		1A2, 3A4 (minor)	
Clarithromycin (all)	3A4	3A4, PGP	
Erythromycin (all)	3A4, PGP	3A4, PGP	
Metronidazole		2C9	
Nafcillin			2C9 (?), 3A4
Quinu-Dalfo		Quinu: 3A4	
Rifampin	PGP		1A2, 2C9, 2C19, 2D6 (Weak), 3A4, PGP
Telithromycin		3A4, PGP	
TMP-SMX	SMX: 2C9 (major), 3A4	SMX: 2C9	
		TMP: 2C8	
Trimethoprim		2C8	
Antifungals			
Fluconazole (400 mg)	3A4 (minor), PGP	2C9, 2C19, 3A4, UGT	
Itraconazole	3A4, PGP	3A4, PGP	
Ketoconazole	3A4	3A4, PGP	
Posaconazole	PGP, UGT	3A4, PGP	
Terbinafine	2D6		
Voriconazole	2C9, 2C19, 3A4	2C9, 2C19 (major), 3A4	
Antimycobacterials (Also Rifampin, above)			
Bedaquiline	CYP3A4		
Ethionamide	3A4 (?)		
Isoniazid	2E1	2C19, 3A4	
Rifabutin	3A4		3A4, UGT
Rifapentine		2C9, 3A4	
Dapsone	3A4		

DRUG	Substrate	Cytochrome P450 interactions Inhibits	Induces
Antiparasitics			
Mefloquine	3A4, PGP	PGP	
Praziquantel	3A4		
Proguanil	2C19 (conversion to cycloguanil)		
Tinidazole	3A4		
Antiretrovirals			
Atazanavir	3A4	1A2, 2C9, 3A4	
Cobicistat	CYP3A4, CYP2D6	CYP3A4, CYP2D6, PGP, BCRP, OATP1B1, OATP1B3	
Darunavir	3A4	3A4	
Delavirdine	2D6, 3A4	2C9, 2C19, 3A4	2C19, 3A4
Efavirenz	2B6, 3A4	2B6, 2C9, 2C19	CYP2C9
Etravirine	CYP3A4, UGT		3A4
Fosamprenavir	2C9, 2C19, 3A4	2C19 (weak)	
Indinavir	3A4, PGP	3A4, PGP	
Lopinavir	3A4	3A4	
Maraviroc	3A4, PGP	2D6	
Nelfinavir	2C9, 3A4, PGP	3A4, PGP	
Nevirapine	2B6, 3A4		3A4
Raltegravir	UGT		3A4
Ritonavir	2D6, 3A4, PGP	2B6, 2C9, 2C19, 2D6, 3A4, PGP	1A2, 1A2 (?), 2C9 (?), PGP (?)
Saquinavir	3A4, PGP	3A4, PGP	3A4, PGP (weak)
Tipranavir	3A4, PGP	1A2, 2C9, 2C19, 2D6	

Refs: Hansten PD, Horn JR. The top 100 drug interactions: a guide to patient management 2012; E. Freeland (WA): H&H Publications; 2010; and package inserts.

TABLE 10A – ANTIBIOTIC DOSAGE* AND SIDE-EFFECTS

CLASS, AGENT, GENERIC NAME (TRADE NAME)	USUAL ADULT DOSAGE*	ADVERSE REACTIONS, COMMENTS (See Table 10B for Summary)
NATURAL PENICILLINS		**Allergic reactions a major issue.** 10% of all hospital admissions give history of pen allergy, but only 10% have allergic reaction if given penicillin. Why? Possible reasons: inaccurate history, waning immunity with age, aberrant
Benzathine penicillin G (Bicillin L-A)	600,000–1.2 million units IM q2–4 wks	response during viral illness. If given **Bicillin C-R IM (procaine Pen + benzathine Pen)** could be reaction to procaine. **Most serious reaction is immediate IgE-mediated anaphylaxis;** incidence only 0.05% but 5–10% fatal. Other
Penicillin G	Low: 600,000–1.2 million units IM per day High: ≥20 million units IV q24h(=12 gm) div q4h	IgE-mediated reactions: urticaria, angioedema, laryngeal edema, bronchospasm, abdominal pain with emesis, or hypotension. All occur within 1 hr of rx. Can form antibody against either the beta-lactam ring or the R-group side chain. **Morbilliform rash after 72 hrs is not IgE-mediated and not serious.**
Penicillin V (250 & 500 mg caps)	0.25–0.5 gm po bid, tid, qid before meals & at bedtime. Pen V preferred over Pen G for oral therapy due to greater acid stability	**Serious late allergic reactions:** Coombs-positive hemolytic anemia, neutropenia, thrombocytopenia, serum sickness, interstitial nephritis, hepatitis, eosinophilia, drug fever. **Cross-allergy to cephalosporins and carbapenems** varies from 0–11%. One factor is similarity, or lack of similarity, of side chains. **For pen desensitization,** see Table 7. For skin testing, suggest referral to allergist. High CSF concentrations cause seizures. Reduce dosage with renal impairment, see Table 17. Allergy refs: AJM 121:572, 2008; NEJM 354:601, 2006.
PENICILLINASE-RESISTANT PENICILLINS		Blood levels ~2 times greater than cloxacillin so preferred for po therapy. Acute hemorrhagic cystitis reported.
Dicloxacillin (Dynapen) (250 & 500 mg caps)	0.125–0.5 gm po q6h before meals	Acute abdominal pain with GI bleeding without antibiotic-associated colitis also reported.
Flucloxacillin[NUS] (Floxapen, Lutropin, Staphcil)	0.25–0.5 gm po q6h 1–2 gm IV q4h	Cholestatic hepatitis occurs in 1/15,000 exposures; more frequently in age > 55 yrs, females and therapy > 2 wks duration. Can appear wks after end of therapy and take wks to resolve (JAC 66:1431, 2011). **Recommendation: use only in severe infection.**
Nafcillin (Unipen, Nafcil)	1–2 gm IV/IM q4-h. Due to > 90% protein binding, need 12 gm/day for bacteremia.	Extravasation can result in tissue necrosis. With dosages of 200–300 mg per kg per day hypokalemia may occur. **Reversible neutropenia (over 10% with ≥21-day rx, occasionally WBC <1000 per mm³).**
Oxacillin (Prostaphlin)	1–2 gm IV/IM q4-h. Due to > 90% protein binding, need 12 gm/day for bacteremia	**Hepatic dysfunction with ≥12 gm per day.** LFTs usually ↑ 2–24 days after start of rx, reversible. In children, more rash and liver toxicity with oxacillin as compared to nafcillin (CID 34:50, 2002).
AMINOPENICILLINS		
Amoxicillin (Amoxil, Polymox)	250 mg–1 gm po tid	IV available in U.K. & Europe. IV amoxicillin rapidly converted to ampicillin. Rash with infectious mono– see Ampicillin.
Amoxicillin extended release (Moxatag)	One 775 mg tab po once daily	Increased risk of cross-allergenicity with oral cephalosporins with identical side-chains: cefadroxil, cefprozil. Allergic reactions, C. difficile associated diarrhea, false positive test for urine glucose with clinitest.
Amoxicillin-clavulanate (Augmentin) AM-CL extra-strength peds suspension (ES-600) AM-CL-ER—extended release adult tabs	See Comment for adult products **Peds: Extra-Strength susp: 600/42.9 per 5 mL.** Dose: 90/6.4 mg/kg div bid. For adult formulations, see Comments IV amox-clav available in Europe	With bid regimen, less clavulanate & less diarrhea. In pts with immediate allergic reaction to AM-CL, ⅓ due to Clav component (J Allergy Clin Immunol 125:502, 2010). Positive blood tests for 1,3-beta D-glucan with IV AM-CL (NEJM 354:2834, 2006). Hepatic dysfunction, usually cholestatic jaundice. AM-CL causes 13–23% of drug-induced liver injury. Onset delayed. Usually mild; rare liver failure (JAC 66:1431, 2011). **Comparison adult Augmentin dosage regimens:** Augmentin 500/125 1 tab po tid Augmentin 875/125 1 tab po bid Augmentin-XR 1000/62.5 2 tabs po bid
Ampicillin (Principen) (250 & 500 mg caps)	0.25–0.5 gm po q6h. 50–200 mg/kg IV/day.	A maculopapular rash occurs (not urticarial), **not true penicillin allergy,** in 65–100% pts with infectious mono, 90% with chronic lymphocytic leukemia, and 15–20% in pts taking allopurinol. Increased risk of true cross-allergenicity with oral cephalosporins with identical side chains: cefaclor, cefprozil, cephalexin, loracarbef. EBV-associated rash does not indicate true penicillin allergy; no rash when challenged.

* NOTE: all dosage recommendations are for adults (unless otherwise indicated) & assume normal renal function.
(See page 2 for abbreviations)

TABLE 10A (2)

CLASS, AGENT, GENERIC NAME (TRADE NAME)	USUAL ADULT DOSAGE*	ADVERSE REACTIONS, COMMENTS (See Table 10B for Summary)
AMINOPENICILLINS (continued)		
Ampicillin-sulbactam (Unasyn)	1.5–3 gm IV q6h; for Acinetobacter: 3 gm (Amp 2 gm/Sulb 1 gm) IV q4h	Supplied in vials: ampicillin 1 gm, sulbactam 0.5 gm or amp 2 gm, sulbactam 1 gm. AM-SB is not active vs pseudomonas. Total daily dose sulbactam ≤4 gm; increasing resistance of aerobic gram-negative bacilli. Sulbactam doses up to 9-12 gm/day evaluated (J Infect 56:432, 2008). See also CID 56:132-133, 2010.
EXTENDED SPECTRUM PENICILLINS. NOTE: Platelet dysfunction may occur with any of the antipseudomonal penicillins, esp. in renal failure patients.		
Piperacillin (Pipracil) (Hard to find PIP alone; usually PIP-TZ)	3–4 gm IV q4–6h (max 24 gm/day). For urinary tract infection: 3 gm IV q4h. See **Comment**	1.85 mEq Na⁺ per gm. See PIP-TZ comment on extended infusion. For P. aeruginosa infections: 3 gm IV q4h.
ANTIPSEUDOMONAL PENICILLINS		
Piperacillin-tazobactam (PIP-TZ) (Zosyn) Prolonged infusion dosing, see **Comment** and Table 10E.	**Formulations:** PIP-TZ: 2/0.25 gm (2.25 gm) PIP-TZ: 3/0.375 gm (3.375 gm) PIP-TZ: 4/0.5 gm (4.5 gm) **Standard Dose (no P. aeruginosa):** 3.375 gm IV q6h or 4.5 gm IV q8h **Standard Dose for P. aeruginosa:** 3.375 gm IV q4h or 4.5 gm IV q6h	Based on PK/PD studies, there is emerging evidence in support of **prolonged infusion** of PIP-TZ. Initial 'loading' dose of 4.5 gm over 30min then 4 hrs later start 3.375 gm IV over 4 hrs q 8h (CrCl>20) or 3.375 gm IV over 4 hrs q12h (CrCl<20) (CID 44:357, 2007; AAC 54:460, 2010). • Cystic fibrosis + P. aeruginosa infection: 360-450 mg/kg/day div q4-6h • P. aeruginosa pneumonia: Combine PIP-TZ with CIP or Tobra. Misc: Assoc false-pos galactomannan test for aspergillus, thrombocytopenia 2.79 mEq Na⁺ per gram of PIP.
Temocillin⁻ᵘˢ	1-2 gm IV q12h.	Semi-synthetic penicillin highly resistant to wide range of beta-lactamases; used to treat beta-lactamase producing aerobic gram-negative bacilli. Source: www.eumedica.be
Ticarcillin disodium (Ticar)	3 gm IV q4-6h.	Coagulation abnormalities common with large doses, interferes with platelet function, ↑ bleeding times; may be clinically significant in pts with renal failure. (4.5 mEq Na⁺ per gm)
Ticarcillin-clavulanate (Timentin)	3.1 gm IV q4-6h.	Supplied in vials: ticarcillin 3 gm, clavulanate 0.1 gm per vial. 4.5-5 mEq Na⁺ per gm. Diarrhea due to clavulanate. Rare reversible cholestatic hepatitis secondary to clavulanate (AYM 156:1327, 1996). In vitro activity vs. Stenotrophomonas maltophilia.
CARBAPENEMS. Review: AAC 55:4943, 2011. **NOTE: Cross allergenicity: In studies of pts with history of Pen-allergy but no confirmatory skin testing, 0-11% had allergic reactions with cephalosporin therapy** (JAC 54:1155, 2004). **In better studies, pts with positive skin tests for Pen allergy were given Carbapenem: no reaction in 99%.** (Allergy 63:237, 2008; NEJM 354:2835, 2006; J Allergy Clin Immunol 124:167, 2009). **Increasing reports of carbapenemase-producing aerobic gram-negative bacilli** (JCM 48:1019, 2010; Ln ID 11:381, 2011; CID 53:49 & 60, 2011).		
Doripenem (Doribax) Ref: CID 49:291, 2009	**500 mg IV q8h (1-hr infusion).** For prolonged infusion, see Table 10E, page 110. Do not use for pneumonia	Most common adverse reactions (≥5%): Headache, nausea, diarrhea, rash & phlebitis. Seizure reported in post-marketing surveillance. Lower serum valproic acid levels. Adjust dose if renal impairment. Somewhat more stable in solution than IMP or MER (JAC 65:1023, 2010, CID 49:291, 2009). FDA safety announcement (01/05/12): Trial of Dori for the treatment of VAP stopped early due to safety concerns. Compared to IMP, patients treated with Dori were observed to have excess mortality and poorer cure rate. **NOTE: Dori is not approved to treat any type of pneumonia; Dori is not approved for doses greater than 500 mg q8h.**
Ertapenem (Invanz)	1 gm IV/IM q24h.	**Lidocaine** diluent for IM use; ask about lidocaine allergy. Standard dosage may be inadequate in obesity (BMI ≥40). Reports of DRESS (drug rash eosinophilia systemic symptoms) Syndrome. Visual hallucinations reported (NZ Med J 122:78, 2009). No predictable activity vs. P. aeruginosa.
Imipenem + cilastatin (Primaxin) Ref: JAC 58:916, 2006	**0.5 gm IV q6h; for P. aeruginosa: 1 gm q6-8h** (see **Comment**)	Most seizure potential of carbapenems, increased dosage in renal failure (esp. elderly) & with CNS disorders. Review of IMP for infection due to P. aeruginosa, increase dosage to 1 gm IV q6-8h & use another agent (CID 49:1881, 2005). Seizure comment, see footnote¹, Table 10B, page 105. Cilastatin blocks enzymatic degradation of imipenem in lumen of renal proximal tubule & also prevents tubular toxicity.

(See page 2 for abbreviations) *NOTE: all dosage recommendations are for adults (unless otherwise indicated) & assume normal renal function.

TABLE 10A (3)

CLASS, AGENT, GENERIC NAME (TRADE NAME)	USUAL ADULT DOSAGE*	ADVERSE REACTIONS, COMMENTS (See Table 10B for Summary)
CARBAPENEMS (continued)		
Meropenem (Merrem)	**0.5–1 gm IV q8h. Up to 2 gm IV q8h for meningitis.** Prolonged infusion in critically ill: If CrCl ≥ 50: 2 gm q8h (over 3hr) q8h. If CrCl 30-49: 1 gm (over 3hr) q8h. If CrCl 10-29: 1 gm (over 3hr) q12h (Inten Care Med 37:632, 2011).	For seizure incidence comment, see Table 10B, page 105. Comments: Does not require a dehydropeptidase inhibitor (cilastatin). Activity vs aerobic gm-neg, slightly ↑ over IMP. activity vs staph & strep slightly ↓, anaerobes: B. ovatus, B. distasonis more resistant to meropenem.
MONOBACTAMS		
Aztreonam (Azactam)	**1 gm q8h–2 gm IV q6h.**	Can be used in pts with allergy to penicillins/cephalosporins. Animal data and a letter raise concern about cross-reactivity with ceftazidime (Infect Dis 7(Suppl4):S613, 1986; Allergy 53:624, 1998); **side-chains of aztreonam and ceftazidime are identical.**
Aztreonam for Inhalation (Cayston)	75 mg inhaled tid x 28 days. Use bronchodilator before each inhalation.	Improves respiratory symptoms in CF pts colonized with P. aeruginosa. Alternative to inhaled Tobra. AEs: bronchospasm, cough, wheezing. SE far, no emergence of other resistant pathogens. Ref: Chest 135:1223, 2009.
CEPHALOSPORINS (1st parenteral, then oral drugs). NOTE: Prospective data demonstrate correlation between use of cephalosporins (esp. 3rd generation) and ↑ risk of C. difficile toxin-induced diarrhea. May also ↑ risk of colonization with vancomycin-resistant enterococci. See Oral Cephalosporins, page 96, for important note on cross-allergenicity.		
1st Generation, Parenteral		
Cefazolin (Ancef, Kefzol)	**1–1.5 gm IV/IM q8h, occasionally 2 gm IV q8h for serious infections, e.g., MSSA bacteremia (max. dose 12 gm/day).**	Do not use into lateral ventricles—seizures! No activity vs. community-associated MRSA. Rare failures (if cefazolin treatment of MSSA bacteremia due to hyperproduction of type A beta lactamase (AAC 53:3437, 2009).
2nd Generation, Parenteral (Cephamycins): More active in vitro vs. ESBL-producing aerobic gram-negative bacilli. Do not use as there are no clinical data for efficacy.		
Cefotetan (Cefotan)	**1–3 gm IV/IM q12h. (max. dose not > 6 gm q24h).**	Disadvantages: ↑ resistance of B. fragilis, B. ovatus, B. distasonis (most common in pelvic infections); do not use for intra-abdominal infections. Methylthiotetrazole (MTT) side chain can inhibit vitamin K activation. Avoid alcohol-disulfiram reaction.
Cefoxitin (Mefoxin)	**1 gm q8h–2 gm IV/IM q6-8h.**	↑ Increasing resistance of B. fragilis isolates.
Cefuroxime (Kefurox, Ceftin, Zinacef)	**0.75–1.5 gm IV/IM q8h.**	Improved activity against H. influenzae compared with 1st generation cephalosporins. See Cefuroxime axetil for oral preparation.
3rd Generation, Parenteral—Use correlates with incidence of C. difficile toxin diarrhea: all are inactivated by ESBLs and amp C cephalosporinase from aerobic gram-negative bacilli.		
Cefoperazone-sulbactam[NUS] (Sulperazon)	Usual dose (Cefoperazone comp) 1–2 gm IV q12h; if larger doses, do not exceed 4 gm/day of sulbactam	In SE Asia & elsewhere, used to treat intra-abdominal, biliary, & gyn. infections. Other uses due to broad spectrum of activity. Possible clotting problem due to side-chain.
Cefotaxime (Claforan)	**1 gm q8-12h to 2 gm IV q4h.**	Maximum daily dose: 12 gm; can give as 4 gm IV q8h. Similar to ceftriaxone but requires multiple daily doses. Often used in healthcare-associated infections, where P. aeruginosa is a consideration. Use may result in ↑ incidence of C. difficile-assoc. diarrhea and/or selection of vancomycin-resistant E. faecium. Risk of cross-allergenicity with aztreonam (same side chain).
Ceftazidime (Fortaz, Tazicef)	**Usual dose: 1–2 gm IV/IM q8-12h.** Prolonged infusion dosing: initial dose: 15 mg/kg over 30 min, then immediately begin: If CrCl > 50: 6 gm (over 24 hr) daily. If CrCl 31-50: 4 gm (over 24 hr) daily. If CrCl 10-30: 2 gm (over 24 hr) daily (AAC 49:3550, 2005; Infect 37:418, 2009).	
Ceftizoxime (Cefizox)	**From 1-2 gm IV q8-12h up to 2 gm IV q4h.**	Maximum daily dose: 12 gm; can give as 4 gm IV q8h. "Pseudocholelithiasis" 2° to sludge in gallbladder by ultrasound (50%), symptomatic (9%) (NEJM 322:1821, 1990). More likely with > 2 gm per day with pt on total parenteral nutrition and not eating (AnIM 115:712, 1991). Clinical significance still unclear but has led to cholecystectomy (JID 177:356, 1995) and gallstone pancreatitis (Ln 17:662, 1998). In pilot study, 2 gm once daily by continuous infusion superior to 2 gm bolus once daily (AAC 59:285, 2007). For Ceftriaxone Desensitization, see Table 7, page 80.
Ceftriaxone (Rocephin)	**1-2 gm once daily.** Commonly used IV dosage in adults: 1-2 gm once daily. Purulent meningitis: 2 gm q12h. Can give IM in 1% lidocaine.	

* NOTE: all dosage recommendations are for adults (unless otherwise indicated) & assume normal renal function.

(See page 2 for abbreviations)

TABLE 10A (4)

CLASS, AGENT, GENERIC NAME (TRADE NAME)	USUAL ADULT DOSAGE*	ADVERSE REACTIONS, COMMENTS (See Table 10B for Summary)
CEPHALOSPORINS (1st parenteral, then oral drugs) (continued)		
Other Generation, Parenteral: All are substrates for ESBLs & ampC cephalosporinase		**Cefepime penetrates to target faster than other cephalosporins.**
Cefepime (Maxipime)	Usual dose: 1-2 gm IV q8-12h. **Prolonged infusion dosing:** Initially: 2 gm IV over 30 min, then immediately begin If CrCl > 60: 6 gm (over 24 hr) daily If CrCl 30-60: 4 gm (over 24 hr) daily If CrCl 11-29: 2 gm (over 24 hr) daily	Active vs P. aeruginosa and many enteric gm-neg bacilli. Enterobacter, Serratia, C. freundii resistant to ceftazidime, cefotaxime. More active vs MSSA than 3rd generation cephalosporins. Neutropenia after 14 days rx (Scand J Infect Dis 42:156, 2010). Prolonged infusion: JAC 57:1017, 2006; Am J Health Syst Pharm 68:319, 2011). Case of red man syndrome reported (AAC 56:6387, 2012).
Cefpirome^a,b (HR 810)	1-2 gm IV q12h	Similar to cefepime. ↑ activity vs enterobacteriaceae. P. aeruginosa, Gm + organisms. Anaerobes: less active than cefoxitin, more than 1st and 2nd generations.
Ceftaroline fosamil (Teflaro)	600 mg IV q12h (1-hr infusion)	Active vs MSSA (not inactivated by AmpC & ESBL enzymes. Approved for MRSA skin and skin structure infections, but not for other MRSA infections. Active in vitro vs. VISA, VRSA. Refs: CID 52:1156, 2011; Med Lett 53:5, 2011.
Ceftobiprole^a,b,c	0.5 gm IV q8h for mixed gm-neg & gm-pos infections. 0.5 gm IV q12h for gm-pos infections	Infuse over 2 hrs for q8h dosing, over 1 hr for q12h dosing. Associated with caramel-like taste disturbance. Active vs. MRSA. Ref.: Clin Microbiol Infections 13(Suppl 2):17 & 25, 2007.
		Cross-Allergenicity: Patients with a history of IgE-mediated allergic reactions to penicillin (e.g., bronchospasm anaphylaxis, angioneurotic edema, immediate urticaria) should not receive a cephalosporin. If the history is a cephalosporin side chain determines cross-reactivity to penicillin, available data suggest a 5-10% risk of rash in such patients. • In pts with history of Pen 'reaction' and no skin testing, 0.2-8.4% react to a cephalosporin (Aller Asthma Proc 26:135, 2006). If positive Pen G skin test, only 2% given a cephalosporin will react. Can predict with cephalosporin skin testing. but not easily available (An N Engl J Med 141:16, 2004; AJM 125:572, 2008). • IgE antibodies against either ring structure or side chains: 80% pts lose IgE over 10 yrs post-reaction (J Aller Clin Immunol 103:918, 1999). Amox, Cefadroxil, Cefprozil have similar side chains; Amp, Cefaclor, Cephalexin, Cephedrine have similar side chains. • If Pen/Ceph skin testing not available or clinically no time, proceed with cephalosporin if history does not suggest IgE-mediated reaction, prior reaction more than 10 yrs ago or cephalosporin side chain differs from implicated Pen. • Any of the cephalosporins can result in **C. difficile toxin-mediated diarrhea/enterocolitis.** The reported frequency of nausea/vomiting and non-C. difficile toxin diarrhea is summarized in Table 10B. There are **few drug-specific adverse effects, e.g.:**
Oral Cephalosporins **1st Generation, Oral**		
Cefadroxil (Duricef) (500 mg caps, 1 gm tabs)	0.5–1 gm po q12h.	**Cefaclor:** Serum sickness-like reaction 0.1–0.5%—arthralgia, rash, erythema multiforme but no adenopathy, proteinuria (Ped Pharm & Therap 125:805, 1994). Appear due to mixture of drug biotransformation and genetic susceptibility.
Cephalexin (Keflex) (250 & 500 mg tabs)	0.25–1 gm po q6h (max 4 gm/day).	
2nd Generation, Oral		
Cefaclor (Ceclor, Ceclor CD) (250 & 500 mg caps)	0.25–0.5 gm po q8h.	**Cefdinir:** Drug-iron complex causes red stools in roughly 1% of pts.
Cefprozil (Cefzil) (250 & 500 mg tabs)	0.25–0.5 gm po q12h.	**Cefditoren pivoxil:** Hydrolysis yields pivalate. Pivalate absorbed (70%) & becomes pivaloyl/carnitine which is renally excreted; 39–63% ↓ **in serum carnitine concentrations.** Carnitine involved in fatty acid (FA) metabolism & FA transport into mitochondria. Effect transient & reversible. Contraindicated in patients with carnitine deficiency or those in whom inborn error of metabolism results in clinically significant carnitine deficiency. Also contains caseinate (milk protein): **avoid if milk allergy** (not same as lactose intolerance). Need gastric acid for optimal absorption.
Cefuroxime axetil po (Ceftin) (250 & 500 mg tabs)	0.125–0.5 gm po q12h.	
3rd Generation, Oral		
Cefdinir (Omnicef) (300 mg cap)	300 mg po q12h or 600 mg po q24h.	
Cefditoren pivoxil (Spectracef) (200 mg tab)	400 mg po bid.	
Cefixime pivoxil (Suprax) (400 mg tab)	0.4 gm po q12-24h.	
Cefpodoxime proxetil (Vantin) (100 & 200 mg tabs)	0.1–0.2 gm po q12h.	**Cefpodoxime:** There are rare reports of acute liver injury, bloody diarrhea, pulmonary infiltrates with eosinophilia.
Ceftibuten (Cedax) (400 mg tab)	0.4 gm po q24h.	**Cephalexin:** Can cause false-neg. urine dipstick test for leukocytes.

* NOTE: all dosage recommendations are for adults (unless otherwise indicated) & assume normal renal function.

(See page 2 for abbreviations)

TABLE 10A (5)

CLASS, AGENT, GENERIC NAME (TRADE NAME)	USUAL ADULT DOSAGE*	ADVERSE REACTIONS, COMMENTS (See Table 10B for Summary)
AMINOGLYCOSIDES AND RELATED ANTIBIOTICS—See Table 10D, page 109, and Table 17A, page 205		
GLYCOPEPTIDES, LIPOGLYCOPEPTIDES, LIPOPEPTIDES		
Teicoplanin^NUS (Targocid)	For septic arthritis—maintenance dose 12 mg/kg per day; S. aureus endocarditis— trough serum levels >20 mg/mL required (12 mg/kg q12h times 3 loading dose, then 12 mg/kg q24h).	Hypersensitivity: fever (at 3 mg/kg 2.2%, at 24 mg per kg 8.2%), skin reactions 2.4%. Marked ↓ platelets (high dose ≥15 mg per kg per day). Red neck syndrome less common than with vancomycin.
Telavancin (Vibativ) Lipoglycopeptide Ref: CID 49:1908, 2009. Med Lett 52(1,3):2010	10 mg/kg IV q24h if CrCl >50 mL/min. Infuse each dose over 1 hr. Adjust dose if wt ≥30% over IBW, see Table 10D.	Vanco treatment failure of MRSA bacteremia associated with Vanco trough concentration <15 µg/mL & MIC >1 µg/mL (CID 56:1536, 2013). Do pregnancy test before therapy. Adverse events: dysgeusia (taste) 33%, nausea 27%, vomiting 14%, headache (3.1%), foamy urine; ↑ creatinine (3.1%); flushing if infused rapidly. In clin trials, evidence or renal injury in 3% telavancin vs 1% vanco. renal injury reported in 1/3 of 21 complicated pts (Lancet ID 67:723, 2012).
Vancomycin (Vancocin) CID 49:325, 2009. Guidelines Ref. See Comments for po dose.	Initial doses based on actual wt, including for obese pts. Subsequent doses adjusted based on measured serum levels. For critically ill pts, give loading dose of 25-30 mg/kg IV then 15-20 µg/mL q8-12h. Target trough level is 15-20 µg/mL. For individual doses over 1 gm, infuse over 1.5-2 hrs. **Dosing for morbid obesity (BMI ≥40 kg/m²):** 30 mg/kg/day divided q8-12h—no dose over 2 gm. Infuse doses of 1 gm or more over 1.5-2 hrs. Check trough levels. Limit maximal single dose to 2 gm. Oral tabs for C. difficile: 125 mg po q24h. Generic drug now available	• MIC values vary with method used, hard to be sure: compare (JCM 49:269, 2011). • With MRSA Vanco MIC = 2 & 4 gm/day IV. AUC/MIC > 400 in 80% with est. risk of nephrotoxicity of 25%. With MIC = 1 & Vanco dose >3 gm/day IV, AUC/MIC > 400 in only 57% (nephrotoxicity risk 35%) (CID 52:969, 2011). • Higher Vanco doses assoc with nephrotoxicity, causal relation unproven: other factors: renal disease, other nephrotoxic drugs; shock/vasopressors, radiographic contrast (AAC 52:1330, 2008; AAC 55:3278, 2011; AJM 123:182e1, 2010). • With MIC >1 or 2 and renal insufficiency, consider other drugs active vs. MRSA: ceftaroline, daptomycin, linezolid, telavancin (regardless of MIC or AUC/MIC), consider other drugs active vs. MRSA: ceftaroline. **PO vanco for C. difficile colitis: 125 mg po q6h.** Commercial po formulation very expensive. Can compound po doses from IV formulation: 5 g. IV vanco + 47.5 mL sterile H₂O (2 gm stevia powder, 0.05 gm stevia powder, 40 mL glycerin and then enough cherry syrup to yield 100 mL. — 50 mg vanco/mL. Oral dose = 2.5 mL q6h po. **Intrathecal dose:** 5-10 mg/day (children & adults) to target CSF concentration of 10-20 mg/mL. **Nephrotoxicity:** with dosing at or above 4 gm/day (AAC 52:1330, 2008; see also CID 49:507, 2009). Concomitant hypertension or administration of aminoglycosides or loop diuretic are risk factors with continuous infusion (JAC 62:168, 2008). **Red Neck Syndrome:** not an allergic rxn but due to histamine release. Other adverse effects: rash, immune thrombocytopenia (NEJM 356:904, 2007), fever, neutropenia, initial report of ototoxicity, IgA bullous dermatitis (CID 38:442, 2004). **Obesity dosing:** Frequent under dosing (AJM 121:515, 2008). For OCL calculation for morbidly obese patient see Table 10D or Am J Health Sys Pharm 66:642, 2009.
		count (JAC 67:727, 2012).
Daptomycin (Cubicin) (Ref on resistance: CID 50:S10, 2010)	**Skin/soft tissue:** 4 mg per kg IV over 2 or 30 minutes q24h. **Bacteremia/right-sided endocarditis:** 6 mg per kg IV over 2 or 30 minutes q24h; up to 12 mg per kg q24h under study. Morbid obesity: base dose on total body weight (J Clin Pharm 45:48, 2005)	**Pneumonia:** Dapto failed to eradicate S. pneumo with a trend toward failure to eradicate S. aureus in trials of CAP (CID 46:1142, 2008). In animal models Dapto failed vs. S. pneumo but efficacious vs. S. aureus. Perhaps because Dapto inactivation by surfactant (JID 191:2149, 2005). In theory, less functional surfactant with necrotizing S. aureus pneumonia; S. pneumo rarely or never cause necrosis (NEJM 355:653, 2006). Disturbing case report of developed S. aureus pneumonia while on dapto (AAC 50:3245, 2006) and in pts given mean dose of 8 mg/kg/day (CID 49:177, 2009). **Dapto** well-tolerated in healthy volunteers at doses up to 12 mg/kg q24h x 14d (AAC 50:3245, 2006) and in pts (CID 50(Suppl 1):S10, 2011). Can occur de novo, after or during Dapto therapy and Nafcillin (CID 53:158, 2011). Concomitant Oxacillin restores Dapto activity (CID 53:158, 2011). **Potential muscle toxicity:** At 4 mg per kg per day, 1 CPK in 2.8% daptio pts & 1.8% comparator-treated pts. Risk increases if min ≥24 mg/mL (CID 53:158, 2011). Suggest weekly CPK. DC Dapto if CPK exceeds 10x normal level or if symptoms of myopathy and CPK >1,000 (5x ULN) (PI 2008, 2010). NOTE: Dapto in not ionically strongly ionized reagents (Hemosil, Recombiplastin, Hemoliance Recombiplastin), can falsely prolong PT & INR (Blood Coag Fibrinolysis 19:32, 2008). **Eosinophilic pneumonia** reported (CID 50:737, 2010; CID 50:e63, 2010).

---

* NOTE: all dosage recommendations are for adults (unless otherwise indicated) & assume normal renal function.

TABLE 10A (6)

CLASS, AGENT, GENERIC NAME (TRADE NAME)	USUAL ADULT DOSAGE*	ADVERSE REACTIONS, COMMENTS (See Table 10B for Summary)
CHLORAMPHENICOL, CLINDAMYCIN(S), ERYTHROMYCIN GROUP, KETOLIDES, OXAZOLIDINONES, QUINUPRISTIN-DALFOPRISTIN		
Chloramphenicol (Chloromycetin)	50-100 mg/kg/day po/IV div q6h (max 4 gm/day)	No oral drug distrib in U.S. Hematologic (↓ RBC—1/3 pts, aplastic anemia 1:21,600 courses). Gray baby syndrome in premature & newborn. Myelotoxid reactions, optic atrophy or neuropathy (very rare), digital paresthesias, minor disulfiram-like reactions.
Clindamycin (Cleocin)	0.15–0.45 gm po q6h. 600–900 mg IV/IM q8h.	Based on number of exposed pts, these drugs are the most frequent cause of **C. difficile toxin-mediated diarrhea.** In most severe form can cause pseudomembranous colitis/toxic megacolon. Available as caps, IV sol'n, topical (for acne) & intravaginal suppositories & cream. Used to inhibit synthesis of toxic shock syndrome toxins.
Lincomycin (Lincocin)	0.6 gm IV/IM q8h.	Risk of C. difficile colitis. Rarely used.
Erythromycin Group (Review drug interactions before use) Azithromycin (Zithromax) Azithromycin ER (Zmax)	**po preps:** Tabs 250 & 600 mg. Peds suspension: 100 & 200 mg per 5 mL. Adult ER suspension: 2 gm. Dose varies with indication, see Table 7. Acute otitis media (page 11), acute exac. chronic bronchitis (page 37), Comm-acq. pneumonia (pages 39–40), & sinusitis (page 50): IV: 0.5 gm per day.	**Motilin:** activates duodenal/jejunal receptors to initiate peristalsis. Erythro (E) and E esters activate motilin receptors and cause uncoordinated peristalsis with resultant anorexia, nausea or vomiting. Less binding and GI distress with azithromycin/clarithromycin. No peristalsis benefit. (JAC 39:307, 2007). Systemic erythro in 1st 2 weeks of life associated with **infantile hypertrophic pyloric stenosis** (J Ped 139:380, 2001). **Frequent drug-drug interactions:** see Table 22, page 217. Major concern is prolonged QT_c interval on EKG. **Prolonged QT_c:** Erythro, clarithro & azithro all increase risk of ventricular tachycardia via increase in QT_c interval. Can be congenital or acquired (NEJM 358:169, 2008). 5 days of azithro increased risk of cardiovascular death (hazard ratio 2.88) compared to amox: estimated 47 additional cardiovascular deaths per 1 million courses. (NEJM 366:1881, 2012).
Erythromycin Base and esters (Erythrocin) IV name: E. lactobionate Clarithromycin (Biaxin) or clarithro extended release (Biaxin XL)	0.25 gm q6h–0.5 gm po/IV q6h; 15–20 mg/kg up to 4 gm q24h. Infuse over 30+ min. 0.5 gm po q12h. Extended release: Two 0.5 gm tabs po per day.	**↑ risk QT_c >500 msec: Risk amplified by other drugs** (macrolides, antiarrhythmics, & drug-drug interactions (see FDA, page 700 for list). Prolonged QT_c can result in torsades de pointes (ventricular tachycardia) and/or cardiac arrest. Refs, CID 43:1603, 2006 & www.torsades.org. **Cholestatic hepatitis** in approx. 1:1000 adults (not children) given E estolate. **Transient reversible tinnitus or deafness** with 24 gm per day of erythro IV in pts with renal or hepatic impairment. Reversible sensorineural hearing loss with Azithro (J Otolaryngol 36:257, 2007). Dosages of oral erythro preparations expressed as base equivalents. With differences in absorption/biotransformation, variable amounts of erythro esters and erythro base have same free erythro serum level, e.g., 400 mg Erythro ethyl succinate is equivalent to 250 mg erythro estolate. Erythro gluceptate can exacerbate symptoms of myasthenia gravis. Approved for treatment of C. difficile toxin-mediated diarrhea. Limited activity vs. normal bowel flora. In trial vs. po Vanco, lower relapse rate vs. non NAP1 strains than Vanco (NEJM 364:422, 2011). Cohort study reported slight ↑ in cardiovascular mortality during 5 days of therapy with azithromycin (NEJM 366:1881, 2012), leading to a drug safety statement by FDA (http://www.fda.gov/Drugs/DrugSafety/ucm304372.htm). Mortality difference did not persist after therapy.
Fidaxomicin (Dificid) (200 mg tab)	One 200 mg tab po bid × 10 days with or without food	
Ketolide: Telithromycin (Ketek) (Med Lett 46:66, 2004; Drug Safety 31:561, 2008)	Two 400 mg tabs po q24h. 300 mg tabs available.	Drug warnings: acute liver failure & serious liver injury post treatment. (AnIM 144:415, 447, & 505; 2006). Visual disturbances: blurred vision & slow accommodation; may cause worsening of **myasthenia gravis (Black Box Warning): Contraindicated in pts with myasthenia gravis.** Neuromuscular blockade & myasthenia complications may be due to inhibition of nicotinic acetylcholine receptor at neuromuscular junction (AAC 54:5399, 2010). Potential QT_c prolongation. Several **drug-drug interactions** (Table 22, pages 217–218) (NEJM 355:2260, 2006).

* NOTE: all dosage recommendations are for adults (unless otherwise indicated) & assume normal renal function.

(See page 2 for abbreviations)

TABLE 10A (7)

CLASS, AGENT, GENERIC NAME (TRADE NAME)	USUAL ADULT DOSAGE*	ADVERSE REACTIONS, COMMENTS (See Table 10B for Summary)
CHLORAMPHENICOL, CLINDAMYCIN(S), ERYTHROMYCIN GROUP, KETOLIDES, OXAZOLIDINONES, QUINUPRISTIN-DALFOPRISTIN (continued)		
Linezolid (Zyvox) (600 mg tab) Review: JAC 66(Suppl4):3, 2011	PO or IV dose: **600 mg q12h.** Available as 600 mg tabs, oral suspension (100 mg per 5 mL), & IV solution. Special populations Refs: Renal insufficiency (J Infect Chemother 17:70, 2011); Liver transplant (CID 42:434, 2006); Cystic fibrosis (AAC 48:281, 2004); Burns (J Burn Care Res 31:207, 2010).	**Reversible myelosuppression:** thrombocytopenia, anemia, & neutropenia reported. Most often after >2 wks of therapy. Incidence of thrombocytopenia after 2 wks of rx: 7/20 osteomyelitic pts; 5/7 pts treated with vanco & then linezolid. Refs: CID 37:1609, 2003 & 38:1058 & 1065, 2004. 6-fold increased risk in pts with ESRD (CID 42:1111, 2006; AAC 50:2042, 2006). **Lactic acidosis; peripheral neuropathy, optic neuropathy:** After 4 or more wks of therapy. Data consistent with time and dose-dependent inhibition of intramitochondrial protein synthesis (CID 42:1578 and 43:180, 2006). **Inhibitor of monoamine oxidase:** risk of severe hypertension if taken with foods rich in tyramine. Avoid concomitant pseudoephedrine, phenylpropanolamine, and caution with SSRIs[1]. **Serotonin syndrome** (fever, agitation, mental status changes, tremors). Risk with concomitant SSRIs: (CID 42:1578 and 43:180, 2006). Other adverse effects: black hairy tongue and acute interstitial nephritis (IDCP 17:61, 2009). **Rhabdomyolysis:** a case of this entity, probably related to linezolid, was reported in a patient receiving linezolid as a component of multi-drug therapy for XDR tuberculosis (CID 54:1624, 2012). **Resistance:** Outbreaks of Linezolid-resistant epidermidis and MRSA due to mobil gene that methylates ribosomal target of Linezolid (CID 50:821, 2010). Resistance due, primarily, to mutation of the 23S rRNA binding site (AAC 56:603, 2012).
Quinupristin + dalfopristin (Synercid) (CID 36:473, 2003)	**7.5 mg per kg IV q8h via central line**	Venous irritation (5%), none with central venous line. Asymptomatic ↑ unconjugated bilirubin. **Arthralgia 2%–50%** (CID 36:476, 2003). **Note:** E. faecium susceptible; E. faecalis resistant. **Drug-drug interactions:** Cyclosporine, nifedipine, midazolam, many more—see Table 22.
TETRACYCLINES		
Doxycycline (Vibramycin, Doryx, Monodox, Adoxa, Periostat) (20, 50, 75, 100 mg tab)	0.1 gm po/IV q12h	Similar to other tetracyclines. ↑ nausea on an empty stomach. Erosive esophagitis, esp. if taken at bedtime; **take with lots of water.** Phototoxicity & photo-onycholysis occur but less than with tetracycline. Deposition in teeth less. Can be used in patients with renal failure. **Comments:** Effective in treatment and prophylaxis for malaria, leptospirosis, typhus fevers.
Minocycline (Minocin, Dynacin) (50, 75, 100 mg cap; 45, 90, 135 mg ext rel tab; IV prep)	**200 mg po/IV loading dose, then 100 mg po/IV q12h** IV minocycline no longer available.	**Vestibular symptoms** (30–90% in some groups, none in others): vertigo 33%, ataxia 43%, nausea 50%, vomiting 3%, women more frequently than men. Hypersensitivity pneumonitis, reversible, ~34 cases reported (BMJ 310:1520, 1995). Can increase **pigmentation** of the skin with long-term use. Comments: Effective vs. other tetracycline-resistant strains and in prophylaxis of meningococcal disease. P. acnes many resistant to other tetracyclines, not to mino. Induced autoimmunity reported in children treated for acne (J Ped 153:314, 2008). Active vs Nocardia asteroides, Mycobacterium marinum.
Tetracycline, Oxytetracycline (Sumycin) (250, 500 mg cap) (CID 36:462, 2003)	**0.25–0.5 gm po q6h, 0.5–1 gm IV q12h**	GI (oral 19%, tetra 4), anaphylactoid reaction (rare), deposition in teeth, negative N balance, hepatotoxicity, enamel agenesis, pseudotumor cerebri/encephalopathy. Outdated drug; Fanconi syndrome. See drug-drug interactions; Table 22. **Contraindicated in pregnancy, hepatotoxicity in mother, transplacental to fetus. Comments: Pregnancy:** IV dosage over 2 gm per day may be associated with fatal hepatotoxicity. (Ref: JAC 66:1431, 2011.)
Tigecycline (Tygacil) Meta-analysis & editorial: Ln ID 11:804 & 834, 2011. Also CID 54:1699 & 1710, 2012. Increased mortality in serious infections compared with alternative antibiotics. Use with caution in serious infections.	**100 mg IV initially, then 50 mg IV q12h with po food, if possible to decrease risk of nausea.** **If severe liver dis. [Child Pugh C]:** 100 mg initially then 25 mg IV q12h	Derivative of tetracycline. High incidence of nausea (25%) & vomiting (20%) but only 1% of pts discontinued therapy due to an adverse event. Details on A-Ss in JAC 62 (Suppl 1):i17, 2008. Pregnancy Category D. Do not use in children under age 18; may cause permanent tooth discoloration and/or inhibit bone growth. Potential reversible catabolic state (elevated BUN) and maybe hyperpigmentation (CID 45:136, 2007). **Tetracycline, minocycline & tigecycline** associated with acute pancreatitis (Int J Antimicrob Agents. 34:486, 2009). Dear Doctor Letter (4/27/09) lower cure rate and higher mortality in pts with VAP treated with tigecycline. Ref: Diag Micro Infect Dis 68:140, 2010. FDA drug safety communication: http://www.fda.gov/Drugs/DrugSafety/ucm224370.htm

[1] **SSRI** = selective serotonin reuptake inhibitors, e.g., fluoxetine (Prozac).

(See page 2 for abbreviations)

* **NOTE:** all dosage recommendations are for adults (unless otherwise indicated) & assume normal renal function.

TABLE 10A (8)

CLASS, AGENT, GENERIC NAME (TRADE NAME)	USUAL ADULT DOSAGE*	ADVERSE REACTIONS, COMMENTS (See Table 10B for Summary)
FLUOROQUINOLONES (FQs): All can cause false-positive urine drug screen for opiates (Pharmacother 26:435, 2006). Toxicity review: Drugs Aging 27:193, 2010.		
Ciprofloxacin (Cipro) and **Ciprofloxacin extended release** (Cipro XR, Proquin XR) (100, 250, 500, 750 mg tab; 500 mg ext rel tab)	Usual Parenteral dose: **400 mg IV q12h** for FQs. Usual oral dose: **400 mg IV q8h** Uncomplicated Urethritis/cystitis (Oral): Dose: **250 mg po bid or CIP XR 500 mg po once daily** Other indications (Oral): **500-750 mg po bid**	FQs are a common precipitant of C. difficile toxin-mediated diarrhea. **Children:** No FQ approved for use under age 16 based on joint cartilage injury in immature animals. Articular SEs in children est. at 2-3% (LnID 3:537, 2003). The exception is anthrax. Pathogenesis believed to involve FQ chelation of Mg++ = damaging chondrocyte interactions (AAC 51:1022, 2007; Int J Antimicrob Agents 33:194, 2009). **CNS toxicity:** Poorly understood. Varies from mild (lightheadedness) to moderate (confusion) to severe (seizures). May be aggravated by NSAIDs. **Gemi skin rash:** 631 recipients for 10 days. Rash appears after 8-10 days of rx. Incidence of rash only 1.5%. Frequency higher with longer rx, age 40, treated 14 days (22.6%). In men, < age 40, treated 14 days, frequency 7.7%. Mechanism unclear. Indication to D/C therapy. Ref: Diag Micro Infect Dis 68:140, 2010.
Gatifloxacin (Tequin) See comments	**200-400 mg IV/po q24h.** (See comment)	**Hypoglycemia/hyperglycemia:** Due to documented hypo and hyperglycemic reactions (NEJM 354:1352, 2006; CID 43:402, 2009, US distribution of Gati ceased in 6/2006. Gati ophthalmic solution remains available.
Gemifloxacin (Factive) (320 mg tab)	**320 mg po q24h.**	**Opiate screen false-positives:** FQs can cause false-positive urine assay for opiates (JAMA 286:3115, 2001; Ann Pharmacotherapy 38:1525, 2004). **Photosensitivity:** See Table 10C, page 108. Rarely, retinal detachment (JAMA 307:1414, 2012). **QT, corrected (QT) interval prolongation:** If QT, (>500 msec or >60 msec from baseline) is considered possible with any FQ. ↑ QTc can lead to torsades de pointes and ventricular fibrillation. Risk low with current marketed drugs. Risk ↑ in women, ↓K+, ↓Mg++, bradycardia. (Refs: CID 43:1603, 2006). Major problem is ↑ risk with concomitant drugs.

Avoid concomitant drugs with potential to prolong QTc such as:

Antiarrhythmics:	Anti-Infectives:	CNS Drugs:	Misc:
Amiodarone	Azoles (not posa)	Fluoxetine	Dolasetron
Disopyramide	Clarithro/erythro	Haloperidol	Droperidol
Dofetilide	FQs (not CIP)	Phenothiazines	Fosphenytoin
Flecainide	Halofantrine	Pimozide	Indapamide
Procainamide	NNRTIs	Quetiapine	Methadone
Quinidine, quinine	Pentamidine	Risperidone	Naratriptan
Sotalol	Protease Inhibitors	Sertraline	Salmeterol
	Telavancin	Tricyclics	Sumatriptan
	Telithromycin	Venlafaxine	Tamoxifen
		Ziprasidone	Tizanidine
	Anti-Hypertensives:		
	Bepridil		
	Isradipine		
	Nicardipine		
	Moxipril		

Updates online: www.qtdrugs.org;
www.torsades.org

Levofloxacin (Levaquin) (250, 500, 750 mg tab)	**250-750 mg po/IV q24h.** For most indications, 750 mg is preferred dose. Potential drug interactions: avoid concomitant dairy products, multivitamins, iron, antacids due to chelation by multivalent cations & interference with absorption	**Tendinopathy:** Over age 60, approx. 2-6% of all Achilles tendon ruptures attributable to use of FQ (ArM 163:1801, 2003). ↑ Risk with concomitant steroids, renal disease or transplant (heart, lung, kidney) (CID 36:1404, 2003). **Chelation:** Risk of chelation of oral FQs by multivalent cations (Ca++, Mg++, Fe++, Zn++). Avoid dairy products, multivitamins (Clin Pharmacokinet 40 (Suppl1) 33:2001). **Allergic Reactions:** Rare (1:50,000): urticaria, anaphylaxis. May be more common with Moxi. 3 pts with Moxi immediate reactions tolerated CIP (Am J Pharmacother 44:740, 2010). **Myasthenia gravis:** Any of the FQs may exacerbate muscle weakness in pts. with myasthenia gravis.
Moxifloxacin (Avelox)	**400 mg po/IV q24h**; Note: no need to increase dose for morbid obesity (JAC 66:2330, 2011). Ophthalmic solution (Vigamox)	**Retinal detachment:** A case-control study from Canada found an association between current (but not recent or past) use of fluoroquinolones and occurrence of retinal detachment (JAMA 307:1414, 2012).
Ofloxacin (Floxin)	**200-400 mg po bid** Ophthalmic solution (Ocuflox)	

* NOTE: all dosage recommendations are for adults (unless otherwise indicated) & assume normal renal function.

(See page 2 for abbreviations)

TABLE 10A (9)

CLASS, AGENT, GENERIC NAME (TRADE NAME)	USUAL ADULT DOSAGE*	ADVERSE REACTIONS, COMMENTS (See Table 10B for Summary)
POLYMYXINS (POLYPEPTIDES)	**Note: Proteus sp., Providencia sp., Serratia sp., B. cepacia are intrinsically resistant to polymyxins.**	
Polymyxin B (Poly-Rx) 1 mg = 10,000 units Avoid monotherapy, see Colistin.	Standard Dose: 15,000–25,000 units/kg/day IV divided q12h **Intrathecal Rx of Meningitis:** 50,000 units/day into CSF daily x 3-4 days, then q48h x 2 weeks.	**Adverse effects: Neurologic:** rare but serious is neuromuscular blockade; other: circumoral paresthesias, extremity numbness, blurred vision, drowsy, irritable, ataxia. **Renal:** reversible acute tubular necrosis. PK study in septic pts: no need to reduce dose for renal insufficiency (CID 47:1298, 2008). Efficacy correlates with AUC/MIC & need maximal daily dose to optimize AUC (JAC 65:2231, 2010)
Colistin, Polymyxin E (Colymycin) All doses are based on mg of Colistin base. Calculated doses are higher than the package insert dosing; need to avoid underdosage in the critically ill. Do not use as monotherapy (combine with carbapenem or rifampin) Dosing formula based on PK study of 105 pts (AAC 55:3284, 2011) Loading dose (AAC 53:3430, 2009) PK/PD studies (AAC 54:4783, 2010 in vitro), JAC 65:1984, 2010 (in vivo).	*(See page 2 for abbreviations)* **LOADING DOSE:** 3.5 (targeted average serum steady state value) x2 x body weight in kg (lower of ideal or actual weight) IV. This will often result in a loading dose of over 300 mg of colistin base. First maintenance dose is given 12 hrs. later. **MAINTENANCE DOSE:** Formula for calculating the daily maintenance dosage: 3.5 (the desired serum steady state concentration) x [(1.5 x CrClₙ +30)] = total daily dose. Divide and give q8h or maybe q12h. The maximum CrClₙ (mL/min) is listed at 475 mgs. **NOTE:** CrClₙ is the Creatinine Clearance (CrCln) normalized (n) for Body Surface Area (BSA) such that the CrCln = CrCl x BSA in m²/1.73 m² Combination therapy is recommended for all pts: Colistin (as above) + [(IMP or MER) or RIF] (based on IBW) **Intrathecal or intraventricular for meningitis:** 10 mg/day **Cystic fibrosis:** 3-8 mg/kg/day q8h **Inhalation therapy:** 50-75 mg IV or 3-4 mL of Saline via nebulizer 2-3x/day	• **GNB Resistance:** Some sp. are intrinsically resistant: Serratia sp., B. cepacia. In vitro and in animal models, gram-negative bacilli rapidly become resistant. Concomitant Tigecycline may attenuate risk of resistance (JAC 60:421, 2007). Synergy with Rifampin or Tigecycline unpredictable. The greater the resistance of GNB to Colistin, the greater the susceptibility to beta-lactams (AM-SB, PIP-TZ, extended spectrum Ceph, maybe carbapenems). • **Caveat:** higher doses of colistin (> 5 mg/kg of ideal body weight per day) are associated with increased risk of nephrotoxicity and should be reserved for critically ill patients (Clin Infect Dis 53:879, 2011). • **Bactericidal activity concentration dependent** but no post-antibiotic effect; do not dose once daily. • **Nephrotoxic:** exact risk unclear, but increased by concomitant nephrotoxins (IV contrast), hypotension, maybe Rifampin. Reversible. • **Neurotoxicity:** Frequent: circumoral paresthesia, vertigo, abnormal vision, contusion, ataxia. Rare: neuromuscular blockade with respiratory failure. • **Caution:** Some international colistimethate products are expressed in IUs. To convert IUs to mg of colistin base: 30,000 IUs colistimethate = 2.4 mg colistimethate base = 1 mg colistin base.
MISCELLANEOUS AGENTS		
Fosfomycin (Monurol) (3 gm packet)	3 gm with water po times 1 dose. For emergency use: single patient IND for IV use. From 17 mgm/day to 400–403/2032.	Diarrhea in 9% compared to 6% of pts given nitrofurantoin and 2.3% given TMP-SMX. Available outside U.S., IV & PO, for treatment of multi-drug resistant bacteria. For MDR-GNB: 6-12 gm/day IV divided q6-8h. Ref: Int J Antimicrob Ag 37:415, 2011.
Fusidic acid**ᴺᵁˢ** (Fucidin, Taksta)	500 mg loading dose then 500 mg po bid US: loading dose of 1500 mg po bid x 1 day, then 60 mg po bid	Activity vs. MRSA of importance. Approved outside the U.S.; currently in U.S. clinical trials. Ref for proposed US regimen: CID 52 (Suppl 7):S520, 2011.
Methenamine hippurate (Hiprex, Urex)	1 gm po bid	Nausea and vomiting, skin rash or dysuria. Overall ~3%. Methenamine requires acid urine (pH ≤5) to liberate formaldehyde. Useful in suppressive therapy; not useful for acute infection. Do not use with sulfonamides. Comment: Do not force fluids; may dilute formaldehyde. Of no value in pts with chronic Foley. If urine pH >5.0, co-administer ascorbic acid (1–2 gm/day). To acidify the urine, cranberry juice (1200–4000 mL per day) has been used; results ±.
Methenamine mandelate (Mandelamine)	1 gm po qid	Do not use concomitantly with sulfonamides (precipitate), or in presence of renal or severe hepatic dysfunction.

* NOTE: all dosage recommendations are for adults (unless otherwise indicated) & assume normal renal function.

TABLE 10A (10)

CLASS, AGENT, GENERIC NAME (TRADE NAME)	USUAL ADULT DOSAGE*	ADVERSE REACTIONS, COMMENTS (See Table 10B for Summary)
MISCELLANEOUS AGENTS (continued)		
Metronidazole (Flagyl) (250, 375, 500 mg tab/cap) Ref.: Activity vs. *B. fragilis* Still drug of choice (*CID 50 (Suppl 1):S16, 2010*).	Anaerobic infections: usually IV **7.5 mg per kg (~500 mg) q6h** (not to exceed 4 gm q24h). With Oral 7½, can **use IV at 15 mg per kg q12h.** If life-threatening, use loading dose of IV 15 mg per kg. **Oral dose: 500 mg qid; extended release tabs** available 750 mg.	**Common AEs:** nausea (12%), metallic taste, "furry" tongue. Avoid alcohol during 48 hrs after last dose to avoid disulfiram reaction (N/V, flushing, GI cramps, dyspnea). Neurologic AEs with high dose/long Rx: peripheral, autonomic and optic neuropathy (*J Child Neurol 21:429, 2006*). Aseptic meningitis, encephalopathy, seizures & reversible cerebellar lesion reported (*NEJM 346:68, 2002*). Also: topical & vaginal gels. Can use IV soln as enema for *C. diff* colitis. Resistant anaerobic organisms: Actinomyces, Peptostreptococci, Peptostreptococci. Once-daily IV dosing of 1500 mg; rational (*NEJM 11/2: standard in Europe: supportive retrospective studies in adults with intra-abdominal infections (*JAC 19:410, 2007*).
Nitazoxanide	See Table 13B, page 152	Absorption 1 with meals. Increased activity in acid urine, much reduced at pH 8 or over. Not effective in endstage renal
Nitrofurantoin macrocrystals (Macrobid, Macrodantin, Furadantin) (25, 50, 100 mg caps)	Active UTI: **Furadantin/Macrodantin 50-100 mg qid x 7 days** OR **Macrobid 100 mg po bid x 7 days** Dose for long-term UTI suppression: **50-100 mg at bedtime**	disease. Nausea and vomiting, peripheral neuropathy, pancreatitis. **Pulmonary reactions** (with chronic rx): **acute** ARDS type. **Chronic desquamative interstitial pneumonia & fibrosis.** Intrahepatic cholestasis & **hepatitis** similar to chronic active hepatitis. Hemolytic anemia in G6PD deficiency. Drug rash, eosinophilia, systemic symptoms (DRESS) hypersensitivity syndrome reported (*Meth J Med 67:147, 2009*). **Contraindicated in renal failure.** Should not be used in infants <1 month of age. Birth defects: increased risk reported (*Arch Ped Adolesc Med 163:978, 2009*).
Rifampin (Rimactane, Rifadin) (150, 300 mg cap)	**300 mg po bid or 600 mg po once daily**	Causes orange-brown discoloration of sweat, urine, tears, contact lens. **Many important drug-drug interactions,** see Table 22. Immune complex flu-like syndrome: fever, headache, myalgias, arthralgia--especially with intermittent rx. Thrombocytopenia, vasculitis reported (*C Ann Pharmacother 42: 727, 2008*). Can cause interstitial nephritis. Risk-benefit of adding RIF to standard therapies for *S. aureus* endocarditis (*AAC 52:2463, 2008*). See also, *Antimycobacterial Agents,* Table 12B, page 138.
Rifaximin (Xifaxan) (200, 550 mg tab)	Travelers diarrhea: **200 mg tab po tid** times 3 days Hepatic encephalopathy: **550 mg tab po bid.** *C. diff* diarrhea as "chaser": **400 mg po bid.** Dose varies with indications. See *Nocardia & Toxoplasmosis*	For traveler's diarrhea and hepatic encephalopathy (*AAC 54:3618, 2010; NEJM 362:1071, 2010*). In general, adverse events equal to or less than placebo.
Sulfonamides [e.g. sulfisoxazole (Gantrisin), sulfamethoxazole (Gantanol), (Truxazole), sulfadiazine]		**CNS:** headache, dizziness. **Derm:** mild rash to life threatening Stevens-Johnson syndrome, toxic epidermal necrolysis, photosensitivity. **Hem:** agranulocytosis, aplastic anemia. **Cross-allergenicity:** other sulfa drugs, sulfonylureas, diuretics, crystalluria (esp. sulfadiazine--need ≥ 1500 mL po fluid/day). **Other:** serum sickness, hemolysis if G6PD def. polyarteritis. SLE reported
Tinidazole (Tindamax)	**Tabs 250, 500 mg.** Dose for giardiasis 2 gm po times 1 with food.	**Adverse reactions:** metallic taste 3.7%, nausea 3.2%, anorexia/vomiting 1.5%. All higher with multi-day dosing. Avoid alcohol during 3 for 3 days after last dose, cause disulfiram reaction, flushing, N/V, tachycardia.
Trimethoprim (Trimpex, Proloprim, and others) (100, 200 mg tab)	**100 mg po bid or 200 mg po q24h.**	**CNS:** drug fever, aseptic meningitis. **Derm:** rash (3-7% at 200 mg/day), photoxocity, Stevens-Johnson syndrome (rare). toxic epidermal necrolysis (rare). **Renal:** 1 K+, 1 Na+, 1 Cl-. **Hem:** neutropenia, thrombocytopenia, methemoglobinemia.
Trimethoprim (TMP)- Sulfamethoxazole (SMX) (Bactrim, Septra, Sulfatrim, Cotrimoxazole) Single-strength (SS) is 80 TMP/400 SMX, double-strength (DS) 160 TMP/800 SMX	**Standard po rx: 1 DS tab bid. P. carinii:** see Table 13A, page 145. rx: (base on TMP **component of 15-20 mg per kg IV per day divided q6h, q8h, or q12h. For shigellosis: 2.5 mg per kg IV q6h**	Adverse reactions in 10%. GI: nausea, vomiting, anorexia. Skin: Rash, urticaria, photosensitive. Reactions may be severe (*Med Lett 44:43, 2000*). Uncommon reactions may represent toxic metabolites of SMX rather than allergy (*Ann Pharmacother 42:381, 1998*). Daily ascorbic acid 0.5–1.0 gm may promote detoxification (*JAIDS 36:1041, 2004*). Rare hypoglycemia. AIDS pts: (*LnID 6:178, 2006*). **Sweet's Syndrome** can occur. TMP competes with creatinine for tubular secretion: serum creatinine can 1; TMP also blocks distal renal tubule secretion of K+, 1 serum K+ in 21% of pts (*AnM 124:316, 1996*). Risk of hyperkalemia increased 7x if concomitant ACE inhibitor (*Arch Int Med 170:1045, 2010*). Discontinuation of renal artery/vein (*JAC 67:1271, 2006*). Combined with pyrimethamine is rx of choice for active treatment of PCP (*JAC 66:1117, 2011*). TMP-SMX contains sulfites and may trigger asthma in sulfite-sensitive pts. Frequent drug use associated of thrombocytopenia. No cross allergenicity with other sulfonamide non-antibiotic drugs (*NEJM 349:1628, 2003*). **For TMP-SMX desensitization, see Table 7, page 80.**

* NOTE: all dosage recommendations are for adults (unless otherwise indicated) & assume normal renal function.

(See page 2 for abbreviations)

TABLE 10A (11)

CLASS, AGENT, GENERIC NAME (TRADE NAME)	USUAL ADULT DOSAGE*	ADVERSE REACTIONS, COMMENTS (See Table 10B for Summary)
Topical Antimicrobial Agents Active vs. S. aureus & Strep. pyogenes (*CID 49:1541, 2009*). **Review of topical antiseptics, antibiotics** (*CID 49:1541, 2009*).		
Bacitracin (Baciguent)	20% bacitracin zinc ointment, apply 1–5 x/day.	Active vs. staph, strep & clostridium. Contact dermatitis occurs. Available without prescription.
Fusidic acid™ ointment	2% ointment, apply tid	Available in Canada and Europe (*Leo Laboratories*). Active vs. S. aureus & S. pyogenes.
Mupirocin (Bactroban)	**Skin cream or ointment 2%: Apply tid times 10 days. Nasal ointment 2%: apply bid times 5 days.**	Skin cream: itch, burning, stinging 1–1.5%; Nasal: headache 9%, rhinitis 6%, respiratory congestion 5%. Not active vs. enterococci or gm-neg bacteria. Summary of resistance: *CID 49:935, 2009*. If large amounts used in azotemic pts, can accumulate polyethylene glycol (*CID 49:1541, 2009*).
Polymyxin B—Bacitracin (Polysporin)	5000 units/gm; 400 units/gm. Apply 1–4x/day	Polymyxin active vs. some gm-neg bacteria but not Proteus sp., Serratia sp. or gm-pos bacteria. See *Bacitracin* comment above. Available without prescription.
Polymyxin B—Bacitracin—Neomycin (Neosporin, triple antibiotic ointment (TAO))	5000 units/gm; 400 units/gm, 3.5 mg/gm. Apply 1–3x/day.	See *Bacitracin* and *polymyxin B* comments above. Neomycin active vs. gm-neg bacteria and staphylococci; not active vs. streptococci. Contact dermatitis incidence 1%; risk of nephro- & oto-toxicity if absorbed. TAO spectrum broader than mupirocin and active mupirocin-resistant strains (*DMID 54:63, 2006*). Available without prescription.
Retapamulin (Altabax)	1% ointment; apply bid. 5, 10 & 15 gm tubes.	Microbiologic success in 90% S. aureus infections and 97% of S. pyogenes infections (*J Am Acad Derm 55:1003, 2006*). Package insert says **do not use for MRSA** (not enough pts in clinical trials). Active vs. some mupirocin-resistant S. aureus strains.
Silver sulfadiazine	1% cream, apply once or twice daily.	A sulfonamide but the active ingredient is released silver ions. Activity vs. gram-pos & gram-neg bacteria (including P. aeruginosa). Often used to prevent infection in pts with 2nd/3rd degree burns. Rarely, may stain into the skin.

(*See page 2 for abbreviations*)   * NOTE: all dosage recommendations are for adults (unless otherwise indicated) & assume normal renal function.

TABLE 10B – SELECTED ANTIBACTERIAL AGENTS—ADVERSE REACTIONS—OVERVIEW

Adverse reactions in individual patients represent all-or-none occurrences, even if rare. After selection of an agent, the physician should read the manufacturer's package insert [statements in the product labeling (package insert)] must be approved by the FDA].

Numbers = frequency of occurrence (%); **++** = significant adverse reaction; **+** = occurs, incidence not available; **0** = not reported; **R** = rare, defined as <1%.

NOTE: Important reactions in bold print. A blank means no data found.

ADVERSE REACTIONS	Dicloxacillin	Nafcillin	Oxacillin	Penicillin G, V	Amoxicillin	Amox-Clav	Ampicillin	Amp-Sulb	Piperacillin	Pip-Taz	Ticarcillin	Ticar-Clav	Doripenem	Ertapenem	Imipenem	Meropenem	Aztreonam	Aminoglycosides (Amikacin, Gentamicin, Kanamycin, Netilmicin[NUS], Tobramycin)	Linezolid	Telithromycin
Rx stopped due to AE					2-4.4			3	3.2	3.2	3		3.4 / 4-8	4	3	1.2	<1		3/1	7/2
Local: phlebitis		++	+	+	+				+		+	+	+	+	3	3	4		1	1
Hypersensitivity																				
Fever		+	+	+	+				+		+		+	+	+	+	2			
Rash	**4**	**4**	**4**	**3**	**5**	**3**	**5**	**2**	**1**	**4**	**3**	**2**	**1-5**	+	+	+	**2**	+	+	
Photosensitivity	0	0	0	0	R	0	0	0	0	0	0	0	R	R	0	0	+			
Anaphylaxis	0	0	R	R	R	R	R	0	R	R	0	0	R	R	0	+	+	+	+	
Serum sickness	0	R	R	4	R		R	+	+	R	R	R	+	+	+	+	+		+	
Hematologic																				
+ Coombs	3	R	R	3	+		+	0	+	+	0	+	R	1	2	2	R		1.1	
Neutropenia	0	+	R	+	+	+	+	+	6	+	0	+	+	+	+	+	+		+	
Eosinophilia	22	22	22	22	2	R	22	22	+	+	R	+	1	+	2	+	8		3-10	
Thrombocytopenia	R	R	R	R	R	R	R	R	+	+	R	R	+	+	+	+	+		(see 10C)	
↑ PT/PTT	0	0	0	R	+	+	+	0	+	+	+	+	+	+	R	R	R			
GI																				
Nausea/vomiting		+			2	3	+	**2**	2	7	1	1	4-12	1	2	4	R		3/1	7/2
Diarrhea	+	0		+	**5**	**9**	**10**	**2**	2	11	3	1	6-11	6	2	5	R		4	10
C. difficile colitis	R	R	R	+	R	R	R	+	+	+	R	R	R	+	+	+	+		+	+
Hepatic: ↑ LFTs	R	R	R	R	R	+	+	+	+	+	+	+	+	6	4	4	+		1.3	+
Hepatic failure	0	0	+	0	0	0	0	0	+	0	0	0	+	R	R	R	0			
Renal: ↑ BUN, Cr	0	0	+	R	R	R	R	R	+	+	R	R	R	+	+	0	0	5-25[2]		
CNS																				
Headache	R	R	R	R	0	0	R	+	R	8	R	R	4-16	2	+	3	+		2	2
Confusion	R	R	R	R	R	+	R	+	+	+	R	R	+	+	+	+	+		+	2

[1] A case of antagonism of warfarin effect has been reported (*Pharmacother 27:1467, 2007*).

[2] Varies with criteria used.

TABLE 10B (1)

PENICILLINS, CARBAPENEMS, MONOBACTAMS, AMINOGLYCOSIDES

ADVERSE REACTIONS	Penicillin G, V	PENICILLINASE-RESISTANT ANTI-STAPH. PENICILLINS — Dicloxacillin	Nafcillin	Oxacillin	AMINOPENICILLINS — Amoxicillin	Amox-Clav	Ampicillin	Amp-Sulb	AP PENS — Piperacillin	Pip-Taz	Ticarcillin	Ticar-Clav	CARBAPENEMS — Doripenem	Ertapenem	Imipenem	Meropenem	Aztreonam	AMINOGLYCOSIDES (Amikacin, Gentamicin, Kanamycin, Netilmicin[NUS], Tobramycin)	MISC. — Linezolid	Telithromycin
CNS (continued)																				
Seizures	R						R						See footnote[3]				+			
Special Senses																				
Ototoxicity																		3–14ᵃ		
Vestibular																		4–6ᵇ		
Cardiac																				
Dysrhythmias																				+
Miscellaneous, Unique (Table 10A)	+	+	+	+	+	+	+	+	+	+	+	+	+	+	+	+	+	+	+	++
Drug-drug interactions, common (Table 22)																+		+	++	+

CEPHALOSPORINS/CEPHAMYCINS

ADVERSE REACTIONS	Cefazolin	Cefotetan	Cefoxitin	Cefuroxime	Cefotaxime	Ceftazidime	Ceftizoxime	Ceftriaxone	Cefepime	Ceftaroline	Ceftobiprole[NUS]	Cefaclor/Cef.ER[5]/Loracarbef[NUS]	Cefadroxil	Cefdinir	Cefixime	Cefpodoxime	Cefprozil	Ceftibuten	Cefditoren pivoxil	Cefuroxime axetil	Cephalexin
Rx stopped due to AE	+	R	+	2	5	2	4	2	1.5	2.7	4			3		2.7	2	2	2	2.2	
Local, phlebitis	5	1		2		2	4	2	1	2	1.9	2									
Hypersensitivity																					
Fever	+	+	+	+		2	+	R	+	2	R	+		R		1.3	+	+	+	R	
Rash	+	2	+	R	2	2	2	R	2	3	2.7	1		R		R	1	R	R	R	1
Photosensitivity	0	0	0	0	R	0	0	0	0	0	0	0		R		R					

[3] **All β-lactams in high concentration can cause seizures** (*JAC 45:5, 2000*). In rabbit, IMP 10x more neurotoxic than benzyl penicillin (*JAC 22:687, 1988*). In clinical trial of IMP for pediatric meningitis, trial stopped due to seizures in 7/25 IMP recipients; hard to interpret as purulent meningitis causes seizures (*PIDJ 10:122, 1991*). Risk with IMP ↓ with careful attention to dosage (*Epilepsia 42:1590, 2001*).
Postulated mechanism: Drug binding to GABA$_A$ receptor. IMP binds with greater affinity than MER.
Package insert, percent seizures: ERTA 0.5, IMP 0.4, MER 0.7. However, in 3 clinical trials of MER for bacterial meningitis, no drug-related seizures (*Scand J Inf Dis 31:3, 1999; Drug Safety 22:191, 2000*).
In febrile neutropenic cancer pts, IMP-related seizures reported at 2% (*CID 32:381, 2001; Peds Hem Onc 17:585, 2000*). Also reported for DORI.
[4] Varies with criteria used.
[5] Cefaclor extended release tablets.

TABLE 10B (2)

CEPHALOSPORINS/CEPHAMYCINS

ADVERSE REACTIONS	Cephalexin	Cefuroxime axetil	Cefditoren pivoxil	Ceftibuten	Cefprozil	Cefpodoxime	Cefixime	Cefdinir	Cefadroxil	Cefaclor/Cef.ER[6]/Loracarbef[NUS]	Ceftobiprole[NUS]	Ceftaroline	Cefepime	Ceftriaxone	Ceftizoxime	Ceftazidime	Cefotaxime	Cefuroxime	Cefoxitin	Cefotetan	Cefazolin
Hypersensitivity *(continued)*																					
Anaphylaxis	R	R				R				R	R	R		R		R		R		+	R
Serum sickness	+	R								≤0.5*											+
Hematologic																					
+ Coombs	+	R	R	R	R	R	R	R	+	R	+	9.8	14	R		R	R	R	2	++	+
Neutropenia	3	1	R		R	R	R			+	+		1	2	4	1	1	1	2	+	3
Eosinophilia	9		R	5	2	R	R			2	+		1	6	6	8	1	7	3	3	
Thrombocytopenia				R							+		+	+	+	+	+	+			
↑ PT/PTT					+								+	+	+	+				+	
GI																					
Nausea/vomiting	2	3	6/1	6	4	4	13	3	2	3	+	4/2	1	R		R	R	R	2	1	1
Diarrhea		4	1.4	3	3	7	16	15	3	2	9/4.8	5	1	3	+	1	1	R	1	4	4
C. difficile colitis		+	+	+	+	+	+	+	+	1–4	<1	+	+	+	+	+	+	+	+	+	+
Hepatic: ↑ LFTs	+	2	R	+	2	4	R	1	3	3	3	2	3	3	0	6	1	3	+	1	1
Renal: ↑ BUN, Cr	+	+	R	R	R	4	+	R	+	+	R	<2	0	1	0	R	0	4	3	0	0
CNS																					
Headache	+	R	2	R	R	1		2		3	4.5		2								0
Confusion	+			R						+											0
Seizures											R		+[7]								0
Special Senses																					
Ototoxicity	0	0	0	0	0	0	0	0	0	0				0	0	0	0	0	0	0	0
Vestibular	0	0	0	0	0	0	0	0	0	0				0	0	0	0	0	0	0	0
Cardiac																					
Dysrhythmias	0	0	+	0	0	0	0	+	0	0								0		0	0
Miscellaneous, Unique *(Table 6A)*	0	0								+		+		+							0
Drug/drug interactions, common *(Table 22)*	0	0	0	0	0	0	0	0	0	0	0							0		0	0

6 Serum sickness requires biotransformation of parent drug plus inherited defect in metabolism of reactive intermediates (*Ped Pharm & Therap 125:805, 1994*).

7 FDA warning of seizure risk when dose not adjusted for renal insufficiency.

TABLE 10B (3)

ADVERSE REACTIONS	MACROLIDES			QUINOLONES						OTHER AGENTS											
	Azithromycin, Reg. & ER[8]	Clarithromycin, Reg. & ER[8]	Erythromycin	Ciprofloxacin/Cipro XR	Gatifloxacin[NUS]	Gemifloxacin	Levofloxacin	Moxifloxacin	Ofloxacin	Chloramphenicol	Clindamycin	Colistimethate (Colistin)	Daptomycin	Metronidazole	Quinupristin-dalfopristin	Rifampin	Telavancin	Tetracycline/Doxy/Mino	Tigecycline	TMP-SMX	Vancomycin
Rx stopped due to AE	1	3		3.5	2.9	2.2	4.3	3.8	4				2.8				3		5	2	13
Local: phlebitis	+												6						2		8
Hypersensitivity																					
Fever		+									+	+	2		++	1		R	7	++	1
Rash	R		+	R	R	1-22[9]		R	2	+	+	+	4		R	+	4	+	2.4	++	3
Photosensitivity	R			R	R	R	+	+	R	+	+	+						+	+	+	0
Anaphylaxis			+	R	R	R	+	R	R	+								+	+	+	
Serum sickness														R				R			
Hematologic																					
Neutropenia	R	1		R	R				1	+	+			+				R			2
Eosinophilia				R				1	1		+							+		+	+
Thrombocytopenia	R	1		R			0.1-1			+	+			R				+		+	+
↑ PT/PTT							+														0
GI																					
Nausea/vomiting	3[10]	3-6	++ 25	5	8/<3	2.7	7.2	7.2	7	+	7	+	6.3	12		+	27/14	+	30/20	3	
Diarrhea	5	3-6	8	2	4	3.6	5	5	4	+	++		5	+		+	7	+	13	3	
C. difficile colitis	+	R		R	R	R	R	R	R	+	++		+			R	R	+			
Hepatic: ↑LFTs	R	+	+	2	R	1.5	0.1-1	R	2		+		R		2	R	4	+	4		0
Hepatic failure	0	R	R				+											+			0
Renal																					
↑ BUN, Cr	+	4		1					R	+	0	++	R	++		+	3	+		+	5
CNS																					
Dizziness, light headedness				R	3	0.8	3	2	3					+		+	3.1		2	3.5	
Headache	R	2		1	4	1.2	6	2	2		+		5	+		+		+	3.5	+	
Confusion	R	+		+	+	0.1-1	0.1-1	R	R					+		+		+			
Seizures	+	+	R	+	+	0.1-1	0.1-1	R	R					+				+			

[8] Regular and extended-release formulations.

[9] **Highest frequency:** females <40 years of age after 14 days of rx; with 5 days or less of Gemi; incidence of rash <1.5%.

[10] Less GI upset/abnormal taste with ER formulation.

TABLE 10B (4)

ADVERSE REACTIONS	MACROLIDES			QUINOLONES						OTHER AGENTS											
	Azithromycin, Reg. & ER	Clarithromycin, Reg. & ER	Erythromycin	Ciprofloxacin/Cipro XR	Gatifloxacin NUS	Gemifloxacin	Levofloxacin	Moxifloxacin	Ofloxacin	Chloramphenicol	Clindamycin	Colistimethate (Colistin)	Daptomycin	Metronidazole	Quinupristin-dalfopristin	Rifampin	Telavancin	Tetracycline/Doxy/Mino	Tigecycline	TMP-SMX	Vancomycin
Special senses																					
Ototoxicity	+		+																		R
Vestibular				0					0									21[11]			
Cardiac																					
Dysrhythmias	+	+	+	R[12]	+[12]	+[12]	R[12]	+[12]	+[12]		R										
Miscellaneous, Unique (Table 10A)	+	+	+	+	+	+	+	+	+	+	+	+	+	+	+	+	+	+	+	+	0
Drug/drug interactions, common (Table 22)	+	+	+	+	+	+	+	+	+	+	+	+	+	+	++	++	+	+	+	+	+

TABLE 10C – ANTIMICROBIAL AGENTS ASSOCIATED WITH PHOTOSENSITIVITY

The following drugs are known to cause photosensitivity in some individuals. There is no intent to indicate relative frequency or severity of reactions. Listed in alphabetical order:

Azithromycin, benznidazole, ciprofloxacin, dapsone, doxycycline, erythromycin ethyl succinate, flucytosine, ganciclovir, gatifloxacin, gemifloxacin, griseofulvin, interferons, lomefloxacin, ofloxacin, pyrazinamide, saquinavir, sulfonamides, tetracyclines, tigecycline, tretinons, voriconazole

---

[11] Minocycline has 21% vestibular toxicity.

[12] Fluoroquinolones as class are associated **with QTc prolongation.** Ref.: *CID* 34:861, 2002.

TABLE 10D – AMINOGLYCOSIDE ONCE-DAILY AND MULTIPLE DAILY DOSING REGIMENS

(See Table 17, page 205, if estimated creatinine clearance <90 mL per min.)

- General Note: dosages are given as **once daily dose (OD)** and **multiple daily doses (MDD).**
- For **calculation of dosing weight in non-obese patients** use **Ideal Body Weight (IBW):**
  - **Female:** 45.5 kg + 2.3 kg per inch over 60 inch height = dosing weight in kg.
  - **Male:** 50 kg + 2.3 kg per inch over 60 inch height = dosing weight in kg.
- **Adjustment for calculation of dosing weight in obese patients** (actual body weight (ABW) is ≥ 30% above IBW): IBW + 0.4 (ABW minus IBW) = adjusted weight (*Pharmacotherapy 27:1081, 2007; CID 25:112, 1997*).
- If CrCl >90 mL/min, use doses in this table. If CrCl <90, uses doses in *Table 17, page 205.*

- For non-obese patients, calculate estimated creatinine clearance (CrCl) as follows:

$$\frac{(140 \text{ minus age})(IBW \text{ in kg})}{72 \times \text{serum creatinine}} = \text{CrCl in mL/min for men.}$$

Multiply answer by 0.85 for women (estimated)

- For morbidly obese patients, calculate estimated creatinine clearance (CrCl) as follows (*AJM 84:1053, 1988*):

$$\frac{(137 \text{ minus age}) \times [(0.285 \times \text{wt in kg}) + (12.1 \times \text{ht in meters}^2)]}{51 \times \text{serum creatinine}} = \text{CrCl (obese male)}$$

$$\frac{(146 \text{ minus age}) \times [(0.287 \times \text{wt in kg}) + (9.74 \times \text{ht in meters}^2)]}{60 \times \text{serum creatinine}} = \text{CrCl (obese female)}$$

DRUG	MDD AND OD IV REGIMENS/ TARGETED PEAK (P) AND TROUGH (T) SERUM LEVELS	COMMENTS For more data on once-daily dosing, see AAC 55:2528, 2011 and Table 17, page 204
Gentamicin (Garamycin), **Tobramycin** (Nebcin)	MDD: 2 mg per kg load, then 1.7 mg per kg q8h P 4–10 mcg/mL, T 1–2 mcg per mL OD: 5.1 (7 if critically ill) mg per kg q24h P 16–24 mcg per mL, T <1 mcg per mL	**All aminoglycosides have potential to cause tubular necrosis and renal failure, deafness due to cochlear toxicity, vertigo due to damage to vestibular organs, and rarely neuromuscular blockade.** Risk minimal with oral or topical application due to small % absorption unless tissues altered by disease.
Kanamycin (Kantrex), **Amikacin** (Amikin)	MDD: 7.5 mg per kg q12h P 15–30 mcg per mL, T 5–10 mcg per mL OD: 15 mg per kg q24h P 56–64 mcg per mL, T <1 mcg per mL	Risk of nephrotoxicity ↑ with concomitant administration of cyclosporine, vancomycin, ampho B, radiocontrast. Risk of nephrotoxicity ↓ by concomitant AP Pen and perhaps by once-daily dosing method (especially if baseline renal function normal). In general, same factors influence risk of ototoxicity.
Streptomycin		
Netilmicin[NUS]	MDD: 2 mg per kg q8h P 4–10 mcg per mL, T 1–2 mcg per mL OD: 6.5 mg per kg q24h P 22–30 mcg per mL, T <1 mcg per mL	**NOTE: There is no known method to eliminate risk of aminoglycoside nephro/ototoxicity. Proper rx attempts to ↓ the % risk.** The clinical trial data of OD aminoglycosides have been reviewed extensively by meta-analysis (*CID 27:816, 1997*). **Serum levels:** Collect peak serum level (PSL) exactly 1 hr after the start of the infusion in the 3rd dose. In critically ill pts, PSL after the 1st dose as volume of distribution and renal function may change rapidly.
Isepamicin[NUS]	Only OD: Severe infections 15 mg per kg q24h, less severe 8 mg per kg q24h	Other dosing methods and references: For once-daily 7 mg per kg per day of gentamicin—Hartford Hospital method (may under dose if <7 mg/kg/day dose), see AAC 39:650, 1995.
Spectinomycin (Trobicin)[NUS]	2 gm IM times 1—gonococcal infections	One in 500 patients (Europe) have mitochondrial mutation that predicts cochlear toxicity (*NEJM 360:640 & 642, 2009*). Aspirin supplement (3 gm/day) attenuated risk of cochlear injury from gentamicin (*NEJM 354:1856, 2006*).
Neomycin—oral	Prophylaxis GI surgery: 1 gm po times 3 with erythro, see *Table 15B, page 193* For hepatic coma: 4–12 gm per day po	
Tobramycin—inhaled (Tobi). See Cystic fibrosis, *Table 1, page 43.* Adverse effects few: transient voice alteration (13%) and transient tinnitus (3%).		
Paromomycin—oral. See *Entamoeba and Cryptosporidia*, *Table 13A, page 141.*		

TABLE 10E: PROLONGED OR CONTINUOUS INFUSION DOSING OF SELECTED BETA LACTAMS

Based on current and rapidly changing data, it appears that prolonged or continuous infusion of beta-lactams is at least as successful as intermittent dosing. Hence, this approach can be part of stewardship programs as supported by recent publications.

A meta-analysis of observational studies found reduced mortality among patients treated with extended or continuous infusion of carbapenems or piperacillin-tazobactam (pooled data) as compared to standard intermittent regimens. The results were similar for extended and continuous regimens when considered separately. There was a mortality benefit with piperacillin-tazobactam but not carbapenems (CID 56:272, 2013). The lower mortality could, at least in part, be due to closer professional supervision engendered by a study environment. On the other hand, a small prospective randomized controlled study of continuous vs. intermittent pip-tazo, ticar-clav, and meropenem found a higher clinical cure rate and a trend toward lower mortality in the continuous infusion patients (CID 56:236, 2013).

DRUG	MINIMUM STABILITY (AT ROOM TEMP)	RECOMMENDED DOSE	COMMENTS
Cefepime	24 hr (8 hr at 37°C)	Initial dose: 15 mg/kg over 30 min, then immediately begin: • If CrCl > 60: 6 gm (over 24 hr) daily • If CrCl 30-60: 4 gm (over 24 hr) daily • If CrCl 11-29: 2 gm (over 24 hr) daily	CrCl adjustments extrapolated from prescribing information, not clinical data. Refs: JAC 57:1017, 2006; Am. J. Health Syst. Pharm. 68:319, 2011.
Ceftazidime	24 hr (8 hr at 37°C)	Initial dose: 15 mg/kg over 30 min, then immediately begin: • If CrCl > 50: 6 gm (over 24 hr) daily • If CrCl 31-50: 4 gm (over 24 hr) daily • If CrCl 10-30: 2 gm (over 24 hr) daily	CrCl adjustments extrapolated from prescribing information, not clinical data. Refs: Br J Clin Pharmacol 50:184, 2000; IJAA 17:497, 2001; AAC 49:3550, 2005; Infect 37: 418, 2009.
Doripenem	4 hr (in D5W) 12 hr (in NS)	• If CrCl ≥ 50: 500 mg (over 4 hr) q8h • If CrCl 30-49: 250 mg (over 4 hr) q8h • If CrCl 10-29: 250 mg (over 4 hr) q12h	Based on a single study (Crit Care Med 36:1089, 2008).
Meropenem	4 hrs	• If CrCl ≥ 50: 2 gm (over 3 hr) q8h • If CrCl 30-49: 1 gm (over 3 hr) q8h • If CrCl 10-29: 1 gm (over 3 hr) q12h	Initial 1 gm dose reasonable but not used by most investigators. Ref: Intens Care Med 37:632, 2011.
Pip-Tazo	24 hr	Initial dose: 4.5 gm over 30 min, then 4 hrs later start: • If CrCl ≥ 20: 3.375 gm (over 4 hr) q8h • If CrCl < 20: 3.375 gm (over 4 hr) q12h	Reasonable to begin first infusion 4 hrs after initial dose. Refs: CID 44:357, 2007; AAC 54:460, 2010. See CID 56:236, 245 & 272, 2013.

TABLE 11A – TREATMENT OF FUNGAL INFECTIONS—ANTIMICROBIAL AGENTS OF CHOICE*

TYPE OF INFECTION/ORGANISM/ SITE OF INFECTION	ANTIMICROBIAL AGENTS OF CHOICE		COMMENTS
	PRIMARY	ALTERNATIVE	
Aspergillosis (A. fumigatus most common, also A. flavus and others) (See NEJM 360:1870, 2009 for excellent review)			
Allergic bronchopulmonary aspergillosis (ABPA) Clinical manifestations: wheezing, pulmonary infiltrates, bronchiectasis & fibrosis. Airway colonization assoc. with ↑ blood eosinophils, ↑ serum IgE, ↑ specific serum antibodies.	Acute asthma attacks associated with ABPA: **Corticosteroids**	Rx of ABPA: **Itraconazole** 200 mg po bid times 16 wks or longer	Itra decreases number of exacerbations requiring corticosteroids with improved immunological markers improved lung function & exercise tolerance (IDSA Guidelines updated CID 46:327, 2008).
Allergic fungal sinusitis: relapsing chronic sinusitis; nasal polyps without bony invasion; asthma, eczema or allergic rhinitis; ↑ IgE levels and isolation of Aspergillus sp. or other dematiaceous sp. (Alternaria, Cladosporium, etc.)	Rx controversial: systemic corticosteroids + surgical debridement (relapse common).	For failures try Itra' 200 mg po bid times 12 mos or flucon nasal spray.	Controversial area.
Aspergilloma (fungus ball)	No therapy or surgical resection. Efficacy of antimicrobial agents not proven.		Aspergillus may complicate pulmonary sequestration.
Invasive, pulmonary (IPA) or extrapulmonary: (See Am J Respir Crit Care Med 173:707, 2006). Post-transplantation and post-chemotherapy in neutropenic pts (PMN <500 per mm³) that may also present with neutrophil recovery. Most common invasive mold infection in transplant pts. Usually a late (≥100 days) complication in allogeneic bone marrow & liver transplantation: High mortality (CID 44:531, 2007). **Typical x-ray/CT lung lesions** (halo sign, cavitation, or Rx based on halo signs on CT associated with better response to Rx & improved outcome. An immunologic test that detects circulating **galactomannan** is available for dx of invasive aspergillosis (Lancet ID 4:349, 2005). Galactomannan detection in the blood relatively insensitive; antifungal rx may decrease sensitivity (CID 40:1762, 2005). One study suggests improved sensitivity when performed on BAL fluid. (Am J Respir Crit Care Med 177:27, 2008). **Fab- PZ & AM-CL.** Numerous other causes of false positive galactomannan tests reported. For strengths & weaknesses of the test see CID 42:1417, 2006.	**Primary therapy** (See CID 46:327, 2008): **Voriconazole** 6 mg/kg IV q12h on day 1; then either (4 mg/kg IV q12h) or (200 mg po q12h for body weight ≥40 kg, but 100 mg po q12h for body weight <40 kg) OR **Alternative therapies:** **Liposomal ampho B** (L-AmB) 3-5 mg/kg/day IV; OR **Ampho B lipid complex** (ABLC) 5 mg/kg/day IV; OR **Caspofungin** 70 mg/day then 50 mg/day thereafter; CR OR **Micafungin**ᴺᴬ 100 mg bid (JAC 64:840, 2009– based on PK/PD study): CR OR **Posaconazole**ᴺᴬ 200 mg qid, then 400 mg bid after stabilization of disease; OR **Itraconazole** capsules 600 mg/day for 3 days, then 400 mg/day (or 2.5 mg/kg of oral solution once daily).		**Voriconazole** more effective than ampho B. Vori, both a substrate and an inhibitor of CYP2C19, CYP2C9, and CYP3A4, has potential for deleterious drug interactions (e.g., with protease inhibitors) and careful review of concomitant medications advisable with prolonged therapy or for patients with possible drug-drug interactions. In patients with CrCl <50 mL/min, the drug should be given orally, not IV, since the intravenous vehicle (SBECD–sulfobutylether-B-cyclodextrin) may accumulate. **Ampho B: not recommended except as a lipid formulation**, either L-AMB or ABLC. 10 mg/kg and 3 mg/kg doses of L-AMB are equally efficacious with greater toxicity of higher dose (CID 2007: 44:1289–97). One comparative trial found much greater toxicity with ABLC than with L-AMB: 34.8% vs 9.4% adverse events and 21.2% vs 2.8% nephrotoxicity (Cancer 112:1282, 2008) Vori preferred as primary therapy. **Casp:** ~50% response rate in IPA, licensed for salvage therapy. Elavirenz, nelfinavir, nevirapine, phenytoin, rifampin, dexamethasone, and carbamazepine, may reduce caspofungin concentrations. **Micafungin:** Favorable responses to micafungin as a single agent in 6/12 patients in primary therapy group and 9/22 in the salvage therapy group of an open-label, non-comparative trial (J Infect 53: 337, 2006). Outcomes no better with combination therapy. Few significant drug-drug interactions. *(Continued on next page)*
Posaconazole superior to Flu or Itra with fewer invasive fungal infections and improved survival in patients with hematologic malignancies undergoing induction chemotherapy (NEJM 356:348, 2007).			

[1] Oral solution preferred to tablets because of ↑ absorption *(see Table 11B, page 124).*

Posaconazole recommendations are for adults (unless otherwise indicated) and assume normal renal function

See page 2 for abbreviations. All dosage recommendations are for adults (unless otherwise indicated) and assume normal renal function

TABLE 11A (2)

TYPE OF INFECTION/ORGANISM/ SITE OF INFECTION	ANTIMICROBIAL AGENTS OF CHOICE		COMMENTS
	PRIMARY	**ALTERNATIVE**	
Aspergillosis *(continued from previous page)*			*(Continued from previous page)*
			Itraconazole: Licensed for treatment of invasive aspergillosis in patients refractory to or intolerant of standard antifungal therapy. Itraconazole (formulated as capsules, oral solution in hydroxypropyl-beta-cyclodextrin (HPCD), and parenteral solution with HPCD as a solubilizer; oral solution and parenteral formulation not licensed for treatment of invasive aspergillosis. 2.5 mg/kg oral solution provides dose equivalent to 400 mg capsules. Parenteral HPCD formulation dosage is 200 mg every 12h IV for 2 days, followed by 200 mg daily thereafter. Oral absorption of capsules enhanced by low gastric pH, erratic in fasting state and with hypochlorhydria; measurements of plasma concentrations recommended during oral therapy of invasive aspergillosis; target troughs concentrations > 0.25 mcg/mL. Itraconazole is a substrate of CYP3A4 and non-competitive inhibitor of CYP3A4 with potential for significant drug-drug interactions. Do not use for azole-non-responders. **Combo therapy:** Uncertain role and not routinely recommended for primary therapy; consider for treatment of refractory disease, although benefit unproven. A typical combo regimen would be an echinocandin in combination with either an azole or a lipid formulation of ampho B.
Blastomycosis *(CID 46: 1801, 2008)* (Blastomyces dermatitidis) Cutaneous, pulmonary or extrapulmonary.	**LAB,** 3-5 mg/kg per day, OR **Ampho B,** 0.7-1 mg/kg per day, **then Itra** 200 mg bid or tid for 1-2 weeks, **then Itra** 200 mg tid for 3 days followed by Itra 200 mg bid for 6-12 months	**Itra** 200 mg tid for 3 days then once or twice per day for 6-12 months for mild to moderate disease. OR **Flu** 400-800 mg per day for those intolerant to itra	Serum levels of **Itra** should be determined after 2 weeks to ensure adequate drug exposure. Flu less effective than itra; role of vori or posa unclear but active in vitro.
Blastomycosis: CNS disease *(CID 50:797, 2010)*	**LAB** 5 mg/kg per day for 4-6 weeks, followed by **Flu** 800 mg per day	**Itra** 200 mg bid or tid; OR **Vori** 200-400 mg q12h	Flu and vori have excellent CNS penetration, perhaps counterbalance their slightly reduced activity compared to Itra. Treat for at least 12 months and until CSF has normalized. Document serum Itra levels to assure adequate drug concentrations. Recent study suggests more favorable outcome with Voriconazole with Voriconazole *(CID 50:797, 2010)*.

[2] **Oral solution preferred to tablets because of ↑ absorption** *(see Table 11B, page 124).*

See page 2 for abbreviations. All dosage recommendations are for adults (unless otherwise indicated) and assume normal renal function

TABLE 11A (3)

Candidiasis: Candida is a common cause of nosocomial bloodstream infection. A decrease in C. albicans & increase in non-albicans species show ↓ susceptibility among candida species to antifungal agents (esp. fluconazole). These changes have predominantly affected immunocompromised pts in environments where antifungal prophylaxis (esp. fluconazole) is widely used. Oral, esophageal, or vaginal candidiasis is a major manifestation of advanced HIV & represents one of the most common AIDS-defining diagnoses. See CID 48:503, 2009 for updated IDSA Guidelines.

TYPE OF INFECTION/ORGANISM/ SITE OF INFECTION	ANTIMICROBIAL AGENTS OF CHOICE		COMMENTS
	PRIMARY	ALTERNATIVE	
Candidiasis: Bloodstream infection **Bloodstream: non-neutropenic patient** Remove all intravascular catheters if possible; replace catheters at a new site (not over a wire). Higher mortality associated with delay in therapy (CID 43:25, 2006).	**Caspofungin** 70 mg IV loading dose, then 50 mg IV daily, OR **Micafungin** 100 mg IV daily, OR **Anidulafungin** 200 mg IV loading dose then 100 mg IV daily.	**Fluconazole** 800 mg (12 mg/kg) loading dose, then 400 mg daily IV OR **PO Lipid-based ampho B** 3-5 mg/kg IV daily; OR **Ampho B** 0.7 mg/kg IV daily; OR **Voriconazole** 400 mg (6 mg/kg) twice daily for 2 doses then 200 mg q12h.	**Fluconazole** recommended for patients with mild-to-moderate illness, hemodynamically stable, with no recent azole exposure. Fluconazole not recommended for treatment of documented C. krusei: use an echinocandin or voriconazole or posaconazole (note: echinocandins have better in vitro activity than either vori or posa against C. glabrata). Fluconazole recommended for treatment of Candida parapsilosis because of reduced susceptibility of this species to echinocandins. Transition from echinocandin to fluconazole for stable patients with Candida albicans or other azole-susceptible species. **Echinocandin** for patients with recent azole exposure or with moderately severe or severe illness, hemodynamic instability. An echinocandin should be used for treatment of Candida glabrata unless susceptibility to fluconazole or voriconazole has been confirmed. Echinocandin may be preferred empirical therapy in centers with high prevalence of non-albicans candida species. A double-blind randomized trial of anidulafungin (n=127) and fluconazole (n=118) showed an 88% microbiologic response rate (119/135 candida species) with anidulafungin vs a 76% (99/130 candida species) with fluconazole (p=0.02) (NEJM 356: 2472, 2007). **Voriconazole** with little advantage over fluconazole (more drug-drug interactions) except for oral step-down therapy of Candida krusei or voriconazole-susceptible Candida glabrata. Recommended **duration of therapy** is 14 days after last positive blood culture. Duration of systemic therapy should be extended to 4-6 weeks for eye involvement. **Fundoscopic examination** within first week of therapy to exclude ophthalmic involvement. Ocular findings present in ~15% of patients with candidemia, but endophthalmitis is uncommon (~2%) (CID 53:262, 2011). Intraocular injections of ampho B may be required for endophthalmitis; echinocandins have poor penetration into the eye. For **septic thrombophlebitis**, catheter removal and incision and drainage of the vein, as needed, are recommended; duration of therapy at least 2 weeks after last positive blood culture.

See page 2 for abbreviations. All dosage recommendations are for adults (unless otherwise indicated) and assume normal renal function

TABLE 11A (4)

TYPE OF INFECTION/ORGANISM/ SITE OF INFECTION	ANTIMICROBIAL AGENTS OF CHOICE		COMMENTS
	PRIMARY	ALTERNATIVE	
Candidiasis: Bloodstream infection (continued)			
Bloodstream: neutropenic patient Remove all intravascular catheters if possible; replace catheters at a new site (not over a wire).	**Caspofungin** 70 mg IV loading dose, then 50 mg IV daily, 35 mg for moderate hepatic insufficiency, OR **Micafungin** 100 mg IV daily; OR **Anidulafungin** 200 mg IV loading dose, then 100 mg IV daily; OR **Lipid-based ampho B** 3-5 mg/kg IV daily.	**Fluconazole** 800 mg (12 mg/kg) loading dose, then 400 mg daily IV or PO, OR **Voriconazole** 400 mg (6 mg/kg) twice daily for 2 doses then 200 mg (3 mg/kg) q12h.	Fluconazole may be considered for less critically ill patients without recent azole exposure. Duration of therapy in absence of metastatic complications is for 2 weeks after last positive blood culture, resolution of signs, and resolution of neutropenia. Perform funduscopic examination after recovery of white count as signs of ophthalmic involvement may not be seen during neutropenia. See comments above for recommendations concerning choice of specific agents.
Candidiasis: Bone and Joint Infections **Osteomyelitis**	**Fluconazole** 400 mg (6 mg/kg) daily IV or PO, OR **Lipid-based ampho B** 3-5 mg/kg daily for several weeks, then oral fluconazole.	An **echinocandin** (as above) or **ampho** B 0.5-1 mg/kg daily for several weeks then oral **fluconazole.**	Treat for a total of 6-12 months. **Surgical debridement** often necessary; **remove hardware** whenever possible.
Septic arthritis	**Fluconazole** 400 mg (6 mg/kg) daily IV or PO, OR **Lipid-based ampho B** 3-5 mg/kg daily for several weeks, then oral fluconazole.	An **echinocandin** or **ampho** B 0.5-1 mg/kg daily for several weeks then oral **fluconazole.**	**Surgical debridement** in all cases; removal of prosthetic joints whenever possible. Treat for at least 6 weeks and indefinitely if retained hardware.
Candidiasis: Cardiovascular infections **Endocarditis** (See Eur J Clin Microbiol Infect Dis 27:519, 2008)	An **echinocandin:** **Caspofungin** 50-150 mg/day; OR **Micafungin** 100-150 mg/day; OR **Anidulafungin** 100-200 mg/day; OR **Lipid-based ampho B** 3-5 mg/kg daily + **5-FC** 25 mg/kg qid	**Ampho B** 0.6-1 mg/kg daily + **5-FC** 25 mg/kg qid	Consider use of higher doses of echinocandins for endocarditis or other endovascular infections. Can switch to **fluconazole 400-800 mg orally in stable patients** with negative blood cultures and fluconazole susceptible organism. See Med 90:237, 2011 for review of Fluconazole for candida endocarditis. Valve replacement strongly recommended, particularly in those with prosthetic valve endocarditis. Duration of therapy not well defined, but treat for at least 6 weeks after valve replacement and longer in those with complications (e.g., perivalvular or myocardial abscess, extensive disease, delayed resolution of candidemia). Long-term (life-long?) suppression with fluconazole 400-800 mg daily for native valve endocarditis and no valve replacement; life-long suppression for prosthetic valve endocarditis if no valve replacement.
Myocarditis	**Lipid-based ampho B** 3-5 mg/kg daily, OR **Fluconazole** 400-800 mg (6-12 mg/kg) daily IV or PO; OR **An echinocandin** (see endocarditis).		Can switch to **fluconazole 400-800 mg orally in stable patients** with negative blood cultures and fluconazole susceptible organism. Recommended duration of therapy is for several months.

See page 2 for abbreviations. All dosage recommendations are for adults (unless otherwise indicated) and assume normal renal function

TABLE 11A (5)

TYPE OF INFECTION/ORGANISM/ SITE OF INFECTION	ANTIMICROBIAL AGENTS OF CHOICE		COMMENTS
	PRIMARY	ALTERNATIVE	
Candidiasis: Cardiovascular infections *(continued)*			
Pericarditis	**Lipid-based ampho B** 3–5 mg/kg daily, OR **Fluconazole** 400–800 mg (6–12 mg/kg) daily IV or PO; OR **An echinocandin** *(see endocarditis)*		Pericardial window or pericardiectomy also is recommended. Can switch to **fluconazole 400–800 mg orally in stable patients** with negative blood cultures and fluconazole susceptible organism. Recommended duration of therapy is for several months.
Candidiasis: Mucosal, esophageal, and oropharyngeal			
Candida esophagitis Primarily encountered in HIV-positive patients	**Fluconazole** 200–400 (3–6 mg/kg) mg IV or PO daily; OR **posaconazole** suspension 400 mg bid x 3 days then 400 mg daily or **voriconazole** 150 mg IV daily, OR **micafungin** 150 mg IV daily, OR **anidulafungin** 200 mg IV loading dose then 100 mg IV daily; OR **Ampho B** 0.5 mg/kg daily.	An azole (**itraconazole** solution 200 mg daily, or **voriconazole** 200 mg q12h).	**Duration of therapy** 14–21 days. IV echinocandin or ampho B for patients unable to tolerate oral therapy. For fluconazole refractory disease, itra (80% will respond), posa, vori, an echinocandin, or ampho B. Echinocandins associated with higher relapse rate than fluconazole. ARV therapy recommended. Suppressive therapy with fluconazole 200 mg 3x/wk for recurrent infections. Suppressive therapy may be discontinued once CD4 > 200/mm³.
Oropharyngeal candidiasis Non-AIDS patient	**Clotrimazole** troches 10 mg 5 times daily; OR **Nystatin** suspension or pastilles qid; OR **Fluconazole** 100–200 mg daily.	**Itraconazole** solution 200 mg daily, OR **posaconazole** suspension 400 mg bid for 3 days then 400 mg daily, or **voriconazole** 200 mg q12h; OR an echinocandin (**caspofungin** 70 mg loading dose then 50 mg IV daily, or **micafungin** 100 mg IV daily, or **anidulafungin** 200 mg IV loading dose then 100 mg IV daily; OR **Ampho B** 0.3 mg/kg daily.	**Duration of therapy** 7–14 days. Clotrimazole or nystatin recommended for mild disease; fluconazole preferred for moderate-to-severe disease. Alternative agents reserved for refractory disease.
AIDS patient	**Fluconazole** 100–200 mg daily for 7–14 days.	Same as for non-AIDS patient, above, for 7–14 days.	Antiretroviral therapy (ARV) recommended in HIV-positive patients to prevent recurrent disease. Suppressive therapy not necessary, especially with ARV therapy and CD4 > 200/mm³, but if required fluconazole 100 mg thrice weekly recommended. Itra, posa, or vori for 28 days for fluconazole-refractory disease. IV echinocandin also an option. Dysphagia or odynophagia predictive of esophageal candidiasis.

See page 2 for abbreviations. All dosage recommendations are for adults (unless otherwise indicated) and assume normal renal function

TABLE 11A (6)

TYPE OF INFECTION/ORGANISM/ SITE OF INFECTION	ANTIMICROBIAL AGENTS OF CHOICE		COMMENTS
	PRIMARY	ALTERNATIVE	
Candidiasis: Mucosal, esophageal, and oropharyngeal *(continued)*			
Vulvovaginitis			
Non-AIDS Patient	**Topical azole therapy: Butoconazole 2%** cream (5 gm) q24h at bedtime x 3 days or 2% cream SR 5 gm x 1; OR **Clotrimazole 100 mg vaginal tabs** (2 at bedtime x 3 days) or 1% cream (5 gm) at bedtime times 7 days (14 days may 1 cure rate) or 100 mg vaginal tab x 7 days or 500 mg vaginal tab x 1; OR **Miconazole 200 mg vaginal suppos** (1 at bedtime x 3 days) or 100 mg vaginal suppos. (q24h x 7 days or 2% cream (5 gm) at bedtime x 7 days. OR **Terconazole 80 mg vaginal tab** (1 at bedtime x 3 days) or 0.4% cream (5 gm) at bedtime x 7 days or 0.8% cream 5 gm intravaginal q24h x 3 days; or tioconazole 6.5% vag. ointment x 1 dose. **Oral therapy: Fluconazole 150 mg** po x 1; OR **Itraconazole 200 mg** po bid x 1 day.	**Recurrent vulvovaginal candidiasis:** fluconazole 150 mg weekly for 6 months.	
AIDS Patient	Topical **azoles** (clotrimazole, buto, mico, tico, or tercon) x3–7d; OR Topical **nystatin** 100,000 units/day as vaginal tablet x14d; OR Oral **flu** 150 mg x1 dose.		For recurrent disease 10-14 days of topical azole or oral flu 150 mg, then flu 150 mg weekly for 6 mos.
Candidiasis: Other infections			
CNS Infection	**Lipid-based ampho B** 3–5 mg/kg daily ± 5-FC 25 mg/kg qid.	**Fluconazole** 400-800 mg (6-12 mg/kg) IV or PO.	Removal of **intraventricular devices** recommended. Flu 400-800 mg as step-down therapy in the stable patient and in patient intolerant of ampho B. Experience too limited to recommend echinocandins at this time. **Treatment duration** for several weeks until resolution of CSF, radiographic, and clinical abnormalities.
Cutaneous *(including paronychia, Table 1, page 28)*	Apply topical ampho B, clotrimazole, econazole, miconazole, or nystatin 3-4 x daily for 7–14 days of terconazole 400 mg po once daily x 14 days. Ciclopirox olamine 1% cream/lotion; apply topically bid x 7–14 days.		
Disseminated candidiasis	**Fluconazole** 400 mg (6 mg/kg) daily, IV or PO; OR **Lipid-based ampho B** 3–5 mg/kg daily; OR An **echinocandin** (as for bloodstream infection).	**Ampho B** 0.5–0.7 mg/kg daily.	**Ampho B** recommended for **unstable patients;** flu in stable patients. **Step-down** to oral flu once patient is stabilized. Other azoles may also be effective. Treatment, usually for several months, should be continued until lesions have resolved and during periods of immunosuppression.
Endophthalmitis • Occurs in 10% of candidemia, thus ophthalmological consult for all pts • Diagnosis: typical white exudates on retinal exam and/or isolation by vitrectomy	**Ampho B**-0.7–1 mg/kg + **Flucytosine** 25 mg/kg qid; OR **Fluconazole** 6-12 mg/kg daily.	**Lipid-based ampho** 3-5 mg/kg daily; OR **voriconazole** 6 mg/kg q12h for 2 doses, then 3–4 mg/kg q12h	**Duration of therapy:** 4-6 weeks or longer, based on resolution determined by repeated examinations. Patients with chorioretinitis only often respond to systemically administered antifungals. Intravitreal amphotericin and/or vitrectomy may be necessary for those with vitritis or endophthalmitis *(Br J Ophthalmol 92:466, 2008; Pharmacotherapy 27:1711, 2007).*

See page 2 for abbreviations. All dosage recommendations are for adults (unless otherwise indicated) and assume normal renal function

TABLE 11A (7)

TYPE OF INFECTION/ORGANISM/ SITE OF INFECTION	ANTIMICROBIAL AGENTS OF CHOICE		COMMENTS
	PRIMARY	ALTERNATIVE	
Candidiasis: Other infections (*continued*)			
Neonatal candidiasis	**Ampho B** 1 mg/kg daily; OR **Fluconazole** 12 mg/kg daily.	**Lipid-based ampho B** 3-5 mg/kg daily.	**Lumbar puncture** to rule out CNS disease, **dilated retinal examination,** and **intravascular catheter removal** strongly recommended. Lipid-based ampho B used only if there is no renal involvement. Echinocandins considered 3rd line therapy. Duration of therapy is at least 3 weeks.
Peritonitis (Chronic Ambulatory Peritoneal Dialysis) See Table 19, page 213.	**Fluconazole** 400 mg po q24h x 2-3 wks; or **caspofungin** 70 mg IV on day 1 followed by 50 mg IV q24h for 14 days; or **micafungin** 100 mg q24h for 14 days.	**Ampho B,** continuous intraperitoneal dosing at 1.5 mg/L of dialysis fluid times 4–6 wks.	Remove cath immediately or if no clinical improvement in 4-7 days.
Candidiasis: Urinary tract infections			
Cystitis Asymptomatic See CID 52:s427, 2011; CID 52:s452, 2011.	If possible, remove catheter or stent. No therapy indicated except in patients at high risk for dissemination or undergoing a urologic procedure.		**High risk patients** include neonates and neutropenic patients; these patients should be managed as outlined for treatment of bloodstream infection. For patients undergoing urologic procedures, flu 200 mg (3 mg/kg) daily or ampho B 0.5 mg/kg daily (for flu-resistant organisms) for several days pre- and post-procedure.
Symptomatic	**Fluconazole** 200 mg (3 mg/kg) daily for 14 days.	**Ampho B** 0.5 mg/kg daily (for fluconazole resistant organisms) for 7-10 days.	Concentration of echinocandins in urine is low; case reports of efficacy versus azole resistant organisms (*Can J Infect Dis Med Microbiol 18:149, 2007; CID 44:e46, 2007*). Persistent candiduria in immunocompromised pt warrants ultrasound or CT of kidneys to rule out fungus ball.
Pyelonephritis	**Fluconazole** 200–400 mg (3–6 mg/kg) once daily orally.	**Ampho B** 0.5 mg/kg daily IV ± **5-FC** 25 mg/kg orally qid.	**Treat for 2 weeks.** For suspected disseminated disease treat as if bloodstream infection is present.
Chromoblastomycosis (*Clin Exp Dermatol. 34:849, 2009*). (Cladophialophora, Phialophora, or Fonsecaea). Cutaneous (usually feet, legs): raised scaly lesions, most common in tropical areas	If lesions small & few, surgical excision or cryosurgery with liquid nitrogen. If lesions chronic, extensive, burrowing: **itraconazole.**	**Itraconazole:** 200–400 mg once daily orally or 400 mg pulse therapy once daily for 1 week monthly for 6-12 months (or until response)[NA].	**Terbinafine**[NA] 500-1000 mg once daily alone or in combination with itraconazole 200-400 mg/d; or **posaconazole** (800 mg/d) also may be effective.

See page 2 for abbreviations. All dosage recommendations are for adults (unless otherwise indicated) and assume normal renal function

TABLE 11A (8)

TYPE OF INFECTION/ORGANISM/ SITE OF INFECTION	ANTIMICROBIAL AGENTS OF CHOICE		COMMENTS
	PRIMARY	ALTERNATIVE	

Coccidioidomycosis (Coccidioides immitis) (IDSA Guidelines 2005: CID 41:1217, 2005; see also Mayo Clin Proc 83:343, 2008)

Primary pulmonary (San Joaquin or Valley Fever):
Pts low risk persistence/complication
Primary pulmonary in pts with † risk for complications or dissemination. Rx indicated:
- Immunosuppressive disease, post-transplantation, hematological malignancies or therapies (steroids, TNF-α antagonists)
- Pregnancy in 3rd trimester
- Diabetes
- CF antibody >1:16
- Pulmonary infiltrates
- Dissemination (identification of spherules or culture of organism from ulcer, joint effusion, pus from subcutaneous abscess or bone biopsy, etc.)

| Mild to moderate severity: Itraconazole solution 200 mg po bid, OR Fluconazole 400 mg po q24h for 3-12 mos | | |

Antifungal rx not generally recommended. Treat if fever, wt loss and/or fatigue in pts with † risk persistence within several wks to 2 mos (see below). Uncomplicated pulmonary in normal host not common in endemic areas (Emerg Infect Dis 12:958, 2006) Influenza-like illness of 1–2 wks duration.

Ampho B cure rate 50–70%. Responses to azoles are similar. Itra may have slight advantage esp. in soft tissue infection. Relapse rates after rx 40%. Relapse rate † if † CF titer ≥1:256. Following CF titers after completion of rx important; rising titers warrant retreatment. **Posaconazole** reported successful in 73% of pts with refractory non-meningeal cocci (Chest 132:952, 2007). Not frontline therapy.

Locally severe or disseminated disease
Ampho B 0.6–1 mg/kg per day x 7 days then 0.8 mg/kg every other day or liposomal ampho B 3-5 mg/kg IV or ABLC 5 mg/kg IV, until clinical improvement (usually several wks or more) then to an oral azole. Rx for at least 1 year. Some use combination of Ampho B & Flu for progressive severe disease; controlled series lacking.
Consultation with specialist recommended: surgery may be required in HIV+ patients or until CD4 >250 & infection controlled. Flu 200 mg po q24h or itra 200 mg po bid (Mucosis 46:42, 2003).

Meningitis: occurs in 1/3 to 1/2 of pts with disseminated coccidioidomycosis

| Adult (CID 42:103, 2006) | Fluconazole 400–1,000 mg po q24h indefinitely. | Ampho B IV as for pulmonary (above) + 0.1–0.3 mg daily intra-thecal (intraventricular) via reservoir device. OR Itra 400–800 mg q24h OR voriconazole (see Comment) | **80% relapse rate, continue flucon indefinitely.** Voriconazole successful in high doses (6 mg/kg q 12h) followed by oral suppression (200 mg po q12h) |
| Child | Fluconazole (po) indefinitely, dose not established, 6 mg per kg q24h used | | |

Cryptococcosis (IDSA Guideline: CID 30:710, 2000). New Guidelines CID 50:291, 2010. Excellent review: Brit Med Bull 72:99, 2005 Risk 57% in organ transplant & those receiving other forms of immunosuppressive agents (EID 13:953, 2007).

| Non-meningeal (non-AIDS) | Fluconazole 400 mg po q24h for 8 wks to 6 mos For more severe disease: Ampho B 0.5–0.8 mg/kg per day IV or Ampho B 0.5–0.8 mg/kg per day IV till response then change to fluconazole 400 mg po q24h for 8–10 wks course | Itraconazole 200–400 mg/day solution q24h for 6-12 mos OR Ampho B 0.3 mg/kg per day IV + flucytosine 37.5 mg/kg po qid times 6 wks | **Flucon alone 90% effective for meningeal and non-meningeal forms.** Fluconazole as effective as ampho B. Addition of **interferon-γ** (IFN-γ•1b 50 mcg per M² subcut, 3x per wk x 9 wks) to liposomal ampho B assoc. with response in pt failing antifungal rx (CID 38: 910, 2004). Posaconazole 400–800 mg also effective in a small series of patients (CID 45:562, 2007; Chest 132:952, 2007) |
| Meningitis (non-AIDS) | Ampho B 0.5–0.8 mg/kg per day IV + flucytosine 37.5 mg/kg po q6h until pt afebrile & cultures neg (~6 wks) (NEJM 301:126, 1979), then stop ampho B/flucyt; start fluconazole 400 mg po q24h x 8-10 wks (less severely ill pt.) Some recommend flu for 2 yrs to reduce relapse rate (Ln 38:297, 1991). Some recommend AMB plus fluconazole as induction Rx. Studies underway. | Itraconazole 37.5 mg/kg po q24h x 8-10 wks (AnIM 113:183, 1990); OR Fluconazole 400 mg po q24h x 8–10 wks (less severely ill pt.) | If CSF opening pressure >25 cm H₂O, repeat LP to drain fluid to control pressure. Outbreaks of C. gattii meningitis have been reported in the Pacific Northwest (EID 13:42, 2007); severity of disease and prognosis appear to be worse than with C. neoformans; initial therapy with ampho B + flucytosine recommended. C. gattii less susceptible to flucon than C. neoformans (Clin Microbiol Inf 14:727, 2008). Outcomes in both AIDS and non-AIDS cryptococcal meningitis improved with Ampho B + 5-FC induction therapy for 14 days in those with neurological abnormalities or high organism burden (PLoS ONE 3:e2870, 2008). |

³ Some experts would reduce to 25 mg per kg q6h

See page 2 for abbreviations. All dosage recommendations are for adults (unless otherwise indicated) and assume normal renal function

TABLE 11A (9)

TYPE OF INFECTION/ORGANISM/ SITE OF INFECTION	ANTIMICROBIAL AGENTS OF CHOICE		COMMENTS
	PRIMARY	ALTERNATIVE	
Cryptococcosis (continued)			
HIV+ /AIDS: Cryptococcemia and/or Meningitis			
Treatment See Clin Infect Dis 50:291, 2010 (IDSA Guidelines). ↓ with ARV but still common presenting OI in newly diagnosed AIDS pts. Cryptococcal infection may be manifested by positive blood culture or positive serum cryptococcal antigen (CRAG; >95% sens). CRAG no help in monitoring response to therapy. With ARV, symptoms of acute meningitis may return: immune reconstitution inflammatory syndrome (IRIS). ↑ CSF pressure (> **250 mm H₂O**) associated with high mortality, lower with CSF removal. If frequent LPs not possible, ventriculoperitoneal shunts an option (Surg Neurol 63:529 & 531, 2005).	**Treatment:** Ampho B 0.7 mg/kg IV q24h + **flucytosine¹** 25 mg/kg po q6h for at least two weeks or longer until CSF is sterilized. See Comment. **Then** **Consolidation therapy:** Fluconazole 400-800 mg po q24h to complete a 10-wk course then suppression (see below). Start Antiretroviral Therapy (ARV) if possible.	**Amphotericin B or liposomal ampho B plus fluconazole** 400 mg PO or IV daily, **OR** **Amphotericin B** 0.7 mg/kg or **liposomal ampho B** 4 mg/kg IV q24h alone. **OR Fluconazole** ≥ 800 mg/day (1200 mg preferred) (PO or IV) **plus Flucytosine** 25 mg/kg po q6h for 4-6 weeks.	Outcome of treatment: treatment failure associated with dissemination of infection & high serum antigen titer, indicative of high burden of organisms and lack of (5FC) use during induction Rx, abnormal neurological evaluation & underlying hematological malignancy. Mortality rates still high, especially in those with concomitant pneumonia (Postgrad Med 121:107, 2009). Early Dx essential for improved outcome (PLOS Medicine 4:e47, 2007). Ampho B + 5FC more rapidly than ampho + flu or ampho + 5FC + flu. Ampho B 1 mg/kg/d alone much more rapidly fungicidal in vivo than flu 400 mg/d (CID 45:76&81, 2007). Use of lipid-based ampho B assoc. with lower mortality compared to ampho B deoxycholate in solid organ transplant recipients (CID 48:1566, 2009). Monitor 5-FC levels: peak 70-80 mg/L, trough 30-40 mg/L. Higher levels assoc. with bone marrow toxicity. No difference in outcome if given IV or po (AAC 51:1038, 2007). Failure of flu may rarely be due to resistant organism, especially if burden of organism high at initiation of Rx. Although 200 mg qd or 400 mg qd of flu median survival 76 & 82 days respectively; authors prefer 400 mg po qd (BMC Infect Dis 6:118, 2006). Trend toward improved outcomes with fluconazole 400-800 mg combined with ampho B versus ampho B alone in AIDS patients (CID 48:1775, 2009). Role of other azoles uncertain: successful outcomes were observed in 14/29 (48%) subjects with cryptococcal meningitis treated with posaconazole (JAC 56:745, 2005). Voriconazole also may be effective. Survival probably improved with ART but IRIS may complicate its use. There is considerable controversy as to the timing of initiation of ART (see CID 50:1532, 2010 and CID 51: 984, 985, 986, 987, 2010). One study suggests higher mortality with initiation of ART within 72 hrs of diagnosis (CID 50:1532, 2010), but the generalization of this study is an issue. Among others, most authorities continue to recommend ART within 2-wks.
Suppression (chronic maintenance therapy): Discontinuation of antifungal can be considered among pts who remain asymptomatic, with CD4 >100–200/mm³ for ≥6 months. Some perform a lumbar puncture before discontinuation of maintenance rx. Reappearance of pos. serum CRAG may predict relapse	**Fluconazole** 200 mg/day po. [If CD4 count rises to >100/mm³ with effective antiretroviral rx., some authorities recommend dc suppressive rx. See www.hivatis.org. Authors would only dc if CSF culture negative.]	**Itraconazole** 200 mg po q12h if flu intolerant or failure No data on Vori for maintenance.	Itraconazole less effective than fluconazole & not recommended because of higher relapse rate (23% vs 4%). Recurrence rate of 0.4 to 3.9 per 100 patient-years with discontinuation of suppressive therapy in 100 patients on ARV with CD4 >100 cells/mm³.

¹ Flucytosine = 5-FC

See page 2 for abbreviations. All dosage recommendations are for adults (unless otherwise indicated) and assume normal renal function

TABLE 11A (10)

ANTIMICROBIAL AGENTS OF CHOICE

TYPE OF INFECTION/ORGANISM/ SITE OF INFECTION	PRIMARY	ALTERNATIVE	COMMENTS
Dermatophytosis (See *Mycopathologia 166:353, 2008*) **Onychomycosis** (Tinea unguium) (*NEJM 360:2108, 2009*) Ciclopirox olamine 8% lacquer daily for 48 weeks; best suited for superficial and distal infections (overall cure rates of approx 30%).	**Fingernail Rx Options:** **Terbinafine** 250 mg po q24h (children <20 kg: 67.5 mg/day, 20–40 kg: 125 mg/day, >40 kg: 250 mg/day) x6 wks (79% effective) OR **Itraconazole** 200 mg po q24h x 3 mos.[NAI] OR **Itraconazole** 200 mg po bid x 1 wk/mo x 2 mos. OR **Fluconazole** 150–300 mg po q wk x 3–6 mos.	**Toenail Rx Options:** **Terbinafine** 250 mg po q24h (children <20 kg: 67.5 mg/day, 20–40 kg: 125 mg/day, >40 kg: 250 mg/day) x 12 wks (76% effective) OR **Itraconazole** 200 mg po q24h x 3 mos (59% effective) OR **Itraconazole** 200 mg bid x 1 wk/mo. x 3–4 mos (63% effective)[NAI] OR **Fluconazole** 150–300 mg po q wk x 6–12 mos (48% effective)[NAI]	
Tinea capitis ("ringworm") (Trichophyton tonsurans, Microsporum canis, N. America; other sp. elsewhere) (*PIDJ 18:191, 1999*)	**Terbinafine** 250 mg po q24h (adults): <20 kg: 67.5 mg/day; 5 mg/kg/day x 4 wks (children).	**Itraconazole** 3–5 mg/kg per day x 4 wks[NAI] **Fluconazole** 6 mg/kg q wk x 8–12 wks. Cap at 150 mg po q wk for adults **Griseofulvin:** adults 500 mg po q24h x 6–8 wks, children 10–20/kg per day until hair regrows.	Durations of therapy for "T" tolerance: treat for approx. twice as long for M. canis. All agents with similar cure rates (60–100%) in clinical studies. Addition of topical ketoconazole or selenium sulfate shampoo reduces transmissibility (*Int J Dermatol 39:261, 2000*)
Tinea corporis, cruris, or pedis (Trichophyton rubrum, T. mentagrophytes, Epidermophyton floccosum) "Athlete's foot, jock itch," and ringworm	**Topical rx:** Generally applied 2x/day. Available as creams, ointments, sprays, by prescription & "over the counter." Apply 2x/day for 2–3 wks. Preclotrimazol: Lotrimin Ultra or Lamisil AT contain butenafine & terbinafine—both are fungicidal.	**Terbinafine** 250 mg po q24h x 2 wks[NAI] OR **ketoconazole** 200 mg po q24h x 4 wks OR **fluconazole** 150 mg po 1x/wk for 2–4 wks[NAI] **Griseofulvin:** adults 500 mg po q24h x 4–8 wks for peds	Keto po often effective in severe recalcitrant infection. Follow for hepatotoxicity; many drug-drug interactions.
Tinea versicolor (Malassezia furfur or Pityrosporum orbiculare) Rule out erythrasma—see Table 1, page 54	**Ketoconazole** (400 mg po single dose)[NAI] or (200 mg po q24h x 7 days) or (2% cream 1x q24h x 2 wks)	**Fluconazole** 400 mg po single dose or **itraconazole** 400 mg po q24h x 3–7 days	Keto (po) times 1 dose was 97% effective in 1 study. Another alternative: **Selenium sulfide** (Selsun). 2.5% lotion: apply as lather, leave on 10 min then wash off. 1/day x 7 day or 3–5x/wk times 2–4 wks
Fusariosis Third most common cause of invasive mould infections, after Aspergillus and Mucorales and related molds, in patients with hematologic malignancies (*Mycoses 52:197, 2009*). Pneumonia, skin infections, bone and joint infections, and disseminated disease occur in severely immunocompromised patients. In contrast to other moulds, blood cultures are frequently positive. *Fusarium solani, F. oxysporum, F. verticillioides* and *F. proliferatum* account for approx. 90% of isolates (*Clin Micro Rev 20: 695, 2007*). Frequently fatal; outcome depends on degree of immunosuppression.	**Surgical debridement** for localized disease. **Lipid-based ampho B** 5–10 mg/kg/d; OR **Ampho B** 1–1.5 mg/kg/d	**Posaconazole** 400 mg po bid with meals (if not taking meals, 200 mg qid); OR **Voriconazole** IV: 6 mg per kg q12h times 1 day, then 4 mg per kg q12h; PO: 400 mg q12h; then 200 mg q12h. See comments.	Most antifungal agents, including echinocandins, *F. solani* and *F. verticillioides* typically are resistant to azoles. *F. oxysporum* and *F. moniliforme* may be susceptible to voriconazole and posaconazole. Role of combination therapy not well defined but case reports of response (*Mycoses 50: 227, 2007*). Outcome dependent on reduction or discontinuation of immunosuppression. Duration of therapy depends on response; long-term suppressive therapy for patients remaining on immunosuppressive therapy.

* **Serious but rare cases of hepatic failure** have been reported in pts receiving terbinafine & should not be used in those with chronic or active liver disease (see *Table 11B, page 126*).
• Use of itraconazole has been associated with myocardial dysfunction and with onset of congestive heart failure.

See page 2 for abbreviations. *All dosage recommendations are for adults (unless otherwise indicated) and assume normal renal function*

TABLE 11A (11)

TYPE OF INFECTION/ORGANISM/ SITE OF INFECTION	ANTIMICROBIAL AGENTS OF CHOICE		COMMENTS
	PRIMARY	ALTERNATIVE	
Histoplasmosis (Histoplasma capsulatum): See IDSA Guideline: CID 45:807, 2007. Best diagnostic test is urinary, serum, or CSF histoplasma antigen: MiraVista Diagnostics (1-866-647-2847)			
Acute pulmonary histoplasmosis	**Mild to moderate disease, symptoms <4 wks:** No rx. If symptoms last over one month: **Itraconazole** 200 mg po tid for 3 days then once or twice daily for 6-12 wks. **Moderately severe or severe: Liposomal ampho B,** 3-5 mg/kg/d or **ABLC** 5 mg/kg/d IV or ampho B 0.7-1.0 mg/kg/d for 1-2 wks, then **itra** 200 mg tid for 3 days, then bid for 12 wks. + **methylprednisolone** 0.5-1 mg/kg/d for 1-2 wks.		Ampho B for patients at low risk of nephrotoxicity.
Chronic cavitary pulmonary histoplasmosis	**Itra** 200 mg po tid for 3 days then once or twice daily for at least 12 mos (some prefer 18-24 mos).		Document therapeutic itraconazole blood levels at 2 wks. Relapses occur in 9-15% of patients.
Mediastinal lymphadenitis, mediastinal granuloma, pericarditis; and rheumatologic syndromes	**Mild cases:** Antifungal rx not indicated. Nonsteroidal anti-inflammatory drug for pericarditis or rheumatologic syndromes. If no response to non-steroidals, **Prednisone** 0.5-1.0 mg/kg/d tapered over 1-2 weeks for 1) pericarditis with hemodynamic compromise, 2) lymphadenitis with obstruction or compression syndromes, or 3) severe rheumatologic syndromes.		
Progressive disseminated histoplasmosis	**Itra** 200 mg po once or twice daily for 6-12 wks for moderately severe to severe cases. If symptoms persist after 12 weeks. **Mild to moderate disease: Itra** 200 mg po bid for 3 days then **itra** 200 mg tid for at least 12 mos **Moderately severe to severe disease: Liposomal ampho B,** 3 mg/kg/d or **ABLC** 5 mg/kg/d for 1-2 weeks then **itra** 200 mg tid for 3 days, then bid for at least 12 mos.		Check itra blood levels to document therapeutic concentrations.
CNS histoplasmosis	**Liposomal ampho B,** 5 mg/kg/d, for a total of 175 mg/kg over 4-6 wks, then **itra** 200 mg 2-3x a day for at least 12 mos.		**Ampho B** 0.7-1.0 mg/kg/d may be used for patients at low risk of nephrotoxicity. Confirm therapeutic itra blood levels. Azoles are teratogenic; itra should be avoided in pregnancy; use a lipid ampho formulation. Urinary antigen levels useful for monitoring response to therapy and relapse Monitor CNS histo antigen, monitor itra blood levels. PCR may be better for Dx than histo antigen. Absorption of itra (check levels) and CNS penetration may be an issue; case reports of success with Fluconazole effective for CNS disease or itra failures. (*Arch Neurology* 2008; *J Antimicro Chemo* 57:1235, 2006) (*Braz J Infect Dis* 12:555, 2008) and Posaconazole (*Drugs* 65:1553, 2005) following Ampho B therapy.
Prophylaxis (immunocompromised patients)	**Itra** 200 mg po daily		Consider primary **prophylaxis in HIV-infected** patients with < 150 CD4 cells/mm³ in high prevalence areas. Secondary prophylaxis (i.e. suppressive therapy) indicated in HIV-infected patients with < 150 CD4 cells/mm³ and other immunocompromised patients in who immunosuppression cannot be reversed

See page 2 for abbreviations. All dosage recommendations are for adults (unless otherwise indicated) and assume normal renal function

TABLE 11A (12)

TYPE OF INFECTION/ORGANISM/ SITE OF INFECTION	ANTIMICROBIAL AGENTS OF CHOICE		COMMENTS
	PRIMARY	ALTERNATIVE	
Madura foot (See *Nocardia* & *Scedosporium*)			
Mucormycosis & other related species—Rhizopus, Rhizomucor, Lichtheimia (CID 54:1629, 2012). Rhinocerebral, pulmonary invasive. Key to successful rx: early dx with symptoms suggestive of sinusitis (or lateral facial pain or numbness); think mucor with palatal ulcers, &/or black eschars, onset unilateral blindness in immunocompromised or diabetic pt. Rapidly fatal without rx. Dx by culture of tissue or stain: wide ribbon-like, non-septated with variation in diameter & right angle branching.	**Liposomal ampho B** 5-10 mg/kg/day; OR **Ampho B** 1-1.5 mg/kg/day.	**Posaconazole** 400 mg po bid with meals (if not taking meals, 200 mg po qid)[NM].	**Combination therapy** of ampho B or a lipid-based ampho B plus caspofungin associated with improved cure rates (100% vs 45%) in one small retrospective study (6 combo therapy patients, 31 monotherapy, historical control patients); ampho B lipid complex (ABLC) monotherapy relatively effective with 80% success rate vs 69% other polyenes (CID 47:364, 2008). Complete or partial response rates of 60-80% in posaconazole salvage protocols (JAC 61, Suppl 1:35, 2008). Resistant to voriconazole: prolonged use of voriconazole prophylaxis predisposes to mucormycosis infections. [1] Total duration of therapy based on response: continue therapy until 1) resolution of clinical signs and symptoms of infection, 2) resolution or stabilization of radiographic abnormalities; and 3) resolution of underlying immunosuppression. Posaconazole for secondary prophylaxis for those on immunosuppressive therapy (CID 48:1743, 2009).
Paracoccidioidomycosis (South American blastomycosis) P. brasiliensis (Dermatol Clin 26:257, 2008; Expert Rev Anti Infect Ther 6:251, 2008). Important cause of death from fungal infection in AIDS patients in Brazil (Mem Inst Oswaldo Cruz 104:513, 2009).	**TMP/SMX** 800/160 mg bid-tid for 30 days, then 400/80 mg/day indefinitely (up to 3-5 years); OR **Itraconazole** (100 or 200 mg orally daily)	**Ketoconazole** 200-400 mg daily for 6-18 months; OR **Ampho B** total dose > 30 mg/kg	Improvement in > 90% pts on itra or keto.[NM] **Ampho B** reserved for severe cases and those intolerant to other agents. TMP-SMX suppression life-long in HIV+.
Lobomycosis (keloidal blastomycosis)/ P. loboi	Surgical excision, clofazimine or itraconazole.		
Penicilliosis (Penicillium marneffei). Common disseminated fungal infection in AIDS pts in SE Asia (esp. Thailand & Vietnam). Invasive.	**Ampho B** 0.5-1 mg/kg per day times 2 wks followed by **Itraconazole** 400 mg/day for 10 wks followed by 200 mg/day po **indefinitely for HIV-infected pts.**	For less sick patients **Itra** 200 mg po tid x 3 days, then 200 mg bid x 12 wks, then 200 mg po q24h; (IV if unable to take po)	3rd most common OI in AIDS pts in SE Asia following TBc and cryptococcal meningitis. Prolonged fever, lymphadenopathy, hepatomegaly. Skin nodules are umbilicated (mimic cryptococcal infection or molluscum contagiosum). Preliminary data suggests vori effective. CID 43:1060, 2006.
Phaeohyphomycosis, Black molds, Dematiaceous fungi (See CID 46:1033, 2009) Sinuses, skin, bone & joint, brain abscess, endocarditis, emerging especially in HSCT pts with disseminated disease. **Scedosporium prolificans,** Bipolaris, Wangiella, Cunularia, Exophiala, Phialemonium, Scytalidium, Alternaria.	**Surgery + itraconazole** 400 mg/day po; duration not defined, probably 6 mo[NM]	Case report of success with **voriconazole ± terbinafine** (Scand J Infect Dis 39:87, 2007); OR **itraconazole + terbinafine** synergistic against S. prolificans. No clinical data & combination could show ↑ toxicity (see *Table 11B, page 124*).	**Posaconazole** successful in case of brain abscess (CID 34:1648, 2002) and refractory infection (Mycosis: 519, 2006). **Notoriously resistant to antifungal rx including amphotericin & azoles.** 44% of patients in compassionate use/salvage therapy study responded to voriconazole (AAC 52:1743, 2008). >80% mortality in immunocompromised hosts.

¹ **Oral solution preferred to tablets because of ↑ absorption** (see Table 11B, page 124).

See page 2 for abbreviations. All dosage recommendations are for adults (unless otherwise indicated) and assume normal renal function.

TABLE 11A (13)

TYPE OF INFECTION/ORGANISM/ SITE OF INFECTION	ANTIMICROBIAL AGENTS OF CHOICE		COMMENTS
	PRIMARY	ALTERNATIVE	
Madura foot (continued)			
Scedosporium apiospermum (Pseudallescheria boydii) (not confused with a true dematiaceous mold) (Medicine 81:333, 2002). Skin, subcut. (Madura foot), brain abscess, recurrent meningitis. May appear after near-drowning incidents. Also emerging especially in hematopoietic stem cell transplant (HSCT) pts with disseminated disease	**Voriconazole** 6 mg/kg IV q12h on day 1, then either (4 mg/kg IV q12h) or (200 mg po q12h for body weight ≥40 kg, but 100 mg po q12h for body weight <40 kg) (AAC 52:1743, 2008). 300 mg bid serum concentrations are subtherapeutic, i.e., <1 mcg/mL (CID 46:201, 2008)	Surgery + **itraconazole** 200 mg po bid until clinically well.⁵ᴺ (Many species now resistant or refractory to Itra); OR **Posa** 400 mg po bid with meals (if not taking meals, 200 mg po qid).	**Resistant to many antifungal drugs including amphotericin.** In vitro voriconazole more active than Itra and posaconazole in vitro (Clin Microbiol Rev 21:157, 2008). Case reports of successful rx of disseminated and CNS disease with voriconazole (AAC 52:1743, 2008). Posaconazole active in vitro and successful in several case reports
Sporotrichosis IDSA Guideline: CID 45:1255, 2007. Cutaneous/Lymphocutaneous	**Itraconazole** po 200 mg/day for 2-4 wks after all lesions resolved, usually 3-6 mos.	If no response, **Itra** 200 mg po bid or **terbinafine** 500 mg po bid & **SSKI** 5 drops (eye drops) tid & increase to 40-50 drops tid	Fluconazole 400-800 mg daily only if no response to primary or alternative suggestions. Pregnancy or nursing: local hyperthermia (see below).
Osteoarticular	**Itra** 200 mg po bid x 12 mos.	**Liposomal ampho B** 3-5 mg/kg/d IV or **ABLC** 5 mg/kg/d IV or **ampho B deoxycholate** 0.7-1 mg/kg IV daily. If response, change to **Itra** 200 mg po bid x total 12 mos.	After 2 wks of therapy, document adequate serum levels of itraconazole.
Pulmonary	If severe, **lipid ampho B** 3-5 mg/kg/d IV or **standard ampho B** 0.7-1 mg/kg IV daily until response, then **Itra** 200 mg po bid. Total of 12 mos.	Less severe: **itraconazole** 200 mg po bid x 12 mos.	After 2 weeks of therapy document adequate serum levels of Itra. Surgical resection plus ampho B for localized pulmonary disease.
Meningeal or Disseminated	**Lipid ampho B** 5 mg/kg IV once daily x 4-6 wks, then—if better—**Itra** 200 mg po bid for total of 12 mos.	AIDS/Other immunosuppressed pts chronic therapy with **Itra** 200 mg po once daily.	After 2 weeks, document adequate serum levels of Itra.
Pregnancy and children	**Pregnancy:** Cutaneous—local hyperthermia. Severe: **lipid ampho B** 3-5 mg/kg IV once daily. **Avoid itraconazole.**	**Children:** Cutaneous: **Itra** 6-10 mg/kg (max of 400 mg) daily. Alternative is **SSKI** 1 drop/kg/day increasing to max of 1 drop/kg or 40-50 drops tid/day, whichever is lowest	For children with disseminated sporotrichosis: Standard ampho B 0.7 mg/kg IV once daily & after response, Itra 6-10 mg/kg IV once daily.

See page 2 for abbreviations. All dosage recommendations are for adults (unless otherwise indicated) and assume normal renal function

TABLE 11B – ANTIFUNGAL DRUGS: DOSAGE, ADVERSE EFFECTS, COMMENTS

DRUG NAME, GENERIC (TRADE)/USUAL DOSAGE	ADVERSE EFFECTS/COMMENTS
Non-lipid amphotericin B deoxycholate (Fungizone): 0.3–1 mg/kg per day as single infusion **Ampho B predictably not active vs. Scedosporium, Candida lusitaniae & Aspergillus terreus** (TABLE 11C, page 127)	**Admin:** Ampho B is a colloida suspension that must be infused in electrolyte-free D5W at 0.1 mg/mL to avoid precipitation. No need to protect suspensions from light. Infusions cause chills/fever, myalgia, anorexia, nausea, rarely hemodynamic collapse/hypotension. Postulated due to proinflammatory cytokines, doesn't appear to be histamine release (Pharmacol 23:966, 2003). Infusion duration usu. 4+ hrs. No difference found in 1 vs 4 hr infus. except chills/fever occurred sooner with 1 hr infus (Ln Med Dose Ranges/Pulmonary reactions (severe dyspnea & focal infiltrates suggest pulmonary edema) assoc with rapid infus. **Severe rigors respond to meperidine (25–50 mg IV)**. If repeated, may pretreat with ibuprofen (200 mg) and heparin (1000 units) had no influence on rigors/fever. If cytokine postulate correct, NSAIDs or high-dose steroids may prove efficacious but their use may risk worsening infection under rx or increased risk of **nephrotoxicity** (i.e. NSAIDs). Clinical side effects ↓ with ↑ age. **Toxicity:** Major concern is nephrotoxic. Manifest initially by kaliuresis and hypokalemia, then fall in serum bicarbonate (may proceed to renal tubular acidosis). ↑ in renal erythropoietin and anemia, and rising BUN/serum creatinine. Hypomagnesemia may occur. Can reduce risk of renal injury by **(a) pre- & post-infusion hydration with 500 mL saline (if clinical status allows salt load)**, **(b)** avoidance of other nephro-toxins, e.g. aminoglycosides, cyclosporine.
Lipid-based ampho B products: **Amphotericin B lipid complex (ABLC)** (Abelcet): 5 mg/kg per day as single infusion	**Admin:** Consists of ampho B complexed with 2 lipid bilayer ribbons. Compared to standard ampho B, larger volume of distribution, rapid blood clearance and high tissue concentrations (liver, spleen, lung). Dosage: **5 mg/kg once daily;** infuse at 2.5 mg/kg per hr; adult and ped. dose the same. Do NOT use an in-line filter. Do not dilute with saline or mix with other drugs or electrolytes.[2] **Toxicity:** Fever and chills in 14–18%; nausea 9%, vomiting 8%; serum creatinine ↑ in 11%; renal failure 5%; anemia 4%; ↓ K 5%; rash 4%. A fatal case of fat embolism reported following ABLC infusion (Exp Mol Path 177:246, 2004).
Liposomal amphotericin B (LAB, AmBisome):1–5 mg/kg per day as single infusion.	**Admin:** Consists of vesicular bilayer liposome with ampho B intercalated within the membrane. Dosage: **3–5 mcg/mL** iV as single dose infused over a period of approx. 120 min. Infusion time can be reduced to 60 min. (see footnote[2]). Tolerated well in elderly pts (J Inf 50:277, 2005). **Major toxicity:** Gen less than ampho B. Nephrotoxicity 18.7% vs 33.7% for ampho B, chills 47% vs 75%, nausea 39.7% vs 38.7%, vomiting 31.8% vs 43.9%, rash 24% both. Ca ↓ 18.4% vs 20.4% vs 25.6%, ↓ K 20.4% vs 25.6%. Acute infusion-related reactions common with liposomal ampho B, 20–40%, 86% occur within 5 min of infusion and chest pain dyspnea, hypoxia and flushing & urticaria near end of 4 hr infusion. All responded to diphenhydramine (1 mg/kg) & interruption of infusion. Reactions may be due to complement activation by liposome (CID 36:1213, 2003).
Caspofungin (Cancidas) 70 mg IV on day 1 followed by 50 mg IV q24H (reduce to 35 mg IV q24h with moderate hepatic insufficiency)	An echinocandin (targets synthesis of β-(1,3)-D-glucan). Fungicidal against candida (MIC <2 mcg/mL) including those resistant to other antifungals & active against aspergillus (MIC 0.4–2.7 mcg/mL). Approved indications for caspo incl: empirical rx for febrile, neutropenic pts; rx of candidemia, candida intraabdominal abscesses, peritonitis, & pleural space infections; esophageal candidiasis; & invasive aspergillosis in pts refractory to or intolerant of other therapies. Serum levels on rec. dosages ≈ peak 12, trough 1.3 (24 hrs) mcg/mL. **Toxicity:** remarkably non-toxic. Most common adverse effect: pruritus at infusion site & headache, fever, chills, vomiting, & diarrhea assoc with inf. ↑ serum creatinine in 8% on caspo vs 21% short-course ampho B in 422 pts with candidemia (N Eng J Med, Oct 12, 2005, online). Drug metab in liver & dosage ↓ to 35 mg in moderate to severe hepatic failure. Class C for preg (embryotoxic in rats & rabbits). See Table 22, page 217 for drug-drug interactions, esp. cyclosporine (hepatic toxicity) & tacrolimus (drug level monitoring recommended). Reversible thrombocytopenia reported (Pharmacother 24:1408, 2004). **No drug in CSF or urine.**
Micafungin (Mycamine) 50 mg/day for prophylaxis post-bone marrow stem cell trans; 100 mg candidemia, 150 mg candida esophagitis.	The 2nd echinocandin approved by FDA for rx of esophageal candidiasis & prophylaxis against candida infections in HSCT recipients. Active against most strains of candida spp. & aspergillus sp. incl those resist to fluconazole such as C. glabrata & C. krusei. No antagonism seen when combo with other antifungal drugs. No dosage adjust for severe renal failure or moderate hepatic impairment. Watch for drug-drug interactions with sirolimus or nifedipine. Micafungin well tolerated & common adverse events incl nausea 2.8%, vomiting 2.4%, & headache 2.4%. Transient ↑ LFTs, BUN, creatinine 2.4%. rare cases of significant hepatitis & renal insufficiency. See CID 42:1171, 2006. **No drug in CSF or urine.**

[1] Published data from patients intolerant of or refractory to conventional ampho B deoxycholate (Amp B d). **None of the lipid ampho B preps (except liposomal ampho B was more effective vs ampho B in rx of disseminated histoplasmosis in 2 wks).** Dosage equivalency has not been established (CID 36:1500, 2003). Nephrotoxicity ↓ with all lipid ampho B preps.

[2] Comparisons between Abelcet & AmBisome suggest higher infusion-assoc. toxicity (rigors) with Abelcet (70% vs 36%) but higher frequency of mild hepatic toxicity with AmBisome (59% vs 38%, p=0.05). Mild elevations in serum creatinine were observed in 1/3 of both (BJ Hemat 103:198, 1998; Focus on Fungal Inf #9, 1999; Bone Marrow Tx 20:39, 1997; CID 26:1383, 1998).

[3] HSCT = hematopoietic stem cell transplant.

See page 2 for abbreviations. All dosage recommendations are for adults (unless otherwise indicated) and assume normal renal function.

TABLE 11B (2)

DRUG NAME, GENERIC (TRADE)/USUAL DOSAGE	ADVERSE EFFECTS/COMMENTS
Andulafungin (Eraxis) For Candidemia: 200 mg IV on day 1 followed by 100 mg/day IV); Rx for EC: 100 mg IV x 1, then 50 mg IV once/d	An echinocandin with antifungal activity (cidal) against candida sp. & aspergillus sp. including ampho B- & triazole-resistant strains. FDA approved for treatment of esophageal candidiasis (EC), candidemia, and other complicated Candida infections. Effective in clinical trials of esophageal candidiasis & in 1 trial was superior to fluconazole in rx of invasive candidiasis/candidemia in 245 pts (75.6% vs 60.2%). Well tolerated, remarkably non-toxic; most common side-effects: nausea, vomiting, ↓ mg, ↓ K, & headache in 11-13% of pts. No dose adjustments for renal or hepatic insufficiency. See CID 43:215, 2006. **No drug in CSF or urine.**
Fluconazole (Diflucan) 100 mg cap 150 mg tabs 200 mg tabs 400 mg IV Oral suspension- 50 mg per 5 mL	IV=oral dose because of excellent bioavailability. **Pharmacology:** absorbed po, water solubility enables IV. For peak serum levels (see Table 9A, page 87). T½ 30hr (range 20-50 hr), 12% protein bound. **CSF levels 50-90% of serum in normals,** 1 in meningitis. No effect on mammalian sterol metabolism. **Drug-drug interactions common,** see Table 22. Side-effects overall 16% (more common in HIV+ pts (21%)). Nausea 3.7%, headache 1.9%, skin rash 1.8%, abdominal pain 1.7%, vomiting 1.7%, diarrhea 1.5%, ↑ SGOT 20%. Alopecia (scalp, pubic crest) in ↑ 2-20% pts (reversible in approx. 6mo). Rare: severe hepatotoxicity (CID 41:301, 2005), exfoliative dermatitis. **Note: Candida krusei and Candida glabrata resistant to Flu.**
Flucytosine (Ancobon) 500 mg cap	AEs. Overall 30%. GI 6% (diarrhea, anorexia, nausea, vomiting); hematologic 22% (leukopenia, thrombocytopenia, when serum level >100 mcg/mL (esp. in azotemic pts)), hepatotoxicity (asymptomatic ↑SGOT, reversible); skin rash 7%, aplastic anemia (rare—2 or 3 cases). False 1 in serum creatinine on EKTACHEM analyzer.
Griseofulvin (Fulvicin, Grifulvin, Grisactin) 500 mg, susp 125 mg/mL	Photosensitivity, urticaria, GI upset, fatigue, leukopenia (rare). Interferes with warfarin drugs. Increases blood and urine porphyrins, should not be used in patients with porphyria. Minor disulfiram-like reactions. Exacerbation of systemic lupus erythematosus.
Imidazoles, topical For vaginal and/or skin use	Not recommended in 1st trimester of pregnancy. Local reactions: 0.5-1.5% dyspareunia, mild vaginal or vulvar erythema, burning, pruritus, urticaria, rash. Rarely similar symptoms in sexual partner.
Itraconazole (Sporanox) 100 mg cap ~10 mg/mL oral solution

IV usual dose 200 mg bid x 4 doses followed by 200 mg q24h for a max of 14 days | **Itraconazole tablet & solution forms not interchangeable, solution preferred.** Many authorities recommend measuring drug serum concentration after 2 wks to obtain highest plasma concentration. To obtain highest plasma concentration, tablet is given with food & acidic drinks (e.g., cola), while solution is taken in fasted state; under these conditions, the peak conc. of capsule is approx. 3 mcg/mL & of solution 5.4 mcg/mL. Peak levels reached faster (2.2 vs 5.1hrs) with solution. **36 of rx plasma concentrations after IV injection (po given). Solution: 200 mg (20 mL) po qd. (do not use to treat meningitis)** (on day 36 of rx). Absorption of caps requires acid environment, reduced when taken with antacids, or in absence of penetration into CSF. Adverse effects: dose-related nausea 10%, diarrhea 8%, vomiting 6%, & abdominal discomfort 5.7%. Allergic rash 8.6%, ↑ bilirubin 6%, edema 3.5%, & hepatitis 2.7% reported. ↑ doses may produce hypokalemia 8% & ↑ blood pressure 3.2%. Delirium, peripheral neuropathy & tremor reported (J Neur Neurosurg Psych 81:327, 2010). **Reported to produce impairment in cardiac function.** Severe liver failure req transplant in pts receiving pulse rx for onchomycosis: FDA reports 24 cases with 11 deaths out of 50 mill people who received the drug prior to 2001. Other concern: as with fluconazole and ketoconazole, is **drug-drug interactions;** see Table 22. Some can be life-threatening. |
Ketoconazole (Nizoral) 200 mg tab	Gastric acid required for absorption—cimetidine, omeprazole, antacids block absorption. In achlorhydria, dissolve tablet in 4 mL 0.2N-HCl, drink with a straw. Coca-Cola ↑ absorption by 65%. CSF levels "none." **Drug-drug interactions important,** see Table 22. **Some interactions can be life-threatening.** Liver toxicity of hepatocellular type reported in about 1:10,000 exposed pts—usually after several days to weeks of exposure. At doses of ≥800 mg per day serum testosterone and plasma cortisol levels fall. With high doses, adrenal (Addisonian) crisis reported.
Miconazole (Monistat IV) 200 mg—*not available in U.S.*	IV miconazole indicated in patient critically ill with Scedosporium (Pseudallescheria boydii) infection. Very toxic due to vehicle needed to get drug into solution.
Nystatin (Mycostatin) 30 gm cream 500,000 units oral tab	Topical: virtually no adverse effects. Less effective than imidazoles and triazoles. PO: large doses give nausea GI distress and diarrhea.

See page 2 for abbreviations. All dosage recommendations are for adults (unless otherwise indicated) and assume normal renal function

TABLE 11B (3)

DRUG NAME, GENERIC (TRADE)/USUAL DOSAGE	ADVERSE EFFECTS/COMMENTS
Posaconazole (*Noxafil*) 400 mg po bid with meals (if not taking meals, 200 mg qid). 200 mg po TID (with food) for prophylaxis. 40 mg/mL suspension. No IV formulation.	An oral triazole with activity against a wide range of fungi refractory to other antifungal rx including: aspergillosis, mucormycosis (variability by species), fusariosis, Scedosporium (Pseudallescheria), phaeohyphomycosis, histoplasmosis, refractory candidiasis, chromoblastomycosis, & refractory coccidioidomycosis. Approved for prophylaxis. **Should be taken with high fat meal for maximum absorption.** Clinical responses in 75% of 176 AIDS pts with azole-refractory oral/esophageal candidiasis. Posaconazole has similar toxicities as other triazoles: nausea 9%, vomiting 6%, abd. pain 5%, headache 5%, diarrhea, ↑ ALT, AST, & rash (3% each). In pts rx for >6 mos., serious side-effects have included adrenal insufficiency, nephrotoxicity, & QTc interval prolongation. Significant drug-drug interactions; inhibits CYP3A4 (see Table 22). Consider monitoring serum concentrations (*See Drugs 65:1552, 2005*)
Terbinafine (*Lamisil*) 250 mg tab	In pts given terbinafine for onychomycosis, rare cases (8) of idiosyncratic & symptomatic hepatic injury & more rarely liver failure leading to death or liver transplant. The drug is **not recommended** for pts **with chronic or active liver disease**; hepatotoxicity may occur in pts with or without pre-existing disease. Pretreatment serum transaminases (ALT & AST) advised & alternate rx used for those with abnormal levels. Rx started on terbinafine should be warned about symptoms suggesting liver dysfunction (persistent nausea, anorexia, fatigue, vomiting, RUQ pain, jaundice, dark urine or pale stools). If symptoms develop, drug should be discontinued & liver function immediately evaluated. In controlled trials, changes in ocular lens and retina reported—clinical significance unknown. Major drug-drug interaction is 100% ↑ in rate of clearance by rifampin. AEs: usually mild, transient and rarely caused discontinuation of rx, % with AE; terbinafine vs placebo: nausea/diarrhea 2.6–5.6 vs 2.9; rash 5.6 vs 2.2; taste abnormality 2.8 vs 0.7. Inhibits CYP2D6 enzymes (see Table 22). An acute generalized exanthematous pustulosis and subacute cutaneous lupus erythematosus reported.
Voriconazole (*Vfend*) IV: Loading dose 6 mg per kg q12h times 1 (then 4 mg per kg q12h) IV for invasive aspergillus & serious mold infections: **3 mg per kg IV q12h** for serious candida infections. Oral: **>40 kg body weight:** 400 mg po q12h, then 200 mg po q12h. **<40 kg body weight:** 200 mg po q12h, then 100 mg po q12h **Take oral dose 1 hour before or 1 hour after eating.** Oral suspension 140 mg per mL). Oral suspension dosing: Same as for oral tabs. Reduce to ½ maintenance dose for moderate hepatic insufficiency	A triazole with activity against Aspergillus sp., **including Ampho resistant strains of A. terreus.** Active vs Candida sp. (including krusei), Fusarium sp., & various molds. Toxicity similar to other azoles/triazoles including uncommon serious hepatic toxicity (hepatitis, cholestasis & fulminant hepatic failure. Liver function tests should be monitored during IV & drug dc'd if abnormalities detected. Rash reported in up to 20%, occ. photosensitivity & rare Stevens-Johnson, hallucinations & **anaphylactoid infusion reactions following IV or po ('altered/enhanced visual perception', blurred or colored visual change or photophobia) within 30-60 minutes. Visual changes resolve within 30-60 min. after administration & are attenuated with repeated doses (do not drive at night for outpatient rx).** Peripheral edema reported in up to 24% of pts. 1 case of QT prolongation with ventricular tachycardia in a 15 y/o pt with ALL reported. **Approx. 21%** experience a transient visual disturbance. Pts rx with repeated doses. Up to 20% or more of pts with subtherapeutic levels with oral administration; check levels for suspected treatment failure, life threatening infections. Steady state serum levels reach 2.5–4 mcg/mL. Pts with subtherapeutic levels may be required to achieve target steady-state drug concentrations of 1–6 mcg/mL. Toxicity similar to other azoles/triazoles including uncommon serious hepatic toxicity (hepatitis, cholestasis & fulminant hepatic failure. IV voriconazole carrier (SBECD-sulfobutylether-β cyclodextrin) may accumulate and may adversely affect nephrotoxicity in renal impaired. (*NEJM 356:348, 2007*). Clinical responses in 75% of 176 AIDS with an impaired renal study did not support the use of voriconazole IV (*CID 54:913, 2012*); hallucinations, hypoglycemia, electrolyte disturbance & pneumonitis attributed to ↑ drug concentrations. Potential for drug-drug interactions high—see Table 22. **NOTE: Not in urine in active form. No activity vs. mucormycosis.**

See page 2 for abbreviations. All dosage recommendations are for adults (unless otherwise indicated) and assume normal renal function

TABLE 11C – AT A GLANCE SUMMARY OF SUGGESTED ANTIFUNGAL DRUGS AGAINST TREATABLE PATHOGENIC FUNGI

Microorganism	Antifungal[1,2,3,4]					
	Fluconazole[5]	Itraconazole	Voriconazole	Posaconazole	Echinocandin[6]	Polyenes
Candida albicans	+++	+++	+++	+++	+++	++
Candida dubliniensis	+++	+++	+++	+++	+++	++
Candida glabrata	±	±	++	++	+++	++
Candida tropicalis	+++	+++	+++	+++	+++	++
Candida parapsilosis[7]	+++	+++	+++	+++	++ (higher MIC)	++
Candida krusei	-	±	++	+	+++	++
Candida guilliermondii	+++	+++	+++	++	++ (higher MIC)	-[8]
Candida lusitaniae	+++	+	++	++	++	-
Cryptococcus neoformans	+++	+	+++	+++	-	++
Aspergillus fumigatus[9]	-	++	+++	+++	++	++
Aspergillus flavus[9]	-	++	+++	+++	++	++ (higher MIC)
Aspergillus terreus[9]	-	±	++	++	++	-
Fusarium sp.	-	-	+++	+++	-	++ (lipid formulations)
Scedosporium apiospermum (Pseudallescheria boydii)	-	-	+++	+++		-
Scedosporium prolificans[10]	-	-	±	±	-	-
Trichosporon spp.	±	+	++	++	-	±
Mucormycosis (e.g. Mucor, Rhizopus, Lichtheimia)	-	-	-	++	-	++ (lipid formulations)
Dematiaceous molds[11] (e.g., Alternaria, Bipolaris, Curvularia, Exophiala)	-	++	+++	+++	-	+
Dimorphic Fungi						
Blastomyces dermatitidis	+	+++	++	++	-	+++
Coccidioides immitis/posadasii	+++	+++	++	++	-	+++
Histoplasma capsulatum	+	+++	++	+	-	+++
Sporothrix schenckii	-	++			-	+++

- = no activity; ± = possibly activity; + = active, 3rd line therapy (least active clinically)
++ = Active, 2nd line therapy (less active clinically); +++ = Active, 1st line therapy (usually active clinically)

1 Minimum inhibitory concentration values do not always predict clinical outcome.
2 Echinocandins, voriconazole, posaconazole and polyenes have poor urine penetration.
3 During severe immune suppression, success requires immune reconstitution.
4 Flucytosine has activity against Candida sp. Cryptococcus sp. and dematiaceous molds, but is primarily used in combination therapy.
5 For infections secondary to Candida sp., patients with prior triazole therapy have higher likelihood of triazole resistance.
6 Echinocandin pharmacodynamics, see JAC 05/1108, 2010.
7 Successful treatment of infections from Candida parapsilosis requires removal of foreign body or intravascular device.
8 Treatment failures reported, even for susceptible strains.
9 Lipid formulations of amphotericin may have greater activity against A. fumigatus and A. flavus (+++).
10 Scedosporium prolificans is poorly susceptible to single agents and may require combination therapy (e.g., addition of terbinafine).
11 Infections from mucormycosis, some Aspergillus sp., and dematiaceous molds often require surgical debridement.

TABLE 12A – TREATMENT OF MYCOBACTERIAL INFECTIONS*

Tuberculin skin test (TST). Same as PPD [Chest 138:1456, 2010]:

Criteria for positive TST after 5 tuberculin units (intermediate PPD) read at 48–72 hours:

- ≥5 mm induration: + HIV, immunosuppressed, ≥15 mg prednisone per day, healed TBc on chest x-ray, recent close contact
- ≥10 mm induration: foreign-born, countries with high prevalence; IVD Users; low income; NH residents; chronic illness; silicosis
- ≥15 mm induration: otherwise healthy

Two-stage to detect sluggish positivity. If 1ˢᵗ PPD + but <10 mm, repeat intermediate PPD in 1 wk. Response to 2ⁿᵈ PPD can also happen if pt received BCG in childhood.

BCG vaccine as child: if ≥10 mm induration, ≥5 yr from country with TBc, should be attributed to M. tuberculosis. In areas of low TB prevalence, TST reactions of ≤18 mm more likely from BCG than TB [CID 40:211, 2005]. Prior BCG may result in booster effect in 2-stage TST [AIM 161:1760, 2001; Clin Micro Inf 10:980, 2005].

Routine anergy testing no longer recommended in HIV+ or HIV-negative patients [JAMA 283:2003, 2000].

Interferon Gamma Release Assays (IGRAs): IGRAs detect sensitivities to M. TBc by measuring IFN-8 release in response to M. TBc antigens. May be used in place of TST in all situations in which TST may be used [MMWR 59 (RR-5), 2010]. Four such tests have now been approved by the U.S. FDA.

- QuantiFERON-TB (QFT) (approved 2001, but discontinued in 2005)
- QuantiFERON-TB Gold (QFT-G) (approved 2005)
- QuantiFERON-TB Gold In-Tube Test (QFT-GIT) (approved 2007)
- T-Spot (approved 2008)

QFT-G, QFT-GIT & T-Spot each measures different aspects of immune response so test results are not always interchangeable. IGRAs are relatively specific for M. TBc and should not cross-react with BCG or most nontuberculous mycobacteria. CDC recommends IGRA over TST for persons unlikely to return for reading TST & for persons who have received BCG. TST is preferred in children age < 5 yrs (but IGRA is acceptable). IGRA or TST may be used without preference for recent contacts of TB with special utility for follow-up testing since IGRAs do not produce "booster effect". May also be used without preference over TBc for occupational exposures. As with TST, testing with IGRAs in low prevalence populations will result in false-positive results [CID 53:234, 2011].
For detailed discussions of IGRAs, see MMWR 59 (RR-5), 2010 and JAMA 308:241, 2012.

Nucleic acid amplification tests (NAAT) can reliably detect M. tuberculosis in clinical specimens 2 or more weeks earlier than conventional cultures. They are particularly useful in detecting M.TBc from smear-positive specimens. Sensitivity lower in smear-negative or extrapulmonary specimens [CID 49:46, 2009. PLoS Medicine 5:e156, 2008]. CDC currently recommends that NAA testing be performed on at least one respiratory specimen from each patient for whom diagnosis of TB is being considered but has not yet been established, and for whom the test result would alter case management or TB control activities [MMWR 58:7, 2009].

Rapid (24-hr or less) diagnostic tests for M. tuberculosis: (1) the Amplified Mycobacterium tuberculosis Direct Test amplifies and detects M. tuberculosis ribosomal RNA; (2) the AMPLICOR Mycobacterium tuberculosis Test amplifies and detects M. tuberculosis DNA. Both tests have sensitivities & specificities >95% in sputum samples that are AFB-positive. In negative smears, specificity remains >95% but sensitivity is 40–77% [MMWR 58:7, 2009; CID 49:46, 2009].

Xpert MTB/RIF is a rapid test (2 hrs) for M. TBc in sputum samples which also detects RIF resistance with specificity of 99.2% and sensitivity of 72.5% in smear negative patients [NEJM 363:1005, 2010]. The test may be effectively used in low resource settings [Lancet online, accessed 4/19/2011]. Current antibody-based and ELISA-based rapid tests for TBc not recommended by WHO because they are less accurate than microscopy ± culture [Lancet ID 11:736, 2011].

SUGGESTED REGIMENS

CAUSATIVE AGENT/DISEASE	MODIFYING CIRCUMSTANCES	INITIAL THERAPY	CONTINUATION PHASE OF THERAPY
I. Mycobacterium tuberculosis exposure but TST negative (household members & other close contacts of potentially infectious cases)	Neonate—Rx essential	INH (10 mg/kg/ day for 3 mos)	Repeat tuberculin skin test (TST) in 3 mos. If mother's smear neg & infant's TST neg & chest x-ray (CXR) normal, stop INH. In UK, BCG is then given [Ln 2:1479, 1990], unless mother HIV+. If infant's repeat TST + &/or CXR abnormal (hilar adenopathy &/or infiltrate), INH + RIF (10–20 mg/kg/day (or SM)) Total rx 6 mos. If mother is being rx, separation of infant from mother not indicated.
	Children <5 years of age—rx 3 mos	As for neonate for rx 3 mos.	If repeat TST at 3 mos is negative, stop. If repeat TST +, continue INH for total of 9 mos. If INH not given initially, repeat TST at 3 mos.
	Older children & adults— Risk 2–4% 1ˢᵗ yr		**I + rx** with INH for 6 mos. (see Category I below).
			No rx if repeat TST negative

* Dosages are for adults (unless otherwise indicated) and assume normal renal function   ¹ **DOT** = directly observed therapy

See page 2 for abbreviations, page 137 for footnotes

TABLE 12A (2)

CAUSATIVE AGENT/DISEASE	MODIFYING CIRCUMSTANCES	SUGGESTED REGIMENS	
		INITIAL THERAPY	ALTERNATIVE
II. Treatment of latent infection with **M. tuberculosis (formerly known as "prophylaxis)** (NEJM 364:1441, 2011) **A. INH indicated due to high-risk**	(1) + tuberculin reactor & HIV+ (risk of active disease 10% per yr. AIDS 170 times †, HIV+ 113 times †). (2) Newly infected persons (TST conversion in past 2 yrs—risk 3.3% 1st yr) (3) Past tuberculosis, not rx with adequate chemotherapy (4) + tuberculin reactors with CXR consistent with non-progressive tuberculous disease (risk 0.5–5.0% per yr) (5) + tuberculin reactors with specific predisposing conditions: illicit IV drug use (MMWR 38:236, 1989), silicosis, diabetes mellitus, prolonged adrenocorticoid rx (>15 mg prednisone/day), immunosuppressive/anti-cancer rx, hematologic diseases (Hodgkin's, leukemia), endstage renal disease, clinical condition with rapid substantial weight loss or chronic under-nutrition, previous gastrectomy (CID 45:428, 2007). (6) + tuberculin reactors due to start anti-TNF-α (alpha) therapy (CID 46:1738, 2008). For management algorithm see Thorax 60:800, 2005. **NOTE: For HIV, see Sanford Guide to HIV/AIDS Therapy &/or JID 196:S35, 2007**	**INH** (5 mg/kg/day, max 300 mg/day for adults; 10 mg/kg/day for children, max to exceed 300 mg/day/day for children). May use 2x/wk INH with DOT (MMWR 52:735, 2003). Optimal duration 9 mos. (includes children). HIV+ at least 9 mos INH regimen, in some cases, 6 mos. may be given for cost-effectiveness (AJRCCM 161:S221, 2000). Do not use 6 mos. regimen in HIV+ persons <18 yrs, or those with fibrotic lesions on chest film (NEJM 345:189, 2001). For current recommendations for monitoring: (MMWR 59:8, 2010). **Rifapentine** (wt-based dose): 10–14 kg: 300 mg; 14.1–25 kg: 450 mg; 25.1–32 kg: 600 mg; 32.1–49.9 kg: 750 mg; 250 kg: 900 mg. Not recommended for children age < 2 yrs, those with HIV/AIDS on ART, pregnant women, or pts presumed infected with INH- or RIF-resistant M. TBc. (MMWR 60:1650, 2011).	If compliance problem: **INH** by DOT 15 mg/kg 2x/wk (max 900 mg) po for 4 mos. Effective as 9 months INH regimen (HIV- and HIV+). **RIF** 600 mg/day po for 4 mos. Effective as 9 mos INH regimen (CID 49:1883, 2009). Meta-analysis suggests 3 mos of INH + RIF may be equiv to "standard" (6–12 mos) INH therapy (CID 40:670, 2005). 3–4 month INH + RIF regimens also as safe and effective as 9 months INH in children (CID 45:715, 2007).
		Rifapentine is as effective as 9 mos. daily INH. Dosages for this regimen: **INH** 15 mg/kg (max. 900 mg).	
		INH (5 mg/kg per day, max. 300 mg per day for adults; 10 mg/kg per day for children) plus **rifapentine** (wt-based) once a week for 12 weeks (65% vs 75% reduction in active disease) 9 mos. is current recommendation. See II. A above for details and alternate x.	Reanalysis of earlier studies favors **INH** prophylaxis (if INH-related, hepatitis case fatality rate <1% and TB case fatality ≥6.7%, which appears to be the case) (AVM 152:2517, 1990). Recent data suggest INH prophylaxis has positive risk/benefit ratio if pts carefully monitored for hepatotoxicity (AVM 127:1051, 1997). Overall risk of hepatotoxicity 0.1–0.15% (JAMA 281:1014, 1999).
B. INH indicated	Age no longer considered modifying factor (see Comments)		
	Pregnancy—Any risk factors (II.A above)	Treat with **INH** as above. For protection for progression of latent to active disease, esp. those who are HIV+ or who have been recently infected, rx should not be delayed even during the first trimester.	
	Pregnancy—No risk factors	No initial rx (see Comment)	Delay rx until after delivery
C. TST positive & drug resistance likely (For data on worldwide prevalence of drug resistance see NEJM 344:1294, 2001; JID 185:1197, 2002; JID 194:479, 2006; EID 13:380, 2007)	INH-resistant (or adverse reaction to INH), RIF-sensitive organisms likely	**RIF** 600 mg per day po for 4 mos. (HIV+ or HIV–)	Rifabutin 300 mg daily is an alternative. Estimate RIF alone has protective effect of 56%; 26% of pts reported adverse effects (only 2157 did not complete 6 mos. rx). 4 months therapy with RIF (10 mg/kg/d) produced fewer adverse effects than 9 months of INH (AIM 149:689, 2008).
	INH- and RiF-resistant organisms likely	Efficacy of all regimens unproven. (**PZA** 25–30 mg per kg per day to max. of 2 gm per day) + **ETB** 15–25 mg per kg per day) times 12 mos.	Delay rx until after delivery (**PZA** 25 mg per kg per day + **levo** 500 mg per day), all po, times 6–12 mos.

See page 2 for abbreviations, page 137 for footnotes   * Dosages are for adults (unless otherwise indicated) and assume normal renal function   **¹ DOT** = directly observed therapy

TABLE 12A (3)

CAUSATIVE AGENT/DISEASE	MODIFYING CIRCUMSTANCES	SUGGESTED REGIMENS						COMMENTS
		INITIAL THERAPY[*]			CONTINUATION PHASE OF THERAPY AND DIRECTLY OBSERVED THERAPY (DOT) REGIMENS (in vitro susceptibility known)			
		SEE COMMENTS FOR DOSAGE AND DIRECTLY OBSERVED THERAPY (DOT) REGIMENS						
		Regimen: in order of preference	Drugs	Interval/Doses[1] (min. duration)	Regimen[*]	Drugs	Interval/Doses[1,2] (min. duration)	Range of Total Doses (min. duration)	

III. Mycobacterium tuberculosis
A. Pulmonary TB
General reference on rx in adults & children: Ln 362:887, 2003; (RR-11), 2003; (2) 40(Suppl.1): S1, 2005. References on transplant & other immuno-compromised: CID 48:1276, 2009; CID 50:S239, 2004. In pts with newly diagnosed HIV and TB, Rx for both should be started as soon as possible (NEJM 362:697, 2010).

Isolation essential Pts with active TB should be isolated in single rooms, not cohorted (MMWR 54(RR-17), 2005). Older observations on infectivity of susceptible & resistant M. Tbc before and after rx (AJRCCM 150:1962) may not be applicable to MDR M. Tbc or the HIV+ individual. Extended isolation may be appropriate. 10% of pts with active susceptible organisms remain culture-pos at day 60 (CID 51:371, 2010).

See footnotes, page 137
USE DOT REGIMENS IF POSSIBLE
(continued on next page)

Modifying circumstances: Rate of INH resistance known to be <4% (drug-susceptible organisms). Modified from MMWR 52 (RR-11), 2003

Initial therapy regimens:

Regimen	Drugs	Interval/Doses (min. duration)
1 (See Figure 1, page 133)	INH, RIF, PZA, ETB	7 days per wk times 56 doses (8 wks) or 5 days per wk times 40 doses (8 wks). Fixed dose combination of INH, RIF, PZA & ETB currently being evaluated (JAMA 305:1415, 2011)
2 (See Figure 1, page 133)	INH, RIF, PZA, ETB	7 days per wk times 14 doses (2 wks), then 2 times per wk times 12 doses (6 wks) or 5 days per wk times 10 doses (2 wks) then 2 times per wk times 12 doses (6 wks)
3 (See Figure 1, page 133)	INH, RIF, PZA, ETB	3 times per wk times 24 doses (8 wks)
4 (See Figure 1, page 133)	INH, RIF, ETB	7 days per wk times 56 doses (8 wks) or 5 days per wk times 40 doses (8 wks)

Continuation phase regimens:

Regimen	Drugs	Interval/Doses (min. duration)	Range of Total Doses (min. duration)
1a	INH/RIF[*]	7 days per wk times 126 doses (18 wks) or 5 days per wk times 90 doses (18 wks)	182-130 (26 wks)
1b	INH/RIF	2 times per wk times 36 doses (18 wks)	92-76 (26 wks)[*]
1c[3]	INH/RFP	1 time per wk times 18 doses (18 wks)	74-58 (26 wks)
2a	INH/RIF	2 times per wk times 36 doses (18 wks)	62-58 (26 wks)
2b[3]	INH/RFP	1 time per wk times 18 doses (18 wks)	44-40 (26 wks)
3a	INH/RIF	3 times per wk times 54 doses (18 wks)	78 (26 wks)
4a	INH/RIF	7 days per wk times 217 doses (31 wks) or 5 days per wk times 155 doses (31 wks)[3]	273-195 (39 wks)
4b	INH/RIF[*]	2 times per wk times 62 doses (31 wks)	118-102 (39 wks)

COMMENTS — Dose in mg per kg (max. q24h dose):

Regimen q24h:	INH	RIF	PZA	ETB	SM	RFB
Child	10-20 (300)	10-20 (600)	15-30 (2000)	15-25	20-40 (1000)	10-20 (300)
Adult	(300)	10 (600)	15-30 (2000)	15-25	15 (1000)	(300)
2 times per wk:						
Child	20-40 (900)	10-20 (600)	50-70 (4000)	50	25-30 (1500)	(300)
Adult	15 (900)	10 (600)	50-70 (4000)	50	25-30 (1500)	5 (300)
3 times per wk (DOT):						
Child	20-40 (900)	10-20 (600)	50-70 (3000)	25-30	25-30 (1500)	NA
Adult	15 (900)	10 (600)	50-70 (3000)	25-30	25-30 (1500)	NA

Second-line anti-TB agents can be dosed as follows to facilitate DOT:
Cycloserine 500-750 mg po q24h (5 times per week)
Ethionamide 500-750 mg po q24h (5 times per wk)
Kanamycin or capreomycin 15 mg per kg IM/IV q24h (3-5 times per wk)
Ciprofloxacin 750 mg po q24h (5 times per wk)
Ofloxacin 600-800 mg po q24h (5 times per wk)
Levofloxacin 750 mg po q24h (5 times per wk)
(CID 21:1245, 1995)

Risk factors for drug-resistant (MDR) TB: Recent immigration from Latin America or Asia or living in area of ↑ resistance (≥4%) or previous rx without RIF; exposure to known MDR TB. Incidence of MDR TB in **US steady** at 0.7%. Increased % of primary drug resistance is particularly high (>25%) in parts of China, India, Thailand, Russia, Estonia & Latvia. ~80% of US MDR cases in foreign born.

(continued on next page)

TABLE 12A (4)

CAUSATIVE AGENT/DISEASE	MODIFYING CIRCUM-STANCES	SUGGESTED REGIMEN[f]	DURATION OF TREATMENT (mos.)[j]	SPECIFIC COMMENTS[a]	COMMENTS
III. Mycobacterium tuberculosis A. Pulmonary TB (continued from previous page)	INH (± SM) resistance	RIF, PZA, ETB (a FQ may strengthen the regimen for pts with extensive disease)	6	(continued from previous page) INH should be stopped in cases of INH resistance. Outcome similar for drug susceptible and INH-mono-resistant strains (CID 48:179, 2009).	(continued from previous page) Note that CIP not as effective as PZA + ETB in multidrug regimen for susceptible TB (CID 22:287, 1996). **Moxifloxacin, and levofloxacin have enhanced activity compared with CIP against M. tuberculosis.** FQ resistance may be seen in pts previously treated with FQ (CID 37:1448, 2003). WHO recommends using moxifloxacin (if MIC ≤ 2) if resistant to earlier generation FQs (AAC 54:4765, 2010). **Linezolid has excellent in vitro activity, including MDR strains** and effective in selected cases of MDR-TB and XDR-TB but watch for toxicity (JAC 64:1119, 2009; CID 50:49, 2010). **Bedaquiline** recently FDA approved for treatment of MDR-TB based on efficacy in Phase 2 trials (NEJM 360:2397, 2009; AAC 56:3271, 2012). Dose is 400 mg once daily for 2 weeks then 200 mg 3x/week for 22 weeks administered as directly observed therapy (DOT), taken with food, and always in combination with other anti-TB meds. Consultation with an expert in MDR-TB management strongly advised before use of this agent.
Multidrug-Resistant Tuberculosis (MDR TB): Defined as resistant to at least 2 drugs including INH & RIF. Pt clusters with high mortality (NEJM 363:1050, 2010).	Resistance to INH & RIF (± SM)	FQ, PZA, ETB, IA, ± alternative agent[f]	18–24	In such cases, extended rx is needed to ↓ the risk of relapse. In cases with extensive disease, the use of an additional agent (alternative agents) may be prudent to ↓ the risk of failure & additional acquired drug resistance. Resectional surgery may be appropriate.	
	Resistance to INH, RIF (± SM), & ETB	FQ (ETB or PZA if active), IA, & 2 alternative agents[f]	24	Use the first-line agents to which there is susceptibility. Add 2 or more alternative agents in case of extensive disease. Surgery should be considered. Survival in pts receiving active FQ & surgical intervention (AJRCCM 169:1103, 2004).	
Extensively Resistant TB (XDR-TB): Defined as resistant to INH & RIF plus any FQ and at least one of the 3 second-line drugs: capreomycin, kanamycin or amikacin (MMWR 56:250, 2007; Ln 379:1879, 2010).	Resistance to RIF	INH, ETB, FQ, supplemented with PZA for the first 2 mos (an IA may be included for the first 2–3 mos. for pts with extensive disease)	12–18	Q24h & 3 times per wk regimens of INH, PZA, & SM given for 3 mos were effective in a BMRC trial (AJRD 115:727, 1977). However, extended use of an IA may not be feasible. It is not known if ETB would be as effective as SM in these regimens. But for more extensive disease &/or to shorten duration (e.g., to 12 mos.), an IA may be added in the initial 2 mos. of rx.	
See footnotes, page 137 Reviews of therapy for MDR TB: JAC 54:593, 2004; Med Lett 1:75, 2009; for XDR-TB, see MMWR 56:250, 2007; NEJM 359:563, 2008	XDR-TB	See Comments	18–24	Therapy requires administration of 4–6 drugs to which infecting organism is susceptible, including multiple second-line drugs (MMWR 56:250, 2007). Increased mortality seen primarily in HIV+ patients. Cure with outpatient therapy likely in non-HIV+ patients when regimens of 5 or more drugs to which organism is susceptible are employed (NEJM 359:563, 2008; CID 47:496, 2008). Successful sputum culture conversion correlates to initial susceptibility to FQs and kanamycin (CID 46:42, 2008). Addition of "later generation" FQ (Levo, Moxi) beneficial on meta-analysis of XDR-TB (CID 51:6, 2010).	

See page 2 for abbreviations; page 137 for footnotes   * Dosages are for adults (unless otherwise indicated) and assume normal renal function   † **DOT** = directly observed therapy

TABLE 12A (5)

CAUSATIVE AGENT/DISEASE; MODIFYING CIRCUMSTANCES	SUGGESTED REGIMENS		COMMENTS
	INITIAL THERAPY	CONTINUATION PHASE OF THERAPY (In vitro susceptibility known)	

III. Mycobacterium tuberculosis

B. Extrapulmonary TB *(continued)*	INH + RIF (or RFB) + PZA q24h times 2 months. Authors add **pyridoxine** 25–50 mg po q24h to regimens that include INH	INH + RIF (or RFB)	6 mos regimens probably effective. Most experience with 9–12 mos regimens. Am Acad Ped (1994) recommends 6 mos rx for isolated cervical adenitis, renal and 12 mos for meningitis, miliary, bone/joint. DOT useful here as well as for pulmonary tuberculosis. IDSA recommends 6 mos for lymph node, pleural, pericardial, disseminated disease, genitourinary & peritoneal TBc; 6-9 mos for bone & joint; 9-12 mos for CNS (including meningeal) TBc. Corticosteroids strongly rec only for pericarditis & meningeal TBc (MMWR 52(RR-11):1, 2003)
C. Tuberculous meningitis Excellent summary of clinical aspects and therapy (including steroids): CMR 21:243, 2008. Also J Infect 59:167, 2009.	INH + RIF + ETB + PZA	May omit ETB when susceptibility to INH and **RIF** established. See Table 9, page 87, for CSF drug penetration. Initial reg of INH + RIF + SM + PZA also effective, even in patients with INH-resistant organisms (JID 192:79, 2005).	3 drugs often rec for initial rx. We prefer 4 (J Infect 59:167, 2009). May sub ethionamide for ETB. Infection with MDR TB↑ mortality & morbidity (CID 38:851, 2004; JID 192:79, 2005). Delay in treatment & abnormal mental status complicate outcome (Medicine 84:351-1741, 2004). PCR of CSF markedly↑ diagnostic sensitivity and provides rapid dx but considerable variability in sensitivity depending on method used (LnID 3:633, 2003). ↓ survival in HIV pts (JID 192:2134, 2005). FQs (Levo, Gati, CIP) may be useful if started early (AAC 55:3244, 2011).
D. Tuberculosis during pregnancy	INH + RIF + ETB for 9 mos		PZA not recommended: teratogenicity data inadequate. Because of potential ototoxicity to fetus throughout gestation (16%), SM should not be used unless other drugs contraindicated. Add **pyridoxine** 25 mg per day for pregnant women on INH. Breast-feeding should not be discouraged in pts on first-line drugs (MMWR 52(RR-11):1, 2003).
E. Treatment failure or relapse: Usually due to poor compliance and/or resistant organisms, or suf pharmacodynamics (drug levels: CID 55:169, 2012).	Directly observed therapy (DOT). Check susceptibilities. (See section III.A, page 130 & below)	INH + RIF (or RFB), q24h times 4 months (total 6 mos.) May treat up to 9 mos in pts with delayed response.	Pts whose sputum has not converted after 5-6 mos = treatment failures. Failures may be due to non-compliance or resistant organisms. Check susceptibilities of original isolates and obtain susceptibility on current isolates. Non-compliance common, therefore institute DOT. If isolate shows resistance, modify regimen to include at least 2 effective agents, preferably ones which pt has not received. Surgery may be necessary. In MDR-TB patients with MDR-TB usually convert sputum within 12 weeks of successful therapy (AnIM 144:650, 2006). NB: patients with delayed or inadequate innate immune responses, bacterial infection and TB progression (JID 204:358, 2011).
F. HIV infection or AIDS-pulmonary or extrapulmonary disease (NOTE: 60-70% of HIV+ pts with TB have extrapulmonary disease.)	INH + RIF (or RFB) + PZA q24h times 2 months. (Authors add **pyridoxine** 25-50 mg po q24h to regimens that include INH)	INH + RIF (or RFB) + PZA q24h times 2 months.	1. Because of possibility of developing resistance to RIF in pts with low CD4 cell counts who receive wkly (or 2x/wk) dosing, 1x/wk RFB & biweekly INH is recom. that such pts receive daily (or min 3x/wk) doses of RFB for initiation & continuation phase of rx (MMWR 51:214, 2002). 2. Clinical & microbiologic response same as in HIV-neg patient although there is considerable variability in outcomes among currently available studies (CID 32:623, 2001). 3. Post-treatment suppression not necessary for drug-susceptible strains. 4. Rate of INH resistance known to be <4% (for↑ rates of resistance, see Section III.A). 5. Adjunctive prednisolone of NO benefit in HIV+ patients with CD4 counts >200 (JID 191:856, 2005) or in patients with TBc pleurisy (JID 190:869, 2004).
Concomitant protease inhibitor (PI) therapy (PI Mechanism: CID 49:1305, 2009). (Medicine 84:43, 2005; JAIDS 49:185, 2008; AJRCCM 162:7, 2001)	**Initial & cont. therapy: INH** 300 mg + RFB (see below for dose) + PZA 25 mg per kg + ETB 15 mg per kg q24h times 2 mos, then INH + RFB times 4 mos (up to 7 mos.)	**Alternative regimen:** INH + SM + PZA q24h treatment 2 mos; then INH + SM + PZA 2-3x per wk for 7 mos. May be used with intermittent INH + SM + PZA May be stopped up to 12 mos in pts with delayed response.	**Comments:** Rifamycins induce cytochrome CYP450 enzymes (RIF > RFP > RFB) & reduce serum levels of concomitantly administered PIs. Conversely, PIs (ritonavir > amprenavir > indinavir = nelfinavir > saquinavir) inhibit CYP450 & cause↑ serum levels of RFP & RFB. If dose of RFB is not reduced, toxicity (esp. uveitis) may occur. Monitoring clinically effective (CID 30:779, 2000). **Although RFB is preferred, RIF can be used** for rx of active TB in pts on regimens containing efavirenz or ritonavir. **RIF should not be administered to pts on ritonavir + saquinavir because drug-induced hepatitis with marked transaminase elevations has been seen in healthy volunteers receiving this regimen** (www.fda.gov).
	PI dosages Nelfinavir 1000 mg q12h or indinavir 1000 mg q8h or amprenavir 1200 mg q12h. Saquinavir standard dose Ritonavir standard dose Lopinavir/ritonavir— standard dose	**RFB Dose** 150 mg q24h or 300 mg intermittently 300 mg q24h or intermittently 150 mg 2x weekly 150 mg 2x per wk	Rifabutin dosing adjustments: For patients on efavirenz, use RFB 450 mg daily. Concomitant use of RFB with saquinavir/ritonavir (CID 48:1471, 2009). Efavirenz TB therapy (CID 48:1752, 2009; CMR 24:351, 2011). Therapy for latent TB less compromised by concomitant RIF than Nevirapine (CID 48:1752, 2009; CMR 24:351, 2011).

See page 2 for abbreviations, page 137 for footnotes * Dosages are for adults (unless otherwise indicated) and assume normal renal function † **DOT** = directly observed therapy

133

TABLE 12A (6)

FIGURE 1 [Modified from MMWR 52(RR-11):1, 2003]

Treatment Algorithm for Tuberculosis

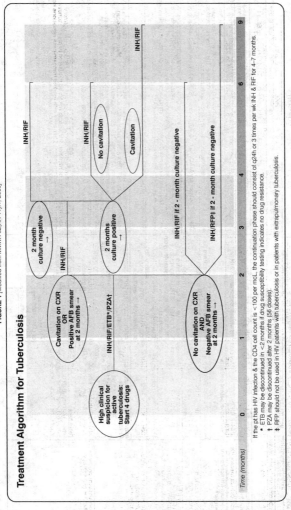

| Time (months) | 0 | 1 | 2 | 3 | 4 | 6 | 9 |

High clinical suspicion for active tuberculosis: Start 4 drugs

Cavitation on CXR OR Positive AFB smear at 2 months →
INH/RIF/ETB*/PZA†

2 month culture negative →
INH/RIF

2 months culture positive →

INH/RIF
No cavitation

INH/RIF
Cavitation

INH/RIF

No cavitation on CXR AND Negative AFB smear at 2 months →

INH/RIF if 2 - month culture negative

INH/RFP‡ if 2 - month culture negative

If the pt has HIV infection & the CD4 cell count is <100 per mcL, the continuation phase should consist of q24h or 3 times per wk. INH & RIF for 4–7 months.
* ETB may be discontinued in <2 months if drug susceptibility testing indicates no drug resistance.
† PZA may be discontinued after 2 months (56 doses).
‡ RFP should not be used in HIV patients with tuberculosis or in patients with extrapulmonary tuberculosis.

See page 2 for abbreviations.

TABLE 12A (7)

CAUSATIVE AGENT/DISEASE	MODIFYING CIRCUMSTANCES	SUGGESTED REGIMENS PRIMARY/ALTERNATIVE		COMMENTS
IV. Other Mycobacterial Disease ("Atypical") (See ATS Consensus: AJRCCM 175:367, 2007; IDC No. Amer 16:187, 2002; CMR 15:716, 2002; CID 42:1756, 2006; EID 17:506, 2011)				
A. M. bovis		INH + RIF + ETB		The M. tuberculosis complex includes M. bovis. All isolates inherently resistant to PZA, 9–12 months of rx used by some authorities. Isolation not required. Increased prevalence of extrapulmonary disease in U.S. born Hispanic populations and elsewhere (CID 47:168, 2008; EID 14:909, 2008; EID 17:457, 2011)
B. Bacillus Calmette-Guerin (BCG) (derived from M. bovis)	Only fever (>38.5°C) for 12–24 hrs.	INH 300 mg q24h times 3 months		Intravesical BCG effective in superficial bladder tumors and carcinoma in situ. With sepsis, consider initial adjunctive prednisolone. Also susceptible to RFB, cipro, oflox, streptomycin, amikacin, capreomycin (AAC 53:316, 2009). BCG may cause regional adenitis or pulmonary disease in HIV-infected children (CID 37:1226, 2003). **Resistant to PZA.**
	Systemic illness or sepsis	INH 300 mg + RIF 600 mg + ETB 1200 mg q24h times 6 mos.		
C. M. avium-intracellulare complex (MAC, MAI), or Battey bacillus) ATS/IDSA Consensus Statement: AJRCCM 175:367, 2007; alternative ref. CID 42:1756, 2006. Anti-tumor necrosis factor-α increases risk of infection with MAI and other non-tuberculous mycobacteria (EID 15:1556, 2009).	**Immunocompetent patients**			See AJRCCM 175:367, 2007 for details of dosing and duration of therapy. Intermittent (tiw) therapy not recommended for patients with cavitary disease, patients who have been previously treated or patients with moderate of severe disease. The primary microbiologic goal of therapy is 12 months of negative sputum cultures on therapy.
	Nodular/Bronchiectatic disease	**Clarithro** 1000 mg tiw or **azithro** 500–600 mg tiw) + **ETB** 25 mg/day + **RIF** 600 mg tiw		**"Classic" pulmonary MAC:** Women 50–75, smokers, COPD. May be associated with hot tub use (Clin Chest Med 23:675, 2002).
	Cavitary disease	**Clarithro** 500–1000 mg/day (lower dose for <50 kg) or **azithro** 250–300 mg/day) + **ETB** 15 mg/kg/day + **RIF** 450–600 mg/day ± **streptomycin** or **amikacin**		**"New" pulmonary MAC:** Women 30–70, scoliosis, mitral valve prolapse, (bronchiectasis), pectus excavatum ("Lady Windermere syndrome") and fibronodular disease in elderly women (EID 6:1576, 2010). May also be associated with interferon gamma deficiency (AJM 113:756, 2002). For cervicofacial lymphadenitis (localized) in immunocompetent children, surgical excision is as effective as chemotherapy (AAC 44:1057, 2007).
	Advanced (severe) or previously treated disease	**Clarithro** 500–1000 mg/day (lower dose for wt <50 kg) or **azithro** 250–300 mg/day) + **ETB** 15 mg/kg/day ± **streptomycin** or **amikacin**		Moxifloxacin and gatifloxacin, active in vitro & in vivo (AAC 51:4071, 2007).
	Immunocompromised pts: Primary prophylaxis—Pt's CD4 count <50–100 cells per mm³. Discontinue when CD4 count >100 per mm³ in response to ART (NEJM 342:1085, 2000; CID 34: 662, 2002) Guideline: AnIM 137:435, 2002	**RFB** 300 mg po q24h **OR** **Azithro** 1200 mg po weekly + **RIF** 300 mg po q24h		RFB reduces MAC infection rate by 55% (no survival benefit); clarithro by 68% (30% survival benefit); azithro by 59% (68% survival benefit) (CID 26:611, 1998). **Many drug-drug interactions,** see Table 22, pages 219, 222. Drug-resistant MAI disease seen in 29–58% of pts in whom disease develops while taking clarithro prophylaxis & 11% of those on azithro but has not been observed with RFB prophylaxis (J Inf 38:6, 1999). Clarithro resistance more likely in pts with extremely low CD4 counts at initiation (CID 27:807, 1998). Need to be sure no active M. TBc (NEJM 335:384 & 428, 1996).
	Immunocompromised pts	**Azithro** 1200 mg po weekly **OR** **Clarithro** 500 mg po bid		
	Treatment Either presumptive dx or after + culture from normally sterile site, usually, sterile body fluids, eg liver	**Clarithro** 500 mg * po bid + **ETB** 15 mg/kg/day +/- **RFB** 300 mg/day po q24h * Higher doses of clari (1000 mg bid) may be associated with ↑ mortality (CID 29:125, 1999)	**Azithro** 500 mg po/day + **ETB** po/day + **RFB** 300–450 mg po/day	Median time to neg. blood culture: clarithro + ETB 4.4 wks vs azithro + ETB >16 wks. At 16 wks, clearance of bacteremia seen in 37.5% of azithro- & 85.7% of clarithro-treated pts (CID 27:1278, 1998). Other ref. suggests similar clearance rates for azithro (46%) vs clarithro (56%) when combined with ETB (CID 31:1245, 2000). Azithro 250 mg po q24h not effective, but azithro 600 mg po q24h as effective as 1200 mg po q24h & yields fewer adverse effects (AAC 43: 2869, 1999).

(continued on next page)

See page 2 for abbreviations; page 137 for footnotes   * Dosages are for adults (unless otherwise indicated) and assume normal renal function   † **DOT** = directly observed therapy

TABLE 12A (8)

CAUSATIVE AGENT/DISEASE	MODIFYING CIRCUMSTANCES	SUGGESTED REGIMENS		COMMENTS
		PRIMARY	ALTERNATIVE	
IV. Other Mycobacterial Disease ("Atypical") (continued)				
C. M. avium-intracellulare complex (continued)				(continued from previous page) Addition of RFB to clarithro + ETB ↓ emergence of resistance to clari ↓, relapse rate & improves survival (CID 37:1234, 2003). Clofazimine not recommended for MAI in HIV+ pts. Drug toxicity: With clarithro, pts had to stop drug 2° to dose-limiting adverse reaction. Combination of clarithro, ETB and RFB led to uveitis and pseudojaundice; result is reduction in max. dose of RFB to 300 mg. Treatment failure rate is high. Reasons: drug toxicity, development of drug resistance, & inadequate serum levels. Serum levels of clarithro ↓ in pts also given RIF or RFB (JID 171:747, 1995). If pt not responding to initial regimen after 2–4 weeks, add one or more drugs.
	Chronic post-treatment suppression—secondary prophylaxis	**Always necessary. (Clarithro or azithro) + ETB 15 mg/kg/day (dosage above)**	**Clarithro or azithro or RFB (dosage above)**	Recurrences almost universal without chronic suppression. However, in patients on ART with robust CD4 cell response, it is possible to discontinue chronic suppression (JID 178:1446, 1998; NEJM 340:1301, 1999).
D. Mycobacterium celatum	Treatment; optimal regimen not defined	**May be susceptible to clarithro, FQ (Clin Microbiol 35:2626, 1997). Susceptible to "like MAI" but often resistant to RIF (JID 178:1571, 1999). Most reported cases received 3 or 4 drugs, usually clarithro + ETB ± CIP ± RFB (EID 9:399, 2003).**		Isolated from pulmonary lesions and blood in AIDS patients (CID 24:144, 1997). Can be confused with M. xenopi (and MAC). Susceptibilities similar to MAC, but highly resistant to RIF (CID 24:140, 1997).
E. Mycobacterium abscessus **Mycobacterium chelonae**	Treatment; Surgical excision may facilitate clarithro rx in subcutaneous abscess and is important adjunct to rx. For role of surgeon in M. abscessus pulmonary disease, see CID 52:565, 2011.	**Clarithro 500 mg po bid times 6 mos. Azithro may also be effective. For serious disseminated infections and amikacin + IMP or cefoxitin for 1°2–8 wks (Clin Micro Rev 15:716, 2002; AJRCCM 175:367, 2007) or add Moxi or Levo (CID 49:1365, 2009).**		M. abscessus susceptible to AMK (70%), clarithro (95%), cefoxitin (70%), CLO, cefmetazole, RFB, FQ, IMP, azithro, cipro, doxy, mino, tigecycline (CID 42:1756, 2006; JIC 15:46, 2009). Single isolates of M. abscessus often not associated with disease. Clarithro-resistant strains now described (J Clin Micro 39:2745, 2001). M. chelonae susceptible to AMK (80%), clarithro, azithro, tobramycin (100%), IMP (60%), moxifloxacin (94%), linezolid (94%) (CID 42:1756, 2006). Resistant to cefoxitin, FQ (CID 24:1147, 1997; AJRCCM 156:S1, 1997). Tigecycline highly active in vitro (AAC 52:4184, 2008; CID 49:1358, 2009).
F. Mycobacterium fortuitum	Treatment; optimal regimen not defined. Surgical excision of infected areas.	**AMK + cefoxitin + probenecid 2–6 wks, then po TMP-SMX, or doxy 2–6 mos. Usually responds to 6–12 mos of oral rx with 2 drugs to which it is susceptible (AAC 46:3283, 2002; Clin Micro Rev 15:716, 2002). Nail salon-acquired infections respond to 4–6 mos of minocycline, doxy, or CIP (CID 38:38, 2004).**		**Resistant to all standard anti-TBc drugs.** Sensitive in vitro to doxycycline, minocycline, cefoxitin, IMP, AMK, TMP-SMX, CIP, oflox, azithro, clarithro, linazolid, tigecycline (Clin Micro Rev 15:716, 2002), but some strains resistant to azithro/clarithro, rifabutin (DMID 39:567, 1997; Clin Micro Rev 14:716, 2002). If susceptible, use 2 agents active in vitro until sputum cultures negative for 12 months (AJRCCM 175:367, 2007).

See page 2 for abbreviations, page 137 for footnotes * Dosages are for adults (unless otherwise indicated) and assume normal renal function † **DOT** = directly observed therapy

TABLE 12A (9)

CAUSATIVE AGENT/DISEASE: MODIFYING CIRCUMSTANCES	SUGGESTED REGIMENS		COMMENTS
	PRIMARY	ALTERNATIVE	
IV. Other Mycobacterial Disease ("Atypical") (continued)			
G. Mycobacterium haemophilum	Regimen(s) not defined. In animal model, **clarithro + rifabutin** effective (AAC 39:2316, 1995). Combination of **CIP + RFB + clarithro** reported effective but clinical experience limited (Clin Micro Rev 9:435, 1996; CID 52:488, 1998). Surgical debridement may be necessary		Clinical: Ulcerating skin lesions, synovitis, osteomyelitis, cervicocolical lymphadenitis in children (CID 41:1569, 2005). Associated with permanent eyebrow makeup (CID 52:488, 2011). Lab: Requires special media to isolate. Sensitive in vitro to: CIP, cycloserine, rifabutin, moxifloxacin. Over ½ resistant to: INH, RIF, ETB, PZA (AnIM 120:118, 1994). For localized cervicocolical lymphadenitis in immunocompetent children, surgical excision as effective as chemotherapy (CID 44:1057, 2007) or watchful waiting* (CID 52:180, 2011).
H. Mycobacterium genavense	Regimen(s) used include ≥2 drugs: **ETB RIF RFB CLO clarithro**. In animal model, **clarithro & RFB** (& to lesser extent amikacin & **ETB**) shown effective in reducing bacterial counts; **CIP** not effective (JAC 42:483, 1998).		Clinical: CD4 <50. Symptoms of fever, weight loss, diarrhea. Lab: Growth in BACTEC vials slow (mean >42 days); may require subculture on solid media. Isolation on Middlebrook 7H11 agar containing 2 mcg per mL myco-bactin J and blood or charcoal still insufficient for in vitro sensitivity testing (J Clin Micro 34:2760, 1992). Survival 1 from 81 to 263 days in pts x rx for at least 1 month with ≥2 drugs (AnIM 155:400, 1995).
I. Mycobacterium gordonae	Regimen(s) not defined, but consider **RIF + ETB + KM or CIP + clarithro**		Frequent colonizer, not associated with disease. In vitro: sensitive to ETB, RIF, AMK, CIP, clarithro, linezolid (AAC 47:1736, 2003). Resistant to INH (CID 14:1229, 1992). Surgical excision
J. Mycobacterium kansasii	Q24h po: **INH** (300 mg) + **RIF** (600 mg) + **ETB** (25 mg per kg times 2 mos., then 15 mg per kg) + **pyridoxine** (50 mg) x 18 mos. (until culture-neg. 12 mos.)	If RIF-resistant, po q24h: **INH** (900 mg) + **ETB** (25 mg per kg) + **sulfamethoxazole** (1 gm tid). Rx until all culture-neg. times 15 mos. (See Comment). **Clari + ETB** also effective in small study (CID 37:1178, 2003)	All isolates are **resistant to PZA**. Highly susceptible to linezolid in vitro (AAC 47:1736, 2003) and to clarithro and moxifloxacin (JAC 55:950 2005). If HIV+ pt taking protease inhibitor, substitute either clarithro (500 mg bid) or RFB (150 mg per day) for INH. Because of variable susceptibility to INH, some substitute clarithro 500–750 mg q24h for INH. Resistance to clarithro reported, but most strains susceptible to clarithro as well as moxifloxacin (JAC 55:950, 2005) & levofloxacin (AAC 48:4562, 2004). Prognosis related to level of immunosuppression (CID 37:584, 2003)
K. Mycobacterium marinum	(**Clarithro** 500 mg bid) or (**minocycline** or **doxycycline** 100–200 mg q24h), or **TMP-SMX** 160/800 mg po bid), or **RIF + ETB** for 3 mos. (AJRCCM 156:S1, 1997; Eur J Clin Microbiol ID 25:609, 2006). Surgical excision.		Resistant to INH & PZA. Also susceptible in vitro to linezolid (AAC 47: 1736, 2003). CIP, moxifloxacin also show moderate in vitro activity (AAC 46:1114, 2002).
L. Mycobacterium scrofulaceum	Surgical excision. Chemotherapy seldom indicated. Although regimens not defined, **clarithro + CLO** with or **without ETB INH RIF strep + cycloserine** have also been used.		In vitro resistant to INH, RIF, ETB, PZA, AMK, CIP (CID 20: 549, 1995). Susceptible to clarithro, strep, erythromycin.
M. Mycobacterium simiae	Regimen(s) not defined. Start 4 drugs as for disseminated MAI		Most isolates resistant to all 1st-line anti-tbc drugs. Isolates then not clinically significant (CID 26: 625, 1998).
N. Mycobacterium ulcerans (Buruli ulcer)	WHO recommends **RIF + SM** for 8 weeks (Lancet 375:664, 2010; Lancet 367:1849, 2006; AAC 51:645, 2007). **RIF + SM** resulted in 47% cure rate (AAC 51:4029, 2007). **RIF + cipro** recommended as alternatives by WHO (CMAJ 31:119, 2009). Recent small studies document similar effectiveness of 4 wks of **RIF + SM** followed by 4 weeks of **RIF + Clarithro** (No relapse in 30 pts) (CID 5294, 2011)		Susceptible in vitro to RIF, strep, CLO, clarithro, CIP, oflox, amikacin, moxi, linezolid, moxifloxacin. Monotherapy with RIF selects resistant mutants in mice (AAC 47:1228, 2003) RIF + moxi, RIF + clarithro, moxi + clarithro similar to RIF + SM in mice (AAC 51:3737, 2007).
O. Mycobacterium xenopi	Regimen(s) not defined (CID 24:226 & 233, 1997). Some recommend a macrolide, **INH + ETB (rifabutin)**; **ETB + SM** (AJRCCM 156:S1, 1997) or **RIF INH ± ETB (rifabutin)** (AAC 45:3229, 2001) but sugg-gests no need to treat in most pts with HIV (CID 37:1250, 2003)		In vitro sensitive to clarithro (AAC 36:2841, 1992) and rifabutin (JAC 39:567, 1997) and many standard antimycobacterial drugs. Clarithro-containing regimens more effective than RIF/INH/ETB regimens in vitro (AAC 45:3229, 2001). FQs, linezolid also active in vitro.
Mycobacterium leprae (leprosy) Classification: CID 44:1096, 2007. Clinical mgmt of leprosy reactions: IDCP 18:235, 2010. Overview: Lancet 11:464, 2011.	There are 2 sets of therapeutic recommendations here: one from USA (National Hansen's Disease Programs [NHDP], Baton Rouge, LA) and one from WHO. Both are based on expert recommendations and neither has been subjected to controlled clinical trial (P. Joyce & D. Scollard, Comns Current Therapy 2004; J Am Acad Dermatol 51:417, 2004).		

Dosages are for adults (unless otherwise indicated) and assume normal renal function **DOT** = directly observed therapy

See page 2 for abbreviations, page 137 for footnotes

TABLE 12A (10)

Type of Disease	NHDP Regimen	WHO Regimen	COMMENTS
Paucibacillary Forms: (Indeterminate, Tuberculoid, Borderline tuberculoid)			Side effects overall 0.4%
Single lesion paucibacillary	Treat as paucibacillary leprosy for 12 months.	**(Dapsone** 100 mg/day (unsupervised) **+ RIF** 600 mg po/day) for 12 months.	
		Single dose ROM therapy: (RIF 600 mg + Oflox 400 mg + Mino 100 mg) (*Lr*: 353:655, 1999).	
Multibacillary forms: Borderline Borderline-lepromatous Lepromatous *See Comment for erythema nodosum leprosum* Rev: *Lancet* 363:1209, 2004	**Dapsone** 100 mg/day **+ CLO** 50 mg/day **+ RIF** 600 mg/day) for 24 mos. **Alternative regimen:** (**Dapsone** 100 mg/day **+ RIF** 600 mg/day **+ Minocycline** 100 mg/day) for 24 mos if CLO is refused or unavailable.	**(Dapsone** 100 mg/day **+ CLO** 50 mg/day (both unsupervised) **+ RIF** 600 mg/day (supervised)) **+ CLO** 300 mg once monthly (supervised)). Continue regimen for 12 months.	Side-effects overall 5.1%. For **erythema nodosum leprosum:** prednisone 60–80 mg/day or thalidomide 100–400 mg/day (*BMJ* 44: 775, 1988; *AJM* 108:487, 2000). Thalidomide available in US at 1-800-4-CELGENE. Altho thalidomide effective, WHO no longer rec because of potential toxicity (*JID* 193:1743, 2006) however the majority of leprosy experts feel thalidomide remains drug of choice for ENL under strict supervision. **CLO (Clofazimine)** available from NHDP under IND protocol; contact at 1-800-642-2477. **Ethionamide** (250 mg q24h) or **prothionamide** (375 mg q24h) may be subbed for CLO. Etanercept effective in one case refractory to above standard therapy (*CID* 52:e133, 2011). Regimens incorporating clarithro, minocycline, RIF moxifloxacin, and/or ofloxacin also show promise (*AAC* 44:2919, 2000; *AAC* 50:1558, 2006). Dapsone monotherapy has been abandoned due to emergence of resistance (*CID* 52:e127, 2011), but older patients previously treated with dapsone monotherapy may remain on lifelong maintenance therapy. Dapsone (or acedapsone[a,b]) effective for prophylaxis in one study (*J Inf* 41:137, 2000). Moxifloxacin highly active in vitro and produces rapid clinical response (*AAC* 52:3113, 2008).

FOOTNOTES:

[1] When DOT is used, drugs may be given 5 days/wk. & necessary number of doses adjusted accordingly. Although no studies compare 5 with 7 q24h doses, extensive experience indicates this would be an effective practice.

[2] Patients with cavitation on initial chest x-ray & positive cultures at completion of 2 mos of rx should receive a 7 mos (31 wks; either 217 doses [q24h] or 62 doses [2x/wk] continuation phase.

[3] 5 day/wk admin is always given by DOT.

[4] Not recommended for HIV-infected pts with CD4 cell counts <100 cells/mcL.

[5] Options 1c & 2b should be used only in HIV-neg. pts who have neg. sputum smears at the time of completion of 2 mos of rx & do not have cavitation on initial chest x-ray. For pts started on this regimen & found to have a + culture from 2 mos specimen, rx should be extended extra 3 mos.

[6] Options 4a & 4b should be considered only when options 1-3 cannot be given.

[7] Alternative agents = ethionamide, cycloserine, p-aminosalicylic acid, clarithromycin, AM-CL, linezolid.

[8] Modified from *MMWR* 52(RR-11):1, 2003. See also *IDCP* 11:329, 2002.

[9] Continuation regimen with INH/ETB less effective than INH/RIF (*Lancet* 364:1244, 2004).

See page 2 for abbreviations, page 137 for footnotes   * Dosages are for adults (unless otherwise indicated) and assume normal renal function   † **DOT** = directly observed therapy

TABLE 12B – DOSAGE AND ADVERSE EFFECTS OF ANTIMYCOBACTERIAL DRUGS

AGENT (TRADE NAME)[1]	USUAL DOSAGE*	ROUTE/[1]* DRUG RESISTANCE (RES) US*[1]	SIDE-EFFECTS, TOXICITY AND PRECAUTIONS	SURVEILLANCE
FIRST LINE DRUGS				
Ethambutol (Myambutol) (100, 400 mg tab)	25 mg/kg/day for 2 mos then 15 mg/kg/day q24h as 1 dose (<10% protein binding) [Bacteriostatic for both extracellular & intracellular organisms]	RES: 0.3% (0-0.7%) po 400 mg tab	**Optic neuritis** (with decreased visual acuity, central scotomata, and loss of green and red perception, peripheral neuropathy and headache (~1%), rashes (rare), arthralgia (rare), hyperuricemia (rare). Anaphylactoid reaction (rare). *Comment:* Primarily used to inhibit resistance. Disrupts outer cell membrane in M. avium with ↑ activity to other drugs.	Monthly visual acuity & red/green with dose >15 mg/kg/day, ≥10% decrease considered significant. Usually reversible if drug discontinued.
Isoniazid (INH) (Nydrazid, Laniazid, Teebaconin) (50, 100, 300 mg tab)	Q24h dose: 5-10 mg/kg/day up to 300 mg/day as 1 dose. 2x/wk dose: 15 mg/kg (900 mg max dose) (<10% protein binding) [Bactericidal to both extracellular and intracellular organisms] Add pyridoxine in alcoholic, pregnant, or malnourished pts.	RES: 4.1% (2.6-8.5%) po 300 mg tab IM 100 mg/mL in 10 mL (IV route not FDA-approved but has been used, esp. in AIDS)	Overall ~1%. Liver. **Hep** (children mild ↑ SGOT, normalizes with continued rx, age <20 yrs rare. 20-34 yrs ↑ 2%, ≥50 yrs ↑ 3%) (also ↑ with q24h alcohol & previous exposure to Hep C (usually asymptomatic—*CID* 36:293, 2003)). May be fatal. With prodromal sx, dark urine do LFTs; discontinue if SGOT >3-5xnormal. **Peripheral neuropathy** (17% on 6 mg/kg per day, less on 300 mg, incidence ↑ in slow acetylators). **pyridoxine 10 mg q24h will decrease incidence**; other neurologic sequelae, convulsions, optic neuritis, toxic encephalopathy, psychosis, muscle twitching, dizziness, coma (all rare); allergic skin rashes, fever, minor disulfiram-like reaction, flushing after Swiss cheese, blood dyscrasias (rare). + antinuclear (20%). **Drug-drug interactions** common (see Table 22).	Pre-rx liver functions. Repeat if symptoms (fatigue, weakness, malaise, anorexia, nausea or vomiting) >3 days (*AJRCCM 152:1705, 1995*). Some recommend SGOT at 2, 4, 6 mos esp. if age >50 yrs. Clinical evaluation every mo.
Pyrazinamide (500 mg tab)	25 mg per kg per day (maximum 2.5 gm per day) q24h as 1 dose [Bactericidal for intracellular organisms]	po 500 mg tab	**Arthralgia, hyperuricemia** (with or without symptoms); hepatitis (not over 2% if recommended dose not exceeded); gastric irritation; photosensitivity (rare).	Pre-rx liver functions. Monthly SGOT, uric acid. Measure serum uric acid if symptomatic gouty attack occurs.
Rifamate*— combination tablet	2 tablets single dose q24h	po (1 hr before meal)	1 tablet contains 150 mg INH, 300 mg RIF	As with individual drugs
Rifampin (Rifadin, Rimactane, Rifocin) (100, 300, 450, 600 mg cap)	10.0 mg per kg per day up to 600 mg q24h as 1 dose (60-90% protein binding) [Bactericidal to all populations of organisms]	RES: 0.2% (0-0.3%) po 300 mg cap (Ciba, Merrell-Dow)	INH/RIF dc'd in ~3% for toxicity, gastrointestinal irritation, antibiotic-associated colitis, drug fever (1%), pruritus with or without skin rash (1%), anaphylactoid reactions in HIV-1 pts, mental confusion, thrombocytopenia (1%), leukopenia (1%), hemolytic anemia, transient abnormalities in liver function. **"Flu syndrome"** (fever, chills, headache, bone pain, shortness of breath) seen if RIF taken irregularly or if q24h dose restarted after an interval of no rx. **Discolors urine, tears, sweat, contact lens an orange-brownish color.** May cause drug-induced lupus erythematosis (*Ln 349: 1521, 1977*).	Pre-rx liver function. Repeat if symptoms. **Multiple significant drug-drug interactions,** see *Table 22.*
Rifater*— combination tablet (See Side-Effects)	Wt ≥55 kg, 6 tablets single dose q24h	po (1 hr before meal)	1 tablet contains 50 mg INH, 120 mg RIF, 300 mg PZA. Used in 1st 2 months of rx (PZA 25 mg per kg). Purpose is convenience in dosing, ↑ compliance. Unit cost 1.58 more. Side-effects = individual drugs.	As with individual drugs. PZA 25 mg per kg
Streptomycin (IV/IM soln)	15 mg per kg IM q24h, 0.75-1.0 gm per day initially for 60-90 days, then 1.0 gm 2-3 times per week (15 mg per kg per day) q24h as 1 dose	RES: 3.9% (2.7-7.6%) IM (or IV)	Overall 8%. **Ototoxicity.** vestibular dysfunction (vertigo); paresthesias; dizziness & nausea (all less in pts receiving 2-3 doses per week); tinnitus and high frequency loss (1%); nephrotoxicity (rare); peripheral neuropathy (rare); allergic skin rashes (4-5%); drug fever. Available from X-Gen Pharmaceuticals, 607-732-4411. Net. re: W—*CID 19:1150, 1994.* Toxicity similar to qd vs tid dosing (*CID 38:1538, 2004*).	Monthly audiogram. In older pts, lower serum creatinine or BUN at start of rx and weekly if pt stable

[1] Note: Malabsorption of antimycobacterial drugs may occur in patients with AIDS enteropathy. For review of adverse effects, see *AJRCCM 167:1472, 2003.*

[2] **RES** = % resistance of M. tuberculosis.   **DOT** = directly observed therapy

* Dosages are for adults (unless otherwise indicated) and assume normal renal function   [1] Dosages in Hispanics, Asians, and patients <10 years old)

§ Mean (range) (higher in Hispanics, Asians, and patients <10 years old)

See page 2 for abbreviations.

TABLE 12B (2)

AGENT (TRADE NAME)[1]	USUAL DOSAGE*	ROUTE[1] DRUG RESISTANCE (RES) US§	SIDE-EFFECTS, TOXICITY AND PRECAUTIONS	SURVEILLANCE
SECOND LINE DRUGS (more difficult to use and/or less effective than first line drugs)				
Amikacin (Amikin) (IV soln)	7.5–10.0 mg per kg q24h [Bactericidal for extracellular organisms]	RES: (est. 0.1%) IM/IV 500 mg vial	See Table 10B, pages 104 & 109	Monthly audiogram. Serum creatinine or BUN weekly if stable
Bedaquiline (Sirturo) (100 mg tab)	Directly observed therapy (DOT): 400 mg once daily for 2 weeks, then 200 mg 3 times weekly for 22 weeks, used in combination with other anti-TB medications	Does not exhibit cross-resistance to other TB drugs; always use in combination with other TB drugs to prevent selection of resistant mutants	Toxicity similar with ol vs dal dosing (CID 38:1538, 2004). Most common: nausea, vomiting, arthralgia, headache. Elevated transaminases. Bedaquiline in clinical trials was administered as one component of a multiple drug regimen, so side-effects were common, yet difficult to assign to a particular drug.	Moderate QTc increases (average of 10-16 ms over the 24 weeks of therapy). Potential risks of pancreatitis, myopathy, myocardial injury, severe hepatotoxicity.
Capreomycin sulfate (Capastat sulfate)	1 gm per day (15 mg per kg per day) q24h as 1 dose	RES: 0.1% (0-0.9%) IM/IV	Nephrotoxicity (36%), ototoxicity (auditory 11%), eosinophilia, leukopenia, skin rash, fever, hypokalemia, neuromuscular blockade.	Monthly audiogram, biweekly serum creatinine or BUN
Ciprofloxacin (Cipro) (250, 500, 750 mg tab)	750 mg bid	po 500 mg or 750 mg ER IV 200–400 mg vial	TB not a FDA-approved indication for CIP. Desired CIP serum levels 4-6 mcg per mL; requires median dose 800 mg (AJRCCM 151:2006, 1995). Discontinuation rates 6–7%. CIP well tolerated (AJRCCM 151:2006, 1995). FQ-resistant M. Tb identified in New York (Ln 345:1148, 1995). See Table 10B, pages 107 & 100 for adverse effects.	None
Clofazimine (Lamprene) (50, 100 mg cap)	50 mg per day (unsupervised) + 300 mg 1 time per month supervised or 100 mg per day	po 50 mg (with meals)	Skin: **pigmentation (pink-brownish black)** 75–100%; dryness 20%, pruritus 5%. GI: abdominal pain 50% (rarely severe leading to exploratory laparoscopy), splenic infarction (VR), bowel obstruction (VR), GI bleeding (VR). Eye: conjunctival irritation, retinal crystal deposits.	None
Cycloserine (Seromycin) (250 mg cap)	750–1000 mg per day (15 mg per kg per day) 2–4 doses per day [Bacteriostatic for both extra-cellular & intracellular organisms]	RES: 0.1% (0-0.3%) po 250 mg cap	Convulsions, **psychoses** (5–10% of those receiving 1.0 gm per day); headache; somnolence; hyperreflexia, increased CSF protein and pressure, **peripheral neuropathy.** 100 mg pyridoxine per day concomitantly. Contraindicated in epileptics.	None
Dapsone (25, 100 mg tab)	100 mg per day	po 100 mg tab	Blood: ↓ hemoglobin (1-2 gm) & ↑ retics (2-12%), in most pts. Hemolysis in G6PD deficiency, ↑ hemolysis due to concomitant atazanavir (AAC 56:4061, 2012). CNS: peripheral neuropathy (rare). Renal: albuminuria, nephrotic syndrome. Erythema nodosum leprosum in pts rx for leprosy (½% 1st year).	None
Ethionamide (Trecator-SC) (120, 250 mg tab)	500–1000 mg per day (15–20 mg per kg per day) 1–3 doses per day [Bacteriostatic for extracellular organisms only]	RES: 0.8% (0-1.5%) po 250 mg tab	**Gastrointestinal irritation** (up to 50% on large dose); goiter, peripheral neuropathy (rare); convulsions (rare); changes in affect (rare); difficulty in diabetes control; rashes; hepatitis; purpura, stomatitis, gynecomastia; menstrual irregularly. Give drug with meals or antacids; 50–100 mg pyridoxine per day concomitantly; SGOT monthly. Possibly teratogenic.	
Moxifloxacin (Avelox) (400 mg tab)	400 mg qd	po 400 mg cap IV	Not FDA-approved indication. Concomitant administration of rifampin reduces serum levels of moxi (CID 45:1001, 2007).	None
Ofloxacin (Floxin) (200, 300, 400 mg tab)	400 mg bid	po 400 mg cap IV	Not FDA-approved indication. Overall adverse effects 11%, 4% discontinued due to side-effects. GI: nausea 3%, diarrhea 1%. **CNS:** insomnia 3%, headache 1%, dizziness 1%.	

See page 2 for abbreviations.

* Dosages are for adults (unless otherwise indicated), and assume normal renal function
§ Mean (range) (higher in Hispanics, Asians, and patients <10 years old)   [1] **DOT** = directly observed therapy

TABLE 12B (3)

AGENT (TRADE NAME)[1]	USUAL DOSAGE*	ROUTE,[1]* DRUG RESISTANCE (RES) US*§	SIDE-EFFECTS, TOXICITY AND PRECAUTIONS	SURVEILLANCE
SECOND LINE DRUGS (continued)				
Para-aminosalicylic acid (PAS, Paser) (Na⁺ or K⁺ salt) (4 gm cap)	4-6 gm bid (200 mg per kg per day) [Bacteriostatic for extracellular organisms only]	RES: 0.8% (0-1.5%) po 450 mg tab (see Comment)	**Gastrointestinal irritation** (10-15%); goitrogenic action (rare); depressed prothrombin activity (rare); G6PD-mediated hemolytic anemia (rare), drug fever, rashes, hepatitis, myalgia, arthralgia. Retards hepatic enzyme induction, may ↓ INH hepatotoxicity. Available from CDC, (404) 639-3670. Jacobus Pharm. Co. (609) 921-7447.	None
Rifabutin (Mycobutin) (150 mg cap)	300 mg per day (prophylaxis or treatment)	po 150 mg tab	Polymyalgia, polyarthralgia, leukopenia, granulocytopenia. Anterior uveitis when given with concomitant clarithromycin; avoid 600 mg dose (NEJM 330:438, 1994). Uveitis reported with 300 mg per day (AnIM 12:510, 1994). Reddish urine, orange skin (pseudojaundice).	None
Rifapentine (Priftin) (150 mg tab)	600 mg twice weekly for 1st 2 mos., then 600 mg q week	po 150 mg tab	Similar to other rifabutins. (See RIF, RFB). Hyperuricemia seen in 21%. Causes red-orange discoloration of body fluids. Note ↑ prevalence of RIF resistance in pts on weekly rx (Ln 353:1843, 1999).	None
Thalidomide (Thalomid) (50, 100, 200 cap)	100-300 mg po q24h (may use up to 400 mg po q24h for severe erythema nodosum leprosum)	po 50 mg tab	**Contraindicated in pregnancy. Causes severe life-threatening birth defects. Both male and female patients must use barrier contraceptive methods (Pregnancy Category X).** Frequently causes drowsiness or somnolence. May cause peripheral neuropathy. (AJM 108:487, 2000). For review, see Ln 363:1803, 2004.	Available only through pharmacists participating in System for Thalidomide Education and Prescribing Safety (S.T.E.P.S.).

See page 2 for abbreviations.   * Dosages are for adults (unless otherwise indicated) and assume normal renal function   [1] **DOT** = directly observed therapy
§ Mean (range) (higher in Hispanics, Asians, and patients <10 years old)

TABLE 13A– TREATMENT OF PARASITIC INFECTIONS

- Artesunate, Diethylcarbamazine (DEC), Melarsoprol, Nifurtimox, Sodium stibogluconate, Suramin are available from the CDC Drug Service. Quinacrine, Iodoquinol, Niclosamide, Paromomycin, Diloxanide, Fumagillin, Miltefosine, Triclabendazole, Spiramycin are available from compounding pharmacies and specialty labs. **See Table 13D for complete contact information for these antiparasitic drugs.**
- The following resources are available through the Centers for Disease Control and Prevention (CDC) in Atlanta. Website is www.cdc.gov. General advice for parasitic diseases other than malaria: (+1) (770) 488-7775 (day), (+1) (770) 488-7100 (after hours). For CDC Drug Service 8:00 a.m. – 4:30 p.m. (after hours): For CDC Drug Service (+1) (404) 639-3670; fax: (+1) (404) 639-3717. See www.cdc.gov/laboratory/drugservice/index.html
- For malaria treatment (+1) (770) 488-7788; treatment (+1) (770) 488-7788, or after hours (+1) (770) 488-7100; toll-free (US) 1-855-856-4713; website: www.cdc.gov/malaria
- **NOTE: All dosage regimens are for adults (unless otherwise indicated) and assume normal renal function.**
- For licensed drugs, suggest checking package inserts to verify dosage and side-effects. Occasionally, post-licensure data may alter dosage as compared to package inserts.
- **Reference with peds dosages: Treat Guide Med Lett 5 (Supp 5):1, 2007.**

INFECTING ORGANISM	SUGGESTED REGIMENS		COMMENTS
	PRIMARY	ALTERNATIVE	
PROTOZOA—INTESTINAL (non-pathogenic: E. hartmanni, E. dispar, E. coli, Iodamoeba butschlii, Endolimax nana, Chilomastix mesnili)			
Balantidium coli	**Tetracycline** 500 mg po qid x 10 days	**Metronidazole** 750 mg po tid times 5 days	Another alternative: **Iodoquinol** 650 mg po tid x 20 days
Blastocystis hominis Need to treat dubious (See Comment). Ref: J Clin Gastro 44:85, 2010.	**Metronidazole** 1.5 gm po 1x/day x 10 days (placebo-controlled trial in J Travel Med 10:128, 2003) or 750 mg po tid x 10 days.	**Alternatives: Iodoquinol*** 650 mg po tid x 20 days or **TMP-SMX-DS**, one bid x 7 days or **Nitazoxanide** 500 mg bid x 3 days	Role as pathogen unclear; may serve as marker of exposure to contaminated food/water.
Cryptosporidium parvum & hominis Treatment is unsatisfactory Ref.: Curr Opin Infect Dis 23:494, 2010.	**Immunocompetent—No HIV: Nitazoxanide** 500 mg po bid x 3 days (expensive)	**HIV with immunodeficiency:** Effective antiretroviral therapy key therapy. **Nitazoxanide** no clinical or parasite response compared to placebo. Salvage regimen: **(azithro** 600 mg po once daily + **paromomycin** 1 gm po bid x 4 wks), continue for immunocompetent for 8 wks (JID 178:900, 1998)	**Nitazoxanide:** Approved in liquid formulation for rx of children & 500 mg tabs for adults who are immunocompetent. Ref.: CID 40:1173, 2005. **C. hominis** assoc. with ↑ risk of joint pain, eye infection, recurrent headache, & dizzy spells (JID 44:915, 2004).
Cyclospora cayetanensis; **cyclosporiasis** (Clin Micro Rev 23:218, 2010)	**Immunocompetent pts: TMP-SMX-DS** tab 1 po bid x 7–10 days. Other options: see Comments.	**AIDS pts: TMP-SMX-DS** tab 1 po bid for up to 3–4 wks. Other options: see Comments.	If sulfa-allergic: **CIP** 500 mg po bid x 7 days but results inconsistent. Anecdotal success with nitazoxanide. Biliary disease described in HIV pts.
Dientamoeba fragilis See AJTMH 82:614, 2010; Clin Micro Infect 14:601, 2008.	**Iodoquinol*** 650 mg po tid x 20 days or **Paromomycin*** 25–35 mg/kg/day po in 3 div doses x 7 days.	**Tetracycline** 500 mg po qid x 10 days + **Iodoquinol*** 650 mg po tid x 10 days OR (**Iodoquinol*** + **Paromomycin***)	**Metronidazole** associated with high failure rates.
Entamoeba histolytica; amebiasis	Reviews: Ln 361:1025, 2003; NEJM 348:1565, 2003.		
Asymptomatic cyst passer	**Paromomycin*** (aminosidine in U.K.) 25–35 mg/kg/day po in 3 divided doses x 7 days OR **Iodoquinol*** 650 mg po tid x 20 days	**Diloxanide furoate*** (Furamide) 500 mg po tid x 10 days.	Note: E. hartmanni and E. dispar are non-pathogenic.
Patient with diarrhea/dysentery; mild/moderate disease. Oral therapy possible	**Metronidazole** 500–750 mg po tid x 7–10 days or **tinidazole** 2 gm po daily x 3 days, followed by: Either **paromomycin*** 25–35 mg/kg/day po divided in 3 doses x 7 days or **Iodoquinol*** 650 mg po tid x 20 days to clear intestinal cysts. See comment.	x 10 days	Colitis can mimic ulcerative colitis, ameboma can mimic adenocarcinoma of colon. **Nitazoxanide** 500 mg po bid x 3 days may be effective (JID 184:381, 2001 & Tran R Soc Trop Med & Hyg 101:1025, 2007).
Severe or extraintestinal infection, e.g., hepatic abscess	**Metronidazole** 750 mg **iv to PO** tid x 10 days or **tinidazole** 2 gm 1x/day x 5 days (high frequency of GI side-effects). See Comment. **Pregnancy: Paromomycin*** 25–35 mg/kg/day po in 3 divided doses x 5–10 days.	x 10 days followed by **paromomycin*** 25–35 mg/kg/day po divided in 3 doses x 7 days or **Iodoquinol*** 650 mg po tid x 20 days.	**Serology positive (antibody present) with extraintestinal disease.**
Giardia lamblia (Giardia duodenalis); **giardiasis**	(**Tinidazole** 2 gm po x 1) OR (**nitazoxanide** 500 mg po bid x 3 days) OR **Albendazole** (400 mg po once daily x5 days or 5 days). **Metro** & **Paromomycin** are alternatives.	**Metronidazole** 250 mg po tid x 5 days (high frequency of GI side-effects). See Comment. **Pregnancy: Paromomycin*** 25–35 mg/kg/day po in 3 divided doses x 5–10 days.	**Refractory pts: (metro 750 mg po + quinacrine 100 mg po)**—both 3x/day x 3 wks (CID 33:22, 2001) or furazolidone 100 mg po qid x 7 days. Nitazoxanide ref.: CID 40:1173, 2005.

* For source of drug, see Table 13D, page 155.

TABLE 13A (2)

INFECTING ORGANISM	SUGGESTED REGIMENS		COMMENTS
	PRIMARY	ALTERNATIVE	
PROTOZOA—INTESTINAL (continued)			
Cystoisospora belli (formerly Isospora belli) (AIDS ref. MMWR 58 (RR-4):1, 2009)	**Immunocompetent: TMP-SMX-DS** tab 1 po bid **Immunosuppressed: TMP-SMX-DS** qid for up to 4 wks. If CD4<200 may not respond.	CIP 500 mg po bid x 7 days is second-line alternative (AnIM 132:885, 2000) OR **Pyrimethamine** 50-75 mg/day + **Folinic acid** 10-25 mg/day (po).	**Chronic suppression in AIDS pts:** either **TMP-SMX-DS** 1 tap po 3x/wk OR tab 1 po daily OR **pyrimethamine** 25 mg/day po + **folinic acid** 10 mg/day po 3x/wk. **CIP** 500 mg po 3x/wk.
Microsporidiosis		For HIV+ pts, antiretroviral therapy key	To obtain fumagillin: 800-292-8773 or www.leiterx.com. Neutropenia & thrombocytopenia serious adverse events.
Ocular: Encephalitozoon hellum or cuniculi, Vittaforma (Nosema) corneae, Nosema ocularum	**Albendazole** 400 mg po bid x 3 wks plus fumagillin eye drops (see Comment).	In HIV+ pts, reports of response of E. hellum to **fumagillin** eyedrops (see Comment).	Dx: Most labs use modified trichrome stain. Need electron micrographs for species identification. FA and PCR methods in development. Peds dose ref: PIDJ 23:915, 2004
intestinal (diarrhea): Enterocytozoon bieneusi, Encephalitozoon (Septata) intestinalis	**Albendazole** 400 mg po bid x 3 wks; peds dose: 15 mg/kg per day into 2 daily doses x 7 days for **E. intestinalis**. Fumagillin equally effective.	Oral **fumagillin 20 mg po tid** reported effective for **E. bieneusi** (NEJM 346:1963, 2002) — see Comment	For Trachipleistophora sp., try itraconazole + albendazole (NEJM 351:42, 2004). Other pathogens: Brachiola vesiculorum & algerae (NEJM 351:42, 2004)
Disseminated: E. hellum, cuniculi or intestinalis, Pleistophora sp. others in Comment	**Albendazole** 400 mg po bid x 3 wks	No established rx for Pleistophora sp.	
PROTOZOA—EXTRAINTESTINAL			
Amebic meningoencephalitis (Clin Infect Dis 51:e7, 2010 (Balamuthia))			
Acanthamoeba sp — no proven rx Rev. FEMS Immunol Med Micro 50:1, 2007. Balamuthia mandrillaris	Success with IV **pentamidine + sulfadiazine + flucytosine** + (either **fluconazole** or **itraconazole**) (FEMS Immunol Med Micro 50:1, 2007). 2 children responded to po rx: **TMP-SMX + rifampin + keto** (PIDJ 20:623, 2001).		For Acanthamoeba keratitis: miltefosine or voriconazole.
Naegleria fowleri >95% mortality. Ref. MMWR 57:573, 2008. Sappinia diploidea	**Pentamidine, Amphotericin B** + (**Fluconazole** or **itraconazole**) or **Liposomal Ampho B** + **Sulfadiazine** + (**Azithro** or **Clarithro**). See CID 51:e7, 2010. **Ampho B** 1.5 mg/kg per day in 2 div doses x 3 days; then 1 mg/kg/day x 6 days plus 1.5 mg/day intrathecal x 2 days; then 1 mg/day intrathecal qod x 8 days. **Azithro + pentamidine + itra + flucytosine** (JAMA 285:2450, 2001)		Anecdotal response to miltefosine.
Babesia microti (US) and **Babesia divergens** (EU) (NEJM 366:366.2397, 2012)	For mild/moderate disease: **Atovaquone** 750 mg po bid + **Azithro** 600 mg po on day 1, then 250-1000 mg po daily for 7-10 days. If relapse, treat x 6 wks & until blood smear neg x 2 wks.	For severe babesiosis: (**Clindamycin** 600 mg po tid + (**quinine** 650 mg po tid) x 7-10 days For adults, can give **clinda** IV as 1.2 gm bid.	Overwhelming infection in asplenic patients. In immunocompromised patients, treat for 6 or more weeks (CID 46:370, 2008). **Consider exchange transfusion if ≥10% parasitemia** (Trans Med Rev 16:239, 2002)
Leishmaniasis (Suggest consultation—CDC (+1) 770 488 7775; see LnID 7:581, 2007; CID 43:1089 2006)			
Cutaneous: Mild Disease (< 4 lesions, none > 5 cm diameter; all lesions in cosmetically sensitive area, none over joints) Otherwise, consider Moderate Disease	**Mild Disease** (< 4 lesions, none > 5 cm): **Paromomycin** ointment bid x 20 days (investigational); cryotherapy (freeze up to 3x with liquid nitrogen); intralesional Antimony 20 mg/kg into lesions weekly x 8-10 wks. Spontaneous resolution in > 50% but may take 6 months (PLoS Negl Trop Dis 4:e628, 2010). Heat therapy ref. see www.thermosurgery.com.	**Moderate Disease:** **Sodium stibogluconate*** (Pentostam) or **Meglumine antimoniate** (Glucantime) 20 mg/kg/day IV/IM x 20 days. Dilute in 120 mL of D5W and infuse over 2 hrs. **Alternative: Fluconazole** 200 mg po daily x 6 weeks (for L. mexicanus, L. panamensis, L. major) x 30 days **Ketoconazole** 600 mg po daily x 30 days (L. mexicanus)	Oral therapy. Topical paromomycin* & other topical treatment only when low potential for mucosal spread; never use for L. braziliensis or L. guyanensis cutaneous lesions. Generic pentavalent antimony varies in quality and safety.

* For source of drug, see Table 13D, page 155.

TABLE 13A (3)

INFECTING ORGANISM	SUGGESTED REGIMENS		COMMENTS
	PRIMARY	ALTERNATIVE	
PROTOZOA—EXTRAINTESTINAL (continued)			
Leishmaniasis, Mucosal (Espundia). Usually due to L. brasiliensis.	**Pentavalent antimony (Sb)** 20 mg/kg/day IV or IM x 28 days of **liposomal amphotericin B** (regimens vary) with total cumulative dose of 20-60 mg/kg or **amphotericin B** 0.5-1 mg/kg IV daily or qod to total dose of 20-40 mg/kg.	No good alternative; variable efficacy of oral Miltefosine: **Miltefosine** 2.5 mg/kg/day (to maximum of 150 mg/day) po divided tid x 28 days (AJTMH 81:387, 2009).	Antimony available from CDC drug service; miltefosine available from Paladin Labs. See Table 13D for contact information.
Visceral leishmaniasis – Kala-Azar – New World & Old World L. donovani: India, Africa L. infantum: Mediterranean L. chagasi: New World	**Liposomal ampho B** FDA-approved in immunocompetent hosts: 3 mg/kg once daily days 1-5 & days 14 & 21. Alternative regimens: 3 mg/kg IV daily on days 1-5 and day 10 or 10 mg/kg on days 1 and 2.	**Standard Ampho B** 1 mg/kg IV daily x 15-20 days OR **Ampho B** x 6-8 wks (total of 15-20 mg/kg) OR **Miltefosine** 2.5 mg/kg/day (max 150 mg/day) x 28 days OR **pentavalent antimony** 20 mg/kg/day IV/IM x 28 days.	In HIV patients, may need lifelong suppression with Amphotericin B q 2-4 wks
Malaria (Plasmodia species) —NOTE: CDC Malaria info— prophylaxis/treatment (770) 488-7788. After hours: 770-488-7100. US toll-free 1-855-856-4713. CDC offers species confirmation and drug resistance testing. Refs: JAMA 297:2251, 2264 & 2285, 2007. Websites: www.cdc.gov/malaria, www.who.int/health-topics/malaria.htm. Review of rapid diagnostic tests: CID 54:1637, 2012.			
Prophylaxis—Drugs require personal protection: screens, nets, 30-35% DEET skin repellent (avoid > 50% DEET) (Med Lett 54:75, 2012), permethrin spray on clothing and mosquito nets. Country risk in CDC Yellow Book.			
For areas free of chloroquine (CQ)-resistant P. falciparum: Central America (west of Panama Canal), Caribbean, Korea, Middle East (most)	CQ phosphate 500 mg (300 mg base) po per wk, starting 1-2 wks before travel, during travel, & 4 wks post-travel or **atovaquone-proguanil (AP)** 1 adult tab per day (1 day prior to, during, & 7 days post-travel. Another option for P. vivax only countries: **primaquine (PQ)** 30 mg base po daily in non-pregnant. G6PD-OK in travelers: >92% effective vs P. vivax (CID 33:1990.) Note: **CQ** may exacerbate psoriasis.	**CQ Peds dose:** 8.3 mg/kg (5 mg/kg of base) po 1 wk up to 300 mg (base) max. dose or **AP** by weight (peds tabs: 11–20 kg, 1 tab; 21–30 kg, 2 tabs; 31–40 kg, 3 tabs; >41 kg, 1 adult tab per day. **Adults:** Doxy or MQ as below.	CQ safe during pregnancy. **The areas free of CQ-resistant falciparum malaria continue to shrink:** See CDC or WHO maps for most current information on CQ resistance. **Doxy AEs:** photosensitivity, candida vaginitis, gastritis.
For areas with CQ-resistant P. falciparum CDC info on prophylaxis (770) 488-7788 or website: www.cdc.gov/malaria & LnID 6:139, 2006	**Atovaquone** 250 mg – **proguanil** 100 mg (Malarone) comb. tablet. 1 per day with food 1–2 days prior to, during, & 7 days post-travel. Peds dose in footnote[1] Malarone preferred for trips of a week, or less: expense may preclude use for longer trips. Native malarone (AP) for prophylaxis/treatment programs in a few countries. Fansidar 1 tab po 3.5 times during pregnancy (Expert Rev Anti Infect Ther 8:589, 2010).	**Doxycycline** 100 mg po daily for adults & children > 8 yrs of age[1]. Take 1-2 days before, during & for 4 wks after travel. **OR** **Mefloquine (MQ)** 250 mg (228 mg base) po once per wk, 1-2 wks before, during, & for 4 wks after travel. Peds dose in footnote[1] **Doxy AEs:** photosensitivity, candida vaginitis, gastritis.	**Pregnancy: MQ current best option.** Insufficient data with Malarone. Avoid doxycycline and primaquine. **Primaquine: Can cause hemolytic anemia if G6PD deficiency present.** **MQ not recommended** if cardiac conduction abnormalities, seizures, or psychiatric disorders, e.g., depression, psychosis. MQ outside U.S.: 275 mg tab, contains 250 mg of base. If used, can start 3 wks before travel to assure tolerability.

[1] **Peds prophylaxis dosages** (Ref.: CID 34:493, 2002): **Mefloquine** weekly dose by **weight** in kg: < 15 = 5 mg/kg; 15-19 = ¼ adult dose; 20-30 = ½ adult dose; 31-45 = ¾ adult dose; >45 = adult dose. **Atovaquone/proguanil** by **weight in kg,** single daily dose using peds tab (62.5 mg atovaquone & 25 mg proguanil): 5-8 kg, ½ tab; 8-10 kg, ¾ tab; 11-20 kg, 1 tab; 21-30 kg, 2 tabs; 31-40 kg, 3 tabs; ≥41 kg, one adult tab. **Doxycycline,** ages ≥8-12 yrs: 2 mg/kg per day up to 100 mg/day. Continue daily x 4 wks after leaving risk area. Side effects: photosensitivity, nausea, yeast vaginitis

* For source of drug, see Table 13D, page 155.

TABLE 13A (4)

INFECTING ORGANISM	SUGGESTED REGIMENS		COMMENTS
	PRIMARY	ALTERNATIVE	

PROTOZOA—EXTRAINTESTINAL/Malaria (Plasmodia species) (continued)

Treatment of Malaria. Diagnosis is by microscopy. Alternative: rapid antigen detection test (Binax NOW): detects 96-100% of P. falciparum and 50% of other plasmodia (CID 49:908, 2009; CID 54:1637, 2012). Need microscopy to speciate. Can stay positive for over a month after successful treatment.

Clinical Severity/ Plasmodia sp.	Region Acquired	Suggested Treatment Regimens (Drug)		Comments
		Adults	Peds	
Uncomplicated/ P. falciparum (or species not identified) Malaria rapid diagnostic test (Binax NOW): CID 54:1637, 2012.	Cen. Amer., west of Panama Canal; Haiti; Dom. Repub., & most of Mid-East **CQ-sensitive** CQ-resistant or unknown resistance. Note: If >5% parasitemia or Hb <7, treat as severe malaria.	CQ phosphate 1 gm salt (600 mg base) po, then 0.5 gm in 6 hrs, then 0.5 gm daily x 2 days. Total: 2500 mg salt **Adults: Atovaquone-proguanil** 1 gm–400 mg (4 adult tabs) po 1x/day x 3 days w/ food R [QS 650 mg po tid x 3 days (7 days if SE Asia)] + [Doxy 100 mg po bid; or tetra 250 mg po qid) or clinda 20 mg/k/d divided tid) x 7 days] OR **Artemether-lumefantrine*** tabs 20/120 mg: 4 tabs po (at 0, 8 hrs) then bid x 2 days (total 6 doses); take with food OR a less desirable adult alternative, mefloquine 750 mg po x 1 dose, then 500 mg po x 1 dose 6-12 hr later. MQ is 2nd line alternative due to neuropsychiatric reaction. Also, resistance in SE Asia.	Peds: CQ 10 mg/k/g of base po; then 5 mg/k/g of base at 6, 24, & 48 hrs. Total: 25 mg/kg base **Peds:** [QS 10 mg/kg po tid x 3 days) + (clinda 20 mg/kg per day div tid)] – both x 7 days. OR [QS (same dose) + tetra (as in Doxy tid) – then 6-12 hrs later 10 mg/kg po]. **Artemether-lumefantrine*** • 5 kg to < 15 kg: 1 tablet po; 120 mg) as a single dose, then 1 tablet again after 8 hours, then 1 tablet every 12 hours for 2 days • 15 kg to < 25 kg (120 mg): 2 tablets (240 mg) as a single dose, then 2 tablets every 12 hours for 2 days • 25 kg to < 35 kg: 3 tablets (60 mg/ 360 mg) as a single dose, then 3 tablets again after 8 hours, then 3 tablets every 12 hrs for 2 days • > 35 kg: as per adult dose.	**Peds dose should never exceed adult dose.** CQ + MQ prolong QTc. **Pregnancy & children:** Can substitute clinda for doxy/tetra: 20 mg/kg per day po div tid x 7 days. In U.S. QS is only available as quinacrine 324 mg capsule, thus hard to use to treat children. **Peds atovaquone-proguanil dose** (all once daily x 3 d) by weight: 5-8 kg: 2 peds tabs; 9-10 kg: 3 peds tabs; 11-20 kg: 1 tablet po; 21-30 kg: 2 adult tabs; 31-40 kg: 3 adult tabs; >40 kg: 4 adult tabs. **Pregnancy:** Quinine + Clindamycin **Note: Oral Artemether-lumefantrine tabs FDA-approved.** IV Artesunate available from CDC Drug Service, see Table 13D, page 155.
Uncomplicated/ P. malariae or P. knowlesi (JID 99: 1107 & 1143, 2009).	All regions – CQ-sensitive	CQ as above adults & peds In South Pacific, beware of P. knowlesi; looks like P. malariae, but behaves like P. falciparum (CID 46:165, 2007).	CQ as above adults & peds In South Pacific	
Uncomplicated/ P. vivax or P. ovale	**CQ-sensitive** (except Papua, New Guinea, Indonesia which are CQ-resistant–see below)	CQ as above + PQ base: 30 mg po daily x 14 days Each primaquine phosphate tab is 26.3 mg of salt and 15 mg of base. 30 mg of base = 2 26.3 mg tabs prim. phos.	**Peds:** CQ as above + PQ base 0.5 mg po once daily x 14 days	PQ used to eradicate latent parasites in liver. **Screen for G6PD def. before starting PQ;** If G6PD deficient dose PQ as 45 mg po once weekly x 8 wks. **Note: rare severe reactions.** Avoid PQ on pregnancy.
Uncomplicated/ P. vivax	**CQ-resistant:** Papua, New Guinea & Indonesia	[QS + (doxy or tetra) + PQ] as above or Artemether-Lumefantrine (same dose as for P. falciparum)	**Peds:** MQ + PQ as above. **Peds** (<8 yrs old): QS alone x 7 days or MQ alone. In either high, add doxy or tetra.	Rarely, acute. Lung injury and other serious complications: LnID 8:449, 2008.

* For source of drug, see Table 13D, page 155.

TABLE 13A (5)

INFECTING ORGANISM	SUGGESTED REGIMENS		COMMENTS
	PRIMARY	ALTERNATIVE	
Clinical Severity/ Plasmodia sp.	Region Acquired	Suggested Treatment Regimens (Drug)	Comments
		Primary—Adults	Alternative & Peds	

PROTOZOA—EXTRAINTESTINAL/Malaria (Plasmodia species) /Treatment of Malaria (continued)

Clinical Severity/ Plasmodia sp.	Region Acquired	Primary—Adults	Alternative & Peds	Comments
Uncomplicated Malaria/Alternatives for Pregnancy Ref: LnID 7:118 & 136, 2007	CQ-sensitive areas	**CQ** as above		Doxy or tetra used if benefits outweigh risks. No controlled studies of AP in pregnancy. If P. vivax or P. ovale, after pregnancy check for G6PD deficiency & give PQ 30 mg po daily times 14 days.
	CQ-resistant P. falciparum	**QS + clinda** as above	If failing or intolerant: **QS + doxy**	
	CQ-resistant P. vivax	**QS** 650 mg po tid x 7 days		
	Intermittent pregnancy treatment (empiric)	Give treatment dose of [Sulfadoxine 500 mg + Pyrimethamine 25 mg (Fansidar) po] at 3 times during pregnancy to decrease maternal & fetal morbidity & mortality		
Severe malaria, i.e., impaired consciousness, severe anemia, renal failure, pulmonary edema, ARDS, DIC, jaundice, acidosis, seizures, parasitemia >5%. One or more of latter. **Almost always P. falciparum.** Ref: NEJM 358:1829, 2008; Science 320:30, 2008.	All regions Note: •Artesunate is effective but not FDA-approved. Available from CDC Drug Service under specific conditions. •IV quinidine rarely available. Possible emergency availability from Eli Lilly.	**Quinidine gluconate** in normal saline: 10 mg/kg (salt) IV over 1 hr then 0.02 mg/kg/min by constant infusion OR 24 mg/kg IV over 4 hrs & then 12 mg/kg IV over 4 hrs q8h. Continue until parasite density <1% & can take po. **QS**: QS 650 mg po tid x 3 days (7 days if SE Asia) + (**Doxy** 100 mg IV q12h x 7 days) OR (**clinda** 10 mg/kg IV load & then 5 mg/kg IV q8h x 7 days)	**Peds: Quinidine gluconate IV**—same mg/kg dose as for adults **PLUS** (**Doxy:** if <45 kg, 4 mg per kg IV q12h; if ≥45 kg, dose as for adults) OR **Clinda**, same mg/kg dose as for adults Artesunate* 2.4 mg/kg IV at 0, 12, 24, 48 hrs. then **Doxy** 100 IV q12h x 7 days (see Comment)	During quinidine IV monitor BP EKG (prolongation of QTc) & blood glucose (hypoglycemia). Consider exchange transfusion if parasitemia >10%. Switch to QS po + (Doxy or Clinda) when patient able to take oral drugs. **Steroids not recommended for cerebral malaria.** If quinidine not available, or patient intolerant or high level parasitemia. **IV artesunate*** available from CDC Malaria Branch (8 hr transport time post-approval). see Table 13D (Ref: CID 44:1067 & 1075, 2007). Substitute Clinda for Doxy in pregnancy.
Malaria—self-initiated treatment: Only for people at high risk. Carry a reliable supply of recommended meds (to avoid counterfeit meds). Use only if malaria is lab-diagnosed and no available reliable meds.		**Artemether-lumefantrine** (20/120 mg tab) 4 tabs po x 1 dose, repeat in 8 hrs, then repeat q12h x 2 days (take with food) OR **Atovaquone-proguanil (AP)** 4 adult tabs (1 gm/400 mg) po x 3 days	**Peds:** Using adult AP tabs po 11–20 kg, 1 tab; 21–30 kg, 2 tabs; 31–40 kg, 3 tabs; >41 kg, 4 tabs. For Peds dosing of Artemether-lumefantrine, see Uncomplicated P. falciparum, page 144.	Do not use for renal insufficiency pts. Do not use if weight <11 kg, pregnant, or breast-feeding. **Artemether-lumefantrine:** sold as Riamet (EU) and Coartem (US & elsewhere).
Pneumocystis carinii pneumonia (PCP). Revised name is **Pneumocystis jiroveci** (yee-row-vek-ee). Ref: JAMA 301:2578, 2009. **Not acutely ill**, able to take po meds. PaO2 >70 mmHg Serum 1,3 B-D Glucan assay has high diagnostic accuracy for PCP (JCM 50:7, 2012).		**TMP-SMX-DS**, 2 tabs po q8h x 21 days) OR (**Dapsone** 100 mg po q24h + **trimethoprim** 5 mg/kg po tid x 21 days) NOTE: Concomitant use of corticosteroids usually reserved for sicker pts with PaO2 <70 (see below)	**Clindamycin** 300–450 mg po q6h + **primaquine** 15 mg base po q24h) x 21 days OR **Atovaquone** suspension 750 mg po bid with food x 21 days	Mutations in gene of the enzyme target (dihydropteroate synthetase) of sulfamethoxazole identified. Unclear whether mutations result in resist to TMP-SMX vs. Dapsone (Ref: CID 27:191, 1998. Dapsone ref: CID 27:191, 1998). **After 21 days, chronic suppression** in AIDS pts (see below—post-treatment suppression).

* For source of drug, see Table 13D, page 155.

TABLE 13A (6)

INFECTING ORGANISM	SUGGESTED REGIMENS — PRIMARY	SUGGESTED REGIMENS — ALTERNATIVE	COMMENTS
PROTOZOA—EXTRAINTESTINAL/Malaria (Plasmodia species)/Treatment of Malaria *(continued)*			
Acutely ill, po rx not possible. PaO_2 <70 mmHg. Still unclear whether antiretroviral therapy (ART) should be started during treatment of PCP (CID 46: 634, 2008).	**Prednisone** (15–30 min. before TMP-SMX): 40 mg po bid times 5 days, then 40 mg q24h times 5 days, then 20 mg q24h times 11 days) + **[TMP 15 mg per kg per day component per kg per day] IV div. q6-8h times 21 days**	**Prednisone** as in primary rx PLUS **[Clinda 600 mg IV q8h) + primaquine 30 mg base po q24h] times 21 days** OR **Pentamidine** 4 mg per kg per day IV times 21 days. Ceprolungan active in animal models (CID 36:1445, 2003)	**After 21 days, chronic suppression in AIDS pts** (see post-treatment suppression). **PCP can occur in absence of HIV infection & steroids** (CID 25:215 & 1997). Wait 4–8 days before declaring treatment failure & switching to clinda + primaquine or adding pentamidine (JAIDS 48:63, 2008).
Primary prophylaxis and post-treatment suppression	Can substitute IV prednisolone (reduce dose 25%) for po prednisone. **TMP-SMX-DS** (or **-SS**): 1 tab po q24h OR (DS 3x/wk) OR **(dapsone** 100 mg po q24h) x3 (NEJM 344:159, 2001).	**Pentamidine** 300 mg in 6 mL sterile water by aerosol q4 wks OR **[dapsone** 200 mg po + **pyrimethamine** 75 mg po + **folinic acid** 25 mg po — **all once a week]** or **atovaquone** (1500 mg po q24h with food)	**TMP-SMX-DS** provides cross-protection vs toxo and other bacterial infections. Dapsone + pyrimethamine protects vs toxo. Atovaquone suspension 1500 mg once daily as effective as daily dapsone (NEJM 339:1889, 1998) or inhaled pentamidine (JID 180:369, 1999)
Toxoplasma gondii (Reference: Ln 363:1965, 2004) **Immunologically normal patients** *(For pediatric doses, see reference)*			
Acute illness w/ lymphadenopathy	No specific rx unless severe/persistent symptoms or evidence of vital organ damage.		
Acq. via transfusion (lab accident) **Active chorioretinitis; meningitis;** severe disease due to steroids or cytotoxic drugs	**[Pyrimethamine** 200 mg po times 1, then 50–75 mg po q24h] + **[sulfadiazine** (see footnote²)/5 + **leucovorin (folinic acid)** 5–20 mg 3x/wk]—see Comment. Treat 1–2 wks beyond resolution of signs/symptoms, continue leucovorin 1 wk after stopping pyri.	Treat as for active chorioretinitis. **[Pyrimethamine + folinic acid]** as above, once po on 3° day, then 50–75 mg po q24h] + **[sulfadiazine** (see footnote²)]	For congenital toxo, toxo meningitis in adults & chorioretinitis, **add prednisone 1 mg/kg/day in 2 div. doses** until CSF protein conc. falls or vision-threatening inflammation subsides. Adjust folinic acid dose by following CBC results. Screen patients with IgM and IgG serology at commercial lab. IgG+/IgM– = remote past infection. IgG+/IgM+ = seroconversion. Suggest consultation with Palo Alto Medical Foundation Toxoplasma Serology Lab: 650-853-4828 or toxlab@pamf.org. Details in Ln 363:1965, 2004. **Consultation advisable.**
Acute in pregnant women. Ref: CID 47:554, 2008.	**If <18 wks gestation at diagnosis: Spiramycin¹*** 1 gm po q8h until 16–18 wks; dc if amniotic fluid PCR is negative. Positive PCR treat as below. **If >18 wks gestation & suspected fetal infection by positive amniotic fluid PCR: [Pyrimethamine** 50 mg q12h x 2 doses, then 50 mg/day + **sulfadiazine** 75 mg/kg x 1 dose, then 50 mg/kg q12h (max 4 gm/day) + **folinic acid** 10–20 mg po daily] for minimum of 4 wks or for duration of pregnancy. Mgmt complex. Combo rx with pyrimethamine + sulfadiazine + leucovorin—see Comment		
Fetal/congenital	**[Pyrimethamine (pyri)** 200 mg x 1 po, then 75 mg/day po) + **sulfadiazine** (Wt based dose: 1 gm if <60 kg, 1.5 gm if ≥60 kg) po q6h] + **folinic acid** 10–25 mg po q24h x30 days (AAC 42:1346, 1996)		
AIDS			
Cerebral toxoplasmosis Ref: MMWR 58(RR-4) 1, 2009	**[Pyrimethamine (pyri)** 200 mg x 1 po, then 75 mg/day po) + **sulfadiazine** (Wt based dose: 1 gm if <60 kg, 1.5 gm if ≥60 kg po q6h)] + **folinic acid** 10–25 mg po q24h] **atovaquone** 750 mg po q6h. Treat 4–6 wks after resolution of signs/symptoms, and then lifelong suppression.	**[Pyri + folinic acid** (as in primary regimen)] + 1 of the following: (1) **Clinda** 600 mg po/IV q6h or (2) **TMP-SMX** 5/25 mg/kg po or IV bid or (3) **atovaquone** 750 mg po q6h.	Use alternative regimen for pts with severe sulfa allergy. MRI-enhancing brain lesions (CT or MRI), if multiple. >85% of pts respond to 7–10 days of empiric rx. Pyri penetrates brain even if no inflammation; folinic acid prevents pyrimethamine hematologic toxicity. Ref: MMWR 58(RR-4) 1, 2009. **Another alternative:** (Dapsone 200 mg po + pyrimethamine 75 mg po + folinic acid 25 mg po) once weekly.
Primary prophylaxis, AIDS pts—IgG toxo antibody + CD4 count <100 per mcL	**TMP-SMX-DS:** 1 tab po q24h or 3x/wk) OR **(TMP-SMX-SS:** 1 tab po q24h)	**[(Dapsone** 50 mg po q24h or 3x/wk) + **(pyri** 50 mg po q wk)] OR **atovaquone** 1500 mg po q24h	

² Sulfonamides for toxo. Sulfadiazine now commercially available. Sulfisoxazole much less effective.

* For source of drug, see Table 13D, page 155.

TABLE 13A (7)

INFECTING ORGANISM	SUGGESTED REGIMENS		COMMENTS
	PRIMARY	ALTERNATIVE	
PROTOZOA—EXTRAINTESTINAL/Toxoplasma gondii/AIDS (continued)			
Suppression after rx of cerebral toxo	(Sulfadiazine 2-4 gm po divided in 2-4 doses/day) + (folinic acid 10-25 mg po q24h). DC if CD4 count 200 x 3 mos	[(Clinda 600 mg po q8h) + (pyri 25-50 mg po q24h)] + (folinic acid 10-25 mg po q24h) OR atovaquone 750 mg po q6-12h	(Pyri + sulfa) prevents PCP and toxo. (clinda + pyri) prevents toxo only. Additional drug needed to prevent PCP
Trichomonas vaginalis	See Vaginitis, Table 1, page 26.		
Trypanosomiasis. Ref.: Ln 362:1469, 2003. **Note: Drugs for African trypanosomiasis may be obtained free from WHO. See Table 13D, page 155, for source information.**			
West African sleeping sickness (T. brucei gambiense)			
Early: Blood/lymphatic	Pentamidine 4 mg/kg IV/IM daily x 7-10 days	In US, free from CDC drug service: Suramin* 100 mg IV (test dose), then 1 gm IV on days 1, 3, 7, 14, & 21	
Late: Encephalitis	Eflornithine* 100 mg/kg q6h IV x14 days (CID 41:748, 2005). Obtain drug from WHO drug service (simarrop@who.int or +41 22 791 1345). Combined with melarsoprol better, see Comment.	Melarsoprol* 2.2 mg/kg per day IV x 10 days (melarsoprol/nifurtimox combination superior to melarsoprol alone (JID 195:311 & 322, 2007).	Combination of IV eflornithine 400 mg/kg/day divided q12h x 7 days, plus nifurtimox 15 mg/kg/day po, divided q8h x 10 days more efficacious than standard dose eflornithine (CID 45:1435 & 1443, 2007; Ln 374:56, 2009).
East African sleeping sickness (T. brucei rhodesiense)			
Early: Blood/lymphatic	Suramin* 100 mg IV (test dose), then 1 gm IV on days 1, 3, 7, 14, & 21	Pods: Suramin* 10-15 mg/kg IV on days 1, 3, 7, 14 & 21	Suramin & Melarsoprol: CDC Drug Service or WHO (at no charge) (see Table 13D).
Late: Encephalitis (prednisolone may prevent encephalitis)	Melarsoprol* From 2-3.6 mg/kg per day IV over 3 days; repeat 3.6 mg/kg after 7 days & for 3rd time at 3.6 mg/kg 7 days after 2nd course	Melarsoprol 2.2 mg/kg/day IV x 10 days (PLoS NTD 6:e1695, 2012)	Early illness; patient waiting for Suramin, use pentamidine 4 mg/kg/day IV/IM x 1-2 doses. Does not enter CSF
T. cruzi—**Chagas disease** or acute American trypanosomiasis. Ref.: LnID 10:566, 2010. For chronic, see Comment.	Benznidazole* 5-7 mg/kg per day po div. 2x/day x 60 days. NOTE: Take with meals to alleviate G-I side effects. Contraindicated in pregnancy.	Nifurtimox* 8-10 mg/kg per day po div. 4x/day after meals x 120 days Ages 11-16 yrs: 12.5-15 mg/kg per day div. qid po x 90 days Children <11yrs: 15-20 mg/kg per day div. qid po x 90 days	Immunosuppression for heart transplant can reactivate chronic Chagas disease (J Card Failure 15:249, 2009). Can transmit by organ/transfusions (CID 49:1534, 2009).
NEMATODES—INTESTINAL (Roundworms)			
Anisakis simplex **(anisakiasis)** Anisakiasis differentiated from Anisakidosis (CID 51:806, 2010). Other: A. physlatry, Pseudoterranova decipiens.	Physical removal: endoscope or surgery. IgE antibody test vs A. simplex may help diagnosis. No antimicrobial therapy.		Anisakiasis acquired by eating raw fish: herring, salmon, mackerel, cod, squid. Similar illness due to Pseudoterranova species acquired from cod, halibut, red snapper.
Eosinophilia? Think Strongyloides, toxocaria and filariasis: CID 34:407, 2005; 42:1781 & 1655, 2006— See Table 13C.			
Ascaris lumbricoides **(ascariasis)** Ln 367:1521, 2006	Albendazole 400 mg po daily x 3 days or mebendazole 100 mg po bid x 3 days	Ivermectin 150-200 mcg/kg po x 1 dose	Review of efficacy of single dose: JAMA 299:1937, 2008.
Capillaria philippinensis **(capillariasis)**	Mebendazole 100 mg po x 1, repeat in 2 wks	Mebendazole 200 mg po bid x 20 days	Albendazole preferred
Enterobius vermicularis **(pinworm)**	Mebendazole 100 mg po x 1, repeat in 2 wks	Pyrantel pamoate 11 mg/kg base to max. dose of 1 gm) po x 1 dose; repeat in 2 wks OR Albendazole 400 mg po x 1 dose	Side-effects in Table 13B, page 154.
Gongylonemiasis (adult worms in oral mucosa)	Surgical removal	Albendazole 400 mg/day po x 3 days	Ref: CID 32:1378, 2001; J Helminth 80:425, 2006.
Hookworm (Necator americanus and Ancylostoma duodenale)	Albendazole 400 mg po daily x 3 days	Mebendazole 100 mg po bid x 3 days OR Pyrantel pamoate 11 mg/kg (to max. dose of 1 gm) po x 3 days	NOTE: Ivermectin not effective. Eosinophilia may be absent but eggs in stool (NEJM 351:799, 2004).
Strongyloides stercoralis **(strongyloidiasis)** (Hyperinfection, See Comment)	Ivermectin 200 mcg/kg per day po x 2 days	Albendazole 400 mg po bid x 7 days : less effective	**For hyperinfections,** repeat at 15 days. For hyperinfection: veterinary ivermectin given subcutaneously or rectally (CID 49:1411, 2009).

* For source of drug, see Table 13D, page 155.

TABLE 13A (8)

INFECTING ORGANISM	SUGGESTED REGIMENS		COMMENTS
	PRIMARY	ALTERNATIVE	
NEMATODES—INTESTINAL (Roundworms) (continued)			
Trichostrongylus orientalis, T. colubriformis	**Pyrantel pamoate** 11 mg/kg (max. 1 gm) po x 1	**Albendazole** 400 mg po x 1 dose	**Mebendazole** 100 mg po bid x 3 days
Trichuris trichura (**whipworm**) (Ln 367:1521, 2006)	**Albendazole** 400 mg po 1x/day x 3 days. Often refractory; multiple courses may be necessary.	**Mebendazole** (100 mg po bid x 3 days or 500 mg once) or **Ivermectin** 200 mcg/kg daily po x 3 days	Cure rate of 55% with one 500 mg dose of **Mebendazole** + one dose of **Ivermectin** 200 mcg/kg (CID 51:1420, 2010).
NEMATODES—EXTRAINTESTINAL (Roundworms)			
Ancylostoma braziliense & caninum; causes **cutaneous larva migrans** (Dog & cat hookworm)	**Albendazole** 400 mg po bid x 3-7 days (Ln ID 8:302, 2008).	**Ivermectin** 200 mcg/kg po x 1 dose/day x 1–2 days (not in children wt < 15 kg)	Also called "creeping eruption," dog and cat hookworm. Ivermectin cure rate 81-100% (1 dose) to 97% (3 doses) (CID 31:493, 2000).
Angiostrongylus cantonensis (**Angiostrongyliasis**); causes eosinophilic meningitis	Mild/moderate disease: Analgesics, serial LPs (if necessary). Prednisone 60 mg/day x 14 days reduces headache & need for LPs.	Adding **Albendazole** 15 mg/kg/day to prednisone 60 mg/day both for 14 days may reduce duration of headaches and need for repeat LPs.	**Do not use Albendazole without prednisone,** see TRSMH 102:990, 2008. Gnathostoma and Baylisascaris also cause eosinophilic meningitis.
Baylisascariasis (Raccoon roundworm); eosinophilic meningitis	No drug proven efficacious. Try po **albendazole,** corticosteroids. Treat for one month.	Peds: 25–50 mg/kg po: Adults: 400 mg po bid with corticosteroids	Steroids ref: CID 39:1484, 2004. Other causes of eosinophilic meningitis: Gnathostoma & Angiostrongylus.
Dracunculus medinensis: **Guinea worm** (CMAJ 170:495, 2004)	Slow extraction of pre-emergent worm over several days		No drugs effective. Oral analgesics, anti-inflammatory drugs; topical antiseptics/antibiotic ointments to alleviate symptoms and facilitate worm removal by gentle manual traction over several days
Filariasis. Wolbachia bacteria needed for filarial development. **Rx with doxy 100-200 mg/day x 6-8 wks**	number of wolbachia & number of microfilaria		
Lymphatic filariasis (**Elephantiasis**): Wuchereria bancrofti or Brugia malayi or B. timori. Ref: Curr Opin Inf Dis 21:673, 2008 (role of Wolbachia).	**Diethylcarbamazine***(DEC) [6 mg/kg/day po in 3 divided doses x 14 days]. DEC x 1 day, DEC 50 mg x 1 day, then 50 mg x 3 day, then 14 day, OR gradual dose increase: day 1-50 mg po, day 2-50 mg po tid, day 3-100 mg tid, day 4 through 12-6 mg/kg po divided tid + **Doxy** 200 mg/day x 6 wks.	Interest in combining albendazole with DEC. **Doxycycline** 200 mg/day x 6 wks PLUS **DEC** + albendazole reduced microfilaremia (CID 46:1385, 2008)	Oncho & Loa loa may both be present. Check peripheral smear: if Loa loa microfilaria present, treat oncho first with ivermectin before DEC for Loa loa.
Cutaneous			
Loiasis. **Loa loa,** eye worm disease	**Diethylcarbamazine** (DEC)*,[a]: Day 1, 50 mg; Day 2, 50 mg tid; Day 3, 100 mg tid; Days 4-21, 8-10 mg/kg/day in 3 divided doses x 21 days. **If concomitant onchocerca, treat onchocerca first.**	**Albendazole** 200 mg po bid x 21 days if still symptomatic after 2 courses of DEC.	If over 5,000 microfilaria/mL of blood, DEC can cause encephalopathy. Might start with albendazole a few days ± steroids, then DEC.
Onchocerca volvulus (**onchocerciasis**) (AJTMH 81:702, 2009)	First give **doxy** 200 mg/day x 6 wks and then **ivermectin:** Single dose 150 mcg/kg po; repeat every 3-6 months until asymptomatic.	DEC is contraindicated	Oncho can cause irreversible eye damage **NOTE: DEC can cause irreversible eye damage if concomitant onchocerciasis.** Goal is reducing burden of adult worms. (Albendazole 400 mg po + Ivermectin 200 µg/kg po) or DEC 6 mg/kg po suppresses microfilaria but no effect on adult worms
Mansonella perstans (dipetalonemiasis)	In randomized trial, doxy 200 mg po once daily x 6 weeks cleared microfilaria from blood in 67 of 69 patients (NEJM 361:1448, 2009).		Efficacy of doxy believed to be due to inhibition of endosymbiont wolbachia. Ivermectin has no activity. Ref: Trans R Soc Trop Med Hyg 100:458, 2006.
Mansonella streptocerca	**Ivermectin** 150 µg/kg x 1 dose.		Chronic pruritic, hypopigmented lesions that may be confused with leprosy. Can be asymptomatic.

[a] May need antihistamine or corticosteroid for allergic reaction from disintegrating organisms

* For source of drug, see Table 13D, page 155.

TABLE 13A (9)

INFECTING ORGANISM	SUGGESTED REGIMENS		COMMENTS
	PRIMARY	**ALTERNATIVE**	
NEMATODES—EXTRAINTESTINAL (Roundworms)/Filariasis (continued)			
Mansonella ozzardi	**Ivermectin** 200 µg/kg x 1 dose may be effective. Limited data but no other option.	Usually asymptomatic. Articular pain, pruritus, lymphadenopathy reported. May have allergic reaction from dying organisms.	
Dirofilariasis: **Heartworms**			
D. immitis, dog heartworm	No effective drugs; surgical removal only option		Can lodge in pulmonary artery → coin lesion. Eosinophilia rare.
D. tenuis (raccoon), D. ursi (bear), D. repens (dogs, cats)	No effective drugs		Worms migrate to conjunctivae, subcutaneous tissue, scrotum, breasts, extremities
Gnathostoma spinigerum			
Cutaneous larva migrans	**Albendazole** 400 mg po q24h or bid times 2 days.	**Ivermectin** 200 µg/kg/day po x 2 days.	Other etiology of larva migrans: Ancylostoma sp., (see page 148)
Eosinophilic meningitis	Supportive care, monitor for cerebral hemorrhage	Case reports of steroid use: both benefit and harm from Albendazole or ivermectin (EIN 17:1174, 2011).	Other causes of eosinophilic meningitis: **Angiostrongylus** (see page 148) & **Baylisascaris** (see page 148)
Toxocariasis (Ann Trop Med Parasit 103:3, 2010)	Rx directed at relief of symptoms as infection self-limited, e.g., **steroids & antihistamines; use of anthelmintics controversial.**		
Visceral larval migrans	**Albendazole** 400 mg po bid x 5 days ± **Prednisone** 60 mg/day	**Mebendazole** 100–200 mg bid times 5 days	Severe lung, heart or CNS disease may warrant steroids (Clin Micro Rev 16:265, 2003). Differential dx of larval migrans syndromes: Toxocara canis & catis, Ancylostoma spp., Gnathostoma spp., Spirometra spp.
Ocular larval migrans	First 4 wks of illness: (Oral **prednisone** 30–60 mg po q24h + subtenon **triamcinolone** 40 mg/wk) x 2 wks (Surgery is sometimes necessary)		No added benefit of anthelmintic drugs. Rx of little effect after 4 wks. Some use steroids (Clin Micro Rev 16:265, 2003).
Trichinella spiralis (**Trichinellosis**) —— muscle infection (Review: Clin Micro Rev 22:127, 2009).	**Albendazole** 400 mg po bid x 8–14 days	**Mebendazole** 200–400 mg po tid x 3 days, then 400–500 mg po tid x 10 days. Concomitant **prednisone** 40–60 mg po q24h	Use albendazole/mebendazole with caution during pregnancy. ↑ IgE, ↑ CPK, ESR 0, massive eosinophilia: >5000/µL
TREMATODES (Flukes) – Liver, Lung, Intestinal. All flukes have snail intermediate hosts; transmitted by injection of metacercariae on plants, fish or crustaceans.			
Clonorchis sinensis (liver fluke)	**Praziquantel** 25 mg/kg po tid x 2 days or **albendazole** 10 mg/kg po per day po x 7 days		Same dose in children
Dicrocoelium dendriticum	**Praziquantel** 25 mg/kg po x 1 day		Ingestion of raw or undercooked sheep liver
Fasciola buski (intestinal fluke)	**Praziquantel** 25 mg/kg po tid x 1 day		Same dose in children
Fasciola hepatica (sheep liver fluke) Fasciola gigantica	**Triclabendazole** once, may repeat after 12-24 hrs. 10 mg/kg po x 1 dose. Single 10 mg/kg po dose effective in controlling endemic disease (PLoS Negl Trop Dis 6(8):e1720).		Alternative: **Bithionol** Adults and children: 30-50 mg/kg (max. dose 2 gm/day) every other day times 10-15 doses. In CDC formulary, efficacy unclear
Heterophyes heterophyes (intestinal fluke) Metagonimus yokogawai (intestinal fluke) Metorchis conjunctis (No Amer liver fluke) Nanophyetus salmincola	**Praziquantel** 25 mg/kg po tid x 1 days		
Opisthorchis viverrini (liver fluke)	**Praziquantel** 25 mg/kg po tid x 2 days		
Paragonimus sp. (lung fluke)	**Praziquantel** 25 mg/kg po bid x 2 days or **Triclabendazole** 10 mg/kg po x 2 doses over 12-24 hrs.		Same dose in children

* For source of drug, see Table 13D, page 155.

TABLE 13A (10)

INFECTING ORGANISM	SUGGESTED REGIMENS		COMMENTS
	PRIMARY	ALTERNATIVE	
TREMATODES (Flukes) – Liver, Lung, Intestinal (continued)			
Schistosoma haematobium: GU bilharzi- asis. (NEJM 346:1212, 2002)	Praziquantel 40 mg/kg po on the same day (one dose of 40 mg/kg or two doses of 20 mg/kg)		Same dose in children.
Schistosoma intercalatum.	Praziquantel 20 mg/kg po on the same day in 1 or 2 doses		Same dose in children
Schistosoma japonicum; Oriental schisto. (NEJM 346:1212, 2002)	Praziquantel 60 mg/kg po on the same day (3 doses of 20 mg/kg)		Same dose in children. Cures 60–90% pts.
Schistosoma mansoni (intestinal bilhariziasis)	Praziquantel 40 mg/kg po on the same day (one dose of 40 mg/kg or two doses of 20 mg/kg)		Praziquantel: Same dose for children and adults. Cures 60–90% pts.
Possible praziquantel resistance (JID 176:304, 1997) (NEJM 346:1212, 2002)			Report of success treating myeloraciculopathy with single po dose of praziquantel, 50 mg/kg, + prednisone for 6 mos (CID 39:1618, 2004).
Schistosoma mekongi	Praziquantel 60 mg per kg po on the same day (3 doses of 20 mg/kg)		Same dose for children
Toxemic schisto; Katayama fever	Praziquantel 20 mg/kg po bid with short course of high dose prednisone. Repeat Praziquantel in 4-6 wks (Clin Micro Rev 16:225, 2010).		Reaction to onset of egg laying 4–6 wks after infection exposure in fresh water.
CESTODES (Tapeworms)			
Echinococcus granulosus (hydatid disease) (PLID 12:871, 2012; Int Dis Clin No Amer 26:421, 2012)	**Liver cysts:** Meta-analysis supports percutaneous aspiration-injection-reaspiration (**PAIR**) + albendazole for uncomplicated single liver cysts. Before & after drainage: **albendazole** ≥60 kg, 400 mg po bid or < 60 kg, 15 mg/kg per day div. bid. with meals. After 1-2 days puncture (P) & needle aspirate (P) cyst content. Instill (I) hypertonic saline (15–30%) or absolute alcohol, wait 20–30 min, then re-aspirate (R) with final irrigation. **Continue albendazole for at least 30 days.** Cure in 96% as comp. to 90% pts with surgical resection. Albendazole ref: Acta Tropica 114:1, 2010.		
Echinococcus multilocularis (alveolar cyst disease) (CCID 776:437, 2003)	**Albendazole** efficacy not clearly demonstrated, can try in dosages used for hydatid disease. Wide surgical resection only reliable rx: technique evolving. Post-surgical resection rx of inoperable. Albendazole for several years (Acta Tropic 1141, 2010).		
Intestinal tapeworms			
Diphyllobothrium latum (fish), Dipylidium caninum (dog), Taenia saginata (beef), & Taenia solium (pork)	Praziquantel 5–10 mg/kg po x 1 dose for children and adults.	Niclosamide [2] 2 gm po x 1 dose	Niclosamide from Expert Compounding Pharm, see Table 13D.
Hymenolepis diminuta (rats) and H. nana (humans)	Praziquantel 25 mg/kg po x 1 dose for children	Niclosamide [2] 2 gm po daily x 7 days	
	NOTE: Treat T. solium intestinal tapeworms, if present, with **praziquantel 5-10 mg/kg po x 1 dose for children & adults.**		
Neurocysticercosis (NCC); larval form of T. solium. Ref: AJTMH 72:3, 2005			
Parenchymal NCC			
"Viable" cysts by CT/MRI Meta-analysis: treatment assoc with cyst resolution, ↓ seizures, and ↓ seizure recurrence. Ref: AnIM 145:43, 2006.	[**Albendazole** ≥60 kg: 400 mg bid with meals or 60 kg: 15 mg/kg per day in 2 div. doses (max. 800 mg/day) + **Dexamethasone** 0.1 mg/kg per day + Anti-seizure medication] — all x 8-30 days. May need anti-seizure therapy for a year	(**Praziquantel** 100 mg/kg per day in 3 div. doses po x 1 day, then 50 mg/kg/d in 3 doses plus **Dexamethasone** 0.1 mg/kg per day ± Anti-seizure medication) — all x 29 days. See Comment	Albendazole assoc. with 46% ↓ in seizures (NEJM 350:249, 2004). Praziquantel less cysticidal activity. Steroids decrease serum levels of praziquantel. NIH reports metronidazole at ≤ 20 mg/kg allows a resolution (Antimicrob Ag Chemo 53:3464, 2009). **Treatment improves prognosis of associated seizures.**
"Degenerating" cysts	**Albendazole + dexamethasone as above**		
Dead calcified cysts	**No treatment indicated**		
Subarachnoid NCC	(**Albendazole + steroids** as above) + shunting for hydrocephalus prior to drug therapy. Ref: Expert Rev Anti Infect Ther 9:123, 2011.		
Intraventricular NCC	Neuroendoscopic removal is treatment of choice with or without obstruction. If surgery not possible, **albendazole + dexamethasone; observe closely for evidence of obstruction of flow of CSF.**		

* For source of drug, see Table 13D, page 155.

TABLE 13A (11)

INFECTING ORGANISM	SUGGESTED REGIMENS		COMMENTS
	PRIMARY	ALTERNATIVE	

CESTODES (Tapeworms)/Neurocysticercosis (NCC) (continued)

Sparganosis (Spirometra mansonoides) Ref.: CID 36:1355, 2003; Ln 363:889, 2004. **NOTE: Due to potential neurotoxicity and risk of aplastic anemia, lindane not recommended.**

Larval cysts; source—frogs/snakes | Surgical resection. No antiparasitic therapy. Can inject alcohol into subcutaneous masses.

ECTOPARASITES, Ref.: CID 36:1355, 2003; Ln 363:889, 2004. **NOTE: Due to potential neurotoxicity and risk of aplastic anemia, lindane not recommended.**

DISEASE	INFECTING ORGANISM			

INFECTING ORGANISM	PRIMARY	ALTERNATIVE	COMMENTS
Head lice Med Lett 51:57, 2009	Pediculus humanus, var. capitis	**Permethrin** 1% lotion: Apply to shampooed dried hair for 10 min.; repeat in 9-10 days. **OR** **Malathion** 0.5% lotion (Ovide): Apply to dry hair for 8-12 hrs, then shampoo. 2 doses 7-9 days apart. **OR** **Spinosad** 0.9% suspension: wash off after 10 min (85% effective). Repeat in 7 days, if needed.	**Ivermectin** 200-400 μg/kg po once, 3 doses at 7 day intervals effective in 95% (JID 193:474, 2006). Topical ivermectin 0.5% lotion, 75% effective. **Malathion:** Report that 1-2 20-min. applications 98% effective (Ped Derm 21:670, 2004). In alcohol—potentially flammable. **Benzyl alcohol:** 76% effective	**Permethrin:** success in 78%. Extra combing of no benefit. Resistance increasing. No advantage to 5% permethrin. **Spinosad** is effective, but expensive. Refs: NEJM 367:1687 & 1750, 2012; Pediatrics 126:392, 2010.
Pubic lice (crabs)	Phthirus pubis	**Pubic hair: Permethrin OR malathion** as for head lice	**Eyelids: Petroleum jelly** applied qid x 10 days **OR yellow oxide of mercury** 1% qid x 14 days	
Body lice	Pediculus humanus, var. corporis	No drugs for the patient. Organism lives in & deposits eggs in seams of clothing. Discard clothing, if not possible, treat clothing with 1% malathion powder or 0.5% permethrin powder. Success with ivermectin in homeless shelter: 12 mg po on days 0, 7, & 14 (JID 193:474, 2006)		
Scabies Refs: MMWR 59(RR-12):89, 2010; NEJM 362:717, 2010.	Sarcoptes scabiei			
Immunocompetent patients		**Permethrin** 5% cream (ELIMITE) under nails (finger and toe). Apply entire skin from chin down to and including under fingernails and toenails. Leave on 8-14 hrs. Repeat in 1-2 wks. Safe for children age >2 mos.	**Ivermectin** 250 μg/kg po x 1. As above, second dose if persistent symptoms **Less effective: Crotamiton** 10% cream, apply x 24 hr, rinse off, then reapply x 24 hr.	Trim fingernails. Reapply cream to hands after handwashing. Treat close contacts; wash and heat dry linens. Pruritus may persist times 2 wks after mites gone.
AIDS and HIV-infected patients (CD4 <150 per mm³), debilitated or developmentally disabled patients **(Norwegian scabies—**see Comments)		For Norwegian scabies: **Permethrin** 5% cream daily x 7 days, then twice weekly until cured. Add **Ivermectin** po (dose in Alternative)	**Ivermectin** 200 mcg/kg po on days 1, 2, 8, 9, 15 (and maybe 22, 29) + **Permethrin** cream.	Norwegian scabies in AIDS pts: Extensive, crusted. Can mimic psoriasis. Not pruritic. Highly contagious—Isolate!
Myiasis	Due to larvae of flies	Usually cutaneous/subcutaneous nodule with central punctum. Treatment: Occlude punctum to prevent gas exchange with petrolatum, fingernail polish, makeup cream or bacon. When larva migrates, manually remove.		

* For source of drug, see Table 13D, page 155.

TABLE 13B - DOSAGE AND SELECTED ADVERSE EFFECTS OF ANTIPARASITIC DRUGS

Doses vary with indication. For convenience, drugs divided by type of parasite; some drugs used for multiple types of parasites, e.g., albendazole.

CLASS, AGENT, GENERIC NAME (TRADE NAME)	USUAL ADULT DOSAGE	ADVERSE REACTIONS/COMMENTS
Antiprotozoan Drugs		
Intestinal Parasites		
Diloxanide furoate[NUS] (Furamide)	500 mg tid x 10 days.	Source: See Table 13D, page 155. Flatulence, N/V, diarrhea. Rarely causes nausea, abdominal cramps, rash, acne.
Iodoquinol (Yodoxin)	Adults: 650 mg po tid (or 30-40 mg/kg/day div. tid); children: 40 mg/kg per day div. tid.	Contraindicated if iodine intolerance (contains 64% bound iodine). Can cause iododerma (papular or pustular rash) and/or thyroid enlargement.
Metronidazole	Side-effects similar for all. See metronidazole in Table 10B, Table 10A, page 102.	
Nitazoxanide (Alinia)	Adults: 500 mg po q12h. Children 4-11: 200 mg susp. po q12h. Take with food. Expensive.	Abdominal pain 7.8%, diarrhea 2.1%. Rev.: CID 40:1173, 2005; Expert Opin Pharmacother 7:953, 2006.
Paromomycin (Humatin), po Aminosidine in U.K.	Up to 750 mg tid (250 mg tabs). Source: See Table 13D.	Headaches, nausea, yellow sclera (resolves after treatment). Aminoglycoside similar to neomycin; if absorbed due to concomitant inflammatory bowel disease can result in oto/nephrotoxicity. Doses >3 g daily are associated with nausea, abdominal cramps, diarrhea.
Quinacrine[xls] (Atabrine, Mepacrine)	100 mg po tid x 5 days. No longer available in U.S.: 2 pharmacies will prepare as a service. (1) Connecticut (+1) 203-785-9818, (2) Californa 800-247-9767	Contraindicated for pts with history of psychosis or psoriasis. Yellow staining of skin. Dizziness, headache, vomiting, toxic psychosis (1.5%), hemolytic anemia, leukopenia, thrombocytopenia, mild disulfiram-like reactions.
Tinidazole (Tindamax)	250-800 mg tabs, with food. Regimen varies with indication.	Chemical structure similar to metronidazole but better tolerated. Seizures/peripheral neuropathy reported. **Adverse effects:** Metallic taste 4-6%, nausea 3-5%, anorexia 2-3%.
Antiprotozoan Drugs: Non-Intestinal Protozoa		
Extraintestinal Parasites[NUS]		
Antimony Compounds[NUS]		
Stibogluconate sodium (Pentostam) from CDC or Meglumine antimoniate (Glucantime—French trade names	For IV use: vials with 100 mg antimony/mL. Dilute selected dose in 50 mL of D5W shortly before use. Infuse over at least 10 minutes.	**AEs in 1st 10 days:** headache, fatigue, elevated lipase/amylase, clinical pancreatitis. After 10 days: elevated AST/ALT/ALK/PHOS. **NOTE: Reversible T wave changes in 30-60%. Risk of QTc prolongation. Renal excretion; modify dose if renal insufficiency. Metabolized in liver; lower dose if hepatic insufficiency.**
Artemether-Lumefantrine, po (Coartem, FDA-approved)	Tablets contain 20 mg Artemether and 120 mg Lumefantrine. Can be crushed and mixed with a few teaspoons of water	Can prolong QTc; avoid in patients with congenital long QTc, family history of sudden death or long QTc, or need for drugs known to prolong QTc (see list under fluoroquinolones, Table 10A, page 102). Artemether induces CYP3A4 and both Artemether & Lumefantrine are metabolized by CYP3A4 (see drug-drug interactions, Table 22A, page 217). Adverse effects experienced by >30% of adults: headache, anorexia, dizziness, arthralgia and myalgia.
Artesunate IV Ref. NEJM 358:1829, 2008	Available from CDC Malaria Branch. 2.4 mg/kg IV at 0, 12, 24, & 48 hrs.	More effective than quinine & safer than quinidine. Contact CDC at 770-488-7758 or 770-488-7100 after hours. No dosage adjustment for hepatic or renal insufficiency. No known drug interactions.
Atovaquone (Mepron) Ref. AAC 46:1163, 2002	Suspension: 1 tsp (750 mg) po bid 750 mg/5 mL	No. pts stopping rx due to side-effects was 9%: rash 22%, GI 20%, headache 16%, insomnia 10%, fever 14%
Atovaquone and proguanil (Malarone) For prophylaxis of P. falciparum; little data on P. vivax. Generic available in US.	**Prophylaxis:** 1 tab po (250 mg + 100 mg) q24h with food **Treatment:** 4 tabs po (1000 mg + 400 mg) once daily with food x 3 days. Adult tab: 250/100 mg; Peds tab 62.5/25 mg. Can be taken with milk or other liquid nutrients. Peds dosage, prophylaxis footnote 1 page 143; treatment see comment, page 144.	Adverse effects in rx trials: Adults—abd. pain 17%, N/V 12%, headache 10%, dizziness 5%. Rx stopped in 1%. Asymptomatic mild ↑ in ALT/AST. Children—cough, headache, anorexia, vomiting, abd. pain. See drug interactions, Table 22, page 217. G6PD-deficient pts. Renal insufficiency contraindicated if CrCl <30 mL per min.

NOTE: Drugs available from CDC Drug Service indicated by "CDC." Call (+1) (404) 639-3670 (or -2888 (Fax). **See Table 13D, page 155 for sources and contact information for hard-to-find antiparasitic drugs.**

TABLE 13B (2)

CLASS, AGENT, GENERIC NAME (TRADE NAME)	USUAL ADULT DOSAGE	ADVERSE REACTIONS/COMMENTS
Antiprotozoan Drugs: Non-Intestinal Protozoa/Extraintestinal Parasites *(continued)*		
Benznidazole (CDC Drug Service)	7.5 mg/kg per day po. 100 mg tabs	Photosensitivity in 50% of pts. GI: abdominal pain, nausea/vomiting/anorexia. CNS: disorientation, insomnia, twitching/seizures, paresthesias, polyneuritis. **Contraindicated in pregnancy**
Chloroquine phosphate (Aralen)	Dose varies—see *Malaria Prophylaxis and rx, pages 143-144.*	Minor: anorexia/vomiting, headache, dizziness, blurred vision, pruritus in dark-skinned pts. Major: protracted rx in rheumatoid arthritis can lead to retinopathy. Can exacerbate psoriasis. Can block response to rabies vaccine. Contraindicated in pts with epilepsy.
Dapsone See Comment re methemoglobinemia	100 mg po q24h	Usually tolerated by pts with rash after TMP-SMX. Dapsone is common etiology of acquired methemoglobinemia (*NEJM 364:957, 2011*). Metabolite of dapsone converts heme iron to +3 charge (no O2 transport) from normal +2. Normal blood level <2. Cyanosis at 10%; headache & fatigue tachycardia, dizziness at 30-40%; acidosis & coma at 60%, death at 70-80%. Low G6PD is a risk factor. Treatment: methylene blue 1-2 mg/kg IV over 5 min x 1 dose.
Eflornithine (Ornidyl) (WHO or CDC drug combine)	200 mg/kg IV (slowly) q12h x 7 days for African trypanosomiasis	Diarrhea in ½ pts, vomiting, abdominal pain, anemia/leukopenia in ½ pts, seizures, alopecia, jaundice, ↓ hearing. Contraindicated in pregnancy
Fumagillin	Eyedrops + po. 20 mg tid. Leiter's: 800-292-6773.	Adverse events: Neutropenia & thrombocytopenia
Mefloquine	One 250 mg tab/wk for malaria prophylaxis; for rx, 1250 mg x 1 or 750 mg & then 500 mg in 6-8 hrs. In U.S., 250 mg tab = 228 mg base, outside U.S., 275 mg tab = 250 mg base	Side-effects in roughly 3%. Minor: headache, irritability, insomnia, weakness, diarrhea. Toxic psychosis, seizures can occur. Do not use with quinine, quinidine, or halofantrine. Rare: Prolonged QT interval and toxic epidermal necrolysis (*Ln 349:101, 1997*). Not used for self-rx due to neuropsychiatric side-effects.
Melarsoprol (Mel B, Arsobal) (CDC)	See Trypanosomiasis for adult dose. Peds: Dose: 0.36 mg/kg IV, then gradual ↑ to 3.6 mg/kg q1-5 days for total of 9-10 doses.	Post-rx encephalopathy (2-10%) with 50% mortality overall, risk of death? 2° to 8-14%. **Pregnancy—No;** teratogenic. Side-effects vary: kala-azar pts, vomiting in up to 40%, diarrhea in 17%; "motion sickness". Other: Heart damage, albuminuria, abdominal pain, vomiting, peripheral neuropathy, Herxheimer-like reaction, pruritus.
Miltefosine (Impavido) (Expert Rev Anti Infect Ther 4:177, 2006)	100-150 mg (approx. 2.25 mg/kg per day) po divided tid x 28 days Cutaneous leishmaniasis 2.25 mg/kg po q24h x 6 wks	Source: See Table 13D, page 155. **Pregnancy—No;** teratogenic. Side-effects: CNS: polyneuritis (1/3), disorientation, insomnia, twitching, seizures. Skin rash. Hemolysis with G6PD deficiency. Daily dose >150 mg can cause severe GI side effects (*Ln 352:1821, 1998*).
Nifurtimox (Lampit) (CDC) (Manufactured in Germany by Bayer)	8-10 mg/kg per day po div. 4 x per day for 90-120 days	Side-effects in 40-70% of pts. GI: abdominal pain, nausea/vomiting. CNS: polyneuritis (1/3), disorientation, insomnia, twitching, seizures. Skin rash. Hemolysis with G6PD deficiency.
Pentamidine (NebuPent)	300 mg via aerosol q month. Also used IM.	Hypotension, hypocalcemia, hypoglycemia followed by hyperglycemia, pancreatitis. Neutropenia (15%), thrombocytopenia. Nephrotoxicity. Others: nausea/vomiting, ↑ liver tests, rash.
Primaquine phosphate	26.3 mg (= 15mg base). Adult dose is 30 mg of base po daily.	In G6PD def. pts, can cause hemolytic anemia with hemoglobinuria, ↓ WBC, ↓ platelets. Can give 5 mg folinic acid per day to ↓ bone marrow depression and not interfere with antitoxoplasmosis effect. Methemoglobinemia. Nausea/abdominal pain if pt. fasting (*CID 39:1336, 2004*). **Pregnancy: No.**
Pyrimethamine (Daraprim, Malocide) Also combined with sulfadoxine as Fansidar (25-500 mg)	100 mg/day, then 25 mg/day. Cost of folinic acid (leucovorin)	Major problem is hematologic: megaloblastic anemia, ↓ WBC, ↓ platelets. Can give 5 mg folinic acid per day to ↓ bone marrow depression and not interfere with antitoxoplasmosis effect. If high-dose pyrimethamine, ↑ folinic acid to 10-50 mg/day. Pyrimethamine + sulfadiazine can cause mental changes due to carnitine deficiency (*AJM 95:112, 1993*). Other: Rash, vomiting, diarrhea, xerostomia.
Quinidine gluconate Cardiotoxicity ref LnID 7:549, 2007	Loading dose of 10 mg (equiv to 6.2 mg of quinidine base) / kg IV over 1-2 hr, then a constant infusion of 0.02 mg of quinidine gluconate / kg per minute. May be available for compassionate use from Lilly.	Adverse reactions of quinidine/quinine similar: (1) IV bolus injection can cause fatal hypotension, (2) hyperinsulinemic hypoglycemia, esp. in pregnancy, (3) ↓ rate of infusion of IV quinidine if QT ↑ 25% of baseline, (4) reduce dose 30-50% after day 3 due to ↓ renal clearance and ↓ vol. of distribution.

NOTE: Drugs available from CDC Drug Service indicated by "CDC." Call (+1) (404) 639-3670 (or -2888 (Fax)). **See Table 13D, page 155 for sources and contact information for hard-to-find antiparasitic drugs.**

TABLE 13B (3)

CLASS, AGENT, GENERIC NAME (TRADE NAME)	USUAL ADULT DOSAGE	ADVERSE REACTIONS/COMMENTS
Antiprotozoan Drugs: Non-Intestinal Protozoa/Extraintestinal Parasites *(continued)*		
Quinine sulfate (Qualaquin) (300 mg salt = 250 mg base).	324 mg tabs. No IV prep. in US. Oral rx of chloroquine-resistant falciparum malaria: 624 mg po tid x 3 days, then (tetracycline 250 mg po qid or doxy 100 mg bid) x 7 days	Cinchonism: tinnitus, headache, nausea, abdominal pain, blurred vision. Rarely: blood dyscrasias, drug fever, asthma, hypoglycemia. Transient blindness in < 1% of 500 pts (*AJM 136:339, 2002*). **Contraindicated if prolonged QTc, myasthenia gravis, optic neuritis or G6PD deficiency.**
Spiramycin (Rovamycin)	1 gm po q8h (see Comment)	GI and allergic reactions have occurred. Available at no cost after consultation with Palo Alto Medical Foundation Toxoplasma Serology Lab: 650-853-4828 or from U.S. FDA 301-796-1600.
Sulfadiazine	1–1.5 gm po q6h.	See Table 10C, page 102, for sulfonamide side-effects.
Sulfadoxine & pyrimethamine combination (Fansidar)	Contains 500 mg sulfadoxine & 25 mg pyrimethamine	Long half-life of both drugs: Sulfadoxine 169 hrs, pyrimethamine 111 hrs allows weekly dosage. In combination, used empirically in pregnancy for intermittent preventative treatment (ITPp) against malaria: dosing at 3 set times during pregnancy. Reduces material and fetal mortality in HIV+. *See Expert Rev Anti Infect Ther 8:589, 2010.* Fatalities reported due to Stevens-Johnson syndrome and toxic epidermal necrolysis. Renal excretion—Caution if renal impairment.
DRUGS USED TO TREAT NEMATODES, TREMATODES, AND CESTODES		
Albendazole (Albenza)	Doses vary with indication. Take with food; fatty meal increases absorption.	**Pregnancy Cat. C**; give after negative pregnancy test. Abdominal pain, nausea/vomiting, alopecia, ↑ serum transaminase. Rare leukopenia.
Bithionol (CDC)	Adults & children: 30–40 mg/kg (to max. of 2 gm/day) po every other day x 10–15 doses	Photosensitivity, skin reactions, urticaria, GI upset.
Diethylcarbamazine (CDC)	Used to treat filariasis.	Headache, dizziness, nausea, fever. Host may experience inflammatory reaction to death of adult worms: fever, urticaria, asthma, GI upset (Mazzotti reaction). **Pregnancy—No.**
Ivermectin (Stromectol, Mectizan) (3 mg tab & topical 0.5% lotion for head lice)	Strongyloidiasis dose: 200 µg/kg/day po x 2 days Onchocerciasis: 150 µg/kg x 1 po Scabies: 200 µg/kg po x 1; if AIDS, wait 14 days & repeat	Mild side-effects: fever, pruritus, rash. In rx of onchocerciasis, can see tender lymphadenopathy, headache, bone/joint pain. Host may experience inflammatory reaction to death of adult worms: fever, urticaria, asthma, GI upset (Mazzotti reaction).
Mebendazole (Vermox)	Doses vary with indication.	Rarely causes abdominal pain, nausea, diarrhea. Contraindicated in pregnancy & children <2 yrs old.
Praziquantel (Biltricide)	Doses vary with parasite; see Table 13A.	Mild: dizziness/drowsiness, N/V, rash, fever. Only contraindication is ocular cysticercosis. Potential exacerbation of neurocysticercosis. Metab-induced by anticonvulsants and steroids; can negate effect with cimetidine 400 mg po tid. Reduce dose if advanced liver disease.
Pyrantel pamoate (over-the-counter)	Oral suspension. Dose for all ages: 11 mg/kg (to max. of 1 gm) x 1 dose	Rare GI upset, headache, dizziness, rash
Suramin (Germanin) (CDC)	Drug powder mixed to 10% solution with 5 mL water and used within 30 min. First give test dose of 0.1 gm IV. Try to avoid during pregnancy.	Does not cross blood-brain barrier; no effect on CNS infection. Side-effects: vomiting, pruritus, urticaria, fever, paresthesias, albuminuria (discontinue drug if casts present). Do not use if renal/liver disease present. Deaths from vascular collapse reported.
Triclabendazole (Egaten) (CDC)	Used for fasciola hepatica liver fluke infection: 10 mg/kg po x 1 dose. May repeat in 12-24 hrs. 250 mg tabs	AEs ≥10%: sweating and abdominal pain. AEs 1-10%: weakness, chest pain, fever, anorexia, nausea, vomiting. Note: use with caution if G6PD def. or impaired liver function.

NOTE: Drugs available from CDC Drug Service indicated by "CDC." Call (+1) (404) 639-3670 (or -2888 (Fax)). **See Table 13D, page 155 for sources and contact information for hard-to-find antiparasitic drugs.**

TABLE 13C – PARASITES THAT CAUSE EOSINOPHILIA (EOSINOPHILIA IN TRAVELERS)

Frequent and Intense (> 5000 eos/mcL)	Moderate to Marked Early Infections	During Larval Migration; Absent or Mild During Chronic Infections	Other
Strongyloides (absent in compromised hosts); Lymphatic Filariasis; Toxocaria (cutaneous larva migrans)	Ascaris; Hookworm; Clonorchis; Paragonimis	Opisthorchis	Schistosomiasis; Cysticercosis; Trichuris; Angiostrongylus; Non-lymphatic filariasis; Gnathostoma; Capillaria; Trichostrongylus

TABLE 13D – SOURCES FOR HARD-TO-FIND ANTIPARASITIC DRUGS

Source	Drugs Available	Contact Information
CDC Drug Service	Artesunate, Benznidazole, Diethylcarbamazine (DEC), Eflornithine, Melarsoprol, Nifurtimox, Sodium stibogluconate, Suramin, Triclabendazole	www.cdc.gov/laboratory/drugservice/index.html (+1) 404-639-3670
WHO	Drugs for treatment of African trypanosomiasis	simarrop@who.int; (+41) 794-682-726; (+41) 227-911-345 francoj@who.int; (+41) 796-198-535; (+41) 227-913-313
Compounding Pharmacies, Specialty Labs, Others		
Expert Compounding Pharmacy	Quinacrine, Iodoquinol, niclosamide	www.expertpharmacy.org 1-800-247-9767; (+1) 818-988-7979
Fagron Compounding Pharmacy (formerly Gallipot)	Quinacrine, Iodoquinol, Paromomycin, Diloxanide	www.fagron.com 1-800-423-6967; (+1) 651-9517
Leiter's Pharmacy	Fumagillin	www.leiterrx.com 1-800-292-0773
Paladin Labs	Miltefosine	www.paladin-labs.com
Victoria Apotheke Zurich	Paromomycin (oral and topical), Triclabendazole	www.pharmaworld.com (+41) 43-344-6060
Fast Track Research	Miltefosine (may be free under treatment IND for cutaneous, mucocutaneous leishmaniasis)	jberman@fasttrackresearch.com
Palo Alto Medical Foundation, Toxoplasma Serology Lab	Spiramycin	(+1) 650-853-4828

TABLE 14A – ANTIVIRAL THERAPY*

For HIV, see Table 14D; for Hepatitis, see Table 14F and Table 14G

VIRUS/DISEASE	DRUG/DOSAGE	SIDE EFFECTS/COMMENTS
Adenovirus: Cause of RTIs including fatal pneumonia in children & young adults and 60% mortality in transplant pts (CID 43:331, 2006). Frequent cause of cystitis in transplant patients. Adenovirus 14 associated with severe pneumonia in otherwise healthy young adults (MMWR 56(45):1181, 2007). **Findings include:** fever, liver enzymes, leukopenia, thrombocytopenia, diarrhea, pneumonia, or hemorrhagic cystitis.	In severe cases of pneumonia or post HSCT: **Cidofovir** • 5 mg/kg IV x 2 wks, then q 2 wks + **probenecid** 1.25 gm/M² given 3 hrs before cidofovir and 3 & 9 hrs after each infusion. • Or 1 mg/kg IV 3x/wk. For hemorrhagic cystitis (CID 40:199, 2005; Transplantation, 2006; 81:1398). Intravesical **cidofovir** (5 mg/kg in 100 mL saline instilled into bladder)	Successful in 3/8 immunosuppressed children (CID 38:45, 2004 & 8 of 10 children with HSCT (CID 41; 1812, 2005). ↓ in virus load predicted response to cidofovir. Ribavirin has mixed activity, appears restricted to group C serotypes. Vidarabine and Gancoiclovir have in vitro activity against adenovirus, but no clinical data. New adenovirus serotype 14 that has more virulence (14a) transmitted from a monkey to researcher and subsequently to members of his family. PLoS Pathog 2011 Jul 14; 7:e1002155.
Coronavirus—SARS-CoV (Severe Acute Respiratory Distress Syn.) A new coronavirus, isolated Spring 2003 (NEJM 348:1953 & 1967, 2003) emerged from southern China & spread to Hong Kong and 32 countries. Bats appear to be a primary reservoir for SARS virus (PNAS 102: 14040, 2005).	Therapy remains predominantly supportive care. Therapy tried or under evaluation (see Comments): • Ribavirin—ineffective • Interferon alfa ± steroids—small case series. • Pegylated IFN-α effective in monkeys. • Low dose steroids alone successful in one Beijing hospital. High dose steroids ↑ serious fungal infections. • Inhaled nitric oxide improved oxygenation & improved chest x-ray (CID 39:1531, 2004).	**Transmission by close contact:** effective infection control practices (**mask [changed frequently]**, eye protection, gown, gloves) key to stopping transmission. Other coronaviruses (HCoV-229E, OC43, NL63, etc.) implicated as cause of croup, asthma exacerbations, & other RTIs in children (CID 40:1721, 2005; JID 191:492, 2005). May be associated with Kawasaki disease (JID 191:499, 2005).
Enterovirus—Meningitis: most common cause of aseptic meningitis	No rx recommended; however, **pleconaril** still under investigation.	No clinical benefit demonstrated in double-blind placebo-controlled study in 21 infants with enteroviral aseptic meningitis (PIDJ 22:335, 2003). Failed to ameliorate symptoms but did have some improvement among those with severe headache (AAC 2006 50:2409-14).
Hemorrhagic Fever Virus Infections: For excellent reviews, see Med Lab Observer, May 2005, p. 16, Lancet Infectious Disease Vol. 6 No 4. **Congo-Crimean Hemorrhagic Fever (HF)** (CID 39:284, 2004) Non-severe, symptoms include N/V, fever, headache, myalgias, & stupor (1/3). Signs: conjunctival injection, hepatomegaly, petechiae (1/3). Lab: ↓ platelets, ↓ WBC, ↑ ALT, AST, LDH & CPK (100%).	Oral **ribavirin, 30 mg/kg** as initial loading dose & 15 mg/kg q6h x 4 days & then 7.5 mg/kg/day x 6 days (WHO recommendation) (see Comment) Antiviral Res 78:125, 2008	3/3 researchers in Pakistan had complete recovery (LnI 346:472, 1995) & 61/69 (88%) with confirmed CCHF in Iran treated pts (7.7 vs. 10.3 days). Shorter time of hospitalization among ribavirin treated pts but no difference in mortality or transfusion needs in study done in Turkey (J Infection 52: 207-215, 2006).
Ebola/Marburg HF (Central Africa) Severe outbreak of Ebola in Angola 308 cases with 277 deaths by 5/3/05 (NEJM 352:2155, 2005; LnID 5:331, 2005). Major epidemic of Marburg virus 2004-2005 in Congo 2004-5 in Angola (NEJM 355:866, 2006)	No effective antiviral rx (J Virol 77: 9733, 2003).	Can infect gorillas & chimps that come in contact with other dead animal carcasses (Science 303:387, 2004). Marburg reported in African Fruit Bat, Rousettus aegyptiacus (PLoS ONE 2: e764, 2007). Marburg virus outbreak revealed 15% seroprevalence among 4549 with confirmed CCHF in Iran (22/33 only selected villages). None recalled any illness similar to Ebola. Seroprevalence among children rises until age 15, then plateaus. Seropositive status correlates to location of fruit bats. PLoS ONE (Feb 9); 5:e9126, 2010
With pulmonary syndrome: Hantavirus pulmonary syndrome, "sin nombre virus"	No benefit from ribavirin has been demonstrated. Early recognition of disease and supportive (usually ICU) care is key to successful outcome.	Acute onset of fever, headache, myalgias, non-productive cough, thrombocytopenia and non-cardiogenic pulmonary edema with respiratory insufficiency following exposure to rodents.
With renal syndrome: Lassa, Venezuelan, Korean, HF, Sabia, Argentinian HF, Bolivian HF, Junin, Machupo	Oral **ribavirin, 30 mg/kg** as initial loading dose & 15 mg/kg q6h x 4 days & then 7.5 mg/kg x 6 days (WHO recommendation) (see Comment)	Toxicity low, hemolysis reported with recovery when treatment stopped. No significant changes in WBC, platelets, hepatic or renal function. See CID 36:1254, 2003.

---

¹ HSCT = Hematopoietic stem cell transplant
* See page 2 for abbreviations.

Dosage recommendations are for adults (unless otherwise indicated) and assume normal renal function.

TABLE 14A (2)

VIRUS/DISEASE	DRUG/DOSAGE	SIDE EFFECTS/COMMENTS
Hemorrhagic Fever Virus Infections *(continued)*		
Dengue and dengue hemorrhagic fever (DHF) www.cdc.gov/ncidod/dvbid/dengue/dengue-hcp.htm Think dengue in traveler to tropics or subtropics (incubation period usually 4-7 days) with fever, bleeding, thrombocytopenia, or hemoconcentration with shock. Dx by viral isolation or serology; serum to CDC (telephone 787-706-2399).	**No data on antiviral rx.** Fluid replacement with careful hemodynamic monitoring critical. Rx of **DHF** with colloids effective: 6% hydroxyethyl starch preferred in 1 study *(NEJM 353:9, 2005)*. Review in *Semin Ped Infect Dis 16: 60-65, 2005.*	Of 77 cases dx at CDC (2001–2004), recent (2-wks) travel to Caribbean island 30%, Asia 17%, Central America 15% *(MMWR 54:556, June 10, 2005)*. 5 pts with severe **DHF** rx with dengue antibody-neg, gamma globulin 500 mg per kg q24h IV for 3-5 days; rapid ↑ in platelet counts *(CID 36:1623, 2003)*. New test approved by FDA in 2011: DENV Detect IgM Capture ELISA test. Has some cross-reactivity with West Nile Virus infection. Should only be used in pts with symptoms c/w Dengue Fever.
West Nile virus (see *AnIM 104:545, 2004*) A flavivirus transmitted by mosquitoes, blood transfusions, transplanted organs *(NEJM 348: 2196, 2003; CID 38:1257, 2004)*, & breast-feeding *(MMWR 51:877, 2002)*. Birds (>200 species) are main host with humans & horses incidental hosts. The US epidemic continues.	**No proven rx to date.** 2 clinical trials in progress: (1) Interferon alfa-N3 *(CID 40:764, 2005)* (this option failing out of favor). (2) IVIG from Israel with high titer antibody West Nile *(JID 188:5, 2003; Transpl Inf Dis 4:160, 2003)*. Contact NIH 301-496-7453, see www.clinicaltrials.gov/show/NCT00068055. Reviewed in *Lancet Neurology 6: 171-181, 2007.*	Usually nonspecific febrile disease but 1/150 cases develop meningoencephalitis, aseptic meningitis or polio-like paralysis *(AnIM 104:545, 2004; JCI 113: 1102, 2004)*. Long-term sequelae (neuromuscular weakness & psychiatric) common *(CID 43:723, 2006)*. Dx by ↑ IgM in serum & CSF or CSF PCR (contact State Health Dept./CDC). Blood supply now tested in U.S. ↑ serum lipase in 11/17 cases *(NEJM 352:420, 2005)*.
Yellow fever	**No data on antiviral rx. Guidelines for use of preventative vaccine:** *(MMWR 51: RR17, 2002)*	Reemergence in Africa & S. Amer. due to urbanization of susceptible population *(Lancet Inf 5:604, 2005)*. Vaccination effective. *(JAMA 276:1157, 1996)*. Vaccine safe and effective in HIV patients, especially in those with suppressed VL, and higher CD4 counts *(CID 48:659, 2009)*. A purified whole-virus, inactivated, cell-culture-derived vaccine (XRX-001) produced using the 17D strain has proven safe and resulted in neutralizing antibodies after 2 doses in a de-escalation, phase I study. *(N Engl J Med 2011 Apr 7; 364:1326)*
Chikungunya fever A self-limited arbovirus illness spread by Aedes mosquito. High epidemic potential.	**No antiviral therapy.** Mice given purified human polyvalent CHIKV immunoglobulins were therapeutic. *(JID 200: 516, 2009)*.	Clinical presentation: high fever, severe myalgias & headache, macular papular rash with occ. thrombocytopenia. Rarely hemorrhagic complications. Dx by increase in IgM antibody.
SFTSV (Severe fever with thrombocytopenia syndrome virus)	**No known therapy.**	New virus in the Bunyaviridae family described in China. Initially thought to be anaplasma infection; serology showed new virus. Possibly transmitted by *Haemaphysalis longicornis* ticks. *(N Engl J Med 2011; 364:1523-32)*
Hepatitis Viral Infections	*See Tables Table 14F (Hepatitis A & B), Table 14G (Hepatitis C)*	

---

* See page 2 for abbreviations. NOTE: All dosage recommendations are for adults (unless otherwise indicated) and assume normal renal function.

TABLE 14A (3)

VIRUS/DISEASE	DRUG/DOSAGE	SIDE EFFECTS/COMMENTS
Herpesvirus infections **Cytomegalovirus (CMV)** Marked ↓ in HIV associated CMV infections & death with Highly Active Antiretroviral Therapy. Initial treatment should optimize ART.	Primary prophylaxis not generally recommended except in certain transplant populations (see below). Preemptive therapy in pts with ↑ CMV DNA titers in plasma & CD4 <100/mm³. Recommended by some: **valganciclovir** 900 mg po q24h (CID 32: 783, 2001). Authors rec: primary prophylaxis be dc if response to ART with ↑ CD4 >100 for 6 mos. (MMWR 53:98, 2004).	Risk for developing CMV disease correlates with quantity of CMV DNA in plasma: each log₁₀ ↑ associated with 3.1-fold ↑ in disease (JCI 101:497, 1998; CID 28:758, 1999). Resistance demonstrated in 5% of transplant recipients receiving primary prophylaxis (J Antimicrob Chemother 65:2628, 2010).
Colitis, Esophagitis, Gastritis Dx by biopsy of ulcer base/edge (Clin Gastro Hepatol 2:564, 2004) with demonstration of CMV inclusions & other pathogen(s).	**Ganciclovir** as with retinitis except induction period extended for 3–6 wks. Responses less predictable than for retinitis. **Valganciclovir also likely effective.** Switch to oral valganciclovir when po tolerated & when symptoms not severe enough to interfere with absorption. Antiretroviral therapy is essential in long term suppression. Alternative: **Cidofovir** 5 mg/kg IV, qwk x 2 wks, followed by administration q2 wks, MUST be administered with **probenecid** 2 gm po 3 hrs before each dose and further 1 gm doses 2 hrs and 8 hrs after completion of the cidofovir infusion. IV saline hydration is essential.	No agreement on use of maintenance; may not be necessary except after relapse.
Encephalitis, Ventriculitis: Treatment not defined, but should be considered the same as retinitis. Disease may develop while taking ganciclovir as suppressive therapy. See Herpes 11(Suppl 12):95A, 2004. "Lumbosacral polyradiculopathy," diagnosis by CMV DNA in CSF	**Ganciclovir**, as with retinitis. **Foscarnet** 40 mg/kg IV q12h another option. Switch to **valganciclovir** when possible. Suppression continued until CD4 remains >100/mm³ for 6 mos. **Alternative: Cidofovir** 5 mg/kg IV, qwk x 2 wks followed by administration q2 wks. MUST be administered with probenecid 2 gm po 3 hrs before each dose and further 1 gm doses 2 hrs and 8 hrs after completion of the cidofovir infusion. IV saline hydration is essential.	About 50% will respond; survival ↑ (5.4 wks to 14.6 wks) (CID 27:345, 1998). Resistance can be demonstrated genotypically.
Mononeuritis multiplex	Not defined	Due to vasculitis & may not be responsive to antiviral therapy
Pneumonia— Seen predominantly in transplants (esp. bone marrow), **rare in HIV.** Treat only when histological evidence present in AIDS & other pathogens not identified. High rate of CMV reactivation in immunocompetent ICU patients; prolonged hospitalizations and increased mortality (JAMA 300:413, 2008).	**Ganciclovir/valganciclovir**, as with retinitis. In bone marrow transplant pts, combination therapy with CMV immune globulin.	In bone marrow transplant pts, serial measure of pp65 antigen was useful in establishing early diagnosis of CMV interstitial pneumonia with good results if ganciclovir was initiated within 6 days of antigen positivity (Bone Marrow Transplant 26:413, 2000). For preventive therapy, see Table 15E.

TABLE 14A (4)

VIRUS/DISEASE	DRUG/DOSAGE		SIDE EFFECTS/COMMENTS

Herpesvirus Infections (continued)

CMV Retinitis
Most common cause of blindness in AIDS patients with <50/mm3 CD4 counts.
19/30 pts (63%) with inactive CMV retinitis who responded to HAART (↑ of ≥60 CD4 cells/mL) developed immune recovery vitreitis (vision ↓ & floaters with posterior segment inflammation —vitreitis, papillitis, & macular changes) an average of 43 wks after rx started (JID 179: 697, 1999).
Corticosteroid rx ↓ inflammatory reaction of immune recovery vitreitis without reactivation of CMV retinitis, either periocular corticosteroids or short course of systemic steroid.

For immediate sight-threatening lesions: Ganciclovir intraocular implant & valganciclovir 900 mg po q24h.
For peripheral lesions: Valganciclovir 900 mg po q12h x14-21d, then 900 mg po q24h for maintenance therapy

Ganciclovir 5 mg/kg IV q12h x 14-21d, then **valganciclovir** 900 mg po q24h
OR
Foscarnet 60 mg/kg IV q8h or 90 mg/kg IV q12h x 14-21d, then 90-120 mg/kg IV q24h
OR
Cidofovir 5 mg/kg IV q wk x 2 wks, then 5 mg/kg every other wk; each dose should be administered with IV saline hydration & oral probenecid
OR
Repeated intravitreal injections with **fomivirsen** (for relapses only, not as initial therapy)

Differential diagnosis: HIV retinopathy, herpes simplex retinitis, varicella-zoster retinitis (NEJM 346:1119, 2002).
Valganciclovir po equal to GCV IV in induction of remission; (NEJM 346:1119, 2002).
Valganciclovir po equal to GCV IV in induction of remission.
Cannot use ganciclovir ocular implant alone as approx. 50% risk of CMV retiniti other eye at 6 mos, & 31% risk visceral disease. Risk ↓ with systemic rx but when contralateral retinitis does occur, ganciclovir-resistant mutation often present (JID 189:611, 2004).
Concurrent systemic rx recommended.
Because of unique mode of action, **fomivirsen** may have a role in pts resistant to other therapies.
Retinal detachments 50-60% within 1 yr of dx of retinitis. (Ophthal 111:2232, 2004)
Equal efficacy of IV GCV & FOS. GCV avoids nephrotoxicity of FOS; FOS avoids bone marrow suppression of GCV. Although bone marrow toxicity may be similar to ganciclovir.
Oral valganciclovir should replace both.

Pts who discontinue suppression therapy should undergo regular eye examination for early detection of relapses!

Post treatment suppression (Prophylactic) if CD4 count <100/mm³: **Valganciclovir** 900 mg po q24h.

Discontinue if CD4 >100/mm³ x 6 mos on ART.

CMV in Transplant patients: See Table 15E. Use of **valganciclovir** to prevent infections in CMV seronegative recipients who receive organs from a seropositive donor & in seropositive receivers has been highly effective (Ln 365:2105, 2005). Pharm Ther 35:676). Extended prophylaxis (up to a year more effective than short term prophylaxis in lung transplant recipients (Ann Intern Med 152:761, 2010).
CMV in pregnancy: Hyperimmune globulin 200 IU/kg maternal weight as single dose during pregnancy (early), administered IV reduced complications of CMV in infant at one year of life. (CID 55: 497, 2012).

Epstein Barr Virus (EBV) — Mononucleosis
(Ln ID 3:131, 2003)

No treatment. Corticosteroids for tonsillar obstruction, CNS complications, or threat of splenic rupture.

Etiology of atypical lymphocytes: EBV, CMV, Hep A, Hep B, toxo, measles, mumps, drugs (Int Pediatr 18:20, 2003)

HHV-6—implicated as cause of roseola (exanthem subitum) & other febrile diseases of childhood (NEJM 352:768, 2005) Fever & rash (documented in transplant pts (JID 179:311, 1999). Reactivation in 47% of 110 U.S. hematopoietic stem cell transplant pts assoc. with delayed monocytes & platelet engraftment (CID 40:932, 2005) assoc. with meningoencephalitis in immunocompetent adults. Diagnosis made by pos PCR in CSF. ↓ viral copies in response to **ganciclovir** rx (CID 40:890 & 894, 2005). Foscarnet therapy improved thrombotic microangiopathy (Am J Hematol 76:156, 2004).

HHV-7—ubiquitous virus (>90% of the population is infected by age 3 yrs). No relationship to human disease. Infects CD4 lymphocytes via CD4 receptor; transmitted via saliva.

HHV-8—The agent of Kaposi's sarcoma, Castleman's disease, & body cavity lymphoma. Associated with diabetes in sub-Saharan Africa (JAMA 289:2770, 2004).

No antiviral treatment. Effective anti-HIV therapy may help.

Localized lesions: radiotherapy, laser surgery or intralesional chemotherapy. Systemic: chemotherapy. Castleman's disease responded to ganciclovir (JID 2006).
& valganciclovir (JID 2006).

* See page 2 for abbreviations. NOTE: All dosage recommendations are for adults (unless otherwise indicated) and assume normal renal function.

TABLE 14A (5)

VIRUS/DISEASE	DRUG/DOSAGE	SIDE EFFECTS/COMMENTS
Herpes simplex virus (HSV Types 1 & 2)		
Bell's palsy	As soon as possible after onset of palsy. **Prednisone** 1 mg/kg po divided bid x 5 days then taper to 5 mg bid over the next 5 days (total of 10 days prednisone) Alternate: **Prednisone** (dose as above) + **Valacyclovir** 500 mg bid x 5 days	Prospective randomized double blind placebo controlled trial compared prednisolone vs acyclovir vs. (prednisolone + acyclovir) vs placebo. Best result with prednisolone: 85% recovery with placebo, 96% recovery with prednisolone, 93% with combination of acyclovir & prednisolone (NEJM 357:1598 & 1653, 2007). **Large meta-analysis confirms: Steroids alone, effective; antiviral drugs alone, not effective; steroids + antiviral drugs, no more effective than steroids alone** (JAMA 302: 985, 2009)
Encephalitis (Excellent reviews: CID 35: 254, 2002). Herpes evidence (EID 9:234, 2003; Eur J Neurol 12:331, 2005; Antiviral Res: 71:141-148, 2006)	**Acyclovir** IV 10 mg/kg IV (infuse over 1 hr) q8h x 14-21 days. Up to 20 mg/kg q8h in children <12 yrs. Dose calculation in obese patients uncertain. To lessen risk of nephrotoxicity with larger doses, seems reasonable to infuse each dose over more than 1 hour.	Acyclovir is the most common cause of sporadic encephalitis. Survival & recovery from **rx imperative.** Mortality rate reduced from >70% to 19% with acyclovir rx. PCR analysis of CSF for HSV-1 DNA is 100% specific & 75–98% sensitive. 8/33 (25%) CSF samples drawn before day 3 were neg. by PCR: neg. PCR assoc. with 1 protein & <10 WBC per mm³ in CSF (CID 36:1335, 2003). All were + after 3 days. Relapse after successful rx reported in 7/27 (27%) children. Relapse was associated with a lower total dose of initial acyclovir rx (285 ± 82 mg per kg in relapse group vs. 462 ± 149 mg per kg, p. <0.03) (CID 30:185, 2000, Neuropediatrics 35:371, 2004).
Genital Herpes: Sexually Transmitted Treatment Guidelines 2010, MMWR 59 (RR-12), 2010.		
Primary (initial episode)	**Acyclovir** (Zovirax or generic) 400 mg po tid x 7–10 days OR -- **Valacyclovir** (Valtrex) 1000 mg po bid x 7-10 days ∙ OR -- **Famciclovir** (Famvir) 250 mg po tid x 7–10 days	↓ by 2 days time to resolution of signs & symptoms, ↓ by 4 days time to healing of lesions, ↓ by 7 days duration of viral shedding. Does not prevent recurrences. For severe cases only: 5 mg per kg IV q8h times 5-7 days.
Episodic recurrences	**Acyclovir** 800 mg po bid **x 2 days** or 400 mg po tid **x 5 days** or **Famciclovir** 1000 mg po bid **x 1 day** or 125 mg po bid x 5 days or **Valacyclovir** 500 mg po bid **x 3 days** or 1 gm po once daily **x 5 days** For HIV patients, see Comment	An ester of acyclovir, which is well absorbed, bioavailability 3-5 times greater than acyclovir. Metabolized to penciclovir, which is active component. Side effects and activity similar to acyclovir. **Famciclovir** 250 mg po tid **equal to acyclovir** 200 mg po 5 times per day. For episodic recurrences in HIV patients: **Acyclovir** 400 mg po tid x 5–10 days or **famciclovir** 500 mg po bid x 5-10 days or **valacyclovir** 1 gm po bid x 5-10 days
Chronic daily suppression	**Suppressive therapy reduces the frequency of genital herpes recurrences by 70–80% among pts who have frequent recurrences (i.e., >6 recurrences per yr) & many report no symptomatic outbreaks.** **Acyclovir** 400 mg po bid, **or famciclovir** 250 mg po bid, **or valacyclovir** 1 gm po q24h; pts with <9 recurrences per yr could use 500 mg po q24h and those with ≥9 recurrences use valacyclovir 1 gm po q24h if breakthrough at 500 mg. For HIV patients, see Comment	For chronic suppression in HIV patients: **acyclovir** 400-600 mg po bid or **famciclovir** 500 mg po bid or **valacyclovir** 500 mg po bid
Genital, Immunocompetent		
Gingivostomatitis, primary (children)	**Acyclovir** 15 mg/kg po 5x/day x 7 days	Efficacy in randomized double-blind placebo-controlled trial (BMJ 314:1800, 1997).
Keratoconjunctivitis and recurrent epithelial keratitis	**Trifluridine** (Viroptic), 1 drop 1% solution q2h (max. 9 drops per day) for max. of 21 days (see Table 1, page 13)	In controlled trials, response % > idoxuridine. Suppressive dx with acyclovir (400 mg bid) reduced recurrences of ocular HSV from 32% to 19% (NEJM 339:300, 1998).
Mollaret's recurrent "aseptic" meningitis (usually HSV-2) (Ln 363:1772, 2004)	No controlled trials of antiviral rx & resolves spontaneously. If therapy is to be given, **acyclovir** (15-30 mg/kg/day) IV or **valacyclovir** 1-2 gm po tid should be used.	Pos. PCR for HSV in CSF confirms dx (EJCMID 23:560, 2004). **valacyclovir** ref: JAC 47:855, 2001.

* See page 2 for abbreviations. NOTE: All dosage recommendations are for adults (unless otherwise indicated) and assume normal renal function.

TABLE 14A (6)

VIRUS/DISEASE	DRUG/DOSAGE	SIDE EFFECTS/COMMENTS
Herpes simplex virus (HSV Types 1 & 2) (continued)		
Mucocutaneous (for genital see previous page)		
Oral labial, "fever blisters":	Start rx with prodrome symptoms (tingling/burning) before lesions show.	Penciclovir (J Derm Treat 13:67, 2002; JAMA 277:1374, 1997; AAC 46: 2848, 2002); Docosanol (J Am Acad Derm 45:222, 2001). Oral acyclovir 5% cream (AAC 46:2238, 2002); Oral famciclovir (JID 179:303, 1999). Topical fluocinonide (0.05% Lidex gel) q8h times 5 days in combination with famciclovir ↓ lesion size and pain when compared to famciclovir alone (JID 181:1906, 2000).
Normal host: See Ann Pharmacotherapy 38:705, 2004; JAC 53:703, 2004	**Drug** · · · · · · **Dose** · · · · · · · **Sx Decrease** **Oral:** Valacyclovir² 2 gm po q12h x 1 day · · 1 day Famciclovir² 500 mg po bid x 7 days · · 2 days Acyclovir³ᵃ 400 mg po 5 x per day (q4h while awake) x 5 days) · · ½ day	
	Topical: Penciclovir 1% cream · · q2h during day x 4 days · · 1 day Acyclovir 5% cream³ · · 5x/day (q3h) x 7 days · · 1½ day See Table 1, page 28	
--- Herpes Whitlow ---		
Oral labial or genital: Immunocompromised		
(includes pts with AIDS) and critically ill pts in ICU setting/large necrotic ulcers in perineum or face. (See Comment)	**Acyclovir** 5 mg per kg IV (infused over 1 hr) q8h times 7 days (250 mg per MP) or 400 mg po 5 times per day times 14–21 days (See Comment if suspect acyclovir-resistant) **OR** **Famciclovir:** In HIV infected, 500 mg po bid for 7 days for recurrent episodes of genital herpes **OR** **Valacyclovir**ᴺᴸ: In HIV-infected, 500 mg po bid for 5–10 days for recurrent episodes of genital herpes or 500 mg po bid for chronic suppressive rx.	**Acyclovir-resistant HSV: IV foscarnet** 90 mg/kg IV q12h x 7 days. Suppressive therapy with famciclovir (500 mg po bid), valacyclovir (500 mg po bid) or acyclovir (400–800 mg po bid) reduces viral shedding and clinical recurrences.
--- Pregnancy and genital H. simplex ---	Acyclovir safe even in first trimester. No proof that acyclovir at delivery reduces risk/severity of neonatal Herpes. In contrast, C-section in women with active lesions reduces risk of transmission. Ref. Obstet Gyn 106:845, 2006.	
Herpes simiae (Herpes B virus): **Monkey bite** CID 35:1191, 2002	**Postexposure prophylaxis:** Valacyclovir 1 gm po q8h times 14 days or acyclovir 800 mg po 5 times per day times 14 days. **Treatment of disease:** (1) CNS symptoms absent: Acyclovir 12.5–15 mg per kg IV q8h or ganciclovir 5 mg per kg IV q12h. (2) CNS symptoms present: Ganciclovir 5 mg per kg IV q12h	Fatal human cases of myelitis and hemorrhagic encephalitis have been reported following bites, scratches, or eye inoculation of saliva from monkeys. Initial sx include fever, headache, myalgias and diffuse adenopathy. Incubation period of 2–14 days (EID 9:246, 2003). In vitro ACV and ganciclovir less active than other nucleosides (penciclovir or 5-ethyldeoxyuridine may be more active; clinical data needed) (AAC 51:2028, 2007).

² FDA approved only for HIV pts
³ Approved (for immunocompromised pts
ᵃ See page 2 for abbreviations. NOTE: All dosage recommendations are for adults (unless otherwise indicated) and assume normal renal function.

TABLE 14A (7)

Herpesvirus Infections *(continued)*

Varicella-Zoster Virus (VZV)

Varicella: Vaccination has markedly ↓ incidence of varicella & morbidity *(NEJM 352:450, 2005; NEJM 353:2377, 2005 & NEJM 356:1338, 2007)*. Guidelines for VZV vaccine *(MMWR 56(RR-4) 2007)*.

VIRUS/DISEASE	DRUG/DOSAGE	SIDE EFFECTS/COMMENTS
Normal host (chickenpox) **Child** (2–12 years)	**In general, treatment not recommended.** Might use oral **acyclovir** for healthy persons at ↑ risk for moderate to severe varicella, i.e., >12 yrs of age; chronic cutaneous or pulmonary diseases; chronic salicylate rx (↑ risk of Reye syndrome). **acyclovir** dose: 20 mg/kg po qid x 5 days (start within 24 hrs of rash).	Acyclovir slowed development and ↓ number of new lesions and ↓ duration of disease in children: 9 to 7.6 days *(PIDJ 21:739, 2002)*. Oral dose of acyclovir in children should not exceed 80 mg per kg per day or 3200 mg per day.
Adolescents; young adults	**Acyclovir** 800 mg po 5x/day x 5–7 days (start within 24 hrs of rash) or **valacyclovir^NAI** 1000 mg po 3x/day x 5 days. **Famciclovir^NAI** 500 mg po 3x/day probably effective but data lacking.	↓ duration of fever, time to healing, and symptoms *(AnIM 130:922, 1999)*.
Pneumonia or chickenpox in 3rd trimester of pregnancy	**Acyclovir** 800 mg po 5 times per day or 10 mg per kg iv q8h times 5 days. Risks and benefits to fetus and mother still unknown. Many experts recommend rx, especially in 3° trimester. Some would add VZIG (varicella-zoster immune globulin).	Varicella pneumonia associated with 41% mortality in pregnancy. Acyclovir ↓ incidence and severity *(JID 185:422, 2002)*. If varicella-susceptible mother exposed and respiratory symptoms develop within 10 days after exposure, start acyclovir
Immunocompromised host	**Acyclovir** 10–12 mg per kg (500 mg per M²) IV q8h times 7 days (infused over 1 hr)	Disseminated ↑ varicella infection reported during infliximab rx of rheumatoid arthritis *(J Rheum 31:2517, 2004)*. Continuous infusion of high-dose acyclovir (2 mg per kg per hr) successful in 1 pt with severe hemorrhagic varicella *(NEJM 336:732, 1997)*. Mortality high (43%) in AIDS pts *(Int J Inf Dis 6:6, 2002)*.
Prevention—Postexposure prophylaxis Varicella deaths still occur in unvaccinated persons *(MMWR 56 (RR-4) 1–40, 2007)*	**CDC Recommendations for Prevention:** Since <5% of varicella but >50% of varicella-related deaths occur in adults >20 yrs of age, the CDC recommends a more aggressive approach in this age group: **1st, varicella-zoster immune globulin** (VZIG) (125 units/10 kg (22 lbs) body weight IM up to a max. of 625 units; minimum dose is 125 units) is recommended for postexposure prophylaxis in susceptible persons at greater risk for complications (immunocompromised such as HIV, malignancies, pregnancy, and steroid therapy) as soon as possible after exposure (<96 hrs). If varicella develops, initiate treatment quickly (<24 hr after rash) with **acyclovir** as below. Some would rx presumptively with acyclovir in high-risk pts. **2nd,** susceptible adults should be vaccinated. Check antibody in adults with negative or uncertain history of varicella (10–30% will be Ab-neg.) and vaccinate those who are Ab-neg. **3rd,** susceptible children should receive vaccination. Recommended routinely before age 12–18 mos. but OK at any age.

* *See page 2 for abbreviations.* NOTE: All dosage recommendations are for adults (unless otherwise indicated) and assume normal renal function.

TABLE 14A (8)

VIRUS/DISEASE	DRUG/DOSAGE	SIDE EFFECTS/COMMENTS
Herpesvirus Infections/Varicella-Zoster Virus (VZV) (continued)		
Herpes zoster (shingles) (See NEJM 342:635, 2000 & 347:340, 2002) **Normal host** Effective therapy most evident in pts >50 yrs. (For treatment of post-herpetic neuralgia, see CID 36: 877, 2003) New vaccine ↓ herpes zoster & post-herpetic neuralgia (NEJM 352: 2271, 2005; JAMA 292:157, 2006). Reviewed in J Am Acad Derm 58:361, 2008.	**[NOTE: Trials showing benefit of therapy: only in pts treated within 3 days of onset of rash]** **Valacyclovir** 1000 mg po tid times 7 days (adjust dose for renal failure) (See Table 17) OR **Famciclovir** 500 mg tid x 7 days. Adjust for renal failure (see Table 17) OR **Acyclovir** 800 mg po 5 times per day times 7–10 days Add **Prednisone** in pts over 50 yrs old to decrease discomfort during acute phase of zoster. Does not decrease incidence of post-herpetic neuralgia. Dose: 30 mg po bid days 1–7, 15 mg bid days 8–14 and 7.5 mg bid days 15–21.	Valacyclovir ↓ post-herpetic neuralgia more rapidly than acyclovir in pts >50 yrs of age: median duration of zoster-associated pain was 38 days with valacyclovir and 51 days on acyclovir (Arch Fam Med 9:863, 2000). Toxicity of both drugs similar (AAC 39:1546, 1995). Time to healing more rapid. Reduced post-herpetic neuralgia (PHN) vs placebo in pts >50 yrs of age: duration of PHN famciclovir 63 days, placebo 163 days. Famciclovir similar to acyclovir in reduction of acute pain and PHN (J Micro Immun Inf 37:75, 2004). A meta-analysis of 4 placebo-controlled trials (691 pts) demonstrated that acyclovir accelerated by approx. 2-fold pain resolution by all measures employed and reduced post-herpetic neuralgia at 3 & 6 mos (CID 22:341, 1996); med. time to resolution of pain 41 days vs 101 days in those >50 yrs. Prednisone added to acyclovir improved quality of life measurements (↓ acute pain, sleep, and return to normal activity) (AnIM 125:376, 1996). In post-herpetic neuralgia, controlled trials demonstrated effectiveness of gabapentin, the lidocaine patch (5%) & opioid analgesic in controlling pain (Drugs 64:937, 2004; J Clin Virol 29:248, 2004). Nortriptyline & amitriptyline are equally effective but nortriptyline is better tolerated (CID 36:877, 2003). Role of antiviral drugs in rx of PHN unproven (Neurol 64:21, 2005) but 8 of 15 pt improved with IV acyclovir 10 mg/kg q8 hrs x 14 days followed by oral valacyclovir 1 gm 3x a day for 1 month (North J Neurol 253:940, 2006).
Immunocompromised host Not severe	**Acyclovir** 800 mg po 5 times per day times 7 days. (Options: **Famciclovir** 750 mg po q24h or 500 mg bid or 250 mg 3 times per day times 7 days **OR valacyclovir** 1000 mg po tid times 7 days, though both are not FDA-approved for this indication)	If progression, switch to IV. RA pts on TNF-alpha inhibitors at high risk for VZV. Zoster more severe, but less post-herpetic neuralgia (JAMA 301:737, 2009).
Severe: >1 dermatome, trigeminal nerve or disseminated	**Acyclovir** 10–12 mg per kg IV (infusion over 1 hr) q8h times 7–14 days. In older pts, ↓ to 7.5 mg per kg. If nephrotoxicity and pt improving, ↓ to 5 mg per kg q8h.	A common manifestation of immune reconstitution following HAART in HIV-infected children (J All Clin Immun 113:742, 2004). For acyclovir-resistant VZV occurs in HIV+ pts previously treated with acyclovir. **Foscarnet** (40 mg per kg IV q8h for 14–26 days) successful in 4/5 pts but 2 relapsed in 7 and 14 days (AnIM 115:19, 1991).

* See page 2 for abbreviations. NOTE: All dosage recommendations are for adults (unless otherwise indicated) and assume normal renal function.

TABLE 14A (9)

Influenza (A & B)

- Refs: http://www.cdc.gov/flu/weekly; http://www.cdc.gov/flu/professionals/antivirals/recommendations.htm
- Guidelines: ACIP (MMWR 60 (RR-1): Jan 21, 2011); IDSA (CID 48:1003–1032, 2009).
- **Novel A H1N1 Swine Flu emerged in Spring 2009 (Science 325:197, 2009). Rapid Test for Influenza may be falsely negative in over 50% of cases of Swine Flu. During epidemic, treatment should be started based on symptoms alone.** Antiviral therapy cost-effective without viral symptoms during influenza season (CID 49:1090, 2009).
- Vaccine info (http://www.cdc.gov/h1n1flu/recommendations.htm).
- **Oseltamivir: Caution: potential for confusion in dosing oral suspension** (NEJM 361:1912, 2009).
- **Pathogenic avian influenza (H5N1)** emerged in poultry (mainly chickens & ducks) in East & Southeast Asia. As of August 30, 2006, 246 laboratory confirmed cases reported in 10 countries with 144 deaths (see www.cdc.gov/flu/avian). Human-to-human transmission reported; most have had direct contact with poultry. Mortality highest in young, age 10–19 (73%), 56% overall and 81.8%, respectively, with high viral load and cytokine storm (Nature Medicine 12:1203, 2006). **Human isolates resistant to amantadine/rimantadine.** Oseltamivir therapy recommended if avian H5N1 suspected. ↑ dose & duration of oseltamivir necessary for maximum effect in mouse model (JID 192:665, 2005; Nature 435:419, 2005).

Virus/Disease	Susceptible to: (Recommended Drug/Dosage):	Resistant to:	Side Effects/Comments
Novel A/H1N1 (Swine)	**Oseltamivir** 75 mg po bid times 5 days (also approved for rx of children age 1–12 yrs, dose 2 mg per kg up to a total of 75 mg bid times 5 days)* **or** **Zanamivir** 2 inhalations (5 mg each) bid for 5 days. *In morbidly obese patient, increase dose of oseltamivir to 150 mg po bid for pts who are severely ill with influenza; consideration may be given to use of oseltamivir at higher doses (150 mg bid) and/or extended courses (eg., ≥ 10 days) (MMWR 58:749, 2009). Safety of high doses not established in pregnancy (http://www.who.int/csr/resources/publications/swineflu/clinical_management_h1n1.pdf).	Amantadine and rimantadine (100%)	**Caution:** do not reconstitute zanamivir powder for use in nebulizers or mechanical ventilators (MedWatch report of death). **For severe, life-threatening disease consider compassionate use IV Peramivir** (Biocryst/Shionogi: investigational) 600 mg IV daily for a minimum of 5 days. For access to compassionate use call 205-369-3262 or website: http://www.biocryst.com/ie and www.shionogi.com. Peramivir is an investigational IV neuraminidase inhibitor with activity against influenza A and B, including H1N1 Swine. In phase II studies a single IV dose (300 or 600 mg) was non-inferior to oseltamivir (75 mg bid x 5 days), time to symptom resolution was 78, 81 and 81.8 hrs, respectively. In a second non-comparative study of pts at high risk for complications of influenza, using daily IV peramivir, the median time to alleviation of symptoms in all 37 pts was 68.6 hrs. In a placebo controlled study, peramivir was significantly better than placebo for both clinical symptoms (fever) and virologic shedding (Antimicrob Agents Chemother 54:4568, 2010).
A/H1N1 (Seasonal) The 2011–12 U.S. seasonal influenza vaccine virus strains are identical to those contained in the 2010–11 vaccine. These include A/California/7/2009 (H1N1)-like, A/Perth/16/2009 (H3N2)-like, and B/Brisbane/60/2008-like antigens. The influenza A (H1N1) vaccine virus strain is derived from a 2009 pandemic influenza A (H1N1) virus	**Oseltamivir** 75 mg po bid times 5 days (also approved for rx of children age 1–12 yrs, dose 2 mg per kg up to a total of 75 mg bid times 5 days)* **or** **Zanamivir** 2 inhalations (5 mg each) bid for 5 days.	Amantadine/ rimantadine (>95% resistant)	**Peramivir IV** alternative agent for serious infection (as above). Pts with COPD or asthma, **potential risk of bronchospasm with zanamivir.** All ↓ duration of symptoms by approx. 50% (1–2 days) if given within 30–36 hrs after onset of symptoms. Benefit influenced by duration of symptoms before rx; initiation of oseltamivir within 1st 12 hrs after fever onset ↓ total median illness duration by 74.6 hrs (JAC 51:123, 2003). ↓ risk of pneumonia (Curr Med Res Opin 21:761, 2005).

* See page 2 for abbreviations. NOTE: All dosage recommendations are for adults (unless otherwise indicated) and assume normal renal function.

TABLE 14A (10)

Virus/Disease	Susceptible to (Recommended Drug/Dosage):	Resistant to:	Side Effects/Comments
Influenza (A & B) (continued)			
A/H3N2 A/H3N2v (swine variant)	Oseltamivir or Zanamivir (as above)	Amantadine/ rimantadine (100% resistant)	**Peramivir** alternative agent for serious infection (as above). New A/H3N2v variant reported in late 2011 (MMWR 60: 1-4, 2011). Transmission from pigs to humans. Most cases in children < 10 yrs old. Responds to neuraminidase inhibitors.
B	Oseltamivir or Zanamivir (as above)	No data	**Peramivir** alternative agent for serious infection (as above).
H5N1 (Avian)	Oseltamivir or Zanamivir (as above)	Amantadine/ rimantadine	**Peramivir** alternative agent for serious infection (as above). Report of increasing resistance in up to 18% of children with H5N1 treated with oseltamivir and less responsive H5N1 virus in several patients. Less resistance to zanamivir so far.
Prevention: Influenza A & B	Give vaccine and if ≥13 yrs age, consider **oseltamivir** 75 mg po q24h or **zanamivir** 2 inhalations (5 mg each) once daily for 5 days for the two weeks following vaccination or for the duration of peak influenza in community or for outbreak control in high-risk populations if vaccination cannot be administered (CID 2009; 48:1003-1032). Avoid Oseltamivir if seasonal H1N1 infection predominates with Oseltamivir resistant strain. (Consider for similar populations as immunization recommendations.)		immunization contraindicated if hypersensitivity to chicken eggs.

VIRUS/DISEASE	DRUG/DOSAGE	SIDE EFFECTS/COMMENTS
Measles While measles rates in the US is at the lowest rates ever (55/100,000) much higher rates reported in developing countries (CID 42:322, 2006). High attack rates in the unvaccinated (CID 47:1143, 2008). Concern about lack of vaccine effectiveness in developing countries (Lancet 373:1543, 2009). Children Adults	No therapy or **vitamin A** 200,000 units po daily times 2 days No rx or **ribavirin** IV: 20-35 mg per kg per day times 7 days	Imported measles on the rise (MMWR 57: 169, 2008). Vitamin A may ↓ severity of measles. ↓ severity of illness in adults (CID 20-454, 1994).
Metapneumovirus (HMPV) A paramyxovirus isolated from pts of all ages, with mild bronchiolitis/bronchospasm to pneumonia. Can cause lethal pneumonia in HSCT pts (Ann Intern Med 144:344, 2006)	**No proven antiviral therapy** (intravenous ribavirin used anecdotally with variable results)	Human metapneumovirus isolated from 6-21% of children with RTIs (NEJM 350:443, 2004). Dual infection with RSV assoc. with severe bronchiolitis (JID 191:382, 2005). Nucleic acid test now approved to detect 12 respiratory viruses (xTAG Respiratory Viral Panel, Luminex Molecular Diagnostics)
Monkey pox (orthopox virus) (see LnID 4:17, 2004) Outbreak from contact with ill prairie dogs. Source likely imported Gambian giant rats (MMWR 42-642, 2003).	**No proven antiviral therapy.** Cidofovir is active in vitro & in mouse model (AAC 46:1329, 2002; Antiviral Res. 57:13, 2003) (Potential new drugs Virol J 4:8, 2007)	Incubation period of 12 days, then fever, headache, cough, adenopathy, & a vesicular papular rash that pustulates, umbilicates, & crusts on the head, trunk, & extremities. Transmission in healthcare setting rare (CID 40:789, 2005; CID 41:1742, 2005; CID 41:1765, 2005)
Norovirus (Nolwalk-like virus, or NLV) Vast majority of outbreaks of non-bacterial gastroenteritis.	**No antiviral therapy.** Replete volume. Transmission by contaminated food, fecal-oral contact with contaminated surfaces, or fomites.	Sudden onset of nausea, vomiting, and/or watery diarrhea lasting 12-60 hours. Ethanol-based hand rubs effective (J Hosp Inf 60:144, 2005).

* See page 2 for abbreviations. NOTE: All dosage recommendations are for adults (unless otherwise indicated) and assume normal renal function.

TABLE 14A (11)

VIRUS/DISEASE	DRUG/DOSAGE	SIDE EFFECTS/COMMENTS
Papillomaviruses: Warts **External Genital Warts**	**Patient applied:** **Podofilox** (0.5% solution or gel): apply 2x/day x 3 days, 4th day no therapy, repeat cycle 4x; OR **Imiquimod** 5% cream: apply once daily ths 3x/wk for up to 16 wks. **Provider administered:** Cryotherapy with liquid nitrogen; repeat q1-2 wks; OR **Podophyllin resin** 10-25% in tincture of benzoin. Repeat weekly as needed; OR **Trichloroacetic acid** (TCA): repeat weekly as needed; OR surgical removal.	**Podofilox:** inexpensive and safe (pregnancy safety not established). Mild irritation after treatment. **Imiquimod:** Mild to moderate redness & irritation. Topical imiquimod effective for treatment of vulvar intraepithelial neoplasms (NEJM 358:1465, 2008). Safety in pregnancy not established. **Cryotherapy:** Blistering and skin necrosis common. **Podophyllin resin:** Must air dry before treated area contacts clothing. Can irritate adjacent skin. **TCA:** Caustic. Can cause severe pain on adjacent normal skin. Neutralize with soap or sodium bicarbonate.
Warts on cervix	Need evaluation for evolving neoplasia.	Gynecological consult advised.
Vaginal warts	Cryotherapy with liquid nitrogen or TCA	
Urethral warts	Cryotherapy with liquid nitrogen or **Podophyllin resin** 10-25% in tincture of benzoin	
Anal warts	Cryotherapy with liquid nitrogen or TCA or surgical removal	Advise anoscopy to look for rectal warts.
Skin papillomas	Topical **α-lactalbumin. Oleic acid** (from human milk) applied 1x/day for 3 wks	↓ lesion size & recurrence vs placebo (p <0.001) (NEJM 350:2663, 2004). Further studies warranted.
Parvo B19 Virus (Erythrovirus B19). Review: NEJM 350:586, 2004. Wide range of manifestation. **Treatment options for common symptomatic infections:**		
Erythema infectiosum	Symptomatic treatment only	Diagnostic tools: IgM and Igb antibody titers. Perhaps better: blood parvovirus PCR.
Arthritis/arthralgia	Non-specific anti-inflammatory drugs (NSAID)	Dose of IVIG not standardized; suggest 400 mg/kg IV of commercial IVIG for 5 or 10 days or 1000 mg/kg IV for 3 days.
Transient aplastic crisis	Transfusions and oxygen	Most dramatic anemias in pts with pre-existing hemolytic anemia.
Fetal hydrops	Intrauterine blood transfusion	Bone marrow shown erythrocyte maturation arrest with giant pronormoblasts.
Chronic infection with anemia	IVIG and transfusion	
Chronic infection without anemia	Perhaps IVIG	
Papovavirus/Polyomavirus		
Progressive multifocal leukoencephalopathy (PML) Serious demyelinating disease due to JC virus in immunocompromised pts.	No specific therapy for JC virus. Two general approaches: 1. In HIV pts: HAART. Cidofovir may be effective. 2. Stop or decrease immunosuppressive therapy.	Failure of treatment with interferon alfa-2b, cytarabine and topotecan. Immunosuppressive natalizumab recently removed from market due to reported associations with PML. Mixed reports on cidofovir. Most likely effective in pts with HAART experience.
BK Virus induced nephropathy in immunocompromised pts and hemorrhagic cystitis	Decrease immunosuppression if possible. Suggested antiviral therapy based on anecdotal data. If progressive renal dysfunction: 1. **Fluoroquinolone** first; 2. **IVIG** 500 mg/kg IV; 3. **Leflunomide** 100 mg po daily x 3 days, then 10-20 mg po daily; 4. **Cidofovir** only if refractory to all of the above (see Table 14B for dose).	Use PCR to monitor viral "load" in urine and/or plasma. Report of cidofovir as potentially effective for BK hemorrhagic cystitis (CID 49:233, 2009).

TABLE 14A (12)

VIRUS/DISEASE	DRUG/DOSAGE	SIDE EFFECTS/COMMENTS
Rabies (see Table 20B, page 215; see MMMWR 54: RR-3:1, 2005, see MMWR 54: RR-1, 2005, CDC Guidelines for Prevention and Control 2006, MMWR/55/RR-5, 2006) Rabid dogs account for 50,000 cases per yr worldwide. Most cases in the U.S. are cryptic, i.e. no documented evidence of bite or contact with a rabid animal (CID 35:738, 2003). 70% assoc. with 2 rare bat species (EID 9:151, 2003). An organ donor with early rabies infected 4 recipients (2 kidneys, liver & artery) who all died of rabies 13 days after transplant (NEJM 352:1103, 2005).	**Mortality 100% with only survivors those who receive rabies vaccine before the onset of illness/symptoms** (CID 36:61, 2003). A 15-year-old female who developed rabies post-bat bite survived after drug induction of coma (NEJM 352:2508, 2005).	Corticosteroids ↑ mortality rate and ↓ incubation time in mice. Therapies that have failed after symptoms develop include rabies vaccine, rabies immune-globulin, rabies virus neutralizing antibody, ribavirin, alfa interferon, & ketamine.
Respiratory Syncytial Virus (RSV) Major cause of morbidity in neonates/infants. Nucleic acid test now approved to detect 12 respiratory viruses (xTAG Respiratory Viral Panel, Luminex Molecular Diagnostics). Ref: CID 56:258, 2013 (immunocompromised host).	Hydration, supplemental oxygen. Routine use of ribavirin not recommended. Ribavirin therapy associated with small increases in O₂ saturation but no consistent decrease in need for mech. ventilation or length of ICU stays. High cost, aerosol administration & potential toxicity (Red Book of Pediatrics, 2006). RNA interference with ALN-RSV01 impedes the expression of nucleocapsid protein of RSV. Study of 85 healthy volunteers showed a significant reduction in RSV infection vs. placebo (Proc Natl Acad Sci U S A 107:8800, 2010).	In adults, RSV accounted for 10.6% of hospitalizations for pneumonia, 11.4% for COPD, 7.2% for asthma & 5.4% for CHF in pts >65 yrs of age (NEJM 352:1749, 2005). RSV caused 11% of clinically important respiratory illnesses in military recruits (CID 41:311, 2005). Palivizumab (Synagis) 15 mg/kg IM once per month November-April. Timing of coverage may need to be adjusted in some regions based on reported cases in the region, as opposed to using fixed dosing schedules (Pediatrics 126:e116, 2010).
Prevention of RSV in: (1) Children <24 mos. old with chronic lung disease of prematurity (formerly broncho-pulmonary dysplasia) requiring supplemental O₂ or (2) Premature infants (<32 wks gestation) and <6 mos. old at start of RSV season or (3) Children with selected congenital heart diseases	**Palivizumab (Synagis)** 15 mg per kg IM q month Nov.-April. Ref: Red Book of Pediatrics, 2006.	Expense argues against its use, but in 2004 approx. 100,000 infants received drug annually in U.S. (PIDJ 23:1051, 2004). Significant reduction in RSV hospitalization among children with congenital heart disease (Expert Opin Biol Ther. 7:1471-80, 2007)
Rhinovirus (Colds) See Ln 361:51, 2003 Found in 1/2 of children with community-acquired pneumonia; role in pathogenesis unclear (CID 39:681, 2004). High rate of rhinovirus identified in children with significant lower resp tract infections (Ped Int Dis 28:337, 2009)	No antiviral rx indicated (Ped Ann 34:53, 2005). Symptomatic rx: • **Ipratropium bromide** nasal (2 sprays per nostril tid) • **Clemastine** 1.34 mg ↓ -2 tab po bid-tid. Avoid zinc products (see Comment).	Six relief: ipratropium nasal spray ↓ rhinorrhea and sneezing vs placebo (AnIM 125:89, 1996). Clemastine (an antihistamine) ↓ sneezing, rhinorrhea but associated with dry nose, mouth & throat in 6-19% (CID 22:656, 1996). Oral **pleconaril** given within 24 hrs of onset reduced duration (1 day) & severity of "cold symptoms" in DBPCT (p <.001) (CID 36:1523, 2003). Echinacea didn't work (CID 38:1367, 2004 & 40:807, 2005)—but to rest. Public health advisory advising that three over-the-counter cold remedy products containing zinc (e.g., Zicam) should not be used because of multiple reports of permanent anosmia (www.fda.gov/Safety/MedWatch/SafetyInformation/SafetyAlertsforHumanMedicalProducts/ucm166996.htm)
Rotavirus: Leading recognized cause of diarrhea-related illness among infants and children world-wide and kills ½ million children annually.	No antiviral rx available; oral hydration life-saving. In one study, **Nitazoxanide** **7.5 mg/kg bid x 3 days** reduced duration of illness from 75 to 31 hrs in Egyptian children. Impact on diarrhea or other parameters not measured (Lancet 368:100, 2006). Too early to recommend routine use (Lancet 368:100, 2006)	Two live-attenuated vaccines highly effective (85 and 98%) and safe in preventing rotavirus diarrhea and hospitalization (NEJM 354:1 & 23, 2006). Contact CDC for information on the two vaccines, RV1 or RV5, for infants (MMWR 58(RR02):-1, 2009)
SARS-CoV: See page 156		
Smallpox (NEJM 346:1300, 2002)	Smallpox vaccine (if within 4 days of exposure) + cidofovir (dosage uncertain but likely similar to CMV (5 mg/kg IV once weekly for 2 weeks followed by once weekly dosing. Must be used with hydration and Probenecid; contact CDC: 770-488-7100). From vaccination: Progressive vaccinia—vaccinia immune globulin may be of benefit. To obtain immune globulin, contact CDC: 770-488-7100. (CID 39:759, 776 & 819, 2004)	
Contact vaccinia: See page 157		
West Nile virus: See page 157		

* See page 2 for abbreviations. NOTE: All dosage recommendations are for adults (unless otherwise indicated) and assume normal renal function.

TABLE 14B - ANTIVIRAL DRUGS (NON-HIV)

DRUG NAME(S) GENERIC (TRADE)	DOSAGE/ROUTE IN ADULTS*	COMMENTS/ADVERSE EFFECTS
CMV (See SANFORD GUIDE TO HIV/AIDS THERAPY)		
Cidofovir (Vistide)	5 mg per kg IV once weekly for 2 weeks, then once every other week. **Properly timed IV prehydration with normal saline & probenecid administration are required with each cidofovir infusion:** 2 gm or 3 hrs before each dose and further 1 gm doses at 2 & 8 hrs after completion of the cidofovir infusion. Renal function (serum creatinine and urine protein) must be monitored prior to each dose (see pkg insert for details). Contraindicated if creatinine >1.5 mg/dL, CrCl ≤55 mL/min or urine protein ≥100 mg/dL.	**Adverse effects: Nephrotoxicity:** dose-dependent proximal tubular injury (Fanconi-like syndrome): proteinuria, glycosuria, bicarbonaturia, phosphaturia, polyuria (nephrogenic diabetes insipidus, Ln 352:413, 1998), acidosis. Use with other nephrotoxic drugs contraindicated; probenecid may decrease 58% use but still highly nephrotoxic. Other toxicities: nausea 69%, fever 58%, alopecia 27%, myalgia 16%, proboenecid hypersensitivity 16%, neutropenia 29%, iritis and uveitis reported; also ↓ intraocular pressure. **Black Box warning.** Renal impairment can occur after ≤2 doses. Contraindicated in pts receiving concomitant nephrotoxic agents. Monitor for ↓ WBC. In animals, carcinogenic, teratogenic; causes ↓ sperm and ↓ fertility. FDA indication only CMV retinitis in HIV pts. **Comment:** Recommended dosage, frequency or infusion rate must not be exceeded. Dose must be reduced if discontinued if changes in renal function occur during rx. For ↑ of 0.3-0.4 mg per dL in serum creatinine, cidofovir dose must be ↓ from 5 to 3 mg per kg; discontinue cidofovir if ↑ of 0.5 mg per dL above baseline or 3+ proteinuria develops (for 2+ proteinuria, observe pts carefully and consider discontinuation).
Foscarnet (Foscavir)	Induction: 90 mg per kg IV over 1.5-2 hours, q12h OR 60 mg per kg, over 1 hour, q8h Maintenance: 90 –120 mg per kg IV, over 2 hours, q24h Dosage adjustment with renal dysfunction (see Table 17).	Use infusion pump to control rate of administration. **Adverse effects: Major toxicity is renal impairment (1/3 of patients)** – ↑ creatinine, proteinuria, nephrogenic diabetes insipidus, ↓K+, ↓Ca++, ↓ Mg++. Toxicity ↑ with other nephrotoxic drugs (ampho B, aminoglycosides or pentamidine (especially severe ↓ Ca++)]. Adequate hydration may ↓ toxicity. Other: headache, mild (100%); fatigue (100%), nausea (80%), fever (25%) CNS: seizures. Hemato: ↓ WBC, ↓ Hgb. Hepatic: liver function tests ↑. Neuropathy. Penile and oral ulcers.
Ganciclovir (Cytovene)	IV: 5 mg per kg q12h times 14 days (induction) 5 mg per kg IV q24h or 6 mg per kg 5 times per wk (maintenance) Dosage adjust. with renal dysfunction (see Table 17)	**Adverse effects: Black Box warnings:** cytopenias, carcinogenicity/teratogenicity & aspermia in animals Absolute neutrophil count dropped below 500 per mm³ in 15%, thrombocytopenia 21%, anemia 6%. Fever 48%, GI 50%, nausea, vomiting, diarrhea, abdominal pain 19%, rash 10%. Retinal detachment 11% (likely due to underlying disease). Confusion, headache, psychiatric disturbances and seizures. Neutropenia may respond to granulocyte colony stimulating factor (G-CSF or GM-CSF). Severe myelosuppression may be ↑ with coadministration of zidovudine or azathioprine. 32% dc/interrupted rx, principally for neutropenia. Avoid extravasation.
Ganciclovir (Vitrasert)	Oral: 1.0 gm tid with food (fatty meal) (250 & 500 mg cap) Intraocular implant, 4.5 mg	Hematologic less frequent than with IV. Granulocytopenia 18%, anemia 12%, thrombocytopenia 6%. GI: same as with IV. Retinal detachment 8%.
Valganciclovir (Valcyte)	900 mg (two 450 mg tabs) po bid times 21 days for induction, followed by 900 mg po q24h. Take with food. Dosage adjustment for renal dysfunction (See Table 17A)	**Adverse effects:** Late retinal detachment (7/30 eyes). Does not prevent CMV retinitis in good eye or visceral dissemination. **Comment:** Replacement every 6 months recommended. A prodrug of ganciclovir with better bioavailability than oral ganciclovir. 60% with food. **Adverse effects:** Similar to ganciclovir.
Herpesvirus (non-CMV) Acyclovir (Zovirax or generic)	Doses: see Table 14A for various indications 400 mg or 800 mg tab 200 mg cap Suspension 200 mg per 5 mL Ointment or cream 5% IV injection Dosage adjustment for renal dysfunction (See Table 17A).	**po:** Generally well-tolerated with occ. diarrhea, vertigo, arthralgia. Less frequent rash, fatigue, insomnia, fever, menstrual abnormalities, acne, sore throat, muscle cramps, lymphadenopathy. **IV:** Phlebitis, caustic with vesicular lesions with IV infusion. CNS (1%): lethargy, tremors, confusion, hallucinations, delirium, seizures, coma—all reversible. Renal: High dose, rapid infusion may crystallize in renal tubules → obstructive uropathy (rapid infusion, dehydration, prior ↓ renal function). With high-dose need adequate pre-hydration and ↓ dose if renal insufficiency and ↑ dose if risk). Adequate hydration may prevent such nephrotoxicity. Hepatic: ↑ ALT, AST. Uncommon: neutropenia, rash, diaphoresis, hypotension, headache, nausea.

* See page 2 for abbreviations. NOTE: All dosage recommendations are for adults (unless otherwise indicated) and assume normal renal function.

TABLE 14B (2)

DRUG NAME(S) GENERIC (TRADE)	DOSAGE/ROUTE IN ADULTS*	COMMENTS/ADVERSE EFFECTS
Herpesvirus (non-CMV) (continued)		
Famciclovir (Famvir)	125 mg, 250 mg, 500 mg tabs. Dosage depends on indication: (see label and Table 14A).	Metabolized to penciclovir. **Adverse effects:** similar to acyclovir; included headache, nausea, diarrhea, and dizziness but incidence does not differ from placebo. May be taken without regard to meals. Dose should be reduced if CrCl <60 mL per min (see package insert & Table 17, page 211). May be taken with or without food.
Penciclovir (Denavir)	Topical 1% cream	Apply to area of recurrence of herpes labialis with start of sx, then q2h while awake times 4 days. Well tolerated.
Trifluridine (Viroptic)	Topical 1% solution: 1 drop q2h (max. 9 drops/day) until corneal re-epithelialization, then dose is ↓ for 7 more days (one drop q4h for at least 5 drops/day), not to exceed 21 days total rx.	Mild burning (5%), palpebral edema (3%), punctate keratopathy, stromal edema. For HSV keratoconjunctivitis or recurrent epithelial keratitis.
Valacyclovir (Valtrex)	500 mg, 1 gm tabs Dosage depends on indication and renal function (see label, Table 14A & Table 17A)	An ester pro-drug of acyclovir that is well-absorbed; bioavailability 3–5 times greater than acyclovir. **Adverse effects** similar to acyclovir (see JID 186:540, 2002). Thrombotic thrombocytopenic purpura/hemolytic uremic syndrome reported in pts with advanced HIV disease and transplant recipients participating in clinical trials at doses of 8 gm per day.
Hepatitis		
Adefovir dipivoxil (Hepsera)	10 mg po q24h (with normal CrCl); see Table 17A if renal impairment. 10 mg tab	Adefovir dipivoxil is a prodrug of adefovir. It is an acyclic nucleotide analog with activity against hepatitis B (HBV) at 0.2–2.5 mM (IC$_{50}$). See Table 9 for Cmax & T½. Active against YMDD mutant lamivudine-resistant strains and in vitro vs. entecavir-resistant strains. To minimize resistance, package insert recommends using in combination with lamivudine for lamivudine-resistant virus; consider alternative therapy if viral load remains >1,000 copies/mL with lamivudine treatment. Primarily renal excretion—adjust dose. No food interactions. Generally few side effects, but **Black Box warning** regarding lactic acidosis/hepatic steatosis with nucleoside analogs and severe exacerbation of hepB on discontinuation; monitoring required after discontinuation. At 10 mg per day potential for delayed nephrotoxicity. Monitor renal function, esp. with pts with pre-existing or other risks for renal impairment. Pregnancy Category C. Hepatitis may exacerbate when treatment discontinued; Up to 25% of pts developed ALT 10 times normal within 12 wks; usually responds to re-treatment or self-limited, but hepatic decompensation has occurred.
Boceprevir (Victrelis)	For HCV genotype 1 800 mg po TID (with food) in combination with pegIFN + RBV*	* Initiate boceprevir 4 weeks after starting pegIFN + RBV. Use response guided therapy (see Table 14A for details). Most common AEs: Fatigue, anemia, nausea, headache, and dysgeusia. Difficult to distinguish between AEs caused by pegIFN or RBV.
Entecavir (Baraclude)	0.5 mg q24h; if refractory or resistant to lamivudine or telbivudine: 1 mg per day. Tabs: 0.5 mg & 1 mg. Oral solution: 0.05 mg/mL. Administer on an empty stomach.	A nucleoside analog active against HBV including lamivudine-resistant mutants. Minimal adverse effects reported: headache, fatigue, dizziness, & nausea reported in 22% of pts. Alopecia, anaphylactoid reactions reported. Potential for lactic acidosis and exacerbation of hepB at discontinuation (**Black Box warning**) as above. Do not use as single anti-retroviral agent in HIV co-infected pts. M184 mutation can emerge (NEJM 356:2614, 2007). Adjust dosage in renal impairment (see Table 17, page 211).

* See page 2 for abbreviations. NOTE: All dosage recommendations are for adults (unless otherwise indicated) and assume normal renal/renal function.

TABLE 14B (3)

DRUG NAME(S) GENERIC (TRADE)*	DOSAGE/ROUTE IN ADULTS*	COMMENTS/ADVERSE EFFECTS
Hepatitis (continued)		
Interferon alfa is available as alfa-2a (Roferon-A), alfa-2b (Intron-A)	For hepC, usual Roferon-A and Intron-A doses are 3 million international units 3x weekly subQ	Depending on agent, available in pre-filled syringes, vials of solution or powder. **Black Box warnings:** include possibility of causing or aggravating serious neuropsychiatric disorders, autoimmune disorders, ischemic events. Withdraw therapy if any of these suspected. **Adverse effects:** Flu-like syndrome is common, esp. during 1st wk of rx: fever 98%, fatigue 89%, myalgia 73%, headache 71%. **Gi:** anorexia 46%, diarrhea 29%. CNS: dizziness 21%. Hemorrhagic or ischemic stroke. Rash 18%, may progress to Stevens Johnson or exfoliative dermatitis. Profound fatigue & psychiatric symptoms in up to ½ of pts (J Clin Psych 64:708, 2003) (depression anxiety, irritability & agitation) can occur. Anti-depressant prophylaxis may help. Inducate. TSH. autoimmune thyroid disorders with ↓ or ↑ thyroidism, hematol: WBC 49%, ↓ Hgb 27%, ↓ platelets 35%. Post-marketing reports of antibody-mediated pure red cell aplasia in patients receiving interferon/ribavirin with erythropoiesis-stimulating agents. Acute reversible hearing loss &/or tinnitus in up to 1/3 (Ln 343:1134, 1994). Optic neuropathy (retinal hemorrhage, cotton wool spots, ↓ in color vision) reported (AIDS 18:1865, 2004). Doses may require adjustment (or dc) based on individual response or adverse events and can vary by product, indication (eg, HCV or HBV) and mode of use (mono- or combination-rx). (Refer to labels of individual products and to ribavirin if used in combination (see Comments for details of use).
PEG interferon alfa-2b (PEG-Intron)	0.5–1.5 mcg/kg subQ q wk	
Pegylated-40k interferon alfa-2a (Pegasys)	180 mcg subQ q wk	
Lamivudine (3TC) (Epivir-HBV)	Hepatitis B dose 100 mg po q24h Dosage adjustment with renal dysfunction (see label). Tabs 100 mg and oral solution 5 mg/mL.	**Black Box warnings:** caution; dose is lower than HIV dose, so must exclude co-infection with HIV before using this formulation; lactic acidosis/hepatic steatosis; severe exacerbation of liver disease can occur on dc. YMDD-mutants resistant to lamivudine may emerge on treatment. **Adverse effects:** See Table 14D.
Ribavirin (Rebetol, Copegus)	For use with an interferon for hepatitis C. Available as 200 mg caps and 40 mg/mL oral solution (Rebetol) or 200 mg and 400 mg tabs (Copegus) (See Comments regarding dosage).	**Black Box warnings:** ribavirin monotherapy of HCV is ineffective; hemolytic anemia may precipitate cardiac events; teratogenic/embryotoxic (**Preg Category X**). Drug may persist for 6 mos, avoid pregnancy for at least 6 mos after end of rx of women or their partners. Only approved for pts with Ccr > 50 mL/min. Also should not be used in pts with severe heart disease or some hemoglobinopathies. ARDS reported (Chest 124:406, 2003). **Adverse effects:** hemolytic anemia (may require dose reduction or dc), dental/periodontal disorders, and all adverse effects of concomitant interferon used (see above). Postmarketing: retinal detachment, ↓ hearing, hypersensitivity reactions. See label for full warning and information. Dose and duration of interferon used, weight, HCV genotype, and combination of rx (mono and/or dc) based on side effects (especially degree of hemolysis, with different criteria in those with/without cardiac disease). For example, initial Rebetol dose with Intron A (interferon alfa-2b) is wt-based: 400 mg am & 600 mg pm with meals. Doses and duration of Copegus with peg-interferon alfa-2a are less in pts with genotype 2 or 3 (800 mg per day divided into 2 doses, for 24 wks) than with genotypes 1 or 4 (1000 mg for wt < 75 kg and 1200 mg per day divided into 2 doses for wt > 75 kg for 48 wks); in HIV/HCV-co-infected pts, dose is 800 mg per day regardless of genotype. (See individual labels for details, including initial dosing and criteria for dose modification in those with/without cardiac disease.)
Telaprevir (Incivek)	For HCV genotype 1 750 mg q8h (with food) in combination with INF+RBV	Must be given in combination with PegIFN/RBV. D/c telaprevir after 12 weeks of rx. Use response guided therapy (see table 14A for details). Most common AEs: **Black Box Warning:** Rash (inc rare Stevens Johnson reaction, DRESS, and TEN, each of which may be fatal), pruritis, nausea, anorexia, headache, fatigue, anemia, insomnia, and depression. Difficult to dissect telaprevir AEs from IFN/ribavirin. An oral nucleoside analog approved for Rx of Hep B. It has ↑ rates of response and superior viral suppression than lamivudine (NEJM 357:2576, 2007). **Black Box warnings** regarding lactic acidosis/hepatic steatosis with nucleosides and potential for severe exacerbation of HepB on dc. Generally well-tolerated with ↓ mitochondrial toxicity vs other nucleosides and no dose limiting toxicity observed (Ann Pharmacother 40:472, 2006; Medical Letter 49:11, 2007). Myalgias, myopathy and rhabdomyolysis reported. Peripheral neuropathy. Genotypic resistance rate was 4.4% by one yr, ↑ to 21.5% by 2 yrs of rx of eKg+ pts. Selects for YMDD mutation like lamivudine. Combination with lamivudine was inferior to telbivudine (Hepatology 45:507, 2007).
Telbivudine (Tyzeka)	600 mg orally q24h, without regard to food. Dosage adjustment with renal dysfunction. Ccr < 50 mL/min (see label). 100 mg per 5 mL solution.	

See page 2 for abbreviations. NOTE: All dosage recommendations are for adults (unless otherwise indicated) and assume normal renal function.

TABLE 14B (4)

DRUG NAME(S) GENERIC (TRADE)	DOSAGE/ROUTE IN ADULTS*	COMMENTS/ADVERSE EFFECTS
Influenza A. Treatment and prophylaxis of influenza has become more complicated. Many circulating strains are resistant to adamantanes (amantadine & rimantadine), while others are resistant to the neuraminidase inhibitor, oseltamivir, but susceptible to adamantane. Resistance to the neuraminidase inhibitor, zanamivir, is very rare, but there are limitations to the use of this inhalation agent. In this rapidly evolving area, close attention to guidance from public health authorities is warranted. In patients severely ill with influenza, combination therapy, higher than usual doses of oseltamivir and/or longer than usual treatment courses may be considered in appropriate circumstances *(MMWR 58: 749-752, 2008)*.		
Amantadine (Symmetrel) **or Rimantadine** (Flumadine)	**Amantadine** 100 mg caps, tabs; 50 mg/mL oral solution & syrup. Treatment or prophylaxis: 100 mg bid; or 100 mg daily if age ≥65 y; dose reductions with Ccr starting at ≤50 mL/min. **Rimantadine** 100 mg tabs, 50 mg/5 mL syrup. Treatment or prophylaxis: 100 mg bid, or 100 mg daily in elderly nursing home pts, or severe hepatic disease, or Ccr ≤10 mL/min. For children, rimantadine only approved for prophylaxis.	**Side-effects/toxicity:** CNS (nervousness, anxiety, difficulty concentrating, and lightheadedness). Symptoms occurred in 6% on rimantadine vs 14% on amantadine. They usually ↓ after 1st week and disappear when drug dc. GI (nausea, anorexia). Some serious side-effects—delirium, hallucinations, and seizures—are associated with high plasma drug levels resulting from renal insufficiency, esp. in older pts, those with prior seizure disorders, or psychiatric disorders. Activity restricted to influenza A viruses.
Influenza A and B—For both drugs, initiate within 48 hrs of symptom onset		
Zanamivir (Relenza) For pts ≥7 yrs of age (treatment) or ≥5 yrs (prophylaxis)	Powder is inhaled by specially designed inhalation device. Each blister contains 5 mg zanamivir. **Treatment:** oral inhalation of 2 blisters (10 mg) bid x 5 days. **Prophylaxis:** oral inhalation of 2 blisters (10 mg) once daily for 10 days (household outbreak) to 28 days (community outbreak).	Active by inhalation against neuraminidase of both influenza A and B and inhibits release of virus from epithelial cells of respiratory tract. Approx. 4–17% of inhaled dose absorbed into plasma. Excreted by kidney but with low absorption, dose reduction not necessary in renal impairment. Minimal side-effects: <3% cough, sinusitis, diarrhea, nausea and vomiting. **Reports of respiratory adverse events in pts with or without airways disease, should be avoided in pts with underlying respiratory disease.** Allergic reactions and neuropsychiatric events have been reported. **Caution: do not reconstitute zanamivir powder for use in nebulizers or mechanical ventilators** (MedWatch report of death). Zanamivir for iv administration is available for compassionate use through an emergency IND application that can be accessed at: http://www.fda.gov/Drugs/DevelopmentApprovalProcess/HowDrugsareDevelopedandApproved/ApprovalApplications/InvestigationalNewDrugINDApplication/default.htm
Oseltamivir (Tamiflu) For pts ≥ 1 yr (treatment or prophylaxis)	For adults: **Treatment,** 75 mg po bid for 5 days; 150 mg po bid has been used for critically ill or morbidly obese patients but this dose is not FDA-approved. **Prophylaxis,** 75 mg po once daily for 10 days to 6 wks. [See label for pediatric weight-based dosing.] Adjust doses for CrCl ≤30 mL/min. 30 mg, 45 mg, 75 mg caps; powder for oral suspension.	Well absorbed (80% bioavailable) from GI tract as ethyl ester of active compound GS 4071. T½ 6–10 hrs; excreted unchanged by kidney. Adverse effects include diarrhea, vomiting, headache. Nausea ↓ with food. Rarely, severe skin reactions (toxic epidermal necrolysis, Stevens-Johnson syndrome, erythema multiforme). **Delirium & abnormal behavior reported** *(CID 48:1003, 2009).*
Respiratory Syncytial Virus (RSV)		
Palivizumab (Synagis) Used for prevention of RSV infection in high-risk children	15 mg per kg IM q month throughout RSV season Single dose 100 mg vial	A monoclonal antibody directed against the F glycoprotein on surface of virus; side-effects are uncommon, occ. ↑ ALT. Anaphylaxis <1/10⁵ pts; acute hypersensitivity reaction <1/1000. Postmarketing reports: URI, otitis media, fever, ↓ plts, injection site reactions. Preferred over polyclonal immune globulin in high risk infants & children.

* See page 2 for abbreviations. *NOTE: All dosage recommendations are for adults (unless otherwise indicated) and assume normal renal function.*

TABLE 14B (5)

DRUG NAME(S) GENERIC (TRADE)	DOSAGE/ROUTE IN ADULTS*	COMMENTS/ADVERSE EFFECTS
Warts (See CID 28:S37, 1999)	Regimens are from drug labels specific for external genital and/or perianal condylomata acuminata only (see specific labels for indications, regimens, age limits).	
Interferon alfa-2b (IntronA)	Injection of 1 million international units into base of lesion, thrice weekly on alternate days for up to 3 wks. Maximum 5 lesions per course.	Interferons may cause "flu-like" illness and other systemic effects. 88% had at least one adverse effect. **Black box warning:** alpha interferons may cause or aggravate neuropsychiatric, autoimmune, ischemic or infectious disorders.
Interferon alfa-N3 (Alferon N)	Injection of 0.05 mL into base of each wart, up to 0.5 mL total per session, twice weekly for up to 8 weeks.	Flu-like syndrome and hypersensitivity reactions. Contraindicated with allergy to mouse IgG, egg proteins, or neomycin.
Imiquimod (Aldara)	5% cream. Thin layer applied at bedtime, washing off after 6-10 hr, thrice weekly to maximum of 16 wks.	Erythema, itching & burning, erosions. Flu-like syndrome, increased susceptibility to sunburn (avoid UV).
Podofilox (Condylox)	0.5% gel or solution twice daily for 3 days, no therapy for 4 days; can use up to 4 such cycles.	Local reactions—pain, burning, inflammation in 50%. Can ulcerate. Limit surface area treated as per label.
Sinecatechins (Veregen)	15% ointment. Apply 0.5 cm strand to each wart three times per day until healing but not more than 16 weeks.	Application site reactions, which may result in ulcerations, phimosis, meatal stenosis, superinfection.

* See page 2 for abbreviations. NOTE: All dosage recommendations are for adults (unless otherwise indicated) and assume normal renal function.

TABLE 14C – AT A GLANCE SUMMARY OF SUGGESTED ANTIVIRAL AGENTS AGAINST TREATABLE PATHOGENIC VIRUSES

ANTIVIRAL AGENT

Virus	Acyclovir	Amantadine	Adefovir Entecavir Lamivudine Tenofovir	Boceprevir Telaprevir	Cidofovir	Famciclovir	Foscarnet	Ganciclovir	αInterferon Or PEG INF	Oseltamivir	Ribavirin	Rimantadine	Valacyclovir	Valganciclovir	Zanamivir
Adenovirus					+			±						±	
BK virus					+										
Cytomegalovirus	±				+++	±	+++	+++					±	+++	
Hepatitis B			+++						+++		±				
Hepatitis C				++++*					+++*		+++*				
Herpes simplex virus	+++					+++	+++						+++		
Influenza A		±***								+++***		±***			+++
Influenza B										+++					+++
JC Virus					+										
Respiratory Syncytial Virus											+				
Varicella-zoster virus	+					+	+	+					+++	+	

* 1st line rx = an IFN + Ribavirin plus either Boceprevir or Telaprevir if Genotype 1
*** High level resistance H1N1 (non-swine) in 2008; Swine H1N1 susceptible.
** not CDC recommended due to high prevalence of resistance

- = no activity; ± = possible activity; + = active, 3rd line therapy (least active clinically)
++ = Active, 2nd line therapy (less active clinically); +++ = Active, 1st line therapy (usually active clinically)

TABLE 14D – ANTIRETROVIRAL THERAPY (ART) IN TREATMENT-NAÏVE ADULTS (HIV/AIDS)

(See the SANFORD GUIDE TO HIV/AIDS THERAPY 2013 for additional information)

The U.S. Dept of Health & Human Svcs (DHHS) provides updated guidelines on a regular basis; the most recent update of the HHS Guidelines was September 2012. These, as well as recommendations for anti-retroviral therapy (ART) in pregnant women and in children, are available at www.aidsinfo.nih.gov. These documents provide detailed recommendations and explanations, and additional alternatives concerning the use of ART. The new Guidelines include: (1) recommendations to start therapy at any CD4 count for asymptomatic patients unless there is a reason to defer treatment; the strength of the recommendation increases with lower CD4 count values; (2) Addition of new sections on HIV and Aging patients and Cost of ART (now included as Table 6(I)). (3) New recommendations for starting ART for those patients presenting with TB. For patients with CD4 counts <50 cells/mm³, ART should be initiated within 2 weeks of starting TB treatment (AI).

- For patients with CD4 counts ≥50 cells/mm³ with clinical disease of major severity as indicated by clinical evaluation (including low Karnofsky score, low body mass index [BMI], low hemoglobin, low albumin, organ system dysfunction, or extent of disease), the Panel recommends initiation of ART within 2 to 4 weeks of starting TB treatment (BI for CD4 count 50–200 cells/mm³ and BIII for CD4 count >200 cells/mm³).
- For other patients with CD4 counts ≥50 cells/mm³, ART can be delayed beyond 2 to 4 weeks but should be started by 8 to 12 weeks of TB therapy (AI for CD4 count 50–500 cells/mm³ and BIII for CD4 count >500 cells/mm³). Note that immune reconstitution syndromes (IRIs or IRIS) may result from initiation of any ART, and may require medical intervention.

The following principles and concepts guide therapy:

- The goal of rx is to inhibit maximally viral replication, allowing re-establishment & persistence of an effective immune response that will prevent or delay HIV-related morbidity.
- Fully undetectable levels of virus is the target of therapy for ALL patients, regardless of stage of disease or number/type of prior regimens.
- The lower the viral RNA can be driven, the lower the rate of accumulation of drug resistance mutations and the longer the therapeutic effect will last.
- To achieve maximal & durable suppression of viral RNA, combinations of potent antiretroviral agents are required, as is a high degree of adherence to the chosen regimens.
- Virologic failure is defined as confirmed virus > 200 c/mL.
- Treatment regimens must be tailored to the individual as well as to the virus.
- Resistance testing (genotype) should be performed prior to the initiation of ARV therapy. Antiretroviral drug toxicities can compromise adherence in the short term & can cause significant negative health effects over time. Carefully check for specific risks to the individual, for interactions between the antiretrovirals selected & between those & concurrent drugs, & adjust doses as necessary for body weight, for renal or hepatic dysfunction, & for possible pharmacokinetic interactions.

A. When to start therapy? (www.aidsinfo.nih.gov)

Guidelines	Any symptoms or CD4 <200/µL	CD4 200-350/µL	CD4 350-500/µL	CD4 >500/µL
IAS-USA: JAMA 308: 387, 2012	Treat	Treat	Treat	Consider Treatment* * No Apparent Harm in treating earlier
DHHS: www.aidsinfo.nih.gov	Treat	Treat	Treat	Treat* * Strength of rating increases as CD4 count decreases

Life Cycle of HIV With Sites of Action of Antiretrovirals

Fusion / Entry	Reverse Transcription	Integration	Maturation
Enfuvirtide Maraviroc	**nRTI** Zidovudine Stavudine Zalcitabine Didanosine Abacavir Lamivudine Tenofovir Emtricitabine **NNRTI** Nevirapine Efavirenz Delavirdine Etravirine Rilpivirine	Elvitegravir/ cobicistat Raltegravir	**Protease Inhibitors** Saquinavir Ritonavir Indinavir Nelfinavir Fos-Amprenavir Lopinavir Atazanavir Tipranavir Darunavir

TABLE 14D (2)

B. **Approach to constructing ART regimens for treatment naive adults.** *(See Guidelines for the Use of Antiretroviral Agents in HIV-1-Infected Adults and Adolescents at www.aidsinfo.nih.gov. for updates and further alternatives.)*

- See Section D for specific regimens and tables which follow for drug characteristics, usual doses, adverse effects and additional details.
- Selection of components will be influenced by many factors, such as:
  - Co-morbidities (e.g., lipid effects of PIs, liver or renal disease, etc)
  - Pregnancy (e.g., avoid efavirenz, particularly in the first trimester when the neural tube is forming —pregnancy class D)
  - HIV status (e.g., avoid nevirapine in women with CD4 >250 and men with CD4 >400)
  - Results of viral resistance testing (recommended for all patients prior to initiation of ART)
  - Potential drug interactions or adverse drug effects; special focus on tolerability (even low grade side effects can profoundly effect adherence)
  - Convenience of dosing

Select 1 drug in *column A* +1 NRTI combination in *column B*	A	Initial Combination Regimen for ARV Naïve Patients	
		B	COMMENTS
Preferred	**NNRTI** • Efavirenz (600 mg/qhs) **Ritonavir-Boosted PI** • Atazanavir/rit (300/100 qd) • Darunavir/rit (800/100 qd) **Integrase Inhibitor** • Raltegravir (400 BID) • Elvitegravir/ Cobicistat (150/150 qd)	Tenofovir / FTC (300/200 qd) FTC = **Emtricitabine** FTC + Tenofovir = **Truvada** FTC + Tenofovir + Efavirenz = **Atripla** FTC + Tenofovir + Elvitegravir/Cobi = **Stribild**	Co-formulations increase convenience, but sometimes prescribing the two components individually is preferred, as when dose adjustments are needed for renal disease. **ATV/r** should not be used in patients who require >20 mg omeprazole equivalent per day. No / little data on Raltegravir + any other nRTI regimens. RTG 600 mg once daily not quite as effective as 400 mg bid. No data on ElVitegravir + cobicistat with other nucleosides.
Alternative	**NNRTI** • Rilpivirine (25 qd) • Etravirine (200 mg bid or 400 mg qd) **Ritonavir-Boosted PI** • Fosamprenavir/rit (1400/100 qd) • Lopinavir/rit (400/100 qd) • Saquinavir/rit (1000/100 bid)	**(in order of preference)** Tenofovir / FTC (300/200 qd) Abacavir/3TC (600/300 qd) Zidovudine/ 3TC (300/150 bid) FTC + TDF + RPV = **Complera/Eviplera**	Viramune XR 400 mg preferred formulation Rilpivirine is best used for patients with VL < 100K. Rilpivirine should not be used with any PPI therapy. Lopinavir Ritonavir should not be used once daily in pregnant women (should only be used twice daily) Etravirine and Rilpivirine are options for some patients who have NNRTI resistance mutations (e.g., K103N) at baseline. Expert consultation is recommended.
Acceptable	**NNRTI** • Nevirapine (400 qd) **Non-boosted PI** • Fosamprenavir (1400 bid) • Atazanavir (400 qd) • *Nelfinavir* (1250 bid) **Boosted PI** • Saquinavir/rit (1000/100 bid)** **CCR5 INHIBITOR** • Maraviroc (300 bid)** ** *Dosing effected by drug-drug interactions*	**(in order of preference)** Tenofovir/FTC (300/200 qd) Abacavir/3TC (600/300 qd) ddI (300) + 3TC (300) or FTC (200)	Nevirapine should be used with caution with ABC owing to possible overlap of idiosyncratic hypersensitivity. Saquinavir associated with prolonged QTc. Boosted PIs can be administered once or twice daily. Non-boosted PIs are typically less preferred than boosted PIs. *Nelfinavir is used most often in pregnant women as an alternative PI. It has inferior virologic responses.* No data on MVC and any NRTIs other than ZDV/3TC.

C. **During pregnancy.** Expert consultation mandatory. Timing of rx initiation & drug choice must be individualized. Viral resistance testing should be strongly considered. Long-term effects of agents unknown. Certain drugs hazardous or contraindicated. *(See Table 8A.)* For additional information & alternative options, see www.aidsinfo.nih.gov.

TABLE 14D (3)

D. Antiretroviral Therapies That Should NOT Be Offered (Modified from www.aidsinfo.nih.gov)

1. Regimens not recommended

	Regimen	Logic	Exception
a.	Monotherapy with NRTI	Rapid development of resistance & inferior antiviral activity	Perhaps ZDV to reduce peripartum mother-to-child transmission. See Perinatal Guidelines at www.aidsinfo.nih.gov and Table 20B, Sanford Guide to HIV/AIDS Therapy
b.	Dual NRTI combinations	Resistance and inferior antiretroviral activity compared with standard drug combinations	Perhaps ZDV to reduce peripartum mother-to-child transmission. See Perinatal Guidelines at www.aidsinfo.nih.gov and Table 8B, Sanford Guide to HIV/AIDS Therapy
c.	Triple-NRTI combinations	Triple-NRTI regimens have shown inferior virologic efficacy in clinical trials: (tenofovir + lamivudine + abacavir) & (didanosine + lamivudine + tenofovir) & others	(Zidovudine + lamivudine + abacavir) or (zidovudine + lamivudine + tenofovir) might be used if no alternative exists.
d.	Double Boosted PIs	Using 2 or more PI agents boosted with ritonavir adds nothing in terms of anti-HIV activity but can add extra toxicity	No exceptions
e.	2 NNRTI agents	Increased rate of side effects. Drug-drug interaction between etravirine and nevirapine and etravirine and efavirenz	No exceptions

2. Drug, or drugs, not recommended as part of antiretroviral regimen

		Logic	Exception
a.	Saquinavir hard gel cap or tab (Invirase), darunavir, or tipranavir as single (unboosted) PI	Bioavailability only 4%, inferior antiretroviral activity	No exceptions
b.	Stavudine + didanosine	High frequency of toxicity, peripheral neuropathy, pancreatitis & mitochondrial toxicity (lactic acidosis). In pregnancy: lactic acid acidosis, hepatic steatosis, ± pancreatitis	Toxicity partially offset by potent antiretroviral activity of the combination. Use only when potential benefits outweigh the sizeable risks.
c.	Efavirenz in pregnancy or in women who might become pregnant	Teratogenic in non-human primates. **Pregnancy Category D—may cause fetal harm**	Only if no other option available; major risk would be 1st trimester (first 4-6 weeks as neural tube is forming in fetus). Note that oral contraceptives alone may not be reliable for prevention of pregnancy in women on ART or other medications (see Safety & Toxicity of Individual Agents in Pregnancy at www.aidsinfo.nih.gov).
d.	Stavudine + zidovudine	Antagonistic	No exceptions
e.	Atazanavir + indinavir	Additive risk of hyperbilirubinemia	No exceptions
f.	Emtricitabine + lamivudine	Same target and resistance profile	No exceptions
g.	Abacavir + tenofovir	Rapid development of K65R mutation; loss of effect	Can avoid if zidovudine also used in the regimen; might be an option for salvage therapy but not earlier lines of therapy.
h.	Tenofovir + didanosine	Reduced CD4 cell count increase; concern of K 65R development	Use with caution. Likely increases ddI concentrations and serious ddI toxicities
i.	Abacavir + didanosine	Insufficient data in naïve patients	Use with caution

E.

1. **Selected Characteristics of Antiretroviral Drugs** (CPE = CSF penetration effectiveness)

Selected Characteristics of Nucleoside or Nucleotide Reverse Transcriptase Inhibitors (NRTIs)

All agents may have Black Box warning: Risk of lactic acidosis/hepatic steatosis. Also, labels note risk of fat redistribution/accumulation with ARV therapy. For combinations, see warnings for component agents.

* CPE (CNS Penetration Effectiveness) value: 1 = Low Penetration; 2 - 3 = Intermediate Penetration; 4 = Highest Penetration into CNS (Letendre, et al, CROI 2010, abs #430)

TABLE 14D (4)

Generic/ Trade Name	Pharmaceutical Prep.	Usual Adult Dosage & Food Effect	% Absorbed, po	Serum T½, hrs	Intracellular T½, hrs	CPE*	Elimination	Major Adverse Events/Comments (See Table 14E)
Abacavir (ABC; Ziagen)	300 mg tabs or 20 mg/mL oral solution	300 mg po bid or 600 mg po q24h Food OK	83	1.5	20	1	Liver metab., renal excretion of metabolites, 82%	**Hypersensitivity reaction:** fever, rash, N/V, malaise, diarrhea, abdominal pain, respiratory symptoms. (Severe reactions may be ↑ with 600 mg dose. **Do not rechallenge! Test HLA-B*5701 before use. See Comment Table 14E.** Studies raise concerns re ABC/3TC regimens in pts with VL ≥ 100,000 (www.niaid.nih.gov/ news/newsreleases/2008/actg5202bulletin.htm). Recent report suggests possible ↑ risk of cardiac event in pts with other cardiac risk factors (D:A:D study group Lancet 2008; updated CROI 2009, LB abst 44).
Abacavir (ABC)/lamivudine (3TC) (Epzicom or Kivexa)	Film coated tabs ABC 600 mg + 3TC 300 mg	1 tab once daily (not recommended)			(See individual components)			(See Comments for individual components) Note: **Black Box warnings** for ABC hypersensitivity reaction & others. Should only be used for regimens intended to include these 3 agents. Black Box warning— limited data for VL >100,000 copies/mL. Not recommended as initial therapy because of inferior virologic efficacy.
Abacavir (ABC)/ lamivudine (3TC)/ zidovudine (AZT) (Trizivir)	Film-coated tabs: ABC 300 mg + 3TC 150 mg + ZDV 300 mg	1 tab po bid (not recommended for wt. <40 kg or CrCl <50 mL/min or impaired hepatic function)						
Didanosine (ddI; Videx or Videx EC)	125, 200, 250, 400 enteric-coated caps; 100, 167, 250 mg powder for oral solution;	≥60 kg Usually 400 mg enteric-coated po q24h 0.5 h before or 2 h after meal. Do not crush. <60 kg: 250 mg EC po q24h. Food ↓ levels. See Comment	30–40	1.6	25–40	2	Renal excretion, 50%	Pancreatitis, peripheral neuropathy, lactic acidosis & hepatic steatosis (rare but life-threatening, esp. combined with stavudine in pregnancy). Retinal, optic nerve changes. **The combination ddI + TDF is generally avoided, but if used,** reduce dose of ddI-EC from 400 mg to 250 mg EC q24h (or from 250 mg EC to 200 mg EC for adults <60 kg). **Monitor for ↑ toxicity & possible ↓ in efficacy of this combination; may result in ↓ CD4.** Possibly associated with noncirrhotic portal hypertension.

TABLE 14D (5)

E. **Selected Characteristics of Antiretroviral Drugs** (CPE = CSF penetration effectiveness)

1. **Selected Characteristics of Nucleoside or Nucleotide Reverse Transcriptase Inhibitors (NRTIs)** *(continued)*

Generic/ Trade Name	Pharmaceutical Prep.	Usual Adult Dosage & Food Effect	% Absorbed, po	Serum T½, hrs	Intracellular T½, hrs	CPE*	Elimination	Major Adverse Events/Comments (See Table 14E)
Emtricitabine (FTC, Emtriva)	200 mg caps; 10 mg per mL oral solution.	200 mg po q24h. Food OK	93 (caps), 75 (oral sol'n)	Approx. 10	39	3	Renal excretion 86%, minor biotransformation, 14% excretion in feces	Well tolerated; headache, nausea, vomiting & diarrhea occasionally, skin rash rarely. Skin hyperpigmentation. Differs only slightly in structure from lamivudine (5-fluoro substitution). **Exacerbation of Hep B reported in pts after stopping FTC.** Monitor at least several months after stopping FTC in Hep B pts; some may need anti-HBV therapy.
Emtricitabine/ tenofovir disoproxil fumarate (TRUVADA)	Film-coated tabs: FTC 200 mg + TDF 300 mg	1 tab po q24h for CrCl ≥50 mL/min. Food OK	92/25	10/17	—	*(See individual components)*	Primarily renal/renal	*See Comments for individual agents* **Black Box warning—Exacerbation of HepB after stopping FTC;** but preferred therapy for those with Hep B.
Emtricitabine/ tenofovir/efavirenz (ATRIPLA)	Film-coated tabs: FTC 200 mg + TDF 300 mg + efavirenz 600 mg	1 tab po q24h on an empty stomach, preferably at bedtime. Do not use if CrCl <50 mL/min	*(See individual components)*					Not recommended for pts <18 yrs. *(See warnings for individual components).* **Exacerbation of Hep B** reported in pts discontinuing component drugs; some may need anti-HBV therapy (preferred anti-Hep B therapy). **Pregnancy category D**- may cause fetal harm. Avoid in pregnancy or in women who may become pregnant.
Emtricitabine/ tenofovir/rilpivirine (COMPLERA/ EVIPLERA)	Film-coated tabs: FTC 200 mg + TDF 300 mg + RPL 25 mg	1 tab po q24h with food			*(See individual components)*	*(See individual components)*		*See individual characteristics.* Preferred use in pts with HIV RNA level <100,000 c/mL. Should not be used with PPI agents.
Lamivudine (3TC, Epivir)	150, 300 mg tabs; 10 mg/mL oral solution	150 mg po bid or 300 mg po q24h. Food OK	86	5–7	18	2	Renal excretion, minimal metabolism	**Use HIV dose, not Hep B dose.** Usually well-tolerated. **Risk of exacerbation of Hep B after stopping 3TC.** Monitor at least several months after stopping 3TC in Hep B pts; some may need anti-HBV therapy.
Lamivudine/ abacavir (Epzicom)	Film-coated tabs: 3TC 300 mg + abacavir 600 mg	1 tab po q24h. Food OK Not recommended for CrCl <50 mL/min or impaired hepatic function	86/86	5–7/1.5	16/20	*(See individual components)*	Primarily renal/ metabolism	*See Comments for individual agents.* **Note abacavir hypersensitivity Black Box warnings** (severe reactions may be somewhat more frequent with 600 mg dose) and 3TC Hep B warnings. Test HLA-B*5701 before use.
Lamivudine/ zidovudine (Combivir)	Film-coated tabs: 3TC 150 mg + ZDV 300 mg	1 tab po bid. Not recommended for CrCl <50 mL/min or impaired hepatic function Food OK	86/64	5–7/ 0.5–3	—	*(See individual components)*	Primarily renal/ metabolism with renal excretion of glucuronide	*See Comments for individual agents* **Black Box warning**—exacerbation of Hep B in pts stopping 3TC

TABLE 14D (6)

E. Selected Characteristics of Antiretroviral Drugs (CPE = CSF penetration effectiveness)

1. Selected Characteristics of Nucleoside or Nucleotide Reverse Transcriptase Inhibitors (NRTIs) (continued)

Generic/ Trade Name	Pharmaceutical Prep.	Usual Adult Dosage & Food Effect	% Absorbed, po	Serum T½, hrs	Intracellular T½, hrs	CPE*	Elimination	Major Adverse Events/Comments (See Table 14E)
Stavudine (d4T, Zerit)	15, 20, 30, 40 mg capsules; 1 mg per mL oral solution	≥60 kg: 40 mg po bid <60 kg: 30 mg po bid Food OK	86	1.2–1.6	3.5	2	Renal excretion, 40%	Not recommended by DHHS as initial therapy because of adverse reactions. **Highest incidence of lipoatrophy, hyperlipidemia, & lactic acidosis of all NRTIs.** Pancreatitis. Peripheral neuropathy. (See didanosine comments.)
Tenofovir disoproxil fumarate (TDF; Viread)— a nucleotide	300 mg tabs	CrCl ≥50 mL/min: 300 mg po q24h. Food OK; high-fat meal ↑ absorption	39 (with food) 25 (fasted)	17	>60	1	Renal excretion	Headache. N/V. **Cases of renal dysfunction reported:** check renal function before using (dose reductions necessary if CrCl <50 cc/min); avoid concomitant nephrotoxic agents. One study found ↑ renal function at 48-wks in pts receiving TDF with a PI (mostly lopinavir/ritonavir) than with a NNRTI (JID 197:102, 2008). Must adjust dose of ddI (↓) if used concomitantly but best to avoid this combination (see ddI Comments). Atazanavir & lopinavir/ritonavir ↑ tenofovir concentrations: monitor for adverse effects. **Black Box warning— exacerbations of Hep B reported after stopping tenofovir.** Monitor several months after stopping TDF in Hep B pts; some may need anti-HBV Rx.
Zidovudine (ZDV, AZT, Retrovir)	100 mg caps, 300 mg tabs; 10 mg per mL IV solution, 10 mg/mL oral syrup	300 mg po q12h. Food OK	64	1.1	11	4	Metabolized to glucuronide & excreted in urine	Bone marrow suppression. GI intolerance. headache, insomnia, malaise, myopathy.

2. Selected Characteristics of Non-Nucleoside Reverse Transcriptase Inhibitors (NNRTIs)

Delavirdine (Rescriptor)	100, 200 mg tabs	400 mg po three times daily. Food OK	85	5.8	3		Cytochrome P450 (3A inhibitor). 51% excreted in urine (<5% unchanged), 44% in feces	Rash severe enough to stop drug in 4.3% ↑ AST/ALT, headaches. **Use of this agent is not recommended.**

TABLE 14D (7)

E. **Selected Characteristics of Antiretroviral Drugs** (CPE = CSF penetration effectiveness)

2. **Selected Characteristics of Non-Nucleoside Reverse Transcriptase Inhibitors (NNRTIs)** *(continued)*

Generic/Trade Name	Pharmaceutical Prep.	Usual Adult Dosage & Food Effect	% Absorbed, po	Serum T½, hrs	Intracellular T½, hrs	CPE*	Elimination	Major Adverse Events/Comments *(See Table 14E)*
Efavirenz (Sustiva) **(Pregnancy Category D)**	50, 100, 200 mg capsules; 600 mg tablet	600 mg po q24h at bedtime, without food. Food may ↑ serum conc., which can lead to ↑ in risk of adverse events.	42	40–55 See Comment	3		Cytochrome P450 (3A mixed inducer/inhibitor). 14–34% of dose excreted in urine as glucuronidated metabolites, 16–61% in feces	Rash severe enough to dc use of drug in 1.7%. High frequency of diverse CNS AEs: somnolence, dreams, confusion, agitation. Serious psychiatric symptoms. Certain CYP2B6 polymorphisms may predict exceptionally high plasma levels with standard doses (CID 45:1230, 2007). False-pos. cannabinoid screen. **Pregnancy Category D—may cause fetal harm—avoid in pregnant women or those who might become pregnant.** Use another method of contraception is 100% reliable). Very long tissue T½. **If rx to be discontinued, stop efavirenz 1–2 wks before stopping companion drugs.** Otherwise, risk of developing efavirenz resistance, as after 1–2 days only efavirenz in blood &/or tissue. Some authorities bridge this gap by adding a PI to the NRTI backbone if feasible after efavirenz is discontinued (CID 42:401, 2006)
Etravirine (Intelence)	100 mg tabs	200 mg twice daily after a meal	Unknown (↓ systemic exposure if taken fasting)	41	2		Metabolized by CYP 3A4 (inducer) & 2C9, 2C19 (inhibitor). Excreted into feces (>90%), mostly unchanged drug.	For pts with HIV-1 resistant to NNRTIs & others. Active in vitro against most such isolates. Rash common, but rarely can be severe. Potential for multiple drug interactions. Generally, multiple mutations are required for high-level resistance. See Table 3C, page 16. Sanford Guide to HIV/AIDS Therapy, for specific mutations and effects. Because of interactions, do not use with boosted atazanavir, boosted tipranavir, unboosted PIs, or other NNRTIs.
Nevirapine (Viramune) Viramune XR	200 mg tabs; 50 mg per 5 mL oral suspension; XR 400 mg tabs	200 mg po q24h x 14 days & then 200 mg po bid (see comments & **Black Box warning**) Food OK. **If using Viramune XR, start the lead in dosing of 200 mg q24h prior to using 400 mg/d**	>90	25–30	4		Cytochrome P450 (3A4, 2B6) inducer. 80% of dose excreted in urine as glucuronidated metabolites, 10% in feces	**Black Box warning—fatal hepatotoxicity.** Women with CD4 >250 esp. vulnerable, inc. pregnant women. Avoid in this group unless benefits clearly > risks (www.fda.gov/cder/drug/advisory/nevirapine.htm). If used, intensive monitoring required. Men with CD4 >400 also at ↑ risk. Rash severe enough to stop drug in 7%, **severe or life-threatening skin reactions** in 2%. Do not restart if any suspicion of such reactions. As with dose escalation period may ↓ skin reactions. As rash is a marker of long-term efficacy, consider continuing companion agents for several days if nevirapine is discontinued

TABLE 14D (8)

E. Selected Characteristics of Antiretroviral Drugs (CPE = CSF penetration effectiveness)

2. Selected Characteristics of Non-Nucleoside Reverse Transcriptase Inhibitors (NNRTIs) *(continued)*

Generic/ Trade Name	Pharmaceutical Prep.	Usual Adult Dosage & Food Effect	% Absorbed, po	Serum T½, hrs	Intracellular T½, hrs	CPE*	Elimination	Major Adverse Events/Comments (See Table 14E)
Rilpivirine (Edurant)	25 mg tabs	25 mg daily with food	absolute bio-availability unknown; 40% lower Cmax in fasted state	50	unknown		Metabolized by Cyp3A4 majority of drug metabolized by liver; 25% excreted unchanged in feces.	QTc prolongation with doses higher than 50 mg per day. Most common side effects are depression, insomnia, headache, and rash. Rilpivirine should not be co-administered with carbamazepine, phenobarbital, phenytoin, rifabutin, rifampin, rifapentine, proton pump inhibitors, or multiple doses of dexamethasone. A fixed dose combination of rilpivirine + TDF/FTC (Complera/Eviplera) is approved. **Needs stomach acid for absorption. Do not administer with PPI.**

3. Selected Characteristics of Protease Inhibitors (PIs).

All PIs: Glucose metabolism: new diabetes mellitus or deterioration of glucose control; possible hemophilia bleeding; hypertriglyceridemia or hypercholesterolemia. Exercise caution re: potential drug interactions & contraindications. QTc prolongation has been reported in a few pts taking PIs; some PIs can block hERG channels in vitro (*Lancet 365:682, 2005*).

Generic/ Trade Name	Pharmaceutical Prep.	Usual Adult Dosage & Food Effect	% Absorbed, po	Serum T½, hrs		CPE*	Elimination	Major Adverse Events/Comments (See Table 14E)
Atazanavir (Reyataz)	100, 150, 200, 300 mg capsules	400 mg po q24h with food. Ritonavir-boosted PIs (atazanavir 300 mg po q24h + ritonavir 100 mg po q24h) with food, is recommended for ART-experienced pts. The boosted dose is also used when combined with either efavirenz 600 mg po q24h (or TDF 300 mg po q24h. If used with buffered ddI, take with food 2 hrs pre or 1 hr post ddI.	Good oral bioavailability; food enhances bioavailability & ↓ pharmacokinetic variability. Absorption ↓ by antacids, H₂-blockers, proton pump inhibitors. Avoid unboosted drug with PIs/H₂-blockers. Boosted drug can be used with or > 10 hr after or > 12 hr after a PPI, as long as limited doses of the acid agents are used (see 2008 *drug label changes*).	Approx. 7		2	Cytochrome P450 (3A4, 1A2 & 2C9 inhibitor) & UGT1A1 inhibitor, 13% excreted in urine (7% unchanged); 79% excreted in feces (20% unchanged)	Lower potential for ↑ lipids. Asymptomatic unconjugated hyperbilirubinemia common; jaundice especially likely in Gilbert's syndrome (*JID 192:1381, 2005*). Headache, rash. GI symptoms. Prolongation of PR interval (1st degree AV block) reported. Caution in pre-existing conduction system disease. Efavirenz & tenofovir ↓ atazanavir exposure: use atazanavir/ritonavir regimen; also, atazanavir + tenofovir concentrations—watch for adverse events. In rx-experienced pts taking TDF and needing H2 blockers, atazanavir 400 mg with ritonavir 100 mg can be given; do not use PPIs. Compared to PIs, increased risk of renal stones, p<0.001 (*CID 55:1262, 2012*).
Darunavir (Prezista)	400 mg, 600 mg tablets	(600 mg darunavir + 100 mg ritonavir) po bid, with food or (800 mg darunavir (two 400 mg tabs) + 100 mg ritonavir) po once daily with food (Preferred regimen in ART naive pts)	82% absorbed (taken with ritonavir). Food ↑ absorption.	Approx 15 hr (with ritonavir)		3	Metabolized by CYP3A and is a CYP3A inhibitor	Once daily dosing regimen mostly in 1st line therapy. Contains sulfa moiety. Rash, nausea, headaches seen. Coadmin of certain drugs cleared by CYP3A is contraindicated (*see label*). Use with caution in pts with hepatic dysfunction. (Recent FDA warning about occasional hepatic dysfunction early in the course of treatment). Monitor carefully, esp. first several months and with pre-existing liver disease. May cause hormonal contraception failure.

TABLE 14D (9)

E. Selected Characteristics of Antiretroviral Drugs (CPE = CSF penetration effectiveness)

3. Selected Characteristics of Protease Inhibitors (PIs). (continued)

Generic/ Trade Name	Pharmaceutical Prep.	Usual Adult Dosage & Food Effect	% Absorbed, po	Serum T½, hrs	CPE*	Elimination	Major Adverse Events/Comments (See Table 14E)
Fosamprenavir (Lexiva)	700 mg tablet; 50 mg/mL oral suspension	1400 mg (two 700 mg tabs) po q12h **OR** po q24h with ritonavir [1400 mg fosamprenavir (2 tabs) + ritonavir 200 mg] po q24h **OR** [1400 mg fosamprenavir (2 tabs) + ritonavir 100 mg] po q24h **OR** [700 mg fosamprenavir (1 tab) + ritonavir 100 mg] po bid	Bioavailability not established. Food OK	7.7 Amprenavir	3	Hydrolyzed to amprenavir, then acts as cytochrome P450 (3A4 substrate, inhibitor, inducer)	Amprenavir prodrug. Contains sulfa moiety. Potential for serious drug interactions (see label). Rash, including Stevens-Johnson syndrome. Once daily not recommended for PI-experienced pts. (1) additional ritonavir needed if given with efavirenz (see label). Booster twice daily regimen is recommended for PI-experienced pts. Potential for PI cross-resistance with darunavir
Indinavir (Crixivan)	100, 200, 400 mg capsules. Store in original container with desiccant	Two 400 mg caps (800 mg) po q8h, without food or with light meal. Can take with enteric-coated Videx. [If taken with ritonavir (e.g., 800 mg indinavir + 100 mg ritonavir po q12h), no food restrictions]	65	1.2–2	4	Cytochrome P450 (3A4 inhibitor)	**Maintain hydration. Nephrolithiasis**, nausea, inconsequential ↑ of indirect bilirubin (jaundice in Gilbert syndrome). ↑ AST/ALT, headache, asthenia, blurred vision, metallic taste, hemolysis. ↑ urine WBC (>100/hpf) has been assoc. with nephritis/ medullary calcification, cortical atrophy.
Lopinavir + ritonavir (Kaletra)	(200 mg lopinavir + 50 mg ritonavir), and (100 mg lopinavir + 25 mg ritonavir) tablets. Tabs do not need refrigeration. Oral solution: (80 mg lopinavir + 20 mg ritonavir) per mL. Refrigerate, but can be kept at room temp. (≤77°F) x 2 mos.	(400 mg lopinavir + 100 mg ritonavir)—2 tabs po bid. Higher dose may be needed in non-rx-naive pts when used with efavirenz, nevirapine, or unboosted fosamprenavir. [Dose adjustment in concomitant drugs may be necessary, see Table 17A]	No food effect with tablets.	5–6	3	Cytochrome P450 (3A4 inhibitor)	Nausea/vomiting/diarrhea (worse when administered with zidovudine), ↑ AST/ALT, pancreatitis. Oral solution 42% alcohol. Lopinavir + ritonavir can be taken as a single daily dose of 4 tabs (total 800 mg lopinavir + 200 mg ritonavir), except in treatment-experienced pts or those taking concomitant efavirenz, nevirapine, amprenavir, or nelfinavir. Possible PR and QT prolongation. Use with caution in those with cardiac conduction abnormalities or when used with drugs with similar effects.
Nelfinavir (Viracept)	625, 250 mg tabs; 50 mg/gm oral powder	Two 625 mg tabs (1250 mg) po bid, with food	20–80 Food ↑ exposure & ↓ variability	3.5–5	1	Cytochrome P450 (3A4 inhibitor)	Diarrhea. Coadministration of drugs with life-threatening toxicities & which are cleared by CYP3A4 is contraindicated. Not recommended in initial regimens because of inferior efficacy; prior concerns about EMS now resolved. **Acceptable choice in pregnant women although it has inferior virologic efficacy than most other ARV anchor drugs.**

TABLE 14D (10)

E. Selected Characteristics of Antiretroviral Drugs (CPE = CSF penetration effectiveness)

3. Selected Characteristics of Protease Inhibitors (PIs). (continued)

Generic/ Trade Name	Pharmaceutical Prep.	Usual Adult Dosage & Food Effect	% Absorbed, po	Serum T½, hrs	CPE*	Elimination	Major Adverse Events/Comments (See Table 14E)
Ritonavir (Norvir)	100mg capsules; 600 mg per 7.5 mL solution. Refrigerate caps but not solution. Room temperature for 1 mo. is OK.	Full dose not recommended (see comments). **With rare exceptions, used exclusively to enhance pharmacokinetics of other PIs, using lower ritonavir doses.**	Food ↑ absorption	3–5	1	Cytochrome P450: 3A4 & 2 d6 inhibitor)	Nausea/vomiting/diarrhea, extremity & circumoral paresthesias, hepatitis, pancreatitis, taste perversion, ↑ CPK & uric acid. **Black Box warning**—potentially fatal drug interactions. Many drug interactions—see Table 22A–Table 22B
Saquinavir (Invirase)—hard gel caps or tabs) + **ritonavir**	Saquinavir 200 mg caps, 500 mg film-coated tabs; ritonavir 100 mg caps	[2 tabs saquinavir (1000 mg)] + 1 cap ritonavir (100 mg)] po bid with food	Erratic; 4 (saquinavir alone). Much more reliably absorbed when boosted with ritonavir.	1–2	1	Cytochrome P450 (3A4 inhibitor)	Nausea, diarrhea, headache, ↑ AST/ALT. Avoid rifampin with saquinavir + ritonavir: ↑ hepatitis risk. **Black Box warning**—Invirase to be used only with ritonavir. Possible QT prolongation. Use with caution in those with cardiac conduction abnormalities or when used with drugs with similar effects.
Tipranavir (Aptivus)	250 mg caps. Refrigerate unopened bottles. Use opened bottles within 2 mos. 100 mg/mL solution	[500 mg (two 250 mg caps) + ritonavir 200 mg] po bid with food.	Absorption low. ↑ with high fat meal. ↓ with Al⁺⁺ & Mg⁺⁺ antacids.	5.5–6	1	Cytochrome 3A4 but with ritonavir, most of drug is eliminated in feces.	Contains sulfa moiety. **Black Box warning—reports of fatal/nonfatal intracranial hemorrhage, hepatitis, fatal hepatic failure.** Use cautiously in liver disease, esp. hepB, hepC; contraindicated in Child-Pugh class B–C. Monitor LFTs. Coadministration of certain drugs contraindicated (see label). **For highly ART-experienced pts or for multiple-PI resistant virus.** Do not use tipranavir and etravirine together owing to 76% reduction in etravirine levels.

4. Selected Characteristics of Fusion Inhibitors

Generic/ Trade Name	Pharmaceutical Prep.	Usual Adult Dosage	% Absorbed	Serum T½, hrs	CPE*	Elimination	Major Adverse Events/Comments (See Table 14E)
Enfuvirtide (T20, Fuzeon)	Single-use vials of 90 mg/mL, when reconstituted. Vials should be stored at room temperature. Reconstituted vials can be refrigerated for 24 hrs only.	90 mg (1 mL) subcut. bid. Rotate injection sites, avoiding those currently inflamed.	84	3.8	1	Catabolism to its constituent amino acids with subsequent recycling of the amino acids in the body pool. Elimination pathway(s) have not been performed in humans. Does not alter the metabolism of CYP3A4, CYP2 d6, CYP1A2, CYP2C19 or CYP2E1 substrates.	Local reaction site reactions 98%, 4% discontinue; erythema/induration ~80–90%, nodules/cysts ~80%. **Hypersensitivity reactions reported** (fever, rash, chills. N/V, ↓ BP, &/or ↑ AST/ALT)—do not restart if occur. Including background regimens, peripheral neuropathy 8.9%, insomnia 11.3%, ↓ appetite 6.3%, myalgia 5%, lymphadenopathy 2.3%, eosinophilia ~10%, ↑ incidence of bacterial pneumonias. Alone offers little benefit to a failing regimen (NEJM 348:2249, 2003).

TABLE 14D (11)

E. **Selected Characteristics of Antiretroviral Drugs** (CPE = CSF penetration effectiveness) (continued)

Generic/ Trade Name	Pharmaceutical Prep.	Usual Adult Dosage	% Absorbed	Serum T½, hrs	CPE*	Elimination	Major Adverse Events/Comments (See Table 14E)
5. Selected Characteristics of CCR-5 Co-receptor Antagonists							
Maraviroc (Selzentry)	150 mg, 300 mg film-coated tabs	Without regard to food: - 150 mg bid if concomitant meds include CYP3A inhibitors including PIs (except tipranavir/ritonavir) and delavirdine (with/without CYP3A inducers) - 300 mg bid without significantly interacting meds including NRTIs, tipranavir/ritonavir, nevirapine - 600 mg bid if concomitant meds include CYP3A inducers, including efavirenz (without strong CYP3A inhibitors)	Est. 33% with 300 mg dosage	14–18	3	CYP3A and P-glycoprotein substrate. Metabolites (via CYP3A) excreted feces > urine	**Black Box Warning–Hepatotoxicity,** may be preceded by rash, ↑ eos or IgE. NB: no hepatotoxicity was noted in MVC trials. Black box inserted owing to concern about potential CCR5 class effect. Data lacking in hepatic/renal insufficiency; ↑ concern with either could ↑ risk of ↓BP. Currently for treatment-experienced patients with multi-resistant strains. **Document CCR-5-tropic virus before use, as treatment failures assoc. with appearance of CXCR-4 or mixed-tropic virus.**
6. Selected Characteristics of Integrase Inhibitors							
Raltegravir (Isentress)	400 mg film-coated tabs	400 mg po bid, without regard to food	Unknown	~9	3	Glucuronidation via UGT1A1, with excretion into feces and urine. (Therefore does NOT require ritonavir boosting)	For both treatment naive patients and treatment experienced pts with multiply-resistant virus. Generally well-tolerated. Nausea, diarrhea, headache, fever similar to placebo. CK↑ & rhabdomyolysis reported, with unclear relationship to drug. Watch for increased depression in those with a history of depression. Low genetic barrier to resistance. Increase in CPK, myositis, rhabdomyolysis have been reported. Rare Stevens Johnson Syndrome.
Elvitegravir + cobicistat + FTC/TDF (Stribild)	150 mg ELV + 150 mg Cobi + 200 mg FTC + 300 mg TDF	one tab daily with or without food	<10%	12.9 (Cobi), 3.5 (ELV)	Un-known	The majority of **elvitegravir** metabolism is mediated by CYP3A enzymes. Elvitegravir also undergoes glucuronidation via UGT1A1/3 enzymes **Cobicistat** is metabolized by CYP3A and to a minor extent by CYP2D6	For both treatment naive patients and treatment experienced pts with multiply-resistant virus. Generally well-tolerated. Use of cobicistat increases serum creatinine by ~ 0.1 mg/dl via inhibition of proximal tubular enzyme; this does not result in reduction in true GFR but will result in erroneous apparent reduction in eGFR by MDRD or Cockcroft Gault calculations. Usual AEs are similar to those observed with ritonavir (cobi) and tenofovir/FTC. *(Lenendre, et al, CROI 2010, abs #430)*

* CPE (CNS Penetration Effectiveness) value: 1 = Low Penetration; 2 - 3 = Intermediate Penetration; 4 = Highest Penetration into CNS *(Letendre, et al, CROI 2010, abs #430)*

TABLE 14E– ANTIRETROVIRAL DRUGS & ADVERSE EFFECTS
(www.aidsinfo.nih.gov)
See also www.aidsinfo.nih.gov; for combinations, see individual components

DRUG NAME(S): GENERIC (TRADE)	MOST COMMON ADVERSE EFFECTS	MOST SIGNIFICANT ADVERSE EFFECTS
Nucleoside Reverse Transcriptase Inhibitors (NRTI) Black Box warning for all nucleoside/nucleotide RTIs: lactic acidosis/hepatic steatosis, potentially fatal. Also carry Warnings that fat redistribution and immune reconstitution syndromes (including autoimmune syndromes) with delayed onset) have been observed		
Abacavir (Ziagen)	Headache 7–13%, nausea 7–19%, diarrhea 7%, malaise 7–12%	**Black Box warning—Hypersensitivity reaction (HR)** in 8% with malaise, fever, GI upset, rash, lethargy & respiratory symptoms most commonly reported; myalgia, arthralgia, edema, paresthesia less common. **Discontinue immediately if HR suspected. Rechallenge contraindicated; may be life-threatening.** Severe HR may be more common with once-daily dosing. **HLA-B*5701 allele** predicts ↑ risk of HR in Caucasian pop., excluding pts with B*5701 ↓ ↑ HR incidence (NEJM 358:568, 2008; CID 46:1111-1118, 2008). DHHS guidelines recommend testing for B*5701 and use of abacavir-containing regimens only if HLA-B*5701 negative. Vigilance essential in all groups. Possible increased risk of MI with use of abacavir had been suggested (JID 201:318, 2010). Other studies found no increased risk of MI (CID 52: 929, 2011). A meta-analysis of randomized trials by FDA also did not show increased risk of MI (www.fda.gov/drugs/drugsafety/ucm245164.htm). Nevertheless, care is advised to optimize potentially modifiable risk factors when abacavir is used.
Didanosine (ddl) (Videx)	Diarrhea 28%, nausea 6% rash 9%, headache 7%, fever 12%, hyperuricemia 2%	**Pancreatitis 1–9%. Black Box warning—Cases of fatal & nonfatal pancreatitis** have occurred in pts receiving ddl, especially when used in combination with d4T or d4T + hydroxyurea. Fatal lactic acidosis in pregnancy with ddl + d4T. Peripheral neuropathy in 20%. 12% required dose reduction. ↑ toxicity and possible ↓ efficacy; may result in ↓ CD4. Rarely, retinal changes or optic neuropathy. Diabetes mellitus and macdodmyolysis reported in post-marketing surveillance. Possible increased risk of MI under study (www.fda.gov/CDER). Non-cirrhotic portal hypertension with ascites, varices, splenomegaly reported in post-marketing surveillance. *See also Clin Infect Dis 49:626, 2009; Amer J Gastroenterol 104:1707, 2009.*
Emtricitabine (FTC) (Emtriva)	Well tolerated. Headache, diarrhea, nausea, rash, skin hyperpigmentation	Potential for lactic acidosis (as with other NRTIs). Also in Black Box—**severe exacerbation of hepatitis B on stopping drug reported—monitor clinical/labs for several months after stopping in pts with hepB.** Anti-HBV rx may be warranted if FTC stopped.
Lamivudine (3TC) (Epivir)	Well tolerated. Headache 35%, nausea 33%, diarrhea 18%, abdominal pain 9%, insomnia 11% (all in combination with ZDV). Pancreatitis more common in pediatrics.	**Black Box warning.** Make sure to use HIV dosage, not Hep B dosage. **Exacerbation of hepatitis B on stopping lamivudine require close clinical/lab monitoring for several months.** **Patients with hepatitis B who stop lamivudine require close clinical/lab monitoring for several months.** Anti-HBV rx may be warranted if 3TC stopped.
Stavudine (d4T) (Zerit)	Diarrhea, nausea, vomiting, headache	**Peripheral neuropathy** 15–20%. Appears to produce lactic steatosis and lipoatrophy/lipodystrophy more commonly than other NRTIs. **Black Box warning—Fatal & nonfatal pancreatitis with d4T + ddl.** Use with TDF generally avoided (but would require dose reduction of ddl) because of ↑ toxicity and possible ↓ efficacy; may result in ↓ CD4. Rarely, retinal changes or optic neuropathy. Diabetes mellitus and macdodmyolysis reported in post-marketing surveillance. **Fatal lactic acidosis/steatosis in pregnant women receiving d4T + ddl.** Fatal and non-fatal lactic acidosis cases can occur in pregnancy. Use with particular caution in patients with risk factors for liver disease, but lactic acidosis can occur even in those without known risk factors. Possible ↑ toxicity if used with ribavirin. Motor weakness in the setting of lactic acidosis mimicking the clinical presentation of Guillain-Barré syndrome (including respiratory failure) (rare).
Zidovudine (ZDV, AZT) (Retrovir)	Nausea 50%, anorexia 20%, vomiting 17%, **headache 62%.** Also reported: asthenia, insomnia, myalgias, nail pigmentation. Macrocytosis expected with all dosage regimens.	**Black Box warning—hematologic toxicity, myopathy. Anemia** (<8 gm, 1%), granulocytopenia (<750, 1.8%), Anemia may respond to epoetin alfa if endogenous epoetin levels are ≤500 mU/ml at baseline (low). Myopathy (rare) with ↑ LDH & CPK. **Black Box warning—co-administration with ribavirin not advised.** Hepatic decompensation may occur in HIV/HCV co-infected patients receiving zidovudine with interferon alfa ± ribavirin.

TABLE 14E (2)

DRUG NAME(S): GENERIC (TRADE)	MOST COMMON ADVERSE EFFECTS	MOST SIGNIFICANT ADVERSE EFFECTS
Nucleoside Reverse Transcriptase Inhibitor (NRTI) Black Box warning for all nucleoside/nucleotide RTIs: lactic acidosis/hepatic steatosis, potentially fatal. Also carry Warnings that fat redistribution and immune reconstitution syndromes (including autoimmune syndromes with delayed onset) have been observed (continued)		
Tenofovir disoproxil fumarate (TDF) (Viread)	Diarrhea 11%, nausea 8%, vomiting 5%, flatulence 4% (generally well tolerated)	**Black Box Warning—Severe exacerbations of hepatitis B reported in pts who stop tenofovir.** Monitor carefully if drug is stopped; anti-HBV rx may be warranted if TDF stopped. Reports of renal injury from TDF, including Fanconi syndrome (CID 37:e174, 2003; J AIDS 35:269,204; CID 42:283, 2006). Fanconi syndrome and diabetes insipidus reported with TDF + ddl (AIDS Reader 19:114, 2009). Modest decline in renal function appears greater with TDF than with NRTIs (CID 51:296, 2010) and may be greater in those receiving TDF with a PI instead of an NNRTI (JID 197:102, 2008; AIDS 26:567, 2012). In a VA study that followed >10,000 HIV-infected individuals, TDF exposure was significantly associated with increased risk of proteinuria, a more rapid decline in renal function and chronic kidney disease (AIDS 26:867, 2012). Monitor Ccr, serum phosphate and urinalysis, especially carefully in those with pre-existing renal dysfunction or nephrotoxic medications. TDF also appears to be associated with increased risk of bone loss. In a substudy of an ACTG comparative treatment trial, those randomized to TDF-FTC experienced greater decreases in spine and hip bone mineral density (BMD) at 96 weeks compared with those treated with ABC-3TC (JID 203:1791, 2011). Consider monitoring BMD in those with history of pathologic fractures, or who have risks for osteoporosis or bone loss.
		TDF redistribution and immune reconstitution can occur with ART
Non-Nucleoside Reverse Transcriptase Inhibitors (NNRTI). Labels caution that fat redistribution and immune reconstitution can occur with ART		
Delavirdine (Rescriptor)	Nausea, diarrhea, vomiting, headache	Skin rash has occurred in 18%, can continue or restart drug in most cases. Stevens-Johnson syndrome & erythema multiforme have been reported rarely, ↑ in liver enzymes in <5% of patients.
Efavirenz (Sustiva)	**CNS side effects 52%;** symptoms include dizziness, insomnia, somnolence, impaired concentration, psychiatric sx, & abnormal dreams; symptoms are worse after 1st or 2nd dose & improve over 2-4 weeks; discontinuation rate 2.6%. Rash 26% (vs. 17% in comparators); discontinuation rate 1.7%. Can cause false-positive urine test results for cannabinoid with CEDIA DAU multi-level THC assay. Metabolite can cause false-positive urine screening test for benzodiazepines (CID 48:1787, 2009).	**Caution:** CNS effects may impair driving and other hazardous activities. Serious neuropsychiatric symptoms reported, including severe depression (2.4%) & suicidal ideation (0.7%). Elevation in liver enzymes. Fulminant hepatic failure reported (see FDA label). **Teratogenicity reported in primates; pregnancy category D—may cause fetal harm, avoid in pregnant women or those who might become pregnant.** NOTE: No single method of contraception is 100% reliable. Barrier + 2nd method of contraception advised, continued 12 weeks after stopping efavirenz. Contraindicated with certain drugs metabolized by CYP3A4. Slow metabolism in those homozygous for the CYP-286 G516T allele can result in exaggerated toxicity and intolerance. This allele is much more common in blacks and women (CID 42:408, 2006). Stevens-Johnson syndrome and erythema multiforme reported in post-marketing surveillance.
Etravirine (Intelence)	Rash 9%, generally mild to moderate and spontaneously resolving; 2% dc clinical trials for rash. More common in women. Nausea 5%.	Severe rash (erythema multiforme, toxic epidermal necrolysis, Stevens-Johnson syndrome & erythema multiforme have been reported rarely, ↑ in liver enzymes Hypersensitivity reactions can occur with rash, constitutional symptoms and organ dysfunction, including hepatic failure (see FDA label). Potential for CYP450-mediated drug interactions. Rhabdomyolysis has been reported in post-marketing surveillance.
Nevirapine (Viramune)	**Rash 37%:** usually occurs during 1st 6 wks of therapy. Follow recommendations for 14-day lead-in period to ↓ risk of rash (see Table 14D). Women experience 7-fold ↑ in risk of severe rash (CID 32:124, 2001). 50% resolve within 2 wks of dc drug & 80% by 1 month, 6.7% discontinuation rate.	**Black Box warning—Severe life-threatening skin reactions reported:** Stevens-Johnson syndrome, toxic epidermal necrolysis, & hypersensitivity reaction w/drug rash with eosinophilia & systemic symptoms (DRESS) (AIM 161:2501, 2001). For severe rashes, dc drug immediately & do not restart. In a clinical trial, the use of prednisone ↑ the risk of rash. **Black Box warning—Life-threatening hepatotoxicity reported,** 2/3 during the first 12 wks of rx. Overall 1% develops hepatitis. Pts with pre-existing ↑ in ALT or AST &/or history of chronic Hep B or C ↑ susceptible (Hepato 35:182, 2002). Women with CD4 >250, including pregnant women, at ↑ risk. Avoid in this group unless no other option. Men with CD4 >400 also at ↑ risk. Monitor pts intensively (clinical & LFTs), esp. during the first 12 wks of rx. If hepatotoxicity, severe skin or hypersensitivity reactions occur, dc drug & never rechallenge.

TABLE 14E (3)

DRUG NAME(S): GENERIC (TRADE)	MOST COMMON ADVERSE EFFECTS	MOST SIGNIFICANT ADVERSE EFFECTS
Non-Nucleoside Reverse Transcriptase Inhibitors (NNRTI) (continued)		
Rilpivirine (Edurant)	Headache (3%), rash (3%) led to discontinuation in 0.1%; insomnia (3%), depressive disorders led to discontinuation in 1%. Increased liver enzymes observed.	Drugs that induce CYP3A or increase gastric pH may decrease plasma concentration of rilpivirine and co-administration with rilpivirine should be avoided. Among these are certain anticonvulsants, rifampicins, PPIs, dexamethasone and St. John's wort. At supra-therapeutic doses, rilpivirine can increase QTc interval: use with caution with other drugs known to increase QTc. May cause depressive disorder, including suicide attempts or suicidal ideation. Overall, appears to cause fewer neuropsychiatric side effects than efavirenz (JAIDS 60;33, 2012).
Protease Inhibitors (PI)	Abnormalities in glucose metabolism, dyslipidemias, fat redistribution syndromes are potential problems. Pts taking PI may be at increased risk for developing osteopenia/osteomalacia. Spontaneous bleeding episodes have been reported in HIV+ pts with hemophilia being treated with PI. Rheumatoid complications have been reported with use of PIs (Ann Rheum Dis 61;82, 2002). Potential of some PIs for QTc prolongation has been suggested (AIDS 365;682, 2005). **Caution for all PIs**—Coadministration with certain drugs dependent on CYP3A or other enzymes for elimination & for which QTc or prolongation levels can cause serious toxicity may be contraindicated. As with other classes, rx may result in immune reconstitution syndromes, which may include early or late presentations of autoimmune syndromes. Taking into account both spontaneous and induced deliveries, a French cohort study demonstrated increased premature births among women receiving ritonavir-boosted PIs as compared with those receiving other antiretroviral therapy, even after accounting for other potential risk factors (CID 54: 1348, 2012).	
Atazanavir (Reyataz)	Asymptomatic unconjugated hyperbilirubinemia in up to 60% of pts, jaundice in 7–9% [especially with Gilbert syndrome (JID 192: 1381, 2005)]. Moderate to severe events: Diarrhea 1–3%, nausea 6–14%, abdominal pain 4%, headache 6%, rash 20%.	Prolongation of PR interval (1st degree AV block in 5-6%) reported; rarely 2° AV block. QTc increase and torsades reported (CID 44;e67, 2007). Acute interstitial nephritis (Am J Kid Dis 44;E81, 2004) and urolithiasis (atazanavir stones) reported (AIDS 20;2131, 2006; NEJM 355;2158, 2006). Potential ↑ transaminases in pts co-infected with HBV or HCV. Severe skin eruptions (Stevens-Johnson syndrome, erythema multiforme, and toxic eruptions, or DRESS syndrome) have been reported.
Darunavir (Prezista)	With background regimens, headache 15%, nausea 18%, diarrhea 20%, ↑ amylase 17%. Rash in 10% of treated; 0.5% discontinuation.	Hepatitis in 0.5%, some with fatal outcome. Use caution in pts with HBV or HCV co-infections or other hepatic dysfunction. Potential for clinically significant rash, including Stevens-Johnson syndrome, toxic epidermal necrolysis, erythema multiforme. Contains sulfa moiety. Potential for major drug interactions.
Fosamprenavir (Lexiva)	Skin rash ~ 20% (moderate or worse in 3–8%), nausea, headache, diarrhea.	Rarely Stevens-Johnson syndrome, hemolytic anemia, angioedema. Prodrug of amprenavir. Contains sulfa moiety. Angioedema, and nephrolithiasis reported in post-marketing experience. Potential increased risk of MI (see FDA label). Angioedema, oral paresthesias, myocardial infarction and nephrolithiasis reported in post-marketing experience. Elevated LFTs seen with higher than recommended doses; increased risk in those with pre-existing liver abnormalities. Acute hemolytic anemia reported with amprenavir.
Indinavir (Crixivan)	↑ indirect bilirubin 10–15% (≥2.5 mg/dl) with overt jaundice especially likely in those with Gilbert syndrome (JID 192: 1381, 2005). Nausea 12%, vomiting 4%, diarrhea 5%. Metallic taste. Paronychia and ingrown toenails reported (CID 32:140, 2001).	**Kidney stones.** Due to indinavir crystals in collecting system. Nephrolithiasis in 12% of adults, higher in pediatrics. Minimize risk with good hydration (at least 48 oz. water/day) (AAC 42;332, 1999). Tubulointerstitial nephritis/renal cortical atrophy reported in association with asymptomatic ↑ urine WBC. Severe hepatitis reported in 3 cases (Ln 349;924, 1997). Hemolytic anemia reported.
Lopinavir/Ritonavir (Kaletra)	GI: **diarrhea** 14–24%, nausea 2–16%. More diarrhea with q24h dosing.	Lipid abnormalities in up to 20–40%. Possible increased risk of MI with cumulative exposure (JID 201;318, 2010). ↑ PR interval, 2° or 3° heart block described. Post-marketing reports of ↑ QTc and torsades: avoid use in congenital QTc prolongation or in other circumstances that prolong QTc or increase susceptibility to torsades. Hepatitis, with hepatic decompensation; caution especially in those with pre-existing liver disease. Pancreatitis. Inflammatory edema of legs (AIDS 16;673, 2002). Stevens-Johnson syndrome & erythema multiforme reported. Note high drug concentration of oral solution. Toxic potential of oral solution (contains ethanol and propylene glycol) in neonates.
Nelfinavir (Viracept)	Mild to moderate **diarrhea** 20%. Oat bran tabs, calcium, or oral anti-diarrheal agents (e.g., loperamide, diphenoxylate/atropine sulfate) can be used to manage diarrhea.	Potential for drug interactions. Powder contains phenylalanine.

TABLE 14E (4)

DRUG NAME(S): GENERIC (TRADE)	MOST COMMON ADVERSE EFFECTS	MOST SIGNIFICANT ADVERSE EFFECTS
Protease Inhibitors (PI) *(continued)*		
Ritonavir (Norvir) **(Currently, primary use is to enhance levels of other anti-retrovirals, because of ↑toxicity, interactions with full-dose ritonavir)**	GI: bitter aftertaste, ↓ by taking with chocolate milk, Ensure, or Advera, nausea 23%, ↓ by initial dose esc (titration) regimen, vomiting 13%, diarrhea 15%. Circumoral paresthesias 5–6%, Dose > 100 mg bid assoc. with ↑ GI side effects & ↑ in lipid abnormalities.	**Black Box** warning relates to many important drug-drug interactions—inhibits P450 CYP3A & CYP2 D6 system—may be life-threatening *(see Table 22A)*. Several cases of iatrogenic Cushing's syndrome reported with concomitant use of ritonavir and corticosteroids, including dosing of the latter by inhalation, epidural injection or a single IM injection. Rarely Stevens-Johnson syndrome, toxic epidermal necrolysis anaphylaxis. Primary A-V block (and higher) and pancreatitis have been reported. Hepatic reactions, including fatalities. Monitor LFTs carefully during therapy, especially in those with pre-existing liver disease, including HBV and HCV.
Saquinavir (Invirase: hard cap, tablet)	Diarrhea, abdominal discomfort, nausea, headache	**Warning—Use Invirase only with ritonavir.** Avoid garlic capsules (may reduce SQV levels) and use cautiously with proton-pump inhibitors (increased SQV levels significant). Use of saquinavir/ritonavir can prolong QTc interval or may rarely cause 2° or 3° heart block; torsades reported. Contraindicated in patients with prolonged QTc or those taking drugs or who have other conditions (e.g., low K+ or Mg+ +) that pose a risk with prolonged QTc interval *(http://www.fda.gov/drugs/DrugSafety/ucm230096.htm, accessed May 25, 2011)*. Contraindicated in patients with complete AV block, or those at risk, who do not have pacemaker. Hepatic toxicity encountered in patients with pre-existing liver disease or in individuals receiving concomitant rifampin. Rarely, Stevens Johnson syndrome.
Tipranavir (Aptivus)	Nausea & vomiting, diarrhea, abdominal pain. Rash in 8–14%, more common in women, & 33% in women taking ethinyl estradiol. Major lipid effects.	**Black Box Warning—associated with hepatitis & fatal hepatic failure.** Risk of hepatotoxicity increased in hepB or hepC co-infection. Possible photosensitivity skin reactions. Contraindicated in Child-Pugh Class B or C hepatic impairment. **Associated with fatal/nonfatal intracranial hemorrhage (can inhibit platelet aggregation).** Caution in those with bleeding risks. Potential for major drug interactions. Contains sulfa moiety and vitamin E.
Fusion Inhibitor		
Enfuvirtide (T20, Fuzeon)	Local injection site reactions (98% at least 1 local ISR, 4% dc because of ISR) (pain & discomfort, induration, erythema, nodules & cysts, pruritus, & ecchymosis). Diarrhea 32%, nausea 23%, fatigue 20%.	↑ Rate of bacterial pneumonia (3.2 pneumonia events/100 pt yrs). **hypersensitivity reactions** ≤1% (rash, fever, nausea & vomiting, chills, rigors, hypotension, & ↑ serum liver transaminases); can occur with reexposure. Cutaneous amyloid deposits containing enfuvirtide peptide reported in skin plaques persisting after discontinuation of drug *(J Cutan Pathol 39:220, 2012)*.
CCR5 Co-receptor Antagonists		
Maraviroc (Selzentry)	With ARV background: Cough 13%, fever 12%, rash 10%, abdominal pain 8%. Also, dizziness, myalgia, arthralgias. ↑ Risk of URI, HSV infection.	**Black box warning—Hepatotoxicity.** May be preceded by allergic features (rash, ↑eosinophilia or ↑IgE levels). Use with caution in ptn with HepB or C. Cardiac ischemia/infarction in 1.3%. May cause ↓BP, orthostatic syncope, especially in patients with renal dysfunction. Significant interactions with CYP3A inducers/inhibitors. Long-term risk of malignancy unknown. Stevens-Johnson syndrome reported post-marketing. Generally favorable safety profile during trial of ART-naive individuals *(JID 201: 803, 2010)*.
Integrase Inhibitors		
Raltegravir (Isentress)	Diarrhea, headache, insomnia, nausea. LFT ↑ may be more common in pts co-infected with HBV or HCV.	Hypersensitivity reactions can occur. Rash, Stevens-Johnson syndrome, toxic epidermal necrolysis reported. Hepatic failure reported. ↑CK, myopathy and rhabdomyolysis reported *(AIDS 22:1382, 2008)*. ↑ of preexisting depression reported in 4 pts; all could continue raltegravir after adjustment of psych. meds *(AIDS 22:1890, 2008)*. Chewable tablets contain phenylalanine.
Elvitegravir (Stribid)	Nausea and diarrhea are the two most common AEs. An increase in serum creatinine of 0.1 - 0.15 mg/dl with use of cobicistat (related to inhibition of prox. tubular enzymes, not a true reduction in GFR).	Same Rx Black Box warnings as ritonavir and tenofovir. Rare lactic acidosis syndrome. Owing to renal toxicity, should not initiate Rx when pre-Rx eGFR is < 70 cc/min. Follow serum creatinine and urinary protein and glucose. Discontinue drug if serum Cr rises > 0.4 mg/dl above baseline value.

TABLE 14F– HEPATITIS A & HBV TREATMENT

Hepatitis A *(Ln 351:1643, 1998)*

1. **Drug/Dosage:** No therapy recommended. If within 2 wks of exposure, IVIG 0.02 mL per kg IM times 1 protective. Hep A vaccine equally effective as IVIG in randomized trial and is emerging as preferred Rx *(NEJM 357:1685, 2007)*.

2. **Side Effects/Comments:** 40% of pts with chronic Hep C who developed superinfection with Hep A developed fulminant hepatic failure *(NEJM 338:286, 1998)*.

HBV Treatment

				When to Treat HBV	
HBeAg status	HBV DNA: "viral load"	ALT	Fibrosis*	Treatment** IFN = interferon; NUC = nucleoside/ tide analogue	Comments
+	> 20,000	< 2xULN	F0 –F2	Observe	Low efficacy with current Rx; biopsy helpful in determining whether to Rx. Lean toward Rx if older age or + Family Hx HCC
+	> 20,000	< 2x ULN	F3-F4	**Treat: IFN or NUC**	**No IFN if decompensated cirrhosis.**
+	>20,000	> 2x ULN	Any	**Treat: IFN or NUC**	INF has higher chance of seroconversion to HBeAg Negative and HBsAg Negative status.
-	< 2000	< 1xULN	Any	Observe	Might Treat if F4; **No IFN if decompensated cirrhosis.**
-	2000-20,000	< 2x ULN	F0 – F2	Observe	
-	2000-20,000	< 2x ULN	F3 – F4	**Treat: NUC or (IFN)**	NUCs favored if HBeAg negative; Treatment duration ill-defined. Certainly > 1 year, likely chronic Rx (indefinitely)
-	> 20,000	> 2xULN	Any	**Treat: NUC or IFN**	NUCs favored if HBeAg negative; Treatment duration chronic / indefinite

Modified from *AASLD HBV Treatment Guidelines (www.aasld.org)*; Lok/ McMahon, Hepatology .2009; 50. p. 1-36
* Liver Biopsy or fibrosure assay is helpful in determining when and how to treat
** Treatment options listed below

Treatment Regimens. Single drug therapy is usually sufficient; combination therapy used with HIV co-infection.

	Drug/Dose	Comments
Preferred Regimens	**Pegylated-Interferon-alpha 2a** 180 µg sc once weekly OR **Entecavir** 0.5 mg po daily OR **Tenofovir** 300 mg po once daily	PEG-IFN: Treat for 48 weeks Entecavir: Do not use Entecavir if Lamivudine resistance present. Entecavir/Tenofovir: Treat for at least 24-48 weeks after seroconversion from HBeAg to anti-HBe. Indefinite chronic therapy for HBeAg negative patients. Renal impairment dose adjustments necessary.
Alternative Regimens	**Lamivudine** 100 mg po once daily OR **Telbivudine** 600 mg po once daily OR **Emtricitabine** 200 mg po once daily (investigational) OR **Adefovir** 10 mg po once daily	These alternative agents are rarely used except in combination. When used, restrict to short term therapy owing to high rates of development of resistance. Not recommended as first-line therapy. Use of Adefovir has mostly been replaced by Tenofovir.
Preferred Regimen for HIV-HBV Co-Infected Patient	**Truvada** (Tenofovir 300 mg + Emtricitabine 200 mg) po once daily + another anti-HIV drug	ALL patients if possible as part of a fully suppressive anti-HIV/anti-HBV regimen. Continue therapy indefinitely.

TABLE 14G– HCV TREATMENT REGIMENS AND RESPONSE

1. **Hepatitis C (HCV) Treatment Setting.** Indications for treatment of HCV must take into account both relative and absolute contraindications. Response to therapy reflects defined terms. Duration of therapy is response guided based on Genotype. Recommended follow-up during and post-treatment.

2. **Indications for Treatment.** Assuming use of Pegylated Interferon (Peg-IFN) + Ribavirin in the regimen: motivated patient, acute HCV infection, biopsy: chronic hepatitis and significant fibrosis, cryoglobulinemic vasculitis, cryoglobulinemic glomerulonephritis, stable HIV infection, compensated liver disease, acceptable hematologic parameters, creatinine < 1.5 (GFR > 50).

TABLE 14G (2)

3. **Contraindications for Treatment.** Contraindications (both relative and absolute) also assume use of Pegylated Interferon (Peg-IFN) + Ribavirin in the regimen.

    a. Relative Contraindications. Hgb < 10, ANC < 1000, PTLs < 50K, hemodialysis and/or GFR < 50, active substance and alcohol use, anticipated poor compliance, untreated mental health disorder, e.g. depression, stable auto-immune disease, Thalassemia and sickle cell anemia, sarcoidosis, HIV co-infection (CD4 < 200, concurrent zidovudine)

    b. Absolute Contraindications. Uncontrolled, active, major psychiatric illness, especially depression; hepatic decompensation (encephalopathy, coagulopathy, ascitis); severe uncontrolled medical disease (DM, CHF, CAD, HTN, TB, cancer); untreated thyroid disease; pregnancy, nursing, child-bearing potential (anticipated pregnancy, no birth control); active untreated autoimmune disease; HIV co-infection (CD4 < 100, concurrent ddI)

4. **Response to Therapy.** Predictors of successful response to therapy include: recent infection with HCV, Genotype 2 or 3 infection, favorable IL-28B haplotype, less severe liver disease on biopsy, HCV viral load < 800,000.

5. **Definitions of Response to Therapy.**

Null	Failure to decrease HCV VL by >2 log at week 12.
Non-Responder	Failure to clear HCV RNA by week 24.
Partial Response	>2 log ↓ HIV RNA by week 12 but not undetectable at week 24.
Early Virologic Response (EVR)	>2 log ↓ at week 12 and undetectable at week 24; **Complete EVR** = undetectable at both week 12 and 24.
Rapid Virologic Response (RVR)	Undetectable by week 4 and sustained through course of Rx
Extended Rapid Virologic Response (eRVR)	New terminology with Direct Acting Agents (DAAs). Undetectable after 4 weeks of DAA treatment (e.g., week 4 for telaprevir or week 8 for boceprevir), with sustained undetectable HCV RNA at weeks 12 and 24.
End of Treatment Response (ETR)	Undetectable at end of treatment.
Relapse	Undetectable at end of therapy (ETR) but rebound (detectable) virus within 24 weeks after therapy stopped.
Sustained Virologic Response (SVR)	CURE! Still undetectable at end of therapy and beyond 24 weeks after therapy is stopped.

6. **HCV Treatment Regimens**

- Biopsy is a 'gold standard' for staging HCV infection and is helpful in some settings to determine the ideal timing of HCV treatment. When not obtained, "non-invasive" tests are often employed to assess the relative probability of advanced fibrosis or cirrhosis.

- Resistance tests: Genotypic resistance assays are available that can determine polymorphisms associated with reduction in susceptibility to some DAAs (Direct Acting Agents, e.g., protease inhibitors). **However, resistance tests are not routinely recommended in pts naïve to Rx and are reserved for selective use in patients who have received prior unsuccessful treatment with a DAA.**

- **IMPORTANT NOTE REGARDING TREATMENT DECISION-MAKING:** Newer drugs are in development. Emerging data suggest a high probability that newer regimens that spare the use of pegylated Interferon (peg-IFN) and/or Ribavirin (RBV) will be successful and available in the next 1-2 years **(or sooner).** Therefore, the timing of the decision to initiate HCV therapy needs to be individualized based on: the patients current clinical status, the viral genotype, the pt's ability to tolerate peg-IFN/RBV based therapies, and the likelihood of disease progression over the next 5 years while newer treatments are developed. The Ultimate Goal for treatment of HCV: no Interferon or Ribavirin, only Direct Acting Agents (DAA).

Genotype	Regimen
All	• Either **Pegylated Interferon (PEG-IFN) alfa 2a** (Pegasys) 180 mcg SQ weekly OR • **PEG-IFN Alfa 2b** (PEG-Intron) 1.5 mcg/kg SQ weekly
	PLUS
2, 3	• Ribavirin 400 mg bid (if using response guided Rx, dose Ribavirin as for Genotype 1, 4)
1, 4	• **Ribavirin** 600 mg bid (wt > 75 kg) OR • **Ribavirin** 400 mg qAM + 600 mg qPM (wt < 75 kg)
	PLUS

1 Only	• **Telaprevir** (Incivek) 750 mg (2 tabs) po tid (with food–not low fat) for 12 wks only
	  ▪ Start immediately with PEG-IFN + Ribavirin at recommended doses
	  ▪ Must stop Telaprevir at week 12 and continue PEG-IFN + Ribavirin for remainder of duration of therapy

	OR

1 Only	• **Boceprevir** (Victrelis) 800 mg (4 caps) po tid (with food–meal or light snack)
	  ▪ Start 4 weeks after starting PEG-IFN + Ribavirin at recommended doses
	  ▪ Continue along with PEG-IFN + Ribavirin for full duration of therapy

WARNINGS:	• **Never use Telaprevir or Boceprevir as monotherapy** • **Never Dose Reduce Either Telaprevir or Boceprevir** • **Never Combine Telaprevir or Boceprevir** • **Never use either drug in sequence owing to shared resistance profiles**

TABLE 14G (3)

7. **Duration of HCV Therapy.** Predictors of SVR: *CID 56:118, 2013.*

Genotype	Response Guided Therapy

2, 3	• If RVR: Treat for 16-24 weeks of total therapy*
	  ▪ Check for SVR at week 40 or 48 depending on duration of therapy (16 or 24 weeks)
	• If EVR: Treat for 24 weeks of total therapy
	  ▪ Check for SVR at week 48
	• If Partial or Null Response: Discontinue therapy at week 12 (treatment failure)

4	• If eRVR or EVR: Treat for 48 weeks of total therapy ▪ Check for SVR at week 72 • If Partial or Null Response: Discontinue at weeks 24 and 12, respectively.

1**	• If eRVR: Continue therapy for 24 weeks (week 28 for boceprevir)
	  ▪ Check for SVR at week 48 (week 52 for boceprevir)
	• IF EVR: Continue therapy for 48 weeks
	  ▪ Check for SVR at week 72
	• If Null, Partial Response, or **NOT complete EVR:** Discontinue therapy at week 12
	  therapy at week 12

* Similar SVR rates for 16 vs. 24 wks but higher relapse with 16 wks of therapy. Re-treatment in such settings usually results in SVR with longer (24 wks) duration.

** Assuming use of Direct Acting Agents (DAA), e.g., Telaprevir or Boceprevir. If DAAs are not being used, treatment duration is the same as for Genotype 4.

TABLE 15A – ANTIMICROBIAL PROPHYLAXIS FOR SELECTED BACTERIAL INFECTIONS*

CLASS OF ETIOLOGIC AGENT/DISEASE/CONDITION	PROPHYLAXIS AGENT/DOSE/ROUTE/DURATION	COMMENTS
Group B streptococcal disease (GBS), neonatal: Approaches to management [CDC Guidelines, *MMWR 59 (RR-10):1, 2010*]:		
	Pregnant women—intrapartum antimicrobial prophylaxis procedures:	**Regimens for prophylaxis against early-onset group B streptococcal disease in neonate used during labor:**
	1. Screen all pregnant women with vaginal & rectal swab for GBS at 35–37 wks gestation (unless other indications for prophylaxis exist—GBS bacteriuria during this pregnancy or previously delivered infant with invasive GBS disease, even then cultures may be useful for susceptibility testing). Use transport medium; GBS survive at room temp. up to 96 hrs. **Rx during labor if swab culture positive.**	**Penicillin G** 5 million Units IV (initial dose) then 2.5 to 3 million Units IV q4h until delivery **Alternative: Ampicillin** 2 gm IV (initial dose) then 1 gm IV q4h until delivery Penicillin-allergic patients:
	2. Rx during labor if previously delivered infant with invasive GBS infection, or if any GBS bacteriuria during this pregnancy.	• Patient not at high risk for anaphylaxis: **Cefazolin** 2 gm IV (initial dose) then 1 gm IV q8h until delivery
	3. Rx if GBS status unknown but if any of the following are present: (a) delivery at <37 wks gestation [see *MMWR 59 (RR-10): 1, 2010* algorithms for preterm premature rupture of membranes] or (b) duration of ruptured membranes ≥18 hrs, or (c) intrapartum temp. ≥100.4°F (≥38.0°C). If amnionitis suspected, broad-spectrum antibiotic coverage should include an agent active vs. group B streptococci.	• Patient at high risk for anaphylaxis from β-lactams: □ If organism is both clindamycin- and erythromycin-susceptible, **or** is erythromycin-resistant, but clindamycin-susceptible confirmed by D-zone test (or equivalent) showing lack of inducible resistance: **Clindamycin** 900 mg IV q8h until delivery
	4. Rx if positive intra-partum NAAT for GBS.	□ If susceptibility of organism unknown, lack of inducible resistance to clindamycin has not been excluded, or patient is allergic to clindamycin: **Vancomycin** 1 gm IV q12h until delivery
	5. Rx not indicated if: negative vaginal/rectal cultures at 35–37 wks gestation or C-section performed before onset of labor with intact amniotic membranes [use standard surgical prophylaxis].	
Neonate (mother given prophylaxis)	See detailed algorithm in *MMWR 59 (RR-10):1, 2010.*	
Preterm, premature rupture of the membranes in Group B strep-negative women	IV **ampicillin** 2 gm q6h + IV **erythromycin** 250 mg q6h) for 48 hrs followed by po **amoxicillin** 250 mg q8h + po **erythromycin** base 333 mg q8h for 5 days. • Decreases infant morbidity (*JAMA 278:989, 1997*). (*Note:* May require additional antibiotics for therapy of specific existing infections)	Antibiotic Rx reduced infant respiratory distress syndrome (50.6% to 40.8%, p = 0.03), necrotizing enterocolitis (5.8% to 2.3%, p = 0.03) and prolonged pregnancy (2.9 to 6.1 days, p <0.001). (In subset in 1 large study (49/49 pts), po erythromycin or improved neonatal outcomes vs placebo (11.2% vs 14.4% poor outcomes, p=0.02 for single births), but not co-AM-CL or both drugs in combination (both assoc. with † necrotizing enterocolitis) (*Lt 357:979, 2001).* (See ACOG discussion, Ob Gyn 102:875, 2003; Practice Bulletin in Ob Gyn 109:1007, 2007; Rev. Obstet Gynecol Can 31:863 & 868, 2009).
Post-splenectomy bacteremia. Likely agents: Pneumococci (90%), meningococci ; H. influenzae type b. Bacteremia due to Enterobacteriaceae, S. aureus, Pseudomonas spp. and rarely P. aeruginosa described. Also at † risk for fatal malaria, severe babesiosis. Ref: Redbook Online, 2009. *Amer Acad Pediatrics.*	**Immunizations:** Ensure admin. of pneumococcal vaccine, H. influenzae B, & quadrivalent meningococcal vaccines at recommended times. In addition, asplenic children with sickle cell anemia, thalassemia, & perhaps others, daily antimicrobial prophylaxis until at least age 5—see *Comments and* Sickle-cell disease (below). Sepsis due to susceptible organisms may occur despite daily prophylaxis (J Clin Path 54:214, 2001).	Antimicrobial prophylaxis until age 5: Amox 20 mg/kg/day or Pen V-K 125 mg bid. Over age 5: Consider Pen V-K 250 mg bid for at least 1 yr in children post-splenectomy. Some recommend prophylaxis for a minimum of 3 yrs or until at least age 18. Maintain immunizations plus self-administer AM-CL with any febrile illness while seeking physician assistance. For self-administered therapy, cefuroxime axetil can be used in the penicillin-allergic pt who is not allergic to cephalosporins; alternatively, respiratory FQ can be considered in beta lactam-allergic pt in appropriate populations. Pen allergy: TMP-SMX or clarithro may be significant in S. pneumo may be significant in some areas, particularly among pen-resistant isolates.

TABLE 15A (2)

CLASS OF ETIOLOGIC AGENT/DISEASE/CONDITION	PROPHYLAXIS AGENT/DOSE/ROUTE/DURATION	COMMENTS
Sexual Exposure Sexual assault survivor (likely agents and risks, see *MMWR 59 (RR-12):1, 2010*). For review of overall care: *NEJM 365:834, 2011*.	[[**Ceftriaxone** 250 mg (IM)] + [**Metronidazole** 2 gm po as single dose] + [(**Azithromycin** 1 gm po once) or (**Doxycycline** 100 mg po bid for 7 days)]	• Obtain expert advice re: forensic exam & specimens, pregnancy, physical trauma, psychological support. • Test for gonococci and chlamydia (NAAT) at appropriate sites. Check wet mount for T. vaginalis (and culture), check specimen for bacterial vaginosis and Candida if appropriate. • Serologic evaluation for syphilis, HIV, HBV, HCV not easily transmitted from sexual activity, but consider test in high-risk circumstances (*MMWR 60:945, 2011*). • Initiate post-exposure protocols for HBV vaccine, HIV post-exposure prophylaxis as appropriate (see *Table 15D*). • Follow-up exam for STDs in 1-2 weeks; retest if prophylaxis not given initially or if symptomatic. • Follow-up serologies for syphilis, HIV, HBV (and HCV if done) at 6 wks, 3 mos and 6 mos. **Notes:** Ceftriaxone is preferred over cefixime for treatment of gonorrhoea; the latter is less effective for pharyngeal infection and strains with decreased susceptibility to cephalosporins are beginning to appear: those with decreased susceptibility to cefixime are more prevalent than those with decreased susceptibility to ceftriaxone (*MMWR 60:873, 2011*). Cefixime 400 mg po once can be used in place of ceftriaxone, if the latter is unavailable (*MMWR 61:590, 2012*). Azithromycin is preferred to doxycycline because it also provides activity against some GC with reduced susceptibility to cephalosporins (*MMWR 60:873, 2011*). In patients highly allergic to cephalosporins, azithromycin 2 gm po once can be used in place of ceftriaxone.
Contact with specific sexually transmitted diseases	See comprehensive guidelines for specific pathogens in *MMWR 59 (RR-10): 1, 2010*.	
Syphilis exposure		Presumptive rx for exposure within 3 mos. as tests may be negative. See *Table 1, page 24*. If exposure occurred > 90 days prior, establish dx or treat empirically (*MMWR 59 (RR-12): 1, 2010*).
Sickle-cell disease. Likely agent: S. pneumoniae (see post-splenectomy, above) Ref.: *2009 Red Book Online, Amer Acad Pediatrics*	Children <5 yrs: **Penicillin V** 125 mg po bid ≥5 yrs: **Penicillin V** 250 mg po bid. (Alternative in children: Amoxicillin 20 mg per kg per day)	Start prophylaxis by 2 mos. (*Pediatrics 106:367, 2000*); continue until at least age 5. When to d/c must be individualized. Age-appropriate vaccines, including pneumococcal, Hib, influenza, meningococcal. Treating infections, consider possibility of penicillin non-susceptible pneumococci.

TABLE 15B – ANTIBIOTIC PROPHYLAXIS TO PREVENT SURGICAL INFECTIONS IN ADULTS*
(*CID 38:1706, 2004; Am J Surg 189:395, 2005; Med Lett 10:73, 2012*)

General Comments:
- To be optimally effective, antibiotics must be started within 2 hrs before surgical incision (*NEJM 326:281, 1992*), preferably ≤ 1 hr before incision for most agents except vancomycin and quinolones (*JAC 58:645, 2006; CID 38:1706, 2004*).
- Most applications employ a single preoperative dose (*Treat Guide Med Lett 7-47, 2009*).
- For procedures lasting > 2 half-lives of prophylactic agent, intraoperative supplementary dose(s) may be required (see *CID 38:1706, 2004 for schedule*).
- Standard regimens may give relatively low tissue levels in pts with high BMI, but implications of this are not clear (see *Surgery 136:738, 2004 for cefazolin; Eur J Clin Pharm 54:632, 1998 for vancomycin; CID 38:1706, 2004 for iv-based dosing*).
- In most cases, prophylaxis is not extended beyond 24 hrs (*CID 38:1706, 2004*).
- Prophylaxis does carry risk: e.g., C. difficile colitis (*CID 46:1838, 2008*)
- Active screening for S. aureus nasal colonization and application of chlorhexidine washes and intranasal mupirocin has been reported as a strategy that decreases surgical site infection in an area of low MRSA prevalence (*NEJM 362:9, 2010*). Avoid contact of chlorhexidine soap with eyes.

Use of Vancomycin:
- For many common prophylaxis indications, vancomycin is considered an alternative to β-lactams in pts allergic to or intolerant of the latter.
- Vancomycin use may be justifiable in centers where rates of post-operative infection with methicillin-resistant staphylococci are high or in pts at high risk for these.

TABLE 15B (2)

- Unlike β-lactams in common use, vancomycin has no activity against gram-negative organisms. **When gram-negative bacteria are a concern following specific procedures, it may be necessary or desirable to add a second agent with appropriate in vitro activity.** This can be done using cefazolin with vancomycin in the non-allergic pt, or in pts intolerant of β-lactams using vancomycin with another gram-negative agent (e.g., aminoglycoside, fluoroquinolone, possibly aztreonam, if pt not allergic; local resistance patterns and pt factors would influence choice).
- Infusion of vancomycin, especially too rapidly, may result in hypotension or other manifestations of histamine release syndrome (*J Cardiothor Vasc Anesth* 5:574, 1991).

TYPE OF SURGERY	PROPHYLAXIS	COMMENTS
Cardiovascular Surgery Antibiotic prophylaxis in cardiovascular surgery has been proven beneficial in the following procedures: • Prosthetic valve • Reconstruction of abdominal aorta • Procedures on the leg that involve a groin incision • Any vascular procedure that inserts prosthesis/foreign body • Lower extremity amputation for ischemia • Cardiac surgery • Permanent Pacemakers (*Circulation 121:458, 2010*)	**Cefazolin** 1-2 gm IV as a single dose or q8h for 1-2 days or **cefuroxime** 1.5 gm IV as a single dose or q12h for total of 6 gm **or vancomycin** 1 gm IV as single dose or q12h for 1-2 days. For pts weighing > 90 kg, use vanco 1.5 gm IV as a single dose or q12h for 1-2 days. Consider **intranasal mupirocin** evening before, day of surgery & bid for 5 days post-op in pts with pos. nasal culture for S. aureus. Mupirocin resistance has been encountered (*CID 49:935, 2009*).	Single infusion just before surgery probably as effective as multiple doses. Not needed for cardiac catheterization or after removal of retrosternal drainage catheters or just a 2ⁿᵈ dose after coming off bypass. Vancomycin may be preferable in hospitals with ↑ freq of MRSA or in high-risk pts (*CID 38: 1555, 2004*), or those colonized with MRSA (*CID 38:1706, 2004*); however, does not cover gm-neg. bacilli, therefore would add cefazolin. Meta-analysis failed to demonstrate overall superiority of vancomycin over β-lactam prophylaxis for cardiac surgery (*CID 38: 1357, 2004*). Intranasal mupirocin ↓ sternal wound infections from S. aureus in 1850 pts: used historical controls (*Ann Thor Surg 71:1572, 2001*); in another trial, it ↓ nosocomial S. aureus infections only in nasal carriers (*NEJM 346:1871, 2002*). One study of 0.12% chlorhexidine gluconate to nares and oral rinse showed ↓ deep surg site and lower resp infections (*JAMA 296:2460, 2006*).
Gastric, Biliary and Colonic Surgery **Gastroduodenal** Gastroduodenal, includes percutaneous endoscopic gastrostomy (high-risk only; see Comments). Biliary, includes laparoscopic cholecystectomy (high-risk only, see Comments).	**Cefazolin** (1-2 gm IV) or **cefoxitin** (1-2 gm IV) or **cefotetan** (1-2 gm IV) or **cefuroxime** (1.5 gm IV) as a single dose (some give additional doses q12h for 2-3 days).	Gastroduodenal: High-risk is marked obesity, obstruction, ↓ gastric acid or ↓ motility. Meta-analysis supports use in percutaneous endoscopic gastrostomy (*Am J Gastro 95:3133, 2000*). Biliary: high-risk: age >70, acute cholecystitis, non-functioning gallbladder, jaundice or common duct stones. With cholangitis, treat as infection, not prophylaxis (*See Table 1, page 17*). (For guidelines of American Soc of Gastrointestinal Endoscopy, see *Gastroint Endosc 67:791, 2008*).
Endoscopic retrograde cholangiopancreato-graphy Controversial: No benefit from single dose piperacillin in randomized placebo-controlled trial, *AntM 125:442, 1996*	No rx without obstruction. If obstruction: **Ciprofloxacin** 500-750 mg po 2 hrs prior to procedure or **PIP-TZ** 4.5 gm IV 1 hr prior to procedure	Most studies show that **achieving adequate drainage** will prevent post-procedural cholangitis or sepsis and no further benefit from prophylactic antibiotics; greatest benefit likely when complete drainage cannot be achieved. Meta-analysis suggested antibiotics may ↓ bacteremia, but not sepsis/cholangitis (*Endoscopy 31:718, 1999*). Oral ciprofloxacin as effective & less expensive but quinolone resistance increasing (*CID 23:380, 1996*). See *Gastroint Endosc 67:791, 2008* for Amer Soc Gastroint Endosc recommendations.
Colorectal	Oral antibiotics for elective surgery (see Comments) **Parenteral regimens** (emergency or elective): [**Cefazolin** 1-2 gm IV + **metronidazole** 0.5 gm IV] (see Comment) or **cefoxitin** or **cefotetan** 1-2 gm IV (if available) or **AM-SB** 3 gm IV or **ERTA** 1 gm IV (*NEJM 355:2640, 2006* study found ertapenem more effective than cefotetan, but association with non-significant ↑ risk of C. difficile).	**Oral regimens: Neomycin + erythromycin.** Pre-op day: (1) 10 am 4L polyethylene glycol electrolyte solution (Colyte, GoLYTELY) po over 2 hr. (2) Clear liquid diet only. (3) 1 pm, 2 pm & 11 pm, neomycin 1 gm + erythro base 1 gm po. (4) NPO after midnight. Alternative regimens have been less well studied: GoLYTELY 1-6 pm, then neomycin 2 gm po → metronidazole 2 gm po at 7 pm & 11 pm. Oral regimen as effective as parenteral; parenteral in addition to oral not required but often used (*Am J Surg 189:395, 2005*). Many used both parenteral + oral regimens for elective procedures (*Am J Surg 189:395, 2005*), but recent ↑ enthusiasm for mechanical bowel preparation. Meta-analysis did not support mech bowel prep in preventing anastomotic leaks with elective colorectal surg (*Cochr Database Syst Rev 1:CD001544, 2009*). Gastroduodenal dosing: Some experts recommend 2 gm for all and 3 gm (if patient weight > 120 kg. Repeat dose 4 hours after 1st dose if patient still in surgery).

Ruptured viscus: See Peritoneum/Peritonitis, Secondary, Table 1, page 47.

TABLE 15B (3)

TYPE OF SURGERY	PROPHYLAXIS	COMMENTS
Head and Neck Surgery *(Am J Otol Rhinol Laryngol 101 Suppl: 16, 1992)*		Antimicrobial prophylaxis in head & neck surg appears efficacious only for procedures involving oral pharyngeal mucosa (e.g., laryngeal or pharyngeal tumor) but even with prophylaxis, wound infection rate can be high *(Head Neck 23:447, 2001)*. Uncontaminated head & neck surg does not require prophylaxis.
Cefazolin 2 gm IV (Single dose) (some add **metronidazole** 500 mg IV *(Treat Guide Med Lett 7:47, 2009)*)		
OR		
Clindamycin 600-900 mg IV (single dose) ± **gentamicin** 1.5 mg/kg IV (single dose) *(See Table 10D for weight-based dose calculation).*		
Neurosurgical Procedures. [Prophylaxis not effective in ↓ infection rate with intracranial pressure monitors in retrospective analysis of 215 pts *(J Neurol Neurosurg Psych 69:381, 2000)*]		
Clean, non-implant; e.g., craniotomy	**Cefazolin** 1-2 gm IV once. Alternative: **vanco** 1 gm IV once; for pts weighing > 90 kg, use vanco 1.5 gm IV as single dose.	Reference: *Ln 344:1547, 1994*
Clean, contaminated (cross sinuses, or naso/oropharynx)	**Clindamycin** 900 mg IV (single dose)	British recommend amoxicillin-clavulanate 1.2 gm IV[a,c] or (cefuroxime 1.5 gm IV + metronidazole 0.5 gm IV)
CSF shunt surgery:	**Cefazolin** 1-2 gm IV once. Alternative: **vanco** 1 gm IV once; for pts weighing > 90 kg, use vanco 1.5 gm IV as single dose.	Meta-analysis suggests benefit *(Cochrane Database 3: CD 005365)*. Randomized study in a hospital with high prevalence of infection due to methicillin-resistant staphylococci showed vancomycin was more effective than cefazolin in preventing CSF shunt infections *(J Hosp Infect 69:337, 2008)*.
Obstetric/Gynecologic Surgery *(See ACOG Practice Bulletin 8 & Gyn 113:1180, 2009 for additional procedures and alternatives)*		
Vaginal or abdominal hysterectomy	**Cefazolin** 1-2 gm or **cefoxitin** 1-2 gm or **cefotetan** 1-2 gm or **cefuroxime** 1.5 gm IV 30 min. before surgery.	1 study found cefotetan superior to cefazolin *(CID 20:677, 1995)*. For prolonged procedures, doses can be repeated q4-8h for duration of procedure. Ampicillin-subbactam is considered an acceptable alternative *(CID 43:322, 2006)*. Treat pts with bacterial vaginosis pre-op.
Cesarean section for premature rupture of membranes or active labor	**Cefazolin** 1-2 gm IV (See Comments).	Prophylaxis decreases risk of endometritis and wound infection. Traditional approach had been to administer antibiotics after cord is clamped to avoid exposing infant to antibiotic. However, recent studies suggest that administering prophylaxis before the skin incision results in fewer surgical site infections *(Obstet Gynecol 115:187, 2010; Amer J Obstet Gynecol 199:301.e1 and 310.e1, 2008)* and endometritis *(Amer J Obstet Gynecol 196:455.e1, 2007)*.
Surgical Abortion (1st trimester)	1st trimester: **Doxycycline** 300 mg po, as 100 mg 1 hr before procedure + 200 mg post-procedure.	Meta-analysis showed benefit of antibiotic prophylaxis in all risk groups. One regimen was doxy 100 mg orally 1 hr before procedure, then 200 mg after procedure *(Ob Gyn 87:884, 1996)*.
Orthopedic Surgery		
Hip arthroplasty, spinal fusion	Same as cardiac	Customarily stopped after "Hemovac" removed. NSIPP workgroup recommends stopping prophylaxis within 24 hrs of surgery *(CID 38:1706, 2004)*.
Total joint replacement (other than hip)	**Cefazolin** 1-2 gm IV pre-op (± 2nd dose) or **vancomycin** 1 gm IV. For pts weighing > 90 kg, use vanco 1.5 gm IV as single dose.	NSIPP workgroup recommends stopping prophylaxis within 24 hrs of surgery *(CID 38:1706, 2004)*. Usual to administer cefuroxime before tourniquet inflation, but a recent study in total knee arthroplasty found dosing cefuroxime 1.5 gm just prior to tourniquet release (+ 2nd dose 6 hr after surgery) was not inferior to dosing before inflation (+ 2nd dose) *(CID 46:1009, 2008)*.
Open reduction of closed fracture with internal fixation	**Ceftriaxone** 2 gm IV or IM once	3.6% (ceftriaxone) vs 8.3% (for placebo) infection found in Dutch trauma trial *(Ln 347:1133, 1996)*. Several alternative antimicrobials can ↓ risk of infection *(Cochrane Database Syst Rev 2010: CD 000244)*.

TABLE 15B (4)

TYPE OF SURGERY	PROPHYLAXIS	COMMENTS
Prophylaxis to protect prosthetic joints from hematogenous infection related to distant procedures (patients with plates, pins and screws only are not considered to be at risk)		• In 2003, the American Academy of Orthopedic Surgeons (AAOS), in conjunction with the American Dental Association and the American Urological Association, developed Advisory Statements on the use of antibiotic prophylaxis to prevent infection of implanted joint prostheses for procedures that may cause bacteremia. (*J Am Dental Assn 134:895, 2003; J Urol 169:1796, 2003*). These AAOS stratified procedures for risk of bacteremia, described patient factors that might place joints at ↑ risk of infection (incl. all pts in first 2 years after insertion), and offered antibiotic options. (See also *Med Lett 47:59, 2005* and *review in Infect Dis Clin N Amer 19:931, 2005*). • A February 2009 *Information Statement* from the AAOS listed patient factors that may ↑ risk of infection, but recommended that antibiotic prophylaxis be considered for any invasive procedure that may cause bacteremia in all patients with a joint replacement (http://aaos.org/about/papers/advistmt/1033.asp). • The editors believe that the latter approach is excessively broad and exposes many to the risks of antibiotics without definite evidence of benefit. As pointed out in guidelines for prevention of endocarditis, transient bacteremias occur with routine daily activities (*Circulation 2007; 116:1736*). • **A recent prospective, case-control study concluded that antibiotic prophylaxis for dental procedures *did not* decrease the risk of hip or knee prosthesis infection (*Clin Infect Dis 50:8, 2010*).** • For patients with prosthetic joints, infections involving tissue to be manipulated surgically should be treated before surgery whenever possible. Prophylaxis with an anti-staphylococcal β-lactam or vancomycin (according to susceptibility of the organism) for procedures involving tissues colonized by staphylococci would be appropriate, as these organisms are common causes of prosthetic joint infections. In other circumstances, decisions must be based on individual judgment, for now. The 2003 documents cited above appear to provide the best information on which to base such decisions.
Peritoneal Dialysis Catheter Placement	**Vancomycin** single 1 gm IV dose 12 hrs prior to procedure	Effectively reduced peritonitis during 14 days post-placement in 221 pts: vanco 1%, cefazolin 7%, placebo 12% (p=0.02) (*Am J Kidney Dis 36:1014, 2000*).
Urologic Surgery/Procedures • See *Best Practice Policy Statement* from Amer. Urological Assoc. (AUA) (*J Urol 179:1379, 2008*) for detailed recommendations on specific procedures/circumstances. • Selection of agents targeting urinary pathogens may require modification based on local resistance patterns; ↑ TMP-SMX and/or fluoroquinolone (FQ) resistance among enteric gram-negative bacteria is a concern.		
Cystoscopy	• Prophylaxis generally not necessary if urine is sterile. However, AUA recommends FQ or TMP-SMX for those with several potentially adverse host factors (e.g., advanced age, immunocompromised state, anatomic abnormalities, etc.) • Treat patients with UTI prior to procedure using an antimicrobial active against pathogen isolated	
Cystoscopy with manipulation	Ciprofloxacin 500 mg po (TMP-SMX 1 DS tablet po may be an alternative in populations with low rates of resistance)	Procedures mentioned include ureteroscopy, biopsy, fulguration, TURP, etc. Treat UTI with targeted therapy before procedure if possible.
Transrectal prostate biopsy	Ciprofloxacin 500 mg po 12 hrs prior to biopsy and repeated 12 hrs after 1st dose. See Comment.	Bacteremia 7% with CiP vs 37% with gentamicin (*AAC 39:1175, 1997*). Bacteremia 0.8% with CiP 30-60 min before procedure was effective in low risk pts; additional doses were given for ↑ risk (*J Urol 168:1021, 2002*). Serious bacteremias due to FQ-resistant organisms have been encountered in patients receiving FQ prophylaxis. Pre-operative prophylaxis should advise patients to immediately report symptoms suggesting infection. Clinicians should advise patients to immediately report symptoms suggesting infection. Although 2nd or 3rd generation Cephalosporins or addition of single-dose gentamicin has been suggested, infections due to ESBL-producing and gent-resistant organisms have been encountered (*Urol 74:332, 2009*).
Other		
Breast surgery, herniorrhaphy	**Cefazolin** 1-2 gm IV pre-op	Benefits of prophylaxis for clean surgical procedures not clear (*Treat Guide Med Lett 7:47, 2009*). Antibiotics may reduce risk of surgical site infection in breast cancer surgery (studies not examining immediate reconstruction), but great variability in regimens selected (*Cochrane Database Syst Rev 2006; (2): CD 005360*). For inguinal hernia repair, one analysis found prophylaxis to be beneficial in repairs with mesh (*J Hosp Infect 62: 427, 2006*), while another concluded that antibiotics may reduce risk of infection in pooled population or in those repaired with prosthetic material (mesh), but that the data are not sufficient to make firm recommendations for or against their use universally (*Cochrane Database Syst Rev 2007; (3): CD 003769*).

TABLE 15C – ANTIMICROBIAL PROPHYLAXIS FOR THE PREVENTION OF BACTERIAL ENDOCARDITIS IN PATIENTS WITH UNDERLYING CARDIAC CONDITIONS*

In 2007, the American Heart Association guidelines for the prevention of bacterial endocarditis were updated. The resulting document (*Circulation 2007; 116:1736-1754 and http://circ.ahajournals.org/cgi/reprint/116/15/1736*), which was also endorsed by the Infectious Diseases Society of America, represents a significant departure from earlier recommendations.

- Antibiotic prophylaxis for dental procedures is now directed at individuals who are likely to suffer the most devastating consequences should they develop endocarditis.
- Prophylaxis to prevent endocarditis is no longer specified for gastrointestinal or genitourinary procedures. The following is adapted from and reflects the new AHA recommendations.
  See original publication for explanation and precise details.

SELECTION OF PATIENTS FOR ENDOCARDITIS PROPHYLAXIS

FOR PATIENTS WITH ANY OF THESE HIGH-RISK CARDIAC CONDITIONS ASSOCIATED WITH ENDOCARDITIS:	WHO UNDERGO DENTAL PROCEDURES INVOLVING:	WHO UNDERGO INVASIVE RESPIRATORY PROCEDURES INVOLVING:	WHO UNDERGO INVASIVE GI OR GU TRACTS:	WHO UNDERGO PROCEDURES INVOLVING INFECTED SKIN AND SOFT TISSUES:
Prosthetic heart valves Previous infective endocarditis Congenital heart disease with any of the following: • Completely repaired cardiac defect using prosthetic material (Only for 1ˢᵗ 6 months) • Partially corrected but with residual defect near prosthetic • Uncorrected cyanotic congenital heart disease • Surgically constructed shunts and conduits Valvulopathy following heart transplant	Any manipulation of gingival tissue, dental periapical regions, or perforating the oral mucosa– **PROPHYLAXIS RECOMMENDED‡** (see *Dental Procedures Regimens* table below) (Prophylaxis is *not* recommended for routine anesthetic injections (unless through infected oral mucosa), dental x-rays, shedding of primary teeth, adjustment of orthodontic appliances or placement of orthodontic brackets or removable appliances.)	Incision or biopsy of respiratory tract mucosa– **CONSIDER PROPHYLAXIS** (see *Dental Procedures Regimens table below*) Or For treatment of established infection– **PROPHYLAXIS RECOMMENDED** (See *Dental Procedures Regimens* table for oral flora, but include anti-staphylococcal coverage when *S. aureus* is of concern)	PROPHYLAXIS is no longer recommended solely to prevent endocarditis, **but the following approach is reasonable:** For patients with enterococcal UTIs • treat before elective GU procedures • include enterococcal coverage in perioperative regimen for non-elective GU For patients with existing GU or GI infections or those who receive peri-operative antibiotics to prevent surgical site infections or sepsis • it is reasonable to include agents with anti-enterococcal activity in perioperative coverage†	Include coverage against staphylococci and β-hemolytic streptococci in treatment regimens

PROPHYLAXIS is no longer recommended solely to prevent endocarditis, but the following approach is reasonable: For patients with enterococcal UTIs treat before elective GU procedures; include enterococcal coverage in perioperative regimen for non-elective GU. For patients with existing GU or GI infections or those who receive perioperative antibiotics to prevent surgical site infections or sepsis it is reasonable to include agents with anti-enterococcal activity in perioperative coverage†

PROPHYLACTIC REGIMENS FOR DENTAL PROCEDURES

SITUATION	AGENT	REGIMEN†
Usual oral prophylaxis	Amoxicillin	Adults 2 gm, children 50 mg per kg, orally, 1 hour before procedure
Unable to take oral medications	Ampicillin²	Adults 2 gm, children 50 mg per kg, IV or IM, within 30 min before procedure.
	Cefazolin³ OR	Adults 2 gm, children 50 mg per kg; orally, 1 hour before procedure.
Allergic to penicillins	Clindamycin OR	Adults 600 mg, children 20 mg per kg, orally, 1 hour before procedure
	Azithromycin or clarithromycin	Adults 500 mg, children 15 mg per kg, orally, 1 hour before procedure.
Allergic to penicillins and unable to take oral medications	Cefazolin³ OR	Adults 1 gm, children 50 mg per kg; IV or IM, within 30 min before procedure
	Clindamycin	Adults 600 mg, children 20 mg per kg; IV or IM, within 30 min before procedure

† Agents with anti-enterococcal activity include penicillin, ampicillin, amoxicillin, piperacillin, vancomycin and others. Check susceptibility (if available). (See *Table 5 for highly resistant organisms*.)
‡ 2008 AHA/ACC focused update of guidelines on valvular heart disease use term "is reasonable" to reflect level of evidence (*Circulation 118:887, 2008*).

---

1. Children's dose should not exceed adult dose. AHA document lists all doses as 30-60 min before procedure.
2. AHA lists cefazolin or ceftriaxone (at appropriate doses) as alternatives here.
3. Cephalosporins should not be used in individuals with immediate-type hypersensitivity reaction (urticaria, angioedema, or anaphylaxis) to penicillins or other β-lactams. AHA proposes ceftriaxone as potential alternative to cefazolin, and other 1ˢᵗ or 2ⁿᵈ generation cephalosporin in equivalent doses as potential alternatives to cephalexin.

TABLE 15D – MANAGEMENT OF EXPOSURE TO HIV-1 AND HEPATITIS B AND C*

OCCUPATIONAL EXPOSURE TO BLOOD, PENILE/VAGINAL SECRETIONS OR OTHER POTENTIALLY INFECTIOUS BODY FLUIDS OR TISSUES WITH RISK OF TRANSMISSION OF HEPATITIS B/C AND/OR HIV-1 (E.G., NEEDLESTICK INJURY)

Free consultation for occupational exposures, call (PEPline) 1-888-448-4911. [Information also available at www.aidsinfo.nih.gov]

General steps in management:
1. Wash clean wounds/flush mucous membranes immediately (use of caustic agents or squeezing the wound is discouraged; data lacking regarding antiseptics).
2. Assess risk by doing the following: (a) Characterize exposure; (b) Determine/evaluate source of exposure by medical history, risk behavior, & testing for hepatitis B/C, HIV; (c) Evaluate and test exposed individual for hepatitis B/C & HIV.

Hepatitis B Occupational Exposure

		Exposure Source	
Exposed Person†	**HBs Ag +**	**HBs Ag–**	**Status Unknown or Unavailable for Testing†**
Unvaccinated	Give HBIG 0.06 mL per kg IM & initiate HB vaccine	Initiate HB vaccine	Initiate HB vaccine
Vaccinated (antibody status unknown)	Do anti-HBs on exposed person: If titer ≥10 milli-International units per mL, no rx If titer <10 milli-International units per mL, give HBIG + 1 dose HB vaccine**	No rx necessary	Do anti-HBs on exposed person: If titer ≥10 milli-International units per mL, no rx If titer <10 milli-International units per mL, give 1 dose of HB vaccine**

† Persons previously infected with HBV are immune to reinfection and do not require postexposure prophylaxis.

For known vaccine series responder (titer ≥10 milli-International units per mL), monitoring of levels or booster doses not currently recommended. Known non-responder (<10 milli-International units per mL) to 1st series HB vaccine & exposed to either HBsAg+ source or suspected high-risk source—rx with HBIG & re-initiate vaccine series or give 2 doses HBIG 1 month apart. For non-responders after a 2nd vaccine series, 2 doses HBIG 1 month apart is preferred approach to new exposure.

If known high risk source, treat as if source were HBsAG positive
** Follow-up to assess vaccine response or address completion of vaccine series.

Hepatitis B Non-Occupational Exposure [see MMWR 54 (RR11 and RR16), 2006; MMWR 59 (RR-10):1, 2010]
Postexposure prophylaxis is recommended for persons with discrete nonoccupational exposure to blood or body fluids. Exposures include percutaneous (e.g., bite, needlestick or mucous membrane exposure to HBsAG-positive blood or sterile body fluids; sexual or needle-sharing contact of an HBsAG-positive person, or a victim of sexual assault or sexual abuse by a perpetrator who is HBsAg-positive. If immunoprophylaxis is indicated, it should be initiated ideally within 24 h of exposure. Postexposure prophylaxis is unlikely to be effective if administered more than 7 days after a parenteral exposure or 14 days after a sexual exposure. The hepatitis B vaccine series should be completed regardless. The same guidelines for management of occupational exposures can also be used for nonoccupational exposures. For a previously vaccinated person (i.e., written documentation of being vaccinated) and no documentation of postvaccination titers a discrete exposure to an HBsAG-positive source, it also is acceptable to administer a booster dose of hepatitis B vaccine without checking titers. No treatment is required for a vaccinated person exposed to a source of unknown HBsAG status.

Hepatitis C Exposure
Determine antibody to hepatitis C for both exposed person &, if possible, exposure source. If source + or unknown and exposed person negative, follow-up HCV testing for HCV RNA (detectable in blood in 1-3 weeks) and HCV antibody (90% who seroconvert will do so by 3 months) is advised. No recommended prophylaxis; immune serum globulin not effective. Monitor for early infection, as therapy may ↓ risk of progression to chronic hepatitis. Persons who remain viremic 8-12 weeks after exposure should be treated with a course of pegylated interferon (Gastro 130:632, 2006 and Hpt 43:923, 2006). See Table 14G. Case-control study suggested risk factors for occupational HCV transmission include percutaneous exposure to needle that had been in artery or vein, deep injury, male sex of HCW, & was more likely when source VL >6 log10 copies/mL.

TABLE 15D (2)

HIV: Occupational exposure management *[Adapted from CDC recommendations; MMWR 54 (RR9), 2005, available at www.cdc.gov/mmwr/indrr_2005.html]*

- The decision to initiate postexposure prophylaxis (PEP) for HIV is a clinical judgment that should be made in concert with the exposed healthcare worker (HCW). It is based on:
  1. Likelihood of the source patient having HIV infection: ↑ with history of high-risk activity—injection drug use, sexual activity with known HIV+ person, unprotected sex with multiple partners (either hetero- or homosexual), receipt of blood products 1978–1985, ↑ with clinical signs suggestive of advanced HIV (unexplained wasting, night sweats, thrush, seborrheic dermatitis, etc.).
  2. Type of exposure (approx. 1 in 300–400 needlesticks from infected source will transmit HIV).
  3. Limited data regarding efficacy of PEP *(Cochrane Database Syst Rev. Jan 24; (1):CD002835, 2007).*
  4. Significant adverse effects of PEP drugs & potential for drug interactions.

  Fluids normally considered low risk for transmission, unless visibly bloody, include: urine, vomitus, stool, saliva, nasal secretions, tears and sputum.

  Substances considered potentially infectious include: blood, tissues, semen, vaginal secretions, CSF, synovial, pleural, peritoneal, pericardial and amniotic fluids; and other visibly bloody fluids.

- If source person is **known positive for HIV** or **likely to be infected** and **status of exposure warrants PEP,** antiretroviral drugs should be started **immediately.** If source person is HIV antibody negative, drugs can be stopped unless **source is suspected of having acute HIV infection.** The HCW should be re-tested at **3–4 weeks, 3 & 6 months whether PEP is used or not** (the vast majority of seroconversions will occur by 3 months; delayed conversions after 6 months are exceedingly rare). Tests for HIV RNA should not be used for dx of HIV infection in HCW because of false-positives (esp. at low titers) & these tests are only approved for established HIV infection [a possible exception is if pt develops signs of acute HIV (mononucleosis-like) syndrome within the 1st 4–6 wks of exposure when antibody tests might still be negative.]

- PEP for HIV is usually given for **4 wks** and monitoring of adverse effects recommended: baseline **complete blood count, renal and hepatic panel** to be **repeated at 2 weeks.** 50–75% of HCW on PEP demonstrates mild side-effects (nausea, diarrhea, myalgias, headache, etc.) but in up to ⅓ severe enough to discontinue PEP. Consultation with infectious diseases/ HIV specialist valuable when questions regarding PEP arise. **Seek expert help in special situations, such as pregnancy, renal impairment, treatment-experienced source.**

3 Steps to HIV Postexposure Prophylaxis (PEP) After Occupational Exposure: *[Latest CDC recommendations available at www.aidsinfo.nih.gov]*

Step 1: Determine the exposure code (EC)

Is source material blood, bloody fluid, semen/vaginal fluid or other normally sterile fluid or tissue (see above)?

* Exceptions can be considered when there has been prolonged, high-volume contact.

TABLE 15D (3)

3 Steps to HIV Postexposure Prophylaxis (PEP) After Occupational Exposure *(continued)*

Step 2: Determine the HIV Status Code (HIV SC)

What is the HIV status of the exposure source?

HIV negative	HIV positive		Status unknown	Source unknown
No PEP	**Low titer exposure:** asymptomatic & high CD4 count, low VL (<1500 copies per mL)	**High titer exposure:** advanced AIDS, primary HIV/high viral load or low CD4 count	HIV SC unknown	HIV SC unknown
	HIV SC 1	HIV SC 2		

Regimens: (Treat for 4 weeks; monitor for drug side-effects every 2 weeks):

Basic regimen: ZDV + 3TC, or FTC + TDF, or as an alternative d4T + 3TC.

Expanded regimen: Basic regimen + one of the following: lopinavir/ritonavir *(preferred)*, or (as alternatives) atazanavir/ritonavir or fosamprenavir/ritonavir. Efavirenz can be considered (except in pregnancy or potential for pregnancy—**Pregnancy Category D**), but CNS symptoms might be problematic. [**Do not use nevirapine**; serious adverse reactions including hepatic necrosis reported in healthcare workers.]

Other regimens can be designed. If possible, use antiretroviral drugs for which resistance is unlikely based on susceptibility data or treatment history of source (if known). Seek expert consultation if ART-experienced source or in pregnancy or potential for pregnancy.

NOTE: Some authorities feel that an expanded regimen should be employed whenever PEP is indicated. Expanded regimens are likely to be advantageous with ↑ numbers of ART-experienced source pts or when there is doubt about exact extent of exposures in decision algorithm. Mathematical model suggests that under some conditions, completion of full course basic regimen is better than prematurely discontinued expanded regimen. However, while expanded PEP regimens have ↑ adverse effects, there is not necessarily ↑ discontinuation.

Step 3: Determine Postexposure Prophylaxis (PEP) Recommendation

EC	HIV SC	PEP
1	1	Consider basic regimen[a]
2	1	Recommend basic regimen[a,b]
1	2	Recommend basic regimen[b]
2	2	Recommend expanded regimen[c]
3	1 or 2	Recommend expanded regimen[c]
1, 2, 3	Unknown	If exposure setting suggests risks of HIV exposure, consider basic regimen[a]

[a] Based on estimates of ↑ risk of infection after mucous membrane exposure in occupational setting compared with needlestick.
[b] Or, consider expanded regimen[c]
[c] In high risk circumstances, consider expanded regimen[c] on case-by-case basis.

Around the clock, urgent expert consultation available from: National Clinicians'
Postexposure Prophylaxis Hotline (PEPline) at 1-888-448-4911 (1-888-HIV-4911) and on-line at
http://www.ucsf.edu/hivcntr

POSTEXPOSURE PROPHYLAXIS FOR NON-OCCUPATIONAL EXPOSURES TO HIV-1

[Adapted from CDC recommendations, MMWR 54 (RR2), 2005, available at www.cdc.gov/mmwr/indrr_2005.html]

Because the risk of transmission of HIV via sexual contact or sharing needles by injection drug users may reach or exceed that of occupational needlestick exposure, it is reasonable to consider PEP in persons who have had a non-occupational exposure to blood or other potentially infected fluids (e.g., semen/rectal secretions, breast milk) from an HIV+ source. Risk of HIV acquisition per exposure varies with the act (for needle sharing and receptive anal intercourse, ≥0.5%; approximately 10-fold lower with insertive vaginal or anal intercourse, 0.05–0.07%). Overt or occult traumatic lesions may ↑ risk in survivors of sexual assault.

For pts at risk of acquisition through non-occupational exposure to HIV-1 source material having occurred ≤72 hours before evaluation, DHHS recommendation is to treat for 28 days with an antiretroviral **expanded regimen**, using expanded regimens (efavirenz (not in pregnancy or pregnancy risk—Pregnancy Category D) + (3TC or FTC) + (ZDV or TDF)) or lopinavir/ritonavir + (3TC or FTC) + ZDV) or one of several alternative regimens (see Table 14D & MMWR 54(RR-2):1, 2005). Failures of prophylaxis have been reported, and may be associated with longer interval from exposure to start of PEP; this supports prompt initiation of PEP if it is to be used.

Areas of uncertainty: (1) expanded regimens are not proven to be superior to 2-drug regimens, (2) while PEP not recommended for exposures >72 hours before evaluation, it may possibly be effective in some cases, (3) when HIV status of source patient is unknown, decision to treat and source patient selection must be individualized based on assessment of specific circumstances.

Evaluate for exposures to Hep B. Hep C (see Occupational PEP above), and bacterial sexually-transmitted diseases (see Table 15A) and treat as indicated. DHHS recommendations for sexual exposures to HepB and bacterial pathogens are detailed in MMWR 55(RR-11), 2006. Nonoccupational exposure to an HBsAg-positive source should receive hepB immune globulin preferably within 24-hours of percutaneous or mucosal exposure to blood or body fluids of an HBsAg-positive person, along with hepB vaccine/with follow-up to complete vaccine series. Unvaccinated or not-fully-vaccinated persons exposed to a source with unknown HepBsAg-status should receive vaccine and complete vaccine series. See MMWR 55(RR-11), 2006 for details and recommendations in other circumstances.

TABLE 15E – PREVENTION OF SELECTED OPPORTUNISTIC INFECTIONS IN HUMAN HEMATOPOIETIC CELL TRANSPLANTATION (HCT) OR SOLID ORGAN TRANSPLANTATION (SOT) IN ADULTS WITH NORMAL RENAL FUNCTION.

General comments: Medical centers performing transplants will have selected approaches which are appropriate to the infections encountered, patients represented and resources available at those sites. Regimens continue to evolve and protocols adopted by an institution may differ from those at other centers. Care of transplant patients should be guided by physicians with expertise in this area.

References:

For HCT: Expert guidelines endorsed by the IDSA, updating earlier guidelines (*MMWR 49 (RR-10):1, 2000*) in: *Biol Blood Marrow Transpl 15:1143, 2009*. These guidelines provide recommendations for prevention of additional infections not discussed in this table and provide more detailed information on the infections included here.

For SOT: Recommendations of an expert panel of The Transplantation Society for management of CMV in solid organ transplant recipients in: *Transplantation 89:779, 2010*. Timeline of infections following SOT in: *Amer J Transpl 9 (suppl 4):S3, 2009*.

OPPORTUNISTIC INFECTION	TYPE OF TRANSPLANT	PROPHYLACTIC REGIMENS
CMV (Recipient + or Donor +/Recipient –)	SOT	**Prophylaxis approach:** • **Kidney, kidney/pancreas, pancreas:** Valganciclovir 900 mg or 450 mg po q24h for 3-6 months. Ref for low dose: *Pharm Ther 35:676, 2010; CID 52:313, 2011*. However, concern has been expressed about possibly greater chance of failure and resistance emerging on low-dose prophylaxis, particularly in D+/R- (CID 52: 322, 2011). Hence, low-dose NOT recommended for D+ /R- patients. Alternative: Ganciclovir iv or po. • **Liver:** Ganciclovir 5 mg/kg iv q24h or Ganciclovir 1 gm po tid for 3-6 months. Valganciclovir^AAA 900 mg po q24h not FDA approved for this indication, but is widely used and recommended as an alternative. • **Lung:** Ganciclovir 5 mg/kg iv q24h (some give this dose bid for 5-7 days initially, before switching to q24h) or Valganciclovir^AAA 900 mg po q24h for ≥ 6 months. Some add CMV immune globulin in selected cases. • **Heart:** Ganciclovir 5 mg/kg iv q24h or Ganciclovir 1 gm po tid or Valganciclovir 900 mg po q24h for 3-6 months. Some add CMV immune globulin in selected cases. • **Intestine:** Ganciclovir 5 mg/kg iv q24h or Ganciclovir^ 1 gm po tid or Valganciclovir 900 mg po q24h for ≥ 6 months. Some add CMV immune globulin in selected cases. **Pre-emptive therapy:** for kidney, liver, pancreas, heart, monitor weekly for viremia (by PCR or antigenemia). If viremia detected, begin treatment doses of Ganciclovir 5 mg/kg iv bid or Valganciclovir 900 mg po bid. Continue treatment until clearing of test for viremia, but for not less than 2 weeks. At that point, either switch to secondary prophylaxis or resume pre-emptive approach. **Comments:** • Expert panel recommendations from which the above are adopted favor prophylaxis approach in highest risk recipients of SOT (*Transplantation 89:779, 2010*). • With anti-viral prophylaxis, onset of CMV disease appearing later; maintain vigilance for possible late-onset CMV disease and treat accordingly. • Anti-lymphocyte therapies increase risk of CMV and may require extension or re-institution of prophylaxis or pre-emptive approach. • CMV immune globulin regimens for lung, heart, liver or pancreas SOT: 150 mg/kg within 72 h of transplant and at 2, 4, 6 and 8 weeks; then 100 mg/kg at weeks 12 and 16.
	HCT	**Pre-emptive therapy:** monitor 2 once weekly from day 10 to 100 for CMV-antigenemia, and start treatment if positive. • **Allogeneic:** Ganciclovir 5 mg/kg iv bid for 7-14 days (induction) then once daily (maintenance) until negative viral tests (minimum treatment 3 weeks total course of induction + maintenance). • **Autologous:** Ganciclovir 5 mg/kg iv bid 7 days (induction), then once daily (maintenance), then once daily (maintenance) until negative viral tests (minimum treatment 2 weeks total course). Oral Valganciclovir^AAA (900 mg po bid induction, then 900 mg po once daily for maintenance) has been used in place of iv Ganciclovir, but is not approved for this indication. • Continue screening after completion of each course. **OR, alternatively:** **Prophylaxis approach:** from engraftment to day 100, Ganciclovir 5 mg/kg iv bid for 5-7 days (induction), then 5 mg/kg once daily (maintenance). **Late CMV reactivation:** certain HCT recipients require screening for CMV reactivation (and pre-emptive treatment) beyond 100 days (for details, *see Biol Blood Marrow Transpl 15:1143, 2009*).

TABLE 15E (2)

OPPORTUNISTIC INFECTION	TYPE OF TRANSPLANT	PROPHYLACTIC REGIMENS
Hepatitis B	SOT	For anti-viral agents with activity against HBV, see *Table 14B, page 169 to 170*. For discussion of HBV hyperimmune globulin in liver transplantation, see *J Viral Hepatitis (Suppl 1): 37, 2007*. Regimens to prevent re-infection after transplantation are evolving (*Liver Transplantation 14 (suppl 2): S23, 2008*).
	HCT	Patients who are anti-HBC positive and anti-HBs positive, but without evidence of active viral replication, can be monitored for ↑LFTs and presence of ↑HBV-DNA, and given pre-emptive therapy at that time. Alternatively, prophylactic anti-viral therapy can be given, commencing before transplant. (See *guidelines for other specific situations: Biol Blood Marrow Transpl 15:1143, 2009*.) These guidelines recommend Lamivudine 100 mg po q24h as an anti-viral.
Herpes simplex	SOT	Acyclovir 400 mg po bid, starting early post-transplant (*Clin Microbiol Rev 10:86, 1997*).
	HCT	Acyclovir 250 mg per meter-squared iv q12h **or** Acyclovir 400 mg to 800 mg po bid, from conditioning to engraftment or resolution or mucositis. For those requiring prolonged suppression of HSV, the higher dose (Acyclovir 800 mg po bid) is recommended to minimize the risk of emerging resistance.
Aspergillus spp.	SOT	Lung/heart/lung transplant: optimal mgmt unknown. Aerosolized lipid Ampho B + oral anti-aspergillus agent used (*Amer J Transpl 4 (Suppl 10):110, 2004; Ann Pharmacother 44:546, 2010*).
	HCT	Posaconazole 200 mg po tid approved for prophylaxis of invasive infection due to Aspergillus spp. and Candida spp. in high-risk, severely immunocompromised patients (eg. HCT with GVHD). In comparative trial in patients with GVHD, Posaconazole was similar to Fluconazole in preventing invasive fungal infections, but was more effective in preventing invasive Aspergillus infection (*NEJM 356:335, 2007*). Retrospective analysis suggests that Voriconazole would have efficacy in steroid-treated patients with GVHD (*Bone Marrow Transpl 45:662, 2010*), but is not approved for this indication.
Candida spp.	SOT	Liver: Fluconazole 400 mg po q24h x 3 mos. High risk pts (re-transplants, dialysis, SBP) (*Transpl 75:2023, 2003*). Fluconazole resistance (*Liver Transpl 12:850, 2006*).
	HCT	Fluconazole 400 mg po or iv once daily from day 0 to engraftment or when ANC consistently >1000, or Posaconazole 200 mg po tid approved for high-risk patients (e.g., with GVHD or prolonged neutropenia), or Micafungin 50 mg iv once daily.
Coccidioides immitis	Any	Fluconazole 200-400 mg po q24h (*Transpl Inf Dis 5:3, 2003; Am J Transpl 6:340, 2006*). See *CID 21:45, 2008* for approach at one center in endemic area; e.g., for positive serology without evidence of active infection. Fluconazole 400 mg po q24h for first year post-transplant, then 200 mg po q24h thereafter.
Pneumocystis jiroveci	SOT	TMP-SMX: 1 single-strength tab po q24h or 1 double-strength tab po once daily for 3 to 7 days per week. Duration: kidney, 6 mos to 1 year (*Amer J Transpl 9 (suppl 3):S59, 2009*); heart, lung, liver: ≥1 year to life-long (*Amer J Transpl 4 (suppl 10): 135, 2004*).
	HCT	TMP-SMX: 1 single-strength tab po q24h or 1 double-strength tab po once daily or once a day for 3 days per week, from engraftment to ≥ 6 mos post transplant.
Toxoplasma gondii	SOT	TMP-SMX (1 SS tab po q24h or 1 DS tab po once daily x 3-7 days/wk for 6 mos post-transplant. (See *Clin Micro Infect 14:1089, 2008*).
	HCT	TMP-SMX: 1 single-strength tab po q24h or 1 double-strength tab po once daily or once a day for 3 days per week, from engraftment to ≥ 6 mos post transplant for seropositive allogeneic transplant recipients.
Trypanosoma cruzi	Heart	May be transmitted from organs or transfusions (*CID 48:1534, 2009*). Inspect peripheral blood of suspected cases for parasites (*MMWR 55:798, 2006*). Risk of reactivation during immunosuppression is variable (*JAMA 298:2171, 2007; JAMA 299:1134, 2008; J Cardiac Fail 15:249, 2009*). If known Chagas disease in donor or recipient, contact CDC for treatment options (phone 770-488-7775 or in emergency 770-488-7100).

TABLE 16 – PEDIATRIC DOSAGES OF SELECTED ANTIBACTERIAL AGENTS*
Adapted from: (1) Nelson's Pocket Book of Pediatric Antimicrobial Therapy 2009,
J. Bradley & J. Nelson, eds., American Academy of Pediatrics, 2009.

DRUG	DOSES IN MG PER KG PER DAY OR MG PER KG AT FREQUENCY INDICATED[1]				
	BODY WEIGHT <2000 gm		BODY WEIGHT >2000 gm		>28 DAYS OLD
	0–7 days	8–28 days	0–7 days	8–28 days	
Aminoglycosides, IV or IM (check levels; some dose by gestational age + wks of life; *see Nelson's Pocket Book, p. 25*)					
Amikacin	7.5 q18–24h	7.5 q12h	10 q12h	10 q12h	10 q8h
Gent/tobra	2.5 q18–24h	2.5 q12h	2.5 q12h	2.5 q12h	2.5 q8h
Aztreonam, IV	30 q12h	30 q8h	30 q8h	30 q6h	30 q6h
Cephalosporins					
Cefaclor					20–40 div tid
Cefadroxil					30 div bid (max 2 gm per day)
Cefazolin	25 q12h	25 q12h	25 q12h	25 q8h	25 q8h
Cefdinir					7 q12h or 14 q24h
Cefepime	30 q12h	30 q12h	30 q12h	30 q12h	150 div q8h
Cefixime					8 as q24h or div bid
Cefotaxime	50 q12h	50 q8h	50 q12h	50 q8h	50 q8h (75 q6h for meningitis)
Cefoxitin		20 q12h			80–160 div q6h
Cefpodoxime					10 div bid (max 400 mg per day)
Cefprozil					15–30 div bid (max 1 gm per day)
Ceftazidime	50 q12h	50 q8h	50 q8h	50 q8h	50 q8h
Ceftibuten					4.5 bid
Ceftizoxime					33–66 q8h
Ceftriaxone	25 q24h	50 q24h	25 q24h	50 q24h	50 q24h (meningitis 100)
Cefuroxime IV	50 q12h	50 q8h	50 q8h	50 q8h	50 q8h (80 q8h for meningitis)
po					10–15 bid (max 1 gm per day)
Cephalexin					25–50 div q6h (max 4 gm per day)
Loracarbef					15–30 div bid (max 0.8 gm per day)
Chloramphenicol IV	25 q24h	25 q24h	25 q24h	15 q12h	12.5–25 q6h (max 2–4 gm per day)
Clindamycin IV	5 q12h	5 q8h	5 q8h	5 q6h	7.5 q6h
po					
Ciprofloxacin[2] po					20–30 div bid (max 1.5 gm per day)
Ertapenem IV	No data	No data	No data	No data	15 q12h (max. 1g/day)
Imipenem[3] IV			25 q12h	25 q8h	15–25 q6h (max 2–4 gm per day)
Linezolid	10 q12h	10 q8h	10 q8h	10 q8h	10 q8h to age 12
Macrolides					
Erythro IV & po	10 q12h	10 q8h	10 q12h	13 q8h	10 q6h
Azithro po/IV	5 q24h	10 q24h	5 q24h	10 q24h	10 q24h
Clarithro po					7.5 q12h (max. 1 gm per day)
Meropenem IV	20 q12h	20 q8h	20 q12h	20 q8h	60–120 div q8h (120 for meningitis)
Metro IV & po	7.5 q24h	7.5 q12h	7.5 q12h	15 q12h	7.5 q6h
Penicillins					
Ampicillin	50 q12h	50 q8h	50 q8h	50 q6h	50 q6h
AMP-sulbactam					100–300 div q6h
Amoxicillin po				30 div bid	25–50 div tid
Amox-Clav po			30 div bid	30 div bid	45 or 90 (AM/CL-HD) div bid if over 12wks
Dicloxacillin					12–25 div q6h
Mezlocillin	75 q12h	75 q8h	75 q12h	75 q8h	75 q6h
Nafcillin, oxacillin IV	25 q12h	25 q8h	25 q8h	37 q6h	37 q6h (to max. 8–12 gm per day)
Piperacillin, PIP-tazo IV	50 q12h	100 q12h	100 q12h	100 q8h	100 q6h
Ticarcillin, TC/CL IV	75 q12h	75 q8h	75 q8h	75 q6h	75 q6h
Tinidazole					> Age 3: 50 mg/kg for 1 dose
Penicillin G, U/kg IV	50,000 q12h	75,000 q8h	50,000 q8h	50,000 q6h	50,000 units/kg per day
Penicillin V					25–50 mg per kg per day div q6–8h
Rifampin IV, po	10 q24h	10 q24h	10 q24h	10 q24h	10 q24h
Sulfisoxazole po					120–150 mg/kg per day div q4–6h
TMP-SMX po, IV; UTI: 8–12 TMP component div bid; Pneumocystis: 20 TMP component div q6h					
Tetracycline po (age 8 or older)					25–50 div q6h (>7yr old)
Doxycycline po, IV (age 8 or older)					2–4 div bid to max of 200 (>7yr old)
Vancomycin IV	12.5 q12h	15 q12h	18 q12h	22 q12h	40 div q6–8h [some start with 15 mg/kg IV q6h (normal renal function)]; 60 for meningitis.

[1] May need higher doses in patients with meningitis: *see CID 39:1267, 2004.*

[2] With exception of cystic fibrosis, anthrax, and complicated UTI, not approved for use under age 18.

[3] Not recommended in children with CNS infections due to risk of seizures.

* *See page 2 for abbreviations*

TABLE 17A – DOSAGE OF ANTIMICROBIAL DRUGS IN ADULT PATIENTS WITH RENAL IMPAIRMENT

- For listing of drugs with NO need for adjustment for renal failure, see *Table 17B*
- Adjustments for renal failure are based on an estimate of creatinine clearance (CrCl) which reflects the glomerular filtration rate.
- **Different methods for calculating estimated CrCl are suggested for non-obese and obese patients.**
  - Calculations for ideal body weight (IBW) in kg:
    - *Men:* 50 kg plus 2.3 kg/inch over 60 inches height.
    - *Women:* 45 kg plus 2.3 kg/inch over 60 inches height.
  - Obese is defined as 20% over ideal body weight or body mass index (BMI) >30

- Calculations of estimated CrCl *(References, see (NEJM 354:2473, 2006 (non-obese); AJM 84:1053, 1988 (obese))*
  - **Non-obese patient**—
    - Calculate ideal body weight (IBW) in kg (as above)
    - Use the following formula to determine estimated CrCl

$$\frac{(140 \text{ minus age}) \times (\text{IBW in kg})}{72 \times \text{serum creatinine}} = \text{CrCl in mL/min for men.}$$
Multiply answer by 0.85 for women (estimated)

  - **Obese patient**—
    - Weight ≥20% over IBW or BMI >30
    - Use the following formulas to determine estimated CrCl

$$\frac{(137 \text{ minus age}) \times [(0.285 \times \text{wt in kg}) + (12.1 \times \text{ht in meters}^2)]}{51 \times \text{serum creatinine}} = \text{CrCl (obese male)}$$

$$\frac{(146 \text{ minus age}) \times [(0.287 \times \text{wt in kg}) + (9.74 \times \text{ht in meters}^2)]}{60 \times \text{serum creatinine}} = \text{CrCl (obese female)}$$

- If estimated CrCl ≥90 mL/min, see *Tables 10C and 10D for dosing.*
- What weight should be used to calculate dosage on a mg/kg basis?
  - If less than 20% over IBW, use the patient's actual weight for all drugs.
  - **For obese patients** (≥20% over IBW or BMI >30)
    - **Aminoglycosides:** IBW + 0.4 (actual body weight minus IBW) = adjusted weight.
    - **Vancomycin:** actual body weight (whether non-obese or obese.
    - **All other drugs:** insufficient data *(Pharmacotherapy 27:1081, 2007).*

- For slow or sustained extended daily dialysis **(SLEDD)** over 6-12 hours, adjust does as for CRRT. For details, see *CID 49:433, 2009; CCM 39:560, 2011.*
- General reference: Drug Prescribing in Renal Failure, 5th ed., Aronoff, et al. (eds) *(Amer College Physicians, 2007 and drug package inserts).*

TABLE 17A (2)

ANTIMICROBIAL	HALF-LIFE (NORMAL/ESRD) hr	DOSE FOR NORMAL RENAL FUNCTION	METHOD (see footer)	ADJUSTMENT FOR RENAL FAILURE Estimated creatinine clearance (CrCl) mL/min >50-90	10-50	<10	HEMODIALYSIS, CAPD	COMMENTS & DOSAGE FOR CRRT
ANTIBACTERIAL ANTIBIOTICS								
Aminoglycoside Antibiotics: Traditional multiple daily doses—adjustment for renal disease								
Amikacin	1.4-2.3/17-150	7.5 mg per kg q12h or 15 mg/kg once daily (see below)	I	7.5 mg/kg q24h or 15 mg/kg once daily	30-50: 7.5 mg/kg q24h 10-30: 7.5 mg/kg q48h	7.5 mg/kg q72h	HEMO: 7.5 mg/kg AD CAPD: 15-20 mg lost per L dialysate per day (see Comment)	High flux hemodialysis membranes lead to unpredictable aminoglycoside clearance, measure post-dialysis drug levels for efficacy and toxicity. With CAPD, pharmacokinetics highly variable—check serum levels. Usual method for CAPD: 2 liters of dialysis fluid placed qid or 8 liters per day (give 8x20 mg lost per L = 160 mg per day ... amikacin supplement per day).
Gentamicin, Tobramycin (Monitor levels)	2-3/20-60	1.7 mg per kg q8h. Once daily dosing below	I	5-7 mg/kg once or 1.7 mg/kg q8h	Same dose for CRRT See Comment for SLEDD dose	1.7 mg/kg q48-72h	HEMO: 3 mg/kg AD. Monitor levels CAPD: 3-4 mg lost per L dialysate per day	Adjust dosing weight for obesity: [ideal body weight + 0.4 (actual body weight – ideal body weight)] (CID 25:112, 1997).
Netilmicin[NUS]	2-3/35-72	2 mg/kg q8h. Once daily dosing below	I	2 mg/kg q8h: or 6.5 mg/kg once daily	Same dose for CRRT	2 mg/kg q48h	HEMO3 mg/kg CAPD: 3-4 mg lost per L dialysate per day	Gent SLEDD dose in critically ill: 6 mg/kg IV q48h starting 30 min before start of SLEDD (SLEDD: q48h Gent). (AAC54:3635, 2010)
Streptomycin	2-3/30-80	15 mg per kg (max. of 1 gm) q24h. Once daily dosing below	I	15 mg/kg q24-72h Same dose for CRRT	15 mg/kg q24-72h Same dose for CRRT	15 mg/kg q72-96h	HEMO: 7.5 mg/kg AD CAPD: 20-40 mg lost per L dialysate per day	

ONCE-DAILY AMINOGLYCOSIDE THERAPY: ADJUSTMENT IN RENAL INSUFFICIENCY (see Table 10D for OD dosing/normal renal function)

Creatinine Clearance (mL per min.)	>80	60-80	40-60	30-40	20-30	10-20	<10-0
Drug	Dose q24h (mg per kg)	Dose q24h (mg per kg)			Dose q48h (mg per kg)	Dose q72h and AD	Dose q48h and AD
Gentamicin/Tobramycin	5.1	4	3.5	2.5	4	3	2
Amikacin/Kanamycin/streptomycin	15	12	7.5		7.5		8 q96h
Isepamicin[NUS]	8	8	8	8 q48h	8	8 q72h	8 q96h
Netilmicin[NUS]	6.5	5	4	2	3	2.5	2

Carbapenem Antibiotics

Doripenem	1/18	500 mg IV q8h	D&I	500 mg IV q8h	≥30 – ≤50: 250 mg IV q8h >10 – <30: 250 mg IV q12h	No data	No data. CRRT ref: AAC 55:1187, 2011.	
Ertapenem	4/>4	1 gm q24h	D	1 gm q24h	0.5 gm q24h (CrCl <30)	0.5 gm q24h	HEMO: Dose as for CrCl <10: if dosed <6 hrs prior to HD, give 150 mg supplement AD	
Imipenem (see Comment)	1/4	0.5 gm q6-8h	D&I	250-500 mg q6-8h	250 mg q6-12h: 0.5-1 gm bid (AAC 49:2421, 2005)	125-250 mg q12h	HEMO: Dose AD CAPD: Dose for CrCl <10	potential for seizures if recommended doses exceeded in pts with CrCl <20 mL per min. See pkg insert, esp. for pts <70 kg
Meropenem	1/6-8	1 gm q8h	D&I	1 gm q8h	1 gm q12h Same dose for CRRT	0.5 gm q24h	HEMO: Dose AD CAPD: Dose for CrCl <10	

Abbreviation Key: Adjustment Method: **D** = dose adjustment, **I** = interval adjustment; **CAPD** = continuous ambulatory peritoneal dialysis; **CRRT** = continuous renal replacement therapy; **HEMO** = hemodialysis; **AD** = after dialysis; "**Supplement**" or "**Extra**" is to replace drug lost during dialysis—additional drug beyond continuation of regimen for CrCl < 10 mL/min.

TABLE 17A (3)

ANTIMICROBIAL	HALF-LIFE (NORMAL/ESRD) hr	DOSE FOR NORMAL RENAL FUNCTION	METHOD (See footer)	ADJUSTMENT FOR RENAL FAILURE — Estimated creatinine clearance (CrCl), mL/min >50-90	10-50	<10	HEMODIALYSIS, CAPD	COMMENTS & DOSAGE FOR CRRT
ANTIBACTERIAL ANTIBIOTICS								
Cephalosporin Antibiotics: DATA ON SELECTED PARENTERAL CEPHALOSPORINS *(continued)*								
Cefazolin	1.9/40-70	1-2 gm q8h	I	q8h	q12h	q24-48h	HEMO: Extra 0.5-1 gm AD CAPD: 0.5 gm q12h	
Cefepime	2.2/18	2 gm q8h (max. dose)	D&I	q8h	2 gm q12-24h Same dose for CRRT	1 gm q24h	HEMO: Extra 1 gm AD CAPD: 1-2 gm q48h	
Cefotaxime, Cefuroxime	1.7/15-35	2 gm q8h	I	q8-12h	q12-24h	q24h	HEMO: Extra 1 gm AD CAPD: 0.5-1 gm q24h	Active metabolite of cefotaxime in ESRD. ↓ dose further for hepatic & renal failure.
Cefotetan	3.5/13-25	1-2 gm q12h	D	100%	1-2 gm q24h Same dose for CRRT	1-2 gm q48h	HEMO: Extra 1 gm AD CAPD: 1 gm q24h	CRRT dose: 750 mg q12h
Cefoxitin	0.8/13-23	2 gm q8h	I	q8h	q8-12h Same dose for CRRT	q24-48h	HEMO: Extra 1 gm AD CAPD: 1 gm q24h	May falsely increase serum creatinine by interference with assay.
Ceftaroline	1.6/-	600 mg IV q12h	D	600 mg IV q12h	30-50: 400 mg q12h 15-30: 300 mg q12h	< 15: 200 mg q12h	HEMO: Extra 1 gm AD CAPD: 200 mg q12h	1-hr infusion for all doses
Ceftazidime	1.2/13-25	2 gm q8h	I	q8-12h	q12-24h Same dose for CRRT	q24-48h	HEMO: Extra 1 gm AD CAPD: 0.5 gm q24h	Since 1/2 dose is dialyzed, post-dialysis dose is max. of 3 gm.
Ceftobiprole	2.9-3.3/21	500 mg IV q8-12h	I	500 mg IV q8-12h	≥30 & ≤50: 500 mg q12h over 2 hrs ≥10 & <30: 250 mg q12h over 2 hrs	No data	No data	
Cefuroxime sodium	1.2/17	0.75-1.5 gm q8h	I	q8h	q8-12h Same dose for CRRT	q24h	HEMO: Dose AD CAPD: Dose for CrCl <10	
Fluoroquinolone Antibiotics								
Ciprofloxacin	3-6/6-9	500-750 mg po (or 400 mg IV) q12h	D	100%	50-75% CRRT 400 mg IV q24h	50%	HEMO: 250 mg po or 200 mg IV q12h CAPD: 250 mg po or 200 mg IV q8h	
Gatifloxacin[NUS]	7-14/11-40	400 mg po/IV q24h	D	400 mg	400 mg, then 200 mg q24h Same dose for CRRT	400 mg, then 200 mg q24h	HEMO: 200 mg q24h AD CAPD: 200 mg q24h	
Gemifloxacin	7/~7	320 mg po q24h	D	320 mg q24h	160 mg q24h	160 mg q24h	HEMO: 160 mg q24h AD CAPD: 160 mg q24h	
Levofloxacin	6-8/76	750 mg q24h IV, PO	D&I	750 mg q24h	20-49: 750 mg q48h	<20: 750 mg once, then 500 mg q48h	HEMO/CAPD: Dose for CrCl <20	CRRT 750 mg once, then 500 mg q48h, although not FDA-approved
Ofloxacin	7/28-37	200-400 mg q12h	D	200-400 mg q12h	200-400 mg q24h Same dose for CRRT	200 mg q24h	HEMO: Dose for CrCl <10, AD CAPD: 300 mg q24h	
Macrolide Antibiotics								
Clarithromycin	5-7/22	0.5-1 gm q12h	D	100%	75%	50-75%	HEMO: Dose AD CAPD: None	CRRT as for CrCl 10-50
Erythromycin	1.4/5-6	250-500 mg q6h	D	100%	100%	50-75%	HEMO/CAPD/CRRT: None	Ototoxicity with high doses in ESRD

Abbreviation Key, Adjustment Method: **D** = dose adjustment; **I** = interval adjustment; **D&I** = dose and interval adjustment; **CAPD** = continuous ambulatory peritoneal dialysis; **CRRT** = continuous renal replacement therapy; **HEMO** = hemodialysis; **AD** = after dialysis; **"Supplement"** or **"Extra"** is to replace drug lost during dialysis – additional drug beyond continuation of regimen for CrCl < 10 mL/min.

TABLE 17A (4)

ANTIMICROBIAL	HALF-LIFE (NORMAL/ ESRD) hr	DOSE FOR NORMAL RENAL FUNCTION	METHOD (see footer)	ADJUSTMENT FOR RENAL FAILURE Estimated creatinine clearance (CrCl) mL/min			HEMODIALYSIS, CAPD	COMMENTS & DOSAGE FOR CRRT
				>50-90	10-50	<10		
ANTIBACTERIAL ANTIBIOTICS *(continued)*								
Miscellaneous Antibacterial Antibiotics								
Colistin (Polymyxin E) Based on 105 pts (AAC 55:3284, 2011) All doses refer to Colistin "base" in mg	<6/≥48	*See Table 10A, page 101 for loading dose and maintenance dose*	D & I	$3.5 \times [(1.5 \times CrCl) = 30]$ = total daily dose of Colistin base. Divide and give q12h. **CrCln** = normalized CrCl based on body surface area (BSA): Pt BSA in m²/1.73m².			**Intermittent Hemodialysis:** • Calculation of dose: 3.5 (30) =105 mg (CrCl is zero). • On days with no hemodialysis, give total daily dose of 105 mg divided bid. • On dialysis days, need to supplement the dose by 50% due to colistimethate filtration by the dialysis membrane. • So, on dialysis days the total dose is 150 mg; divide and give half the dose during the last hour of hemodialysis and the second half 12 hours later.	**CAPD:** • 160 mg q24h (unable to locate modern CAPD data) **CRRT:** • For average serum steady state concentration of 3.5 µg/mL, the total daily dose is 672 mg; the dose is divided and given q12h. **The dose is necessarily high due to removal of drug by the dialysis membranes.** Rationale: 3.5 µg/mL as the targeted serum level × 192 mg for each 1 µg/mL of targeted serum level = total daily dose, i.e., 3.5 × 192 = 672. *See AAC 55: 3284, 2011 for data.*
Daptomycin	9.4/30	4-6 mg per kg per day	I	4-6 mg per kg per day	CrCl <30, 4-6 mg per kg q48h CRRT: 8 mg/kg q48h (CCM 39:19, 2011)		HEMO & CAPD: 6 mg per kg q48h (during or after q48h dialysis if possible). If next planned dialysis is 72 hrs away, give 9 mg/kg (AAC 55:1677, 2011)	
Linezolid	5-6/6-8	600 mg po/IV q12h	None	600 mg q12h	600 mg q12h **Same dose for CRRT**	600 mg q12h AD	HEMO: As for CrCl <10 CAPD & CRRT: No dose adjustment	Accumulation of 2 metabolites—risk unknown (JAC 56:172, 2005)
Metronidazole	6-14/7-21	7.5 mg per kg q6h	D	100%	100% **Same dose for CRRT**	50%	HEMO: Dose as for CrCl <10 AD CAPD: Dose for CrCl <10	
Nitrofurantoin	0.5/1	50-100 mg	D	100%	Avoid	Avoid	Not applicable	
Sulfamethoxazole (SMX)	10/20-50	1 gm q8h	I	q12h	q18h	q24h	HEMO: Extra 1 gm AD CAPD: 1 gm q24h	
Teicoplanin^NUS	45/62-230	6 mg per kg per day	I	q24h	Same dose for CAVH q48h	q72h	HEMO: Dose for CrCl <10 CAPD: Dose for CrCl <10	
Telithromycin	10/15	800 mg q24h	D	800 mg q24h	600 mg q24h (<30 mL per min.)	600 mg q24h	HEMO: 600 mg AD CAPD: No data	If CrCl <30, reduce dose to 600 mg once daily. If both liver and renal failure, dose is 400 mg once daily
Televancin	7-8/17.9	10 mg/kg q24h	D&I	10 mg/kg q24h	30-50: 7.5 mg/kg q24h	**<30:** 10 mg/kg q48h	No data	No data
Temocillin		1-2 gm q12h	I	1-2 gm q12h	1-2 gm q24h	1 gm q48h	HEMO: 1 gm q48h AD CAPD: 1 gm q48h	

Abbreviation Key: Adjustment Method: **D** = dose adjustment; **I** = interval adjustment; **D&I** = to replace drug lost during dialysis – additional drug beyond continuation of regimen for CrCl < 10 mL/min. **HEMO** = hemodialysis; **AD** = after dialysis; **"Supplement"** or **"Extra"** is to replace drug lost during dialysis – additional drug beyond continuation of regimen for CrCl < 10 mL/min.

TABLE 17A (5)

ANTIMICROBIAL	HALF-LIFE (NORMAL/ ESRD) hr	DOSE FOR NORMAL RENAL FUNCTION	METHOD (see footer)	ADJUSTMENT FOR RENAL FAILURE Estimated creatinine clearance (CrCl) mL/min			HEMODIALYSIS, CAPD	COMMENTS & DOSAGE FOR CRRT
				>50-90	10-50	<10		
ANTIBACTERIAL ANTIBIOTICS *(continued)*								
Trimethoprim (TMP)	11/20-49	100-200 mg q12h	I	q12h	>30: q12h; 10-30: q18h; **Same dose for CRRT**	q24h	HEMO: Dose AD; CAPD: q24h	CRRT dose: q18h
Trimethoprim-sulfamethoxazole-DS (Doses based on TMP component)								
treatment (based on TMP component)	As for TMP	5-20 mg/kg/day divided q6-12h	D	No dose adjustment	30-50: No dose adjustment; 10-29: Reduce dose by 50%	Not recommended; but if used: 5-10 mg/kg q24h	Not recommended; but if used: 5-10 mg/kg AD; CRRT: 5-7.5 mg/kg q8h	
TMP-SMX Prophylaxis	As for TMP	1 tab po q24h or 3 times per week	No change	100%	100%	100%		
Vancomycin[1]	6/200-250	1 gm q12h	D&I	1 gm q12h	1 gm q24-96h	1 gm q4-7 days	HEMO: For trough conc of 15-20 µg/mL, give 15 mg/kg if next dialysis in 1 day; give 25 mg/kg if next dialysis in 2 days; give 35 mg/kg if next dialysis in 3 days *(CID 53:124, 2011)*	CAVH/CVVH: 500 mg q24-48h. New hemodialysis membranes ↑ clear. of vanco; **check levels**
Penicillins								
Amoxicillin	1/5-20	250-500 mg q8h	I	q8h	q8-12h	q8-12h	HEMO: Dose AD; CAPD: 250 mg q12h; CRRT: q8h	IV amoxicillin not available in the U.S. CRRT dose: q8-12h q8-12h
Amoxicillin/ Clavulanate[2]	1.3 AM/1; 5-20/4	500/125 mg q8h (see Comments)	D&I	500/125 mg q8h	250-500 mg AM component q12h	250-500 mg AM component q24h	HEMO: Dose AD; extra dose after dialysis	If CrCl <30 per mL **do not use** 875/125 or 1000/62.5 AM/CL
Amoxicillin ext. rel. tabs	1.5/?	775 mg once daily	Once daily	Once daily	CrCl <30, no data, avoid usage	CrCl <30, avoid usage	HEMO: As for CrCl <10; extra dose after dialysis	
Ampicillin (AM)/ Sulbactam(SB)	1 (AM)/1 (SB); 9 (AM)/10 (SB)	2 gm AM + 1 gm SB q6h	I	q6h	q8-12h	q24h	HEMO: Dose AD; CAPD: 2 gm AM/1 gm SB q24h	CRRT dose: 1.5 AM/0.75 SB q12h
Aztreonam	2/6-8	2 gm q8h	D	100%	50-75% **Same dose for CRRT**	25%	HEMO: Extra 0.5 gm AD; CAPD: Dose for CrCl <10	Technically is a β-lactam antibiotic.
Penicillin G	0.5/6-20	0.5-4 million U q4h	D	100%	75% **Same dose for CRRT**	20-50%	HEMO: Dose AD; CAPD: Dose for CrCl <10	1.7 mEq potassium per million units. ↑s potential of seizure. 10 million units per day max. dose in ESRD.
Piperacillin	1/3.3-5.1	3-4 gm q4-6h	I	q4-6h	q6-8h **Same dose for CRRT**	q8h	HEMO: 2 gm q8h plus 1 gm extra AD; CAPD: Dose for CrCl <10	1.9 mEq sodium per gm

[1] If renal failure, use EMIT assay to measure levels; levels overestimated by RIA or fluorescent immunoassay.

[2] Clavulanate cleared by liver, not kidney. Hence as dose of combination decreased, a deficiency of clavulanate may occur *(JAMA 285:386, 2001)*.

Abbreviation Key: Adjustment Method: **D** = dose adjustment, **I** = interval adjustment; **CAPD** = continuous ambulatory peritoneal dialysis; **CRRT** = continuous renal replacement therapy; **HEMO** = hemodialysis; **AD** = after dialysis; **"Supplement"** or **"Extra"** is to replace drug lost during dialysis – additional drug beyond continuation of regimen for CrCl < 10 mL/min.

TABLE 17A (6)

ANTIMICROBIAL	HALF-LIFE (NORMAL/ ESRD) hr	DOSE FOR NORMAL RENAL FUNCTION	METHOD (see footer)	ADJUSTMENT FOR RENAL FAILURE Estimated creatinine clearance (CrCl), mL/min >50-90	10-50	<10	HEMODIALYSIS, CAPD	COMMENTS & DOSAGE FOR CRRT
ANTIBACTERIAL ANTIBIOTICS (continued)								
Pip (P)/Tazo(T)	0.71-1.2 (both)/2-6	3.375 - 4.5 gm q6-8h	D&I	100%	2.25 gm q6h <20t q8h **Same dose for CRRT**	2.25 gm q8h	HEMO: Dose for CrCl <10 + extra 0.75 gm AD CAPD: 4.5 gm q12h; CRRT: 2.25 gm q6h	
Ticarcillin	1.2/13	3 gm q4h	D&I	1-2 gm q4h	1-2 gm q8h **Same dose for CRRT**	1-2 gm q12h	HEMO: Extra 3.0 gm AD CAPD: Dose for CrCl <10	5.2 mEq sodium per gm
Ticarcillin/ Clavulanate[2]	1.2/11-16	3.1 gm q4h	D&I	3.1 gm q4h	3.1 gm q8-12h **Same dose for CRRT**	2 gm q12h	HEMO: Extra 3.1 gm AD CAPD: 3.1 gm q12h	See footnote[2]
Tetracycline Antibiotics								
Tetracycline	6-10/57-108	250-500 mg qid	I	q8-12h	q12-24h **Same dose for CRRT**	q24h	HEMO/CAPD/CAVH: None	Avoid in ESRD
ANTIFUNGAL ANTIBIOTICS								
Amphotericin B & Lipid-based ampho B	24h-15 days/unchanged	Non-lipid: 0.4-1 mg/kg/day ABLC: 5 mg/kg/day LAB: 3-6 mg/kg/day	I	q24h	q24h **Same dose for CRRT**	q24h	HEMO/CAPD/CRRT: No dose adjustment	For ampho B, toxicity lessened by saline loading; risk amplified by concomitant cyclosporine A, aminoglycosides, or pentamidine
Fluconazole	37/100	100-400 mg q24h	D	100%	50%	50%	HEMO: 100% of recommended dose AD CAPD: Dose for CrCl <10	CRRT: 200-400 mg q24h
Flucytosine	3-6/75-200	37.5 mg per kg q6h	I	q12h	q12-24h **Same dose for CRRT**	q24h	HEMO: Dose AD CAPD: 0.5-1 gm q24h	Goal is peak serum level >25 mcg per mL and <100 mcg per mL
Itraconazole, po soln	21/25	100-200 mg q12h	D	100%	100% **Same dose for CRRT**	50%	HEMO/CAPD: oral solution: 100 mg q12-24h	
Itraconazole, IV	21/25	200 mg IV q12h	-	200 mg IV bid	Do not use IV itra if CrCl <30 due to accumulation of carrier, cyclodextrin			
Terbinafine	36-200/?	250 mg po per day	-	q24h	Use has not been studied. Recommend avoidance of drug			
Voriconazole, IV	Non-linear kinetics	6 mg per kg IV q12h times 2, then 4 mg per kg q12h	-	No change	If CrCl <50 mL per min., accum. of IV vehicle (cyclodextrin). Switch to po or DC For CRRT: 4 mg/kg po q12h			
ANTIPARASITIC ANTIBIOTICS								
Pentamidine	3-12/73-18	4 mg per kg per day	I	q24h	q24h **Same dose for CRRT**	q24-36h	HEMO: 4 mg/kg q48h AD CAPD: Dose for CrCl<10	
Quinine	5-16/5-16	650 mg q8h	I	650 mg q8h	650 mg q8-12h **Same dose for CRRT**	650 mg q24h	HEMO: Dose AD CAPD: Dose for CrCl <10	Marked tissue accumulation

Abbreviation Key: Adjustment Method: **D** = dose adjustment, **I** = interval adjustment, **D&I** = dose & interval adjustment, **CAPD** = continuous ambulatory peritoneal dialysis; **CRRT** = continuous renal replacement therapy; **HEMO** = hemodialysis; **AD** = after dialysis; "**Supplement**" or "**Extra**" is to replace drug lost during dialysis – additional drug beyond continuation of regimen for CrCl < 10 mL/min.

TABLE 17A (7)

ANTIMICROBIAL	HALF-LIFE (NORMAL/ESRD) hr	DOSE FOR NORMAL RENAL FUNCTION	METHOD (see footer)	ADJUSTMENT FOR RENAL FAILURE Estimated creatinine clearance (CrCl), mL/min >50-90	10-50	<10	HEMODIALYSIS, CAPD	COMMENTS & DOSAGE FOR CRRT
ANTITUBERCULOUS ANTIBIOTICS (See http://11ncc.ucsd.edu/TB)								
Amikacin/ Streptomycin (see page 205)								
Bedaquiline	24-30	ND	400 mg po qd x 2 wks, then 200 mg tiw x 22 wks	No adjustment for mild-moderate renal impairment; use with caution if severe renal impairment or ESRD				
Capreomycin		15 mg/kg q24h	I	15 mg/kg q24h	CrCl <30: 15 mg/kg	15 mg/kg AD 3x/wk	HEMO: 15 mg/kg AD 3x/wk	
Cycloserine		10-15 mg/kg/day in 2 div doses	I	10-15 mg/kg/day in 2 div doses	CrCl 10-20: 10-15 mg/kg q12-24h	10-15 mg/kg q24h	HEMO: 10-15 mg/kg AD 3x/wk	
Ethambutol	4/7-15	15-25 mg per kg q24h	I	15-25 mg/kg q24h	15 mg/kg q24-36h **Same dose for CRRT For CrCl 10-20:** 15-25 mg/kg q24-48h	15-25 mg/kg q48h	HEMO: 20 mg/kg 3x/wk AD CAPD: 25 mg/kg q48h	If possible, do serum levels on dialysis pts.
Ethionamide	2.1/?	250-500 mg q12h	D	100%	100%	50%	HEMO/CAPD/CRRT: No dosage adjustment	
Isoniazid	0.7-4/8-17	5 mg per kg per day (max. 300 mg)	D	100%	100%	100%	HEMO: Dose AD CAPD/: Dose for CrCl <10	
Pyrazinamide	9/26	25 mg per kg q24h (max. dose 2.5 gm q24h)	D	25 mg/kg q24h	25 mg/kg q24h **Same dose for CRRT For CrCl 10-20:** 25 mg/kg q24-48h	30 mg per kg 3x/wk	HEMO: 25 mg/kg 3x/wk AD CAPD: No reduction	
Rifampin	1.5-5/1.8-11	600 mg per day	D	600 mg q24h	300-600 mg q24h **Same dose for CRRT**	300-600 mg q24h	HEMO: No adjustment CAPD/: Dose for CrCl <10	Biologically active metabolite
ANTIVIRAL AGENTS For ANTIRETROVIRALS (See CID 40:1559, 2005)								
Acyclovir, IV	2-4/20	5-12.4 mg per kg q8h	D&I	100% q8h	100% q12-24h	50% q24h	HEMO: Dose AD CAPD/: Dose for CrCl <10	Rapid IV infusion can cause ↑ Cr. CRRT dose: 5-10 mg/kg q24h.
Adefovir	7.5/15	10 mg po q24h	I	10 mg q24h	10 mg q48-72h	10 mg q72h	HEMO: 10 mg q week AD	CAPD: No data; CRRT: Dose?
Amantadine	12/500	100 mg po bid	I	q12h	q24-48h	q 7 days	HEMO/CAPD: Dose for CrCl<10/	CRRT: Dose for CrCl 10-50
Atripla	See each drug	200 mg emtricitabine + 300 mg tenofovir + 600 mg efavirenz		Do not use if CrCl <50			HEMO/CAPD: Dose for CrCl<10/	

Cidofovir **Complicated dosing**—see package insert

[a] Ref: *Transplantation* 80:1086, 2005
Abbreviation Key: Adjustment Method: **D** = dose adjustment, **I** = interval adjustment; **CAPD** = continuous ambulatory peritoneal dialysis; **CRRT** = continuous renal replacement therapy; **HEMO** = hemodialysis; **AD** = after dialysis, "**Supplement**" or "**Extra**" is to replace drug lost during dialysis – additional drug beyond continuation of regimen for CrCl < 10 mL/min.

TABLE 17A (8)

ANTIMICROBIAL	HALF-LIFE (NORMAL/ESRD) hr	DOSE FOR NORMAL RENAL FUNCTION	METHOD (see footer)	ADJUSTMENT FOR RENAL FAILURE — Estimated creatinine clearance (CrCl), mL/min >50-90	10-50	<10	HEMODIALYSIS, CAPD	COMMENTS & DOSAGE FOR CRRT
ANTIVIRAL AGENTS For ANTIRETROVIRALS[*]								
ANTIRETROVIRALS (continued)								
Induction	2.5/unknown	5 mg per kg once per wk for 2 wks	I	5 mg per kg once per wk for 2 wks	Contraindicated in pts with CrCl ≤ 55 mL/min.			Major toxicity is renal. No efficacy, safety, or pharmacokinetic data in pts with moderate/severe renal disease.
Maintenance	2.5/unknown	5 mg per kg q2wks	I	5 mg per kg q2wks	Contraindicated in pts with CrCl ≤ 55 mL/min.			
Didanosine tablets[*]	0.6-1.6/4.5	125-200 mg q12h buffered tabs / 400 mg q24h enteric-coated tabs	D	200 mg q12h / 400 mg q24h	125-200 mg q24h	<60 kg: 150 mg q24h; >60 kg: 100 mg q24h. **Do not use EC tabs**	HEMO: Dose AD CAPD/CRRT: Dose for CrCl <10 / HEMO/CAPD: Dose for CrCl <10	Based on incomplete data. Data are estimates. *If <60 kg & CrCl <10 mL per min, do not use EC tabs.*
Emtricitabine (CAPS)	10/>10	200 mg q24h	I	200 mg q24h	30-49: 200 mg q48h; 10-29: 200 mg q72h	200 mg q96h	HEMO: Dose for CrCl <10	*See package insert for oral solution.*
Emtricitabine + Tenofovir	See each drug	200-300 mg q24h	I	No change	30-50: 1 tab q48h	CrCl <30: Do not use		
Entecavir	128-149/?	0.5 mg q24h	D	0.5 mg q24h	0.15-0.25 mg q24h	0.05 mg q24h	HEMO/CAPD: 0.05 mg q24h	Give after dialysis on dialysis days
Famciclovir	2.3-3/10-22	500 mg q8h	D&I	500 mg q8h	500 mg q12-24h	250 mg q24h	HEMO: Dose AD CAPD: No data	CRRT: Not applicable
Foscarnet (CMV dosage). Dosage adjustment based on est. CrCl divided by wt (kg)	Normal half-life (T½) 3 hrs with terminal T½ 18-88 hrs. T½ very long with ESRD	Induction: 60 mg/kg IV q8h x 2-3 wks; Maintenance: 90-120 mg/kg/day IV		*See sub-table below (CrCl mL/min per kg body weight—only for Foscarnet)*			<0.4: Do not use	*See package insert for further details*
Ganciclovir IV:	3.6/30	Induction 5 mg per kg q12h IV	D&I	70-90: 5 mg per kg q12h; 50-60: 2.5-5.0 mg per kg q24h	25-49: 2.5 mg per kg q24h; 10-24: 1.25 mg/kg q24h	1.25 mg per kg 3 times per wk	HEMO: Dose AD CAPD: Dose for CrCl <10	
		Maintenance 5 mg per kg q24h IV	D&I	2.5-5.0 mg per kg q24h	0.6-1.25 mg per kg q24h	0.625 mg per kg q24h 3 times per wk	HEMO: 0.6 mg per kg AD CAPD: Dose for CrCl <10	
po:		1 gm tid po	D&I	0.5-1 gm tid	0.5-1 gm q24h	0.5 gm 3 times per week	HEMO: 0.5 gm AD	
Maraviroc	14-18/No data	300 mg bid	D&I	300 mg bid	300 mg bid	300 mg bid		Risk of side effects increased if concomitant CYP3A inhibitor
Lamivudine	5-7/15-35	300 mg po q24h	D&I	300 mg po q24h	50-150 mg po q24h	25-50 mg po q24h	HEMO: Dose AD; CAPD: Dose for CrCl<10; CRRT: Dose for CrCl <10 mL/min.	CRRT: 100 mg 1st day; then 50 mg/day.

CrCl (mL/min per kg body weight—only for Foscarnet)

	>1.4	>1-1.4	>0.8-1	>0.6-0.8	>0.5-0.6	>0.4-0.5	<0.4
Induction: 60 mg/kg	60 q8h	45 q8h	50 q12h	40 q12h	60 q24h	50 q24h	Do not use
Maintenance	120 q24h	90 q24h	65 q48h	105 q48h	80 q48h	65 q48h	Do not use

[*] Ref. for NRTIs and NNRTIs: Kidney International 60:821, 2001

Abbreviation Key: Adjustment Method D = dose adjustment; I = interval adjustment; **CAPD** = continuous ambulatory peritoneal dialysis; **CRRT** = continuous renal replacement therapy; "**Supplement**" or "**Extra**" is to replace drug lost during dialysis – additional drug beyond continuation of regimen for CrCl < 10 mL/min.
HEMO = hemodialysis; **AD** = after dialysis;

212

TABLE 17A (9)

ANTIMICROBIAL	HALF-LIFE (NORMAL/ ESRD) hr	DOSE FOR NORMAL RENAL FUNCTION	METHOD (see footer)	ADJUSTMENT FOR RENAL FAILURE Estimated creatinine clearance (CrCl), mL/min			HEMODIALYSIS, CAPD	COMMENTS & DOSAGE FOR CRRT
				>50-90	10-50	<10		
ANTIVIRAL AGENTS For ANTIRETROVIRALS *(continued)*								
Oseltamivir, therapy	6-10/>20	75 mg po bid – treatment	I	75 mg q12h	**30-50:** 75 mg bid <**30:** 75 mg once daily	No data	HEMO: 30 mg non-dialysis days[5]; CAPD: 30 mg once per week	Dose for prophylaxis if CrCl <30: 75 mg once daily; CRRT: 75 mg po bid
Peramivir		600 mg once daily	P&I	600 mg q24h	**31-49:** 150 mg q24h **10-30:** 100 mg q24h	100 mg (single dose) then 15 mg q24h	HEMO: 100 mg (single dose) then 100 mg 2 hrs AD (dialysis days only)	CRRT: http://www.cdc.gov/h1n1flu/eva/peramivir.htm
Ribavirin	Use with caution in patients with creatinine clearance <50 mL per min.							
Rimantadine, po	13-65/Prolonged	100 mg bid po	I	100 mg bid	100 mg q24h-bid	100 mg q24h	HEMO/CAPD: No data	Use with caution, little data
Stavudine, po	1-1.4/5.5-8	30-40 mg q12h	D&I	100%	50% q12-24h	≥60 kg: 20 mg per day <60 kg: 15 mg per day	HEMO: Dose as for CrCl <10 AD; CAPD: No data; CRRT: Full dose	
Stribild		1 tab daily	I	If CrCl < 70: contraindicated	If CrCl < 50: discontinue			
Telbivudine	40-49/No data	600 mg po daily	I	600 mg q24h	**30-49:** 600 mg q48h <**30:** 600 mg q72h	600 mg q96h	HEMO: As for CrCl <10 AD	
Tenofovir, po	17/?	300 mg q24h	I	300 mg q24h	**30-49:** 300 mg q48h **10-29:** 300 mg q72-96h	No data	HEMO: 300 mg q7d or after 12 hrs of HEMO[6]	
Valacyclovir	2.5-3.3/14	1 gm q8h	D&I	1 gm q8h	1 gm q12-24h **Same dose for CRRT**	0.5 gm q24h	HEMO: Dose AD; CAPD: Dose for CrCl <10	CAVH dose: As for CrCl 10-50
Valganciclovir	4/67	900 mg po bid	D&I	900 mg bid	450 mg q24h to 450 mg every other day **Same dose for CRRT**	DO NOT USE	See package insert	
Zalcitabine	2/>8	0.75 mg q8h	D&I	0.75 mg q8h	0.75 mg q12h	0.75 mg q24h	HEMO: Dose AD; CAPD: No data	CRRT dose: As for CrCl 10-50
Zidovudine	1.1-1.4/1.4-3	300 mg q12h	D&I	300 mg q12h	300 mg q12h **Same dose for CRRT**	100 mg q8h	HEMO: Dose for CrCl <10 AD; CAPD: Dose for CrCl <10	

[5] HEMO wt-based dose adjustments for children age >1 yr (dose after each HEMO): ≤15 kg: 7.5 mg; 16-23 kg: 10 mg; 24-40 kg: 15 mg; > 40 kg: 30 mg *(CID 50:127, 2010).*

[6] Acute renal failure and Fanconi syndrome reported.

Abbreviation Key: Adjustment Method: **D** = dose adjustment, **I** = interval adjustment, **CAPD** = continuous ambulatory peritoneal dialysis, **CRRT** = continuous renal replacement therapy; **HEMO** = hemodialysis; **AD** = after dialysis; "**Supplement**" or "**Extra**" is to replace drug lost during dialysis -- additional drug beyond continuation of regimen for CrCl < 10 mL/min.

**TABLE 17B – NO DOSAGE ADJUSTMENT WITH RENAL INSUFFICIENCY
BY CATEGORY***

Antibacterials		Antifungals	Anti-TBc	Antivirals	
Azithromycin	Minocycline	Anidulafungin	Ethionamide	Abacavir	Lopinavir
Ceftriaxone	Moxifloxacin	Caspofungin	Isoniazid	Atazanavir	Nelfinavir
Chloramphenicol	Nafcillin	Itraconazole oral solution	Rifampin	Darunavir	Nevirapine
Ciprofloxacin XL	Polymyxin B	Ketoconazole	Rifabutin	Delavirdine	Raltegravir
Clindamycin	Pyrimethamine	Micafungin	Rifapentine	Efavirenz	Ribavirin
Doxycycline	Rifaximin	Voriconazole, **po only**		Enfuvirtide[1]	Saquinavir
Linezolid	Tigecycline			Fosamprenavir	Tipranavir
				Indinavir	

[1] Enfuvirtide: Not studied in patients with CrCl < 35 mL/min. DO NOT USE

TABLE 18 – ANTIMICROBIALS AND HEPATIC DISEASE: DOSAGE ADJUSTMENT*

The following alphabetical list indicates antibacterials excreted/metabolized by the liver **wherein a dosage adjustment
may be indicated** in the presence of hepatic disease. Space precludes details; consult the PDR or package inserts for
details. List is **not** all-inclusive:

Antibacterials		Antifungals	Antivirals[§]	
Ceftriaxone	Nafcillin	Caspofungin	Abacavir	Indinavir
Chloramphenicol	Rifabutin	Itraconazole	Atazanavir	Lopinavir/ritonavir
Clindamycin	Rifampin	Voriconazole	Darunavir	Nelfinavir
Fusidic acid	Synercid**		Delavirdine	Nevirapine
Isoniazid	Telithromycin***		Efavirenz	Rimantadine
Metronidazole	Tigecycline		Enfuvirtide	Ritonavir
	Tinidazole		Fosamprenavir	Stribild

[§] Ref. on antiretrovirals: *CID* 40:174, 2005   ** Quinupristin/dalfopristin   *** Telithro: reduce dose in renal & hepatic failure

TABLE 19 – TREATMENT OF CAPD PERITONITIS IN ADULTS*
(Periton Dial Int 30:393, 2010)[2]

EMPIRIC Intraperitoneal Therapy: Culture Results Pending *(For MRSA see footnote[3])*

Drug		Residual Urine Output	
		<100 mL per day	>100 mL per day
(Cefazolin or Vanco) +	Can mix in same bag	1 gm per bag, q24h	20 mg per kg BW per bag, q24h
Ceftazidime		1 gm per bag, q24h	20 mg per kg BW per bag, q24h

Drug Doses for SPECIFIC Intraperitoneal Therapy—Culture Results Known. NOTE: Few po drugs indicated

Drug	Intermittent Dosing (once per day)		Continuous Dosing (per liter exchange)	
	Anuric	Non-Anuric	Anuric	Non-Anuric
Amphotericin B	NA	NA	MD 1.5 mg	NA
Ampicillin	250–500 mg po bid	ND	No LD, MD 125 mg	ND
Amp-sulbactam	2 gm q12h	ND	LD 1 gm, MD 100 mg	LD 1 gm, MD ↑ 25%
Cefazolin	15 mg per kg	20 mg per kg	LD 500 mg, MD 125 mg	LD 500 mg, ↑ MD 25%
Cefepime	1 gm in one exchange/day	1.25 gm	LD 500 mg, MD 125 mg	LD 500 mg, ↑ MD 25%
Ceftazidime	1000–1500 mg	ND	LD 500 mg, MD 125 mg	LD 500 mg; ↑ MD 25%
Ciprofloxacin	500 mg po bid	ND	LD 50 mg, MD 25 mg	ND
Daptomycin			LD 100 mg, MD 20 mg	LD 500 mg, ↑ MD 25%
Fluconazole	200 mg q24h	ND	200 mg q24h	ND
Gentamicin	0.6 mg per kg	↑ dose 25%	Not recommended	Not recommended
Imipenem	1 gm in one exchange q12h	ND	LD 250 mg, MD 50 mg	LD 250 mg, ↑ MD 25%
Itraconazole	100 mg q12h	100 mg q12h	100 mg q12h	100 mg q12h
Metronidazole	250 mg po bid	ND	250 mg po bid	ND
TMP-SMX	160/800 mg po bid	ND	LD 320/1600 mg po, MD 80/400 mg po q24h	ND
Vancomycin	15–30 mg per kg q3–7 days	↑ dose 25%	LD 1 gm; MD 25 mg	LD 1 gm, ↑ MD 25%

CAPD = continuous ambulatory peritoneal dialysis
Indications for catheter removal: 1) Relapse with same organism within 1 mo; 2) Failure to respond clinically within 5 days;
3) Exit site and tunnel infection; 4) Fungal peritonitis; 5) Fecal flora peritonitis (suggests bowel perforation).

[1] Ref. for NRTIs and NNRTIs: *Kidney International* 60:821, 2001
[2] **All doses IP unless indicated otherwise.**
LD = loading dose, **MD** = maintenance dose, **ND** = no data; **NA** = not applicable—dose as normal renal function.
Anuric = <100 mL per day, **non-anuric** = >100 mL per day
[3] **Does not provide treatment for MRSA.** If gram-pos cocci on gram stain, include vanco.
* *See page 2 for other abbreviations*

TABLE 20A – ANTI-TETANUS PROPHYLAXIS, WOUND CLASSIFICATION, IMMUNIZATION

Clinical Features	WOUND CLASSIFICATION	
	Tetanus Prone	Non-Tetanus Prone
Age of wound	> 6 hours	≤ 6 hours
Configuration	Stellate, avulsion	Linear
Depth	> 1 cm	≤ 1 cm
Mechanism of injury	Missile, crush, burn, frostbite	Sharp surface (glass, knife)
Devitalized tissue	Present	Absent
Contaminants (dirt, saliva, etc.)	Present	Absent

(From ACS Bull. 69:22,23, 1984, No. 10)

IMMUNIZATION SCHEDULE

History of Tetanus Immunization	Dirty, Tetanus-Prone Wound		Clean, non-Tetanus-Prone Wound	
	Td[1,2]	Tetanus Immune Globulin	Td[1,2]	Tetanus Immune Globulin
Unknown or < 3 doses[3]	Yes	No[4]	Yes	No
3 or more doses	No[4]	No	No[5]	No

References: *MMWR 39:37, 1990; MMWR 46 (SS-2):15, 1997; MMWR 61:468, 2012; general vaccine considerations, MMWR 60 (RR-2):1, 2011; and general immunization schedule, MMWR 61:1, 2012.*

---

[1] Td = Tetanus & diphtheria toxoids, adsorbed (adult). For adult who has not received Tdap previously, substitute one dose of Tdap for Td when immunization is indicated *(MMWR 61::468, 2012)*.

[2] For children < 7 years, use DTaP unless contraindicated; for persons ≥ 7 years, Td is preferred to tetanus toxoid alone, but single dose of Tdap can be used if required for catch-up series.

[3] Individuals who have not completed vaccine series should do so.

[4] Yes, if > 5 years since last booster

[5] Yes, if > 10 years since last booster

TABLE 20B – RABIES POSTEXPOSURE PROPHYLAXIS

All wounds should be cleaned immediately & thoroughly with soap & water. This has been shown to protect 90% of experimental animals![1]

Postexposure Prophylaxis Guide, United States, 2012

(MMWR 57 (RR-3): 1, 2008; http://wwwnc.cdc.gov/travel/yellowbook/2012/chapter-3-infectious-diseases-related-to-travel/rabies.htm)

Animal Type	Evaluation & Disposition of Animal	Recommendations for Prophylaxis
Dogs, cats, ferrets	Healthy & available for 10-day observation	Don't start unless animal develops sx, then immediately begin HRIG + vaccine
	Rabid or suspected rabid	Immediate HRIG + vaccine
	Unknown (escaped)	Consult public health officials
Skunks, raccoons, bats,* foxes, coyotes, most carnivores	Regard as rabid	Immediate vaccination
Livestock, horses, rodents, rabbits; includes hares, squirrels, hamsters, guinea pigs, gerbils, chipmunks, rats, mice, woodchucks	Consider case-by-case	Consult public health officials. Bites of squirrels, hamsters, guinea pigs, gerbils, chipmunks, rats, mice, other small rodents, rabbits, and hares **almost never** require rabies post-exposure prophylaxis.

* Most recent cases of human rabies in U.S. due to contact (not bites) with silver-haired bats or rarely big brown bats but risk of acquiring rabies from non-contact bat exposure is exceedingly low (*CID 48:1493, 2009*). For more detail, see *CID 30:4, 2000; JAVMA 219:1687, 2001; CID 37:96, 2003 (travel medicine advisory); Ln 363:959, 2004; EID 11:1921, 2005; MMWR 55 (RR-5), 2006.*

Postexposure Rabies Immunization Schedule

IF NOT PREVIOUSLY VACCINATED

Treatment	Regimen[2]
Local wound cleaning	**All postexposure treatment should begin with immediate, thorough cleaning of all wounds with soap & water.**
Human rabies immune globulin (HRIG)	20 units per kg body weight given once on day 0. If anatomically feasible, the full dose should be infiltrated around the wound(s), the rest should be administered IM in the gluteal area. If the calculated dose of HRIG is insufficient to inject all the wounds, it should be diluted with normal saline to allow infiltration around additional wound areas. HRIG should **not** be administered in the **same syringe**, or into the **same anatomical site** as vaccine, or more than 7 days after the initiation of vaccine. Because HRIG may partially suppress active production of antibody, no more than the recommended dose should be given.[3]
Vaccine	Human diploid cell vaccine (HDCV), rabies vaccine adsorbed (RVA), or purified chick embryo cell vaccine (PCECV) 1 mL **IM (deltoid area[4])**, one each days 0, 3, 7, 14[5].

IF PREVIOUSLY VACCINATED[6]

Treatment	Regimen[2]
Local wound cleaning	All postexposure treatment should begin with immediate, thorough cleaning of all wounds with soap & water.
HRIG	HRIG should **not** be administered
Vaccine	HDCV or PCEC, 1 mL **IM (deltoid area[4])**, one each on days 0 & 3

CORRECT VACCINE ADMINISTRATION SITES

Age Group	Administration Site
Children & adults	**DELTOID[4]** only (**NEVER** in gluteus)
Infants & young children	Outer aspect of thigh (anterolateral thigh) may be used (**NEVER** in gluteus)

---

[1] From *MMWR 48:RR-1, 1999; CID 30:4, 2000*; B. T. Matyas, Mass. Dept. of Public Health.

[2] These regimens are applicable for all age groups, including children.

[3] In most reported post-exposure treatment failures, only identified deficiency was failure to infiltrate wound(s) with HRIG (*CID 22:228, 1996*). However, several failures reported from SE Asia in patients in whom WHO protocol followed (*CID 28:143, 1999*).

[4] The **deltoid** area is the **only** acceptable site of vaccination for adults & older children. For infants & young children, outer aspect of thigh (anterolateral thigh) may be used. Vaccine should **NEVER** be administered in gluteal area.

[5] Note that this is a change from previous recommendation of 5 doses (days 0, 3, 7, 14 & 28) based on new data & recommendations from ACIP. Note that the number of doses for persons with altered immunocompetence remains unchanged (5 doses on days 0, 3, 7, 14 & 28) and recommendations for pre-exposure prophylaxis remain 3 doses administered on days 0, 7 and 21 or 28 (*MMWR 59 (RR-2), 2010*).

[6] Any person with a history of pre-exposure vaccination with HDCV, RVA, PCECV; prior post-exposure prophylaxis with HDCV, PCEC or rabies vaccine adsorbed (RVA); or previous vaccination with any other type of rabies vaccine & a documented history of antibody response to the prior vaccination.

TABLE 21 SELECTED DIRECTORY OF RESOURCES

ORGANIZATION	PHONE/FAX	WEBSITE(S)

ANTIPARASITIC DRUGS & PARASITOLOGY INFORMATION *(CID 37:694, 2003)*

CDC Drug Line	Weekdays: 404-639-3670	http://www.cdc.gov/ncidod/srp/drugs/drug-service.html
	Evenings, weekends, holidays: 404-639-2888	
DPDx: Lab ID of parasites		www.dpd.cdc.gov/dpdx/default.htm
Gorgas Course Tropical Medicine		http://info.dom.uab.edu/gorgas
Malaria	daytime: 770-488-7788	www.cdc.gov/malaria
	other: 770-488-7100	
	US toll free: 855-856-4713	
Expert Compound. Pharm.	800-247-9767/818-787-7256	www.uniquerx.com
World Health Organization (WHO)		www.who.int
Parasites & Health		www.dpd.cdc.gov/dpdx/HTML/Para_Health.htm

BIOTERRORISM

Centers for Disease Control & Prevention	770-488-7100	www.bt.cdc.gov
Infectious Diseases Society of America	703-299-0200	www.idsociety.org
Johns Hopkins Center Civilian Biodefense		www.jhsph.edu
Center for Biosecurity of the Univ. of Pittsburgh Med. Center		www.upmc-biosecurity.org
US Army Medical Research Institute of Inf. Dis.		www.usamriid.army.mil

HEPATITIS B

Hepatitis B Foundation		www.hepb.org, www.natap.org

HEPATITIS C *(CID 35:754, 2002)*

CDC		www.cdc.gov/ncidod/diseases/hepatitis/C
Individual		http://hepatitis-central.com
		www.natap.org
Medscape		www.medscape.com

HIV

General		
HIV InSite		http://hivinsite.ucsf.edu
Johns Hopkins AIDS Service		www.hopkins-aids.edu
		www.natap.org
Drug Interactions		
Johns Hopkins AIDS Service		www.hopkins-aids.edu
Liverpool HIV Pharm. Group		www.hiv-druginteractions.org
Other		http://AIDS.medscape.com
Prophylaxis/Treatment of Opportunistic Infections; HIV Treatment		www.aidsinfo.nih.gov

IMMUNIZATIONS *(CID 36:355, 2003)*

CDC, Natl. Immunization Program	404-639-8200	www.cdc.gov/vaccines/
FDA, Vaccine Adverse Events	800-822-7967	www.fda.gov/cber/vaers/vaers.htm
National Network Immunization Info.	877-341-6644	www.immunizationinfo.org
Influenza vaccine, CDC	404-639-8200	www.cdc.gov/vaccines/
Institute for Vaccine Safety		www.vaccinesafety.edu

OCCUPATIONAL EXPOSURE, BLOOD-BORNE PATHOGENS (HIV, HEPATITIS B & C)

National Clinicians' Post-Exposure Hotline	888-448-4911	www.ucsf.edu/hivcntr

Q-T$_c$ INTERVAL PROLONGATION BY DRUGS

		www.qtdrugs.org

SEXUALLY TRANSMITTED DISEASES

		www.cdc.gov/std/treatment/TOC2002TG.htm
	Slides: http://www.phac-aspc.gc.ca/slm-maa/slides/index.html	

TRAVELERS' INFO: Immunizations, Malaria Prophylaxis, More

Amer. Soc. Trop. Med. & Hyg.		www.astmh.org
CDC, general	877-394-8747/888-232-3299	http://wwwn.cdc.gov/travel/default.asp
CDC, Malaria:		www.cdc.gov/malaria
Prophylaxis		http://www.cdc.gov/travel/default.asp
Treatment	770-488-7788	www.who.int/health topics/malaria
MD Travel Health		www.mdtravelhealth.com
Pan American Health Organization		www.paho.org
World Health Organization (WHO)		www.who.int/home-page

VACCINE & IMMUNIZATION RESOURCES *(CID 36:355, 2003)*

American Academy of Pediatrics		www.cispimmunize.org
CDC, National Immunization Program		www.cdc.gov/vaccines/
National Network for Immunization Information		www.immunizationinfo.org

TABLE 22A – ANTI-INFECTIVE DRUG-DRUG INTERACTIONS

Importance: ± = theory/anecdotal; + = of probable importance; + + = of definite importance
To check for interactions between more than 2 drugs, see: http://www.drugs.com/drug_interactions.html
and http://www.healthline.com/druginteractions

ANTI-INFECTIVE AGENT (A)	OTHER DRUG (B)	EFFECT	IMPORT
Abacavir	Methadone	↓ levels of B	+ +
Amantadine (Symmetrel)	Alcohol	↑ CNS effects	+
	Anticholinergic and anti-Parkinson agents (ex. Artane, scopolamine)	↑ effect of B: dry mouth, ataxia, blurred vision, slurred speech, toxic psychosis	+
	Trimethoprim	↑ levels of A & B	+
	Digoxin	↑ levels of B	±
Aminoglycosides—parenteral (amikacin, gentamicin, kanamycin, netilmicin, sisomicin, streptomycin, tobramycin)	Amphotericin B	↑ nephrotoxicity	+ +
	Cis platinum (Platinol)	↑ nephro & ototoxicity	+
	Cyclosporine	↑ nephrotoxicity	+
	Neuromuscular blocking agents	↑ apnea or respiratory paralysis	+
	Loop diuretics (e.g., furosemide)	↑ ototoxicity	+ +
	NSAIDs	↑ nephrotoxicity	+
	Non-polarizing muscle relaxants	↑ apnea	+
	Radiographic contrast	↑ nephrotoxicity	+
	Vancomycin	↑ nephrotoxicity	+
Aminoglycosides—oral (kanamycin, neomycin)	Oral anticoagulants (dicumarol, phenindione, warfarin)	↑ prothrombin time	+
Amphotericin B and ampho B lipid formulations	Antineoplastic drugs	↑ nephrotoxicity risk	+
	Digitalis	↑ toxicity of B if K⁺ ↓	+
	Nephrotoxic drugs: aminoglycosides, cidofovir, cyclosporine, foscarnet, pentamidine	↑ nephrotoxicity of A	+ +
Ampicillin, amoxicillin	Allopurinol	↑ frequency of rash	+ +
Artemether-lumefantrine	CYP3A inhibitors: amiodarone, atazanavir, itraconazole, ritonavir, voriconazole	↑ levels of A; ↑ QTc interval	+ +
	CYP2D6 substrates: flecainide, imipramine, amitriptyline	↑ levels of B; ↑ QTc interval	+ +
Atazanavir	See protease inhibitors and Table 22B		
Atovaquone	Rifampin (perhaps rifabutin)	↓ serum levels of A; ↑ levels of B	+
	Metoclopramide	↓ levels of A	+
	Tetracycline	↓ levels of A	+ +

Azole Antifungal Agents [**Flu** = fluconazole; **Itr** = itraconazole; **Ket** = ketoconazole; **Posa** = posaconazole; **Vor** = voriconazole; + = occurs; **blank space** = either studied & no interaction OR no data found (may be in pharm. co. databases)]

Flu	Itr	Ket	Posa	Vor	OTHER DRUG (B)	EFFECT	IMPORT
+	+				Amitriptyline	↑ levels of B	+
+	+	+		+	Calcium channel blockers	↑ levels of B	+ +
	+			+	Carbamazepine (vori contraindicated)	↓ levels of A	+ +
+	+	+	+	+	Cyclosporine	↑ levels of B, ↑ risk of nephrotoxicity	+
	+	+			Didanosine	↓ absorption of A	+
	+	+	+	+	Efavirenz	↓ levels of A, ↑ levels of B	+ + (avoid)
	+	+	+	+	H₂ blockers, antacids, sucralfate	↓ absorption of A	+
+	+	+	+	+	Hydantoins (phenytoin, Dilantin)	↑ levels of B, ↓ levels of A	+ +
	+	+			Isoniazid	↓ levels of A	+
	+	+	+	+	Lovastatin/simvastatin	Rhabdomyolysis reported; ↑ levels of B	+ +
				+	Methadone	↑ levels of B	+
+	+	+	+	+	Midazolam/triazolam, po	↑ levels of B	+ +
+	+			+	Oral anticoagulants	↑ effect of B	+ +
+	+			+	Oral hypoglycemics	↑ levels of B	+ +
			+	+	Pimozide	↑ levels of B—**avoid**	+ +
	+			+	Protease inhibitors	↑ levels of B	+ +
	+	+	+	+	Proton pump inhibitors	↓ levels of A, ↑ levels of B	+ +
+	+	+	+	+	Rifampin/rifabutin (vori contraindicated)	↓ levels of B, ↓ serum levels of A	+ +
	+				Rituximab	Inhibits action of B	+ +
			+	+	Sirolimus (vori and posa contraindicated)	↑ levels of B	+ +
+		+	+	+	Tacrolimus	↑ levels of B with toxicity	+ +
+		+			Theophyllines	↑ levels of B	+
		+			Trazodone	↑ levels of B	+ +
+					Zidovudine	↑ levels of B	+

TABLE 22A (2)

ANTI-INFECTIVE AGENT (A)	OTHER DRUG (B)	EFFECT	IMPORT
Bedaquiline	Rifampin	↓ levels of A	++
	Ketoconazole	↑ levels of A	+
Caspofungin	Cyclosporine	↑ levels of A	++
	Tacrolimus	↓ levels of B	++
	Carbamazepine, dexamethasone, efavirenz, nevirapine, phenytoin, rifampin	↓ levels of A; ↑ dose of caspofungin to 70 mg/d	++
Chloramphenicol	Hydantoins	↑ toxicity of B, nystagmus, ataxia	++
	Iron salts, Vitamin B12	↓ response to B	++
	Protease inhibitors—HIV	↑ levels of A & B	++
Clindamycin (Cleocin)	Kaolin	↓ absorption of A	++
	Muscle relaxants, e.g., atracurium, baclofen, diazepam	↑ frequency/duration of respiratory paralysis	++
	St John's wort	↓ levels of A	++
Cobicistat	See Stribild, below		
Cycloserine	Ethanol	↑ frequency of seizures	+
	INH, ethionamide	↑ frequency of drowsiness/dizziness	+
Dapsone	Atazanavir	↑ levels of A - Avoid	++
	Didanosine	↓ absorption of A	+
	Oral contraceptives	↓ effectiveness of B	+
	Pyrimethamine	↑ in marrow toxicity	+
	Rifampin/Rifabutin	↓ serum levels of A	+
	Trimethoprim	↑ levels of A & B (methemoglobinemia)	+
	Zidovudine	May ↑ marrow toxicity	+
Daptomycin	HMG-CoA inhibitors (statins)	Consider DC statin while on dapto	++
Delavirdine (Rescriptor)	See Non-nucleoside reverse transcriptase inhibitors (NNRTIs) and Table 22B		
Didanosine (ddI) (Videx)	Allopurinol	↑ levels of A—**AVOID**	++
	Cisplatin, dapsone, INH, metronidazole, nitrofurantoin, stavudine, vincristine, zalcitabine	↑ risk of peripheral neuropathy	+
	Ethanol, lamivudine, pentamidine	↑ risk of pancreatitis	+
	Fluoroquinolones	↓ absorption 2° to chelation	+
	Drugs that need low pH for absorption: dapsone, indinavir, itra/ ketoconazole, pyrimethamine, rifampin, trimethoprim	↓ absorption	+
	Methadone	↓ levels of A	++
	Ribavirin	↑ levels ddI metabolite—**avoid**	++
	Tenofovir	↑ levels of A **(reduce dose of A)**	++
Doripenem	Probenecid	↑ levels of A	++
	Valproic acid	↓ levels of B	++
Doxycycline	Aluminum, bismuth, iron, Mg++	↓ absorption of A	+
	Barbiturates, hydantoins	↓ serum t/2 of A	+
	Carbamazepine (Tegretol)	↓ serum t/2 of A	+
	Digoxin	↑ serum levels of B	+
	Warfarin	↑ activity of B	++
Efavirenz (Sustiva)	See non-nucleoside reverse transcriptase inhibitors (NNRTIs) and Table 22B		
Elvitegravir	See Stribild, below		
Ertapenem (Invanz)	Probenecid	↑ levels of A	++
	Valproic acid	↓ levels of B	++
Ethambutol (Myambutol)	Aluminum salts (includes didanosine buffer)	↓ absorption of A & B	+
Etravirine	See non-nucleoside reverse transcriptase inhibitors (NNRTIs) and Table 22B		

Fluoroquinolones (**Cipro** = ciprofloxacin; **Gati** = gatifloxacin; **Gemi** = gemifloxacin; **Levo** = levofloxacin; **Moxi** = moxifloxacin; **Oflox** = ofloxacin)

Cipro	Gati	Gemi	Levo	Moxi	Oflox	NOTE: Blank space = either studied and no interaction OR no data found		
						Antiarrhythmics (procainamide, amiodarone)	↑ Q-T interval (torsade)	++
+	+		+	+	+	Insulin, oral hypoglycemics	↑ & ↓ blood sugar	++
+						Caffeine	↑ levels of B	+
+					+	Cimetidine	↑ levels of A	+
+					+	Cyclosporine	↑ levels of B	±
+	+		+	+	+	Didanosine	↓ absorption of A	++

TABLE 22A (3)

ANTI-INFECTIVE AGENT (A)	OTHER DRUG (B)	EFFECT	IMPORT

Fluoroquinolones *(continued)*

Cipro	Gati	Gemi	Levo	Moxi	Oflox	NOTE: Blank space = either studied and no interaction OR no data found		
+	+	+	+	+	+	Cations: Al+++, Ca++, Fe++, Mg++, Zn++ (antacids, vitamins, dairy products), citrate/citric acid	↓ absorption of A (some variability between drugs)	+ +
+						Methadone	↑ levels of B	+ +
+	+				+	NSAIDs	↑ risk CNS stimulation/seizures	+ +
+			+		+	Phenytoin	↑ or ↓ levels of B	+
+	+	+			+	Probenecid	↓ renal clearance of A	+
+						Rasagiline	↑ levels of B	+ +
				+		Rifampin	↓ levels of A (CID 45:1001, 2007)	+ +
+	+	+	+		+	Sucralfate	↓ absorption of A	+ +
+						Theophylline	↑ levels of B	+ +
+						Thyroid hormone	↓ levels of B	+ +
+						Tizanidine	↑ levels of B	+ +
+			+	+	+	Warfarin	↑ prothrombin time	+

Ganciclovir (Cytovene) & **Valganciclovir** (Valcyte)	Imipenem	↑ risk of seizures reported	+
	Probenecid	↑ levels of A	+
	Zidovudine	↓ levels of A, ↑ levels of B	+

Gentamicin	See Aminoglycosides—parenteral		

Imipenem & Meropenem	BCG	↓ effectiveness of B – avoid combination	+ +
	Divalproex	↓ levels of B	+ +
	Ganciclovir	↑ seizure risk	+ +
	Probenecid	↑ levels of A	+ +
	Valproic acid	↓ levels of B	+ +

Indinavir	See protease inhibitors and Table 22B		

Isoniazid	Alcohol, rifampin	↑ risk of hepatic injury	+ +
	Aluminum salts	↓ absorption (take fasting)	+ +
	Carbamazepine, phenytoin	↑ levels of B with nausea, vomiting, nystagmus, ataxia	+ +
	Itraconazole, ketoconazole	↓ levels of B	+
	Oral hypoglycemics	↓ effects of B	+

Lamivudine	Zalcitabine	Mutual interference—do not combine	+ +

Linezolid (Zyvox)	Adrenergic agents	Risk of hypertension	+ +
	Aged, fermented, pickled or smoked foods —↑ tyramine	Risk of hypertension	+
	Clarithromycin	↑ levels of A	+ +
	Rasagiline (MAO inhibitor)	Risk of serotonin syndrome	+
	Rifampin	↓ levels of A	+ +
	Serotonergic drugs (SSRIs)	Risk of serotonin syndrome	+ +

Lopinavir	See protease inhibitors		

Macrolides [**Ery** = erythromycin; **Azi** = azithromycin; **Clr** = clarithromycin; + = occurs; **blank space** = either studied and no interaction OR no data]

Ery	Azi	Clr			
+		+	Carbamazepine	↑ serum levels of B, nystagmus, nausea, vomiting, ataxia	+ + (avoid w/ erythro)
+		+	Cimetidine, **ritonavir**	↑ levels of B	+
+			Clozapine	↑ serum levels of B, CNS toxicity	+
		+	**Colchicine**	↑ **levels of B (potent, fatal)**	+ + (avoid)
+			Corticosteroids	↑ effects of B	+
+		+	Cyclosporine	↑ serum levels of B with toxicity	+
+	+	+	Digoxin, digitoxin	↑ serum levels of B (10% of cases)	+
		+	Efavirenz	↓ levels of A	+ +
+		+	Ergot alkaloids	↑ levels of B	+ +
		+	Linezolid	↑ levels of B	+ +
+		+	Lovastatin/simvastatin	↑ levels of B; rhabdomyolysis	+ +
+			Midazolam, triazolam	↑ levels of B, ↑ sedative effects	+
+		+	Phenytoin	↑ levels of B	+
+		+	Pimozide	↑ Q-T interval	+ +
+		+	Rifampin, rifabutin	↓ levels of A	+
+		+	Tacrolimus	↑ levels of B	+ +
+		+	Theophylline	↑ serum levels of B with nausea, vomiting, seizures, apnea	+ +
+		+	Valproic acid	↑ levels of B	+
+		+	Warfarin	May ↑ prothrombin time	+
		+	Zidovudine	↓ levels of B	+

TABLE 22A (4)

ANTI-INFECTIVE AGENT (A)	OTHER DRUG (B)	EFFECT	IMPORT
Maraviroc	Clarithromycin	↑ serum levels of A	++
	Delavirdine	↑ levels of A	++
	Itraconazole/ketoconazole	↑ levels of A	++
	Nefazodone	↑ levels of A	++
	Protease Inhibitors (not tipranavir/ritonavir)	↑ levels of A	++
	Anticonvulsants: carbamazepine, phenobarbital, phenytoin	↓ levels of A	++
	Efavirenz	↓ levels of A	++
	Rifampin	↓ levels of A	++
Mefloquine	ß-adrenergic blockers, calcium channel blockers, quinidine, quinine	↑ arrhythmias	+
	Divalproex, valproic acid	↓ level of B with seizures	++
	Halofantrine	Q-T prolongation	++ (avoid)
Meropenem	See Imipenem		
Methenamine mandelate or hippurate	Acetazolamide, sodium bicarbonate, thiazide diuretics	↓ antibacterial effect 2° to ↑ urine pH	++
Metronidazole Tinidazole	**Alcohol**	Disulfiram-like reaction	+
	Cyclosporin	↑ levels of B	++
	Disulfiram (Antabuse)	Acute toxic psychosis	+
	Lithium	↑ levels of B	++
	Oral anticoagulants	↑ anticoagulant effect	++
	Phenobarbital, hydantoins	↑ levels of B	++
Micafungin	Nifedipine	↑ levels of B	+
	Sirolimus	↑ levels of B	+
Nelfinavir	See protease inhibitors and Table 22B		
Nevirapine (Viramune)	See non-nucleoside reverse transcriptase inhibitors (NNRTIs) and Table 22B		
Nitrofurantoin	Antacids	↓ absorption of A	+

Non-nucleoside reverse transcriptase inhibitors (NNRTIs): For interactions with protease inhibitors, see *Table 22B*.
Del = delavirdine; **Efa** = efavirenz; **Etr** = etravirine; **Nev** = nevirapine

Del	Efa	Etr	Nev	Co-administration contraindicated (See package insert)		IMPORT
+		+		Anticonvulsants: carbamazepine, phenobarbital, phenytoin		++
+		+		Antimycobacterials: rifabutin, rifampin		++
+				Antipsychotics: pimozide		++
+	+	+		Benzodiazepines: alprazolam, midazolam, triazolam		++
+	+			Ergotamine		++
+	+	+		HMG-CoA inhibitors (statins): lovastatin, simvastatin, atorvastatin, pravastatin		++
+		+		St. John's wort		++
				Dose change needed:		
+				Amphetamines	↑ levels of B—**caution**	++
+		+	+	Antiarrhythmics: amiodarone, lidocaine, others	↓ or ↑ levels of B—**caution**	++
+	+	+	+	Anticonvulsants: carbamazepine, phenobarbital, phenytoin	↓ levels of A and/or B	++
+	+	+	+	Antifungals: itraconazole, ketoconazole, voriconazole, posaconazole	Potential ↓ levels of B, ↑ levels of A	++ (avoid)
+				Antirejection drugs: cyclosporine, rapamycin, sirolimus, tacrolimus	↑ levels of B	++
+			+	Calcium channel blockers	↑ levels of B	++
+		+	+	Clarithromycin	↑ levels of B metabolite, ↑ levels of A	++
+		+	+	Cyclosporine	↑ levels of B	++
+		+	+	Dexamethasone	↓ levels of A	++
+	+	+	+	Sildenafil, vardenafil, tadalafil	↑ levels of B	++
+			+	Fentanyl, methadone	↑ levels of B	++
+				Gastric acid suppression: antacids, H-2 blockers, proton pump inhibitors	↓ levels of A	++
	+	+	+	Methadone, fentanyl	↓ levels of B	++
	+		+	Oral contraceptives	↑ or ↓ levels of B	++
+	+	+	+	Protease inhibitors—see *Table 22B*		
+	+	+	+	**Rifabutin, rifampin**	↑ or ↓ levels of rifabutin; ↓ levels of A—**caution**	++
+	+	+	+	St. John's wort	↓ levels of B	++
	+	+	+	Warfarin	↑ levels of B	++

ANTI-INFECTIVE AGENT (A)	OTHER DRUG (B)	EFFECT	IMPORT
Pentamidine, IV	Amphotericin B	↑ risk of nephrotoxicity	+
	Pancreatitis-assoc drugs, eg, alcohol, valproic acid	↑ risk of pancreatitis	+
Piperacillin	Cefoxitin	Antagonism vs pseudomonas	++
Pip-tazo	Methotrexate	↑ levels of B	++
Polymyxin B	Curare paralytics	Avoid: neuromuscular blockade	++

TABLE 22A (5)

ANTI-INFECTIVE AGENT (A)	OTHER DRUG (B)	EFFECT	IMPORT
Polymyxin E (Colistin)	Curare paralytics	Avoid: neuromuscular blockade	++
	Aminoglycosides, Ampho B, Vanco	↑ nephrotoxicity risk	++
Primaquine	Chloroquine, dapsone, INH, probenecid, quinine, sulfonamides, TMP/SMX, others	↑ **risk of hemolysis in G6PD-deficient patients**	++

Protease Inhibitors—Anti-HIV Drugs. (Atazan = atazanavir; **Darun** = darunavir; **Fosampren** = fosamprenavir; **Indin** = *indinavir;* **Lopin** = lopinavir; **Nelfin** = nelfinavir ; **Saquin** = saquinavir; **Tipran** = tipranavir). For interactions with antiretrovirals, *see Table 22B* **Only a partial list—check package insert**

Also see http://aidsinfo.nih.gov
To check for interactions between more than 2 drugs, see:
http://www.drugs.com/drug_interactions.html and http://www.healthline.com/druginteractions

Atazan	Darun	Fosampren	Indin	Lopin	Nelfin	Saquin	Tipran			
								Analgesics:		
							+	1. Alfentanil, fentanyl, hydrocodone, tramadol	↑ levels of B	+
	+			+		+	+	2. Codeine, hydromorphone, morphine, methadone	↓ levels of B *(JAIDS 41;563, 2006)*	+
+	+	+	+	+	+		+	**Anti-arrhythmics: amiodarone, lidocaine, mexiletine, flecainide**	↑ levels of B; **do not co-administer or use caution** *(See package insert)*	++
	+			+	+	+	+	**Anticonvulsants: carbamazepine, clonazepam, phenobarbital**	↓ levels of A, ↑ levels of B	++
+		+	+				+	Antidepressants, all tricyclic	↑ levels of B	++
+	+						+	Antidepressants, all other	↓ levels of B; do not use pimozide	++
	+							Antidepressants: SSRIs	↓ levels of B - avoid	++
								Antihistamines	**Do not use**	++
+	+	+	+	+	+		+	**Benzodiazepines, e.g., diazepam, midazolam, triazolam**	↑ **levels of B—do not use**	++
+	+	+	+	+	+	+	+	Calcium channel blockers (all)	↑ levels of B	++
+	+			+	+	+	+	Clarithro, erythro	↑ levels of B if renal impairment	+
+	+		+	+	+	+		Contraceptives, oral	↓ levels of A & B	++
	+	+		+			+	Corticosteroids: prednisone, dexamethasone	↓ levels of A, ↑ levels of B	+
+	+	+	+	+	+	+	+	Cyclosporine	↑ levels of B, monitor levels	+
						+		Digoxin	↑ levels of B	++
+	+	+	+	+	+	+	+	Ergot derivatives	↑ **levels of B—do not use**	++
		+	+		+	+		Erythromycin, clarithromycin	↑ levels of A & B	+
			+			+	+	Grapefruit juice (> 200 mL/day)	↓ indinavir & ↑ saquinavir levels	++
+	+	+	+	+	+	+	+	H2 receptor antagonists	↓ levels of A	++
+	+	+	+	+	+	+	+	**HMG-CoA reductase inhibitors (statins): lovastatin, simvastatin**	↑ levels of B	++
+								Irinotecan	↑ **levels of B—do not use**	++
	+	+	+	+	+	+	+	Ketoconazole, itraconazole, ? vori.	↑ levels of A, ↑ levels of B	+
+	+	+	+	+	+	+	+	Posaconazole	↑ levels of A, no effect on B	++
			+					Metronidazole	Poss. disulfiram reaction, alcohol	+
			+					Phenytoin *(JAIDS 36;1034, 2004)*	↓ levels of A & B	++
+	+	+	+	+	+	+	+	**Pimozide**	↑ **levels of B—do not use**	++
+	+		+	+	+	+		Proton pump inhibitors	↓ levels of A	++
+	+	+	+	+	+	+	+	Rifampin, rifabutin	↓ levels of A, ↑ levels of B **(avoid)**	++ **(avoid)**
+	+	+	+	+	+	+	+	Sildenafil (Viagra), tadalafil, vardenafil	Varies, some ↑ & some ↓ levels of B	++
+	+	+	+	+	+	+	+	**St. John's wort**	↓ **levels of A—do not use**	++
+	+	+	+	+	+	+	+	**Sirolimus, tracrolimus**	↑ levels of B	++
+								Tenofovir	↓ levels of A—add ritonavir	++
	+		+	+				Theophylline	↓ levels of B	+
	+						+	Warfarin	↑ levels of B	+
Pyrazinamide								INH, rifampin	May ↑ risk of hepatotoxicity	±
Pyrimethamine								Lorazepam	↑ risk of hepatotoxicity	+
								Sulfonamides, TMP/SMX	↑ risk of marrow suppression	+
								Zidovudine	↑ risk of marrow suppression	+
Quinine								Digoxin	↑ digoxin levels; ↑ toxicity	++
								Mefloquine	↑ arrhythmias	+
								Oral anticoagulants	↑ prothrombin time	++
Quinupristin- dalfopristin (Synercid)								Anti-HIV drugs: NNRTIs & PIs	↑ levels of B	++
								Antineoplastic: vincristine, docetaxel, paclitaxel	↑ levels of B	++
								Calcium channel blockers	↑ levels of B	++
								Carbamazepine	↑ levels of B	++
								Cyclosporine, tacrolimus	↑ levels of B	++

TABLE 22A (6)

ANTI-INFECTIVE AGENT (A)	OTHER DRUG (B)	EFFECT	IMPORT
Quinupristin-dalfopristin (Synercid) *(continued)*	Lidocaine	↑ levels of B	++
	Methylprednisolone	↑ levels of B	++
	Midazolam, diazepam	↑ levels of B	++
	Statins	↑ levels of B	++
Raltegravir	**Rifampin**	**↓ levels of A**	++
Ribavirin	Didanosine	↑ levels of B → toxicity—**avoid**	++
	Stavudine	↓ levels of B	++
	Zidovudine	↓ levels of B	++
Rifamycins (rifampin, rifabutin) Ref.: *ArIM* 162:985, 2002 **The following is a partial list of drugs with rifampin-induced ↑ metabolism and hence lower than anticipated serum levels:** ACE inhibitors, dapsone, diazepam, digoxin, diltiazem, doxycycline, fluconazole, fluvastatin, haloperidol, moxifloxacin, nifedipine, progestins, triazolam, tricyclics, voriconazole, zidovudine *(Clin Pharmacokinetic 42:819, 2003).*	Al OH, ketoconazole, PZA	↓ levels of A	+
	Atovaquone	↑ levels of A, ↓ levels of B	+
	Beta adrenergic blockers (metoprolol, propranolol)	↓ effect of B	+
	Caspofungin	↓ levels of B—increase dose	++
	Clarithromycin	↑ levels of A, ↓ levels of B	++
	Corticosteroids	↑ replacement requirement of B	++
	Cyclosporine	↓ effect of B	++
	Delavirdine	↑ levels of A, ↓ levels of B—**avoid**	++
	Digoxin	↓ levels of B	++
	Disopyramide	↓ levels of B	++
	Fluconazole	↑ levels of B	+
	Amprenavir, indinavir, nelfinavir, ritonavir	↑ levels of A (↓ dose of A), ↓ levels of B	++
	INH	Converts INH to toxic hydrazine	++
	Itraconazole, ketoconazole	↓ levels of B, ↑ levels of A	++
	Linezolid	↓ levels of B	++
	Methadone	↓ serum levels (withdrawal)	+
	Nevirapine	**↓ levels of B—avoid**	++
	Oral anticoagulants	Suboptimal anticoagulation	++
	Oral contraceptives	↓ effectiveness; spotting, pregnancy	+
	Phenytoin	↓ levels of B	+
	Protease inhibitors	**↓ levels of A, ↑ levels of B— CAUTION**	++
	Quinidine	↓ effect of B	+
	Raltegravir	↓ levels of B	++
	Sulfonylureas	↓ hypoglycemic effect	+
	Tacrolimus	**↓ levels of B**	++
	Theophylline	↓ levels of B	+
	TMP/SMX	↓ levels of A	+
	Tocainide	↓ effect of B	+
Rimantadine	*See Amantadine*		
Ritonavir	*See protease inhibitors and Table 22B*		
Saquinavir	*See protease inhibitors and Table 22B*		
Stavudine	Dapsone, INH	May ↑ risk of peripheral neuropathy	±
	Ribavirin	↓ levels of A—**AVOID**	++
	Zidovudine	Mutual interference—do not combine	++
Stribild (Elvitegravir & Cobicistat components) *(See Emtricitabine & Tenofovir for other components)*			
Elvitegravir	Antacids	↓ levels of A	++
Cobicistat	Antiarrhythmics & digoxin	↑ levels of B	++
Cobicistat	Clarithromycin, telithromycin	↑ levels of B	++
Cobicistat & Elvitegravir	Carbamazepine, phenobarbital, phenytoin	↓ levels of A – **AVOID**	++
Cobicistat	SSRIs, TCAs, trazodone, antidepressants	↓ levels of A – **AVOID**	++
Cobicistat	Itraconazole, ketoconazole, voriconazole	↑ levels of B	++
Cobicistat	Colchicine	↑ levels of B – lower dose	++
Elvitegravir & Cobicistat	Rifabutin, rifapentine	↓ levels of A – **AVOID**	++
Cobicistat	Beta blockers	↑ levels of B	++
Cobicistat	Calcium channel blockers	↑ levels of B	++
Cobicistat & Elvitegravir	Dexamethasone	↓ levels of A	++
Cobicistat	Bosentan	↑ levels of B	++
Cobicistat	HMG-CoA reductase inhibitor, sirolimus	↑ levels of B	++
Cobicistat	Cyclosporine, tacrolimus	↑ levels of B	++
Cobicistat	Neuroleptics	↑ levels of B	++
Cobicistat	PDE5 inhibitors, e.g., Sildenafil, vardenafil, tadalafil	↑ levels of B – **AVOID**	++
Cobicistat	Benzodiazepines	↑ levels of B	++
Cobicistat	Ergot derivatives	↑ levels of B – **AVOID**	++
Cobicistat	Cisapride	↑ levels of B – **AVOID**	++
Cobicistat & Elvitegravir	St. John's wort	↑ levels of B – **AVOID**	++

TABLE 22A (7)

ANTI-INFECTIVE AGENT (A)	OTHER DRUG (B)	EFFECT	IMPORT
Sulfonamides	Beta blockers	↑ levels of B	++
	Cyclosporine	↓ cyclosporine levels	+
	Methotrexate	↑ antifolate activity	+
	Oral anticoagulants	↑ prothrombin time; bleeding	+
	Phenobarbital, rifampin	↓ levels of A	+
	Phenytoin	↑ levels of B; nystagmus, ataxia	+
	Sulfonylureas	↑ hypoglycemic effect	+
Telithromycin (Ketek)	Carbamazine	↓ levels of A	++
	Digoxin	↑ levels of B—do digoxin levels	++
	Ergot alkaloids	↑ levels of B—avoid	++
	Itraconazole; ketoconazole	↑ levels of A; no dose change	+
	Metoprolol	↑ levels of B	++
	Midazolam	↑ levels of B	++
	Oral anticoagulants	↑ prothrombin time	+
	Phenobarbital, phenytoin	↓ levels of A	++
	Pimozide	↑ levels of B; QT prolongation—AVOID	++
	Rifampin	↓ levels of A—avoid	++
	Simvastatin & other "statins"	↑ levels of B (↑ risk of myopathy)	++
	Sotalol	↓ levels of B	++
	Theophylline	↑ levels of B	++
Tenofovir	Atazanavir	↓ levels of B—add ritonavir	++
	Didanosine (ddI)	↑ levels of B (reduce dose)	++
Terbinafine	Cimetidine	↑ levels of A	+
	Phenobarbital, rifampin	↓ levels of A	+
Tetracyclines	See Doxycycline, plus:		
	Atovaquone	↓ levels of B	+
	Digoxin	↑ toxicity of B (may persist several months—up to 10% pts)	++
	Methoxyflurane	↑ toxicity; polyuria, renal failure	+
	Sucralfate	↓ absorption of A (separate by ≥2 hrs)	+
Thiabendazole	Theophyllines	↑ serum theophylline, nausea	+
Tigecycline	Oral contraceptives	↓ levels of B	++
Tinidazole (Tindamax)	See Metronidazole—similar entity, expect similar interactions		
Tobramycin	See Aminoglycosides		
Trimethoprim	Amantadine, dapsone, digoxin, methotrexate, procainamide, zidovudine	↑ serum levels of B	++
	Potassium-sparing diuretics	↑ serum K+	++
	Repaglinide	↑ levels of B (hypoglycemia)	++
	Thiazide diuretics	↓ serum Na+	+
Trimethoprim-Sulfamethoxazole	Ace inhibitors	↑ serum K+	++
	Amantadine	↑ levels of B (toxicity)	++
	Azathioprine	Reports of leukopenia	+
	Cyclosporine	↓ levels of B, ↑ serum creatinine	+
	Loperamide	↑ levels of B	+
	Methotrexate	Enhanced marrow suppression	++
	Oral contraceptives, pimozide, and 6-mercaptopurine	↓ effect of B	+
	Phenytoin	↑ levels of B	+
	Rifampin	↑ levels of B	+
	Warfarin	↑ activity of B	+
Valganciclovir (Valcyte)	See Ganciclovir		
Vancomycin	Aminoglycosides	↑ frequency of nephrotoxicity	++
Zalcitabine (ddC) (HIVID)	Valproic acid, pentamidine (IV), alcohol, lamivudine	↑ pancreatitis risk	+
	Cisplatin, INH, metronidazole, vincristine, nitrofurantoin, d4T, dapsone	↑ risk of peripheral neuropathy	+
Zidovudine (ZDV) (Retrovir)	Atovaquone, fluconazole, methadone	↑ levels of A	+
	Clarithromycin	↓ levels of A	±
	Indomethacin	↑ levels of ZDV toxic metabolite	+
	Nelfinavir	↓ levels of A	++
	Probenecid, TMP/SMX	↑ levels of A	+
	Rifampin/rifabutin	↓ levels of A	++
	Stavudine	Interference—DO NOT COMBINE!	++
	Valproic Acid	↑ levels of A	++

TABLE 22B – DRUG-DRUG INTERACTIONS BETWEEN NON-NUCLEOSIDE REVERSE TRANSCRIPTASE INHIBITORS (NNRTIs) AND PROTEASE INHIBITORS
(Adapted from Guidelines for the Use of Antiretroviral Agents in HIV-Infected Adults & Adolescents; see www.aidsinfo.nih.gov)

NAME (Abbreviation, Trade Name)	Atazanavir (ATV, Reyataz)	DARUNAVIR (DRV, Prezista)	Fosamprenavir (FOS-APV, Lexiva)	Indinavir (IDV, Crixivan)	Lopinavir/Ritonavir (LP/R, Kaletra)	Nelfinavir (NFV, Viracept)	Saquinavir (SQV, Invirase)	Tipranavir (TPV)
Delavirdine (DLV, Rescriptor)	No data	No data	**Co-administration not recommended**	IDV levels ↑ 40%. Dose: IDV 600 mg q8h; DLV standard	Expect LP levels to ↑. No dose data	NFV levels ↑ 2X; DLV levels ↑ 50%. Dose: No data	SQV levels ↑ 5X. Dose: SQV 800 mg q8h; DLV standard	No data
Efavirenz (EFZ, Sustiva)	ATV AUC ↓ 74%. Dose: EFZ standard; ATV/RTV 300/100 mg q24h with food	Standard doses of both drugs	FOS-APV levels ↓. Dose: EFZ standard; FOS-APV 1400 mg + RTV 300 mg q24h or 700 mg FOS-APV + 100 mg RTV q12h	Levels: IDV ↓ 31%. Dose: IDV 1000 mg q8h; EFZ standard	Level of LP ↓ 40%. Dose: LP/R 533/133 mg q12h, EFZ standard	Standard doses	Level: SQV ↓ 62%. Dose: SQV 400 mg + RTV 400 mg q12h	No dose change necessary
Etravirine (ETR, Intelence)	↑ ATV & ↑ ETR levels.	Standard doses of both drugs	↑ levels of FOS-APV.	↓ level of IDV.	↑ levels of ETR, ↓ levels of LP/R.	↑ levels of NFV.	↓ ETR levels 33%. SQV/R no change. Standard dose of both drugs.	↓ levels of ETR, ↑ levels of TPV & RTV. **Avoid combination.**
Nevirapine (NVP, Viramune)	Avoid combination. ATZ increases NVP concentrations > 25%. NVP decreases ATZ AUC by 42%	Standard doses of both drugs	Use with caution. NVP AUC increased 14% (700/100 Fos/rit; NVP AUC inc 29% (Fos 1400 mg bid)	IDV levels ↓ 28%. Dose: IDV 1000 mg q8h or combine with RTV; NVP standard	LP levels ↓ 53%. Dose: LP/R 533/133 mg q12h; NVP standard	Standard doses	Dose: SQV + RTV 400/400 mg both q12h	Standard doses

TABLE 23 – LIST OF GENERIC AND COMMON TRADE NAMES

GENERIC NAME: TRADE NAMES	GENERIC NAME: TRADE NAMES	GENERIC NAME: TRADE NAMES
Abacavir: Ziagen	Efavirenz/Emtricitabine/Tenofovir: Atripla	Nitrofurantoin: Macrobid, Macrodantin
Abacavir + Lamivudine: Epzicom	Elvitegravir + Cobicistat + Emtricitabine	Nystatin: Mycostatin
Abacavir + Lamivudine + Zidovudine:	+ Tenofovir: Stribild	Ofloxacin: Floxin
Trizivir	Emtricitabine: Emtriva	Oseltamivir: Tamiflu
Acyclovir: Zovirax	Emtricitabine + tenofovir: Truvada	Oxacillin: Prostaphlin
Adefovir: Hepsera	Emtricitabine + tenofovir + rilpivirine:	Palivizumab: Synagis
Albendazole: Albenza	Complera	Paromomycin: Humatin
Amantadine: Symmetrel	Enfuvirtide (T-20): Fuzeon	Pentamidine: NebuPent, Pentam 300
Amikacin: Amikin	Entecavir: Baraclude	Piperacillin: Pipracil
Amoxicillin: Amoxil, Polymox	Ertapenem: Invanz	Piperacillin/tazobactam: Zosyn,
Amoxicillin extended release: Moxatag	Etravirine: Intelence	Tazocin
Amox./clav.: Augmentin, Augmentin	Erythromycin(s): Ilotycin	Piperazine: Antepar
ES-600; Augmentin XR	*Ethyl succinate*: Pediamycin	Podophyllotoxin: Condylox
Amphotericin B: Fungizone	*Glucoheptonate*: Erythrocin	Polymyxin B: Poly-Rx
Ampho B-liposomal: AmBisome	*Estolate*: Ilosone	Posaconazole: Noxafil
Ampho B-lipid complex: Abelcet	Erythro/sulfisoxazole: Pediazole	Praziquantel: Biltricide
Ampicillin: Omnipen, Polycillin	Ethambutol: Myambutol	Primaquine: Primachine
Ampicillin/sulbactam: Unasyn	Ethionamide: Trecator	Proguanil: Paludrine
Artemether-Lumefantrine: Coartem	Famciclovir: Famvir	Pyrantel pamoate: Antiminth
Atazanavir: Reyataz	Fidaxomicin: Dificid	Pyrimethamine: Daraprim
Atovaquone: Mepron	Fluconazole: Diflucan	Pyrimethamine/sulfadoxine: Fansidar
Atovaquone + proguanil: Malarone	Flucytosine: Ancobon	Quinupristin/dalfopristin: Synercid
Azithromycin: Zithromax	Fosamprenavir: Lexiva	Raltegravir: Isentress
Azithromycin ER: Zmax	Foscarnet: Foscavir	Retapamulin: Altabax
Aztreonam: Azactam, Cayston	Fosfomycin: Monurol	Ribavirin: Virazole, Rebetol
Bedaquiline: Sirturo	Fusidic acid: Taksta	Rifabutin: Mycobutin
Boceprevir: Victrelis	Ganciclovir: Cytovene	Rifampin: Rifadin, Rimactane
Caspofungin: Cancidas	Gatifloxacin: Tequin	Rifapentine: Priftin
Cefaclor: Ceclor, Ceclor CD	Gemifloxacin: Factive	Rifaximin: Xifaxan
Cefadroxil: Duricef	Gentamicin: Garamycin	Rilpivirine: Edurant
Cefazolin: Ancef, Kefzol	Griseofulvin: Fulvicin	Rimantadine: Flumadine
Cefdinir: Omnicef	Halofantrine: Halfan	Ritonavir: Norvir
Cefditoren pivoxil: Spectracef	Idoxuridine: Dendrid, Stoxil	Saquinavir: Invirase
Cefepime: Maxipime	INH + RIF: Rifamate	Spectinomycin: Trobicin
Cefixime^{NUS}: Suprax	INH + RIF + PZA: Rifater	Stavudine: Zerit
Cefoperazone-sulbactam:	Interferon alfa: Intron A	Stibogluconate: Pentostam
Sulperazon^{NUS}	Interferon, pegylated: PEG-Intron,	Silver sulfadiazine: Silvadene
Cefotaxime: Claforan	Pegasys	Sulfamethoxazole: Gantanol
Cefotetan: Cefotan	Interferon + ribavirin: Rebetron	Sulfasalazine: Azulfidine
Cefoxitin: Mefoxin	Imipenem + cilastatin: Primaxin,	Sulfisoxazole: Gantrisin
Cefpodoxime proxetil: Vantin	Tienam	Telaprevir: Incivek
Cefprozil: Cefzil	Imiquimod: Aldara	Telavancin: Vibativ
Ceftaroline: Teflaro	Indinavir: Crixivan	Telbivudine: Tyzeka
Ceftazidime: Fortaz, Tazicef, Tazidime	Itraconazole: Sporanox	Telithromycin: Ketek
Ceftibuten: Cedax	Iodoquinol: Yodoxin	Temocillin: Negaban, Temopen
Ceftizoxime: Cefizox	Ivermectin: Stromectol, Sklice	Tenofovir: Viread
Ceftobiprole: Zeftera	Kanamycin: Kantrex	Terbinafine: Lamisil
Ceftriaxone: Rocephin	Ketoconazole: Nizoral	Thalidomide: Thalomid Thiabendazole:
Cefuroxime: Zinacef, Ceftin	Lamivudine: Epivir, Epivir-HBV	Mintezol
Cephalexin: Keflex	Lamivudine + abacavir: Epzicom	Ticarcillin: Ticar
Cephradine: Anspor, Velosef	Levofloxacin: Levaquin	Tigecycline: Tygacil
Chloroquine: Aralen	Linezolid: Zyvox	Tinidazole: Tindamax
Cidofovir: Vistide	Lomefloxacin: Maxaquin	Tipranavir: Aptivus
Ciprofloxacin: Cipro, Cipro XR	Lopinavir/ritonavir: Kaletra	Tobramycin: Nebcin
Clarithromycin: Biaxin, Biaxin XL	Loracarbef: Lorabid	Tretinoin: Retin A
Clindamycin: Cleocin	Mafenide: Sulfamylon	Trifluridine: Viroptic
Clofazimine: Lamprene	Maraviroc: Selzentry	Trimethoprim: Primsol
Clotrimazole: Lotrimin, Mycelex	Mebendazole: Vermox	Trimethoprim/sulfamethoxazole:
Cloxacillin: Tegopen	Mefloquine: Lariam	Bactrim, Septra
Colistimethate: Coly-Mycin M	Meropenem: Merrem	Valacyclovir: Valtrex
Cycloserine: Seromycin	Mesalamine: Asacol, Pentasa	Valganciclovir: Valcyte
Daptomycin: Cubicin	Methenamine: Hiprex, Mandelamine	Vancomycin: Vancocin
Darunavir: Prezista	Metronidazole: Flagyl	Voriconazole: Vfend
Delavirdine: Rescriptor	Micafungin: Mycamine	Zalcitabine: HIVID
Dicloxacillin: Dynapen	Minocycline: Minocin	Zanamivir: Relenza
Didanosine: Videx	Moxifloxacin: Avelox	Zidovudine (ZDV): Retrovir
Diethylcarbamazine: Hetrazan	Mupirocin: Bactroban	Zidovudine + 3TC: Combivir
Diloxanide furoate: Furamide	Nafcillin: Unipen	Zidovudine + 3TC + abacavir:
Doripenem: Doribax	Nelfinavir: Viracept	Trizivir
Doxycycline: Vibramycin	Nevirapine: Viramune	
Efavirenz: Sustiva	Nitazoxanide: Alinia	

TABLE 23 (2)
LIST OF COMMON TRADE AND GENERIC NAMES

TRADE NAME: GENERIC NAME	TRADE NAME: GENERIC NAME	TRADE NAME: GENERIC NAME
Abelcet: Ampho B-lipid complex	Garamycin: Gentamicin	Rifadin: Rifampin
Albenza: Albendazole	Halfan: Halofantrine	Rifamate: INH + RIF
Aldara: Imiquimod	Hepsera: Adefovir	Rifater: INH + RIF + PZA
Alinia: Nitazoxanide	Herplex: Idoxuridine	Rimactane: Rifampin
Altabax: Retapamulin	Hiprex: Methenamine hippurate	Rocephin: Ceftriaxone
AmBisome: Ampho B-liposomal	HIVID: Zalcitabine	Selzentry: Maraviroc
Amikin: Amikacin	Humatin: Paromomycin	Septra: Trimethoprim/sulfa
Amoxil: Amoxicillin	Ilosone: Erythromycin estolate	Seromycin: Cycloserine
Ancef: Cefazolin	Ilotycin: Erythromycin	Silvadene: Silver sulfadiazine
Ancobon: Flucytosine	Incivek: Telaprevir	Sirturo: Bedaquiline
Anspor: Cephradine	Intelence: Etravirine	Sklice: Ivermectin lotion
Antepar: Piperazine	Intron A: Interferon alfa	Spectracef: Cefditoren pivoxil
Antiminth: Pyrantel pamoate	Invanz: Ertapenem	Sporanox: Itraconazole
Aptivus: Tipranavir	Invirase: Saquinavir	Stoxil: Idoxuridine
Aralen: Chloroquine	Isentress: Raltegravir	Stribild: Elvitegravir + Cobicistat +
Asacol: Mesalamine	Kaletra: Lopinavir/ritonavir	Emtricitabine + Tenofovir
Atripla: Efavirenz/emtricitabine/tenofovir	Kantrex: Kanamycin	Stromectol: Ivermectin
Augmentin, Augmentin ES-600	Keflex: Cephalexin	Sulfamylon: Mafenide
Augmentin XR: Amox./clav.	Ketek: Telithromycin	Sulperazon^NUS: Cefoperazone-
Avelox: Moxifloxacin	Lamisil: Terbinafine	sulbactam
Azactam: Aztreonam	Lamprene: Clofazimine	Suprax: Cefixime^NUS
Azulfidine: Sulfasalazine	Lariam: Mefloquine	Sustiva: Efavirenz
Bactroban: Mupirocin	Levaquin: Levofloxacin	Symmetrel: Amantadine
Bactrim: Trimethoprim/sulfamethoxa-	Lexiva: Fosamprenavir	Synagis: Palivizumab
zole	Lorabid: Loracarbef	Synercid: Quinupristin/dalfopristin
Baraclude: Entecavir	Macrodantin, Macrobid: Nitrofurantoin	Taksta: Fusidic acid
Biaxin, Biaxin XL: Clarithromycin	Malarone: Atovaquone + proguanil	Tamiflu: Oseltamivir
Biltricide: Praziquantel	Mandelamine: Methenamine mandel.	Tazicef: Ceftazidime
Cancidas: Caspofungin	Maxaquin: Lomefloxacin	Teflaro: Ceftaroline
Cayston: Aztreonam (inhaled)	Maxipime: Cefepime	Tegopen: Cloxacillin
Ceclor, Ceclor CD: Cefaclor	Mefoxin: Cefoxitin	Tequin: Gatifloxacin
Cedax: Ceftibuten	Mepron: Atovaquone	Thalomid: Thalidomide
Cefizox: Ceftizoxime	Merrem: Meropenem	Ticar: Ticarcillin
Cefotan: Cefotetan	Minocin: Minocycline	Tienam: Imipenem
Ceftin: Cefuroxime axetil	Mintezol: Thiabendazole	Timentin: Ticarcillin-clavulanic acid
Cefzil: Cefprozil	Monocid: Cefonicid	Tinactin: Tolnaftate
Cipro, Cipro XR: Ciprofloxacin &	Monurol: Fosfomycin	Tindamax: Tinidazole
extended release	Moxatag: Amoxicillin extended release:	Trecator SC: Ethionamide
Claforan: Cefotaxime	Myambutol: Ethambutol	Trizivir: Abacavir + ZDV + 3TC
Coartem: Artemether-Lumefantrine	Mycamine: Micafungin	Trobicin: Spectinomycin
Coly-Mycin M: Colistimethate	Mycobutin: Rifabutin	Truvada: Emtricitabine + tenofovir
Combivir: ZDV + 3TC	Mycostatin: Nystatin	Tygacil: Tigecycline
Complera: Emtricitabine + tenofovir +	Nafcil: Nafcillin	Tyzeka: Telbivudine
rilpivirine	Nebcin: Tobramycin	Unasyn: Ampicillin/sulbactam
Crixivan: Indinavir	NebuPent: Pentamidine	Unipen: Nafcillin
Cubicin: Daptomycin	Nizoral: Ketoconazole	Valcyte: Valganciclovir
Cytovene: Ganciclovir	Norvir: Ritonavir	Valtrex: Valacyclovir
Daraprim: Pyrimethamine	Noxafil: Posaconazole	Vancocin: Vancomycin
Dificid: Fidaxomicin	Omnicef: Cefdinir	Vantin: Cefpodoxime proxetil
Diflucan: Fluconazole	Omnipen: Ampicillin	Velosef: Cephradine
Doribax: Doripenem	Pediamycin: Erythro. ethyl succinate	Vermox: Mebendazole
Duricef: Cefadroxil	Pediazole: Erythro. ethyl succinate +	Vfend: Voriconazole
Dynapen: Dicloxacillin	sulfisoxazole	Vibativ: Telavancin
Edurant: Rilpivirine	Pegasys, PEG-Intron: Interferon,	Vibramycin: Doxycycline
Emtriva: Emtricitabine	pegylated	Victrelis: Boceprevir
Epivir, Epivir-HBV: Lamivudine	Pentam 300: Pentamidine	Videx: Didanosine
Epzicom: Lamivudine + abacavir	Pentasa: Mesalamine	Viracept: Nelfinavir
Factive: Gemifloxacin	Pipracil: Piperacillin	Viramune: Nevirapine
Famvir: Famciclovir	Polycillin: Ampicillin	Virazole: Ribavirin
Fansidar: Pyrimethamine +	Polymox: Amoxicillin	Viread: Tenofovir
sulfadoxine	Poly-Rx: Polymyxin B	Vistide: Cidofovir
Flagyl: Metronidazole	Prezista: Darunavir	Xifaxan: Rifaximin
Floxin: Ofloxacin	Priftin: Rifapentine	Yodoxin: Iodoquinol
Flumadine: Rimantadine	Primaxin: Imipenem + cilastatin	Zeftera: Ceftobiprole
Foscavir: Foscarnet	Primsol: Trimethoprim	Zerit: Stavudine
Fortaz: Ceftazidime	Prostaphlin: Oxacillin	Ziagen: Abacavir
Fulvicin: Griseofulvin	Rebetol: Ribavirin	Zinacef: Cefuroxime
Fungizone: Amphotericin B	Rebetron: Interferon + ribavirin	Zithromax: Azithromycin
Furadantin: Nitrofurantoin	Relenza: Zanamivir	Zmax: Azithromycin ER
Fuzeon: Enfuvirtide (T-20)	Rescriptor: Delavirdine	Zovirax: Acyclovir
Gantanol: Sulfamethoxazole	Retin A: Tretinoin Retrovir: Zidovudine (ZDV)	Zosyn: Piperacillin/tazobactam
Gantrisin: Sulfisoxazole	Reyataz: Atazanavir	Zyvox: Linezolid

INDEX OF MAJOR ENTITIES

Bold numbers indicate major considerations. Antibiotic selection often depends on modifying circumstances and alternative agents.

234

ISBN 978-1-930808-74-4